Nicholas Monsarrat was born in L of a distinguished surgeon. He was educated at Winchester, then at Trinity College, Cambridge, where he studied law. He gave up law to earn a meagre living as a freelance journalist while he began writing novels. His first novel to receive significant attention was *This is the Schoolroom* (1939). It is a largely autobiographical 'coming of age' novel dealing with the end of college life, the 'Hungry Thirties', and the Spanish Civil War.

During World War Two he served in the Royal Navy in corvettes in the North Atlantic. These experiences were used in his best-known novel, *The Cruel Sea* (1951) and made into a film starring Jack Hawkins.

In 1946, he became a director of the UK Information Service, first in Johannesburg, then in Ottawa. Other well-known novels include *The Kapillan of Malta, The Tribe That Lost Its Head,* and its sequel, *Richer Than All His Tribe,* and *The Story of Esther Costello.*

He died in August 1979 as he was writing the second part of his intended three-volume novel on seafaring life from Napoleonic times to the present, *The Master Mariner.*

Nicholas
Monsarrat

❖

THE TRIBE THAT LOST ITS HEAD

HOUSE OF
STRATUS

The sign of the fish came to Pharamaul nearly two thousand years ago, brought perhaps by an apostle of Christ, wrecked on the northern extremity of that tear-shaped island five hundred miles off the south-west coast of Africa. The sign of the fish, a secret means of recognition for the persecuted Christians, stayed in the island of Pharamaul long after the religious teachings of the castaway had disappeared in the mists of time. With it remained certain hallowed words of the gospel, now perverted in the savage rituals of a pagan tribe. In this year of grace the Sign of the Fish in Pharamaul became the symbol of revolt and obscene death.

FOREWORD

The Tribe That Lost Its Head is a work of fiction. None of its characters portrays any 'real life' person whatsoever, either living or dead. There is no country quite like Pharamaul, anywhere in the world. There is no Governor like Sir Elliott Vere-Toombs, no Resident Commissioner like Andrew Macmillan.

In particular, there is no ministry anything like the Scheduled Territories Office. Its nearest relative would be a synthesis of the Foreign Office, the Commonwealth Relations Office, the Colonial Office, and the Ministry of Works – in fact, a unique hybrid.

N M

The Island of Pharamaul

Insert map shows the position of Pharamaul I. in relation to the Continent of Africa

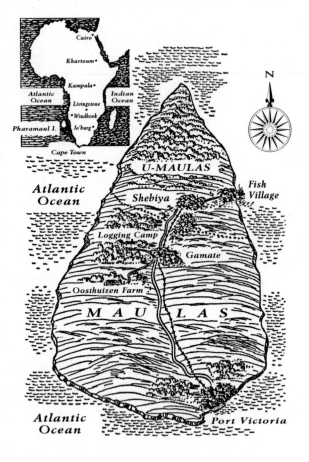

CHAPTER ONE

❖

The plane – a shabby old Dakota – bumped twice in the noonday heat, then settled down on its steady course. Windhoek was left behind, a dusty town set in arid scrub desert: presently the plane crossed the South-West African coastline, and headed out over a pale blue, hazy sea – due west for Pharamaul.

The pilot checked his instruments, held up a thumb to the navigator behind him, set the automatic pilot on 270 degrees, and then relaxed, leaning back in his worn leather seat out of reach of the overhead sun. Windhoek Airport to the Island of Pharamaul – it was a trip he had made thirty-seven times in this year alone. Course due west, distance six hundred miles, flying time three hours and ten minutes, ETA 1530 hours – he could have done it in his sleep. Perhaps one day he *would* do it like that, and see if anybody noticed.

Behind him, the four passengers relaxed also, stretching their legs, occasionally glancing out of the side windows. After the glaring heat and dust of their short inter-plane stop at Windhoek, the shadowless Atlantic below them looked gratefully cool.

Four people in the passenger compartment was less than one-fifth of the Dakota's available complement. It meant

1

privacy and a sense of well-being, as well as comfortable elbow-room. For a variety of reasons, the four passengers were all glad of these things.

Tulbach Browne of the *Daily Thresh* – seasoned traveller of a thousand flights, some epoch-making, very few entirely wasted – went through his usual short-flight, take-off routine. He pressed his ear-drums, and swallowed until his throat was comfortable; popped two dramamine tablets in his mouth, and washed them down with a swig from a tiny, palm-sized flask of whisky; exchanged his scuffed shoes for worn carpet slippers with his monogram upon the toecaps; unbuckled his belt; and patted his bulging breast pocket, which held passport, money, tickets, press card, and notebook, all clipped into one untidy bundle.

Lastly, he looked at his watch, to check the take-off time. If this were early, HAPHAZARD TIMING OF LOCAL AIRLINE would be the phrase; if late, PILOT'S TAKE-IT-OR-LEAVE-IT ATTITUDE might suffice. Once, when exact adherent to the timetable had made Tulbach Browne miss his plane, it had been CIVIL SERVICE MENTALITY MAKES BOAC LAUGHING STOCK. His world had ammunition to suit every mood.

On this occasion, the plane was eleven minutes behind schedule. WINDHOEK AIR SCANDAL seemed indicated. Or even TULBACH BROWNE IN NEVER-NEVER LAND – THE FACTS. For just now, his mood was one of irritation.

Tulbach Browne of the *Daily Thresh* was a small wizened man with sandy hair and a look of permanent disdain. No physical distinction marked him out from the next hundred men to be passed in the street: his face ordinary, rather ugly, his body spare and average, his manner unimpressive. He had known all these things for a very long time: since the age of twenty-two, in fact, when a girl he was busy mauling in a taxi suddenly snapped: 'If I have to be pawed like this, I'd rather it was done by someone attractive.' He had never forgotten that moment: but, in fact, it had served him well.

For now, a quarter of a century later, he was forty-seven – and he had got back at that girl, and at everyone else who had ever overlooked or snubbed him: an impressive total of human beings. As Tulbach Browne of the *Daily Thresh* he was a 'by-line' correspondent most of the way round the world. As Tulbach Browne, he had made a global reputation, and made it in three ways: first by following Northcliffe's advice and giving himself a 'memorable' name: secondly, by learning every detail of his trade; and last and most important, by supplying, copiously, the sort of comment that the *Daily Thresh* lived on.

There had been other things – plenty of luck, and one spectacular piece of bad faith, were among them – but basically, consistent ill nature had been the touchstone.

Competition on the *Daily Thresh*, in this respect, was very high: the paper had at least two staff writers, one of them a woman, who in normal circumstances would have carried off any palm. But Tulbach Browne was in a class by himself. No one could so adroitly 'interpret' the news, no one else could touch him at invective, innuendo, spite, and making plain truth into cloudy lies. Above all, no one could so triumphantly have it both ways at once.

If a politician talked pleasantly, he was ingratiating. If he tried to preserve a serious manner, he was pompous or sulky. A popular author had mere mob-appeal, a 'literary' one was unreadable. A rich man was ostentatious, a poor one seedy; a woman of any elegance at all became 'mink-draped', 'dripping with diamonds', a 'hot-house product' … As with people, so with affairs. A well-organized event was 'slick presentation' – but there was very little that earned even this qualified praise. With few exceptions, Tulbach Browne reported disaster, inefficiency, bad faith. His verdict on the Everest triumph was 'a *Boy's Own Paper* exploit'. His record of the Royal Tour of Canada had been a positive cataract of mistakes and embarrassments which had given universal offence from coast to coast – and a matchless boost to the *Daily Thresh*.

The *Daily Thresh* knew exactly what people liked to read. They preferred things going wrong, Authority with a red face, awkward pauses. Tulbach Browne served up all these things, from all four corners of the world.

Now he was going to Pharamaul, and he was irritated because it was probably a waste of time. (There was also the fact that no one in Windhoek seemed to have heard his name before.) The trip was really a fill-in after his South African tour: he had just 'done' South Africa – seven days, three thousand miles, three stories. The story about the priest who was the 'conscience of South Africa' – whatever that meant. Tulbach Browne had made him sound like a shoddy Messiah on the make. The story about the rich women in furs, giggling as the champagne corks popped, spending enough on a single meal to keep a negro family alive for a month. That had been a natural. And the story about the fascist government heading for a blood bath. That had been easy too.

Now he was going to Pharamaul – for a couple of days, anyway. His office had cabled him something about the local chief coming back from Oxford to take over the tribal chieftainship. ('RUSH CHIEFWARDS RETURNING PHARAMAUL EXOXFORD' had been the actual text.) There might be a story there, particularly if something went wrong and he could flay the Civil Service, British administration, the snob colour bar … Otherwise the time was likely to be wasted.

But what a god-forsaken part of the world this was, anyway. Tulbach Browne stretched, yawned, glanced round him. This beaten-up old plane was symptomatic of the whole thing. There were twenty-one seats, and only three other people besides himself: an old guy who looked like a Colonial civil servant, a young one who might have been anything, and a nigger in the back row.

The Dakota's pilot looked sideways and downwards, craning his neck to watch the sea. There was a ship far below them, heading westwards like the plane: a ship no bigger than a toy, with twin arcs of tiny ripples spreading out on either side of it, and a white wake like a thread of wool astern. It looked at peace and at ease, lazily traversing the vast mill-pool of the South Atlantic.

That was the life, the pilot thought enviously, leaning back in his seat again: plodding along at ten knots, not worrying, dropping the anchor when you got there – no screwed-up navigation, no crosswind on a sodden airfield, no thousands of feet to fall, no trouble at all … Those horn-pipe types had it easy.

He took a paper bag from his side pocket and began, resentfully, to munch an apple.

Two seats behind Tulbach Browne, the old guy who looked like a Colonial civil servant reached out a hand and drew towards him a shabby briefcase. It was of black leather, monogrammed with the Royal arms and the Royal cypher, and battered from twenty years' careless handling in hot climates. It was a Civil Service briefcase, and (as Tulbach Browne had surmised) its owner was a civil servant. Andrew Macmillan, CMG, Resident Commissioner at Gamate, native capital of the Principality of Pharamaul, was returning to duty after twelve weeks' leave in England.

Twelve weeks' leave sounded a long time, though not if one had saved up for it, a day here and a week there, for seven years. In that case, and particularly at the start of such a holiday, twelve weeks' leave seemed no more than a swift, grateful respite after a dusty servitude. But twelve weeks' leave was a long time, Andrew Macmillan had discovered, when, after a fortnight in Oxfordshire with some distant relatives, and a week in London on his own, he realized that he was longing for nothing but to get back to Pharamaul …

Such nostalgia was fantastic, when London had so much to offer, when he had looked forward to the trip so eagerly. The Residency at Gamate was hot, damp, ant-infested, ill-appointed; the servants were lazy, the work repetitive and often dull. His hunger for these things was ridiculous, yet it was a fact. Pharamaul, where he had spent nearly all his working life, Pharamaul which he knew to its last dried-up water-course, its last muddy dam – Pharamaul was his home, and only there could he be happy.

Perhaps this had always been true, perhaps it had grown as any other easeful habit grows. Macmillan was fifty-seven, solid, greying, severe. He had soldiered for a while, in the old days: then he had gone to Pharamaul as a young, energetic Assistant District Officer; and in Pharamaul he had stayed, for the next thirty-five years – first as District Officer at Gamate, the native capital, then transferring to Shebiya, a hundred miles to the north, then completing the requisite term as secretary to the Governor down at Port Victoria, and finally, back in Gamate, assuming the top job of Resident Commissioner.

He knew the whole country – knew it, loathed it, and loved it. He knew the chief tribe, the Maulas, and if he did not loathe them or love them either, he felt for them as a benevolent father feels whose backward sons will never quite grow up, never really leave the nursery. He knew more about the Maulas than the Maulas did themselves: he had known their chiefs, and the men who wanted to be chiefs, and the sly men, and the contented ones, and their relatives, and their quarrels, and their exiles, and their treacheries. He was wedded to the Principality –

'Macmillan of Pharamaul' could have been his title, like Clive of India, Rhodes of Southern Africa. He belonged to it, and to nowhere else.

It had been a hard, dedicated life, a life of endeavour, patience, and little reward. Now he was fifty-seven: he had three modest letters after his name, three more years of service to go, and, when these were run, a pension of thirty-eight eightieths of his salary of £1,750 a year, to live on. When he retired, he would still remain in Pharamaul – a week of playing the awkward, forlorn tourist in London had been enough to decide that. He had no children: his wife had died a decade earlier; he had only one home, and only one family – a hundred and twenty thousand of them. Perhaps the proof of that lay between his hands, in the papers he had drawn out of his briefcase.

It was the manuscript of his book, the book that had occupied all his few spare moments for the last fifteen years, and was still a long way from completion. '*The Principality of Pharamaul*', he read on page one, as he had read a thousand times before. '*The Principality of Pharamaul …*' Was it, after all, an adequate title? In the old days, he knew, it would certainly have been more comprehensive. 'The Principality of Pharamaul,' it would then have read, 'Its Flora and Fauna, with some account of the Principal Tribes (Maulas and U-Maulas), Their Customs and Genealogy, as Seen and Described by Andrew Macmillan, CMG, sometime Her Majesty's Resident Commissioner at Gamate, Native Capital of the Principality …' That might cover it, though it still left out the small, embryo fishing industry near Shebiya …

But how he cherished them, how he had worked for them, how ridiculously he was bound to the whole lazy, dirty, shiftless, stupid collection, and the dry, dusty, straggling mud village where most of them lived. 'The Principality of Pharamaul' – he read again, for the thousandth time, his first ground-out, laboured-over paragraph, – 'came into official existence on the fifteenth day of April 1842, by Royal Decree' – (and, in a footnote underneath, '6 Victoria, Cap 107.') 'A company of Her Majesty's Footguards having been brought in to quell an insurrection which threatened British trading interests, both at Port Victoria and in the interior, they stayed to ensure public order; and thereafter a Lieutenant-Governor, Sir Hugo Fortescue-Hambleton, was appointed (in the words of the proclamation) "to re-establish the rule of law, inculcate the principles of good administration, and work towards such degree of self-determination as the inhabitants' best endeavours, and Her Majesty's Government, may from time to time decide." From that moment, Pharamaul was a British Protectorate under the Crown.

'Pharamaul (latitude 5° East, longitude 22°50' South) is an island some three hundred miles long …' Macmillan sat back, contented at last. He was going home, and this was the home he was going to. He would arrive in time to welcome a new chief, a youngster who had been fifteen years old the last time they had met; but a new chief was nothing to Pharamaul, and nothing to Macmillan either. He had seen them come, and seen them go.

Life went on – not good, not bad, but sufficient; and his own life with it. One day the Maulas would be able to look after themselves; but that day was a long way ahead, and in the meantime it was his appointed job to take care of them.

The navigator, a tall, pale young man with a look of studious detachment, tapped the pilot on the shoulder, and handed him a slip of paper. On it was written a single sentence: 'Halfway there.' Pharamaul Airlines wasted neither time nor money on refinements. No flight information sheet, listing everything from the present ground-speed to the weather awaiting them on arrival, was ever passed aft. No hostess handed round barley sugar, or bent to adjust a safety belt, or discussed life with the eager executive in the rear seat. No stewards served complimentary bottles of Pol Roger '47. A pilot flew the plane, a navigator worked out the position, and tended the radio; at the appropriate moment, he wrote 'Halfway there' on a page torn from his notebook, and passed it up to his chief.

Reading the message now, the Dakota's pilot nodded, raised a thumb, relaxed in his seat again. He knew already that they were halfway there, because the cockpit clock showed one-thirty-five, and on this trip things worked on time, and on nothing else. They were thus at the central point of their journey, the point of no return.

The point of no return ... It had a fine, heroic sound, recalling a score of rotten films, a hundred radio dramas. From this moment, there could be no turning back. From this moment, if anything went wrong, they must press on regardless of danger. The pilot (usually Errol Flynn) must set his teeth, clench his moustache, and endure to the end. Suspended in mortal peril, five thousand feet above a hungry ocean, with three hundred miles behind them, three hundred ahead, they could only mutter 'Roger ... Out ...' and prepare to dice with death. The Wright Brothers gazed down on them from heaven, Charles Lindbergh sat by their side. God the Co-pilot looked over their shoulder, blinking at the unaccustomed dials.

The Dakota's pilot yawned widely, glanced once more at the empty sea, and began to trim his nails.

Across the aisle from Andrew Macmillan – and sometimes eyeing him speculatively, like a lonely stranger in a bar – sat the young man who might have been anything. Tulbach

Browne's estimate was accurate, as it usually was. David Bracken, recent recruit to the Scheduled Territories Office, newly appointed to the Governor's staff at Pharamaul, had not so far settled in any recognizable mould. This was his first overseas job in government service, and he was not yet acclimatized to any of it.

His cards, freshly minted by Smythson's of Bond Street in accordance with standing instructions for officers proceeding overseas, read: 'Mr David Bracken, Secretary, Government Secretariat, Pharamaul'; without such identification, he could have passed for any other kind of young man – journalist, embryo businessman, soldier going on leave, junior barrister on circuit. He was young, fair-haired, pleasant-looking, strongly built: his grey flannel suit became him, his blue tie was negligent and yet appropriate, his brown suede ankle-boots – an affectation on many other men – seemed in his case the right thing to wear.

The ankle-boots were indeed the real clue: if Tulbach Browne had seen them, he would have said 'Brothel-creepers', and classed the young man as an ex-Army type, with a bit of time spent in the Western Desert or in Italy. He would, once more, have been right.

From the career point of view, David Bracken had been caught out by the war, though he wasn't complaining about it and did not really mind. In 1943, when he should have been going to Oxford, he was landing at Salerno: on his twentieth birthday he was in the turret of a tank on the outskirts of Rome: on his twenty-first, in 1945, he was celebrating peace in Paris.

Now, ten years later, he found it hard to say how that decade of peace had really been spent, and if well or ill. He had idled for two years in the Army of Occupation in Berlin: then he had gone up to Oxford after all, to take up normal life where he had left it off. But Oxford at the age of twenty-three, with four years of soldiering and a captaincy in the Royal Armoured Corps behind him, was not the same as Oxford at eighteen, alongside a host of other young men fresh from school. The other young men had been there, of course; but, though he played out his full three years, he had found it impossible to mix with them on anything but the most superficial terms – they always made him feel about a hundred years old, and at times he could not help showing it ... There had followed two years in London, reading for the Bar – but that hadn't worked out either: an excursion into the publishing world, which had left him with a diminished regard for literature, as well as several hundred pounds the poorer; and now this.

'This' was a product of many things: uncertainty, boredom, incipient dedication, a wish to work for something more than a set sum of money every month. If he had been told, a few years earlier, that he would end up as a civil servant, he would have scoffed at the idea – a drab cocoon of cups of tea and pale buff forms could never be his world. But he had discovered the reality to be very different, and now he was committed to it, and he was undeniably glad that this was so.

He had found, as a new recruit in London, that civil servants worked long and thankless hours in dingy surroundings; and that most of them did their particular job, not because it was the best job they could get in a competitive world, but because they believed in it. He found, as far as the Scheduled Territories Office was concerned, that a few people, grossly overworked, dealt with a fantastic number of different human beings, and a huge area of the world's surface – and dealt with them faithfully, carefully, and incorruptibly. He found that he wanted to be part of this service – that it assuaged something within himself that only war in a good cause had hitherto satisfied. He found that he could take all the public derision that seemed to go with the label 'civil servant', if the truth were as rewarding and fulfilling as it had turned out to be.

Now, on his way to Pharamaul, he was hesitant, a little nervous, and happy. His first posting overseas posed a lot of problems, not least the problem of quitting himself well. He had a lot of ideas on colonialism, a lot of ideas on the colour question, a lot of views on British administration, a lot of prejudices, a lot of political preconceptions. Whether they would work out in the field, within the framework he had accepted, was problematical. It would all be very new.

He took out of his pocket a small white booklet, labelled: 'Scheduled Territories Office: Sub-Equatorial Territories', and turned once more to a page he had scanned many times before. It was headed 'Principality of Pharamaul', and it read:

> 'Governor and Commander-in-Chief: Sir Elliott
>   Vere-Toombs, KBE
> Aide-de-Camp: Captain H G Simpson, OBE, RN
> Secretary (Political): A Purves-Brownrigg, CMG
> Secretary: L M Stevens
> Secretary (designate): D Bracken, MC
> Assistant Secretary: Miss N Steuart
> Resident Commissioner (Gamate): A Macmillan, CMG
> District Commissioner (Gamate): G L T Forsdick
> Agricultural and Livestock Officer (Gamate): H J
> Llewellyn
> District Officer (Shebiya): T V Ronald
> Security: Captain K Crump, MC, Royal Pharamaul
> Police.'

He liked, especially, 'Secretary (designate): D Bracken, MC' ... But the total list was a lot of people to get to know – though not a lot of people to administer an island of thirty thousand square miles, and the lives of a hundred and twenty thousand people.

The pilot handed over to the navigator – 'Take it, Joe' was the executive word of command – and, opening the door at the rear of the cockpit, walked aft through the gently swaying aircraft towards the toilet. Usually there were a lot of passengers, and he spoke to none of them; on this occasion there were only four, and he felt safe in acknowledging their presence without fear of getting tied up for half an hour. He nodded cheerfully to the first two: to the third, a youngish chap, he grinned and called out: 'OK?'

'Fine,' said the young man. He leant forward, raising his voice against the engine noises and the vibration. 'When do we get in?'

'About an hour more … We're pretty well on time.'

David Bracken looked up at the pilot's medal ribbons, and said, 'I see you were Battle of the Atlantic.'

'Coastal Command,' said the pilot.

'Ever get to Italy?'

The pilot shook his head. 'No. The sun never shone on us. Based on Londonderry, nearly all the war. Convoys.'

Bracken nodded. It was a different war, and he knew nothing about it. He said, 'It's been a nice quiet trip,' and the pilot smiled, straightened up, and started to move aft again.

To the last passenger, a young negro in a blue serge suit, he was prepared to nod also. But the last passenger was looking out of the window, with an unhappy black face that discouraged any approach. The pilot, shrugging, passed on.

The last passenger, seeing out of the corner of his eye the pilot moving away, turned from the window again. He had been looking away on purpose, because he did not know whether the pilot would nod to him or not, and he did not want to put it to the test. Dinamaula, son of Simaula, grandson of Maula, Hereditary Chieftain of Pharamaul, Prince of Gamate, Son of the Fish, Keeper of the Golden Nail, Urn of the Royal Seed, Ruler and Kingbreaker, Lord of the Known World – Dinamaula had been afraid of being cut.

Such a thought, such an action, would have been inconceivable for him thirty-two hours earlier; because thirty-two hours earlier he had been five thousand miles away, in England, where the air was casually kinder, the feeling vaguely benign, the colour spectrum blurred. But in the intervening time Dinamaula had crossed many frontiers, and a blue sea, and the whole brooding length of Africa. The journey had been an education in the delicate shading of man's regard for man, such as nothing else in his life had so far given him.

Thirty-two hours earlier, and five thousand miles away, he had been a young chief-designate – Chief Dinamaula, head of some tribe in Africa ('or somewhere – be nice to him, anyway'), a free man in a fine city, free to walk into a considerable number of selected hotels in London, free to sit down and order a meal costing as much as a pound, in any restaurant that had no particular table-reservation plan. Free to traverse any street, and hardly be stared at at all: free to book a room at any seaside hotel, and to claim it (in lots of places all round the coast) with scarcely any embarrassment; free to be interviewed ('Chief Dinamaula on the Threat of Communism'), free to broadcast ('Chief Dinamaula on Hookworm in Tanganyika'), free to revisit Oxford ('Six Hundred Overseas Students in Record Rally'). In England he had been a Chief.

Two thousand miles further south, in Kano, Nigeria, he had also been a Chief – a Chief of a foreign state, in a country where such chiefs had recently been allowed to take the reins: a black Chief in a black man's playground. A Deputation of Honour had met him on the airfield, and borne him off for an hour's talk, an hour's slow coffee drinking, an hour's elaborate courtesy. His hosts, rulers of their own free land, had been far too polite even to hint that Dinamaula, Chief of a British Protectorate, was still firmly under tutelage, and of lesser account than they. They had talked instead of land reform, taxes, cattle-culling, rain … In Kano it had been wonderful.

Another two thousand miles further on, at Livingstone, in the Rhodesias, he had been a chief – a black man in a country where an uncertain black–white partnership was groping for the outlines of the future. No deputation here, no recognition – but instead, the modest fellowship of a normal transit-stop. He had drunk his coffee side by side with the next two people off the plane – a white lawyer *en route* for Cape Town, a white American destined for a job in the Copper Belt. There had been no special ease, and no unease either. Each thought his own thoughts, each lit his own cigarette.

In Windhoek – last town in Southern Africa, before taking off for Pharamaul – he had been a chief. 'Non-European Lounge', said the notice, with an accompanying arrow; and when, feeling thirsty, he had turned away, and lined up at the fly-blown counter with the rest of the passengers, and asked for a cup of coffee, the girl's indicative hand had looked like the arrow – pointing off-stage, pointing always somewhere else. Presently, ashamed, he had reached the end of that arrow, and had found the sort of room he had expected – small, dusty, labelled 'Non-Europeans – *Nie Blankes*' in forbidding Gothic script. Part of him thought that perhaps this clear label was better than England's dubious *bonhomie*, part of him revolted, at so concise a discrimination.

15

He had wished that someone would interview him at that moment: 'Chief Dinamaula on Colour Bar' ... Then he had strayed into the wrong lavatory. '*Slegs Vir Blankes*' said the label this time: 'Whites Only' – and he hadn't noticed it in time, and the station janitor had pointed it out to him, in choice phrases drawn from a long history of Teutonic superiority; and then, at the word of command, he had got into the aircraft, and sat in the rear seat without being told to, and looked steadfastly out of the window. In this part of the world, he was an African chief.

It was the first time in seven years that he had been conscious, not that he was black – for the point was driven home a hundred times a day, even in so flattering a climate as London – but that he was inferior.

Examining his inward thoughts, he found that he had been completely knocked off his balance – which, at the age of twenty-two, was mortifying and ridiculous. But perhaps twenty-two was no very advanced age, if the preceding seven years had been spent far away from one's own country, in the kindly air of England ... Dinamaula had left his home at Gamate when he was fifteen years old, in pursuit of a plan, proposed by the Administration and backed by his father, for educating him completely in England. He had been to a great public school – almost the first, and certainly the strictest discipline he had ever known; he had been to Oxford, and had graduated with a passable Law degree; now his father was dead, and he was returning to Pharamaul to claim his inheritance.

He was by now somewhat uncertain of the latter, too ... Pharamaul he remembered as a rough, featureless country, cultivated haphazardly on principles as old as the plough itself, devoted for the most part to stringy scrub cattle and enormous flocks of goats. Gamate, when he was born, had been (and doubtless still was) an untidy straggle of mud huts, sprawling like dusty beehives across two valleys and sheltering over a hundred thousand people – and many more goats; and the people themselves he knew to be largely backward, unenterprising folk, degenerating in the northern parts to a simple, uncontrollable savagery.

They were like children – Dinamaula had no illusions about the fact: smart, flip children in the south, round the slums of Port Victoria: dull, cloddish children at Gamate: cruel, magic-ridden children in the wild north. None of them in the least resembled an Oxford graduate with a degree in Law; at a London party, among the tea cups and the glasses and the clipped political talk and the strangely adoring women, they would have stood out as ragged, brutish, undeniably dirty.

When his Chelsea friends argued about immediate self-government for Pharamaul (with proportional representation, a second, consultative chamber, a loaded ballot in the rural areas) they were thinking of Dinamaula himself, not of the backward, peasant Maulas at Gamate (who did not know what a vote was) or the jungle U-Maulas up country (who could not have told a loaded ballot from a poisoned arrow).

His London friends did not understand about these people, or they shut their eyes to them, or they wanted to wave a wand and turn them all, in the course of a single weekend, into completely emancipated, skilled mechanics earning time-and-a-half on Saturdays. Dinamaula *did* know about them; his eyes were fully, sometimes fearfully open, and he wanted to do something about it – something about everything.

He was their chief, their father; he had journeyed into far lands, seen buildings as tall as ten trees, heard magic voices coming from a box on a table. A table was a thing of wood, square, like so ... He was their chief, their father. Let him then play the man.

Dinamaula became aware that someone was standing above him; and he looked up, to find that one of his three fellow passengers – an oldish, smallish, nondescript man in a rumpled seersucker suit – had paused by his seat. As he raised his eyebrows inquiringly: 'Hallo!' said Tulbach Browne. 'Just stretching my legs ... Is this your first trip?'

Dinamaula smiled, recognizing in the stranger's look and tone the basic English just to demonstrate broadmindedness. This man would really have preferred to talk to one of the two other white passengers aboard the plane: therefore he had chosen the only negro.

'No,' he answered. 'I've flown before ... Won't you sit down?' Tulbach Browne eased himself into the vacant chair, and extended his hand. 'I'm Tulbach Browne of the *Daily Thresh*.'

Dinamaula usually read the *Daily Telegraph*, but he had heard of Tulbach Browne. 'I'm happy to meet you,' he said formally. 'Of course I know your name well. Mine is Dinamaula.'

Tulbach Browne nodded, not really hearing. 'Going home?'

'Yes. Pharamaul is my home. At Gamate, the capital. Are you coming to write about' – he was on the point of saying 'them', but he changed it to – 'us?'

Tulbach Browne grinned. 'If there's anything interesting to write. I've just been in South Africa.'

'A troubled country,' said Dinamaula correctly.

'It's a screwed-up mess ... Ever spent any time there?'

'No.'

'Lucky for you. They don't like nig – negroes in South Africa.'

'Pharamaul is different,' said Dinamaula.

'I wonder.'

'I know.' Dinamaula was suddenly annoyed: he could never decide which was the worst – the man who said 'nigger' and meant it, or the man who didn't say 'nigger', but felt it, and covered up that feeling by a spurious comradeship. This man was another barbarian … 'I know,' he repeated. 'I am Chief Dinamaula.'

'Chief …' Tulbach Browne looked at him, instantly wary, instantly working. 'You must be – you've been at Oxford.'

Dinamaula inclined his head. 'Yes.' Normal words would not come. He said stiltedly, almost biblically: 'I am that man.'

Tulbach Browne looked sideways at Dinamaula again. He saw now a tall, slim, good-looking negro: with neat clothes, a lightish skin, an air of courage and breeding. It could be *real* material … He said, briskly: 'This is a very lucky meeting,' and set himself to stir, to probe, and to lay bare.

Far ahead of them, a smudge of purple rose up out of the sea, topped by a wavering cloudline at its nearer edge. The Island of Pharamaul was now their new horizon.

The Dakota's pilot nodded to himself, recognizing for the hundredth time the shape of Pharamaul from nearly a hundred miles away – vague, undefined, only a little darker than the sea itself. It began slowly to fill the whole western edge of their world, attaining birth as a new land, where for hours before there had been nothing but empty ocean. He wondered, as he had wondered scores of times since reading a magazine article during the war, whether Pharamaul could be the lost Atlantis that so many ancients had sworn to. It was only a little bit to the south.

He disengaged the automatic pilot, throttled back slightly, and leaning forward started the aircraft on a very slow, very gentle descent to sea level. Behind him the navigator began talking, monotonously, into a hand microphone. His lips formed a continuous muttering chain of the words 'Port Victoria Tower ... Port Victoria Tower ...' But as yet, only a faint crackling answered him. Awaiting them, prone in the afternoon heat, Pharamaul still slept.

The plane had suddenly tilted and jerked, and two of the passengers, who had been reading, looked up, and then caught each other's eye; and now, after four or five quick questions at the end of a two-hour silence, they were suddenly in tune. Spanning a quarter of a century, both ex-soldiers, both civil servants, both bound to the same task, Andrew Macmillan and David Bracken now shared an identical world.

'You're replacing Morrison.' Macmillan grinned. 'He wasn't much good.'

'Why not?'

'Usual Government House disease. Nothing to do, too much duty-free liquor.'

'You're up at Gamate?'

'Yes. The Residency has always been there. That's where we do all the work.'

'What's it like?'

'Hot. Dusty. Half asleep, except after the harvest – then they're drunk all the time. There's a lot of routine stuff – poll tax, inspection of cattle, soil conservation, inoculation, trying to knock some sense into their thick heads.'

'What are the Maulas like, as a tribe?'

'Backward. Some of them just down from the trees. But we look after them, all right.'

'Are they –' David Bracken searched for the right word, – 'are they capable of managing their own affairs? Is there any sort of political advancement?'

Andrew Macmillan stared, then shook his head. 'You've got to forget all that stuff. They're just simple, backward children. We look after them.'

'But what are we doing about it?'

'About what?'

'About their being backward. About teaching them to run their own country.'

'They could never run their own country.'

'But in the future?'

'The future is a long way ahead. It may come: there are one or two bright sparks already. But not now. Now, we teach them not to over-graze their lands, not to keep too many goats, not to doctor themselves with dried toadskin and manure, not to kill a man because he takes someone else's wife, not to let rainwater run to waste, not to do anything drastic about twins … I can't think of much else. It's a slow process. It's mostly "not". But we look after them.'

'And schools?'

'There's a school. Damned good one. New. Cost us three thousand pounds. And a mission – Father Schwemmer. And a town band. And a hotel of sorts. And a native tax office. And a tribal management committee. And a little hospital … Gamate is all right.'

'How many people there?'

'A hundred thousand. It's the native capital. And about three men and a boy to run the whole show. I've been there for over thirty years.'

'You must love it.'

'Well …'

'I'm looking forward to seeing it, anyway.'

'Better bring your oldest clothes.'

At about the same time, five seats behind them in the rear of the plane, Tulbach Browne was saying to Dinamaula:

'That's an interesting idea of yours. I've always thought that modern methods of farming, and – er – water conservation, could transform a backward economy almost overnight. The trouble is, of course, to get the officials moving … Do you anticipate a lot of obstruction?'

'That I do not know.' Dinamaula smiled hesitantly. 'You must remember that I've been away for seven years. I'm not in touch with what Government has been doing. And then, of course, my own people – not all of them can understand these things, not all of them are ready for such changes.'

'You mean, there's a conservative element who would resist anything that might threaten their own position in the tribe.'

'Conservative, yes. Backward, perhaps.'

'Reactionary?'

Dinamaula sighed. Already he was tired of this man, who clung and sucked like a blue-grass tick, and, when questioning, slid the answering words upon one's own tongue. He said, 'There are many things to be taken care of. We shall see.'

The warning sign: 'Fasten your seat belts', glowed suddenly from up ahead. Tulbach Browne sat up, preparing to go back to his seat.

'I'd like to come up to Gamate and see you, as soon as you've settled in.'

'You will be welcome,' answered Dinamaula politely. 'We live simply, of course. I hope you won't be disappointed.'

'I'll look forward to it.'

The Dakota turned northwards on a slow banking curve, preparing for its run-in. The whole lower half of Pharamaul now lay before them, framed by sparkling sea, emerging into detail – the rim of surf round the coastline, the smoke over the waterfront at Port Victoria, the dark rolling country that swept northwards till it vanished into haze.

The island was shaped like a huge black tear, pendulous, swelling, ready – centuries ahead – to drop from the Equator.

CHAPTER TWO

❖

If Tulbach Browne had noticed that Pharamaul was shaped like a tear, he would have muttered: 'Damned appropriate, too,' and inserted at least a paragraph about this unhappy black nation which, born of brutality and commercial lust, still wept bitterly for its century-long enslavement. He would have been wrong. Pharamaul had had a normal history: slow, tentative, advancing here, retreating there, bloodied at times by strife, cruelty, and greed; but normal – normal for Africa.

Like countless other parts of the inhabited globe, Pharamaul owed its entire existence, as a country, to Great Britain; otherwise, as India or the West Indies or enormous stretches of Africa, it would have remained a global nonentity, eternally torn by strife, weakened by disease and indolence, and condemned to remain in the jungle shadows for another three or four hundred years. But Pharamaul had been lucky – as Andrew Macmillan's first paragraph had tried to indicate.

At the turn of the last century, intermittent trade had given Pharamaul the only status it seemed likely to enjoy. Its salt fish had sustained the endurance (and tortured the thirst) of passing mariners: its groundnuts had been pressed for oil and rough cattle feed; and the cattle themselves, though no prizewinners for looks or condition, had provided a modest export quota of hides and just-eatable beef. In addition, a little slavery, centred on the dark interior, had buttressed the prosperity of Bristol and Liverpool. Thus Pharamaul, when Queen Victoria took the throne, had been an authentic part of the African pattern: a debased and negative tributary which made a few men rich, a few more men contented in hard employment, and innumerable others doomed to permanent subjection.

Then it had a stroke of luck – and once more, the pattern followed countless other patterns south of the Equator. Tribal strife, which hitherto had been tolerated and possibly encouraged as a convenient bloodletting, at last threatened something which was important and even sacred to the outside world: the free flow of trade. Bands of tribesmen from the interior, having conquered all opponents, within their immediate view, roamed southwards and began to challenge the white settlers moving inland from the coast. This, of course, was serious … Men who had access to the right ear in the city of London spoke the appropriate word: Britain intervened, intent as always on the preservation of life and limb, however remote, however unworthy. The usual warship was sent, the usual regiment plodded ashore, cursing the sun and gesticulating at the flies. They did the best they could, their foes being enteric, heat, dust, and swarming black warriors of undoubted valour and patent skill. Soon, it became clear that the forces of law and order would have to stay where they were for an indefinite time.

It was part of a very old process, a process that had extended and made safe many other boundaries of the known world. Great Britain, having arrived to pacify and discipline, remained to educate and administer.

It cost her the lives of innumerable younger sons of clergymen and merchants, as well as adventurous types unemployable in any other sphere; it paid (again, like India) a very small tribute in terms of trade and treasure. It was just another part of the British Empire, annexed haphazard, and remaining under guard ever afterwards. For since the tribal feuds continued, authority moved north, intent on extending the safety of its frontiers; soon, the whole of Pharamaul had come under the loose dominion of Britain, whose dedicated exiles moved in to work, sweat, rule, exist, and die, generation by generation, little knowing that they were fulfilling an historic role, even as they cursed their fate, and stared biliously at their wives.

Then, in counter-dominion, a black dynasty emerged in Pharamaul, impelled to power by a dominant tribe. They called themselves the Maulas, after their newest and strongest chief, a bloody ruffian called Maula, whose pattern of command was later to be copied by such diverse characters as Stalin, Villa, Dingaan, Kemal Atatürk and Hitler. Maula – Maula the Great – brought order to a troubled country: making laws which had to be kept, killing off all challengers to his rule, exiling the break-away, discontented tribe of U-Maulas (literally, 'Not Maulas') to the miserable jungle that lay to the north of Gamate.

Maula the Great might have done a lot of other things: he might conceivably have marched on Port Victoria, where a supine British governor was eking out his declining years with overt drinking bouts and furtive excursions to the black brothel quarter. But instead, Maula came under the influence of a travelling missionary father from South Austria; spent much time with a brilliant, godlike District Commissioner called Hayes – the kind of man who, time and again, emerged to dedicate his entire sweating life to Britain's overseas dominion; fell in love with British rule and a garish photogravure of Queen Victoria, and survived to attend her Diamond Jubilee in 1897.

His son, Simaula, saw the crowning of King George V; his grandson, Dinamaula, had, as a wide-eyed young man of nineteen, viewed the coronation of Queen Elizabeth II from a modest seat half hidden behind a pillar in Westminster Abbey.

The country which this Dinamaula was now to rule had never become rich: the sun burned too hotly, farming methods were too wasteful, the Maulas themselves too indolent and dull. But under the British wing, it had prospered wonderfully, when compared with the savagery and chaos from which it had sprung. In the last hundred years, pacification had brought trade, trade had brought settlers, settlers had geared up the whole economy of the island, to something like a European level. In Port Victoria, there was now a modern abattoir, to handle the cattle coming down from the Gamate plains: a big logging camp up north, on the fringe of the U-Maula country, kept the Port Victoria sawmills busy most of the year round. A scheme for fish canning, on the coast near Shebiya's 'Fish Village', was even now grinding through its governmental paperwork stage, towards actuality.

Pharamaul's position on the Cape trade route gave it obvious strategic importance: as a result, an oiling and bunkering station had been added to the port, and a small repair dockyard which had done useful work in two world wars. Now tourists came, to spend a few weeks in guaranteed sunshine: easy-life settlers enjoyed the cheap living and the unlimited servants: hard-working immigrants disembarked to carve a life from this blossoming economy; civil servants arrived to shoulder the dreary burden of administration in a hot climate.

Formal government sat at Port Victoria: the Governor's white stone mansion dominated the residential quarter, the Secretariat crouched in its shade: downtown, a town council of solid citizens dealt with the drains, housing, harbour pollution, street lighting, public health, and four civic celebrations a year – Armistice Day, Empire Day, the Queen's Birthday, and Pharamaul's own Foundation Day on April 15th.

Field government was centred two hundred miles away to the north, at the end of Pharamaul's only railway line. There, at Gamate, sat a Resident Commissioner in whose charge were a hundred thousand souls, concentrated in one of the biggest 'native villages' south of the Equator.

Government of any sort faded north of Gamate, where the dry ranchlands gave place to jungle, and the Maulas to the U-Maulas. A single District Officer – one of Andrew Macmillan's staff – camped out at Shebiya, the U-Maula capital: his only link was a radio schedule, his only strength a white skin and a twelve-bore shotgun.

Such was the present pattern, built up over the years. The Principality of Pharamaul was the end result of contribution – contribution for a variety of reasons. Britain had come to annex, and remained to administer. Farmers and traders had opened the country up, and taken their substantial cut: other devoted men had served out their time, with no cut at all. It was one of many such patterns that encircled and enriched the globe.

For the natives themselves, of course, the process of advancement had been slow. Intellectual opinion in London always saw Pharamaul as a product of reactionary and oppressive rule from Whitehall, and called fiercely for progress in all directions – like the valiant strategists who had demanded a 'second front' so early in 1942. But progress, measurable progress, had in fact reared its pretty head … Health, agriculture, water conservation, the general standard of living – all had improved under a century of British rule.

At least three decimating tropical diseases had been eradicated, despite murderous opposition from Maula medical opinion. Literacy, starting at nil in 1842, had now reached thirty per cent – worse than England, immeasurably better than the rest of Africa. Fewer children died in infancy, fewer mothers, their loins smeared with cow dung, their ears assailed by incantations, succumbed to childbirth. Drought, held in check by careful water conservation, struck once every ten years, instead of every other year. Soil clung to the earth, instead of washing seawards in the muddy suppuration that meant ruin to men and animals alike.

Law ruled: thieves and murderers were often caught: fathers whose daughters had been raped now found it at least worthwhile to file a complaint. Here and there, a Maula student attained a level of education comparable with the white world outside, and was sent to Britain (at the expense of the British taxpayer) to be taught the plays of Aeschylus and the maxims of leadership and responsibility. Once there, of course, he was likely to be taken up, lionized, and reassigned to mediocrity by professional enthusiasts who wanted to wave a wand and give Pharamaul its 'freedom' – regardless of whether it was yet fitted to handle that delicate and explosive commodity.

Most of these students reacted and went to the bad. If they stayed in London, they frittered away their lives as disgruntled expatriates on the fringe of the Communist party; if they returned to Pharamaul, they became mutinous near-gangsters, preying on the locations of Port Victoria. Some few of them managed to keep their heads.

Such a one was Dinamaula. He had had his share of lionization, he had met many men like Tulbach Browne, ready to prime him to discontent for the sake of a story, and many women, ready for almost anything in their missionary pursuit of One World. But he had also met, in Oxford and London, older men of greater sense and balance. On returning to take up his inheritance, he was, apart from a nostalgic ambition to improve, almost uninfected by what many others had found a lethal overdose of civilization.

II

Tulbach Browne of the *Daily Thresh*, sweating in the humid cage that was Port Victoria's best hotel, his fingers slippery on the typewriter keys, had already, within twenty-four hours, filed his first Pharamaul story. It was, in its airtight assumption of wisdom, its question-begging, and its incontestable malice, one of his best efforts, and tailored to the *Daily Thresh* pattern like a whore to a bed.

'Yesterday,' wrote Tulbach Browne, 'I had the privilege of talking to one of the most remarkable young men ever to come out of Africa. He is Dinamaula, descendant of a long line of Maula strong men, a gifted African now returning from a brilliant career at Oxford to assume the chieftainship of the Principality of Pharamaul.

'He does so at a difficult moment, and his chieftainship is likely to be a mockery of the word.

'Life has moved on, even in this entrenched backwater of British administration; men like Dinamaula – and there are, thank God, many such – have heard of democracy, progress, science, even if the local Civil Service moguls can't tell these things from the holes in their inkpots, and he is keen – burningly, crusadingly keen – to apply these things to his own country.

'Dinamaula has virile plans, which he outlined to me in an inspiring three-hour session on board the plane to Pharamaul, for the expansion, reform, and development of his beloved homeland: blessings too long denied to this forgotten corner of a backward continent.

'Will he succeed? I do not know, and Dinamaula, for all his fresh enthusiasm and undoubted talent, does not know either.

' "I do not know," he told me, in his attractive, musical voice, "whether there will be any obstruction from officials, when my far-reaching plans for agricultural and political development become known.

' "There are reactionary elements in the tribe, too," he warned me, "who may resist change." His dark eyes flashed. "But they will be taken care of."

'But can he succeed, this lineal descendant of a dynasty of chiefs who have constantly prodded their British "masters" from indolence to intermittent activity? That is the question which is being guardedly discussed, at this very moment, in a hundred back-street hovels, a hundred miserable mud huts in this derelict, disgraceful corner of the British Empire.

'The proud, dispossessed Maulas hope against hope that it may be so. Myself, I take leave to doubt it. Indeed, nothing that I have seen of British officialdom so far, indicates that there is any possibility of Dinamaula finding a sympathetic ear. He, of course, though chief's blood runs strong in his veins, is beyond the pale, where Pharamaul's shopworn white "society" is concerned.

'It is typical of this place that I could not even take him to the local club for an evening "sun-downer". The club, like every thing else in Port Victoria, is rubber-stamped: "White Men Only".

'Pharamaul, tonight, is hot and sticky. Officialdom, tonight and every night, is cold – and sticky. But still the other Pharamaul waits, brooding in patient silence, for Dinamaula to assume the mantle of chief, and to bring them hope for the future. He is, indeed, their only hope.

'His plans are far-reaching, statesmanlike, eminently wise. His chance of forcing them through, in the face of

British officials worried about nothing worse than their next pay-increment, their next shipment of cheap gin from London, are slim – slim as this young and gallant chief himself.

'TOMORROW: The Cocked Hat Brigade of Pharamaul.'

III

Sir Elliott Vere-Toombs, KBE, Governor and Commander-in-Chief of the Principality of Pharamaul, sat behind a leather-topped desk at one end of his study. It was a large room, pine-panelled, floridly carpeted: it was well-proportioned and lofty, the best room in the Secretariat. But, for all that, it was still a hot, humid, and airless box: the fingers of the sun pierced the slatted blinds, the fans whirred and chattered unceasingly, striving against the motionless, languid air. This was an afternoon in Pharamaul – torrid, sleepy, defeating.

Sir Elliott drew a faded khaki handkerchief from his sleeve, and mopped his brow. He was a small spare man, with a high beaked nose and a prim mouth: his dry wrinkled skin and bleached hair proclaimed that heat was no stranger to him. Indeed, heat – often murderous heat – had always beset the long pathway of his official life: the heat of Bengal, Kenya, Ceylon, the West Indies, Hong Kong – all those places to which England exiled her pro-consuls, with orders to maintain the Queen's Peace, no matter what the temperature. He was sixty-one: Pharamaul would be his last bout with the subtropics. After that, the genteel breezes of Bournemouth, the neat chills of Cheltenham, would be his portion until he died. On an afternoon such as this, with the thermometer at an unequivocal ninety-eight degrees, one might be forgiven for looking forward to the change ... His grey Palm Beach suit wilting against his small body, the Governor opened a drawer at the side of his desk.

On the pad before him lay a six-page draft despatch beginning: 'My Lord, I have the honour to submit a report bearing upon the import position in the Principality – ' a despatch so detailed, so pedestrian, and so damnably dull that he could bear to look at it no longer. Within the drawer, secure from anyone's sight save his own, lay his stamp collection. Guiltily, warily, Sir Elliott concentrated on that.

It was an oddly varied collection, containing only the stamps of those countries in which Sir Elliott had served; he had started it as a young man at the outset of his career, when sixteen months in the tropical heat of the Ivory Coast, with nothing whatever to do, had dictated the need for a hobby. Sometimes the sections were small, when promotion had moved him on swiftly: sometimes, as in the case of Hong Kong, a setback in his career had at least resulted in a hundred-percent philatelic coverage. It was sad to think that the collection was now so near its end.

But there were still gaps in the Pharamaul pages that must be filled; missing were such gems as the surcharged Cape Triangulars of 1860, the overprinted South West Africans of 1882, the rare inverted Pharamaul Black of 1890. Sir Elliott was sure that these were to be found, somewhere in Port Victoria (he never cheated by buying from the Stanley Gibbons catalogue); somewhere there must be collections of old letters, old receipts, old legal documents that would fill these gaps for him. It would be disastrous to leave before they came to light.

His hot, gentle fingers smoothed the pages. He dreamed of attic discoveries until there was a knock on the door, when swiftly and furtively he closed the drawer again, and turned back to the despatch. He was thus respectably discovered when the door opened.

It opened slowly, and the girl who presently emerged did so at a very deliberate pace indeed. She knew all about the Governor's stamp collection: she was young enough to find it funny, warm-hearted enough to think it pathetic. And not for the world would she have embarrassed such a nice old poppet ... Nicole Steuart, at the age of twenty-four, finding herself not only the best-looking girl in thirty thousand tropical square miles, but also entangled in a strange, dry-as-dust job in this imperial backwater, still wanted neither to trade on the one, nor to lose the other.

She was young, happy, and interested, in this odd, man-made, protocol-ridden world which yet seemed to be doing good rather than bad ... If it meant nursing old Sir Elliott, and not noticing when he had a lazy spell and sneaked off to his stamp collection, then she could still handle it – any time.

As she came forward, the Governor sighed, as much for her loveliness as for the interruption. If only the world were blessed with mint-condition Pharamaul Blacks, and girls as beautiful as this one, *and nothing else* ... He smiled a tired smile, and said, 'Yes, Nicole?'

This was a Christian-name Secretariat: it was really too hot for anything more formal.

'It's Mr Bracken, Sir Elliott. You said you'd see him. He's here now.'

'Very well.' His smile reappeared, this time less automatic. 'What's he like?'

Nicole Steuart smiled back. 'All right ... They're all the same when they're new, aren't they?'

'What a very disillusioned remark! What are they *all* like?'

'Oh – young – keen – nervous – feeling the heat, wanting to please.'

Sir Elliott coughed, reminding himself that Nicole Steuart (Higher Executive Officer) was talking about Mr

Bracken (Acting Principal). There was, or should have been, a world of difference.

'I'll ring,' he said, formally. 'I just want to – er – finish this despatch.'

'Yes, Sir Elliott.'

Nicole Steuart withdrew, not at all abashed. The formal tone, she knew, was part of the drill, made necessary by the fact that she herself was a lot of conflicting things – pretty, a junior secretary, a machine, a privileged young woman. It should have been confusing, but all it added up to was the job she liked … She shut the door carefully behind her, and said to the waiting young man: 'He's busy at the moment … Not for long, though. Won't you sit down?'

David Bracken, caught between the agonizing cross-fires of a first interview with the Governor, and the nearness of a girl whose fresh beauty, dark hair, and candid shapeliness had knocked him flat, answered foolishly: 'Yes, please.'

Alone again, the Governor reread for the third time the pen-and-ink letter that was nearly as interesting as the stamp collection – the letter from the Permanent Under-Secretary in Whitehall.

It was good to see Andrew Macmillan here, [*wrote the Permanent Under-Secretary*]. What an admirable man he is, and what a lot he knows about Pharamaul! But we all thought he looked over-done, rather below par, even at the end of his leave. Don't work him too hard, will you? He's much too good to lose.

I enjoyed, also, a long talk with Dinamaula, just before he left London. I think he will be all right – he is able and pleasant, perhaps a little on the visionary, corner-cutting side, but he has resisted Chelsea-ization to a satisfactory degree. As you know, the Oxford career was far from brilliant, and he only just scraped a pass-degree; but the same could be said of a lot of us! I fear the Cherwell and the High – not to speak of the Randolph Hotel – exhibit far too many counter-attractions.

However, Dinamaula seems keen to get to work, and he should be useful in livening up some of your old tribal conservatives.

As you will have seen from the postings, I am sending you a young man, David Bracken, to take Morrison's place. He is a "Late Entry", but has caught on to the work here quickly, and we all liked him. He should do well.

Take care of yourself. My regards to Kitty.

The Governor sighed again. It was a hot day for seeing people, and he had already had long sessions both with Macmillan and Dinamaula. Macmillan he trusted like his own right hand: Dinamaula had puzzled him. It might be true that England had not spoilt him, but it had certainly put his head in the clouds, as far as Pharamaul was concerned. He had talked, for example, of rehousing at Gamate, of drainage schemes, of cattle registration – things which the Maulas themselves still scorned and resisted, with the same unbroken front as they had shown for at least a hundred years. The progress to be made there, even with the best will in the world on both sides, must always be at a snail's pace …

It was to be hoped that Dinamaula was not going to unsettle everything, at the outset of a new chieftainship. The latter, in itself, was likely to be disturbing enough, with an Old Gang of regents to be seen off the premises, and youth installed at the helm.

But Macmillan had said, 'Everything will be all right. He's new, that's all.' Macmillan knew what he was talking about ... Sir Elliott pressed the bell, for David Bracken to be shown in.

Their interview lasted an hour, and was unexpectedly satisfactory to both sides. The Governor knew how to talk to young men: a lifetime spent in such jobs as this, with a shifting staff arriving, serving out their time, and leaving again in two or three or four years, had given him a ready-made vocabulary of inquiry, assessment, and inspiration. He found that he liked this particular young man: he was a trifle more mature than the run-of-the-mill entry, a trifle less ready to take opinion on trust; but that was the way of the world nowadays, and presumably the Scheduled Territories Office must choose its recruits from contemporary human beings ... Bracken, on his side, was disarmed by a man who he knew had had a distinguished career (and, on one occasion in Bengal, a notably brave one) in the service of his country, but who could still talk in simple and direct terms of a beginner's problems in administration. Sir Elliott Vere-Toombs might look like a typical old cup of tea from the higher strata of the Colonial Civil Service: he might be a figure of fun to a newspaperman or a cartoonist; but he had two rare and patent qualities – honesty and devotion – which should never be sold short on any market.

Only once, across a chasm of thirty years, did they discover a measure of disagreement.

The operative word had been 'self-determination'.

'Don't you think, sir,' asked David Bracken at one point, when they had been discussing other parts of Africa, 'that a place like Pharamaul is bound to fall into the pattern of the rest of this part of the world?'

'Of course.' The Governor raised his eyebrows. 'It is part of the pattern already. It's not in Africa, of course, but it's close enough to the coast – like Madagascar on the other side – to take its colour from the mainland.'

'That means, then – self-determination.'

'Self-determination?' The Governor sniffed at the word like an amiable inquisitor. 'It depends what you mean by that very elastic term.'

'I meant, like the Gold Coast, or perhaps parts of the Rhodesias – progress towards independence.'

'My dear fellow,' said the Governor, leaning back again, 'that is *not* what self-determination means to me.'

'But, sir, you said they're part of the same pattern.'

'Certainly. But the pattern is the most varied one in the world. The whole of Africa is a pattern – a pattern of change, variety, frequent anomaly. What is appropriate in one part is unthinkable in another. What is appropriate for one *man* would be laughable for his brother across the street ... Self-determination means, to *me*, that a particular people – like the Maulas – will be encouraged to do the very best they can with their own resources and at their own level of development. You can't hurry the thing up, and you certainly can't apply a different set of rules or an advanced programme, just because somewhere else, in a totally different part of Africa, there are some negroes who could knock spots off most lawyers or politicians in the outside world.' He drew breath. 'Africa contains eleven million square miles, and a hundred and fifty million people. Pharamaul is an infinitesimal part of it – say, point one per cent. It *has* self-determination – together with the continuing help it needs from us. But to give it the same self-determination – ' Bracken was aware that the words were taking on a derisive significance, ' – as a country like Nigeria, would ruin it overnight.'

David Bracken smiled. It was the only thing to do. 'Things will stay much as they are, then?'

'I hope so.' The Governor looked at him, alert for radical nonconformity, and yet aware that this young man was searching for an equitable formula for all the world – as he himself had searched, thirty years before. 'I hope so … The thing works, David.' (The Christian name was like a membership card for the only club one wanted to join.) 'They really are a backward lot, as you'll discover before long. Occasionally they throw up a first-class man: old Maula himself was a very considerable statesman, though a complete barbarian in many other ways, and Dinamaula may become the same sort of character, in good time. But basically, they are – ' the Governor hesitated: the word 'savages' had been on his tongue, but it was not quite appropriate. 'They are very simple people. We will have to help them, for a very long while.'

'That was what Macmillan said on the plane.'

'A wise man, Macmillan … Now let's see about your office, and things like that. My secretary will take you round.'

IV

David Bracken closed the door behind him.

'Feeling better?' asked Nicole Steuart.

'Fine,' answered Bracken – and he meant it. He looked at the girl: she was as pretty as he remembered, even when sitting behind a desk so strewn with papers, files, letters, cables, and typing paraphernalia that she seemed like part of a chaotic filing system herself. 'He – the Governor said you'd show me round.'

Nicole Steuart nodded. 'We'll do that … Where were you before this?'

'London.' He perched on the arm of a chair, and looked down at her. It was an agreeable view. 'Is it always as hot as this?'

'This isn't so bad. It's nearly spring, after all … Where before London?'

'Nowhere. I was new.' He began to be nettled, by this cool-looking girl who could survive a temperature of ninety-plus, to put him through the hoop. 'What about you?'

Nicole smiled. 'I'm new, too. I came out here on a holiday, two years ago.'

'Oh?'

'I liked it.' She stared at him. 'Loved it, in fact. I asked for a job here. There was a lot of discussion, people turned a few somersaults, and then they gave me a job.'

'What did you like about it?'

'It's worthwhile. There are plenty of places like Pharamaul, I suppose, only I hadn't heard of them. People need our help. We give it to them. No strings attached. It's something we've been doing for hundreds of years.' She was very pretty, very serious. 'It's worthwhile,' she repeated. 'That's what one thinks, all the time.'

'But do we do enough for them?'

'All we can.'

'Things could move a good deal faster, surely?'

'I used to think that. Now I'm not so sure. Africa's a slow continent. Speed could ruin everything. When you've been here a bit longer, you'll understand that.'

'You've only been here two years.'

She smiled again, less warmly. 'It's longer than two hours.'

There was something between them already – not an antagonism, but a readiness to do battle. She's very pretty, he thought, but she has these opinions ... At the same moment, Nicole was thinking, a little incoherently: nice-looking, prejudiced, ready-made ideas, a bit priggish, but he's here for a long time ... She stood up.

'Let's walk round,' she said. 'You'd better meet the rest of the staff.'

They walked round. It was a somewhat confused process, not aided by the oppressive heat, and the fact that the Secretariat was an untidy jumble of rooms, thrown together as the need for expansion had dictated during the last fifty years. David Bracken met a lot of girls in the cypher room. He met the Governor's Social Secretary – a forbidding woman who looked at him as if he were trying to graduate from the Garden Party List to the Dinner Party Pool. He met some more girls in a room labelled: 'Typists. Leave This Door Open.' He met a man called Stevens, a secretary at the same level as himself. He met a booming character whose cheerful sweating face owed much to the heat, more to pink gin – Captain Simpson, the Naval aide-de-camp. He met the Political Secretary, Purves-Brownrigg, and thought, after a few moments: oh God, one of those.

'So glad you got here safely,' said Purves-Brownrigg, as if Bracken had hacked his way through a dozen enemy columns to reach Port Victoria. 'Nicole, darling, you look *ravishing*. So cool, too.'

Purves-Brownrigg himself looked pre-eminently cool: his dove-grey lightweight suit was immaculate, his fair hair a miracle of neatness.

'I'm Aidan Purves-Brownrigg,' he said, holding out a slim hand. 'The only Foreign Office type among you rough Scheduled people … Did you have a nice journey?'

'Very,' said Bracken shortly. Already he was uncomfortable, ill at ease in this off-colour setting. He remembered too vividly other people like this one – Foreign Office attachés, BBC executives, literary characters, all swimming round London like elegant angel-fish in a heated bowl – only the angel-fish had teeth. Because if you were not another angel-fish, the circuit suddenly closed; the literary page was found to be made up, the file you wanted had gone astray, the broadcasting

programme was already scheduled for six months ahead …
I don't *really* mind them, he thought confusedly: it's not
their fault, and they can be damned amusing company; but
when they pull the trade union stuff, and starve you out if
you won't join the club, then I'm ready to start sweating
and flogging like Colonel Blimp himself …

He said, 'It was a comfortable journey. I was on the same
plane as Macmillan.'

'How lovely for you,' said Purves-Brownrigg. 'Such a
stalwart old character.'

Bracken looked at him, not sure whether this was going
to be tolerable. Why were people like this sent to represent
Britain in rugged outposts like Pharamaul, when they were
so much better off as back-room boys in Paris or Rio or
Washington? Who did the posting? Who handled the
recruitment? What diplomatic nest of – he pulled himself
up, aware that this must be showing in his face. Then he
nodded. 'He seems to know everything there is to know
about Pharamaul.'

'My dear, he's an *encyclopaedia*. A *hundred* volumes.'

'Why didn't you like him?' demanded Nicole, when this
door was shut in turn.

'Not my type,' said David.

'I think men are really awful.'

'We don't have to like them … What does it matter to
you, anyway?'

'Because it's so ridiculous to be prejudiced. Because
Aidan's a sweet person who does a tremendous amount of
good here.'

'Good Lord!' said David. 'Who does he do it to?'

'He's very good company – not *dull*, and talking shop all
the time, like everyone else.'

'People can be good company, and still be normal.'

'That's not the point.'

He turned to her suddenly. 'Look, there's a lot more to it than that. I've seen this thing in operation on a very different plane, where unless you're a practising homosexual you can starve before they'll print a line you write, give you the smallest job, let you say two lines in a play – things like that. I just happen to feel strongly about it, that's all, and I'm not likely to change my mind, just because you tell me there are a few good ones. I *know* that. Let's leave it.'

'All right.' She was surprised, somewhat taken aback by an unexpected crispness in his manner, and surprised also at the way she reacted to it. Here was a young man who at least knew his own mind. That was a nice change, anyway … 'All I meant was, Aidan has talent, and he works hard. It's a pity to write him off, for other reasons.'

'I won't do that … Whom haven't I seen?'

'That's the lot, I think. The rest are up at Gamate. You'll meet some of the wives this evening.'

'What's the form on this dinner party?'

'It's to welcome you as a new member of the family. The Governor always gives one.'

'Will you be there?'

'No. There's a daughter.'

David grinned. 'What's the form *there*?'

'I'll look forward to hearing your views.'

V

David Bracken found himself, by the time he went to bed that night, with very few views that could be put into communicable words. He had been travelling for nearly forty hours, without sleep of any sort: light-headed from swift movement, heat, and a frieze of new faces, he swam through an evening of formal entertainment which left him high and dry on the shores of a very different world.

Through it all, Nicole Steuart's face persisted, like an obstinate reminder of sanity … The Governor, he found, kept considerable state: behind each chair at dinner, a servant in a long, yellow, ankle-length robe stood sentinel, while other servants brought food, removed plates, served wine, all under the eye of a tail-coated butler who could have stepped fresh from a Calvert's whisky advertisement … There were ten guests at dinner: there must have been, at a rough calculation, fifteen servants on duty, while behind the scenes, to produce the iced *consommé*, fillet of sole, *duck à l'orange*, ice cream, and coffee, a round dozen other individuals must have been toiling.

It was pleasant, it was luxurious, it befitted a storybook ideal of a Government House dinner party. Obviously it gave substantial employment, and if it made anyone unhappy, that unhappiness was not apparent. After martinis, sherry, champagne, and cognac, only a nonconformist conscience could be troubled by such an evening, although it could have been duplicated in very few parts of the world, and bore as much relation to England as white to black.

In England, of course, there would have been a lot of argument about it: waste of the taxpayers' money, debasement of fellow human beings, stuffed shirt diplomacy, idle luxury – the democratic viewpoint would have been hammered home with total denunciation. Seeing it in action, David Bracken wasn't sure of the truth. Supposedly the Governor had to entertain. Supposedly it must be done in a certain style, because he was, after all, the senior representative of Her Majesty in this part of the world. The Governor of Pharamaul couldn't dine off Bovril and a boiled egg: he couldn't tell his wife to do the cooking; he couldn't wait at table, or do the washing up afterwards. And it was no good asking 'Why not?' thought David, sipping champagne, rebutting an imaginary member of the Labour Party: that was the way it was, in this corner of the Empire.

Of course, man for man, there were far too many servants, and theirs was – fatal adjective – a non-productive form of employment: they should have been making furniture or aircraft, at attractive piecework rates, and knocking off at six o'clock each evening, free as birds in the upper ether. But suppose they liked being servants? – Suppose it was the thing they did best of all, suppose they did not find it in the least degrading, and would have felt insecure, unhappy, even disgraced, if they could not serve in this glittering household? How did one square that with full employment in a welfare state?

David became aware that fatigue, wine, and introspective thought were making of him a less than satisfactory guest, and he pulled himself together. Whatever social justice dictated, they were all grouped round this table, anyway: ten guests, fifteen servants, a smoothly running kitchen, a damned good dinner, and a dangerous amount to drink. Someone else – not he – could work out the ethics.

It was, as Nicole Steuart had said, a family occasion. The Governor, erect, birdlike in a white dinner jacket and a frilled shirt, sat at the head of the table: on his right was Mrs Simpson, wife of his naval aide-de-camp, on his left Mrs Stevens, wife of one of his secretaries. Opposite him, Lady Vere-Toombs presided, with so easy a charm, so automatic a dispensation of words and attention, that she might have been a senior actress walking through a dress rehearsal, keeping her all for the real performance later that night. She had Captain Simpson and Stevens flanking her: the numbers were made up by Aidan Purves-Brownrigg, the Social Secretary whom David had met earlier that day, and Anthea Vere-Toombs, the Governor's daughter.

They were all behaving very much in character, it seemed to David, surveying them as strangers who had already acquired distinctive labels. Captain Simpson boomed his self-assurance, and gulped his drinks enthusiastically. His wife, foreseeing the day when she would be an Admiral's lady (or know the reason why) talked to Aidan Purves-Brownrigg with an intensity of condescension which gave him little chance to shine. Mrs Stevens, a shy, dull woman with an exceptionally severe hairstyle, listened dutifully and said little; her husband, who was feeling his way after a recent promotion, hung upon the words of Lady Vere-Toombs as if she were a stewardess explaining lifeboat drill at the height of an emergency.

The Social Secretary looked about her, half confidently, because she had arranged this party, and half challengingly, as if it might be thought that she had used this advantage to force her way into it. She was a middle-aged lady, a distant cousin of Lady Vere-Toombs who was now a permanent part of their household.

That left Anthea Vere-Toombs, and Anthea Vere-Toombs, David's neighbour at table, had come as something of a shock to him. She was a tall, haggard blonde, demonstrably in her middle thirties, who for some reason affected the eager solicitation of a streetwalker in her teens. She was slim, good-looking, well made up; her roving eye belonged, for the evening, to David Bracken, but there was no doubt that it was roving. He found himself wondering a lot of things. He wondered how the Governor, a correct figure, and Lady Vere-Toombs, a benign despot, had managed to produce so dubious an offspring – even thirty-five years ago. He wondered why she had never got married. He wondered if her lascivious bearing was as obvious to the others as it was to himself. He wondered how many lovers she had had, and how they were recruited, and if such an undertaking were a necessary qualification for advancement in this arm of the service. He wondered at the fact that, so early in their acquaintance, her left thigh was already keeping up a warm, unrelenting pressure against his own leg.

Conversation was not general: ten people grouped round a large table was too big a party for that. Like a bad Shakespearean play, with many loaded asides, it added up to a very discursive plot indeed.

The Governor was talking about some stamps he had recently discovered. He had heard about an octogenarian trader who had died, up in the bush country south of Gamate. His effects were to be sold by auction; and among them was a lot of old correspondence, dating back fifty and sixty years. The Governor had bought it, together with a job lot of books, newspapers, and magazines. Enshrined among those musty letters was an almost complete set of the Pharamaul 'Jubilee' issue of 1897!

Mrs Stevens, who had four children at home and could hardly keep her eyes open, said, 'How lovely for you! I'd love to see them, some time.' Mrs Simpson remained silent. This had no conceivable connexion with her husband's becoming an Admiral within the next two years – all that was left of his promotion zone – and was therefore unclassifiable.

Lady Vere-Toombs was talking, reprovingly, about the Metropolitan Bishop of Port Victoria, an aged but enterprising black prelate whose latest sideline – a lucrative trade in forged Ethiopian passports – was causing scandal to the faithful and a certain lofty embarrassment to the Government Secretariat itself. If you had an Ethiopian passport, the Bishop contended, you need not pay the Pharamaul poll tax – you need not even acknowledge the existence of the British Government at all. Such was the argument, and, at an inclusive fee of ten shillings, it was proving a popular one. It must somehow be stamped on without hurting anyone's feelings.

Captain Simpson, his face a turkey-cock red above his white bemedalled mess jacket, said, 'If I had my way, we'd send in a couple of policemen, and clean the whole thing up in half an hour.'

Stevens, the secretary, fingered his distorted bow tie, and murmured: 'There are certain administrative difficulties in the way of that, I'm afraid.'

Aidan Purves-Brownrigg, tired of Mrs Simpson's martial pronouncements, talked to the Social Secretary.

'I just love your jade ornaments,' he said. 'Such a subtle colour – and such a lot of them, too.'

The Social Secretary looked down her nose. 'They were my mother's,' she confided. 'She always said they were terribly valuable. Do you think so?'

Purves-Brownrigg bent towards them, his face a few inches from her *décolletage*. He was slightly drunk.

'It's difficult to tell,' he said at last. 'But I like their setting.'

'They have no setting,' said the Social Secretary, puzzled.

'This is their setting,' answered Purves-Brownrigg. He waved his hand over her bosom, like a guide exhibiting a mortal battlefield to the tourists. 'It's absolutely unapproachable!'

'Why, Mr Purves-Brownrigg!' said the Social Secretary. 'And you on the staff, too!'

Anthea Vere-Toombs talked to David Bracken. Their legs still clung together steadily and stickily. Perhaps, thought David, she thinks it's the leg of the table. But when he tried to withdraw, her thigh followed his with hungry persistence.

'I wish we were in London,' said Anthea Vere-Toombs.

'Don't you like it here?'

'Oh, it's all right ...' The bosom of her gown gaped towards him suddenly, revealing a formidable display of bare flesh. Cavernous, he thought, somewhat bemused: caverns – though scarcely measureless to man ... He focused his eyes and his attention again, to hear her say: 'But think of *London* on a night like this! We could be dancing at the Ambassadors!'

'That would be lovely,' said David with difficulty.

Her leg pressed his searchingly. 'Do you like dancing?' She seemed to be asking quite a different question, but David decided that the answer had better be the same.

'I like it very much.'

'I *adore* it!' She seemed about to throw herself into his arms. David saw that Purves-Brownrigg was watching them under lowered lids. He wondered if Anthea Vere-Toombs were really off her head, and if everyone present knew about it, and hoped for the best on occasions like this. He said, groping for the edges of her problem: 'How long have you been out here?'

When the ladies withdrew, the gentlemen talked about stamps, Dinamaula, the regulations governing sick leave for civil servants, and the railway line between Port Victoria and Gamate. In the drawing-room, the ladies discussed the servant problem and the prevailing heat. When they reassembled, the pattern altered in accordance with some predetermined set of rules, of which David was ignorant, and he found himself on a deep sofa, talking to Lady Vere-Toombs. She was kind, authoritative, and efficient: four questions about his family, two about his past service, one about his living quarters (not yet organized), and she had assimilated the outlines of his whole life to date. Thereafter she talked, easily yet with a crisp determination, about Bengal, Hong Kong, and Ceylon.

At half past ten, six servants brought in trays containing whisky, orange juice, and iced water; punctually at eleven, as the clock chimed, Mrs Simpson caught her husband's eye, stood up, and said, 'It really has been delightful.'

The family party was over.

VI

David walked back with Aidan Purves-Brownrigg, downhill into Port Victoria. It was an easy half-mile, with the curve of the bay on their left hand, and the lights of the harbour and the town to draw them on. The chief heat of the day was gone, but the night air still hung languidly. Purves-Brownrigg was making for his flat, David for Port Victoria's run-down, crumbling Hotel Bristol, where he would have to stay for at least a week before he could move into something more permanent.

Feeling the need for fresh air, they had refused two lifts on their way home – in Captain Simpson's old and raucous Bentley, and in the Stevens' family-size Austin. David Bracken hoped that he was not thereby jeopardizing his reputation: Pharamaul was, obviously, a small world. But he felt, in his easy after-dinner mood, that Nicole Steuart might be right about Purves-Brownrigg. When all was said about him, he was lively and entertaining company.

As they strolled downhill, along the dusty, unlit coast road that led to town, Purves-Brownrigg disposed of their late dinner companions, with an unfaltering malice that David knew very well would, in other circumstances, have been applied just as readily to himself. He did not mind.

'I like the old gentleman,' said Purves-Brownrigg. (It was his invariable term for the Governor.) 'He's getting a bit past it, of course: there'll be a large blond wig for him in the diplomatic bag, any time now ... You wouldn't think, to look at him, that he once *defied the mob* in Bengal – not just mowing them down, like that *odious* General Dyer, but waving his stick, like Gordon at Khartoum, till they all just *melted* away.'

'I've never heard the details of that.'

'Give the old gentleman time,' said Purves-Brownrigg. 'You'll hear them ... The Governess is the end, of course – so good-hearted and forceful and boring, plodding on and on like arsenic and old lace without the arsenic. And that Mrs Simpson! ... *What* those sailors have to put up with! It'll be a happy release when the gallant captain is made into an admiral, and she can relax ... But then, I suppose, she'll want to *joust* with the Mountbattens.'

'Will Simpson be made an admiral?'

'They've got to keep their numbers up ... Actually he's a rather pathetic old party – I like him. His great-great-uncle was one of Nelson's captains, and my dear he *dreams of action* the whole time. And all the action he gets is Mrs Simpson.'

'Why do we have a naval aide, anyway?'

'It's lost in the mists of time,' said Purves-Brownrigg. 'But Pharamaul used to be a strategic place – I suppose it still is, with those *criminal* South Africans beating their chests – and so the dear Lords of the Admiralty gave it a permanent naval background. It's better than those *awful* soldiers with bare knees, anyway.'

They were nearing the town now: the air took on a thicker, brinier smell: the lights multiplied, the heat grew oppressive again: the last trams – pride of Port Victoria since 1902 – ground their way reverberatingly towards the terminus.

'What about the Stevens?' asked David.

'Pathetic, aren't they? He's *so* hard-working, it makes me *ill* to watch him. And all those *filthy* children – four of them, all wearing each other's cast-off clothes. My dear, I swear to you there's one pair of khaki shorts that's been passing from hand to hand for seven years. And what she looks like, poor soul – that hairdo is obviously straight out of the Kennel Club Magazine – do this with your wire-haired terrier, and win *first* prize.'

'You really are a bastard,' said David, without rancour, almost admiringly. 'People can't help it if they're poor and ugly.'

'They can't help it,' agreed Purves-Brownrigg. 'But it should all be *hidden away* … And then there's that girl …'

'The daughter?'

'The *monster* … *What* you two were doing at dinner, I'd hate to set down in print. I didn't *dare* look under the table. She might have been holding *anything* … She's really illegal!'

'She seemed a little unstable,' said David.

'Anthea will end up in jail,' said Purves-Brownrigg decisively. 'I can just see it happening … My dear, she *devours* men – never gives them a moment's peace. The man whose place you've taken – a great beefy *athlete* of a man – can't remember his name – '

'Morrison.'

'Yes, Morrison. *Scottish*. You'd have thought he had everything, as far as Anthea was concerned: he weighed about two hundred pounds, he had muscles like *iron bands*, he had a wife who was ill all the time … We all hoped he was *just* the thing, and would wind up with a CBE, if not a knighthood.'

'What happened?'

'My dear, he had to go to hospital … He used to come into the office every morning, positively tottering with fatigue, and then the phone would ring, and he'd have to *crawl* across to Government House again … In the end he was shipped out with the most chronic prostate trouble … I believe they've given him three years in London to recuperate.'

'What goes on now? She must be lonely.'

'Oh, we all do our bit.' Purves-Brownrigg grinned suddenly. 'Even me … But I gather you've been elected. Truly, I gave a sigh of relief when you walked in this morning. At least you can be on call for public holidays.'

David laughed. 'That's not what I came out for.'

'Little you know … There'll be a *long* letter for you in the morning, all about her glands.'

Now they were in downtown Port Victoria itself: the cobbled streets were full of late traffic, the sidewalks were crowded. Men – black men and white – lurched out of taverns, huddled into doorways, pursued a level course for home. There were shops – fly-blown shops with Coca-Cola and stale buns, shoddy shops with cheap clothing, leather belts, checked caps, smarter shops with trunks and nylon underclothes. There was a set of traffic lights. There was a flickering green sign saying: 'Hotel Bristol. Lounge Bar. Open All Night.'

'This is your hovel,' said Purves-Brownrigg. 'I hope you're fixed up with something else.'

'Next week, probably,' answered David. 'I'm hoping to get a flat halfway up the hill, overlooking the harbour.'

'Sounds like Broadlands,' said Purves-Brownrigg.

'It is,' said David. 'What's the form?'

'All right,' said Purves-Brownrigg. 'A bit antiseptic. They saved *plenty* of money on the decorations. But you'll be travelling about a good deal, anyway.'

'I start next week. Gamate first, and then right on up to Shebiya.'

'You might enjoy it.' Purves-Brownrigg, slowing down for their farewell, looked at him sideways. Now he was suddenly less flippant, less affected. 'Don't be disappointed,' he said.

'In what?'

'In us. We can't have looked much, at that bloody dinner. But the thing works. Pharamaul is a funny country. Hot, backward, dull. In some moods, I could *stamp* on it, blot it out, throw it away with the cigarette ends and the bottletops. But it grows on you. All we do is run it as best we can.'

'I'm not disappointed,' said David Bracken, untruthfully.

'The thing works,' Purves-Brownrigg repeated. 'It's a second-rate secretariat, but it covers the ground ... This isn't Paris or Washington, after all ... I think you'll do all right here. The ladies will tear you to ribbons, of course, but you mustn't mind that.'

'What ladies?' asked David, confused.

'The LADIES. They meet every morning for tea, and bitch madly about everything. There's really nothing else for them to do – except for Anthea Vere-Toombs, and she does it *all* the time. But you mustn't mind it if several *odious* remarks find their way back to you.'

'Are they all like that?'

Purves-Brownrigg, holding out his hand, laughed suddenly. 'Oh, no! *She's* all right. Pretty, too ... Nicole's a lovely name, don't you think?'

CHAPTER THREE

❖

It was good, thought Andrew Macmillan, to be back home in Gamate. The shabby old Residency had never felt more comfortable, more private, more welcoming.

If London – sixty hours away – had seemed strange and lonely, Macmillan had found Government House at Port Victoria stranger still, as he always did. There was something about the GH gang that had seemed twenty times removed from reality … He had whipped through it with the minimum of delay, side-stepping a scheduled dinner party, forgoing a night at the 'Bristol', even though he had felt, on landing, desperately tired and strained. A long session with the Governor, an exchange of greetings with that odd character Aidan Purves-Brownrigg, a word with that hearteningly pretty girl Nicole Steuart – and he had climbed aboard the evening train and straightway fallen asleep. Now, after fourteen hot, harassed, and dusty hours in the wooden coach, he was home at last.

He sat at ease on the Residency's wide, cool *stoep*, his feet on a second chair, his old clothes – khaki slacks, khaki shirt, frayed canvas shoes – feeling like the only uniform he would ever care to wear. The Residency, set on a hillside overlooking Gamate, commanded a superb view: the town itself sprawled untidily over its two valleys, with a slow cloud of smoke and dust drifting across it; but beyond were fifty miles of pleasant green plain, and beyond that the encroaching bush, and the purple foothills of the U-Maula country.

Here, two hundred miles north of Port Victoria, at the end of the rickety, single-line railway, here was absolute peace, absolute simplicity; here was Macmillan's own kingdom, benignly ruled, benignly enjoyed: here all problems were safely within his own hands, all doubts resolved by his own will and strength.

He sighed, stretched, crossed his feet, sipped his coffee. The sun slipped a little lower in the sky, lengthening the shadows in the Residency garden, turning to dusty gold all the grass-thatched roofs of all the hundreds of huts within his view. Beyond the fly-screen, insects crawled and buzzed. Presently, gratefully, Andrew Macmillan slept.

He was awakened by the shuffling of feet on the worn boards of the *stoep*. Halfway between sleep and not-sleep, he was reminded of his wife, years ago, shuffling into their bedroom with the breakfast tray, on countless dawns of the past when dawn had meant duty, work, a journey to be taken. And yet it could not be his wife. Then he was reminded of Johannes, his servant of more than a quarter of a century, Johannes who was as much a part of his life as anything else in Pharamaul – and he opened his eyes, and it was Johannes.

'Jah, *barena*,' said Johannes.

Macmillan looked at him. Johannes was his own age, fifty-seven, but he seemed much older, as all negroes did: on his spare flesh the white housecoat hung limply, and the grey hair above the wrinkled face was now sparse and thin. His life is my life, thought Macmillan, still struggling for clarity: we are both old – two old men of Gamate, bound to each other till the grave takes one, or both, and brings that binding to an end. In the old days, Johannes had been a fledgling houseboy, young, eager, disobedient; then a trusted servant, looking after the flat in Port Victoria; and now the wheel had come full circle, and they were just two old men, back home in Gamate, near the tomb, near their long rest … He stirred, and sat up, throwing off these foolish thoughts. He was the Resident Commissioner, Johannes was his senior houseboy: that was all.

'Johannes,' he said, firmly.

'Yes, *barena*,' repeated Johannes. 'Six o'clock, *barena*. I wake you.'

'Dinner,' said Macmillan, collecting himself. 'Three *barenas* – Mr Forsdick, Mr Llewellyn, Captain Crump.'

'Yes, *barena*.'

'What's in the larder?'

'Chicken, *barena*. Wife kill this morning.'

'My chicken?'

'Wife's chicken, *barena*.'

'What happened to my chickens? Six of them.'

'All *barena*'s chickens die, two three weeks.'

The squeeze was so obvious that Macmillan felt impelled to do battle. But then he relaxed again. He had been away for twelve weeks, after all. Various malpractices were bound to have crept in … A little time ago, he would have tracked those six chickens to their several resting-places, and dealt out justice over their dishonoured bones. Now he did not mind so much. Men must live, black men and white. Johannes, in thirty years, had earned many chickens, much forgiveness.

'What besides chicken?' he asked.

'Peaches, *barena*. Yellow peaches. Yellow *tin* peaches.'

'All right … And soup.'

'No soup, *barena*. Tins no good. I throw away, two three weeks.'

'Soup, damn you. Find one tin. Mushroom soup.'

Johannes sighed, shaking his head. 'I look hard, *barena*. Perhaps one tin left in cupboard.'

Macmillan nodded. Soup was on the table. 'Soup,' he said. 'Fried chicken. Potatoes. Peaches. Cream.'

'No cream, *barena*.'

'Cream.'

'No cream in all Gamate. Cows sick. Hot weather.'

It had the rustic ring of truth. 'All right,' said Macmillan again. 'Coffee afterwards. In two hours.' He held up two fingers. 'Two.'

'Yes, *barena*.'

'When the *barenas* come, bring ice and whisky and beer.'

'Yes, *barena*.' Johannes stood waiting, shifting from one foot to another, his old face creased and uncertain. He had a thing to say, and he must say it before he left.

'What is it, Johannes?'

'*Barena* have good holiday?'

'Fine, Johannes. But it's nice to be back.'

The old black face broke suddenly into a smile. Johannes nodded, accepting a welcome cue. He said, with all the honesty in the world: 'It's good to have you here again, *barena*.'

Presently Macmillan saw them approaching across the patchy, burnt-down lawn which was the playground of ticks and white ants: two men, dressed alike in khaki slacks, but wearing ties as a sign of evening formality. They were Forsdick, his District Commissioner in Gamate, and Llewellyn, the agricultural officer who covered the whole Maula territory. They drew near, and it was as if the cares of office, the burden of administration, were closing in on him after a brief respite. They had both been busy elsewhere when his train arrived that morning: the message he had left for them – 'Dinner Tonight, no wives, eight o'clock' – had been the limit of the protocol attending his return. Now they were here, establishing the fact of his formal presence. From now on, the load was his again.

He watched them as they neared him. Forsdick, who (if he could keep away from the whisky bottle) might one day succeed him, was fortyish, plump, red-faced, sweating; he walked heavily, as if his large ungainly body must be carefully steered from point to point. Macmillan, trying to remember him from twelve weeks ago, wondered if Forsdick's face had really been as florid, as moonlike, as it appeared now. Surely he must have stepped up his consumption, in the interval ... Llewellyn was the same as he had always been: a small swarthy Welshman, morose, overworked, single-minded in his pursuit of a thriving Pharamaul. What he knew about crops, cattle, water, and disease was phenomenal; what he knew about anything else was sometimes, for Macmillan, a matter for ribald speculation. But perhaps that was the kind of agricultural officer one needed.

He stood up as they reached the *stoep*, and opened the fly-screened door.

Forsdick said: 'Hallo, Andrew.'

Llewellyn said: 'Good evening, sir.'

Macmillan observed that here, also, things were unchanged. Forsdick's voice was slightly slurring, as was usual any time after five o'clock in the evening; Llewellyn was in low spirits, and showed it. He had been in low spirits when Macmillan had left Gamate, twelve weeks earlier. Then, it had been something to do with an outbreak of contagious abortion. Macmillan wondered what it was this time. He was certainly going to know before very long.

He motioned them past him on to the *stoep*. 'Come in,' he said. 'Nice to see you. Where's Crump?'

'Glued to the radio,' said Forsdick. His voice was fruity, blurred, thickened by twenty years of one-more-for-luck, one-for-the-road, one-for-the-swing-of-the-door. He worked extremely hard at his job, he had a nagging wife whom he loathed: he drank to balance the one and to escape from the other. 'There's something coming through for us,' he continued. 'On the eight o'clock police schedule – prefaced urgent and confidential.'

'Government House in a flap again,' said Llewellyn caustically. 'Nothing else to do all day. They've probably lost the file on the New Year's Honours List … Did you spend any time down there, sir?'

'The minimum,' answered Macmillan briefly. By and large, he felt the same way about Government House, but he could not join his staff in their frequent bouts of condemnation. Discipline was involved – the chain of command – there had to be a Government House, anyway … Johannes shuffled in with the whisky, the beer, the ice, and the glasses, and Macmillan poured in silence – a stiff peg for Forsdick, beer for Llewellyn. 'They've got a new man to replace Morrison – chap named Bracken.'

'What like?' asked Forsdick, sniffing his drink.

'OK … Brand new, of course … Cheers …'

'Down the hatch.'

They all drank.

'How was London?' asked Forsdick, after a pause.

'Fine,' answered Macmillan. He felt he had to add something. 'Lots of traffic … I saw some shows.'

'You can keep London,' said Llewellyn, his sing-song voice still on a sombre key. 'Like a circus, that place is.'

That was enough about London. The long leave was over. London was past, swallowed up in the mist. Only Gamate was real.

'How are things here?' asked Macmillan.

Now they talked as they had talked on hundreds, even thousands of other evenings in the past: it was straight-cut shop, the kind of thing they talked best, the thing they really understood. Gamate was much the same. The harvest was coming to an end, the taxes were starting to dribble in. There had been an epidemic of blue-tongue disease up near the U-Maula border. (So that was it, thought Macmillan – and wondered, not for the first time, why the crosses that Llewellyn had to bear always had such odd names.) One of the Native Treasury staff had been caught stealing postal orders, and had been sacked. There had been a row up at the logging camp, fifty miles to the west, and a man had been 'chopped'. The culprit was now awaiting trial in Port Victoria jail. There was a new translator in the office, who showed signs of being useful. Father Schwemmer, who ran the Gamate Mission, had been complaining about immorality.

'Why, especially?' asked Macmillan, interested.

'One of his altar boys took a girl into the vestry.'

'Well, well.'

'And a lot of *other* altar boys were invited to look on.'

Macmillan laughed. 'It sounds as though he needed some new altar boys.'

'He's sacked the lot, and started from scratch again. But he wants us to do something about it.'

'You can't make *that* illegal,' said Macmillan. 'Especially not in Gamate. Social life would come to a complete standstill.'

Finally, there had been a deputation that morning from the Council of Regents – the two uncles, and one cousin, of Dinamaula, who had ruled the Maula tribe for the past year, ever since Dinamaula's father had died.

'How *are* those wicked uncles?' asked Macmillan, interested afresh.

'It was rather curious,' said Forsdick slowly. His glass was empty again, and Macmillan motioned to him to fill it. With his back turned, Forsdick went on: 'Of course, they know quite well they're on their way out – they were only carrying on till Dinamaula finished at Oxford, and they're not going to quarrel about handing over ... At least, I don't think so ...' He turned. 'But they said – ' he wrinkled his brow, searching for the exact words, 'they said they wanted to be sure there would be no great changes.'

'Why should there be?' asked Macmillan.

'They wouldn't tell me. When I pressed the point, they got a bit vague, and then old Seralo started talking about the importance of carrying on the tribal customs. You know his usual line; he fires it off every time we put a bit of gravel on the roads. But at the end, he said, "We have *heard* – "' Forsdick stressed the word, ' " – *heard* talk of new things."'

Macmillan shrugged. 'I should say he was making that up. New chief, new things – it's a natural line of thought. They're probably worrying about some little racket they're running, which Dinamaula will now take over.'

Llewellyn said, 'Stands to reason they don't *want* to give up.'

Forsdick shook his head. 'I don't know. It sounded as though they were on to something. You know the way they hear things.'

In spite of himself, Macmillan was inclined to agree. The Maulas *did* hear things, by some scarcely credible grapevine which could, for example, infiltrate from Port Victoria to Gamate and beyond, in a matter of hours; a grapevine which could out-distance any traveller, any horseman, any voice on the radio. Macmillan had encountered it many times in the past. When the previous Governor, old Lord Mountstephen, had died while on leave *in London*, Johannes had told him about it at breakfast – a full hour before he himself got the 'Priority' cable from Port Victoria ... It was something that one came to accept, where Pharamaul was concerned.

He shook his head, aware of uneasiness. It was as if he had suddenly sniffed the wind of the future, and found that there was borne upon it the faint scent of far-off trouble. 'New things', in Gamate, almost always meant complication and disturbance.

He said, 'When does Dinamaula arrive?'

'Tomorrow night,' said Forsdick. 'He's coming by truck from Port Victoria.'

Llewellyn, who was long-sighted, suddenly raised his head and pointed to a small dust cloud, stirring far down the hill towards Gamate.

'Here's Crump,' he said. 'That's the police jeep.'

In silence they watched the jeep climbing steadily towards them: it was now a dark spot at the foot of a yellow cloud of dust, gradually taking shape as it drew near. Presently it disappeared behind a fold of the hill, while the yellow cloud still hung in space, unexplained, mysterious. Then, borne towards them on the quiet evening air, its engine suddenly sounded very loud, and the jeep bumped over the last few yards, and appeared between the white gateposts. As it stopped, its dust cloud drifted gently away and was lost in the dusk. A khaki-clad figure sprang out, and walked briskly towards them.

Captain Crump of the Royal Pharamaul Police was a burly, cheerful Irishman who seemed to be laughing nearly all the time. He laughed in his office, he laughed on the telephone, he laughed when he submitted a report, however grave it might be; Macmillan had once watched him laughing happily as he led a riot squad into action, clubs swinging against spears and knives, five years ago at the time of the big tax troubles. Later he had smiled broadly throughout the court proceedings. It was not an assumed cheerfulness. Crump was young, strong, fond of his job, possessed of a total belief in the excellent native police force which he himself had built up. He had a young

63

and pretty wife, a Military Cross from the last war, an assured future. What else should one do but laugh … Crump knew Gamate and the surrounding country, and the tribal feuds, and the good and the bad men, nearly as well as did Macmillan himself, and the latter found him invaluable.

Now he saluted, a broad grin on his face, and said, 'Sir!'

'Hallo, Keith,' said Macmillan. 'Nice to see you again … Have a drink?'

Crump laughed, and said, 'I will that!' and strode through the door of the *stoep* as if he were going to arrest the lot of them. Though he was in khaki like the three others, his khaki was different: immaculate tunic-shirt, creased shorts, a belt and holster, puttees, polished bush-boots … One of Crump's more printable Maula nicknames meant 'The Shining Soldier'.

While Macmillan poured him a drink, the others greeted the police captain, without a great deal of cordiality. Llewellyn did not like him, because Crump was a tall Irishman instead of a small Welshman: Crump did not like Forsdick, because Forsdick drank too much, was always out of condition, and made sheep's eyes at his (Crump's) wife. But they all acknowledged two things in each other: their efficiency, which was never in question, and their basic interdependence, which was obvious. The administration, the discipline, and the health of man and beast, all needed an interlocking team, with a man of Macmillan's calibre to see fair play and step in if need be. They had such a team in Gamate, and they knew that they were lucky in having it.

Crump realized that there were a lot of things worse than a perpetual hangover and a roving eye, if one worked as hard as Forsdick – and each of them in turn found the same sort of dispensation for the others.

Macmillan turned with the drink. 'Here you are ... What was in the telegram?'

Crump reached inside his tunic pocket, and brought out a folded pink flimsy. 'It's about Dinamaula. He's been taking to the newspapers.'

'Has he indeed?' said Forsdick. 'What about?'

'Progress in Pharamaul,' answered Crump. He was laughing again. 'He wants to improve everything.' Then he drank, and fell silent as Andrew Macmillan, looking down at the pink telegram, started to speak.

'It's from GH,' he said, 'passing on a telegram from London ... "Urgent and Confidential",' he read. ' "Following telegram has been received from Secretary of State. Begins:

' "This morning's *Daily Thresh* carries lengthy and tendentious interview with Dinamaula by Tulbach Browne, DT special correspondent to Southern Africa who is now in Port Victoria. In reported interview, Dinamaula expressed dissatisfaction with slow progress in territory, government handling of Maula affairs, and said he was determined to introduce reforms whatever the opposition. There was also reference to reactionary tribal elements who would be taken care of. Following is quotation.

' "Quote Dinamaula's plans are far-reaching, statesmanlike, eminently wise. His chance of forcing them through, in the face of British officials worried about nothing worse than their next pay increment, their next shipment of cheap gin from London, are slim dash slim as this young and gallant chief himself Unquote.

' "Resident Commissioner, Gamate, should be instructed to interview Dinamaula and impress on him the necessity of working for a smooth, orderly change-over in tribal administration. In particular, criticism of government officials by chief-designate, and further publicity of this sort, should be avoided. Telegram Ends.

'"Following for Macmillan. Please take action indicated in last paragraph, and report urgently to me."'

There was only a very brief silence after Macmillan had finished reading. Then Crump laughed, slapping his bare thigh, and said, 'I had a lot of fun decyphering that telegram.'

Llewellyn, snorting, muttered: 'Damn' sauce ... What does he know about it? He was naught but a kid when he left here.'

Said Forsdick, musingly: 'By God, I wish gin *was* cheap.'

Macmillan was frowning to himself. This was the trouble he had smelt from far away, the disturbing element moving towards Gamate. He was not angry, because he knew Gamate, and the sort of place it was, and what it must sound like to an outsider – even an outsider who was a Maula himself. One could think a lot of things about Gamate, without stepping too far beyond the facts. But that was not to say that everything could be cured overnight ... He looked down at the telegram again, and then at Forsdick.

'This was what Seralo meant,' he said.

'Eh?' said Forsdick, who was sinking into a pleasant daydream of his own. 'Seralo?'

'When he came to see you this morning, with the other Regents. He told you they had heard talk of new things. This was it.'

'But how could it have reached here so quickly?' asked Llewellyn incredulously.

'You know how they hear things,' said Macmillan. 'It just got here, that's all.'

'Of course,' said Crump, cheerfully, 'you can't believe all you read in the newspapers. Dinamaula probably never said the half of it.'

'Maybe not,' said Forsdick. 'But half is quite enough.'

'Naught but a kid,' repeated Llewellyn. 'Those bloody Oxford and Cambridge students! They're enough to ruin any man.'

'Dinamaula's twenty-two now,' said Macmillan. He was marshalling his thoughts. 'He's been away for seven years. He's probably picked up one or two ideas, and he got talking about them to this reporter chap. It'll be different when he sees Gamate.' He frowned again. 'It had better be!'

Crump had taken the telegram from Macmillan, and was rereading it. ' "Reactionary tribal elements",' he quoted. 'He's got something there ... By God, he ought to have my job, and try to knock some sense into these old jokers.'

'You know, the Regents aren't going to like this at all,' said Forsdick slowly. The whisky was taking hold, and he was now nicely balanced between the serious and the careless. 'They'll think it's aimed at them.'

'*I* don't like it,' answered Macmillan crisply. 'I think it's aimed at *me* ... "Determined to introduce reforms whatever the opposition" ... I've been in this territory thirty-five years. I know what reforms it needs, and how fast we can go, and what they'll stand for, without everything coming apart at the seams. I don't want a young chap who's never really lived here, except as a kid, coming in and stirring up a lot of trouble.'

'It may be all newspaper talk,' said Crump again.

'*Any* talk is likely to set things off. You know what happens when they start to grumble, and imagine a new set of grievances, and take sides ... The harvest is pretty well finished, too, which means that they've got nothing to do but sit around and argue the toss.' He looked at Crump. 'You'll have to get your boys to work, Keith. Find out what's cooking.'

By 'boys' he meant not the uniformed police, but the unofficial arm of Crump's small force – the tale-bearers, listeners, spies, informers who clung furtively to the edge of officialdom: who slipped into the office when the coast was clear at dusk, who sidled up to the window to speak to the cook, or leant over a thorn fence to talk to the gardener. Much news, much necessary warning, came to Crump in this fashion. It was often the only way to keep a grip on things, in a territory where a policeman's uniform was the signal for silence, and an official 'detective' could gather only innocuous gossip – and lies.

'I'll do that,' said Crump.

'And I want to see Dinamaula as soon as he arrives. Send a messenger down.'

'Better make it a formal invitation, Andrew,' said Forsdick gently. 'Cup of tea at the Residency.'

'Why?'

'He's the chief-designate, after all. Just arrived to take over. It's – ' he gestured, ' – it's an important moment for Gamate. There's been a lot of talk, a lot of excitement, the kids are all practising songs of welcome … You can't just send the waggon for him, with a police corporal hanging on to the tailboard.'

'All right.' Macmillan grinned suddenly. He never minded this sort of correction from his staff. It was the *total* of knowledge and experience which was important … He winked at Crump. 'Put on your medals, and give him my compliments. But see that he gets here.'

There was a shuffling sound behind them, and the dining-room door opened slowly, creaking on its hinges.

Johannes, in a clean white housecoat, came forward, looking important and anxious.

'Soup on table, *barena*,' he said.

'Dinner is served,' corrected Macmillan automatically.

'Dinner served,' said Johannes. 'Soup on table.'

II

The truck, a tough, grimy old Chevrolet whose speedometer had long ago stuck at 86,000 miles, roared northwards towards Gamate, racing its own dust cloud. The road, freshly ploughed after the last rains, was now a pitted yellow ruin again, with twin tyre-tracks deeply gashed along its whole length: wedded to these tracks like some crazy old tram, the truck swayed, lurched, pounded, rattled unceasingly. In the front seat, Dinamaula gripped the forward edge of the dash, and stared at the unfolding ribbon of the road. By his side, his cousin Zuva Katsaula drove carelessly, his hands loose on the wheel, his wide mouth grinning and talkative.

The sun was high, the countryside brown and shimmering: the widow-birds that fluttered across their path, plunging against the long weight of their tail-feathers, were like messengers greeting them with garlands. The road led steadily northwards, past valleys, over the shoulders of hills, skirting round huge weathered boulders and mealie patches and hut circles; now and then a child waved, a woman looked up from her riverside washing, an old man, stately under his beehive hat, raised a hand in greeting. It was Dinamaula's own country, and he was remembering it and loving it and mourning its barren dustiness. Could this be really all? … He wiped the sweat from his forehead, knowing that it *was* all, and that for good or ill it was his.

Zuva Katsaula paused in his talk, and pointed to a hillcrest a dozen miles ahead; a hillcrest having the shape of a woman's nipple, erect, outlined against the pale sky.

'Breast Hill,' said Zuva, with a grin. 'Remember? It's the halfway mark. Oh, brother!'

Dinamaula nodded without answering, and then shifted slightly to look sideways at his companion. Already he did not like this Zuva, whom he had not met for a long time. They had been together at Oxford, and then Zuva, a few months older than himself, had left university, and gone to London. There, it was clear, he had found strange companions. Now they were returning to Gamate together, but they were divided men, for all that.

Zuva was small, dapper, smiling, dressed in grey check trousers and a yellow coat with brown shoulderpads and curious lapels. 'My zoot coat,' he had said, in answer to Dinamaula's query when they had met at Port Victoria. 'Pretty keen number, eh? Straight from Hollywood. Oh, baby! ...' No, Dinamaula did not like this Zuva, who had returned to Pharamaul a month earlier, and had met him at Port Victoria airfield with four companions who formed a ragged shiftless bodyguard at his back. All wore dark spectacles, thick-soled shoes, black hats with wide brims. One of them had an empty shoulder-holster strapped under his coat.

Though that meeting and greeting had been formal enough, yet Zuva had somehow brought to it a quality of snide, derisive toughness that Dinamaula disliked intensely. He and Zuva had made different friends at Oxford, and they had not seen each other for more than a year; even so, Zuva seemed to have strayed a fantastic way from the tribal pattern ... He was mean-eyed, he was slick, he dressed like an actor in a negro musical comedy. His talk was strange, pattering like rain, hitting suddenly like hail: his manner was flip and arrogant, aping a score of old, nameless film stars. Dinamaula was ashamed of him, and sad for his father ... When Zuva had told off one of his 'bodyguard' to look after Dinamaula's luggage, the young man had answered: 'OK, Fingers!'

'What is this "Fingers"?' asked Dinamaula later.

Zuva grinned, tossing back his head. 'Oh, the boys all call me that.'

Dinamaula did not like it at all. This man by his side was not 'Fingers', or anything else; he was Zuva Katsaula, his own blood relation, his friend from boyhood. How much could a man change? ... Dinamaula wanted no 'Fingers' in Pharamaul, no zoot suits, no alien pattern of foolishness.

Certainly he wanted no such talk as Zuva Katsaula had talked, that first night in Port Victoria, before they set out on the journey to Gamate.

How much could a man change? On that night, Dinamaula had sat with Zuva and his circle of friends, in a squalid dive in downtown Port Victoria, drinking *kaffir*-beer laced (illegally) with raw potato-spirit; he had sat watching and thinking of Zuva Katsaula – of their shared past, their dividing present, their split future. For that future must surely be split ... The talk had run in curious circles, as if they were each in turn taking pains to probe Dinamaula's spirit and feeling. But the thoughts behind the probing were all Zuva's thoughts – of that, Dinamaula was sure. Zuva had collected these friends round himself, as soon as he returned to Pharamaul; he must have told them of London, of other friends to be found there, of political matters, of all the promise that could lie in the future, if only one were tough and alert.

It was not exactly communism: indeed, it was scarcely a recognizable creed at all. It was all confused – as yet. Zuva had picked up, from somewhere, a kind of gangster independence of spirit, and had clothed it in the violent jargon of old movies, and the supple double-talk of political Oxford, and the vicious sub-humanity of Soho's café world. He had collected these immediate followers who thought the same way; there were many others, apparently, who saw through the same eyes, heard with the same ears.

It was not communism. It seemed to include no white men, nor any sense of tribal hierarchy either: it included only personal power for whomever could grasp it. It was the Maula Freedom Party, it was Democracy for Pharamaul, the Free Gamate Movement, Social Brotherhood ... The titles varied. So did the aims. So did the methods. It was a thing just beginning, they said. What did the new chief think of it?

They had sipped their heady beer, eyeing him across the chipped rims of their glasses. Dinamaula had thought for a long time, his guarded face impassive in the lamplight. Then he said, 'I have come back to be chief of my people. I will rule as my father ruled.'

His words seemed to hang upon the air, unacceptable, doomed to be rejected.

'But there must be progress,' said Zuva after a pause.

Dinamaula nodded. 'Yes. But according to our accustomed pattern.'

At that, a sigh had gone round the room, a fading of tension. Dinamaula knew then that he had failed to pass some test of theirs, and knew also that there would be no more talk of this sort, while he was still in their company. They had found out exactly where he stood, without greatly committing themselves. He was on one side, they on another. All such thoughts must now turn inwards.

He sipped and swallowed, his throat rebelling against the fierce, too-crude spirit. Presently Zuva said, 'There will be great rejoicing in Gamate, when you return.'

Great rejoicing ... Dinamaula realized, at that moment, how definite was the cleavage that had been established between them. If Zuva, his cousin, had felt able to count on him as one of their own circle, he would have used his own dubious jargon. He would have said 'a hell of a blind', he would have said 'a big night', or 'a wild party', or 'a riot'. But 'great rejoicing' belonged to the old Maula world, the simple world of Gamate. It was Dinamaula's language, not Zuva's. By that single formal phrase, Zuva had recognized his category, and assigned him to it.

Now they sat side by side, driving together along the dusty road that led into the future. Dinamaula's own role was clear: he was to assume the chieftainship, the tribal mantle that had been awaiting him, ever since he had been a small boy, playing on the spill-way of the Gamate dam with this same Zuva. Zuva's role was not clear. He wished to change things – as did Dinamaula. But he wished to change them according to some pattern, some tradition that could be violent and was certainly alien. 'Freedom for Pharamaul' might mean anything, from political justice to political tyranny. Zuva would be close by Dinamaula's side, as his rank entitled him; he might pay lip service, lip homage, but there was a pattern of Maula scheming and treachery which he might well revive at the same time. Perhaps, in the dark future, it would mean exile or death for one or the other of them.

Dinamaula sighed, eyeing the road winding into the hills, and the gaunt scrub-cattle grazing on the nearby slopes, and the sun now beginning to dip towards the west. He did not truly wish to be back in Oxford, or living anonymously in London. He wished to acquit himself well and honourably as chief, and this was likely to be very much harder than he had hoped.

It was a great night in Gamate; a night which, starting decorously enough with ceremonial greetings to the chief-designate, worked itself up to a wild saturnalian pitch such as the town had not witnessed for many a year.

The Maulas were excited and happy, and happiness for them meant simple things – huge crowds thronging the hard-trodden tribal meeting place, the *aboura*, much talking underneath the thorn trees, much laughter and drinking and jostling: children running here and there, squealing, chasing each other: lovers wrestling and writhing in the shadows between the huts: old people shaking their heads, then joining in the fun: long speeches, long songs, long feasting. The Maulas had turned from work to play, with the best will in the world. It was a great night; the harvest was nearly done, and their young chief had come back from far lands, to be their father again.

Soon there would be an even greater night – the night that Dinamaula was formally enthroned. But, meanwhile, this night was a night of special meaning also.

First, for Dinamaula, there were the formal greetings, out of sight of the crowd: a ceremonial welcome from the Regents and the headmen of the tribe.

They had all sat at a table within the Gamate schoolhouse; outside, on the *aboura*, the sounds of excitement and revelry were already mounting, but here all was grave and courteous and ordained by custom.

Old Seralo, the senior Regent and brother of Dinamaula's own father, had the place of honour at the head of the table. He was an old man now, past his best, and his head and lips trembled as he went through the prescribed forms of welcome; but he was wise as well as old, and Dinamaula found comfort in sitting next to him, knowing that he had brought patience and rectitude to the task of regency. The Chair of Rule had lost no honour during the past year ... Next to him was the second uncle, Zuva's father, by name Katsaula, a tall, thin man of the middle years, grave and unsmiling, the historian of the tribe, known for his insistence upon the old forms and the old customs.

Opposite him sat the third Regent, Puero, another cousin of Dinamaula's: a fattish, gross man, this, always drinking and drawing up to table, a man moreover who had broken tribal custom by taking a fourth wife while the first was still living. But his blood entitled him to his place of honour.

Him, Dinamaula did not like: his eyes sat too deep in his creased flabby face, and they moved aside too quickly when they were met. This was the one with whom Zuva would talk, behind the reed screens, long after nightfall … But old Seralo he honoured and loved, and Katsaula he respected. These three had ruled the tribe for the past year, changing nothing, advancing nothing, doing no harm. Now, about to give place, they greeted Dinamaula with gravity and slow ceremonial, while round them the others – Zuva himself, and Dinamaula's witless half-brother Chaamaula, and the head priest with his robes, and the head doctor with his weird necklaces, and all the appointed headmen of Gamate – the others watched and nodded and spoke in their turn, bringing honour to the fortunate moment and the chosen man.

When they were all seated, Seralo spoke first, according to the custom: gross ill-luck would attend any who had the bad manners to intrude upon this pattern.

'Oh Dinamaula,' said Seralo, his old lips trembling, his eyes fixed on a distant point. 'Oh Dinamaula, greetings and blessings upon you.'

'Old uncle, I see you,' answered Dinamaula formally. He had thought that he might be nervous or forgetful, but the words and the shape of the occasion returned to him with blessed assurance. 'I greet you in my turn.'

'Oh Dinamaula,' said Seralo, his voice gathering strength, 'son of Simaula, grandson of Maula –' the company drew breath, sighing 'Ah-h-h-h' at the august and fearful name – 'Hereditary Chieftain of Pharamaul, Prince of Gamate, Son of the Fish, Keeper of – ' his voice faltered.

'Keeper of the Golden Nail,' prompted the second Regent, Katsaula, the historian, the formalist. 'Keeper of the Golden Nail.'

'Keeper of the Golden Nail,' Seralo continued. 'Urn of the Royal Seed, Ruler and Kingbreaker, Lord of the Known World – oh Dinamaula, we greet you.'

'Old Uncle, I see you,' repeated Dinamaula, with the same formality. The list of titles had fallen oddly upon his ears, and momentarily he wondered what his Oxford friends would have thought of them. But now he was not at Oxford, now he was home in Gamate ... 'I see you, and I thank you.'

'Dinamaula,' said Seralo, 'we are glad that you have returned to your own people. We are glad that you will soon reign as our chief. Each of us in turn will tell of this gladness.'

At a sign, the second Regent, Katsaula, took up the thread of ceremonial.

'Oh Dinamaula,' said Katsaula, the historian, enunciating with care, as if he read from some old book; 'we greet you, and we are glad. Rule well in accordance with the custom and the law.'

'Oh Dinamaula,' said Puero, the fat, the gross, his eyes shifting from side to side, 'we greet you. Be welcome in Gamate.'

'Oh Dinamaula,' said Zuva, 'my cousin, my brother, be welcome. You and I have seen far countries together' – a second, uncertain sigh went round the table, at this pushful variation upon the pattern – 'and now you have returned. Be welcome.'

'Oh Dinamaula,' said Chaamaula, the half-brother, the foolish lolling one, reacting to Katsaula's sharp elbow under his ribs, 'oh Dinamaula, be welcome.'

'Oh Dinamaula,' said the head priest. 'Blessings on your head and your feet. Think and walk with God. Be welcome.'

Thus the ritual, thus the thread of greeting. When they were all done, Dinamaula took up the burden of answer.

'Old Uncle,' he began, bowing to Seralo, 'and you others, I thank you. I am happy to have returned from far countries. This is my home, and here I will stay. When I come to reign on the throne of my father' – he bowed again to Seralo, who still nominally maintained his state in the Chair of Rule – 'I will deal honourably between all men, dispensing justice, listening to all complaints, caring for the poor. I greet you, and I thank you.'

At that, the company relaxed. The principal formality was over. Now, if they wished, they might talk at ease.

For some moments, however, there was no ease. It was an awkward occasion. None of them, save Zuva, had seen Dinamaula for seven years: at that time, he had been a youth, still moving freely within the women's huts; now he was a man, and soon to be their chief. They were all citizens of Gamate, used to each other's ways, ruled by custom and the prescribed forms; Dinamaula came fresh from the outside world, a world that held many strange things, a world that might have changed him altogether. Beyond the ritual greetings, there seemed at the moment little common ground between them.

But fortunately, there came an interruption to break the tension in the easiest way possible – with laughter. A small black face appeared at one of the windows, with eyes growing saucer-wide at the sight of the august company; a childish voice said, 'Ow! ...' on a sustained note of awe; and then the head ducked down again, and vanished instantly, and running feet were heard, pattering away into the darkness. Katsaula looked grave at the interruption, but the others laughed.

'The children, at least, have not changed,' said Dinamaula.

'Nothing has changed, my son,' said old Seralo, a smile still on his lips. 'You will find your home as it was in the old days.'

'It is indeed my home,' said Dinamaula, answering some slight question in the old man's voice. 'I have travelled far, but Gamate is my home.'

'That is well,' said Seralo.

'We have heard much of your studies,' said Katsaula. 'A knowledge of the law is a fine thing for a ruler.'

'How are matters in England?' asked Puero, the fat and sly. He used a polysyllabic Maula word meaning 'the-distant-country-of-our-mother', a word that had been handed down from far Victorian days. 'We have heard talk of changes.'

'Certainly there have been changes,' answered Dinamaula. 'But there is still truth and justice and care for the poor.'

'No changes for us in Gamate,' said Puero. Dinamaula saw him exchange a swift glance with Zuva, a flicker of understanding, and wondered if that would be the beginning of secret things between them … 'Here, all is the same, from father to son, and to son's son also.'

'We want no changes,' said Katsaula austerely.

'But the world moves on,' said Zuva. 'Perhaps we must move too … A new chief is another step into the future.'

Dinamaula saw that they were all looking at him, expectantly waiting. Now, clearly, was the time to show what was in his mind; whatever he said in the next few moments would be taken up, as carefully as gleaned corn during a poor harvest, by the Regents and the priest and the doctor and the headmen, and would find its way by a thousand tongues and a thousand ears, till all the men of all Pharamaul had heard it, and pondered it, and understood it.

Speaking gravely and slowly, he said: 'Remember I am the son of Simaula, and grandson of the great Maula. I will rule as they ruled. Whatever changes are to come will be just and fair. I will take thought for the people, and the cattle, and the crops. I will work with white Government, as in the past, to make the tribe prosperous, and to punish evil-doers. But there will be no great changes.' He looked at Puero, and then at Zuva. 'It may be that we can improve upon the past, and learn from it, as our fathers did before us. But my mind is not hungry for power, nor for new things. I will rule as my father ruled. That is all.'

By any standard, it was as good a speech as he could have made. Though it was sincere, yet it took account of all his audience, giving each man a whispered hint of what he wanted to hear, or a guarded warning against excessive zeal. To the old men, he had promised continuity and the rule of law: to the forward-thinking, he held out the prospect of changes – not great changes (these he had denied, for the benefit of Zuva and Puero) but changes such as would advance the common good of the tribe. There could be nothing more, that any true friend of the dynasty could ask for … Ease now returned to the room; men sat back in their chairs, content both with the moment and the future.

Seralo, the oldest and the wisest, found words to round off the scene.

'My son,' he said, rising slowly to his feet, 'you have spoken well, and we thank you … Now let us have no more of these heavy matters. The people are waiting outside, on the *aboura*. Show yourself to them.'

79

Katsaula, careful always for the forms and the customs, said, 'Seralo will lead you out to the people. It would be fitting to say a few words of greeting.'

Dinamaula rose in his turn. 'I thank you,' he said. 'Now let us go.'

Dinamaula was to remember that night, for all the rest of his life. The scene outside was already fantastic: when he appeared on the rough *stoep*, the crowd on the *aboura* seemed to move towards him as though impelled by a giant hand. But the throng was orderly; the old men stood in the front ranks, and behind them the young warriors, singing and chanting, and then, behind them again, in accordance with the custom, the women waited in groups under the thorn trees, waving, calling in shrill tones to their welcome chief. When he raised his hand, and spoke, it was to an electric silence; when he ceased speaking, a great shout of recognition and homage rose up under the sky.

He looked across the heads of the crowd that filled the open space of the *aboura*. He saw, with amusement and without annoyance, that there was a police truck standing a little to one side, under a single thorn tree, with the black policemen smiling widely in his direction, and the white policeman watching the scene at ease, free from care. At that moment, he wanted to unite all men, black and white, in one happy bond. He took the hand of the nearest old man in the front rank, and pressed it, and gave the ceremonial greeting: '*Ahsula!*' – 'Peace!'

The word was taken up. Other men pressed forward to clasp his hand in turn. '*Ahsula!*' called the younger men at the back. The women repeated it, in the further darkness, and then the children, making a jingle out of it – '*Ahsula, Dinamaula! Ahsula, Dinamaula!*' At his side, Seralo, his old face shaking with deep emotion, said, 'Let them sing for you. Let them dance for you.'

First the children sang, a song of peace and welcome, their piping voices sounding reedy-clear under the stars. Then the young men of his own age group – called, by custom, the Dinamaula Regiment – danced a tribal dance, with stamping, and mock killing, and many of the contortions of love, while the young women under the trees went 'Aieeh! ...' and moved their own bodies in time with the beat. Then it was time to feast.

At the long trestle-tables under the thorn trees, Dinamaula and his party ate and drank with lusty appetite. His own mother came to serve him, leaning on his shoulder, smiling, humble, with tears falling down her cheeks at the wonder of the moment. 'My son, my chief,' she whispered, tendering him the dish of prime chopped mutton, helping him with warm and generous hands just as she had done when he was a small boy; and he leant back and touched her trembling arm, and said, 'My mother, I am come home – I thank you,' and gave her a smile that dried her ready tears, and then caused fresh ones to flow. Katsaula, the man of history, pledged his health in a cup of fierce liquor, using old phrases from the past, and new greetings. Seralo pledged him, his lips trembling on the lip of the bowl. Zuva pledged him, his eyes mocking and over-bold; and then the fat Puero, already far gone in his cups.

His mother came again to his elbow, to ask if he needed more food. Round him, the crowds at the other tables began to shout and sing. The children, struggling against sleep, ran from table to table, laughing, eating, snatching, upsetting the cups and the plates. At a signal from Katsaula, a choir of young women advanced, their hips swinging, their bright eyes roving among the young men, and sang a lascivious song – yet a song hallowed by custom – which began: '*Oh Dinamaula, we would give you many sons*'. Old Seralo laughed with glee, Katsaula listened carefully for any variation, Zuva made off into the darkness between the huts with a comely twisting girl, Puero rolled under the trestle-table, and began to snore. After the singing, one of the young girls, not the prettiest, advanced with a dish of olives, and bent over his shoulder, her breast heavy on his arm.

'My Lord,' she said. 'Take, eat.'

'This is Miera,' said Katsaula. 'The daughter of my brother, who died at the time of the bad sickness. She has been chosen.'

'Chosen?' asked Dinamaula, alert. The girl was not comely, and her body, hot from the dancing, was acrid, and shining with sweat. 'How, chosen?'

'Chosen for this honour,' said Katsaula swiftly. He indicated the dish of olives. 'She gives you the last food of the night, according to the custom.'

The girl was still leaning against him. He felt the lower part of her body pressing into the small of his back, like an animal nuzzling. Her wiry hair was plastered with ochre mud, her jaw heavy; between her massive breasts, the sweat ran generously. Something within him revolted – at the girl's animal readiness, at the greasy bowls of mutton, the fierce liquor, the whole noisy uproar that filled the *aboura*. Before, it had been decorous and honourable; now it was suddenly repellent in its crudity.

He said, with difficulty: 'Miera, I thank you,' and took two olives, and bit into one of them. He saw Katsaula eyeing him askance, and he turned again to the girl, and said, 'They have chosen you well.'

He felt her swelling groin seeking the soft parts of his back again, and suddenly he could endure it no more, and he stood up, and nodded to Seralo, and said formally: 'Old Uncle, I have journeyed far. It is time for sleep.'

Sleep came to him on laggard steps. His hut was roomy and the couch of skins was soft, but the hot air of the night seemed to press heavily upon him. His brain was filled with many tangled thoughts, and with liquor also. He thought of what he wanted to do in Gamate, and of what lay in his path. He thought of his mother, who could only approach him as a servant. He thought of the girl Miera, and of the clear intention that she was to be his bride.

He remembered what he had said to the man in the plane – that he wanted to change things – and he knew that this was true. Yet he did not want to change them by violence. He wanted Pharamaula to be something like England – secure, kindly, benign. He wanted a better life for the tribe, yet with no overthrow of the past. He wanted to get married – his liquor-hot body moved at the thought – yet he wanted no girl such as Miera, stupid and uncouth and without grace. There had been another girl in the choir of welcome, a slim girl with a light skin and breasts of small and pointed excellence – but probably she too would be not much more than a willing animal, in bed or out of it.

He listened to the sounds outside on the *aboura*, where the feasting and the drinking were far from done. The last party he had attended had been at the Savoy in London, when he had danced with a blonde girl who had talked coolly of politics and travel and music, and had seemed also to beg his body to invade hers, taking for granted a ready torrent of virility. And so it had proved … How could he change his people and his country, so that all things were clean, all things were handsome, all things were pleasant and up-to-date?

The sounds outside were still raucous and intrusive. Presently, when the girl Miera crept into his hut, he feigned sleep. He could smell the heat of her loins, imagine their moist readiness. But that was not what he wanted, in Gamate or anywhere else. When she withdrew again, wordless, cautious as an animal moving among humans, he turned over and stared in despair at the laced reeds of the roof above his head.

He wanted many things. While some of them were here in Gamate, and some were in England, others still eluded the cloudy confusion of his brain.

III

Tulbach Browne of the *Daily Thresh* sat deep in an old leather armchair in the smoking room of the Pharamaul Club, waiting for Lou Strogoff, the American consul.

Tulbach Browne was bored, irritable, and out of sorts. He did not like Port Victoria, which was hot and dirty: he did not like the way people managed to enjoy life, even on a tropical island; especially he did not like the Hotel Bristol, where the bathwater smelt of the drains, the butter swam in its own rancid fat, and the service was so grudging and so sketchy that he had already lost his temper on half a dozen occasions.

He did not like it, but he had to stay. For the *Daily Thresh* had taken a fancy (not surprisingly) to the stories he was sending, and wanted plenty more of the same sort.

He did not even like the Pharamaul Club, where he was now a temporary member. Listening to the inane conversation going on round him, he renewed his hatred of anything of which he was not fully a part.

His fellow members were mostly large hearty men, burned by the sun, flushed by whisky, beer, pink gin, sherry, port, and rum cocktails. They read the London *Times* air-mail edition, five days old), the *Tatler* and the *Illustrated London News* (by surface mail, six weeks in arrears), and talked about themselves. They were business men, planters, lumber executives, importers, immigrants, rich and poor idlers; sometimes they were even civil servants, most hated category of all. As he listened now, his back turned to the beer-swilling gang which had taken possession of one corner of the smoking-room, Tulbach Browne wanted to set it all down in acid prose, and put it on the wire straightway.

There had been some sort of altercation with one of the native wine stewards.

'Bolshy bastard!' said a thick fruity voice.

'If there's anything I *particularly* dislike,' said another, 'it's a surly club servant.'

'Where's the complaints book? This bloody club gets worse and worse.'

'I'll write a note to Splinter Woodcock.'

'Yes. Splinter will fix him.'

'Rot. Splinter couldn't fix a dripping tap.'

'Could *you*, old boy? – could *you*?'

Roars of laughter, drowning all other sounds.

'Steward! Where's that bloody black oaf got to now?'

'*Barena*?'

'Bring another round – and for Christ's sake hop to it!'

'Yes, *barena*.'

'Bolshy bastard.'

'Splinter Woodcock will fix him.'

Tulbach Browne sat on, sipping his whisky-sour, staring at the spotted mezzotint above the mantelpiece – inevitably, the 'Death of Nelson'. He had spent much of the past week in the club, which was marginally better than the Bristol; it had not endeared him to anyone save Strogoff, the American consul – and even he seemed to have caught the prevailing Pharamaul infection. It was really extraordinary that an American who had spent twenty years in a British protectorate could still like the British.

Tulbach Browne had done other things, too. He had called on the Governor, asked him three questions about local administration, and one about Dinamaula, and had set it all down in 'The Cocked Hat Brigade'. He had written a piece about the club itself, a blistering six hundred words headed 'The Gin Drinkers of Pharamaul', which would probably be in tomorrow's *Daily Thresh*. He had gone twice to a local negro cinema, and had been surprised by the kind of films – exclusively sex, crime, and Western horse-operas, some of them not less than twenty years old – which the film exhibitors seemed to think were fit entertainment for these simple people. But he had not thought that worth a story. Not for the *Daily Thresh*.

Instead, he had written the one about the humble and degraded blacks toiling inhuman hours for the white man, and existing on a handful of mealie-rice a day; and he had met four friends of a man named Zuva Katsaula, a forward-thinking African who apparently headed a movement called the 'Freedom for Pharamaul Party', and had written them up in glowing terms ('There are Statesmen at the Bottom of the Pack'), as four of the only future saviours of the country. These had all been straight-cut *Daily Thresh* stories, easy to write, easier still to print.

But now he was bored again, waiting to go up to Gamate, waiting also for Lou Strogoff – and here was Lou Strogoff, that unlikely man who still admired the British-in-exile, walking through the smoking-room doorway towards him.

Lou Strogoff had been a surprise, when they had first met, a couple of days earlier. 'American consul' usually meant a forceful, brash, *faux-bonhomme* character, inclined to woo like a politician or bluster like a suspect gambler before the TV cameras; inclined, indeed, to give a continuous performance as an American consul. 'Lou Strogoff' had sounded just that. But instead he had turned out to be an oldish, scholarly man, nearer sixty than fifty; soft-spoken, firm, and humorous. He had lived twenty years in Pharamaul, and he was content to stay there till he died.

'But don't quote me on that,' he had added at their first meeting. 'If the State Department hear about it, they'll have me climbing icebergs in Greenland. The foreign service is a great institution – if they just let you stay still in one place.'

Now, as he came forward, greeting one or two friends on the way, he was smiling.

'Still here?' he asked. 'I thought you newspaper fellows never stopped so long in any country. Don't tell me you've fallen for Port Victoria?'

'No,' said Tulbach Browne, somewhat sourly. 'That has not happened. It's just that I've got one or two stories to cover before going up to Gamate.'

'More about the Cocked Hat Brigade?' asked Strogoff innocently.

Tulbach Browne stared. 'How has that got back to you so quickly?'

'We have a very good intelligence system, answered Strogoff blandly. 'It's modelled on the British ...'

They ordered drinks, and sipped them slowly. The pine-panelled room was cool after the heat of the day, and, as the crowds thinned towards the dinner hour, quiet also.

'Didn't you agree with the article?' asked Tulbach Browne presently.

Lou Strogoff smiled. 'No, sir ... I agree that the British wear cocked hats, I agree that the British *act* cocked hats, and sometimes are cocked hats. But I don't agree that it's wrong, for a place like this.' He stared at his drink. 'You're ruling a backward people here. It's something you've done very successfully for hundreds of years – something we Americans are only just learning for ourselves, the hard way. You've got to make your Governor, and all the others, *look* like rulers. If that means cocks' feathers, white uniforms, and plenty of dog, there's no harm in it. It suits Pharamaul.'

'But it's treating the Maulas like children.'

'Most of them *are* children.'

'You know,' said Tulbach Browne, 'I'm surprised you feel like that. I should have thought an American would have seen the silly side of what we're doing in places like this.'

'I used to think that way,' agreed Strogoff amiably. 'I used to pray for a bit of honest American democracy, just to ease the situation. But when you've been here as long as I have ...' His voice tailed off. 'Give the Maulas democracy,' he continued, 'that is, full social and political equality, and you'll have the worst mess you can think of. In the first place, they wouldn't know what to do with it; in the second, the process of finding out would be very painful and completely chaotic; and thirdly, there are just enough smart operators among the Maulas – especially here in Port Victoria – to take advantage of the sudden grant of freedom, and run it as a personal racket.'

'Then we must teach them how to handle it properly.'

'You *are* teaching them. But slowly. When I first came here, back in the mid-thirties, there were no Maulas at all on the town council. The idea would have been unthinkable. Now there are three; three, out of twenty-four. They're not particularly good, because they're so *very* conservative. They don't believe in drains, cavity walls, public wash-houses, diphtheria immunization. However, they *are* learning.'

'But this place,' interjected Tulbach Browne, going off on another tack. He waved his hand round the smoking-room. 'There were some people here earlier – great beefy beery sods, bawling out one of the servants. You can't run a country on that sort of basis.'

'Were they drunk?' asked Strogoff.

'They weren't particularly sober, I'll admit. It seems to be the local disease.'

'If you're a white man, and you have to live in a tropical climate, that's sometimes the only way to endure it.'

'But it was all so crude.'

'Most people in bars and smoking rooms behave in much the same way, don't you think? They're not all like that, anyway, even in Port Victoria – which isn't true Pharamaul. True Pharamaul is up north, in Gamate. There are only a few white men there, and they're very different.'

'Local tin gods, I suppose,' said Tulbach Browne, sneeringly.

Strogoff looked at him. 'It makes a good title for your next piece,' he said quietly, 'but it's not an accurate one. If they're white farmers, they run their places on a paternalistic basis which has worked very well for a couple of hundred years. If they're traders, they give a fair deal – otherwise they wouldn't last six months. When the Maulas run a boycott, they run a boycott … And if they're officials, they do the damnedest job – combined father, mother, policeman, judge, and wetnurse, three hundred and sixty-five days a year – for less than we pay a second-rate soft-goods salesman back home. A damned sight less … Mr Browne.' He said, relaxing, 'I'm *for* this country, and the people that run it. If you want to write an interesting piece, write one about an expatriate American consul on the brink of the grave, who admires the British colonial system.'

Tulbach Browne, who was not without humour, smiled in answer. 'Hell, I want to keep *some* reputation for sanity! The *Daily Thresh* doesn't buy that kind of fairy tale.'

'Then try to sell it to them.' Strogoff raised his hand, and a white-coated servant advanced, collected their empty glasses, and made soft-footed for the service hatch to the bar. 'When are you going up to Gamate?'

'In a couple of days,' answered Tulbach Browne. 'And I warn you. I'm not taking anything on trust. I'm going to see for myself.'

'It's the best way,' said Lou Strogoff equably. 'If you can really use your eyes, the way God meant you to.'

'How do you mean?'

'Not with rose-coloured spectacles. Not with dirt-coloured, either. Not with spectacles at all, in fact. Just with the eyes. It's not easy. But it has been done.'

IV

The LADIES were dealing out destruction at their usual morning meeting, over tea in the Ladies' Annexe to the Pharamaul Club. As always, they were carefully dressed for the occasion; they wore gay hats with flowers, gloves with frilly wrists, large white shoes like boats. They were Mrs Simpson, wife of the naval aide; Mrs Stevens, wife of the First Secretary; Mrs Rogers, wife of the Port Victoria bank manager; Miss Cafferata, an old resident and the principal hanger-on at Government House; and Mrs Burlinghame, whose husband imported kaffir-blankets on a very large scale.

There were two strong points in this interlocking team: Mrs Simpson, who had the edge from the social point of view, and Mrs Burlinghame, who scored her hits and pulled her weight by sheer vitriolic accomplishment. Mrs Rogers had an undoubted advantage, because she had access, by no very indirect means, to the state of everyone's bank balance or overdraft; Miss Cafferata, a severe spinster of fifty-five, suffered from the fact that, when sexual matters were touched on (approximately two mornings in every three), she had to feign a coyness she did not feel, and an ignorance she was bound to profess.

Mrs Stevens, much junior in rank, and also the mother of four children (four was too many, except for those wretched Catholics who couldn't help themselves) – Mrs Stevens mostly kept silent. She knew her place, and the others knew it too. In the Civil Service, a very long uphill climb lay ahead of her.

The subject this morning, as on many mornings in the past, was Anthea Vere-Toombs.

'But what I don't understand,' said Miss Cafferata, drawing her tussore skirt closer round her legs, 'is why her parents don't put a stop to it. I am a great deal at Government House, as you all know. I am sure Sir Elliott and Lady Vere-Toombs – ' she enunciated the names with prodigious clarity, like a proof-reader for *Burke's Peerage*, ' – would never countenance this sort of behaviour.'

'Perhaps they don't know about it,' said Mrs Rogers.

Mrs Simpson snorted. 'Don't see how they can miss it,' she said scornfully. 'Not if the other night at dinner is anything to go by.'

'What actually happened?' asked Mrs Burlinghame. 'I heard she lost control altogether.'

'We've got this new man in the office, David Bracken,' said Mrs Simpson in explanation. She sniffed. 'He's all right, I suppose, if you like those amateur ex-Army types. He was sitting next to Anthea. My dear, he never got a bite to eat! She was practically crawling in his lap.'

'It's time that girl got married,' said Mrs Rogers. 'One day it'll be too late.'

Miss Cafferata looked down her nose. 'What do you mean, too late?'

'I mean, she'll go too far,' said Mrs Rogers stoutly.

'Of course,' said Mrs Burlinghame, launching out at a brilliant tangent, 'she has a great deal of *freedom*. I mean, she can go away *any* time, for *months* if she likes. Do you remember that *long* holiday she took, after she and James Morrison *apparently* had that quarrel?'

The others digested this. Then Mrs Rogers asked, 'You mean, she can go away to recuperate?' Mrs Burlinghame nodded. 'Yes. She went to Johannesburg, didn't she? They say the doctors there are wonderful.'

Mrs Simpson drew in her breath with a sharp hiss. 'She'd better be careful. I believe the South African police are very hot about that sort of thing.'

'What sort of thing?' asked Miss Cafferata.

'Never you mind,' said Mrs Burlinghame, playing up to the popular mystique surrounding Miss Cafferata. 'You're much too young to know.'

'What about this David Bracken?' asked Mrs Rogers. 'Is he married?'

'Apparently not,' said Mrs Simpson. 'But I fancy he's already looking elsewhere.'

'Where?' asked several ladies together.

'Inside the office,' answered Mrs Simpson.

'That's the Steuart girl, I suppose,' said Mrs Burlinghame. 'A bit wishy-washy, I should say, compared with our Anthea.'

'But of course they're working side by side all the time.'

'As long as it's only side by side,' said Miss Cafferata, and giggled wildly.

'Why, Jean!' said Mrs Burlinghame. 'You naughty old thing! What will you be saying next?'

'Wouldn't he prefer a more experienced type?' asked Mrs Rogers.

'Everyone's experienced these days,' remarked Mrs Simpson darkly.

'Would you say,' asked Miss Cafferata, 'that the Steuart girl was *experienced*?'

'My husband says,' said Mrs Stevens, so unexpectedly that they all looked at her, 'that she's very good in the office.'

There was a silence.

'How very interesting,' said Miss Cafferata.

'Do they work together?' asked Mrs Burlinghame.

'No,' answered Mrs Stevens, already regretting her interruption. 'They're in different rooms.'

'Sounds like a hotel,' said Mrs Burlinghame coarsely. 'You know – one of those hotels.'

'Bracken's room is next door to hers,' said Mrs Simpson. 'He changed offices. Don't ask me why.'

'Anthea will have to watch out.'

'Oh, she's got a trick or two up her sleeve.'

'It's not her sleeve I'm thinking of.'

'I heard that Bracken asked her to look at his new flat, the very next morning.'

'Perhaps she'll be taking another trip to Johannesburg before long.'

'Of course, she's getting a bit *old* now.'

'She'd better not count on it.'

The door opened, diplomatically slow, and Anthea Vere-Toombs came in.

'Hallo,' she said. 'Hope I'm not too late for tea.'

'You're just in time,' said Mrs Simpson. 'We were hoping you'd be able to come along.'

'You're always welcome,' said Mrs Rogers. 'What a *pretty* hat!'

'Busy this morning, dear?' asked Miss Cafferata, when Anthea had settled herself.

'Yes, fairly.'

'That's nice,' said Miss Cafferata. 'Enjoy yourself when you're young. That's what we've just been saying.'

CHAPTER FOUR

❖

Within the mid-Victorian bastion of the Scheduled Territories Office, the Whitehall traffic scarcely penetrated; the massive walls were too thick, the double windows too securely bolted, the curtains, perhaps, too dusty. Most of the offices were dreary and dark; the lights burned unceasingly, winter and summer, shedding a wan light on the wan people working within, and infuriating the Ministry of Works, who had to pay the bill and replace the burnt out bulbs. It was one of the oldest ministries in London, and certainly the darkest and shabbiest. It administered large tracts of the earth's surface, and huge sections of its population; itself, it looked like an abandoned orphanage.

It had only two bright spots amid the gloom: the entrance hall, where visitors from the farthest corners of the globe drew breath before plunging into the drab entrails within; and the office of the Permanent Under-Secretary, which he himself – being a forthright man with a habit of getting his own way – had caused to be redecorated when he took over. That had been seven years ago; and the ensuing argument with the Ministry of Works still raged from one end of Whitehall to the other. But the result – a bright room, of pleasing proportions, with a lofty ceiling and solid comfortable furniture – justified all arguments and calmed all criticisms.

The Permanent Under-Secretary for the Scheduled Territories sat at his desk, clearing up his papers before going home. It was seven o'clock, and it had been a long day. In the last nine hours, he had attended a sticky Cabinet meeting, presided at two inter-office committees, and bargained successfully with three cheese-paring vultures from the Treasury; approved a new constitution for some seven hundred square miles of Central Africa, and made a policy decision affecting two million people in the British West Indies; lost an argument with the Navy about the cost of sending two destroyers on a goodwill mission to the Far East, and won a battle with the Army about some deserters who had assaulted a Deputy High Commissioner in Pakistan; dictated a long minute on recruiting in the universities, for the benefit of his Establishments Division; reproved an assistant secretary, reassured an information officer; and had his hair cut, in preparation for a Foreign Office reception for some South American delegates to UNESCO, later that evening.

It had meant a long and exacting day, but not too long and exacting for Sir Hubert Godbold, the Permanent Under-Secretary. Godbold was one of the ablest civil servants in the country, knowledgeable, tough, and untiring. He could have made a fortune in industry, commerce, or any kind of large-scale administration; instead, he made £4,500 a year (less £2,061 income tax) as a senior civil servant, with some five years to go before the retiring age. He had headed the Scheduled Territories Office for seven years; he had weathered a dozen crises – international, internal, financial, political, and unclassifiable; he could work most of his staff off their feet, and he could still find time to say goodbye to an old Office Messenger who was being pensioned off, or talk to a twenty-year old District Officer who was worried about his wife.

Godbold was only one of a number of overworked, nearly anonymous, incorruptible men, of all-embracing competence, who supervised the lives of one hundred and three million people, and were known, collectively and derisively, as civil servants. He was only one, but luckily he was one of the best.

Now, as he sat at his nearly clear desk, there was a knock at the door, and Crossley, one of his assistant under-secretaries, came in, a sheaf of files under his arms. One part of Sir Hubert Godbold's mind – the free-ranging, human part – thought: oh God, what does this careerist bastard want now? The other part – the trained, assiduous part – knew that it must be something that needed dealing with, without delay; otherwise Crossley, a prudent operator, would not have bothered him with it, at seven o'clock on a Friday evening.

Crossley was small, inscrutable, and industrious; he was forty, which was young for an assistant under-secretary, and he had made his way in the Scheduled Territories Office by an admixture of bluff, hard work, manipulation, and genuine talent, which Godbold – no stranger to any of these attributes – was forced to admire. There were lots of Crossleys in the Civil Service; they were not the least useful part of it. One saw through them, one used their undoubted gifts, and one often watched them reach the heights.

Sometimes they tripped up on the way, and were heard of no more; a man could be too clever, too servile, too wrapped up in office politics, too adept at doing hatchet jobs on his contemporaries. But Crossley would probably reach those heights – and in the meantime, he held down a full-time post with full-time enthusiasm and competence.

'Yes, Crossley?' said the Permanent Under-Secretary.

'Sir,' said Crossley, advancing with his files, 'there's a PQ on Pharamaul.'

'Oh ...' Godbold took the proffered papers, and looked at the top one, clipped on to the outside of the file. It was a foolscap sheet of blue–grey draft paper; it was headed: 'Parliamentary Question: Principality of Pharamaul: Mr Price-Canning.'

'*That* man,' said Godbold, with feeling. 'It's those damned *Daily Thresh* articles, I suppose.' He adjusted his spectacles and read slowly, aloud:

'Notice has been given of the following Parliamentary Question, to be asked by Mr Emrys Price-Canning (Ind Lib South Oxford), next Tuesday, September 22nd. "*To ask the Secretary of State for the Scheduled Territories* whether his attention has been drawn to various statements of policy recently made by Dinamaula Maula, chief-designate of the Maula Tribe in the Principality of Pharamaul; whether he is in agreement with such statements; and whether he can give an assurance that the plans outlined in these statements will receive the sympathetic consideration of Her Majesty's Government, and will not be obstructed by government officials in the Principality itself."'

Godbold sat back in his chair again. He had had a great deal to think about, and to do, on that day already; he wanted, if possible, to save himself further thought, further pre-digestive reading. Knowing Crossley, and counting on him, he said: 'Refresh my memory.'

To the staff of the Scheduled Territories Office, it was a familiar phrase, and Crossley was ready for it.

'Sir,' he began again, scarcely glancing at his notes, 'you remember there have been these four articles on Pharamaul by Tulbach Browne in the *Daily Thresh*. Three of them aren't really important – they're the usual thing about our reactionary colonial policy, and the slowness and stuffiness of officials on the spot, and the backwardness of the Maulas – '

'But part of the build-up,' interjected Godbold.

'Part of the build-up, certainly … It was the first one that we sent a telegram about: that was the reported interview with Dinamaula, to the effect that he had a lot of reforms which he wanted to put through, but that he didn't give much for his chances, because he was likely to be obstructed.'

'By the Maulas, as well as our own people.'

'Yes, sir. We telegraphed the Governor, asking for Macmillan to have a word with Dinamaula, and we got an answer yesterday that Macmillan had seen Dinamaula, and had issued a general warning. Now there's this.'

'Any connexion?'

'I shouldn't say so, sir. There's hardly been time. I should think Price-Canning is acting on his own. You know the way he works.'

The Permanent Under-Secretary considered the matter. He did indeed know the way that Emrys Price-Canning worked, whether inside the House or out of it. Price-Canning the never-sleeping conscience of England, Price-Canning the shrine of liberal thought, Price-Canning the soldiers friend, Price-Canning the champion of the underdog, Price-Canning the black man's shield and buckler, Price-Canning the – there was really no end to it.

Godbold knew Price-Canning personally, of course; there was hardly a senior civil servant who did not. The man was everywhere: he spoke with fluent violence, and he was always sure of a good press, from any paper to the left of the *Daily Telegraph*, together with a two-column cut of his beak nose and shock of hair in full cry after the scent of fascist tyranny … His nuisance value was enormous. Mostly he was wrong – wrong-headed, wrongly advised, factually wrong; but this never stopped him from kicking up the maximum of fuss, and making the maximum of noise about it.

Once, years ago, he had actually Righted an Injustice – something to do with an old soldier's pension rights. Since then, he had never looked back. And now, here he was again, rescuing the Maulas from the foul clutches of British officialdom.

Godbold considered a little further. The whole thing could blow over, because Pharamaul was in the main a prosperous, well-administered country, and Dinamaula, when they had had their farewell interview, had seemed sensible and co-operative. On the other hand, the *Daily Thresh* articles had attracted a lot of attention; and Tulbach Browne and Emrys Price-Canning, if they ever came into purposeful collaboration, could give the Scheduled Territories Office a very uncomfortable time.

It seemed to call for a bromide answer: a bromide, with certain safeguards. It was Godbold's job to advise the Minister (who would have to answer the question in the House of Commons) on the best way of dealing with it; knowing his Minister, he wanted to give him the best ammunition available.

'We'd better play it safe,' he said, and waited.

One of Crossley's odd accomplishments was a knowledge of shorthand. He took out his pencil in readiness.

'Something like this,' continued Godbold. ' "Yes, sir, I have seen a newspaper report of the statements in question … While Her Majesty's Government is in full agreement with the views expressed, in so far as they refer to the desirability of the general advancement of the people of Pharamaul, it deprecates an *ex parte* statement of this nature, made by a chief-designate who has not yet assumed office ... There has been, and will be, no obstruction of any sort from HM officials on the spot."'

'*Full* agreement, sir? He went a bit far.'

'All right – general agreement ... Supplementaries?'

Crossley consulted his notes. 'Price-Cannning will probably ask what we're doing to further Dinamaula's plans for development.'

' "Such plans have not yet been officially communicated to HM Government."'

'If and when they are?'

' "I cannot answer a hypothetical question of this nature."'

Both Godbold and Crossley enjoyed this game. 'Are we sincere,' Crossley continued, 'in our professions of willingness to advance the cause of political and cultural development in this area?'

' "HM Government's policy in Pharamaul continues in accord with general colonial advancement throughout this and other areas, and naturally envisages all practicable developments."'

'Did Dinamaula communicate his views before leaving London?'

Godbold paused at that one. Price-Canning might never reach it, in his quest for knowledge; in fact, if he felt like having a slack day, he might never ask any supplementaries at all. But once more, the Minister must have the requisite ammunition to deal with any eventuality.

' "Before leaving London,"' Godbold intoned, while Crossley wrote busily, ' "the chief-designate had a cordial interview with the Permanent Under-Secretary, at which – "' he paused, ' " – at which no specific plans for Maula development were discussed."'

'Has HM Government full confidence in Dinamaula as the future chief of the Maulas?'

Now there was the longest pause of all. That, if Price-Canning ever got to it, was the trick question, because it sought guarantees for the future, the future that might go wrong. It was impossible to give any official commitment, in a sphere which was still a matter of guesswork. Dinamaula, a few years from now, might be a very different person.

' "Her Majesty's Government," ' dictated Godbold at last, ' "has every confidence that Dinamaula, when he assumes the chieftainship, will co-operate with the Pharamaul authorities in pursuance of joint plans for the administration of the Principality." '

Crossley smiled. It was a good answer, a damned good answer: above all, it contained that weasel word 'co-operate', which begged every question in sight. If things went smoothly, then obviously Dinamaula must be co-operating; if there were difficulties, then he was not. It was the sort of answer Crossley hoped to give himself a dozen years from now.

Godbold approved the answer much less himself. 'It's a trick answer,' he explained candidly, 'to a trick question. We don't say that we approve of him in every respect; we approve of him if he co-operates. You see?'

'Oh yes, sir,' answered Crossley, enthusiastically. 'I see.'

Godbold did not like his assistant under-secretary at that moment, but there was no point in showing it. He relaxed in his chair again.

'Smooth all that out,' he said briefly. 'Get it typed. I'll see it before it goes to the Minister.'

The Minister for the Scheduled Territories, Lord Lorde – son of so aged a marquess that the prospect of inheritance had long since ceased to occupy his mind – was probably Britain's most reassignable statesman.

Having, as a young man, failed to qualify for the Army, the Foreign Office, the Law, the higher ranks of the business world, or even the then embryonic British Broadcasting Corporation, he had entered politics at a comparatively early age. His father, although possessing what the London *Times* euphemistically called 'a great gift for silence' – he had made only one speech in thirty-seven years in the House of Lords – had a discreet word with this man, a friendly talk with that; and thereafter Lord Lorde had progressed from ministry to ministry, never remaining long enough to make a serious mark (successive Prime Ministers being far too prudent to risk that), but on the other hand never giving a performance so utterly forlorn as to disqualify him completely from public office.

Usually, he was assigned to the Secretaryship of whatever ministry was likely to remain in the doldrums for some considerable time to come. He had been Minister of War at a time of stagnant peace. He had been First Lord of the Admiralty when the drive was for bigger and better aircraft. He had been Minister of Fuel during the very hottest weather, Minister of Transport during a long winter when heavy snow forced all rail and road traffic to a virtual standstill. He had been Secretary of State for Air up till the very year it became obvious that the heavier-than-air machine had come to stay.

As each new appointment was announced, *The Times* always said: 'Lord Lorde brings to an exacting task the virtues of a fresh mind.'

Lord Lorde was a tall, mournful man, known to the popular Press as 'the hop-pole'. It was reported that one famous prime minister had once remarked, in a fit of exasperation: 'And I'd like to see the beggar hop! ...' Now he was Minister for the Scheduled Territories, normally a quiet billet concerned with Britain's minor acquisitions of the past – small backward countries that were non-profitable, non-ambitious: mandated territories: protectorates that had slipped into Britain's lap during Victorian days, and had lain there ever since.

In the ordinary course of events, the particular office-holder did not greatly matter. The Ministry was run by the Permanent Under-Secretary, in any case; and when the Permanent Under-Secretary was a man of Godbold's calibre, the Minister could have been an ageing long-horned toad, for all the difference it made. But just occasionally, some development in the Scheduled Territories attracted the public attention. When Lord Lorde got up, papers in hand, on that Tuesday afternoon, to answer his oral questions in the House of Commons, he found himself wondering uneasily if this were one of those rare moments of history. Godbold had been particularly insistent that he stick to his brief.

Hansard carried it thus:

62. *Mr Emrys Price-Canning* asked the Secretary of State for the Scheduled Territories whether his attention has been drawn to various statements of policy recently made by Dinamaula Maula, chief-designate of the Maula tribe in the Principality of Pharamaul; whether he is in agreement with such statements; and whether he can give an assurance that the plans outlined in these statements will receive the sympathetic consideration of Her Majesty's Government, and will not be obstructed by government officials in the Principality itself.
The Secretary of State for the Scheduled Territories (Lord Lorde): Yes, sir. I have seen a newspaper report of the statements in question. While I am in general agreement with the views expressed, in so far as they

refer to the desirability of contributing to the advancement of the people of Pharamaul, I deprecate an *ex parte* statement of this nature, made by a chief-designate who has not yet assumed office. There will, of course, be no obstruction from government officials on the spot.

Mr Emrys Price-Canning: Am I to understand from my right hon. Friend's reply that government officials in Pharamaul will assist Chief Dinamaula in his various projects?

Lord Lorde: Yes, sir, if in the opinion of Her Majesty's government such projects are conducive to the general well-being of the Maula tribe.

Mr Emrys Price-Canning: Who will be the judge of that?

An Hon. Member: Order.

Lord Lorde: The government officials on the spot will naturally act in accordance with the broad general policy of Her Majesty's government as regards the colonial peoples, and will as usual concert their plans with those of the reigning chief of the Maulas, in advancing the best interests of his tribe.

Mr Emrys Price-Canning: Arising out of that reply, can the Minister say what will happen if there is a clash of opinion as regards such plans?

Lord Lorde: I cannot answer a hypothetical question of that nature.

Mr Emrys Price-Canning: My right hon. Friend mentioned in the course of his reply that he deprecated *ex parte* statements made by the chief-designate. Surely the chief-designate is the best possible person –

Hon. Members: Order.

Mr Speaker: Hon. members must not make speeches at this time.

Mr Emrys Price-Canning: I apologize, sir. I have a further supplementary question to put. Has the Minister's displeasure with such *ex parte* statements been communicated to Chief Dinamaula, and if so, by whom, and with what result?

Lord Lorde: The Resident Commissioner, Gamate, had an interview with the chief-designate, at which it was indicated that such public statements were entirely unsuitable in the circumstances, and that a serious view might be taken if there were further publicity of this kind. (Interruption.)

Mr Emrys Price-Canning: Muzzling. Hypocrisy. We say we want to advance these people, and yet as soon as one of their chiefs has the guts to –

Hon. Members: Order.

Mr Speaker: The hon. member for South Oxford must not make these statements during the time set aside for oral questions.

Mr Emrys Price-Canning: I call on the Minister to tell me what he will do if these muzzling tactics, this bullying, results in –

Hon. Members: Order.

Mr Speaker: The hon. member is out of order in making these charges during a supplementary question.

Mr Emrys Price-Canning: Sir, I am trying to get at the truth.

Lord Lorde: And I am doing my best to assist my hon. Friend.

Mr Emrys Price-Canning: Nonsense. You're covering up for a bunch of fascist jacks-in-office.

Hon. Members: Withdraw.

Lord Lorde: My hon. Friend is pleased to be offensive.

Mr Emrys Price-Canning: Not half so offensive as the spectacle of a British government department using

all its authority to jump on a wretched native chief
who –

(Confused Interruptions.)

Hon Members: Order. Withdraw.
Lord Lorde: We have to safeguard our declared
principles, and the continuation of –
Mr Emrys Price-Canning: You have to safeguard your
job, and your six-foot sense of superiority, and that's
about all there is to it.
Hon. Members: Withdraw.
Mr Speaker rose.
Mr Speaker: The hon. member must withdraw that
remark.
Mr Emrys Price-Canning: I will withdraw nothing.
Mr Speaker: The hon. member will withdraw, and
resume his seat.
Mr Emrys Price-Canning: I will do nothing of the sort.
This is rank injustice.
Mr Speaker: If the hon. member does not withdraw, I
must name him.
Mr Emrys Price-Canning: Go ahead.
Hon. Members: Name. Name.
Mr Speaker: I name the hon. member for South
Oxford.
The Lord President of the Council: I beg to move, "that
Mr Emrys Price-Canning be suspended from the
service of the House."

Question put, and agreed to.

'UPROAR IN HOUSE,' said the *Daily Thresh*. 'MP SUSPENDED.
"BULLYING AND MUZZLING" IN PHARAMAUL. See "Rank
Injustice" in *Spotlight*, page 4.'

II

David Bracken was glad to be bidding a temporary goodbye to Port Victoria, even though the long and uncomfortable journey to Gamate, and on up to Shebiya, was not in itself an attractive prospect. But Port Victoria during the past week had been unbearably hot; the last days of September were always the worst here, when the heat and smell and humid languor of incipient spring reached their least tolerable point.

He was even, at this stage, somewhat under-employed; naturally, there could not be a great deal for him to do in the Secretariat until he had explored the country and met some of the people he was administering. It was difficult, for example, to compose the first half of a despatch about the effects of *lobola* upon the grazing in the northern Gamate plains, when he scarcely knew whether *lobola* were a disease, an animal, or an illegal method of farming … A long time must elapse, he knew, before he got a real grip on the problems of this country; but in the meanwhile it was good to be making a start, good to be moving instead of sitting still in melting indolence.

When Nicole Steuart put her head round the door of his room, he realized that there was only one thing he was sorry to leave, in Port Victoria.

Smiling, she said: 'Still busy?'

'No, I'm about finished.' David Bracken stood up, and gestured towards a chair. 'Come in.'

She sat down, with the grace and economy of movement which characterized almost everything she did. Her skirt swung like weighted drapery, slow and somehow poetic … Aware that he was falling into agreeably bad habits, David had taken a solemn oath, earlier in the week, that he would not stare either at her face or her body, whenever she came into his office; but when, for the hundredth time since then, he found himself breaking both aspects of the undertaking, he did not feel unduly guilty. After all, he was going to be away for a whole week ... Nicole became conscious of his frank eyes upon her; the half of her that was gently beginning to welcome this, warred unsuccessfully with the other, stricter half, and she sat back, and said coolly: 'I suppose you're packed, and everything?'

David, behind his desk again, nodded. 'Yes. All ready. I hope that odd-looking train won't be too uncomfortable.'

'It always has been, whenever I've made the trip.'

'When were you last in Gamate?'

'About six months ago. It doesn't change much ...' Her thoughts were wandering, as they frequently and mortifyingly did nowadays. With an effort she continued: 'There's been some sort of row in Parliament about Dinamaula. The telegram's just coming through.'

'What kind of row?'

'Price-Canning was suspended for being rude to the SOS.'

David Bracken grinned. 'It must be rather tempting.'

She frowned. 'Silly, though. It doesn't do any good. If Price-Canning really wants to help people like the Maulas, there are better ways of doing it.'

'Oh, Price-Canning's all right. He focuses people's attention.'

'On Price-Canning.'

'Well, at least he stirs things up.'

'That's not always the best thing to do with "things".'

He grinned again. 'I know we don't agree,' he said, falsely apologetic. 'I'll *try* to see it your way. I'm new, you know. Still championing the underdog.'

She looked at him, frowning once more. David Bracken could still annoy her enormously, when he was in this satiric mood that had an element of priggishness about it.

He really *did* believe that all black men were downtrodden, and all white men – except men like Price-Canning – usurpers or colonial despots. He really *did* believe that one side was right all the time, and the other side wrong. He really *had* taken Anthea Vere-Toombs up to his flat, like Mrs Stevens had told her under the strict seal of secrecy. He really must have done a lot of peculiar things there – Anthea was like that – it was a damned shame – Nicole Steuart pulled herself together, and stood up. She had wanted to stay much longer, but it wasn't working out the way she had hoped. That was something that often happened, with David Bracken.

'You'll get over it,' she said briefly. 'It usually takes people about six months.' Then, near the door, she heard herself, with a kind of appalled satisfaction, add jauntily: 'Don't forget to say goodbye to Anthea.' Then she was gone.

David Bracken stared at her shapely retreating back, feeling very foolish. It was just what he had faithfully promised to do.

They were not yet lovers, though David Bracken could scarcely understand why. It was as Aidan Purves-Brownrigg had forecast, on the first evening that he had seen David and Anthea together – David had been elected. The fact that he had not yet taken up his option was a minor triumph of defence over attack.

'Take care of yourself,' said Anthea now, between clinging kisses. They were sitting in her parked car, in the twilight, on the dark road that led to the station; at her insistence, they had set out a full hour before his train was due to leave, and there seemed no doubt in anyone's mind as to how the spare time was to be employed. 'I'll miss you all the time. Will you miss me?'

'Of course,' answered David, glad of a chance to catch his breath. The whole thing was really rather sad. Anthea was distinctly attractive, and demonstrably available. The fact that he did not want her at all was due to a lot of things that were just bad luck. They ranged from a prudent disinclination to seduce the boss's daughter (if the word 'seduce' could be stretched so far) to an unwillingness to accept the role of fly to this clambering spider. They were a very long list of excuses, and Nicole Steuart was involved in most of them.

'You don't sound as though you'll miss me,' said Anthea, pouting. The shoulder strap of her evening gown threatened to cover her shoulder again, and she manoeuvred it down adroitly. 'Don't you think of me at all?'

'Of course I do.'

'When? At night?'

'Oh yes,' agreed David. 'Especially at night.'

She wriggled. 'Why "especially"?'

David paused. The correct answer was, 'Because most men think of women at night, and I don't yet want to think of Nicole like that, so I think of you instead.' But the correct answer was not the answer to give, on this or any other occasion. He temporized. 'It seems to suit you,' he said finally. 'You and the dark somehow go together.'

'You darling!' she said ecstatically. 'When you come back, we'll have to do something about that.' She snuggled up to him, as if he were back already. 'You do want me, don't you?'

'Who wouldn't?'

'I certainly want you. I wish I were a man. It's all so much easier.'

David gulped. 'Why?'

'Oh, we have to hide things all the time.'

If she really believes that, David thought, it's going to take a brave man to contradict her. That man was not himself … He turned and kissed her again, seeing no point in not doing so, and she pushed herself swiftly within his arms, her breast urgent and hungry.

She murmured: 'Have you ever done it in cars?'

'No,' said David promptly.

There was a long and thoughtful pause.

'Old slow-coach,' she chided fondly.

The clock on the dash still showed about twenty minutes to train time. He did not really know what to do. His hand strayed down over her bared breast, meeting only ready acceptance, and then he thought: No, I'm damned if I will, and he sighed, as if it were the saddest thing in the world, and said, 'We'll have to be going, I'm afraid.'

'We've still got time.'

There seemed little doubt that this would be true, for her. Nor, at this late stage, would he have much to worry about himself. Desire warred with all the other factors, and started to overcome them – and then, blessedly, a single wavering light at the far end of the road began to approach their car, a bicycle light that brightened with wonderful deliberation and slowness; and by the time it was level with them, and the rider, a tattered old man with a fowl under one arm, had bowed in greeting and said, 'Jah, *barena*,' and pedalled creakily past, the moment was gone, and the clock had moved forward three minutes, and David sat up and said: 'What a pity. It really *is* time to move.'

Anthea sighed, and straightened up in her turn. She smiled at him, her face softened with desire, her breath still fast.

'I don't like old men on bicycles.'

'They're often the biggest nuisance in the world.'

'It would have been lovely.'

'It certainly would.'

'Next time?'

'Yes,' said David. 'I shouldn't wonder at all.'

'Goodbye,' she said. 'Take care of yourself.'

If it had been Nicole Steuart, he thought – though of course it couldn't have been – but *if* it had been Nicole Steuart, he would have answered: I'll take care of myself because I love you, and want to marry you, and I'll come back for that reason. Or at least he would have wished to say such words ... They still wouldn't have been lovers, because Nicole wouldn't have been like Anthea, and he wouldn't have wanted her to be, and he wouldn't have minded waiting, either – in fact, it wouldn't have seemed like waiting at all. He looked at Anthea, and was sorry for her, and angry with himself. He wanted to tell her that there would never be a next time, but he wasn't even sure of that. There would always be a next time, until he had fixed things with Nicole. But then it would be all right.

The moment, which had seemed funny and mildly scandalous, had now turned sour and stale. He did not in the least want this old-fashioned garrison hack ... He said shortly: 'I'll take care of myself,' and waited, in self-despising impatience, for Anthea to start the car.

The many discomforts of that long train journey to Gamate – the heat, the noise, the rough movement of the train on the narrow track, the rougher berth with its prickly grey blankets – all these things, as well as the shoddy goodbye session with Anthea, were forgotten next morning, when David awoke to his first fabulous dawn in Africa.

He awoke to it with a mouth sourly thick with whisky – there had been nothing else to do, the previous night, and no one to talk to – and a head heavy from the close air of the compartment. But the pale light through the slatted blind beckoned him insistently: his watch showed that the time was still short of five o'clock, but outside was the emerging day. He raised the blind, and turned over on one shoulder to look out. Then he sat up straight in his narrow berth. He was looking towards the east, and the east was about to set Pharamaul on fire.

As far as his eye could reach, the rolling plain stretched away to the horizon. The sunrise was imminent: the grasslands and the rocky outcrops now had a strange uncertain colour – grey from the night, gold from the dawn. Above them, a pale sky was already drawing streaky orange light from the invisible sun. The train was running, with lumbering deliberation, through deserted country: there was a smell of Africa – burnt grass, hot earth – and a look of Africa too. As yet, there was nothing in view save a vast plain, and a conical hill on the horizon, and a world waiting for the day.

As he watched, the conical hill turned from black to purple. The dew and the spider-webs on the grassland started to gleam. A circle of huts came into view: grey, sleepy, motionless except for the first thin wisp of smoke climbing with true ascent into the upper air. Then suddenly the golden edge of the sun swam up from the far horizon, and all the drab colours changed to the colours of hope and warmth – grey to silver, purple to blue, black to red. David stared entranced as the plains of Pharamaul rose instantly to the new day.

Presently the train slowed, and ground to a stop at a rough siding – no more than two lines of track instead of one, a water-tower for the thirsty engine, a clearing with a few huts and a single frame house. David threw on some clothes, and climbed down from the train, glad to stretch his legs. In the cold dawn, the sun quickly gained power and warmth.

He walked forward to the engine. Black faces peered at him from masked windows: other figures climbed down stiffly. Away to the north, a thickening plume of grey smoke marked the southbound train which would pass them at this point. From the caboose next to the engine, one of the train crew smiled at him, and handed down a thick mug of coffee. Sipping it, watching the other train approaching, turning to stare at the sky and the limitless plain around him, listening to the *veld* dawn and the quickening birdsong, David Bracken forgot the past night, and Anthea Vere-Toombs, and even Nicole, and fell in love with Pharamaul.

It was foolish, it was unreal, yet it seemed inevitable. All he had to fall in love with was this near-deserted siding set in the middle of a brown, dusty plain: some goats, some peering children: a white engineer coming out of a frame house: the sun climbing the sky; and a railway line leading north into the haze, and south into a shadowy blankness, as far as the eye could reach. There was some gritty coffee to cheer him, an off-duty fireman to smile at: the splash of water from the rusty water-tower: a dog sniffing at a thorn tree, a million ants crawling and hurrying on their pathway of destruction. That was all there was, to a dawn in Pharamaul; and yet the moment had a beauty amid a simple entrancement that left him breathless.

He remembered now a man back in London, a world traveller, who had told him confidently: 'Once you come to that part of the world, and see what it has to offer, you'll never want to leave it again.' Andrew Macmillan had talked the same way, with the same look of dedication. Now David saw it with his own eyes, and smelt it, and drank it in; and he felt that he could have settled down in the small frame house on the edge of the siding, and there lived out his days in absolute peace.

That feeling was doubly confirmed, eight hours later, in Gamate itself.

Forsdick, the District Commissioner, met him at the station; sweating in the noonday heat, his khaki shirt wilting, his florid face a ruddy purple under the tan.

'How do?' he said, advancing a solid hand. It was a long time since David had heard the homely, North-country phrase. 'Did you have a good trip?'

'Fine,' answered David. 'This train's a bit on the old-fashioned side, though.'

'Hasn't changed for forty years,' said Forsdick. He looked at David. 'I'm Forsdick, District Commissioner. Macmillan's away up country for today. Otherwise he'd have been here. You're staying with him tonight, of course.'

David was aware of a slight edge of apology in the other man's voice, and felt vaguely flattered. He was to learn later that this was the outlook of most field officers towards the central Secretariat – they cursed it, sneered at it, made jokes about it, but they did respect it none the less, as the only fountainhead of promotion and advancement. Thus David himself, with a Government House label attached to him, was automatically accorded the full treatment whenever he went on tour.

Driving back through the dusty, winding track that served as Gamate's main street, Forsdick pointed out the town's meagre features – the hospital, the mission, the hotel, the school. All round them as they drove were crowds of people, and huts close-pressed together, and wandering herds of goats. Their driver blew his horn almost continuously, while children skipped out of the way, and women turned to grin, and old men under the eave-shadows raised their hands, palm outwards, in formal greeting.

'I thought you'd like to come back home for a spot of lunch,' said Forsdick. 'Then we might go down to the office again, to have a look-see.'

'I'd like that,' answered David cordially. He was turning this way and that, in utmost fascination, shielding his eyes against the fierce sun, drinking in the movement and the variety round them. A dog barked, and bit at the car wheels: an old man raised his hat: some girls with pots on their heads giggled and nudged each other. Then they were through the main part of the town, and heading for Forsdick's bungalow, halfway up the hill towards the Residency.

Mrs Forsdick met them at the door. She was a tall severe woman in a faded print dress, her complexion ruined by sunlight and dry heat, her manner brusque. She had hardly greeted David before she turned on her husband.

'You'd better go and change your shirt, George,' she said. 'That one's not fit to be seen. I'm sure Mr Bracken – ' she smiled meaningly, ' – isn't used to things like that.'

Forsdick went off with a muttered word of apology.

'George has been here such a long time,' said Mrs Forsdick, as if in explanation. 'Perhaps we'll be moving on, some day. I hope it won't be too long.'

'Where would you like to go to?'

'Port Victoria,' answered Mrs Forsdick promptly. 'They seem to enjoy themselves all right, down there.' She recollected herself. 'I mean, I think George could do a Government House job without much trouble.'

'I'm sure he could,' said David.

Forsdick called from an inner room: 'How about giving him a drink?'

'That's exactly what I'm doing!' shouted Mrs Forsdick, who had so far shown no sign of anything of the sort. 'You hurry up with your changing.'

When her husband came back, she said: 'Lunch is just about ready. But I suppose you want a drink, all the same.'

'Yes,' said Forsdick. 'Any complaints?'

Lunch, served in a shabby room furnished throughout in yellow pickled oak, turned out to be a very uncomfortable meal. It was clear that the Forsdicks loathed each other, and that their marriage was sustained on his side by alcohol, and on hers by continuous, ill-tempered nagging.

While the flies buzzed at the window, the houseboy slopped in and out on bare feet, and the cold mutton was succeeded by tinned pineapple, the two of them renewed, in a score of ways, their lifelong battle. Any topic that Forsdick raised was promptly squashed by his wife. When he remarked (inaccurately) that the mutton tasted good, she countered: 'Much obliged to you!' with savage irony. When he got up to pour himself some more beer, she called out: 'Steady on, George! You've got to work this afternoon, haven't you?'

'It's good weather for drinking,' said David pacifically.

'Seems it's always good weather for that,' said Mrs Forsdick, with a glance at her husband.

'Cheer up, old girl,' said Forsdick, with heavy facetiousness. He was, in fact, slightly drunk already, and David could scarcely blame him for it. 'Only two more years before our long leave.'

'Where will you go for that?' asked David.

'To my wife's mother in Dorking,' said Forsdick, and guffawed loudly.

'George!' said Mrs Forsdick in furious tones.

'I was telling him where we'll spend our long leave,' said Forsdick coldly.

'Well, you needn't tell him like that.'

'I've never been to Dorking,' said David, at a loss for a subject of conversation.

'You haven't lived,' said Forsdick.

'George!' said his wife again.

Forsdick winked at David, though his face was sullen. 'Can't do a thing right today.'

'Coffee in the lounge,' said Mrs Forsdick. 'Then I have to go out.'

'Never a dull moment,' said Forsdick, and staggered slightly as he rose.

'What do you mean?' asked his wife curtly.

'You're always on the go,' said Forsdick. 'What is it, this time?'

'Bridge,' said Mrs Forsdick.

Coffee was brought in, thin, tasteless, already poured into flower-patterned cups with chipped rims.

'How about a brandy?' asked Forsdick.

'After *lunch*?' exclaimed Mrs Forsdick in astonishment.

'Oh, for Christ's sake!' said Forsdick.

'George,' said Mrs Forsdick. 'I'd like to show you something in the other room.'

Perhaps the most fearful thing about their exchanges was that they seemed to be nothing out of the ordinary. David, driving down to the office with Forsdick half an hour later, had expected apologies, or at least some degree of embarrassment; instead, Forsdick merely said, 'The old girl's on the rampage today,' and went on to talk of other things. It was clear that every lunch was like the lunch they had just had, and probably every dinner also, and that it had been like that for upwards of twenty years, and that this was the accepted pattern for the future.

There must, David decided, be something about life in Gamate, to make up for it.

III

Exactly what there was in Gamate, to charm the heart, subdue all restlessness, and erase all marital horrors, was made clear to David during the next four days. He talked, watched, wandered at will through this curious town which was unlike anything he had ever seen before; he learned the pattern of administration, the delicate balances of care and discipline that kept a backward people happy, the sense of hope and order that made people like Andrew Macmillan, and Forsdick, and Captain Crump, and Llewellyn the agricultural officer, content with their lot, even while they cursed their servitude. He learned the importance of water in a dry land, the paramountcy of tradition to a people who wrote nothing down, whose only rule was a remembered rule.

First there was Forsdick – competent, industrious, salving his intolerable home life with work, whisky, and a rueful sense of humour.

'I've been here a long time,' said Forsdick, leaning back in his tipping chair, his feet on his desk, his thin hair above the ruddy face moving in the breeze from the electric fan. 'Too long, probably, but that's the way it goes … You can't learn this job without living with it. You can't live with it without getting absorbed in details.' He waved his hand over his desk, where there must have been twenty or more files awaiting his attention; their titles stood out like dull inscriptions on a neglected tomb – *Cattle Culling: Local Orders and Reports – Office Administration: Grade II Clerks, Advancement – Pay and Subsistence, District of Shebiya – Maula Headmen: Minutes of Meetings – Gamate Dam: Recorded Water Levels, 1923-1943.* 'And when you get absorbed in the details,' Forsdick went on, 'you just can't see the overall pattern. Luckily Andrew Macmillan carries the whole thing in his head.'

'He must be a remarkable man,' said David.

'He's all that,' agreed Forsdick, 'I only hope …' He looked uncomfortable for a moment. 'One of these days, if all goes well, I'll be taking over from him. I only hope I can do it half as well.'

'But you like the prospect?'

'Of course.' They were both drinking whisky, though it was scarcely five o'clock in the afternoon, and Forsdick sipped deeply at his glass. 'There are only two things wrong with this sort of life,' he said candidly. 'This – ' he gestured with his glass, ' – which becomes a necessity after a while, unless you're a superman like Andrew; and what the women have to put up with.' Alcohol was freeing his tongue. 'It's not much of a life for them, whichever way you look at it ... You saw Grace at lunchtime ... They slave away for years on end – heat all the time, dust and dirt all over the place, no one to talk to, no friends left in England when they go on leave. They read what other women are doing in the newspapers, they see the dresses, and the perfumes, and the washing machines, and the new kinds of frozen food, and all the gadgets, in the magazines ... They read how Rita Hayworth has four husbands in a row, each richer and better-looking than the last: they read about easy divorce, mink coats, women who persuade Kinsey that they have five orgasms every night ... Then they wait patiently at home, with the heat and the flies and the ants all over the house, for chaps like me to come back and tell them about a damned funny thing that happened with a Grade One Sub Translator in the office that afternoon. By God, if I were a service wife in a place like Gamate, I'd run amok with an axe!'

'That rarely seems to happen,' said David. He was already astonished at Forsdick, whom he had thought a dull, beefy clod of a man, without a thought in his head beyond whisky and the next set of files that needed attention. Apparently there were reactions of some subtlety behind that florid brow ... Aware of condescension in his mind, David hastened to right the wrong. 'But I suppose women do have the worst of the deal.'

'Of course they do,' said Forsdick, 'and that's why you can't blame them ... They wait, not only on that afternoon, and for a hundred afternoons just like it, but for the next twenty years as well, so that one day they can move a quarter of a mile up the hill to the Residency, and be the wife of the Resident Commissioner, and have a new set of ants in the kitchen, and even fewer people to talk to.' He drank again, and suddenly winked at David. 'Sorry,' he said. 'It's nice to see a new face ... I just get like this, once in a while.'

Suddenly, David liked Forsdick very much. 'What's the answer?' he asked. 'I mean, why do all of you stick to it?'

'The women stick to it because they signed on for it,' answered Forsdick. 'At the age of eighteen, they waltz down the aisle with a clean-limbed young genius who's just got his first job in the Scheduled Territories service, and who's going to be the Governor of Pharamaul, with a handle to his name, in record time. Twenty years later, their husbands have moved up exactly two grades in the service, and someone else – usually a complete stranger who's never heard of Pharamaul – has the handle and the Governorship. We stick to it, because we like it. It's as simple as that. We make our homes here, we get to know the country, we have a few good friends – black and white – a few men we can trust, a few chiefs and headmen who learn very slowly to trust us in turn, and tell us their troubles, and look to us for help when things go wrong. We get a tribal nickname – ' Forsdick smiled. 'Mine is "Good Man with Bottle" – a bit ambiguous, don't you think? ... We like the country and it becomes our life, and pretty soon we're unfitted for anything else, and somehow it doesn't matter a damn, because the life here has everything we want, and everything we deserve.'

There was a short silence between them, while the fan whirred, and the flies droned, and a black face appeared round the door and then instantly withdrew. But it must have been a silence that Forsdick did not like, or was ashamed of, for after a moment he spoke again.

'Everything we deserve,' he repeated. 'It sounds like some damned Russian play ... Of course,' he went on, his voice slurring, 'I can understand women flying off the handle after they've had that sort of life for years on end,

but that doesn't mean that it's not bloody annoying! ...
Some of them are all right, of course. You'll be meeting
Mrs Crump later on. Wife of our policeman.'

'Pretty?'

'Just right.' He smacked his lips. The alcohol was
beginning to catch up. 'Now if I had that one, to tell my
troubles to ...'

'You can't have them all,' said David, embarrassed, and
therefore turning facetious.

'No,' said Forsdick, winking grossly. 'But you can have a
damned good try, eh?'

Then there was Johannes, Andrew Macmillan's old
servant, standing beside David's chair in the cool of the
evening waiting on the *stoep* for Macmillan to return from
his day's tour. Johannes talked little, and then only in
answer to a question; but his silences were like his
movements – grave, deliberate, and somehow informative.
This, David knew instinctively, was what the older
generation of Maulas was like. Without doubt there were
thousands of men in Gamate just like Johannes, binding
the tribe together with the absolute authority of tradition
and ritual.

Johannes, grey, slow-moving, wrinkled, bent to place a
glass of cool beer on the table at David's side. Then he
straightened up, and sighed, expelling his breath in formal
completion of this service, and said, 'Jah, *barena!*'

'Thank you, Johannes,' said David.

'Jah, *barena.*'

On the far edge of the lawn, the four red-jerseyed
convicts who were working in Macmillan's garden, under
the care of a native warder armed with a spear, gossiped in
undertones as they weeded. All four squatted on their
haunches in the same neat way, moving a half-step forward
from time to time as their task progressed. The warder, a
fat smiling man, was staring down the valley. Sometimes,

when the voices behind him rose unduly, he called
something out over his shoulder, without looking round,
and the talk stilled again. The sun was westering, losing its
heat.

David pointed towards the convicts. 'All bad men?' he
asked.

Johannes grinned, shaking his head. 'Not very bad,
barena. Sometimes they make mistake.'

'What kind of mistake?'

'Drink too much, take other man's wife.'

'Oh.'

'Fight too hard, kill other man.'

'Oh,' said David again.

'Forget to pay taxes.'

David decided that he would rather not know to which
category the quartet in the garden belonged, though clearly
it was all one to Johannes. He sipped his beer reflectively.
At his side, Johannes polished an ashtray with the edge of
his apron.

'Is this your home?' David asked presently.

'*Barena*?'

David waved his arm round. 'Is this your home? Were
you born in Gamate?'

'Jah, *barena*. Live here twenty, thirty years.'

'How old are you, Johannes?'

'Don't know, *barena*. Same as Commissioner. Thirty
years.'

'But the Commissioner is nearly sixty.'

'Ow! ...' said Johannes, impressed. 'Sixty. Ow ...'

The warder in charge of the convicts turned towards the
garden again, and called out something. The four convicts
straightened up, smiling and murmuring, and came
together in a bunch. The warder shouldered his spear,
waved towards Johannes, and called out another, longer
sentence. Then the small group shuffled off down the

drive, and out of sight. The sun, now very low in the west, flashed momentarily on the blade of the spear as the warder set off down the hill behind his charges.

'What did he say?' asked David, interested.

'He said: "Time to put children to bed," ' answered Johannes.

David laughed. 'That's one way of looking at it. But I suppose they could be dangerous.'

'*Barena?*'

'They could try to run away.'

Johannes shook his head. 'No place to run, *barena*. They run home, police come and fetch them again.'

'But their friends could hide them.'

'No friends like that.'

'They could go into the bush, then.'

'Police find them all the time.'

'But suppose – ' began David, and paused. He did not want to pose too complicated a question, but the idea of a rule of law so all-powerful intrigued him. 'But suppose people in the town wanted to help them to escape?'

Johannes shook his head again. 'Men break law, they go to prison. No one help them to escape.' He was frowning: clearly he wanted to express a definitive version of the pattern ingrained in his mind. 'Law good,' he said at last. 'Break law, bad. No one help bad men.'

Apparently it was as simple as that.

Crump, the young Irish police captain, was a cheerful escort, and their tour of Gamate by jeep was an engaging and sometimes hilarious affair. The canvas hood of the jeep warded off the sunlight, and their brisk movement – for Crump was a determined driver with an authoritative hand on the horn – meant coolness and relief from the oppressive atmosphere. They made their way through the teeming centre of the town, pausing momentarily on the edge of the tribal meeting ground, the *aboura*, while a procession of tiny schoolchildren crossed it in a long straggling crocodile, singing and chattering.

'What's going on?' asked David.

'It's a meeting of welcome for Dinamaula,' answered Crump. It was typical of him, thought David, that he automatically knew the answer. 'They'll sing outside his hut, and then he'll come out and pat a few of them on the head. Have you heard them sing?'

'No.'

'It really wrings your heart,' said Crump unexpectedly. 'Particularly at night, in the lamplight ... They sing a song called *Ekartha i Maula* – 'The Land of Maula is my Home', a sort of children's national anthem. You feel they must all be angels, even though you know damn' well that they're a bunch of tough little bastards who'll rifle the poor-box, just as soon as your back's turned.'

Crump started up the jeep again, and they took the winding road that led out of the town, and towards the Gamate dam. The small khaki car with the police pennant created a stir of interest wherever it went: the older men saluted Crump with open hand, the women turned to stare, the children tried to pat the jeep's side as it ground along in low gear. David had an impression of respect in all this notice: respect, and affection too. But when he spoke the thought, Crump only laughed.

'Oh, they're law-abiding enough – the older ones, at least. But they don't like policemen – no one likes policemen.' He laughed again. The fact did not worry him, because he knew he had right and honour on his side. 'They behave themselves because it's expensive and uncomfortable if they don't. If it ever came to a showdown, more people would rally to our side than would dare to take a chance and get tough. At least – ' he added, frowning, ' – that's the situation at present.'

David showed his surprise. 'Could it alter?'

'Oh yes. They're like that, you know: quiet, logical, and friendly, until something – some damned silly thing that you and I wouldn't give tuppence for – gets under their skin. Then they change. Sometimes they change horribly. There's no warning at all. One day they're good, next day they're murdering, looting savages.'

'Has that ever happened here?'

Crump nodded, giving his attention to a sharp turn in the road, with a frieze of goats blocking its edges. 'Not recently. We had a big tax row, about five years ago. It started because some new receipt forms were printed on green paper – it's an unlucky colour. I lost two of my chaps, torn to bits back there on the *aboura* … And there were some horrible things in the old days, before the present dynasty got properly settled in. The U-Maulas – that's the exiled lot, up north round Shebiya – are still pretty cruel.'

'What about people like Johannes – the older men?'

'Very conservative – they're settled in their ways, and don't want to know about anything else. You can usually trust them. Though Johannes is up to all sorts of rackets, of course.'

'What kind of rackets?' asked David, intrigued.

Crump grinned. 'Oh, they're harmless enough. But being the Resident Commissioner's head boy is a terrific job, in a place like this. He can recommend people for work, in the house or the garden. He can squeeze a small commission whenever he goes shopping at a certain store, or threaten to go somewhere else instead. He can pretend to fix things with the RC – it wouldn't cut any ice with a man like Andrew, but no one's to know that for certain. It's all pretty harmless, as I said – not direct swindling, not like auctioning off the empties, or cheating on the eggs and the milk. But we did have to stop one thing.'

'What was that?'

'We found he was selling Andrew's bathwater, a half-pint at a time, as a fertility charm ... That may be all right for the Aga Khan, but we can't have that sort of thing in Gamate.'

They were now level with the dam: under the fringe of trees at the water's edge the cattle stood, in groups of twenty or thirty, cross-bred Afrikanders with ungainly humps weighting their shoulders. The water level was low, and trampled to yellow mud at its margin; the whole dam, a mile across, shimmered in the afternoon heat, and far beyond it the purple U-Maula hills completed a picture of rustic, spacious peace.

'Does the dam ever go dry?' asked David.

'About once every ten years,' Crump answered. 'It's a very old dam – we've added to it over the years, of course, but Andrew says that it figures in old sketches and writings, as far back as 1500. That's one thing that never changes in this part of the world – water, and the need to store it up.'

The fierce heat gained on them as soon as the jeep stood still, bringing with it a cloud of flies. Crump, in shorts and bush tunic, seemed unaffected by it, but David was glad when he put the jeep into gear again, and they turned for home. Crump now drove by a rough back road, traversing the rim of one of Gamate's containing hills; it gave them an all-embracing view of the whole straggling town, with its thousands of huts, its milling people and animals, and the haze of smoke and dust that lay over it.

'Looks just like Dublin, from one of the hills outside,' said Crump surprisingly. 'Once people start living together in clumps, they certainly poison the atmosphere.'

The jeep descended slowly, braking for the sharp curves, skidding on the dry, corrugated track. Presently they were back on the other side of the *aboura*. Crump's sharp eyes, searching endlessly as they moved past huts and mealie-patches, lighted on two men sitting close together under a thorn tree.

'You were talking about the older generation,' he said. 'There are two of the younger …' His tone was acid. 'That's Dinamaula's cousin, Zuva, and one of the Regents, Puero. The worst one.'

He blew an authoritative note on the horn, and the two men, a few yards away, raised their heads. They gave a perfunctory salute, and Crump returned it just as briefly.

'Bastards,' he said, without heat, as the jeep passed.

'What's the trouble?'

'They're cooking something up,' answered Crump. 'I don't know what it is, yet, but I'll find out one of these days. Puero has always been pretty much of a thug, on the discontented fringe of the Maulas, even though he is one of the Regents. Zuva's just come back from England, full of all sorts of ideas. He's got a lot of gangster pals, down in Port Victoria. He and Puero were bound to get together, sooner or later.'

'What can they do?' asked David.

'They're cooking something up,' Crump repeated. 'Things are quiet just now – maybe too quiet. Perhaps it's time for a row … You saw that interview that Dinamaula gave to the newspapers. If they wanted to start building up on that, there could be plenty of trouble.'

'Would Dinamaula join in?'

'Depends on how he's handled,' answered Crump. 'Andrew – ' he began to say something, and then stopped. 'Well, we'll see.' He nodded his head, towards a girl walking slowly up the road towards them, an ugly, flat-faced girl with a thick ungainly figure. 'That's the bride,' he said. 'Miera Katsaula. Not my cup of tea at all.'

'What bride?'

'Dinamaula's. You know how they fix these things up, whether it's in Pharamaul or in London … She's the niece of Katsaula, one of the Regents. They seem to have picked on her to marry Dinamaula. Only he doesn't like the idea.'

David grinned. 'Now how do you know that?'

'We had a man under the bed.' Crump laughed aloud. 'As a matter of fact, that's damn' nearly true ... Dinamaula was meant to sleep with her, the night he arrived, only it didn't take, and everyone's very shocked.'

'Shocked?'

'Oh yes. If the girl comes into your room, you've got to do the right thing, haven't you?'

'Well, you said it was like London.'

They both laughed again. The jeep drew level with the girl, who looked at them with sullen eyes. Crump leaned out and called, *'Ahsula!'*, the Maula greeting, and Miera gave the open-hand salute, without speaking. The jeep rolled on across the *aboura*, and towards the Gamate Hotel.

'I can see Dinamaula's point of view,' said Crump. 'She really is a tough-looking babe.'

'Can't he pick someone else?'

'I hope so. There are plenty of pretty ones to choose from.' Crump braked the jeep, bringing it to a standstill before the one storey, frame-built Gamate Hotel. 'Thirsty work,' he said. 'Let's join the gang for a sundowner.'

The bar of the Gamate Hotel was a plain square room, sparsely furnished with wickerwork tables and chairs, and having a long open counter at one end; the 'gang' who gathered there nightly, and were now in full possession of the premises, were alike in many things – in dress, in thirst, in tenor of conversation. David, entering with Crump, recognized the Forsdicks sitting at one end of the long bar – she grim, he flushed and talkative; standing next to them was Llewellyn, the Welsh agricultural officer, with his diminutive wife, and two girls in nurses' uniforms, and a huge blond man introduced as Oosthuizen – the only white farmer in the district.

'I'm South African, originally,' said Oosthuizen, in answer to David's query. 'Cape Dutch, about five generations ago. We've had our place – ' he jerked his head sideways, towards some far horizon to the south, ' – for nearly a hundred and fifty years. That's why we've been allowed to keep it, I suppose. All the rest was stolen by the British Government and given to the niggers.' He grinned towards Llewellyn; it was evidently a long-standing joke between them. 'But I'm not moving.'

'We'll get you out, one of these days,' said Llewellyn darkly.

'I've got five sons,' said Oosthuizen, laughing. 'The eldest is looking round for a girl already. I reckon you'll have to wait a bit.'

David found a glass of beer thrust in his direction, and the man behind the bar nodded towards him and held out his hand. 'I'm Fellows,' he said, in self-introduction. He was a small bald man with heavy shoulders, an ex-boxer by the look of him. 'I run this place … Glad to see a new face.'

'Biggest robber in town,' commented Oosthuizen, amiably.

'Now, then,' said Fellows. 'Don't talk like that when Captain Crump's in the bar. I've got a licence to lose.'

'Thanks for reminding me,' said Crump, turning round swiftly. 'I'll review that licence in the morning. It's likely to cost you a packet.'

The conversation continued in this strain throughout most of the session – the men 'joshing' each other determinedly, the women seemingly amused by it. One of the nurses caught David's eye, and moved nearer to him.

'I'm from the hospital,' she said. 'Are you coming over to see us?'

'I'd like to.'

'Don't you!' Forsdick called out. 'You'll be carried out feet first, once these little girls get their hands on you.' He squeezed the shoulder of the second nurse. 'Isn't that right, sweetheart?'

'George!' said Mrs Forsdick. 'Stop pawing.'

'I haven't even started yet,' said Forsdick, guffawing. He turned his head towards Crump. 'Your wife coming in tonight?'

'I hope so,' said Crump coldly.

'So do I.' Forsdick winked at David. 'Wait till you see her. She's a peach!'

'My wife's having a baby,' said Oosthuizen. 'Otherwise she'd be here.'

'How many will that make?' asked the nurse, pertly.

'Nine,' answered Oosthuizen, grinning.

'For Heaven's sake! When are you going to stop?'

'Eleven. That makes a cricket team, you know. It's the least I can do in a British protectorate.'

The noise in the bar was considerable. Fellows, the landlord, poured drinks continuously, thrusting them across the counter with a wide sweep of his arm. All the tables were full, the men in dusty khaki, the women in slacks or creased print dresses. Another glass was pushed into David's hand.

'What about paying for this?' he asked Crump.

'We square it all up at the end. Probably we'll each put five bob in the kitty. It's a local rule we've worked out. We never stand a complete round ourselves – lots of the chaps can't afford it, particularly on a night like this, when there are twenty or thirty people in the bar, who all know each other.'

'But who are they, exactly?'

'All sorts …' Crump looked round the room. 'Oosthuizen farms near here, of course. The girls are from the hospital … That one teaches in the school … The people in the corner work on the railway: those others are down from the logging camp near Shebiya. That depressed-looking chap is the postmaster ... Then there are all our own people and their wives, and the medical staff, and local traders, and commercial travellers working their way through the territory. It all adds up.'

'Quite a community.'

'It's a friendly sort of place,' said Crump thoughtfully. 'We're all doing the same sort of job – running this part of the country, as best we can. You get to think of it as a sort of communal enterprise.'

'What about the Maulas themselves? Can they buy drink here?'

Crump shook his head. 'No. They're not allowed alcohol. At least, that's the general rule. I don't mind the chief or the Regents buying an occasional bottle for themselves – Fellows knows that. But the ordinary tribespeople are barred.'

'I should damn' well think so!' said Oosthuizen, overhearing. 'Man, they get drunk enough on that filthy native beer they brew, without giving them anything stronger! Natives can't take hard liquor – it just drives them crazy. I let my niggers break out once a year, at Christmas. It takes about a week to get them back into shape again.'

Someone called to Oosthuizen from further down the bar, and he turned away.

'What's he like?' asked David in a low tone. 'As an employer, I mean.'

'First class,' answered Crump, 'though you mightn't think it, to hear him talk. He employs about five hundred natives, all told – it's a very big farm. He looks after them well, houses them properly, gives them plots of land to farm on their own account. His wife doctors them, and keeps an eye on the women and the kids. It's like a big, spread-out family. It's the South African pattern, really.'

'Is it?' asked David, surprised.

'Oh yes! You don't want to believe all you read in the newspapers ... I expect there are some bad farms in South Africa, but there are some damned good ones as well. I've got a cousin, farming up in the Northern Transvaal. All his neighbours work the same system as Oosthuizen – the white man's the boss, but he's the father as well. If anything goes wrong, he's the one that takes over, and puts it all right again.'

A very pretty dark girl appeared suddenly at his side, and squeezed his arm. Crump exclaimed: 'Molly, darling!' and introduced her as his wife. David found himself understanding Forsdick's patent interest in Mrs Crump. In a drab and dusty town, among tired, run-of-the-mill women, she glowed like candlelight at dusk. He thought suddenly of Nicole, and decided he would ask her to marry him as soon as he got back to Port Victoria. Even making allowances for the half-dozen beers he had drunk, it still seemed a wonderful idea.

'Darling,' said Mrs Crump presently. 'I think you-know-who is going to make a move in my direction. What about it?'

Out of the corner of his eye, David saw that Forsdick was indeed looking towards them, and seemed on the point of joining their party. Crump stood back briskly from the counter.

'I've had my whack,' he said. 'Let's get going.'

It was neatly done. By the time that Forsdick had downed his drink, extricated himself from the bar, and crossed the room, the Crumps had said goodbye and were already through the outer door. Forsdick, blinking, looked round him foolishly.

'What happened?' he asked. 'She was here a moment ago.'

'They had to go,' said David.

'Avoiding me, eh?'

'Oh no, I don't think so.'

'They say it's a good sign,' said Forsdick, who was by now considerably drunk. 'If women run away from you, it means they don't trust themselves. Haven't you heard that?'

'I've heard it,' said David cautiously.

'Have a drink,' said Forsdick, 'and we'll discuss the whole thing from that angle.'

Father Schwemmer, the missionary, was weeding his garden when David called on him. He was a small man, not young, of brisk yet gentle manner: his hair was close-cropped, on the Teuton model, his rusty-brown cassock much in need of repair. Yellow dust lay thick on his cracked boots, and thick also on the mission-house garden; the house itself, brick daubed with clay, was shabby and neglected. Yet his eyes, as he raised them at David's step, were friendly and full of hope, and his handclasp warm.

'Mr Bracken, sir,' he said. 'I was informed that you were in Gamate. Welcome to my house.'

His choice of words, as well as his accent, proclaimed that English was not his mother tongue; and presently, as they talked on the shaded steps of the mission house, Father Schwemmer touched on this, as if it were something he had often had to explain.

'Naturally I am German,' he said, with curious formality. 'This is a German teaching order. A Catholic order – you would call it RC, would you not? Its foundation was in Strasbourg, many hundreds of years ago.'

'How long have you been here?'

134

'Thirty years, perhaps.' He smiled, a shy smile. 'Time passes swiftly in Gamate … We are not rich, as you see. But the mission itself was established on this very piece of land, in the year 1782.' He caught David's eye, and smiled again. 'We Germans, as you know, have a passion for detail and order. If I could not say, exactly like that, "the year 1782", I should feel very much disgraced.'

'You must have some interesting records,' said David. He sipped at the glass of cool beer which Father Schwemmer had poured for him, and looked around him – at the tumbledown house, the arid, carefully-tended garden, the small chapel attached to the main building. High above his head, a copper bell with a frayed rope hung ready for its next summons to the flock. The lifetime of poverty and faith was movingly apparent. 'Was it your order which brought Christianity to Pharamaul?'

Father Schwemmer shook his head. 'I wish I could say that this was so. But it would not be true. It is also a very curious story. You do not know this country, Mr Bracken? But you have seen maps?'

'Yes,' answered David. 'And of course I've read a lot about it.'

'To the north of here – ' Father Schwemmer pointed towards the U-Maula hills, ' – lies Shebiya. That is the other capital, the home of the exiles. Near it, on the coast, is a place marked "Fish Village".'

'Yes,' said David again. 'I remember.'

'Do you know how it received its name?'

David looked surprised. 'From the fish, I suppose.'

'From *a* fish,' corrected Father Schwemmer. 'You will find the story in our records. When the first missionary of our order arrived in Gamate, and then travelled to Shebiya, he found traces of Christianity there already. There was a kind of – ' he waved his hand, ' – a race memory of Christian teaching. This was in 1782, as I have said. But

135

already there was a tradition handed down, a tradition going back into the very mists of time, the story of a Saviour who was the son of a virgin, and who was crucified, and whose followers were later persecuted for their faith. There was even something more. There was the fish, the fish that gave the village its name.'

'I don't understand,' said David.

'That first missionary attended one of their meetings – ' he smiled, ' – their nearly Christian meetings. He found that one of their special rituals was to draw the outline of a fish in the sand, and then rub it out quickly. But that was not a new ritual; that was how the very early Christians – in the first and second century, fifteen hundred years before our missionary was born – used to recognize each other secretly. They would stand in the marketplace, so – ' he stood up, on the sandy path below the doorstep, ' – and draw the outline of a fish with their foot, so.' He drew a fish, with the toe of his cracked boot. 'They would do it as if idly, and then rub it out.' His foot moved, and the sand was smooth again. 'That was their secret way of finding out if the man they spoke to was a Christian. They drew a fish, because the Greek word for fish was Ichthus, and the Greek letters of that word stand for "Jesus Christ, the Son of God, the Saviour".'

David kept silent. The odd, potent story, related in precise accents by this shabby priest, had moved him very much.

'There have been many strange happenings in Africa,' said Father Schwemmer, 'and many wonderful things. But that is one of the strangest. It means that perhaps in the first century after Christ, a wandering preacher, or an escaped slave, or a traveller who was a convert, or an apostle of whom we know nothing, made his way from Rome or Greece, perhaps by sea, perhaps by way of Asia Minor, and travelled all the way down Africa, and then took ship for Pharamaul, and was cast ashore near Shebiya. There he taught the natives what he knew of the life of Our Lord, and taught them also to draw a fish – the secret sign of hope and redemption. And so the place where he landed was called Fish Village. It is still called that, after nineteen hundred years, and they still draw the fish when they come to worship.'

Silence fell between them when Father Schwemmer stopped speaking. It was a good story, thought David, a story rounded and complete: a story in which faith, legend, and drama were nicely blended. Insufficiently briefed on Bible history, he wondered if that first-century traveller could possibly have been St Paul. Surely he had voyaged in Asia Minor: surely he had been 'cast ashore' somewhere ... David sipped his beer again, and Father Schwemmer looked down at the patch of sandy earth on which he had drawn the fish, as if he hoped to see its outlines re-emerging of their own miraculous accord. In his present mood of easy acceptance, David would not have been surprised.

'You will visit that part of the country?' asked Father Schwemmer presently.

With an effort David recalled himself to the twentieth century. 'Yes, the day after tomorrow. I'm driving up to Shebiya with Captain Crump.'

'A fine man,' commented Father Schwemmer.

There was another long pause.

'That was a wonderful story,' said David. 'I shall remember it.'

'It is stories like that,' said Father Schwemmer, 'that make one happy to be in Pharamaul. Though I cannot say that the fish they draw in Shebiya means the same now as the fish that I would draw. There, they are very simple, very savage. Sometimes I wonder if I am teaching them something, or if they are teaching me – something altogether different.'

'Do you go there often?'

'Every two months. We have a small mission house, much neglected. But the District Officer, Mr Ronald, is another fine man. You will see him very soon.'

'Do you think,' asked David, speaking carefully, 'that we are doing all we can, in Pharamaul? It's an old pattern of administration. Is it still the best?'

Father Schwemmer did not answer immediately. He was looking round him – first at the poorly-tended mission house, then at the hill slope leading down to the *aboura*, then to the hills beyond. A man moving nearby caught his eye, and Father Schwemmer followed his progress. The man, a tall half-naked figure, was walking slowly past the front gate: in his wake, a woman heavily burdened plodded with weary patience, her ragged blanket trailing, and behind her walked a child, a boy-child switching at grass-heads with a thin stick. The man raised his hand in formal greeting: the woman shuffled on without lifting her eyes; the child disregarded them all.

The yellow dust settled in their wake. This was Father Schwemmer's parish, and if he had striven to change it in any way, the change must have seemed a slow one.

'Mr Bracken,' he said finally, 'I cannot answer your question, though I have been here thirty years, and I am not the first of our faith to live and work here.' He gestured round him. 'In Pharamaul, in Gamate, all this seems natural and unchangeable. Up the hill, out of sight, the white man rules. Here, near my gate, the black man lives. The white man rules wisely, the black man obeys and lives a hard, dull life. In most parts of the world, the white man obeys and lives a hard, dull life … But in New York, at the United Nations, all this is called evil, and men from other countries tell us that the pattern is bad, that the white man must go away, and the black man must rule his own life.'

Father Schwemmer paused, his eyes on the far hills, his old cassocked body hanging slack and uncertain. Finally he smiled. It was not a happy smile.

'Perhaps somewhere between these two,' he said, 'with the white man *ready* to leave, the black man *ready* to rule – perhaps that is the fair answer. But the fair answer is for tomorrow, not today.'

'We shall not be here tomorrow,' said David, after an uneasy pause.

'No,' said Father Schwemmer. 'That is one thing certain. We shall not be here, on that tomorrow. All we can do is make today a day that leads towards it.'

The formal meeting with Dinamaula and the three Regents was a constrained and queerly uneasy affair. David, by arrangement, met them all in the schoolroom, where the Regents themselves had welcomed Dinamaula on his first arrival; when he walked into the room, he had the impression that they had been quarrelling, or at least discussing something which had left them totally divided in thought. Old Seralo, the senior Regent, greeted him with quavering ceremonial: Katsaula, the man of ritual and history, used the single, prescribed word: '*Ahsula!*' Fat Puero smirked and held out his hand; Dinamaula himself preoccupied and morose, said: 'Nice to see you again, Mr Bracken,' as one Oxford graduate to another. When David sat down, it was as if he were joining, tardily, a board meeting at which each of his fellow directors had secret, incommunicable reservations about every item on the agenda.

Their exchanges were brief, pointed, and unreal. Even for an occasion which was, at best, a formal recognition of his new appointment, it was an awkward session. And at its end, it was nearly disastrous.

'Sir,' began Seralo, bowing in his direction, 'we are happy to welcome the new secretary. We remember Mr –' he groped, ' – Mr Morrison. We hope you will be happy in our country.'

'I never met Mr Morrison,' said David, determinedly loquacious. 'But I know he enjoyed his time in Pharamaul, and I'm sure that I shall do the same.' He turned towards Dinamaula. 'We were on the same plane, Chief,' he said. 'But I didn't know it was you.'

Dinamaula grinned, a quick, mirthless grin in a guarded face. 'I wondered who you thought it was.'

'I was talking to Mr Macmillan,' said David. 'He was on that plane, too.'

'Yes,' said Dinamaula.

'We neither of us knew it was you,' said David, persisting on a point which seemed to contain the seeds of embarrassment. 'No one told us you were likely to be on the same plane.' He smiled companionably. 'You know what Government departments are like. They never brief each other on what they're doing until at least a week later.'

'I do not know,' said Dinamaula, 'but I am sure that it is so.'

After a moment of silence, Puero, the junior Regent, with the air of a careless man who has nothing to lose, said: 'How long will you be staying in Gamate, Mr Bracken?'

'I leave tomorrow,' answered David. 'I'm driving up to Shebiya with Captain Crump.'

'Shebiya,' said Seralo, and sighed.

'With Captain Crump,' said Puero, faintly impudent.

'Mr Bracken,' said Katsaula, 'Shebiya is very different from Gamate. This is the capital of our country, and here we live quietly and work with Government. In Shebiya it is different. There is a man there, Gotwela, an exile – '

'My cousin,' said Seralo, sadly. 'My own cousin.'

'A man,' continued Katsaula, 'who does many strange things. He has the name of chief – chief of the U-Maulas. You will meet him. He is not a Maula – ' Katsaula's tone was hard and unforgiving. 'He has forsaken the tribe … Here, we obey the law, and remember our fathers. In Shebiya it is different.'

'I am sure,' said Puero, smooth and sarcastic, 'that Mr Bracken knows all these things. He knows how we obey the law.'

'We obey the law,' repeated Seralo, almost automatically.

'Gotwela also obeys the law.' Puero seemed to be speaking from some inner compulsion to provoke and sting. 'Otherwise, of course, Government would punish him.'

David had a sudden impression that, of the four other men in the room, the two youngest were laughing at him, and the two eldest were unfriendly or disapproving. It was a moment of some discomfort, with which he was scarcely equipped to deal. He was here to meet and to greet; not to take on a fresh set of problems at one stroke, problems whose outlines he could not yet comprehend.

'Of course, I've read a little about the U-Maulas,' he said, trying for stiffness in his voice. 'And I want to see as much of the country as I can.'

Silence fell again. Dinamaula was looking out of the window, Puero whistling between his teeth. Presently Seralo coughed, and said: 'Please take back our greetings to His Excellency the Governor.'

David nodded.

'Our greetings and our loyalty,' amended Katsaula.

'Certainly I will,' said David.

'Tell him that all is well with the tribe, and with Gamate. Tell him that the harvest – '

'Old Uncle!' said Dinamaula, turning suddenly.

'Yes?'

'Remember I am soon to be chief.'

There was an embarrassed silence.

'Why do you say that?' asked Seralo at length, quavering.

'Greetings we send,' said Dinamaula. David suddenly noticed that he was speaking under great tension. 'Messages about the tribe and the future should wait till later, till I am proclaimed as chief.'

In the constrained silence that closed in again round the harsh words, David thought swiftly. Now it was clear that his arrival in the schoolroom had been preceded by some definitive family quarrel – Seralo's embarrassment, Katsaula's shocked surprise, and the look of sardonic toughness on Puero's face, were all witness to this. The fact that Dinamaula had so far broken custom as to allow the quarrel to intrude upon a formal occasion, pointed to its bitterness – a bitterness now amply reflected in his taut face. There could be no quick resolving of such a moment, David realized, nor would it be seemly for him to try for one … He stood up.

'I have to go, I'm afraid,' he said awkwardly. 'I'm glad that we could meet. I'll be back in Gamate in about a week.'

It was a feeble leave-taking, with no grace and little merit to it. David's last impression was of Puero's eyes meeting his, and of the other man's derisive contempt. The phrase 'making his escape' occurred to him. Behind his back, behind the closed door, furious voices rose as soon as he left the room …

Lastly, David talked with Andrew Macmillan, and learned much from him; learned, among other things, the likely reason for the 'family quarrel' that had so nearly got out of hand.

'I had Dinamaula up here, a couple of days ago,' said Macmillan, after David had described the occasion in detail. 'That was probably the start of it. I choked him off – gave him a real flea in his ear.'

'Oh,' said David, surprised. The crude, schoolboyish phrases seemed somehow out of keeping with the job of Resident Commissioner, though this might not be so. 'Why was that? What happened?'

'London were steamed up about that newspaper interview, as you know.' The two of them were sitting at ease on the Residency *stoep*, drinking their coffee, staring at the same horizon – an orange-purple crest that topped the skyline as the sun dipped far below it. The air was cool and peaceful, the garden deeply quiet in the dusk. 'I got him up here,' Macmillan went on, narrowing his eyes. 'Told him we didn't like it. He started to argue the toss. Told *me* he'd say anything he liked, to any newspaperman he met.' Macmillan grinned. 'I hit the roof.'

'But was the interview true?' asked David. '*Did* he say all those things?'

'That's the damned silly part of it. He didn't. At least, he may have talked a bit about progress and development – no harm in that, either – but he didn't say anything as definite or as tough as Tulbach Browne made out. I believe him there, of course: most of those Press boys are liars through and through. But then Dinamaula said that although he hadn't talked exactly that way, he saw no harm in it. He "stood on his right" – ' Macmillan mimicked, savagely, the sea-lawyer's phrase, ' – he stood on his right to plan future development, and discuss it freely with anyone. That was when I administered the rocket.'

'How did he take it?'

'Turned sulky,' said Macmillan. 'Got up and left, in fact. I suppose he called the Regents together, and told them. That was what the row was about.'

'But how?' asked David, puzzled. 'Why should they disagree about it?'

Andrew Macmillan shifted his weight, relaxing more deeply in his chair. He seemed old and tired, and yet all-competent still. Even to sit with him in Gamate seemed to solve half of Gamate's problems.

'It's a bit complicated,' he said, 'but not as complicated as all that. The Regents are divided, two to one, on a great many things. Seralo and Katsaula are traditionalists. They want nothing changed. Puero is a progressive – and a prize bastard as well, though that's neither here nor there. But if Dinamaula came back and said that he'd been reprimanded by me, and explained why, the Regents would take sides automatically. Seralo and Katsaula would be very shocked, and tell Dinamaula he'd got what was coming to him. Puero would try to persuade him he was badly treated, and egg him on to do the same thing again, only more so. Then there's young Zuva …'

'Is he still here?'

'No, he's back in Port Victoria, chewing the rag with his gangster chums. At least, that's what Keith Crump tells me …' Macmillan paused before going on. 'It's a curious set-up, and likely to become more so, so you'd better get it straight. As I said, the two old boys are conservative. Puero is a radical. Dinamaula is halfway in between – at present. But Zuva is something else again. Maybe he doesn't know himself what he's playing with, but it's a damned dangerous movement that he's trying to get under way. He wants the black man in, and the white man out – *now* … Perhaps the nearest thing to it would be to say that it's the Pharamaul version of Mau Mau.'

A chill wind seemed to invade the garden as Macmillan finished speaking, an uneasy breath of fear and evil. The syllables 'Mau Mau' seemed to float in the air round them, promising a bloody end to their peace. They were alien syllables, of course; they had never yet touched Pharamaul, and had been stemmed, with killing and bitter hatred, in other parts of Africa. But the 'Pharamaul version' could precipitate equal horror, equally murderous excess, equal reprisal ... David turned to look at Andrew Macmillan: the older man was staring ahead of him, seeing many other things besides the garden and the fading sunset. But suddenly he was smiling as well.

'There's always something, isn't there?' he said unexpectedly. 'This country has had a pretty rough history, one way and another, like most of the mainland. It's quiet for twenty years, and then everything flames up, and then it turns quiet again. The thing to do,' he said reflectively, 'is to enjoy the quiet times, and make the most of them, and be ready for the crisis when it comes.'

'*Are* we ready?' asked David, still under the spell of foreboding.

Macmillan jerked his head, in derision. 'As ready as we can be,' he answered, almost contemptuously, 'with two men and a boy to run thirty thousand square miles, a hundred and twenty thousand people ... Work it out for yourself. Apart from the Government House circus down at Port Victoria, I've got one police captain, Crump, one District Commissioner, Forsdick, and one livestock officer, Llewellyn, here in Gamate. I've got a District Officer, Tom Ronald, a hundred miles away, up at Shebiya. There's another policeman, a sub-inspector, in Port Victoria itself. And that's the lot. If it's spread any thinner, anywhere in the world, I'd like to hear about it.' He laughed, still not seeming to take it seriously. 'The funny thing is, it *is* spread thin, all over the world, and it still works. I don't know how we do it.'

'But we do,' said David, stoutly.

'Oh yes. That's what we're paid for.' Macmillan grinned, relaxing further. 'Let's have a drink, and then bed. You've got an early start to make tomorrow.'

'I'm really looking forward to it.'

Macmillan nodded. 'It's rough country. Some of it nearly jungle, in fact. Shebiya is like this – ' he waved his hand round, ' – but not so crowded, and a good deal less civilized. Gotwela, the chief, is a real ruffian ...' He mused, his hands behind his head, as Johannes, who must have been listening at the screen-door, shuffled in with the drink-tray. 'If Zuva,' he said – and his voice seemed distant and detached, ' – if Zuva really wants to start that bloody business, he won't waste any time down at Port Victoria, with a lot of no-good *tsotsies* in zoot suits. He'll join up with Gotwela. That's the character who *really* wants to murder every white man in Pharamaul.'

IV

The jeep, heavily laden, crawling like some brown industrious beetle from hill to small hill, made its slow way northwards. It left the Gamate plains, traversed the encroaching bush, climbed steadily, then forsook the flat grasslands altogether, for the deeper, heavy-pressing jungle that guarded the approaches to the U-Maula country. The road it followed, a rough track sodden with fresh rain, was often no more than an ochre ribbon of swampland winding through fronded wilderness.

Besides David Bracken and Crump, the jeep held their luggage, and a sack of mail, and tools such as pick-axes and spades, and a forty-gallon drum of fresh water. It carried extra petrol, in three battered jerricans, and a two-way radio set, and some corrugated iron sheeting for the Shebiya mission house, and finally a black police corporal who clung to this piled freight like a child to a bucking pony. For these three men, the jeep was their moving fortress, never to be left for long, never to be abandoned.

The jeep, like a small ship on passage through dubious waters, made its way northwards, sometimes fast, mostly slow and labouring: first the grassland was forgotten, and then the thin bush with its staring cattle; and then the thick forest received them, so that their advance was without trace. As soon as they had passed, all evidence of life, all movement, was swallowed up at the same time. No friend could follow them here, no rescuer plot their course … Now they moved through a silent land, a land which had awaited their passing for a hundred years, and yet thought nothing of it; a land inscrutable in its blank denial of welcome. Too careless or too treacherous to threaten, it received them with an impassive air that seemed to mask the very claws of danger.

Perhaps, thought David, looking round him at this untenanted wall of leaf and rank grass, unhealthily green, perhaps it was only his broken night, and those wicked syllables 'Mau Mau', that induced in him a sense of fear and foreboding: but certainly, as they ground their slow track from one horizon to another, and slid down small precipices ending in some shallow, eroded water-course, and churned a level way through clinging mud, and then set their front wheels at one more hill, one more slope of road hacked from dank jungle and dripping trees, certainly the U-Maula country was an unknown country, somewhat less than innocent, something short of human.

Their journey of ninety-odd miles took more than five hours: they stopped many times – to top up their boiling radiator, to refill the petrol tank, to eat and stretch their legs, to take the midday police schedule on the radio, and once, towards the end of their journey, to check their guns. It was a slow determined progress, of men leaving the friendly plains they knew, and entering a hostile keep. The jeep crawled like an insect, edged forward as an armoured truck which penetrates new country lately held by the enemy; but the new country seemed old country also, perhaps the oldest country in the world, old as the oldest bones of foully murdered men, old as sin itself.

Crump, as usual, proved himself a cheerful companion, though at the start of their journey he seemed preoccupied, even morose. 'I never like leaving Molly behind at Gamate,' he had volunteered suddenly. 'Forsdick's a nice chap – works like a demon – but he's getting to be a bit of a bore ... He rang me up this morning, and said – ' Crump mimicked with rare, surprising cruelty, ' – "Don't you worry! I'll take *good* care of Mrs Crump, while you're away!"'

'It's all talk,' said David.

'Sure thing ... But I don't like it, either way. Oh well,' Crump sighed, and settled back in the driving seat of the jeep, 'it won't be long before we're back.'

Later, when they were well within U-Maula territory, David had asked, 'How often do you make this journey?'

'About once a month,' answered Crump. 'We've got a police post up at Shebiya – a corporal and four of the chaps. This lad behind – ' he jerked his head, where their passenger clung to the small mountain of luggage with stolid, stubborn persistence, ' – is the relief. He'll do a month up there.'

'Will there be anything for him to do?'

Crump shrugged. 'You never know. It's been quiet now for a long time. Of course, there's always stock theft, and a murder or two, and a bit of rape on the side.' He grinned. 'You can't expect it to be like an English village. But

Gotwela has the thing pretty well sewn up. When he cracks the whip, they jump. Saves us a lot of trouble.'

'If you can trust *him*.'

'I wouldn't trust him a short yard on a bright sunny day,' said Crump crisply. 'He'd murder his own mother, if it would do him any good. In fact, he did just that, a couple of years ago, only we couldn't pin it on him … But what I meant was, he really does keep order. It's not always our sort of order, but it's near enough to it, for us not to worry. You've got to weigh the thing up. On balance, Gotwela comes out just on the right side. He's a crook, a murderer, and a very cruel man. But he rules the U-Maulas, and we rule him, and so the thing *works*. It wouldn't look too good on paper, in black and white, but here – ' Crump raised a hand momentarily from the bucking steering wheel, and gestured round him at the forbidding, near-jungle landscape which disputed their passage continuously, ' – here it's just about all right. At the moment.'

'You said that before,' commented David presently. It was the time when they stopped, ten miles short of Shebiya, and Crump had been at pains to check their small armoury – the rifle clipped lengthwise under the dash, his own Luger, and David's ancient .45 Webley which he had borrowed from Captain Simpson, the naval aide. 'Do you mean that things could really change so quickly?'

'This is Africa,' answered Crump, releasing and then snapping home the magazine of his pistol. 'Anything can happen … I always do this – ' he patted the smooth, oily stock of the Luger, ' – because I might have to use it in a hurry. Gotwela keeps a tight rein, but some of his lads are still trigger-happy. They're likely to take a pot shot at whatever they see moving. If it turns out to be a police jeep with one police captain, one Government House secretary, and one corporal, so much the better. You could hardly ask for a nicer target, could you?'

David laughed. 'Where do they get the guns?'

'Smuggled. Stolen. Inherited. We have a drive now and again, and bring a few in. A little time ago we got a musket – a genuine, old-style, powder-horn musket with a barrel like an ear trumpet. I reckon we did the owner a pretty good turn by taking it away from him. But he didn't see it that way.'

David laughed again. 'But are there any modern ones?'

'Yes,' said Crump, broodingly, 'there are. Some of the stuff left lying about in the western desert, and in East Africa, found its way down here. God knows how. We picked up a Bren, only the other day.' He sighed. '"Army surplus" covers a lot of funny things. But they're not so funny when they get to a place like this.'

The tremendous, quivering salute which the corporal in charge of the police post tore off, as soon as he caught sight of Crump, seemed to argue a welcome level of morale, in this corner of Shebiya, at least. But that level was not maintained elsewhere …

The town, much smaller than Gamate, was nearly deserted when they drove through it, although it was late afternoon, the traditional time of meeting and gossip. Instead of throngs of people, men and women, children and goats, blocking the pathways or crossing from hut to hut, only a few figures squatted in doorways, turning to look at the jeep as it passed, turning away again as soon as their glum curiosity was satisfied. Instead of movement and life, there was a brooding quietness: no one rose to greet them, no women turned to laugh, no children touched the jeep as it passed, or played last-across-the-road with giggling devilment. Shebiya was like the jungle track they had left behind them: it had been waiting for their party, it had known that they were near, and it now received them with the sullen face of indifference. Only in the police post, with its flag flapping taut at the masthead, its neat pathways whitewashed along their borders, was there a rift in Shebiya's lowering mask. But there, all was order, discipline, and grinning welcome.

Crump spent some time inside the post, while David, glad to stretch his legs, stood by the jeep. A few men passed him, without greeting or glance. Mostly they were ragged in their trailing blankets, but a few wore ancient army greatcoats of tattered khaki, with epaulettes unbuttoned and awry – army surplus from some much older war. Then a waggon drawn by a span of six gaunt oxen creaked by them, stopping a little way ahead, blocking the road. Its driver, a small wizened man under a yellowing, beehive straw hat, remained hunched over the reins, his long whip lying idly across the backs of his team.

Crump came out of the police post, looking pleased, stepping briskly, smart in his freshly laundered bush tunic. He glanced at the ox-waggon, still blocking their way. He leant over and blew a long blast on the jeep's horn. The driver did not stir. After a moment, Crump called something over his shoulder, and two black policemen came running down the pathway.

Crump pointed. The two policemen began to shout at the driver, and one of them, gesturing, made as if to climb up to his seat. The driver, still motionless, watched the latter carefully. It seemed that, once level with him, the policeman would shake him, or push him from his place. But at the last moment, the driver raised his long whip, and brought it down, very slowly, almost derisively, on the backs of his two leading oxen. The ox-waggon started forward again, moving with sarcastic deliberation out of their path.

'They try it on,' said Crump briefly, as he climbed into his place again. 'Then they give way, as slowly as they can. Shebiya is like that.'

'But suppose he didn't get out of the way?' asked David, disturbed by the incident. Against the background of Shebiya's gloomy, shut-in air, the driver's sullen compliance had taken on a quality of menace, difficult to ignore.

'He'd come up before Tom Ronald, at the next summary court,' answered Crump. 'Tom would tell him that he mustn't block the roads with his waggon. The driver would say that he didn't see us, or that he thought there was room to get by, or he was just going to move when the policemen shouted, and he thought they wanted him for something … Tom would caution him not to do it again. That's all.'

'But wouldn't it be better to put it on a legal basis? – arrest the man for obstruction, or whatever it is, to teach him a lesson?'

Crump shook his head. 'No. That's what he really wanted, in a way, so we don't give it him. If we'd hauled him in, on the spot, my chaps would have had all the bother of moving the waggon themselves. Then the driver would have complained that one of his oxen had gone lame, through being handled by a ham-handed policeman, or that one of the waggon wheels had been forced over a big stone, and he was going to sue Government for a hundred pounds …' Crump grinned, throwing it all away. 'They try it on,' he repeated. 'The best thing to do is the simplest – take it in your stride, solve it then and there. When you're dealing with children, nursery tactics are always the best.'

'What were the policemen saying, anyway?'

'They were calling the driver, among other things, a stupid, lazy son of a bitch,' said Crump succinctly. 'Must have given them a lot of pleasure. He's their uncle.'

David was not entirely sure what he had expected Tom Ronald, the District Officer, to be like; in the back of his mind, affected by the strange secret country they were in, he had had a vague picture of an oldish man, huge, of legendary strength and endurance, who ruled the U-Maulas with tremendous authority, and whose name alone – 'Great White Father', or some such – made murderers kill themselves outright, and thieves throw away their spoil in despair ... The man who strolled towards them as the jeep drew up before the frame bungalow, was laughably different. He was young – twenty-two or three – cheerful, and thickset, with a fair skin and curly hair: an ex-footballer, thought David, probably given to hearty reminiscence and endless glasses of beer after the game. He was not surprised when Tom Ronald's first words of greeting turned out to be: 'What ho, chaps! Glad you got here in one piece. I bet you're about ready to wet the old whistle!'

Since the conversation continued, throughout the process of introduction and their entry into the house, on the same level, David found himself hoping, for many reasons, that Tom Ronald was not really as simple and schoolboyish as he sounded. But he found such thoughts evaporating, as time went by. Ronald was indeed a simple character, immature, young for his years: but behind the 'What ho!' and the 'Cheers, chaps!' and the residual inanity of a minor public school in England, lay something else of a different quality altogether, something strong and tough and competent.

Tom Ronald might not fit the 'Great White Father' mould, thought David, as he listened to the other man giving Crump a slangy, nonchalant account of recent happenings in Shebiya; but he certainly knew his territory, and what was going on in it. While David listened to this account, he looked round the room in which they sat. It was something like the Forsdicks' sitting-room, shabby, comfortable, the furniture supplied from stock by the

Office of Works, the woodwork painted throughout in that morbid hue known as Government Beige. The whole house, indeed, was in the same style – cheaply built, crudely decorated, cared for or neglected by a succession of District Officers working out their time in this lonely corner of the world. Outside, the sun bore fiercely down on straggling flower beds, and a lawn marred by bare brown patches, and integrated armies of ants intent on destroying everything wrought by the hand of man … Then his ear was caught by something that Tom Ronald was saying.

'I think we've got a new secret society in Shebiya,' he remarked, offhandedly. 'There have been a lot of meetings lately, and some drilling, out on the hillside. Something to do with fish. They call themselves the Fish Men. Don't know if there's anything in it.'

Crump nodded. 'My chaps at the police post were saying the same thing. But there's always been that fish emblem in Pharamaul, hasn't there? One of the old Maula titles is "Son of the Fish", after all.'

Ronald scratched his chin doubtfully. 'Maybe. That's a religious thing, isn't it? But this seems to be different. Now they've started drawing fishes all over the place. Like a political slogan. There was one on my front gate, the other day.' He laughed. 'Did I give the garden boy hell for it! … But this seems to be different,' he repeated. 'We had half a dozen new people in the village, last week. They also called themselves Fish Men. But *they'd* trekked up from Port Victoria.'

Crump echoed the last words: 'Port Victoria?' in a tone of the utmost surprise, and David felt his stomach give a sudden, uneasy heave. The word 'fish' recalled his conversation with Father Schwemmer, and the dark barbaric world which the latter had conjured from the past. Now, it seemed, there were other Fish Men – not religious Fish Men, but political Fish Men. He recalled also Andrew Macmillan, talking of Mau Mau, and of the ideas that could be stirring in Zuva's brain, and of what Zuva might do if he ever joined hands with Gotwela. He felt the foreboding twinge gripping him again, as Crump said: 'You'd better keep your eye on that. I may as well tell you that I'm looking for something of the sort – a piece of a puzzle that I can't quite fit in. We've had secret societies before, of course, and they've usually petered out. But Zuva, down in Port Victoria, is about ready to start something. I don't want him joining up with the U-Maulas. We're likely to have quite enough trouble with Dinamaula in Gamate, as it is.'

'What's the gen there?' asked Tom Ronald. 'Isn't he going to behave like mother's best boy?'

'No,' said Crump. 'That's the short answer, and it's the only one I can give you, at the moment. But you might let me know if Puero, the Regent, ever shows up here. He's another one who's feeling the spring.'

An agreeable feminine voice behind them asked: 'Who's feeling the spring?' and they all stood up as Tom Ronald's wife entered the room.

Cynthia Ronald was another surprise. Once more, David had had a picture in his mind, a picture drawn from the reality of Tom Ronald's own appearance. Since Tom Ronald had turned out to be a rugger type, his wife was likely to be a female rugger type to match – a wind-blown, *retroussée* blonde with her hair done up in a scarf, drinking her husband level, beer for beer, reading the maps for him as their MG toured southern England during their home leave … Cynthia Ronald, in fact, was tall, dark, and attractive in a distinctly indoor way. When she repeated the words 'Feeling the spring' they seemed to have a personal connotation. When she placed her slim hands on Tom Ronald's shoulders, it was as if she were rehearsing the prelude to an embrace which would take place immediately their visitors were out of the house. David Bracken found her disturbing: she had an unabashed sexuality so clearly reserved for her husband that no spectator could remain entirely free of jealousy.

She said: 'Hallo, Keith,' to Crump, and then: 'Thank God for a new face!' to David himself. Then she perched on the arm of her husband's chair, showing a startling amount of leg in the process, and said: 'Break it up, boys. The world will keep till tomorrow. Let's all have a drink.'

It suddenly seemed an excellent idea. Later, after a surprisingly good dinner, they all played Animal Grab with an ancient, dog-eared pack of cards, till it was time to go to bed. David had no doubt at all in his mind as to which of them was going to sleep the softest. No wonder Tom Ronald, as he had proclaimed several times already, liked his isolated assignment in Shebiya. On these terms, it hardly counted as isolation.

They stayed for three days in Shebiya: days of exploration, inquiry, and a certain tension. The town itself was small, not much more than a clearing in the jungle. One road led south to Gamate, the rough road by which they had come: one road led past Tom Ronald's house, and then eastwards to Fish Village on the coast – temporarily cut off, owing to heavy rains and a washed-out culvert; a third, smaller track wandered westward, to no particular place, and then petered out in a solid, impenetrable wall of vegetation. No known pathway led north: there, the close-knit trees crowded in, the jungle multiplied into a swarming profusion of bush, fronded creepers, dank undergrowth, and clouds of insects, and civilization thinned or thickened into nothing again.

Together, Crump and David Bracken sampled all that Shebiya had to offer. They had a day's shooting, by jeep along the westward track, and then by foot into the hills, where they bagged a brace of bush partridge, and a small duiker – Pharamaul's speediest and prettiest species of buck. They spent an afternoon in the dusty Shebiya courtroom, where they heard Tom Ronald, unaccustomedly severe and stern, try eleven cases, ranging from an allegation of carnal knowledge of a female minor (reluctantly dismissed for lack of evidence) to the aggravated theft of a blanket (six cuts and a week in jail).

They visited the mission house, a dilapidated shack which clearly needed an early call from Father Schwemmer. On its outer walls, the fish emblem now blossomed in uneasy variety – sometimes daubed with paint, sometimes smeared in charcoal, here and there scored with a knife. David, without success, tried to think of it as a votive tribute to Father Schwemmer's gospel message. They toured Shebiya itself, but there was nothing in Shebiya for them: nothing to watch, nothing to enjoy, little to disapprove of. Here, life went on at so plodding a pace, wearing so sullen a mask, that the very act of watching it seemed a pointless exercise. If the U-Maulas were really content with their sub-human lot, then even to observe it long enough to label it sub-human, was boorish and intrusive.

Their last call in Shebiya, on the eve of their departure, was a formal visit to Gotwela, chief of the U-Maulas. Perhaps it was as well that they had kept this call until the end of their stay; otherwise, thought David, it might well have spoilt their three days in this territory.

Gotwela, when at last he appeared, after a mortifying delay, in the doorway of his hut, proved to be a gross, dirty, ruffianly man of undoubted presence. He was tall, yet his enormous paunch and fat bare thighs gave him an illusion of squat ungainliness. He wore the *simbara*, the ceremonial lion-skin which, outmoded in Gamate, still served as a mark of eminence in Shebiya. As he emerged into the sunlight, blinking under heavy brows, he staggered slightly, and free-flowing sweat started from his face and neck. Gotwela, David diagnosed without difficulty, had only recently woken up, and he had a severe hangover on top of it.

It seemed, however, that he kept some state, on a savage plane that was not reassuring. A tall lithe warrior, also wearing the *simbara*, and carrying a polished spear, preceded Gotwela's appearance; two others, similarly clad and armed, ranged themselves at his side as soon as he took his stand. The strange, crudely-arrayed group of four faced the two white men for some moments, without speech and without movement, caught in a static posture of collision, like some old print portraying the last few seconds before an act of historic violence. Especially was the tall gross figure in the centre, swaying gently, pouring with sweat, frowning under iron brows, a figure of menace. Then Crump spoke, '*Ahsula!*' he said formally. 'I am glad to see you, Chief.'

Gotwela raised his hand, and his bodyguard, copying him, lifted their spears. The broad blades caught the sun, flashing as if in warrant of their murderous intent. Gotwela blinked again, and shook his heavy head as though to rid it of its caul of sweat. Then, insolently detached, he looked beyond Crump, noting the jeep and its attendant policeman. He smiled, widening his thick, cruel lips with sardonic slowness. Then he spoke in turn, in a throaty voice, '*Ahsula!* ... Captain Crump ... We are honoured by this visit.'

The three men of the bodyguard grounded their spears on the dusty forecourt of the hut. Then they looked intently ahead of them – perhaps at the jeep, perhaps at the policeman, perhaps at the nearest margin of the forest. But they did not look at Crump or David Bracken.

'I am glad to see you well, Chief,' answered Crump curtly. His trim, tough figure drew virtue from the other man's ungainly squalor, and he seemed to be making the most of it. 'This is Mr Bracken, a new officer of Government. I have brought him with me, to see Shebiya.'

Gotwela nodded briefly, but he did not answer. The bodyguard still stared ahead, oblivious of the sun, the flies, the voice of the police captain. Only their spears were taut and ready. Foolishly, David tried to calculate how long it would take him to reach the jeep, if those spears began to tremble and to lift … He heard Crump speak again: 'I hope that all is well here, Chief.'

'All is well.' Gotwela's voice, deep and coarse, seemed to emerge from his chest in disinterested, uncaring agreement. It was as if he were saying to Crump, directly: '*All was well before you came. All will be well as soon as you have gone. Do not stay.*'

'The cattle?' asked Crump.

'The cattle are well.'

'The crops?'

'The crops are gathered.'

'The rain?'

'We have been fortunate.'

There was a pause. Crump frowned as if displeased. Gotwela gathered a loose fold of his *simbara* and flung it over his shoulder. The bodyguard looked ahead, their spears unmoving. Crump raised his head again.

'What is this of the fish?' he asked brusquely.

But Gotwela was staring back at him, cool, unsurprised. 'Fish?' he repeated.

'We have heard talk of fish.'

Gotwela shook his head. 'I know no fish.'

Unexpectedly, Crump moved. With the polished toe of his boot he drew the fish emblem in the sandy soil – two

159

curved lines, coming to a point at one end, crossing at the other. Then he gestured downwards.

'That is the fish I speak of.'

David saw that the three men of the bodyguard were no longer looking ahead: they were staring down at what Crump had drawn in the sand, and their eyes had lost their veil of blankness. From them, he looked again at Gotwela, but Gotwela was giving no ground. He faced Crump unblinkingly, his heavy head erect, his gross body solid as rock. He said again: 'I know no fish.'

Crump sighed, not at a loss, but as if he realized that this road was barred and he must find another one. Between himself and Gotwela, the fish emblem remained, as though to mark a dark century of cleavage. If Crump would only lift his foot again, thought David, and rub it out, perhaps all would be well, now and in the future ... He saw that Crump, instead, was preparing to take his leave, and that the bodyguard were raising their spears once more, in formal, ironic farewell. He heard Crump say curtly: 'I am watching this fish,' and Gotwela answer: 'I know no fish,' with equal curtness.

The ugly riddle seemed to be rearing up monstrously behind David's back, as he walked down the pathway towards the jeep. But no weapon smote him deep between his shoulder-blades, no spear cleft his skull; only Crump's voice saying, in one breath, '*Ahsula!* Farewell,' and in another, nearer by a few unhurried paces: 'Bloody old murderer! He knows all about it,' seemed to tell of their defeat, and of a thousand wicked years that could lie between one man and another.

Not until the jeep began to move, and they were fifty yards away, did David, shamefacedly, realize his utter relief.

Cynthia Ronald was playing clock golf, by herself, on the patchy brown lawn, when David Bracken came out to say goodbye to her. It seemed an inane occupation for a pretty girl: much was going to waste here, David thought, as he drew near and found himself admiring her figure once more; and then he thought again, and the fact that she was playing this vicarage-garden game, thousands of miles from its natural setting in rural England, was somehow attractive and endearing. Exile in Shebiya, even exile with the man you loved, must need something like clock golf to restore it to normality ... He smiled as she glanced up, and said: 'You look very expert ... It's about time for me to go, I'm afraid.'

'It's been wonderful having you.' She let the putter fall to the ground, and faced him. 'We love it here, but it's nice to see someone new for a change.'

'Don't you ever get lonely?'

She smiled. 'Now and again. But there's lots to do. And we have visitors quite often, after all. Father Schwemmer and Keith Crump turn up every month or so – Andrew Macmillan comes sometimes. Now there's you.' She smiled again. 'And of course I have a nice husband.'

'It boils down to that, doesn't it?'

'Pretty well.'

'Even though you're really quite different, you and he.'

'Oh, I know that.' She looked away, as if it were not something which she wished to discuss, and then she said: 'Everyone says so. It doesn't make any impression at all ... Have you met Mr Forsdick yet?'

'Yes, indeed. I imagine he said it, too.'

'Almost immediately. Poor man. I expect he suffers all the time, at home ... But he doesn't bother me now.'

David grinned. 'I'm sure he tried to.'

'Almost immediately,' she repeated. 'He said: "Where did you get those bedroom eyes?" and I said: "In my bedroom," and he actually blushed!' She giggled. 'After that he was much nicer.'

'It was a fair answer,' said David judiciously. He thought of Nicole Steuart, and of seeing her again quite soon, and he said suddenly, out of the blue: 'It's about time I got married myself.'

'You do that,' said Cynthia Ronald immediately. 'It's the very best thing you can do. And then you can bring her here to see us.'

'How much longer have you got in Shebiya?'

'About two years. But we really do like it here. It grows on you.'

The police jeep drew up at the front gate, and Crump waved to him, signalling his readiness. At the same moment, Tom Ronald came down the steps of his bungalow.

'Time to go, I'm afraid,' said David again.

'Darling, isn't it wonderful?' said Cynthia Ronald, linking her arm through her husband's. 'David's going to get married, and bring his wife up to see us.'

'Good show!' said Tom Ronald.

'Wait a minute,' said David, laughing. 'I haven't even asked her yet.'

'You ask her,' said Ronald. 'Soon as you can. I really recommend it.'

'It's all very well for you two.'

'Yes,' said Cynthia Ronald, 'it's all very well.'

When, after cheerful goodbyes, the jeep moved off down the road, David's last sight of them was as they stood arm-in-arm, in the middle of their lawn, waving farewell. They seemed so natural a pair, so naturally happy, that Shebiya itself shed its gloom as long as they were within view, and became, briefly, a secure and contented place.

But that illusion did not survive even the beginning of the return journey. By the time the jeep had traversed the sullen town, and was grinding downhill through close-pressing trees, security and contentment had ebbed to nothing again. Shebiya was Shebiya, and no happy human pair could alter its fundamental pattern of mutinous fear and threat. Indeed, with the laborious, disappearing miles, Tom Ronald and his wife lost stature alarmingly, shrinking down to the level of hostages, left behind in dubious country, and barely, guiltily remembered from behind the barricade of safety.

CHAPTER FIVE

❖

When Tulbach Browne of the *Daily Thresh* arrived in Gamate, he did not immediately make contact with Dinamaula. Being an experienced newspaperman, he saved the best to the last, knowing well that the delay was likely to give him a better story in the end. Before he saw Dinamaula, he wanted to see the place where he lived, and the people he lived with, and the Maulas whom he ruled, and the white men who, in a truer sense, ruled the Maulas and Gamate and Dinamaula himself as well. Armed thus, and with his prejudices sharpened, he hoped to come upon Dinamaula with a dozen barbed inquiries that would tie his series of stories up into one neat, poisonous bundle.

His headquarters was now the Gamate Hotel, and from there he foraged diligently, a small figure in a seersucker suit and a broad-brimmed hat, intent on the murder of fact. What the Maulas themselves thought of him was never recorded, though he did slip into their tribal legend, much later, as a cloudy figure who had brought trouble and bloodshed to Gamate at a fearful moment in its history – a sort of fore-running Wicked Wizard who never returned to witness the working-out of the curse he had laid on the town. Maula children of a later generation were to know him as 'White Man with Forked Tongue'. In their games, he was the butt, the figure of fun who might, in certain circumstances, spoil everything and emerge as the grisly victor.

But just now he was Tulbach Browne; and as Tulbach Browne he gave Gamate a thorough going-over. He went everywhere – in the hotel, on the *aboura*, touring the outlying districts, calling at the Residency, hanging round the tribal office, knocking on any door, saluting any man, bribing any child. He had a car at his disposal, a hired car from Port Victoria, with a grinning driver who had never had it so good ... In the first week, which included a sudden dart back to Port Victoria in order to file a confidential despatch to his paper, Tulbach Browne's taxi bill was £125.

No one on the *Daily Thresh* would have complained that this sum was wasted. The piece he did on 'Gamate's Tin Gods' was alone worth the money ... It stemmed from a half-hour talk with Llewellyn, the agricultural officer, and a longer call on Andrew Macmillan up at the Residency. From the latter, Tulbach Browne had returned with the inward smile and the itching fingers that only a typewriter could assuage.

Macmillan had received him, as he did all his visitors, sitting on the *stoep* that overlooked the Residency garden, and the broad vista of Gamate that lay below it. The four red-jerseyed convicts were still at work on one corner of the lawn, under the occasional eye of the fat warder with the spear, and it was this that gave Tulbach Browne his first question.

'Do those lads earn any extra money for working here?' he asked offhandedly, as soon as Macmillan had poured their drinks.

'No,' answered Andrew Macmillan shortly. He had had a long day already, and only a Government House directive about 'making himself available to the Press' had reconciled him to this interview. Indeed, recalling that directive (which mentioned 'due caution and reserve' in its second paragraph) he would scarcely have received Tulbach Browne at all – and certainly not at this hospitable level – had it not been for the tradition of welcome that was an essential part of Gamate, and innumerable places like it. In such towns, sprouting like grateful flowers in a desert, the dusty traveller must always be cared for, the weary stranger refreshed. Andrew Macmillan had entertained hundreds of such visitors at the Residency – officials, tourists, priests, traders. Tulbach Browne was part of a moving frieze of guests, as inevitable as the ants in the garden outside … 'We don't pay them anything extra,' he went on, explanatorily. 'It's included in their normal prison routine. They're all hard-labour convicts.'

'But you have to pay for their time, of course?'

'No,' said Macmillan again.

'Sounds like forced labour,' said Tulbach Browne.

'It's nothing of the sort,' said Macmillan tartly. 'They've got to work somewhere. They would much rather be doing garden work, out-of-doors, than sweating away at breaking rocks or digging drains, down at the prison. You just ask them.'

'Well,' said Tulbach Browne jovially, 'it means that you get four gardeners for free, anyway.'

'It's not my garden,' said Macmillan. 'It belongs to Government.'

There was a short pause. Tulbach Browne stared ahead of him, pursing his lips, already well pleased. There would be no need to take notes, at this rate … The phrase 'Slave labour would probably improve *your* garden, too,' and 'Nice work if you can get it – for nothing' swam briefly before his eyes.

He said: 'I suppose there was a lot of excitement when Dinamaula got back here?'

'There was the usual party,' answered Macmillan, rather wearily. 'Dinamaula was a good excuse for it.'

'I see you take a rather detached view of the whole thing,' said Tulbach Browne, eyeing him. *'Blasé overlord'*, he thought, slipping into sub-headings. *'Godlike eminence ...'* Aloud, he continued, 'But a new chief is something special, after all.'

'Certainly he's something special, and I don't take a detached view at all.' Macmillan felt himself getting nettled, realized that it was foolish and possibly dangerous, and took a pull at his self-control. 'It's part of my job to see that that sort of occasion doesn't get out of hand.'

'You mean, they're allowed to celebrate, as long as the party doesn't get too rough?'

'Yes,' said Macmillan, and added: 'Like London on Boat-race night.'

Tulbach Browne steered away from the reasonable comparison. 'It must be very satisfying,' he commented, 'to be able to organize people's lives so completely.' He saw Macmillan opening his mouth to protest, and he chipped in quickly: 'Ah well, it's over and done with, anyway ... Have you seen Dinamaula yourself?'

'Yes,' answered Macmillan. 'I had him up here.'

'Had him up?' repeated Tulbach Browne carefully.

'Yes. I wanted to talk to him.'

'Anything special?'

'About his interview with you.'

'Yes?'

'I didn't like it.'

'Why not?'

'I thought he went too far.'

'Did you tell him so?'

'Yes.'

'You mean, you read the riot act?'

'Yes.'

Tulbach Browne sighed. This was so much better than he had hoped that he was inclined to leave it at that. But he wanted one more phrase, if possible, to complete this particular section.

'How did Dinamaula take it?' he asked.

Macmillan laughed. 'You'd better ask him,' he said. 'I'm not a mind-reader.'

'Doesn't it matter to you, then?'

'No,' said Macmillan, and then corrected himself. 'It matters, of course, but it's not really important. There are certain rules in a territory like this. They have to be obeyed, whether a man is a chief or a herd-boy.'

'That's what you told Dinamaula? Toe the line, or else?'

'There's no "or else",' said Macmillan hardly. 'It's just "Toe the line", as far as I'm concerned.'

Now there was another pause, a much longer one, while the insects renewed their attack on the flyscreen doors, and the sun cast shadows longer by the breadth of a finger, and the four convicts, squatting economically on their thin shanks, advanced a pace or two towards the edge of the lawn. Macmillan, passing his hand over his face, became conscious of three things – that he was tired as he had never been tired before, that he had spoken far too emphatically about something that had really had a softer outline altogether, and above all that he was not doing well with a man whom he must regard as an adversary.

He was mortifyingly aware that Tulbach Browne, and others like him from the slick world of newspapers, could make rings round him, when it came to the subtle realm of question-and-answer: he himself might be Andrew Macmillan, a Resident Commissioner with thirty-five years' service and limitless experience in his own field, but that still left him in the parish-pump class, when set against the giant background of a world-travelling special correspondent. A part of him was ashamed of this inadequacy, a part of him resented fiercely the immense care, the lifelong cherishing that had gone into his humdrum job, while a man like Tulbach Browne could always earn ten times his salary by tapping out a few sentences for tomorrow's newspaper.

It was unfair. Something was totally wrong. He wanted to be too tired to care, but even that was not true. In forty years, he had never been too tired to wish to quit himself well.

Tulbach Browne was aware of nothing but pleasure. He had come in search of a peg on which to hang his 'Tin Gods of Gamate' article, an article he had planned to write ever since he had heard of Macmillan's name and reputation, down at Port Victoria. Instead of a single peg, he already had a whole row of them, ranging from the 'forced labour' idea that would go down particularly well with impoverished amateur gardeners in England, to Macmillan's curt, brash remark about his ultimatum to Dinamaula. The expression 'Toe the line' would alone prompt a dozen infuriated protest meetings on Chelsea's coffee-coloured fringe. A man like Emrys Price-Canning, for example, could wring torrents of righteous invective from every tainted syllable. With luck, indeed, he would be doing just that, twenty-four hours from now ...

A phrase from his own personal armoury, 'Hit them while you can,' occurred to Tulbach Browne, and he put down his glass, and said, 'Going back to that interview ... What exactly was it that you didn't like?'

'Quite a lot of things.' Macmillan's voice was now subdued, measurably more careful. 'But most of all, as I said, Dinamaula's remarks about progress ... It's really not his job to issue statements about what he's going to do in this territory, before he's even taken over as chief. Anyway, his ideas may be altogether wrong. We're not complete fools up here, you know.'

'No,' said Tulbach Browne.

'I've worked for thirty-five years in Pharamaul. I've got a pretty good idea of what ought to be done here, and the sort of progress we ought to make. Dinamaula isn't even twenty-three yet, and he's been away for the last seven years. On the face of it, it's not likely that he can do the job that I can.' He considered this last sentence for a moment, realized that it sounded condescending, and tried to improve on it, somewhat lamely. 'You've got to learn to walk before you can run.'

'And you think that Dinamaula doesn't know how to walk yet?'

'He's young,' answered Macmillan, almost apologetically. 'He's got a lot of ground to make up.'

Smoothly, without perceptible intent, Tulbach Browne turned the conversation. 'I was talking to Llewellyn, your agricultural man, a bit earlier. He was saying that he had a lot of trouble, persuading the Maulas to thin out their herds – to go for quality rather than quantity.'

Macmillan, glad to be on what seemed safer ground, nodded. 'They have this idea,' he said, 'that the more head of cattle a man has, and the more goats and sheep running about the place, the richer he is. What they don't take into account is what these enormous mixed herds do to the grazing. They ruin it, in fact, and the cattle suffer in the process. We have to show them that a hundred prime head of cattle, on a rich pasture, is a much bigger asset than five hundred half-starved animals, trying to live off grazing land that has been cropped nearly bare.'

'How do you *show* them?' asked Tulbach Browne equably.

'We limit the number of head of cattle a man can own. At least, we try to. It's a tricky business. It's tied up with tribal custom, and prestige, and the dowry system, and half a dozen things like that.'

'But it's their capital, after all, isn't it? It's their savings, the only thing they can own. Can you force them to accept that limitation?'

'Certainly.'

'Do you?'

'Yes.'

Tulbach Browne grinned – a grin his friends would have recognized. 'So it's "toe the line", even where farming is concerned?'

Macmillan suddenly awoke – too late – to the tenor of the conversation.

'It's for their own good,' he said.

'Very likely,' said Tulbach Browne. 'But put yourself in their position. Or rather, transfer the whole thing to England. Would you tell an English farmer that he could only own a hundred cows? Would you tell an English investor that he could only save a thousand pounds?'

'This isn't England,' said Macmillan.

'No,' said Tulbach Browne. 'By God, it isn't!'

For the second time, Macmillan had the abject sense of having been fundamentally outwitted. In his inner mind, he knew once more that the thing was unfair: that one set of rules – in England – did not fit another set of people – here in Pharamaul. An English farmer was not a Maula herdsman: hundreds of years divided them, years of learning, years of development, years of science, selective breeding, communal discipline. He knew all these things, and yet when he tried to explain them, he sounded either pompous or brutal … But he tried once more, aware of making a special effort, aware of an unaccustomed pleading in his voice.

'This isn't England,' he repeated. 'Ideas that are automatically accepted there, have to be made a matter of enforcement in Pharamaul. Give an Englishman an entirely free hand, and he won't make a fool of himself; he knows enough not to abuse his freedom. Do the same thing here, and God knows what would happen … It's true of a lot of things besides farming. They're just not ready to run their own lives.'

'Perhaps not from your point of view,' said Tulbach Browne hardly. He was pressing home an advantage which had somehow been offered him on a plate, and he was not disposed to hesitate in his attack. 'But it's just possible,' he went on ironically, 'that a man like Dinamaula might be qualified to lead his people towards self-government. He might be the man destined to take the next step.'

Macmillan shook his head. 'They're not ready for it …' He looked at Tulbach Browne, hating and fearing him. 'I hope that no one tries to tell them that they are.'

'Meaning me?'

Suddenly Macmillan became conscious of his position, his age, and his authority, and he regretted none of them. All he felt was a grim resentment. 'Yes, meaning you,' he snapped. 'You don't know what you're stirring up, you don't know what you're talking about. You've jumped into this thing like a whore at a christening. If you write about the Maulas as though they could take charge of their own affairs tomorrow, if you talk to them on those lines, if you try to persuade them that they can do without us – ' he tapped his chest, ' – it'll be the worst day's work you've ever done.'

'I'm a reporter,' said Tulbach Browne austerely.

'I wish that were true,' said Macmillan bitterly. 'But I think you're something more. I think you're a promoter … You want to promote a story here, regardless of what it costs. I tell you – ' he had stopped being surprised at himself, and was riding high and reckless, conscious only of the triumphant clarity of his thoughts, ' – you're playing with something you know nothing about. Let it alone. It works. Leave it that way.'

'Sounds like "Anything for a quiet life",' said Tulbach Browne. 'Is that your motto?'

'There are plenty of worse things,' answered Macmillan. 'There could come a day when a quiet life will seem the most precious thing that Gamate ever had.'

'Precious for whom?'

'Everyone. Black. White. You. Me. Them.' Macmillan smiled, unable to hold his mood. 'Look,' he said, 'we're getting in too deep, and obviously we don't agree. How about another drink?'

'Not for me,' said Tulbach Browne, rising. 'I've got to work.' He sounded like a prim man fallen among sinners, a dietitian at a barbecue. 'Thanks for giving me the interview.'

'I work, too,' said Macmillan, leaning back again. Now he didn't give a damn, and he knew it was dangerous, and he didn't give a damn for that either. 'But not all the time.'

'Lucky you,' said Tulbach Browne spitefully, moving towards the door.

'Yes,' said Macmillan, to his retreating back. 'Lucky me ... Goodbye.'

II

Too competent and too cold-blooded for anger, Tulbach Browne dismissed Andrew Macmillan from his mind, as soon as he had filed his first Gamate despatch. Not for the first time, he turned the page on the immediate past, conscious that he had acquitted himself well, conscious that this field of endeavour, if left to lie fallow for a season, might yield an ever richer prize in due course. He had wanted to snipe at officialdom in Gamate – to snipe, to wound, and to lay low. With the filing of 'Gamate's Tin Gods', he felt that he could rest on those particular laurels. In this lavishly-endowed area, there were plenty more to be gained, without driving up the hill to the Residency again. That premium journey would keep.

His next call was on Father Schwemmer and to Tulbach Browne, in his mood of acid optimism, there was no reason to suppose that a poor priest, struggling to continue his ministry in the face of blind prejudice and official obstruction, would produce a dividend less rich.

But Father Schwemmer was not really profitable: Father Schwemmer, indeed, was a considerable disappointment. Tulbach Browne, drawing on his experience of the hired priests who regularly declaimed in the columns of the *Daily Thresh*, had expected a man of the same calibre – a professional Christian, a man whose sense of mission had long overtopped his faith, a man who could not wait to tell you of the crucifix perennially itching between his shoulder-blades. There was one such man, very close to the *Daily Thresh* throne, known as 'Christ's Election Agent' … But Father Schwemmer was none of these things. Father Schwemmer was something that Tulbach Browne had not met before, and could not recognize.

It was clear, from the very beginning, that there was no common ground between them. Tulbach Browne, surveying the tumbledown mission house and the neglected garden, had talked in accents of reproachful sympathy of the frustrations of serving in so humble a vineyard. Father Schwemmer, who was feeling happy because his list of confirmation candidates for the current year was longer – by three elusive small boys – than last year's, countered with so contented an expression of hope and faith, that Tulbach Browne (product of a grim Unitarian home) wondered if he had been paid to act the part … It was the same all the way down the list. When Tulbach Browne talked of poverty and injustice, Father Schwemmer spoke of simple happiness. When Tulbach Browne remarked on the backwardness of the Maulas,

Father Schwemmer praised their patient enterprise, sure to bear fruit in the near future. When Tulbach Browne used a word such as 'emancipation', Father Schwemmer first asked, apologetically, for a simpler term, and then talked at length about the slow, due process of advancement, and the virtues of the pace of the ox.

Only once did the interview show promise – the kind of promise that Tulbach Browne was hoping for; and that was when the prospects of the new chieftainship were mentioned.

'Do you expect,' Tulbach Browne had asked, switching like some resourceful hound from a scent that had failed to another one that promised a fresh quarry over the hill, 'that there'll be any trouble when Dinamaula takes over?'

'Trouble?' repeated Father Schwemmer warily. After half an hour's talk, his simple mind had grasped what the other man was doing. His visitor was fishing for trouble, employing in the process a series of questions that seemed to Father Schwemmer intrusive and indeed impertinent. The old man did not want to help his questioner, but he did not want to fail in his duty either. 'Trouble? No, we need not anticipate that.'

'I suppose the dynasty is pretty well established now. There's not much chance of an opposition party.'

'There is always such a chance,' said Father Schwemmer, striving for accuracy. 'Pharamaul is not completely peaceful. It is a country of surprises.'

'What sort of a surprise could there be?

Father Schwemmer looked at him. 'Mr Browne, if we knew that, it would not be a surprise, would it?'

Tulbach Browne smiled bleaky, aware of opposition none the less effective for being thus delicately, gently placed in his path. He tried once more.

'I mean, could it possibly happen that Dinamaula might have a rival? – that someone would try to beat him to it?'

'Beat him to it?'

'Take over the chieftainship before he did.'

Father Schwemmer sighed. He had hoped to fill this hour, the hour before his weekly, sometimes unruly Bible Class, with meditation, or with what so often took its place nowadays – gentle, forgetful sleep; but clearly this was not to be. The man watching him was too intrusive, the questions he asked too searching and too vital, too closely tied to his beloved Pharamaul, his own Gamate. For the sake of truth, for the very love of Christ, he must gird up his loins and give of his best ... He stood up, and said, surprisingly, 'Mr Browne, I would like you to come for a short walk with me.'

'Certainly,' answered Tulbach Browne, momentarily off his guard; and then, 'Where to? I'm pretty busy with – '

'A short walk,' interrupted Father Schwemmer, with the gentlest touch of authority in the world. 'It will take us perhaps ten minutes. It will take us to the tomb of the Maulas.'

'All right,' said Tulbach Browne unwillingly. 'That's something I haven't seen yet.' He grinned. 'What's it like, anyway? All same Taj Mahal, eh?'

'You will see for yourself,' answered Father Schwemmer, and, gravely courteous, ushered his visitor out into the garden again, and down the path. Tulbach Browne, blinking against the sunlight, accepted his escort with awkward, grudging readiness.

They set off on their dubious journey, first across the *aboura*, then up a winding hill leading to the outskirts of the town. They were not a well-assorted pair, though they were both small men of slight build. While Tulbach Browne trotted industriously, Father Schwemmer walked with even, level strides; while the newspaperman seemed inquisitive and wary, the priest was contented; while the seersucker suit caught the attention, the dusty brown *soutane* appeased the eye. They were like two contrasting characters in a simple, centuries-old morality play: the one portraying goodness and grace, the other the classic figure of impiety. If they went on a journey together, it could only involve a fleeting companionship, destined traditionally for dissolution.

They climbed the hill, pausing sometimes to look back at the town: gradually the huts thinned out, and the people who greeted Father Schwemmer with open hand, and stared curiously at Tulbach Browne, became fewer as their advancing steps followed the upward path. Soon they were near the crest of the hill, and making their way along a bare, rocky ridge, lined with thorn and scrub, that led towards a solitary outcrop. Then they turned a corner, and came upon the place of the tombs.

The burial ground lay in ominous, forbidding silence, clasped within a fold of the hill; one side of it was open, looking towards the purple U-Maula mountains, the rest was enclosed by solid ramparts of rock. A ring of sad cypress trees stood for ever sentinel over this solemn plot; at their foot, the green turf flourished briefly in a wilderness of stone and weathered rock. A broken wire fence surrounded the graveyard: inside were only three graves – one large and ornate, the others smaller. Two goats raised their heads at the sound of footsteps, and shambled away from them, in disgruntled alarm. The sun bore down, the wind in the cypress trees sighed thinly against the silence. The whole place had an air of neglected honour, like a battlefield from some secondary, unhistoric war, long fallen out of military favour.

The two men crossed the fence and drew near to the graves; the priest still moving surely, Tulbach Browne looking about him in irritated uncertainty. The largest grave, overgrown, weatherbeaten, green with lichen, had the simple legend: 'Maula the Great', outlined in deeply-etched, German-gothic script. Another grave nearby said: 'Simaula, Son of Maula'. A third, much smaller, with a marble figure of an angel child at its head, was labelled: 'Akamaula, Son of Maula. Aged one year. Whom the Gods love, die young'. That was all there was, in the burial place of the Maulas.

Tulbach Browne watched the priest moving from grave to grave, bending, touching, as if he were on loved and familiar ground. He watched the cypress cones fluttering in the wind, and the goats returning to crop the green turf, and he looked again at the lettering on the tombs, and the far-off U-Maula hills, and he drew nothing from all this, and he came close to the priest again, and said, awkwardly, 'What a curious place.'

The old priest looked at him, his hand still caressing the largest tombstone. 'Yes,' he said. 'It is certainly curious. You will have noticed the most curious thing about it.'

'What is that?' asked Tulbach Browne.

'The three graves.'

Tulbach Browne shrugged. 'Nothing much to any of them.'

'The *three* graves.' Father Schwemmer accented, slightly, the second word. Then he started again. 'Mr Browne, this is the family burial place of a whole dynasty, a dynasty that has ruled in Gamate for over a hundred years. This man – ' he indicated the grave of Maula the Great, ' – did not die till 1900. He had eleven sons. These are two of them, buried here. Akamaula was the infant son of his old age, who died of smallpox while Maula was still alive. Simaula was his fourth son, and succeeded to the chieftainship when Maula died. Simaula himself had eight sons – ' Father Schwemmer paused, and sighed. 'Of course, there were many daughters, but daughters are of no account to this tribe. But Maula and Simaula between them had nineteen sons. That is why I said it was curious.'

'I still don't understand,' said Tulbach Browne. The sun was giving him a headache, the silence was getting on his nerves, and he was struggling with unmanageable facts and figures. He wanted to say, *They're a lot of bloody niggers anyway, what the hell do I care where they're buried*, but he felt that he would be cheated if he got no more than irritation from this day and this hot, dusty climb. 'What's it all about?'

'There could be twenty-one people, in this burial place of the Maulas. There are only three. There you have the history of the tribe.'

Tulbach Browne waited.

'The rest,' continued Father Schwemmer, 'were claimants to the chieftainship, or might have become so. They are not buried here. God knows where they are buried. They were driven from Gamate, killed, exiled, poisoned, rooted out. There is a tribal custom that anyone of royal blood who dies by violence, or strangely, must be buried elsewhere. He cannot lie in the chiefs' burial place. That is why we have three graves here, and only three graves. Maula the Great, and his fourth son Simaula who succeeded him, and the little child who never grew up to become a challenge to his father.'

'Simaula was lucky,' said Tulbach Browne flippantly.

'Simaula was clever,' corrected Father Schwemmer. 'While he was still a young man, and after his three elder brothers had been killed, he feigned madness, and wandered off towards the U-Maula country, and disappeared. He only came back when Maula himself was on his deathbed.'

'But it's ridiculous,' said Tulbach Browne, suddenly waking up. 'It's a pure savagery!'

'You asked me about the Maula dynasty, and whether it was well established,' said Father Schwemmer, smiling. 'I brought you up here to give you your answer.'

179

'But it's ridiculous,' said Tulbach Browne again. 'Why didn't we do something? We ought to keep better order! We ought to control things … You can't let people just run wild like that.'

'Some would say,' answered Father Schwemmer, deceptively mild, 'that that is the meaning of self-determination.'

Tulbach Browne looked at him sharply, not sure whether the other man was making fun of him, He said, half to himself: 'But they can't be allowed to behave like that. It's a damned disgrace! It simply means we haven't taught them properly.'

'It means many more things,' said Father Schwemmer. 'It means also that we have not taught them for long enough. It means that they are simple, savage children who must remain in the nursery. It means that we, the white teachers, cannot go away from here, not for a long time. It means,' said Father Schwemmer, looking down at the graves, and up at the cypress trees, and then at Tulbach Browne, 'that there is enough strife and discord and danger in Pharamaul already, with no help from outside. So every man who lives here, and every man who comes here, must guard his tongue and his thoughts, in case he should add to that strife, and make bad things worse, and perhaps even leave Pharamaul with blood on his hands.'

'It means that to you,' said Tulbach Browne tartly.

'Yes,' answered Father Schwemmer, his hand gentle on the tomb again, 'it means that to me.'

III

Next stop, the Gamate Hotel – a likely fishing ground for a man whose beckoning smile and baited welcome concealed so delicately the barb of the hook … Tulbach Browne found himself at home in the Gamate Hotel, as he had been at home in countless other hotels, all the way across the world; before very long, he was the ideal stranger in the bar – hail-fellow with newcomers, ready with drinks all round, making friends as another man might make slick, contriving shadows on the wall. But beneath the surface, he was watchful all the time, and from at least three people he drew a notable dividend towards the contribution he was seeking in Pharamaul.

First there was David Bracken, on his way down from Shebiya, spending by chance a single evening in Gamate. David knew Tulbach Browne well by reputation; aware of what he was doing, he was wary with the other man, taking great care to give him no opening. But his care did not save him from providing Tulbach Browne with one spectacular, infinitely quotable phrase.

They had been talking, naturally, of Shebiya, and the way it was run, and the simple near-savagery that marked its walled-up way of life. David described the Ronalds, and the happiness they obviously found in their strange home, and the inconclusive visit to Gotwela. The latter, he commented, was not a reassuring figure.

'What's he really like?' asked Tulbach Browne. 'He's the local chief, isn't he?'

Round them the bar was, as usual, noisy and full of business. Fellows, the landlord, pushed out the drinks with a will, and the men in their drab, dusty khaki, and the women in long-accustomed print, gossiped and drank and stared. Footsteps slurred on the rough boards, laughter rose high at the bar counter; faces now familiar to David – the Forsdicks, Llewellyn, Captain Crump who was still his cheerful chauffeur, the pretty nurses from the hospital – swam successively into view, then faded again. He concentrated, with a slight effort, on what Tulbach Browne was saying.

'Gotwela's the local chief,' David answered, 'in a slightly undercover way. He rules the U-Maulas. They're a breakaway tribe. The Maulas here, of course, don't really recognize them as a subdivision, but they don't do anything about it. We work with Gotwela. It seems to be effective.'

'It's a compromise, then?'

'Something like that.'

'And Gotwela himself?'

'Large. Tough. Not exactly civilized.'

Tulbach Browne smiled. 'You make him sound a rather odd character.'

'He's all that,' agreed David carelessly. 'In fact, when you first meet him, he's like something out of the zoo.'

Then, also in the Gamate bar, there was George Forsdick: Forsdick (by ill-chance) at his most unreliable, Forsdick at seven o'clock in the evening, flushed with whisky, hating his wife, eyeing the girls: Forsdick, for better or worse the District Commissioner.

'The trouble with you chaps,' said Forsdick, sticking a solid thumb into Tulbach Browne's brittle chest, 'is that you write such a lot of tripe. I expect you're paid damn' well for it,' he continued, handsomely, slurringly, 'but that doesn't cut much ice with us chaps on the spot. *We* know the sort of game you're playing.'

'What game is that?' Tulbach Browne inquired.

'Looking for a scandal. Writing a lot of tripe.'

'Dear me,' observed Tulbach Browne pleasantly, 'you don't seem to like the Press.'

Forsdick's thumb advanced again. 'You can say that again.' He roared with sudden laughter, spilling his drink. 'That's what the Yanks say. You can say that again.'

'What does it mean?' asked Tulbach Browne, with deceptive patience.

'Christ!' exclaimed Forsdick. 'I thought you chaps knew everything.'

'Oh no,' said Tulbach Browne.

'Then why do you do it?' asked Forsdick belligerently.

'Do what?'

'Write a lot of tripe?'

'I don't agree that we do.'

'You wrote a lot of tripe about Dinamaula.' The thumb came out again, like the classic blunt instrument of all stories of violence. 'You wrote a lot of tripe about Andrew Macmillan. You can't deny it.'

'I do deny it,' said Tulbach Browne, though without emphasis.

'One of the best fellows in the world,' continued Forsdick, unheeding, 'and you go and write a lot of tripe about him … Have a drink,' he commanded, 'and try and be a good chap. In the future. Just by way of a change.'

'Nothing more for me, thanks,' said Tulbach Browne.

'Try and be a good chap,' Forsdick persisted. 'It's not really difficult. Just stop writing a lot of tripe.'

'Aren't you the District Commissioner?' asked Tulbach Browne, closing in.

'You know bloody well I am,' said Forsdick. 'I may not get a lot of money for it. But I don't write tripe.'

'Nor do I.'

'Try and be a good chap,' Forsdick repeated.

'You're in charge here?' asked Tulbach Browne.

'Yes. And don't write a lot of tripe about me. It'll get you nowhere.'

'I don't want to get anywhere.'

'You can say that again,' said Forsdick, bellowing with laughter again, 'because you're not getting anywhere.'

'You don't like the Press?'

'Not my cup of tea.'

'What about Dinamaula?'

'Dinamaula,' answered Forsdick, with rare, unfortunate, distinct enunciation, 'is getting too big for his boots.' Then, for the last time, his thumb jabbed in Tulbach Browne's breastbone. 'In the interests of truth,' he said, 'that's not quite true.'

'Why not?'

'Because,' said Forsdick, struggling with sudden mountainous laughter again, 'he doesn't wear boots ... So if you're writing some more tripe about Dinamaula, don't mention boots ... Just a barefoot boy,' he said, with a kind of drunken poetry in his voice, 'getting too big for the boots he hasn't got.'

'Interesting,' said Tulbach Browne.

'Fascinating ... Have another drink.'

'Nothing more,' said Tulbach Browne, 'for me.'

Looking back on it – as Tulbach Browne did, with rare delight, many times afterwards – it seemed to him that it was that moment of that evening in the Gamate Hotel which somehow gave the signal for everything in Pharamaul to go wonderfully, irrevocably wrong. Hitherto – again in retrospect – he had been playing with the story, fiddling about, merely amusing himself; he had been able to provoke Dinamaula a little, on the plane to Port Victoria, he had enjoyed some easy, knock-down fun with the Governor, and the rest of the well bred turnip-heads at the Pharamaul Club; he had found it possible to prick Andrew Macmillan into an encouraging display of indiscretion.

But now, as he stood at ease in the bar, these preliminary swings regained their modest perspective, and he realized that there was much more to come, and the path of history seemed suddenly to take a new, ecstatic, and disgusting turn. Like a gourmet of deeply perverted taste, who could enjoy only entrails and excrement, Tulbach Browne sniffed the air of harlotry, drawing deep down into his lungs a beloved corruption. He knew, with true instinct, that the story he had come to find was now very near to him.

David Bracken had given him a superbly quotable phrase; Forsdick, less than sober, had left him ample room for attack. Soon he would see Dinamaula, and Dinamaula, beyond doubt, would crown with degraded spices this stinking dish.

He looked about him, seeking a bridge between promise and outcome, and he found it in Oosthuizen, Oosthuizen the farmer, who was nearest to him as Forsdick turned away.

They had already been introduced. 'So you're a farmer,' said Tulbach Browne, picking it up at random. 'Must be interesting. How many people do you have working for you?'

'About five hundred.' Oosthuizen had spent some time in the bar already, but, as with most big men, alcohol took a very slow toll of his senses. The seven glasses of beer he had drunk had induced no more than a careless contentment. He leant against the bar counter, his blond head and enormous frame jutting like a lighthouse from some friendly promontory. 'That is, including the women and the *klonkies*.'

'The what?'

'The kids. They do a good day's work too, leading the plough-oxen or running errands.'

'What do you pay them for that?'

Oosthuizen stared, confronted by total ignorance. 'Man, you must be crazy! They live on my land, they eat my mealies. I don't have to pay them.'

'Sounds like the feudal system,' said Tulbach Browne.

'Yes,' said Oosthuizen, 'and a bloody good system too!'

Fellows, the landlord who had been a boxer, pushed a drink across the counter, and said: 'Compliments of the District Commissioner.'

'Thanks,' said Tulbach Browne automatically, his hand curling round the glass. He looked negligently about the room. 'Pretty crowded tonight ... Does Dinamaula ever come in here?'

'Dinamaula?' repeated Oosthuizen, uncomprehendingly.

'The new chief ... He's been in Gamate quite a few days.'

'He doesn't come in here,' said Fellows simply.

'Why not?'

Fellows shrugged. 'He just doesn't, that's all. He can come round to the hatch at the side door, any time he likes, and I'll serve him, quick enough. Beer, brandy, whatever he wants. The DC has said that's all right.'

'But why not in here?' persisted Tulbach Browne.

'Do you want him in here?' asked Oosthuizen, with emphasis. 'All chums together, eh?'

'That's not the point,' answered Tulbach Browne. 'Why shouldn't he come in here, if he feels like it? This is British territory, isn't it? There's no colour bar. Why shouldn't he drink with us?'

'It's not the way things are done here, that's all,' said Fellows. He was ill at ease, swabbing the bar heavily without looking at it, aware of a new, uncomfortable element within touching distance. 'This bar is reserved for white people. Liquor isn't sold to blacks, anyway, though the Regents can have what they want. *That's* the way it's done in Gamate.'

'But it means there's a colour bar,' insisted Tulbach Browne.

'All right,' said Oosthuizen, suddenly much larger and nearer. 'It means there's a colour bar. What the hell do you know about it? Have you ever seen a nigger with a couple of hard drinks inside him? Man, he'd have your guts to darn his socks with …'

'I don't like that word nigger.'

'I don't like that word nigger,' Oosthuizen mimicked savagely. 'All right, call him something else. Call him – ' he drew, laboriously, on some remembered newspaper phrase, ' – call him a man with a slight difference of pigmentation. Know what that means? It means he's a Maula, and Maulas don't drink with whites in this territory. It's not a new rule, it's an old custom. You want to change it? Don't change it. You'll be starting something that someone else will have to finish.'

'I still say,' said Tulbach Browne patiently, 'that in British territory, there shouldn't be a colour bar. Dinamaula should be as free to come into this room as I am.'

'You can't have that,' said Fellows stoutly. 'And it's no good covering it up with a lot of talk about democracy, and what they do in London. You just can't have Dinamaula coming into the bar here, mixing with people.'

'Isn't Dinamaula "people"?'

'He's black, Mr Browne. This is a hotel for whites. He can't come in here.'

Tulbach Browne faced him, aware of the other man's broad shoulders, aware also of his basic simplicity. This, also, was likely material … He looked from Fellows to Oosthuizen. He was alone among large tough men, of demonstrable strength. He turned aside, smiling. To himself he murmured: 'What'll you bet? What'll you bet?' Aloud, he said, cheerfully, dismissively: 'Time I bought us all a drink.'

IV

Dinamaula lay in the oppressive twilight of his hut, thinking the dire thoughts of solitude. He had spent much of the last few days in the same place and the same employment: lying on a bed of skins, enduring the bright heat of the day and the sticky gloom of the night, staring at the spiders' webs that festooned the reed thatching overhead: drinking beer, eating mealie-porridge, smoking, refusing visitors, thinking, waiting; knowing, in his own mind, that he was so far from the picture of a young chief claiming his inheritance, that many people – his mother, his allotted bride, his uncle Seralo, his brothers of the Dinamaula Regiment – could only fall silent or shed tears at the sight.

Himself, he shed no tears; he carried within his breast a hard stone, a stone of unrest, hatred, disappointment. Ever since he arrived in Gamate, his inheritance had seemed shoddy and not worth the burden of assumption. Ever since he had seen Andrew Macmillan, up at the Residency, it had all turned to bitter pantomime.

I am Dinamaula, he thought, stirring once more to full wakefulness, watching with startling hatred the ants swarming over the soiled plates of his last untouched meal. I am Dinamaula, Chieftain of Pharamaul, Prince of Gamate, Urn of the Royal Seed, Keeper – the fatuous phrases rolled from his loaded brain, as false and discountable as some late-hour banquet introduction, mouthed for a drunken audience by a soberly calculating man. I am Dinamaula, at home at last in Gamate, the established seat of power. I am the centre of that power. But look at me.

What was the good – so his thoughts spun, and wandered, and returned to their dreary core – what was the good of leaving Gamate, and going to Oxford, and making friends and taking a law degree and patiently learning to live in a white and western community, if one had to come back to this? Back to this squalor, this dirt, this ignorance.

Back to this huge problem that was really, by many other standards, so negligible. Back to this confusion.

After a week at home, Dinamaula knew well the outlines of this confusion: knew them, recognized them, and hated them. He had come back to a land that he should never have left, because his leaving and returning was going to make no difference at all. At Oxford, he had talked hungrily of freedom and democracy. The words now were meaningless. In England, he had talked of love, marriage, companionship. The words were futile, in the plane, *en route* for the island of Pharamaul, he had talked of progress. The word was blasphemous.

After a week, he knew what he was up against. He had met the whole range of Maula thought, from left to right – Christ! how did one label it? – from new to old, from volatile to moribund. There were old men like Seralo, the senior Regent, wanting no change.

There were middle men, who wished to swim with the stream, but not to hurry it. There were ambitious men like Puero, who looked for profit and advancement. There were fringe men like Zuva, who wanted violence. There were tens of thousands of Maulas, who did not even know what they hoped for. There was a loutish girl, Miera, who wanted (because she had been so ordered) to share his bed.

There was himself, in the middle of all this, and strangely, tragically, wanting nothing of any aspect of it. What he wanted had not yet appeared on any horizon of any country. He was the man in the middle, the classic figure of fun, the dupe, the one you laughed at. He was in the middle. And by God, if Andrew Macmillan was anything to judge by, the man in the middle occupied the lowest stool of all!

Even now, a week after his interview with the Resident Commissioner, thoughts of rage and mutiny could overtop all other thoughts. He could not truly say that he had been treated like a child – for children usually encountered love and understanding. Instead, he had been treated like some farmyard adolescent who, having found out for himself the facts of life, had to be gagged and bound and bundled out of sight, in case his goatish blood drove him to experiment in a newly discovered but private world.

He liked Macmillan – that was the annoying part. He knew that the other man was solid, dependable, full of knowledge, trustworthy. He wanted to be admitted to such thoughts, to share such company. Instead, he had been 'interviewed', as he had been interviewed on countless occasions in England – by customs men, by men in the Scheduled Territories Office, by Oxford dons, by policemen, club secretaries, women, fellow undergraduates. He had been inspected, weighed, found wanting, almost before he had entered the Residency. Then he had been instructed, in the minutest detail – what to do next, what not to do, what corridors to walk down, what friends to make, what pastures to avoid. He had been told, above all, to behave himself.

Macmillan – the man he liked and admired – had used inexcusable phrases. Dinamaula remembered one of them especially. 'I don't propose,' Macmillan had said, looking at him as if he were a probationary servant in some great patrician house, 'to lose any sleep, just because there's a new chief. *Gamate will survive it.*' And when Dinamaula had kept silent, mortified, taken aback, Macmillan had added: 'You've had your fun with the newspapers, but you'd better talk sense to me!'

Now Dinamaula lay in darkness, enduring the heat, watching the spiders, thinking the thoughts of mutiny and despair. He was still thinking such thoughts when Tulbach Browne sent a message, asking – with expressions of respect and hesitation – if he might be allowed to talk to the chief.

'As a matter of fact,' said Tulbach Browne, nodding sagely, 'Macmillan told me about that himself. Said he'd had you up to the Residency, and read the riot act – whatever that means. Said he told you that you'd have to toe the line. Did he really say that?'

It was an hour later, and, for Tulbach Browne, time to make a move.

'Yes,' said Dinamaula sombrely, 'that was what he said.'

'But it's extraordinary. After all, you're the chief.'

'Not yet.'

Tulbach Browne looked at him, staring across the shadows of the hut. 'But you're going to be.'

'I hope so.'

Tulbach Browne hesitated, wondering whether to pursue a new and crucial line of thought. He decided against it. He had enough in view, as it was; if there were anything in the novel prospect that Dinamaula had opened up, it would certainly keep. Instead, he ground out his cigarette on the beaten-earth floor of the hut, and said: 'I was very surprised when Macmillan told me about the interview. It sounded almost as if he was proud of it.'

'He is a strong man,' said Dinamaula.

'Or thinks he is … He's not the only one, either. I was in the Gamate Hotel, a couple of days ago. You know, they've got some funny ideas there.'

'Who have?'

'People I met. Farmer called Oosthuizen. Bracken, the new man at Government House. Forsdick. And the man behind the bar – can't remember his name – '

'Mr Fellows,' said Dinamaula.

'Fellows. He was *very* vocal … He actually told me,' said Tulbach Browne carefully, 'that you couldn't go in there and have a drink.'

Dinamaula was silent.

'Now that, to me,' said Tulbach Browne, looking at his fingernails, 'is an extraordinary idea. Here we are, in British territory. There's no difference – or there ought to be no difference – between the Gamate Hotel, and a pub in Piccadilly. I don't suppose,' he went on, 'that you ever had any trouble, getting a drink in London?'

'No,' said Dinamaula.

'But here you are, *in your own town*, and there are people boasting – because that's what it sounded like – actually boasting that the Gamate Hotel is reserved for whites only, with a colour bar that they're going to preserve at all costs.'

'It is the custom,' answered Dinamaula briefly.

'Well, I think it's a rotten one.'

'None the less, it has come to be accepted.'

'By you?'

'I have only just returned to Gamate.'

'It might be a good moment,' said Tulbach Browne, 'to make a few changes.'

Dinamaula looked at him. In his special mood of introspective despair, he had been paying less than full attention to the trend of the newspaperman's questions; he had thought them frivolous and ill-connected. Now he became aware of where they were leading, and he felt dangerously stirred by the knowledge. It was part of his sudden vulnerability. He was sad and lonely; his self-esteem had been laid raw; here was a fellow human being, a white man, who cared about such things, who treated him as he had often been treated in London and Oxford, who was unequivocally on his side.

He felt himself being carried along on a wave of predestined action, a Grecian surge of fate and drama. There was a step to be taken, a step into the unknown, a step that would show Macmillan, and people like him, that 'chief' was a fact, not a word.

But he hesitated, needing persuasion. He said, slowly: 'Why are you so interested in all this?'

Tulbach Browne shrugged his shoulders. 'I'm interested, like a lot of other people, in what goes on in the world. Here's something damned queer that people ought to know about – a straight, open colour bar operating in a British protectorate. It needs putting right.'

'Much needs putting right.'

'True. But in this case, I feel like making a start on it.'

'How?'

'A lot of people in Gamate say you can't get a drink at the hotel. I say you can.'

'So?'

'Come with me to the Gamate Hotel.'

Dinamaula shivered suddenly, though the day was hot and the hut airless. Tulbach Browne was looking at him, waiting for his answer – Tulbach Browne who had nothing to lose either way, who would contrive a story out of success or a story out of failure. Dinamaula knew that he was being used by an unscrupulous man, a man who had, during the past hour, alternately flattered, derided, and provoked him; but he knew also that he would go through with it, for many reasons unconnected with Tulbach Browne, reasons of blood and anger that needed no alien prompting. Though he answered, frowning: 'But we know perfectly well what will happen,' he was already preparing to rise to his feet.

V

It was about noon, and there were not many people in the bar of the Gamate Hotel, when Dinamaula followed Tulbach Browne through the doorway and up to the counter. The sun shone through the muslin-curtained windows, falling upon the rough board floor, traversing the dust that hung over the wicker chairs and tables, gleaming on the serried rows of bottles that stood ready behind the bar. It could have been a cheerful scene, but somehow it missed cheerfulness and settled for a shabby utility. Dinamaula, surveying it swiftly, thought: Good God, can't I even come in *here*? ... He was trembling, and he walked behind Tulbach Browne as if the other's determined, bustling figure could draw a veil over his presence. But though he was trembling, he was not sorry to be there.

Almost light-headed, he found himself remembering the men who had fought upon St Crispin's Day. This was another such battlefield ... Bloody and mortal though it might prove, yet it was not an occasion to miss, in any country, any century.

Fellows, from his station behind the bar, saw them coming: Fellows, and Llewellyn the agricultural officer, who was sipping a quick beer at the end of the counter, and Oosthuizen the farmer. Their reactions were characteristic. Llewellyn, a small man, grew noncommittally watchful; Oosthuizen stiffened and stared, scarcely believing his eyes. Fellows reddened, and the hand swabbing down the bar hesitated and then clenched in sudden tension. There were half a dozen other people at the tables; slowly awakening to the incredible, they nudged each other, and ceased to speak, and waited.

There was a deep silence all over the room as Tulbach Browne said, 'Two beers, please.'

Fellows, now a fiery red, stared back at him, his small blue eyes very prominent. Gazing narrowly and carefully, he seemed to be taking in only one figure, though no one present in the room could be unaware that two men had passed between the tables, and up to the bar. Then Fellows shook his head.

'Sorry, Mr Browne.'

'What?' said Tulbach Browne.

'I can't serve you.' Dinamaula, his black face expressionless, had now ranged himself at Tulbach Browne's side, leaning against the bar, and Fellows glanced at him for a quick moment, at last acknowledging his presence, before coming back to Tulbach Browne again.

'Why not?' asked Tulbach Browne, civilly enough.

'You know why not,' said Fellows curtly.

Round them the silence grew into a pall of expectancy.

'I want two beers,' said Tulbach Browne in even tones. 'One for me, one for my friend. I'm staying in the hotel. You can't refuse to serve me.'

'I'll serve you,' said Fellows, heavy breathing. 'But I can't serve the chief.'

'Why not?' repeated Tulbach Browne.

'You know bloody well why not!' This time it was Oosthuizen, solid and formidable, who broke in to take up the argument. 'Because he's not allowed in here. That's why not!'

'I wasn't speaking to you,' said Tulbach Browne briefly.

'I *was* speaking to you,' said Oosthuizen, with dangerous emphasis. 'Man, you've got a bloody cheek, bringing him in like this!'

'Two beers,' said Tulbach Browne.

A man at a table behind them called: 'Throw them both out!'

Dinamaula plucked gently at Tulbach Browne's arm. 'Let us go,' he said. He was now unexpectedly calm, free from anger, free from shame. He had known it would be like this. It was the custom, no more, no less. He did not mind – though perhaps he would mind later.

'We're not going,' said Tulbach Browne. 'Not before we get a drink.'

Fellows shook his head once more. 'I can't serve you in the bar.' His tone grew pleading. 'But there's a nice private room. Just through the curtain. I'll serve you both there, right away.'

'I want two beers,' said Tulbach Browne. 'Here in the public bar.'

'No,' said Fellows.

'You heard him,' said Oosthuizen.

At the back of the room they were now standing up – not menacing, but wishing to be ready for whatever might happen next. Tulbach Browne looked round him, his lip curling. Then he turned to Fellows again.

'Let's get this thing quite definite,' he said. 'I'm staying in the hotel. I've ordered two drinks. You say you won't serve them here, but you will serve them in a private room, out of sight. Why?'

In the silence that followed, an unexpected voice intervened.

'Chief,' called Llewellyn.

Dinamaula turned towards him politely. 'Yes, Mr Llewellyn?'

'I don't think you ought to do this.'

'You're too bloody right!' said Oosthuizen belligerently. Llewellyn tapped his fingers on the bar. 'Let's keep it decent,' he said, with an authority odd in so small a man. He looked at Dinamaula again. 'Mr Fellows is quite right, and you know he is. It's not the custom here. If Mr Browne wants to drink with you, he should take you through into the private room.'

'He shouldn't want to, anyway,' said Oosthuizen.

Tulbach Browne shook his head, denying all this out of hand. 'I want two beers,' he said. 'Here and now. Do I get them, or don't I?'

Ranged side by side, the black man and the white man waited. Then, after a long prickling silence, Fellows said: 'No.'

'You're refusing to serve me?'

'Yes.'

Dinamaula touched his arm again, and this time Tulbach Browne was ready to move. He said: 'All right, then,' and turned slowly away from the bar, and made for the door, holding Dinamaula lightly by the elbow to guide him out. A man called out: 'Bloody sauce!' as they passed, and a woman: 'Well, that's the first time I've ever seen *that!*' As Tulbach Browne and Dinamaula walked through the door again, conversation broke out in full spate behind them, bringing to a historic scene the astounded comment of the witnesses.

They walked a few paces from the hotel to the southern edge of the *aboura*, before they said goodbye to each other. For some reason, it now seemed inappropriate for them to remain together. Dinamaula wanted to think. Tulbach Browne wanted to write. Both were private undertakings.

'Sorry about all that,' said Tulbach Browne at length.

'It is no matter,' answered Dinamaula. His eyes were downcast, as the rawness of defeat and shame started to flood in again. 'It was what we both expected. It is the custom.'

'Stupid bastards! I'll see that people hear about it, though – don't you fear!'

'It is the custom.'

Tulbach Browne looked across the *aboura*, narrowing his eyes against the fierce midday sun. It was the hour after the hour of eating, and few people stirred; even the scrawny, questing goats were indolent, crowding into the shade of every hut. Behind them, the Gamate Hotel presented to the world, and especially to them, a blank, satirical face.

'You're staying on in Gamate?' asked Tulbach Browne after a pause.

'Oh yes,' answered Dinamaula. 'There are a lot of things to be seen to. Then there is the ceremony of taking over as chief.'

'When will that be?'

Dinamaula gestured vaguely. 'A month. Two months.' He smiled briefly and bitterly. 'It is very elaborate.'

'I'd like to be here for that.'

There was a longer pause between them. A man came down the steps of the Gamate Hotel, looked at them for a moment, and then strode off towards his car. It was easy to fancy arrogance and contempt in his striding ... From the opposite side of the *aboura*, a woman left one hut, walked a few yards, and went into another. Tulbach Browne, long-sighted, recognized her.

'That was Miera,' he said.

'Yes,' said Dinamaula.

Tulbach Browne smiled a clubman's smile. 'I've heard a lot of talk.'

'Talk?'

'About your marrying her.'

Dinamaula shook his head. He was thinking of other things; he was thinking of Oosthuizen saying, 'You shouldn't want to drink with him, anyway,' and Fellows saying: 'No.' Almost to himself, he murmured, 'I shall not marry Miera.'

'But you *will* marry?' prompted Tulbach Browne.

'I hope so.'

'Anyone special in mind?'

Dinamaula was still thinking of other things, things further away, things rounded and far more happy. He remembered a party at Oxford, a hectic party that ended in canoes, at dawn, along the sightless riverbank. He remembered another, more sedate affair, in a private room at Claridges in London. No one had said 'No,' on either occasion ... He raised his eyes to Tulbach Browne, scarcely seeing him, aware only of pain and loneliness. He said, scarcely thinking, voicing the thin fabric of a random thought: 'No one special. As a matter of fact, I'd like to marry a white girl.'

CHAPTER SIX

❖

The LADIES, secure in the stuffy haven of the annexe to the Pharamaul Club in Port Victoria, were mulling it all over. They were, as usual, Mrs Simpson, wife of the naval aide: Mrs Rogers, wife of the Port Victoria bank manager; Miss Cafferata, an old resident and the principal hanger-on at Government House; Mrs Burlinghame, whose husband imported *kaffir*-blankets on a very large scale; and Anthea Vere-Toombs.

It was uncomfortably hot. Tea was served, and an assortment of small, sweating cakes, while they waited for Mrs Stevens, wife of the First Secretary, to complete their circle.

'A little bird told me,' remarked Miss Cafferata, with unrivalled archness, 'that *someone* is due back in Port Victoria tonight.' She looked at Anthea Vere-Toombs, who was gloomily sipping milkless, sugarless tea, and wishing it were a martini. 'A little bird told me,' said Miss Cafferata. 'But of course I don't know if it's true.'

'That makes two little birds,' said Anthea. 'They ought to get together and lay an egg … Who's coming back?'

'Someone beginning with D,' answered Miss Cafferata.

'Dinamaula,' said Mrs Burlinghame.

There was a general laugh. Dinamaula was now a frequent subject of discussion in Port Victoria, much of it libelous, all of it unflattering.

Miss Cafferata shook her head. 'No, not that man. Heaven preserve us! ... Someone in the office.'

'David,' said Mrs Rogers brightly. 'Of course! David Bracken.'

'Right,' said Miss Cafferata. 'And *another* little bird,' she went on, looking as if, in spite of all precautions, these birds kept fluttering, uncontrollably, out of her handbag, 'just whispered to me that *someone* will be very pleased to see him.'

'It'll be nice to talk to him again,' said Anthea, grasping the proffered nettle. 'This town's getting a bit dull.'

'You're not the only one who thinks that,' said Mrs Simpson, in a deep naval voice.

'Huh?' said Anthea. There was between her and Mrs Simpson a long-standing and very cordial dislike which neither tried to dissemble. 'Who else is in this act, besides these damned birds?'

'Someone else in the office,' answered Mrs Simpson. 'Someone else who'll also be glad to see David Bracken back again.'

'That Steuart girl,' said Miss Cafferata.

'Oh, her!' said Mrs Burlinghame.

'You'll have to watch out,' said Mrs Simpson sweetly to Anthea. 'Pretty tough competition there.'

'I'm not competing,' said Anthea briefly.

'Oh, don't give up, darling,' said Mrs Simpson. 'Youth isn't everything. I've found that out.'

'Tell us,' said Anthea, 'from memory.'

'Of course,' said Mrs Rogers, under the impression that she was smoothing things out, 'lots of men are quite capable of making love to two people at once.'

'Capable is the word,' said Mrs Burlinghame.

'I once read about a man,' said Miss Cafferata, leaning forward, 'who was caught in bed with *three* girls. In Liverpool. Even the police were shocked. But,' she added, on a note of disappointment, 'they were all sisters.'

'Now where on earth did you read that?' asked Anthea, intrigued in spite of a rising temper.

'Probably in the *Ladies' Home Companion*,' said Mrs Simpson.

Anthea smiled. 'That's really quite funny,' she said, 'for you.'

It was clearly time to change all available subjects.

'I wonder,' observed Miss Cafferata, 'where Mrs Stevens is. It's not like her to be so late. Our little party doesn't seem the same without her.'

As if the change of subject had been the signal for a general interruption, one of the club servants approached their table, intent on his task of collecting, emptying, and restoring ashtrays. He was a Maula youth, not more than fifteen, clad in the traditional ankle-length yellow robe topped by a red tarboosh: his bare feet, scratched and calloused, fell solidly on the pinewood floor. Anthea Vere-Toombs, from force of habit, watched his progress. The boy, murmuring almost without words, looking at no one, reached between Mrs Rogers and Mrs Simpson, emptied the ashtray that stood on their table into a tin canister, polished it with a duster, and restored it to its position. He was deft, preoccupied, unaware of his surroundings; if the five women at the table had been naked, he would not have noticed it. When he had finished, he straightened up, murmured again, and prepared to move on to the next table.

Anthea suddenly said: 'Boy!'

The youth turned, considerably startled. '*Barenala?*' he said. He was good-looking, clean, spare in his movements, and ready to be terrified.

'Matches,' said Anthea.

'*Barenala?*' said the boy, confused.

'Bring matches,' said Anthea.

The boy shook his head, embarrassed and uncomprehending. He picked up the ashtray again, and gave it an extra polish. It was clear that he knew no word of English. He waited in patent discomfort.

'It doesn't matter,' said Anthea, after a pause.

'*Barenala?*'

'Oh, for Christ's sake!' said Anthea irritably.

The boy smiled, unaccountably relieved, showing wonderful teeth in a smooth, youthfully patrician face. He leant forward, shifted the ashtray a few inches, and said, carefully, 'Thank.'

Then he moved away again.

'Well, I must say!' said Miss Cafferata, indignantly. 'If they can't understand plain English, what *is* the good of them?'

'Servants,' said Mrs Burlinghame. 'Don't tell me!'

'Maybe I should never have started that,' said Anthea jocularly.

'No,' said Mrs Simpson.

'I wonder where Mrs Stevens is,' said Miss Cafferata again.

'Probably hasn't paid her club dues,' said Mrs Burlinghame. 'I believe the committee is very strict.'

'You mean, they'd stop her at the door?' asked Miss Cafferata.

'That's the rule,' said Mrs Simpson.

'What sort of salary does Mr Stevens get?' inquired Mrs Rogers. As the wife of the Port Victoria bank manager, she knew the answer better than most people; but she wanted the topic to be established as the crucial one.

'I'm sure I don't know,' said Miss Cafferata delicately.

'Eleven hundred and fifty pounds a year,' said Mrs Simpson. 'Plus local allowances, of course.'

'It ought to be enough,' said Mrs Rogers judiciously.

'Of course, there are all those children,' said Miss Cafferata.

'Whose fault is that?' asked Mrs Burlinghame.

'Mr Stevens, *we hope*,' said Anthea.

'But if she really hasn't paid her club subscription,' said Mrs Rogers, 'won't there be a terrible scandal?'

'I hope so,' said Mrs Simpson. 'I've no patience with that sort of thing.'

'If,' said Mrs Burlinghame, authoritatively, 'people can't afford a certain standard of life, they shouldn't try to pretend that they can.'

'*Noblesse oblige*,' said Miss Cafferata.

'My favourite character,' said Anthea. 'Thought he'd died years ago.'

'What?' asked Mrs Simpson.

'Joke,' said Anthea.

'One of your best,' said Mrs Simpson acidly. 'Personally, I don't really think it's a joking matter.'

'Will they have to give up the tennis club as well?' asked Miss Cafferata.

The door at the far end of the lounge opened, and Mrs Stevens – small, nervous, sketchily dressed – advanced towards them.

'Why, darling!' said Mrs Rogers. '*How* we've missed you!'

'Did you have any trouble getting in?' asked Miss Cafferata.

'Trouble?' repeated Mrs Stevens uneasily.

'Sit down, dear,' said Mrs Burlinghame. 'Have a nice cup of tea. And don't worry about anything. I,' she said fondly, 'am in the chair.'

II

Stevens, the First Secretary, sat at his desk overlooking the forlorn Secretariat garden, adding up the small figures in his cheque book and the diminutive entries in his savings account. It was something he forced himself to do at the end of every month, though it gave him no satisfaction and often brought on a fierce headache. Since the birth of their fourth child, earlier that year, he had found that he was spending, each month, a few pounds more than the total amount of his salary, thus nibbling into his infinitesimal savings at a steady rate. In the end, it could only mean one thing. And that one thing – debt, or a bank overdraft – was going to become even more pressingly complicated, in the near future.

The Stevens had a boy of twelve, a girl of nine, a boy of four, and a girl of six months. Soon the elder boy would have to go to school, in England, and then the elder girl. Both these things would happen long before Stevens himself became due for promotion again. They would entail the outlay of money which he simply had not got. Unless something unforeseen happened, he was surely cornered.

It was a problem he had discussed long and often with his wife, but discussion never brought them any answer, nor any breath of comfort. There was nothing they could cut down, no further economy to be squeezed from the bare gentilities of living. They scarcely entertained at all. On clothes they spent a minimum, on personal pleasures nothing at all. (The last of those pleasures, the subscription to the Reprint Society, had been cancelled at the beginning of the year.) On the other hand, insurance payments had to be kept up, food bills met, the modest allowance to his mother in England regularly despatched. His wife, with four children to cook and clean for, had to have domestic help on at least two days of each week …

The answer was always the same. If you were a civil servant, in a junior grade, you couldn't have four children. Perhaps you couldn't even have one. Certainly you couldn't give four of them any sort of education, any social graces, any kind of a treat. Not on £1,150 a year.

As on countless occasions in the past, Stevens cast about him for a way out of the *impasse*. He could save a few pounds a year if he gave up his pipe. It was, in truth, the last indulgence left for him to forgo. He could send his children to elementary schools in England. With that, as far as the boys were concerned, would vanish any chance of their following him into the Civil Service – something he had set his heart on … He could tell his mother that they simply could not afford to send her the monthly allowance. He could pocket his pride, and ask his younger brother – a successful jobbing plumber in Newcastle – for a few pounds a month, repayable when he was promoted. He could earn another £25 'language allowance' if he devoted every evening, for the next half-year, to learning Maula. And that was really all.

Presently, near despair, he closed his cheque book and his savings account book, clipped them together with a rubber band, and put them in the top left-hand drawer of his desk, along with his tobacco pouch, his box of calling cards, his tin of sugar for tea, his bottle of aspirin, and his Benares paper-knife. From there he looked out across the garden, and the trim driveway edged by drooping cannas and dun-coloured lawns. It was hot, deserted, endlessly serenaded by crickets. At its further margin, Government House stood as it had stood for the last hundred years – gleaming white, solidly set, imposing in spite of its haphazard architecture.

His shabby, rumpled suit clinging to him stickily, Stevens began a habitual daydream – the one with himself as the Governor of Pharamaul, receiving the Queen on her first ceremonial visit to the Principality.

He had just bowed, and murmured: 'Lady Stevens will be delighted, Your Majesty,' when there was a factual interruption, by a far more credible character. Lady Vere-Toombs came down the front steps of Government House, preceded by a white butler and a black footman, and greeted with a deep bow by her Maula chauffeur. She stepped into the official car, a large, old-fashioned, funereal Humber, and was conveyed slowly away down the drive. Gradually peace returned to the courtyard; the crickets, recovering, began their irritating song again.

With a sigh for the pleasures of an unattainable world – wishing he had a bigger car than an Austin Eight, wishing he could afford a new suit for himself, better kitchenware for his wife, a bicycle for his eldest boy – Stevens pressed the bell to summon his typist. Then he reached towards the pile of files that crowded his IN-tray, and picked off the top one.

'ESTIMATES,' he read. '*Division into "Administrative" and "Operational" sub-heads*. Please refer to Scheduled Territories Office circular telegram numbered ...'

He became, unwillingly, immersed.

III

Captain Simpson, RN, the naval aide-de-camp, had nothing whatever to do. Since the day was Thursday, he was in uniform – Number Tens, freshly laundered and pressed, spotlessly white, his medal ribbons standing out from his jacket like brilliant tropical plumage, his golden aiguillettes sweeping down from his shoulder like the silken rope-ties at the corner of an Empire sofa. He sat at his desk, in his office down the corridor from Stevens; a trim, tough, and formidable figure, reading of the exploits of one of his ancestors in a new biography of Admiral Lord Nelson.

He had nothing to do because, despite a bluff and somewhat stolid appearance, he was accustomed to work swiftly and accurately; and the work he had to do in Pharamaul would not have occupied a newly joined midshipman for more than one hour out of any normal fore-noon watch. Captain Simpson attended the Governor upon formal occasions: he gave the requisite number of predetermined dinner parties; and he wrote an occasional despatch on such subjects as offshore fishing, harbour pollution, ceremonial visits by Portuguese, French, and South African naval officers, and the state of efficiency of the Port Victoria dockyard, which remained reassuringly constant.

Apart from that, his time was his own; and time hung heavy as lead, moved slow as pitch, through the fingers of a man accustomed to handle ships and men in action, and whose last command – more than ten years ago – had been a crack destroyer flotilla guarding the eastern flank of the Normandy beach-head.

The present job, in fact, was a joke: one of several naval jokes which were inevitable in the peacetime life of the Royal Navy. All he was doing in Pharamaul was waiting: polishing off the negligible work, putting up with a grumbling wife, keeping his fingers crossed; waiting, and sweating it out for the next assignment.

There were two more years of his captaincy to run, before the tide bore him out of the promotion zone. If the luck fell one way, he would be retired; if the other, he would re-emerge as Rear-Admiral Simpson, with a whole range of new jobs to go to, a wife (thank God) at last contented and appeased, and a career fit to be commended

to the four other admirals who figured, so dauntingly, on
his family tree.

He turned to the biography of Nelson again, greedily
imbibing the valiant spectacle of the past.

Nelson, [he read] had to take one of two courses. He
could lie offshore, blockading the mouth of the
estuary, isolating the French ships, but wasting
precious time; or he could do what his own valour,
and the spirit of the age demanded – sail in, fight, and
destroy. He chose, with scarcely a day's delay, the
latter alternative.

His chief problem was, of course, the fort which
commanded the entrance to the harbour. Its guns
were accurate, its troops wakeful, its commander
clearly a man of courage; as long as it remained in
action, his sailors could never penetrate under its fire
and come to grips with the French fleet. The fort, in
fact, must be silenced. This would involve a cutting-
out expedition, by armed and determined men carried
in small boats, who would creep inshore at nightfall,
put the fort and its guns out of action, and then give
the signal for the main attack.

To command this expedition – destined to become
a classic of its kind – he chose Lieutenant (later
Admiral) Hereward Simpson, who had served for
three years under his command, and had already given
ample proof of his resource, seamanship, and daring.

Lieutenant Simpson took seventy men (including
forty marines) in three boats – a whaler, a longboat,
and a light skiff …

Captain Simpson sighed, laying down the book, looking
vacantly into space. He knew the story by heart, and now
he found that he could scarcely bear to read it again, even

in this new and attractive version. For him, life had been like that, on a few occasions during the Normandy invasion; it had been like that in Norway, in 1940; it had been like that, very many years ago, when he was a midshipman on the China Station. Now it was not like that at all. Now it was a phoney job in a phoney country, a job conducted on paper (when it was conducted at all), and for the rest merely endured.

He stared on, in blessed, frustrated release: seeing long-boats, and skiffs, and forts, and cutlasses, and his great-great-great-uncle Hereward Simpson; not seeing Pharamaul at all.

IV

For David Bracken, his journey down from Gamate, and his return to the Secretariat, were like coming home again. He had been away for ten days: he had travelled less than a thousand miles: but there was a family atmosphere about the office that ensured a feeling of welcome as soon as he stepped inside. By contrast with the strange world of Shebiya and the Maula country, Port Victoria was like a Christmas fireside.

On the big square desk in his office he found so many files that he decided not to look at any of them for at least half a day. Only one of them was tabbed 'IMPORTANT'; common sense told him that if it had really been important, it would have been marked 'IMMEDIATE' ... There were also four notes from Anthea Vere-Toombs, dark green, deckle-edged, addressed in that flamboyant handwriting that seemed to express a swooping determination. He opened the first one. It read: 'Ring me up *instantly* when you arrive. *Longing* for you. X X X Anthea.' He forbore to open any of the others. Instead, he went on a tour of the Secretariat. It seemed natural that he should keep Nicole Steuart's office till the last.

The Governor was out when David inquired for him. 'But I know he wanted to see you,' said his secretary brightly, with just sufficient deliberation in her voice to lend it an overtone of threat.

'Anything special?' asked David, vaguely disquieted.

'I'm sure I don't know,' answered the secretary. It was clear that she did know, and David, moving on, wondered what might have gone wrong in his absence. He could not think of anything.

Stevens, the First Secretary, seemed preoccupied – indeed, rather sad; he said: 'You seem to have had some excitements,' as if David had left him behind to complete an intricate series of household chores, thereby depriving him of a longed-for treat.

'Excitements?' queried David.

'With the Press,' answered Stevens, rather fussily. 'There have been a lot of telegrams. You'll see them all on the file.'

'Tulbach Browne of the *Daily Thresh* was hanging about in Gamate.'

'So we gathered,' said Stevens.

'I believe he saw Andrew Macmillan and Dinamaula.'

'So we gathered,' said Stevens again.

'Was there anything in the papers about that?'

'Yes. It's all on the file.'

'Oh.' David laughed, rather uncertainly. 'Perhaps that's what H E wants to see me about.'

'Possibly.' Stevens looked at him, peering short-sightedly. 'Glad you got back, anyway. There's a lot of stuff coming in all the time. And a joint meeting of the Advisory Council and the Board of Control, next week.'

'Oh,' said David again. It sounded important.

'I expect we'll have to go through all that rigmarole about direct participation again.'

'Yes,' said David. 'I expect we will.'

'There's always something.'

Captain Simpson, the naval aide, was, by contrast, very cheerful; he greeted David as if the latter had just returned from a commando raid with all the prisoners and all the information that anyone could wish for. His voice when he said: 'Pretty rough country up there, I remember,' had a manly ring that seemed to come from another world altogether. Then it was the turn of the Social Secretary, who looked at his dusty clothes with cold dislike, and said, 'Dinner on Monday week, Mr Bracken. To meet Sir Digby Tute. Black tie. And there's the garden party on November 6th. I've sent cards for both.'

'Garden party?' asked David, surprised.

'Yes,' said the Social Secretary. 'His Excellency gives two every year. This is the spring garden party.'

'What do we wear?'

'Morning dress,' answered the Social Secretary, in acid disdain. 'Or a short black coat would do.' She did not sound as if it would do at all. 'Four p.m. till six.'

'How very formal,' said David.

'It is the spring garden party,' said the Social Secretary.

Then he looked in on Aidan Purves-Brownrigg, who greeted him with considerable fervour.

'*How* we've missed you!' said Aidan Purves-Brownrigg. 'The place has been like a *desert!* And poor Anthea has been *grovelling!*'

'Why should that be?' asked David uneasily.

'You must have *whetted* her appetite,' said Purves-Brownrigg. 'Did you?'

'No,' said David.

'Well anyway,' observed Purves-Brownrigg, 'she's ready to take the bit between her legs.'

David said nothing. He foresaw a long series of complications and he wanted to escape them – to escape into tranquillity and gentleness, with someone like Nicole. No, not with 'someone like Nicole'. With Nicole herself.

Then Aidan Purves-Brownrigg's next words, interrupting his daydream, brought him up short.

'My dear,' said Aidan, 'we've been *inundated* with furious telegrams from London! The poor cypher-girls have been turning handsprings! What *have* you and Andrew been saying to that *odious* Tulbach Browne?'

David's heart sank. 'Nothing special,' he answered. 'Why?'

'The *Daily Thresh* has been full of it,' said Aidan. 'At least two *poisonous* articles, each one worse than the last. Making out Andrew as an absolute monster. And you sounded like *Caligula*, at the very least.'

'Me?' said David, confused. 'I don't understand.'

Eagerly Aidan Purves-Brownrigg went into details, exhibiting in the process a formidable memory for exact quotation which (David realized) was probably one of the reasons why he prospered at the Foreign Office. There had, he said, been two articles so far about affairs in Gamate, following on the ones which had already been sent from Port Victoria. The first had been 'Gamate's Tin Gods', which dealt mainly with Andrew Macmillan and the cattle question; and the second, a long piece called 'Toe-the-Line Democracy', which recorded interviews with Father Schwemmer, Oosthuizen the farmer, Forsdick, and David himself.

'The first one was bad enough,' observed Aidan. 'Tulbach Browne said that Andrew ran the place like a *prison* or a barracks, using unpaid convict labour in his own garden; that new ideas were obviously stirring all over Pharamaul, but that the local officials just wanted to sit on the safety valve; and that Andrew had openly said that his motto was anything for a quiet life. He said that Andrew had *sneered* at Dinamaula for being too young and inexperienced to take over responsibility, when the real trouble was that Dinamaula was treated like a backward child – and so were all his people. He said that the number of cattle – "the life-blood of the Maulas" – was forcibly limited by decree, to conform to the *tidy* minds of the local civil servants. That's a phrase I really liked.'

'Good heavens!' said David, impressed. 'No wonder there's a lot on the file.'

'That article was bad enough,' repeated Aidan, with some relish, 'but Tulbach Browne really went to town in the second one ... He said that poor old Father Schwemmer was pretty well ga-ga, and didn't realize how much harm his Christian humility was doing to the progress of the Maulas. He said that Oosthuizen was operating a *complete* forced-labour system for children on his farms, and had openly boasted about the colour bar in Gamate. He said that Forsdick had insulted him, and threatened the freedom of the Press, and *sneered* at Dinamaula for being poor and backward. He hinted that Forsdick had been drunk at the time – not that that really helped matters much.'

'My God!' said David.

' "Dinamaula",' quoted Aidan from memory, ' "is richer than ten average District Commissioners, as Mr Forsdick knows and perhaps resents. But then, Dinamaula is black." Very tasty ... And *you*, of course,' he grinned at David, 'were particularly quotable.'

David felt his stomach dropping like a stone. 'What about me?'

'Don't you remember what you said about Gotwela?' asked Aidan with interest.

'No. Not exactly.'

'Tulbach Browne did ... "I thought that Gamate could show me no more surprises",' intoned Aidan, from his copious memory. ' "I was wrong ... It was my misfortune, later that night, to hear Gotwela, one of the oldest and most respected of the local chiefs, described by Mr Bracken, a junior British official, as being 'like something out of the zoo'. I felt, at the moment, that I had had enough of so-called official circles in Gamate. I would not blame Gamate for feeling the same".'

'But Gotwela's not a respected chief at all!' said David in anguish. 'He's a complete thug!'

'What does that matter?' asked Aidan. 'Tulbach Browne made him sound like the old Prince Consort, and he made *you* sound like a boorish clot. That's all that the story needed.'

'What did the Governor say about it?'

'I thought the old gentleman would have a heart attack,' said Aidan frankly. 'We got all this by telegram from London, and I had to bring the file in ... He's better now, of course. I told him it was all the result of *unscrupulous* reporting.'

'Thanks,' said David gratefully.

'Which it is, of course ... But all the same,' he looked at David, suddenly much more serious, and more competent, 'I think we'd better be ready for it in the future.'

'But what can one do?' asked David.

'There's a well-known operation,' answered Aidan Purves-Brownrigg, lapsing into character again, 'used by those dear soldiers, known as closing the ranks. We'd better copy it.'

'How do you mean?'

'No more stray interviews with that *criminal* Browne. No more friendly drinks with the Press. We must all stick together, keep quiet together, and work to repair the damage.'

'Do you think there'll be any more trouble?'

Purves-Brownrigg sat back in his chair, lounging elegantly. His dove-grey suit became him like a faultless uniform. 'From a long experience,' he said, 'in such plague-spots as Egypt and Persia, such global *slums* as Syria and Trieste, I should say that here in Pharamaul we were only just beginning.'

'Oh,' said David inadequately.

'I feel it in my bones,' said Purves-Brownrigg, ' – and I *have* bones – that a page of particularly *sordid* history is about to be written. Politicians will burst their buttons, Pressmen will fuse their typewriters, heads will roll. I don't want them to be *our* heads.'

'We're so handicapped,' said David, after a pause.

Aidan smiled. 'As long as you realize the fact,' he said, 'and as long as you believe that, handicapped or not, we can still win because we're *right*, all is not lost … In the meantime, isn't it about time you saw Nicole?'

'How is she?' asked David.

'Never better. And thirsting for you, I shouldn't wonder. Waste *no* more time.'

Nicole was indeed waiting for him, in her shabby, sun-plagued office: looking cool, looking lovely, looking just the girl he had been vividly remembering, during many hours of many days of his trip. David found himself suddenly, ecstatically glad to be face to face with her again; indeed, it was difficult for him, seeing her after a ten-day separation, not to stride forward and take her in his arms. It would have been a natural end to much loneliness, much anxiety, much sensual denial. But instead, daunted by her coolness and his own sense of inadequacy, he said, 'Hallo! I just got back.'

'You didn't.' She was smiling, slightly breathless, but more ready with words than he was. 'You got back at least half-an-hour ago. I have spies all over the building. It's not very flattering.'

'I had to go round the office.'

'How *is* the office?'

'All right.' He sat down on the edge of her desk, lighting a cigarette, his hand unsteady. 'Actually, *not* all right. Aidan was telling me about Tulbach Browne and the *Daily Thresh*.'

'Didn't you know?'

'No. I seem to have made rather a fool of myself. We all did, in fact. I suppose you read the telegrams?'

'Yes,' said Nicole. Now she was composed and competent, sitting back in her chair, behind a desk that made few concessions to femininity. Only the vase of pale Iceland poppies battled incongruously with the files and the telephones and the array of pens and pencils. 'It wasn't really surprising. They can always catch you out, if you're not on your guard.'

'I should have been on my guard.'

'But you didn't *know*. Next time will be different ... How was Gamate, otherwise?'

'Wonderful. All that I expected ... The journey up was like discovering the whole of Africa in a few hours.'

Nicole nodded. 'That's the way I remember it ... And Shebiya?'

'It's a funny thing about that place,' answered David, after a pause. 'It gave me the shivers at first – it's so crude and savage, so secret. I saw a cannibal behind every tree ... But – we stayed with the Ronalds. Obviously *they* didn't have that feeling at all. They were entirely happy in Shebiya, completely satisfied with living there.'

'I think they'd be entirely happy anywhere,' said Nicole, smiling.

'I suppose so ... But I got the idea – or perhaps it's just developed later – that I could be happy there, too. It needn't be a frightening place at all, once one got over the strangeness, because there's so much worthwhile work to be done.' He looked at her. 'Could you be happy there?'

Nicole felt herself colouring slightly. 'I don't know. I hadn't thought of it … We all went up there last year, on tour with the Governor.' She giggled. 'Aidan loathed every minute of it, of course. And he found a snake curled up in his sleeping bag. Quite a harmless snake, but he wasn't to know that.'

'I'd like to have seen that.'

'It was worth seeing … Yes, I suppose one *could* be happy in Shebiya.'

With you, David murmured to himself. With you, anywhere. Aloud, his voice sounding unnaturally gruff, he said, 'But I *didn't* like Gotwela.'

She smiled again. 'So I read.' She gestured towards a file on her desk. 'There was another telegram in this morning. Another article by Tulbach Browne.'

'Oh God!' said David. 'What was it this time?'

'About not getting a drink in the Gamate Hotel.' As David frowned, she went on, 'It must have happened just about the time you left. Apparently he took Dinamaula into the bar, and they refused to serve him.'

'Pity,' observed David.

She looked at him squarely. 'Do you think they *should* have let Dinamaula have a drink there?'

'I don't know. I just can't make up my mind about it. I meant that the whole thing was a pity … What did Tulbach Browne have to say?'

Nicole leant forward towards the file, her breast and shoulders admirably outlined against the desk. From where he sat, David stared entranced.

'It's a long telegram,' she answered. 'You can read it later. Mostly it's about the Press reaction to the earlier stories, and a couple more questions in Parliament. Emrys Price-Canning is in full cry again … Then it goes on to quote the *Daily Thresh* report of the hotel incident. "Baiting of Dinamaula continues",' she read. '"Colour bar in British hotel on British soil" ... Then London ask us for our own version. We rang up Gamate a couple of hours ago. Andrew Macmillan simply said that it wasn't the custom for the chief or any of the Regents to come into the bar, and that Dinamaula knew this perfectly well, but had gone through with it, obviously egged on by Tulbach Browne. He said they were offered a private room to have a drink in, but they refused.' She looked up. 'We sent it all off to London straight away. That bit about the private room is a good point.'

David frowned. 'I wish we didn't need "good points".'

After a moment, she said gently: 'It *wouldn't* be a good idea to have mixed drinking in Gamate, would it? Even if the Maulas were allowed alcohol?'

A few weeks in Pharamaul had given David the beginnings of the same feeling, but he was not yet ready to acknowledge it. Instead, he said, 'It's very complicated ... I suppose it means another row in Parliament, anyway.'

'Almost inevitably.'

'And more telegrams.'

'Lots more.'

He had a sudden conviction that there were many better things to think about, at this moment.

'Let's forget the whole thing, just for now.'

'All right,' she agreed.

'Will you have dinner with me?'

'Certainly,' said Nicole.

'Where can we go?'

'There are two or three places, all rather bad.'

'Let's try them one by one.'

'Or I could cook for you myself.'

'How do you feel about that?' asked David hesitatingly, after a pause.

'Perfectly happy,' answered Nicole, with composure. 'Come along at seven o'clock. If you like, you can contribute a bottle of wine.'

'I'll do that,' he said, with secret, serious joy. 'Red or white?'

'Red for me.'

'Red for me, too.'

V

Sir Elliott Vere-Toombs, Governor and Commander-in-Chief of Pharamaul, sat behind his desk, beset by major and minor problems. Being a methodical man, a man of the kind which, a hundred years earlier, had rendered many a Victorian home virtually uninhabitable by meticulous dissection of the housekeeping books – being a methodical man, he had listed these problems as soon as he arrived in his office that morning. Now, neatly written on a pad in front of him, was a numbered schedule of the things that awaited his thought and action. It read:

(1) Anthea
(2) Pharamaul 1/– Mauve, block of four.
(3) Garden party
(4) Dinner for Tute
(5) Rolls-Royce
(6) Despatch on tunny
(7) Coelacanth
(8) Dinamaula
(9) T Browne, D Thresh.

To a stranger, such a schedule would have been largely incomprehensible: to the Governor, it represented all the current pleasures and evils of his official life. As his eye traversed the list, swift thought supplied the details, clothing the bare bones of each item with plaguing elaboration.

Anthea meant that he was seriously worried about his daughter, whom Lady Vere-Toombs had at breakfast gone so far as to describe as 'our problem child', and whom he himself was beginning to regard, with innocent amazement, as something quite beyond either his experience or his control. It seemed that Anthea had had too much to drink the evening before, had wept and screamed half the night, had declared, in one breath, that unless she married David Bracken she would kill herself and in another, that she wouldn't be seen dead in his company. It was all very discouraging. In the past, her education alone had financially crippled Sir Elliott for at least fifteen years. Apparently it was still far from complete.

Pharamaul 1/– Mauve represented temptation in its purest form. It was a stamp, or rather, a block of four stamps, which Sir Elliott coveted beyond anything else in the world. They had been offered to him by a dealer in London, at the bargain price of £750. If he bought them, he would not only be throwing money away. He would be breaking a lifelong rule, of only collecting the stamps which he had personally acquired in the various countries he had served in. But those stamps he had to have.

Garden Party was the next big social event at Government House. His social secretary would naturally see to the details. But there were various policy decisions – whether to hire a marquee, or to trust the weather, whether to serve drinks to selected guests after six o'clock, whether to invite the backsliding Metropolitan Bishop of Port Victoria – which called for urgent thought.

Dinner for Tute was a tricky matter of arrangement. Sir Digby Tute, a visitor to the island with Liberal Party connexions, wanted to meet prominent Maulas. It couldn't be done – not at dinner, anyway. *Rolls-Royce* was another temptation, this time at the official level. Sir Elliott wanted a Rolls-Royce as an office car, instead of the old Humber, and had recently advanced a battery of arguments directed to this end. London didn't agree, and had countered, maddeningly, with a long questionnaire about repairs to the Humber's differential. *Despatch on tunny* was a dull, overdue item that now cried out for attention.

Coelacanth was dangerous, but attractive. Word had been received that a local Maula fisherman had caught one of these prehistoric fish, which were now known to have reappeared off the African coast. If the story was to be believed, swift action was necessary – the story, and the fish, were already forty-eight hours old. If it were a coelacanth, later ichthyologists might well label it Coelacanth Vere-Toombs … But if it was a hoax or a mistake, the Governor could hardly justify the expenditure of public money on acquiring 40 lb of decayed fish which would presently turn out to be something mortifyingly different, like cod or dogfish.

Dinamaula and T Browne were, of course, related items. Dinamaula was a complete new problem in himself, and Tulbach Browne was due in this very office in ten minutes' time.

The Governor sighed, gradually shedding prehistoric fish, and stamps, and his dubious daughter, and concentrating on the real problem: the new chieftainship, the Press in London, the worry in Gamate. He was no stranger to worry: he had worried in Singapore, worried in Bengal, worried in South America. He had had to reprieve a hated murderer in Kenya, quell a huge-scale riot in one of the Indian States, organize famine relief in Ceylon, try a revolting case of child-rape (with religious complications) in the West Indies. In forty years of official life, he had conquered or shelved or circumnavigated almost every human problem stemming from misbehaviour, emotion, or disaster.

But Gamate was different. Gamate was exceptionally complicated; above all, Gamate was artificial and unnecessary, the product of misunderstanding, unpreparedness, and newspaper sensationalism. One of the people responsible for the Gamate situation was even now waiting in his ante-room, and the Governor was not sure how to deal with him. He was feeling old and tired. Basically, he wanted nothing except his stamps, and a Rolls-Royce for the offices and to see Anthea settled down with some nice young fellow belonging to a good regiment.

His secretary knocked at the door, and announced: 'Mr Tulbach Browne, sir.'

It was an awkward meeting; indeed, between men so dissimilar, ranged face to face across such contested and dividing ground, it could hardly be otherwise. The Governor saw Tulbach Browne as an impudent intruder, who had already, in an earlier interview, asked a number of extremely odd questions and then written a story ('The Cocked Hat Brigade') just about as unpleasant and inaccurate as it could possibly be. There had been other stories, both from Port Victoria and from Gamate, not less offensive; the Governor had hoped, after reading them, that their author would at least leave him alone in the future. Really, the man must have a skin like a rhinoceros ...

Tulbach Browne, for his part, saw the Governor as he had always seen him, and men like him, whether he had met them or not – as a titled jack-in-office, reactionary, stupid, and dull. What else could a Colonial Governor be? – the type hadn't changed since mid-Victorian days, and their ideas hadn't changed either. It was the duty of papers such as the *Daily Thresh* to let a little air into cobwebbed corners such as this: a little air, a little sunlight, a little touch of derision and malice. It was down this sort of drain, their readers must be reminded, that so large a slice of their income tax went, producing showy luxury at the top, Civil Service bumbling in the middle, misery and frustration at the bottom. The *Daily Thresh* wanted that sort of story, and he, Tulbach Browne, was without peer at writing it.

From opposite sides of the desk, they regarded each other with cordial dislike, tempered to a hot day and the demands of civility.

'Well, we meet again,' said the Governor, after the first exchange of greetings. 'I hope you enjoyed your trip north?'

'Very much,' answered Tulbach Browne. 'I found out a lot that I didn't know before.'

The Governor considered this at leisure before replying: 'I'm delighted to hear it.'

It was meant to be mildly ironic, but to Tulbach Browne, in his present mood, it sounded something more than that – sarcastic, almost challenging. He decided, having nothing to lose, to close with the enemy.

'Yes,' he said, 'there were a lot of things about Gamate that I never suspected before. It's like another world … I suppose you've heard what they're calling the bar at the Gamate Hotel now?'

'The bar?' repeated Sir Elliott, surprised. 'What bar?'

'The ordinary bar. The lounge. It's got a new name.'

'What name?' asked Sir Elliott.

'The Colour Bar,' answered Tulbach Browne, and grinned. 'Good, don't you think?'

'I don't understand,' said the Governor stiffly. 'What has the colour bar got to do with it?'

'Because of Dinamaula,' answered Tulbach Browne. 'He couldn't get a drink there.'

Light broke in. 'Oh!' said the Governor. He thought the pun in atrocious taste, but he was not going to acknowledge the fact. No further ammunition of any sort was going to be supplied, on this or any other occasion. Instead, he sat back, and remarked, reasonably: 'I believe there *was* some slight unpleasantness, the other day. I'm sure it's all forgotten now.'

Little you know! thought Tulbach Browne, with contempt and hatred sourly thickening on his tongue, so that it almost overflowed into speech. Bloody upper-class double-talk! he thought, twisting in his seat, his skin prickling; bloody fatuous lah-di-dah idiocy, that could use a phrase like 'some slight unpleasantness' for the biggest official balls-up since Pontius Pilate … The colour bar incident at the Gamate Hotel hadn't been 'some slight unpleasantness'; it had been the best story yet to come out of Pharamaul, enough to rock a dozen shoddy thrones, a score of Colonial Governors. He looked across at Sir Elliott, sitting spare and erect in his white suit, behind a desk elegantly bare of papers. He'd find out, thought Tulbach Browne, relaxing gradually, aware of the futility of anger when his own position was so strong and so promising. He'd find out – 'some slight unpleasantness' would grow, and expand, and infect, and start to smell, and finally burst like a neglected corpse over the whole damned island … He relaxed further, settling in his wicker chair, and said: 'No doubt … It was something new to me, that was all … I met a lot of interesting people up there. The Resident Commissioner, Macmillan. He struck me as very strict. And David Bracken, your new secretary.'

'I read your articles,' said Sir Elliott, noncommittally.

'Bracken made an extraordinary remark about the U-Maula chief, Gotwela.'

'I read your articles,' said the Governor again.

225

Tulbach Browne, a resilient man, smiled. 'It sounds as though you didn't like them.'

'I thought they were exaggerated, and therefore inaccurate,' said the Governor curtly.

'How exaggerated?' asked Tulbach Browne.

'It's easy,' said the Governor, 'to pick out one phrase, and isolate it, and use it as a peg to hang a lot of other things on. But I don't think it makes for honest reporting.'

'Are you accusing me of dishonesty?' asked Tulbach Browne swiftly.

'I'm not making any accusations,' answered the Governor. He had known that this would be a wearisome business, and he was tired of it already; but he had agreed to the interview, and it must take its course. 'I simply think that it's unfair to pick one phrase out of its context.'

' "Like something out of the zoo",' said Tulbach Browne musingly. 'It was an unfortunate expression to use.'

'I agree,' said Sir Elliott. 'I've already talked to Mr Bracken about it.'

Tulbach Browne brightened. 'Would you call that an official rebuke?'

'Well,' said the Governor. He recalled the interview with David, at which he had cautioned: 'You *must* be careful when you're talking to these Press fellows,' and David had said: 'I'm very sorry, sir,' and he himself dismissing it, had answered: 'Things will settle down again before long.' It was not an official rebuke, and yet it amounted to something very near to it. He tried to get the thing clear.

'Not a rebuke,' he said judiciously. 'A correction, shall we say.'

'You *corrected* Mr Bracken?'

'I thought he spoke hastily, ill-advisedly.'

'And you told him so?'

'Yes.'

'Doesn't that amount to a rebuke?'

'In a sense, yes.'

Tulbach Browne sighed, conscious once more of the futility of officialdom. Why not say straight out that Bracken had been given a rocket? ... But he had won his point, if he cared to use it: '*Governor Rebukes Own Official*' was a good enough headline, unless there was something better to come. With the feeling that he was now about halfway through the interview, perhaps on a descending slope, he set himself to probe a little further.

'I had a number of talks with Dinamaula,' he said, with innocent readiness. 'An interesting man ... Of course, I've interviewed him before. You know that he has these ideas for development, and so forth?'

'Most people in Pharamaul have ideas of that sort.'

'Have they?' Tulbach Browne affected considerable interest. 'What other people besides Dinamaula have them?'

'The Regents in Gamate. A lot of young men here in Port Victoria. Even Gotwela ... Development, advancement, is always in the air, in a country like this.'

'Does it draw any inspiration from outside?'

'I don't think so. They hear what's going on in various parts of Africa, of course. But mostly it's a home-grown movement.'

'Any evidence of communist penetration?' asked Tulbach Browne alertly.

The Governor shook his head decisively. 'Communism makes no headway with the Maulas. How could it? It's directly opposed to all they feel, all they've been taught, all their tribal pattern. I think that's true for most of Africa, also. The tribal system is a feudal system, basically – hereditary chiefs, an inner ring of nobles and counsellors, a mass of people who simply obey. It's an *accepted* pattern, and it suits them. The whole idea of communism – that is, the overthrow of the hereditary ruling class, and subsequent dictatorship by the masses – would be anathema to a simple people like the Maulas. They could only see something disgraceful in it, something unholy ... Communism isn't the danger, either here or in the rest of Africa. Certainly there's a black nationalism, gradually gaining ground. But it's not communism, or anything like it.'

The reasoned, scholarly voice was not what Tulbach Browne wanted to hear; quickly he lost interest, quickly he switched his approach.

'Very interesting,' he observed. 'Of course, there are a number of different views on that question ... You were saying that a lot of people in Pharamaul had plans for its development, as well as Dinamaula. Does that include your own officials?'

'Naturally.'

'You mean that they would back Dinamaula up?'

'Not necessarily,' answered the Governor.

'Why not?'

'His ideas might be too ambitious, or they might not be the best thing for the country.'

'Who is to judge that?' asked Tulbach Browne.

'The Government of Pharamaul.'

Tulbach Browne smiled, unpleasantly. 'In fact, what Dinamaula thinks and says isn't really important.'

'I didn't say that ... He can be of the very greatest help to us. I hope that he will be. But one man can't impose his views on the whole country.'

Tulbach Browne's smile broadened perceptibly. 'Surely one man *does*?'

'What man?'

'You,' said Tulbach Browne.

The Governor shook his head, almost in despair. 'I am not one man,' he explained laboriously. 'I represent the Scheduled Territories Office, which in turn represents the will of Parliament, which represents the British people. I'm not a dictator. I simply carry out official policy.' He pointed a thin finger towards Tulbach Browne. '*Your* policy.'

'Count me out,' said Tulbach Browne, relapsing into flippancy. 'I want no part of it.'

'That attitude,' remarked the Governor stiffly, 'if I may say so, is responsible for a good many of our troubles, all over the world.'

At that, Tulbach Browne, recognizing that the boom was about to be lowered, rose to take his leave. He had got nothing much from the interview, save to round off his own impressions of the Pharamaul situation so far; but the loss of time was not serious, and he was keeping in reserve – in fact, he would write it that very morning, as soon as he got back to his hotel – a story that would make all the other stories fade into the negligible background. He had got nothing much from the interview, except a vague annoyance, and a confirmation of his estimate of Colonial Governors. It's lucky, he thought, that they're paid a good deal less than I am. Otherwise it really would be a swindle ...

Perhaps it was this sense of irritated superiority that made him decide to fire a parting shot. Ordinarily, he would not have indulged himself in so juvenile an inclination, which often boomeranged alarmingly; but he found that he wanted to score a final point, and in this case it seemed that he ran little risk in so doing. By the time this old buffer was ready to go into action, his own story would be all over the *Daily Thresh*'s front page ... Thus, when he reached the door, and turned to say goodbye, Tulbach Browne made his last throwaway sentence a memorable one.

'I expect you've heard,' he said, 'that Dinamaula wants to marry a white girl.'

Sir Elliott Vere-Toombs, who had been thinking, with pleasure, that a good deal of the morning still remained to him, did not register the weight and meaning of this sentence for some minutes. When he did so, frowning, he decided that he must have misheard Tulbach Browne. The man must have said something quite different: perhaps he had said 'the *right* girl' – which was a laudable enough ambition ... The Governor shook his head, conscious of deafness, old age, gradually failing powers. On his way back to his desk he wondered momentarily why Tulbach Browne had brought the subject up in any case; and then, with conscious, dutiful relief, he turned to more important things.

VI

In the lounge of the Pharamaul Club, a row was under discussion, as it had been for many days past. It was a very special row – in fact, there had been nothing like it, in scope and fury, since the Ladies' Annexe row that had split the club from top to bottom in 1933. Indeed, in the opinion of some of the older members, this was really a bigger row than the Ladies' Annexe row, because it involved so many people who were on the Committee, including Twotty Wotherspoon, the chairman of the House Committee itself.

Basically, as everyone knew by now, it was a row between Twotty Wotherspoon and Splinter Woodcock. But of course, there was a lot more to it than that. Anyone who knew anything about the inner workings of the Pharamaul Club knew that it went a lot deeper ... It had been boiling up for a long time, and it was going to spread. In fact, already the women were taking a hand in it. Mrs Wotherspoon had hinted that she was going to boycott the tennis finals. The Woodcock girl was talking about a club referendum (there had only been one, in the whole history of the club since 1892). Mrs Burlinghame had actually torn a page out of the ladies' Suggestion Book. There was going to be another first-class row about *that*.

And Binkie Buchanan, whose car had been involved in the original argument, had threatened to resign altogether – *from everything*.

Tulbach Browne, waiting in one corner of the crowded lounge for Lou Strogoff, the American consul, to join him for a pre-lunch drink, listened to the discussion with irritated attention. He was quite unable to determine what it was all about, even after half-an-hour's close eavesdropping; occasionally he turned his head, to identify a new speaker, but the new speaker never seemed to have anything new to say. Tulbach Browne surveyed them all with spiteful contempt. Just you wait, he thought, as he had thought when he had been with the Governor. Just you wait – I'll give you something to talk about …

'Splinter Woodcock was wrong.'

'Depends how you look at it, old boy.'

'He shouldn't have said it in the first place.'

'Twotty Wotherspoon shouldn't have said what *he* said.'

'Depends how you look at it.'

'Binkie Buchanan has a perfect right to park his car wherever he wants to.'

'Except blocking the chairman's enclosure.'

'Well, yes.'

'But there was no need for Twotty to take a strong line. This *is* a club, after all.'

'What's that got to do with it?'

'There's too much of that sort of thing.'

'But you've got to have *rules*.'

'I still say Splinter Woodcock was wrong.'

'Besides, going back to the original argument, what does it really matter if someone lights a cigarette before half past one at lunchtime? No one ever bothers about that nowadays.'

'A lot of people don't like cigarette smoke all over their lunch. I don't, for one.'

'If the House Committee is appealed to, they have to stick to the rules.'

'But this is a *club*. Not a bloody girls' school.'

'Well, of course, if you're going to take that line, old man.'

'What other line is there to take?'

'Binkie Buchanan's car uses up too much room, anyway.'

'For Christ's sake, there's no law against a club member having a Rolls-Royce! Not yet, anyway.'

'Pity he doesn't keep it properly clean, though.'

'You've got a point there, old boy. There's nothing I like less than a dirty Rolls.'

'The point is that the rules are made to be obeyed.'

'Or scrubbed out, and rewritten altogether.'

'I say, old boy, steady on!'

'Sounds a bit bolshy to me.'

'No, I think he's got a point there.'

'We wouldn't have had any of this, if Twotty hadn't taken such a strong line in the first place.'

'What else could he do?'

'I'd like to tell you in detail.'

'Steady on, old man!'

'I still say Splinter Woodcock was wrong.'

It was something of a relief when Lou Strogoff arrived.

They had not met for some weeks, and Tulbach Browne was curious to know how the other man would greet him; in the intervening time, things had moved on in Pharamaul, and the position of special correspondent to the *Daily Thresh* had acquired a particular local significance, the sort of thing likely to arouse strong feelings among most of the white population of the island.

Indeed, Tulbach Browne had heard a rumour, a few days earlier, that he was to be asked to resign his temporary membership of the Pharamaul Club, because of what he had written about the Governor. Perhaps the idea had been lost in the later Twotty-Wotherspoon-Splinter-Woodcock-Binkie-Buchanan holocaust.

But in any case, it was somewhat disconcerting that Lou Strogoff made no mention of any of these things, and that his manner when they met was as bland, courteous, and noncommittal as ever. Their talk continued for some minutes before Tulbach Browne felt constrained to bring the question up.

'I had quite a time in Gamate,' he remarked cheerfully, bridging a pause in their conversation. 'There was a fantastic incident at the hotel there.'

'I read your article,' said Lou Strogoff, in much the same tone as the Governor had used, earlier that morning.

'Weren't you surprised?' asked Tulbach Browne.

'I've been to Gamate before,' answered Lou Strogoff gravely. 'I know the set-up there.'

'But you don't agree with it, surely?'

'I agree with people making their own rules, and abiding by them, as long as they don't hurt other people. That's my brand of democracy.'

'But there's a colour bar!' said Tulbach Browne disgustedly.

'You can call it that,' agreed Lou Strogoff. 'It's not the only one in the world. In this case, it means nothing worse than that the white people in Gamate want to drink, and meet each other, in their own surroundings. Why shouldn't they? It's something you yourself do every day in London.'

'I drink in a Fleet Street pub,' said Tulbach Browne stoutly. 'Anyone can come in there, as long as he's got the price of a pint of beer.'

Lou Strogoff sipping his Manhattan, cocked an eye at him. 'Any negroes come in?'

'One or two.'

'Suppose it was one or two *hundred*. Suppose you and the city editor of the *Daily Thresh* were the only white men who could ever find room to have a drink.'

'It's not that sort of pub,' said Tulbach Browne sulkily.

'It's not that sort of world,' corrected Lou Strogoff. 'Land's sakes, there's nothing to be ashamed of, in wanting to mix with your own kin!'

'There's nothing to be ashamed of, in wanting to break down the colour bar system, either.'

Lou Strogoff nodded, eminently reasonable. 'Sure thing … No one's stopping you, Mr Browne. You can bring negroes into your Fleet Street pub, as many as you like. And you can go and drink in lots of negro nightclubs in New York or Paris – if they want to let you in. Some of them don't, you know … What you can't do is take a negro into the Gamate Hotel, because the majority there is against you. Equally, what you can't do is have dinner at the Periscope Grill up in Harlem, because the majority is against you there also.'

'What sort of a dive is that?' asked Tulbach Browne contemptuously.

'Very select,' answered Lou Strogoff dryly. 'The only white man allowed in is the man who collects the trash. You can't park within a hundred yards of it, unless you've got a great big yellow fishtail Cadillac convertible … I can tell you, it's right outside *my* income bracket.'

Tulbach Browne smiled briefly and irritably, no longer enjoying the conversation, or considering it worth pursuing. That was the worst thing about Lou Strogoff, and all other expatriate Americans – and expatriate Englishmen, for that matter: they lost sight of the fundamental truths, they could settle down quite happily in a home-made paradise served by unlimited cheap black labour; they seemed to think that they had a right to enjoy themselves, no matter how much that right clashed with accepted opinion in their own homeland, no matter how dated, how reactionary that enjoyment was … He swallowed his drink with an air of dismissal, and made as if to stand up.

'How about lunch?' he asked. 'I've got a story to file, some time this afternoon.'

Lou Strogoff, courteous as ever, rose to his feet. 'Certainly,' he agreed. 'Now that you remind me, I've got a whole raft of papers, waiting for me back at the office … What's your latest story?'

Tulbach Browne smiled thinly, preceding him into the dining-room. 'The best one yet,' he said, over his shoulder. 'Though I suppose *you* would call it sensational, or unscrupulous, or something like that.'

'It sounds very interesting,' said Strogoff, without great attention. He was examining the stacked rows of cheeses, ranging from Stilton to Port Salut, on the centre table, and looking forward to the part of his lunch that he chiefly enjoyed.

'I hope you'll think so … It goes off this afternoon, anyway. And after that I've got a date with the editor of the *Times of Pharamaul.*'

VII

William Ewart O'Brien, the editor and proprietor of the *Times of Pharamaul* (weekly, 5d), was engaged in an intricate game of three-pack Pelman patience when Tulbach Browne was announced. Being one of the old school (as he liked to describe himself) he did all things with an air of patrician elegance; thus now, whenever he dealt himself a fresh card, he shot his cuffs with formal determination, and the face above the old-fashioned four-in-hand bow tie assumed a senatorial gravity. He surveyed his cards as Napoleon may well have surveyed his troops before the battle of Austerlitz; when he laid an ace upon a king, he might have been repositioning a platoon of the Old Guard ... Nearer seventy than sixty, he was neat, spare, and spruce; his grey tussore suit belonged to another, more spacious generation, his formidable eyebrows proclaimed a self-confident Roman distinction. The fact that he was sitting in a drab Port Victoria office on a hot afternoon, killing time between one appointment and another, was a sad commentary on the twentieth century.

William Ewart O'Brien should have been reviewing his troops beneath the shadow of Ciudad Rodrigo, or disposing, once and for all, of the Irish Question before a crowded House of Lords. But he was, alas, the editor of *The Times* of Pharamaul, and he had nothing whatever to do.

The *Times of Pharamaul*, founded in 1887 under a masthead which featured the Union Jack and the words 'For God, Queen, and the Golden Rule', imposed no greater strain on William Ewart O'Brien than it had done on his father, Richard Cobden O'Brien, its founder and first editor. The price had gone up, by one penny, in the succeeding seventy years, the number of pages had gone down; otherwise, it was indistinguishable from the paper which had first brought the news of the Boer War ('Kruger's Treacherous Assault') to the citizens of Port Victoria, two or three generations earlier.

It still featured an editorial on Free Trade and the need for brotherhood and peace, in most issues: it still carried, each week, the Government House Circular, and a list of ships which had called at Port Victoria, and a section labelled 'Farming Intelligence', and advertisements for paraffin-oil stoves and backache pills. It still detailed excessive temperatures, two-headed calves, Maula violence and incompetence, local drought. It was still the only relatively up-to-date newspaper available on the island. Above all, it still afforded the present editor, William Ewart O'Brien, an air of personal consequence and a standing in the community which he could scarcely otherwise have attained.

As editor, he had a staff of six, an ancient flat-bed press, a faithful clientele, and no competition. He wrote one editorial for each issue, presided at a weekly, somewhat artificial 'policy meeting', called occasionally upon the senior advertisers, and held daily court at the Pharamaul Club. The paper was carried, in the commercial sense, by the customary essential sideline, jobbing printing – the regular production of letterheads, circulars, posters, catalogues, and handbills, without which the *Times of Pharamaul* would have died overnight.

All in all, it gave William Ewart O'Brien modest pleasure, a twice yearly invitation to Government House, an adequate income, and few headaches. But it did not always satisfy. Occasionally it even palled … Now, for instance, on this hot, lowering afternoon, the *Times of Pharamaul* suddenly seemed less thunderous, less valiant, less essential to the onward surge of humanity, than it might have been. Perhaps because it was the spring of the year, perhaps because there was so little news, perhaps because he had once again overheard someone at the club speak of the paper as 'the local rag', William Ewart O'Brien found little pleasure in editorship, none at all in Pelman patience. He wanted something significant to happen, if possible before they went to press in four hours, certainly before he himself died …

It was for all these reasons, compounded of boredom, faintly persisting ambition, and professional snobbery, that he welcomed the arrival of Tulbach Browne.

He knew the other man well by reputation, naturally; in the ordinary course of events he would have talked slightingly of the Yellow Press, and dismissed Tulbach Browne, with old-fashioned and inaccurate scorn, as a penny-a-liner. But he knew in his heart that these things were not true. Tulbach Browne of the *Daily Thresh* was a foreign correspondent of undoubted fame and patent skill. The fact that he was paying a formal call, after due notice, on the *Times of Pharamaul*, was the biggest thing that had happened to the paper since August 1914, when the Kaiser had been burned in effigy on their own front steps, and the German Consul-General, arriving to protest against the action, had slipped and broken his thigh in the shadow of the statue of Kitchener of Khartoum.

William Ewart O'Brien rose, with courtly grace, as Tulbach Browne came in.

'My dear Mr Browne,' he intoned impressively, 'this is indeed an honour! Our little backwater here – ' he gestured round the panelled room, whose walls were covered from top to bottom with yellowing photographs, mysterious caricatures, and printed handbills announcing very old operas, ' – is not often honoured by a visit from one of the great men of the newspaper world!'

It was a friendly greeting, even a moving one. Tulbach Browne had been prepared for anything, from the traditional broken-down drunk, with a marginal Fleet Street background and a sodden, diminishing future, to some bright boy on the make, yearning for the magic touch of a world scoop. William Ewart O'Brien came as a surprise, though Tulbach Browne was able to place him immediately. One of the old school, he thought derisively. So much the better. There was more than one school nowadays, and the curricula were a good deal tougher.

But he decided to play it straight. He wanted one single thing from this funny old relic, and he was going to get it.

'Well, sir!' he answered, on a hearty note. 'I don't know about "great men". I suppose you must be just about the senior editor south of the Equator, yourself. I've been wanting to pay you a visit for a long time.'

They talked in this agreeable strain for some minutes, mutually flattering, mutually gallant. O'Brien thought the other man was merely paying a courtesy call; in fact, Tulbach Browne was waiting for an appropriate moment to put his suggestion, the suggestion that was going to round out his current blitz on Pharamaul. His private aim was simple. Having just cabled the 'marriage to white girl' story to the *Daily Thresh*, he wanted to put it squarely on the local map as well. That way, it would not be buried, or merely rumoured around Pharamaul in some garbled version. It would be here in black and white, for all to see in their own newspaper, for every somnolent clot in the Principality to read and to react to. It would make its mark far more decisively than any second-hand report from far away. It would surely lead to other stories …

Halfway through the interview, Tulbach Browne made his move.

'I've just been filing a story,' he said importantly. 'A big story – in fact, the biggest I've found here yet. It's all here – ' he patted the yellow cable flimsies which he had drawn from his inside pocket, ' – and I've checked it and rechecked it. Perhaps you'd care to read it?'

'I should be very glad to,' answered O'Brien, somewhat mystified. 'Not now, of course,' said Tulbach Browne. 'We don't want to spoil a pleasant session with *work*, do we?' He grinned, with sudden, oily *bonhomie*. 'But take a look at it later on. I thought you might like to use it yourself.'

'I'm afraid – ' began William Ewart O'Brien warily.

Tulbach Browne waved an expansive hand. 'It's all yours,' he said. 'You can have full second rights, on a purely complimentary basis, if you like. I don't mind telling you,' he went on, 'that I've really enjoyed myself on the island. I feel I owe it something. I've absolutely no objection to your running this story – *if* you like it – under my by-line, and with my compliments.'

'I'm sure I shall like it,' said O'Brien, re-exerting an antique charm.

'Read it, anyway,' said Tulbach Browne negligently. 'It's one of the biggest things I've done.'

'But you've written a great many big stories,' remarked O'Brien, theatrically impressed.

'Well, I had to come to Pharamaul for the biggest.' Tulbach Browne now rose, leaving the yellow carbon copies on the desk between them. 'Give me a call later – or better still, meet me at the club for a drink. I'd like to talk to you about the paper, anyway,' he went on weightily. 'You must have to contend with a lot of difficulties. But I admire what you're doing, very much.'

'We all try our best,' said O'Brien modestly.

'It's a very fine best,' said Tulbach Browne. 'Now let me see. When do you go to press?'

'Tonight at six.' O'Brien fingered the cable sheets, taking in a word here and there. He saw 'Dinamaula' and 'marriage' and 'sensation'. He could hardly wait to read it. 'This would be just in time,' he said, almost to himself.

'A very satisfactory tie with the Old Country, incidentally,' said Tulbach Browne. 'It will be in tomorrow morning's *Daily Thresh* in London. If you decide to run it, people will be able to read it in Pharamaul, at just about the same time.' He looked at the other man narrowly. 'Why, you'll scoop the whole of Africa! ... Not for the first time, I'm sure. But you'll do it again. And it's a very big story.'

When Tulbach Browne was gone, William Ewart O'Brien read the story. He read it slowly, with increasing excitement, from the first sentence – 'Tonight in Pharamaul, speculation is mounting about the white bride whom Dinamaula has declared he will bring back to the dusty, teeming village in the heart of his kingdom' – down to the last one: 'Whoever the girl may be, she promises a new, spectacular page in Pharamaul history'.

He read it with his fingers curling, and his old face creased by doubt; he read it with appalled, interior satisfaction. He was on the inside now, right in the middle, possessed of a secret that the whole world was waiting for. The *Times of Pharamaul* would carry the story a full day earlier than *The Times* of London … He had a genuine, huge-scale scoop here on his desk – the greatest scoop in the history of the paper. He believed it utterly, in all its shameful detail, its promise of embarrassment and clamour. He believed it because it was signed by Tulbach Browne.

Of course – he wavered only for a moment – it could not be suppressed. As editor, he had a duty to the public, a duty to Pharamaul, that far outweighed any other consideration. The story would appal everyone at the club, appal everyone in Port Victoria. Indeed, it appalled him … But the obligation to publish was plain and unequivocal.

Such a story could have only one headline, in forty-eight-point Roman, the largest type ever used on the front page of the *Times of Pharamaul*:

'CHIEF DINAMAULA TO MARRY WHITE WOMAN'

CHAPTER SEVEN

❖

'Sir,' said Aidan Purves-Brownrigg, in formal tones, 'whether the story's true or not, it's bound to have tremendous repercussions, all over the territory.'

'You really think so?' asked the Governor fretfully. 'Suppose there's nothing in it? Suppose it's just another newspaper story?'

Aidan shook his head, coaxing his way from point to point, feeling like an eddy of tide gently lapping and seeping over a humped patch of sand. 'True or not, people are going to believe it. To begin with, anyway. That means that we've got to be ready for anything.'

'You really think so?' repeated the Governor. 'Shouldn't we – ah – await developments? See what London has to say, and so forth?'

'No, sir.'

The Governor sighed. He was not at his best on this hot and humid morning. He felt cornered – cornered by the heat, cornered by his desk, cornered by his Political Secretary. He would have faced anything in the world rather than the story in this morning's *Times of Pharamaul* – the story that now lay before him on his desk. It was an absurd story, of course; if there had been anything in it – if Dinamaula had ever had the faintest idea of marrying a white girl – then Andrew Macmillan would have told him about it, long ago … But Aidan Purves-Brownrigg was right in one respect, of course, as he usually was; true or false, the story was sure to attract a certain amount of attention. That could only mean, at the very minimum, more newspapermen, more telegrams from London, more meetings and reports. Really, there was no end to this business.

The Governor sighed again, feeling himself caught at a sad disadvantage. He was aware that he would probably have felt somewhat harassed this morning, in any case; he was feeling excessively guilty about the stamps – the Pharamaul 1/– Mauve block of four – which he had bought after a brief wrestling match with his conscience. He was also feeling some £750 the poorer … Now there was this – and now there was Aidan, advising him (as was his undoubted duty), urging him to action, making the hot day a compulsive cage with only one escape.

'What do you suggest?' he asked presently, when he had forced himself to face the next turn of the path.

'Just a general state of preparedness, sir. First, we want to find out if the story's true. Andrew is seeing Dinamaula today, as you know. He'll be telling us all about that. But whatever happens, there's still the Press. I think they'll come crowding in … We ought to warn the staff, here and in Gamate, not to say anything that might make matters worse.'

'We've done that before, surely.'

'It's time for a reminder, sir.'

'Yes … Very well.'

'And you really ought to hold a Press conference, sir. That is, if a lot of reporters turn up.'

At that the Governor started, looking at Aidan with incredulous eyes, like an animal surprised in a thicket which had seemed, until that moment, utterly secure. The words 'Press conference' contained for him the elements of everything he most disliked – publicity, awkward questions, the barb of quick thinking, the prospect of embarrassment. He lowered his eyes, looking away, playing elaborately with the ornamental blotter on his desk. Presently he said: 'I'd like to think about that. I hardly consider the moment is opportune.'

Now it was Aidan's turn to sigh. He had expected that answer, knowing the man he was dealing with, knowing the way the old gentleman's mind worked. To the Governor, the Press was always the enemy, the alien intruder, the one factor that a civil servant should never be called upon to grapple with. The prospect of meeting them in the mass must be *agony* … The Governor might be everything else – an expert administrator, a man of action, a good man with a despatch, a superb man with minute and counter minute, an engaging man at a party. But he was not a Press conference man, and obviously he didn't intend to become one. Nor could Aidan hope to effect a transformation, now or in the future. Nor (to see it fairly) was there any reason why he should.

'Very well, sir. Perhaps it will keep. But I think we ought to warn people again, about giving interviews.'

'No interviews at all, eh?' said the Governor, relief in his voice, sighting the safe ground ahead.

'Not exactly, sir. We shouldn't refuse to see them. That would be worse than anything. But we all ought to tell roughly the same story. If you like, sir,' said Aidan, rising, 'I'll put up a draft.'

'Yes, do that, there's a good fellow … Not more than two paragraphs, I think, don't you?' The Governor mused, his impulses agreeably channelled at last, his brain meshing gently and smoothly into something he really understood. 'First, a warning against too much freedom of expression. Then, on the other hand, a reminder that there must be a readiness to meet these people, and to talk fully and frankly about – er – our various problems in this part of the world. I think we should avoid,' he went on easily, leaning back, looking at the ceiling, welcoming the words as they multiplied readily upon his tongue, ' – we should avoid laying down any hard and fast rules, where the Press is concerned. After all, you and Andrew Macmillan and the others are hardly children … On the one hand, in view of the publicity that this affair has attracted already, we have to avoid – er – adding fuel to the flames. On the other hand, we have nothing to hide, and we must make that fact plain.'

'Yes, sir,' said Aidan.

'It's really a matter of common sense,' said the Governor, feeling better already. 'As regards the marriage, we must wait and see what Andrew has to report. I imagine it will all blow over, in any case. As regards developments in the Territory, and so forth, we must be guided by our general policy. We all know what we're trying to do here.'

'Yes, sir,' said Aidan.

'General guidance,' concluded the Governor. 'A warning, and also a reminder that we're living, alas, in the twentieth century. I'll leave it to you.'

'I'll put up a draft, sir,' repeated Aidan, on a lower note. It would be just another bloody bromide, he thought despairingly, with the second paragraph neatly cancelling out the first, and the bemused recipients left precisely as they were before. But it might do some *good*, if he could slip a few words by …

'Might be very valuable training for the staff,' said the Governor unexpectedly. Free of the threat of a full-dress Press conference, he now saw the whole thing in vaguer, more philosophical terms. 'Meeting the Press on their own ground. Absolute frankness. Yet reserve as well … Must keep in with the fourth estate, eh?'

'Yes, sir. We *must* keep in with them.'

'But perhaps,' added the Governor hopefully, 'no one will be very much interested.'

II

The first time in its entire history that Pharamaul Airlines had had to lay on extra flights, to cope with a sudden rush of traffic, had been in 1947, when a rumour of a gold-strike (stemming from the rich assay reports arriving from all over the Orange Free State) had brought prospectors scurrying half across the world to inspect, assess, and finally reject the island's mineral possibilities.

The second occasion was the *Daily Thresh* account of Dinamaula's marriage plans.

The story attracted visitors from many corners of the world, intrigued by this exotic news item which promised so many things to so many different men. They came like flies in summer, settled like locusts, voyaged like detribalized ants. Commercial travellers came, from many parts of Africa, drawn by the magnet of a new name upon the map. Political observers came, eager to observe. Tourists queued for priority bookings, mad for a glimpse of the mysterious hinterland, the savage heart of this untamed island.

American cruise-addicts came, working to a minutely planned schedule. Englishmen came, to catch the sun, adjust their income tax, and escape their own climate. Germans came, to dissect: Frenchmen, to comment and to satirize: Scandinavians, to bring back travellers' tales. Suddenly accredited South American diplomats arrived, to fornicate in sepia and to peddle duty-free liquor.

There was a delegation (unofficial) from the blacklisted section of the United Nations Economic and Social Council; there was a dusky commission of inquiry (official) from Portuguese East Africa. Sailors came, glad of a new port of call: soldiers, to examine the terrain; airmen, to explore the prospects of carving fresh landing strips from the living earth, and to get drunk in lax surroundings.

A coal-black, gleaming bishop came from the Gold Coast: a uranium prospector from Canada: an Indian agitator only one jump ahead of innumerable deportation orders. The Vice-President of the United States of America made a two-day detour from his current global itinerary; the Vice-President of the Society for the Prevention of Cruelty to Animals arrived, hot-foot from Angola, certain of finding Christ's work to do among the four-footed heathen. A deputation from the Tokio Junior Chamber of Commerce alighted like small, hissing geese, pecking avidly for commercial worms.

Drunkards came, and derelict whores from Johannesburg: beggars from Israel, and charity operators from the suburbs of Los Angeles: flagpole sitters, and stranded touring companies, and Australian confidence men, and certified lecturers for the English-Speaking Union.

Above all, beyond all, five members of the world's Press arrived, to join Tulbach Browne upon his noisome, private battlefield. They were not a fair cross-section, because this was not really a fair story. It was a story best exploited by men of marginal integrity; and these five were the sort of people, representing the sort of newspapers, eternally attracted by such tainted game.

It was in the shabby, run-down bar of the Hotel Bristol that the Press contingent first gathered after their arrival, greeting Tulbach Browne with a wary, thin-spread camaraderie as false as porcelain teeth. They were John Raper of the *Globe*, Axel Hallmarck of *Clang*, Pikkie Joubert of the South African News Service, and the famous, two-woman photographic team from *Glimpse Magazine*, Clandestine Lebourget and Noblesse O'Toole.

Surveying them, drinking with them, talking glibly without giving a thing away, Tulbach Browne was secretly flattered. A bigger bunch of bastards, male and female, concentrated in one area, one could hardly hope to find; and it was his own story that had brought them there ... He was not at all worried about the newly-hatched competition. The beauty of this thing was that there was lots of material for everyone, with no need for crowding. He himself had excellent contacts, and a long start; therefore he could afford a generous margin of normal human conduct. Whatever the others wrote, whatever they stirred up, it was still his story, and he had a proprietary clutch upon it that would be a long time a-dying.

Meanwhile, it was interesting to recall, in precise terms, exactly why each of these correspondents had come post-haste to Pharamaul.

John Raper of the *Globe* was there because the *Globe* (Sundays only, circulation 8,000,000) was preoccupied with sex, and this story promised a copulative dividend of no mean proportions. The dear old *Globe* (thought Tulbach Browne, sipping his beer, and eyeing the hard-bitten, red-faced sexual gladiator that was John Raper, their senior executioner): the dear old *Globe* – where would it be, without schoolmaster and boy, actor and club servant, youth and older woman, clergyman and niece? ... The *Globe* wanted the Dinamaula story because it scented big trouble there; like most other newspapers, it liked things to go wrong, but above all it liked them to go wrong from the sexual angle, and Pharamaul was one place on the earth's surface where they might go wrong in a very big way indeed.

Many diverse elements were grist to the *Globe*'s specialized mill; the trouble, indeed, was in finding space for them all, without crowding out the racing news or stubbing a toe on the comic strips. The English village girl of fifteen landed with an American bastard – preferably negro: the politician 'surprised in night attire' at some dubious hotel: the Maniac who carved it up and ate it: the film star whose fifth husband (an embarrassed pervert) charged her with insatiable sexual appetite: anything stemming from indecent exposure, attempted molestation, high-class adultery, sexual aberration – all these were *Globe* stories, retailed for the fearful joy of eight million readers, on every Sunday morning of every week, month, and year.

John Raper was their star performer. No one could match him, when it came to dishing up the details; no one could write 'intimacy took place on nineteen different occasions', or 'witness described certain incidents in a nearby Lover's Lane', with greater relish, more explicit euphemism. He had been trained in a tough school, and he looked on the Dinamaula assignment as something approaching a graduation exercise.

Clang magazine was something else again. Whereas the *Globe* recorded disasters ranging only from breast to mid-thigh, *Clang* had a broader ambition. Its aims were succinct, and ruthlessly pursued: to exalt America, to assist at the liquidation of the British Commonwealth, and to sell a lot of copies. It peddled its transatlantic vindictiveness to six million people a week, in thirteen different languages. It told of things going wrong, with slanted, adjectival spite; it was, for week after week, year after year, a brilliant essay in ill will.

No target was too mean, no man too honest and sincere, to escape the editorial side-swipe. If the Queen of England toured Canada, meeting thousands of happy people, acquitting herself with absolute grace, that was not news. If the Queen of England, touring Canada, permitted herself the shadow of a weary yawn on the outskirts of Calgary in a temperature of ninety-eight degrees, that was. The incident would be photographed, the fleeting moment headlined. '*Monarch Bored, Romps Past Dignitaries*' would be the very least that the occasion would produce.

Clang was also strong on sex: not as strong as the *Globe*, which specialized, but still strong. One week in three, a half-naked murderess surrendered to the police ('see cut'): one week in two, a TV star exhibited a neckline plunging to the limit of a 21-inch screen: one week in one, a roving whore from Hollywood told all ('We're just very good friends') about the current stallion from the studio stable. *Clang* treated sex from the American, powder-room standpoint; that is, as something comic, competitive, hygienic, or violent. If there was any love in the world, *Clang* knew it could only be illicit, mercenary, or perverted.

Above all, *Clang* produced the answer to everything. If oil ceased to flow from Saudi Arabia (after an intricate, eighty-year-old dispute), *Clang*-man X solved it in two paragraphs – one derisive, one threatening. If Russia stalled at the United Nations, *Clang*-man Y laid bare the facts, and dictated the solution. If South Africa grew restive, *Clang*-man Z told her to behave, in three sentences, eleven *Clang*-honoured adjectives, all of Olympian finality. Beyond everything else, *Clang* knew the answer to all the problems of the British Commonwealth, all the varied, patently unnecessary complications stemming from the simple association of six hundred million people in forty different countries.

It might look difficult, to an outsider; *Clang* took you inside, and showed you that it was not. After a column and a half, charging bad faith, reactionary practices, colonial stuffiness, and Limey inefficiency, every reader could progress contentedly to the next section ('*Medical: Cancer Can Be Cured*'), with the complete assurance that if only the British would give up their forlorn, mutton-headed efforts at organization, would acknowledge the dusty, dreary error of their ways, would abdicate forthwith, and hand everything over to the natural heirs of the New World, then all would be well.

It was, of course, inevitable that *Clang* should send a man to Pharamaul, since the story promised a rich *macedoine* of sex, misfortune, ill will, and British mismanagement. What was surprising was that they should send Axel Hallmarck, a recruit so new that he could only just be forging his basic weapons of spite and derision. But possibly the fact that he was on probation would make him eager to please … Axel Hallmarck was a spry, slim young man with wiry crew-cut hair and a nominally creaseless nylon suit. He was poor, just out of college, ambitious, and energetic. He could write. He had a list of adjectives as long and as tainted as a leprous beggar's arm. He was almost certain to make good.

Tulbach Browne, who heard all the bad news, had heard of Axel Hallmarck. He was prepared to acknowledge him as a likely operator in the same field, a field that had room for a hundred harlots of either sex. The *Daily Thresh*, publishing six days a week, had less time than *Clang*, a weekly magazine, to polish the apple of discord and serve it up as simmering deep-dish pie. But it did a rough job well, and Tulbach Browne had no objection to sharing the kitchen, splitting the chores, and going shares on the tips. There were always plenty of customers crowding round the hatch.

Pikkie Joubert, and the South African News Service, were in a different category, serving another hatch altogether … The South African News Service had a legitimate interest in Pharamaul. True, it was not part of their own country – and loosely worded phrases that seemed to make it so, or which took the tie for granted, always drew strong reactions from the Pharamaul Club. But it *was* part of the same area, part of the interleaved atlas of Africa that made up one big, hemispheric pattern. The SANS, which covered southern Africa, and was relayed also to London, would report the Dinamaula story straight: that is, as a news story that affected very many people, black and white, between the Gold Coast and Cape Town.

Its reporting would not be slanted, save in one particular: it would take it for granted that most people in South Africa would dislike the idea of a mixed marriage, and it might add to that the parallel idea that a mixed marriage had become possible in Pharamaul only because of some inherent weakness in British colonial thinking and administration.

Pikkie Joubert was no star: he was a run-of-the-mill wire-service reporter, with a football record so dazzling that half a dozen solid South African concerns – from the Transvaal Chamber of Mines to the sugar industry in Natal – had automatically offered him employment as soon as he stopped running and kicking. He had joined the South African News Service because his uncle – the fabulous Japie Joubert, who played for Western Province from 1923 to 1930 – had been at school with the managing director. He was called Pikkie because the use (or the adoption) of that endearing diminutive was a South African tribal custom. All his friends – perhaps in an effort to seem popular, perhaps in the simple pursuit of being loved – employed the same tenderized version of their proper Christian names. Francis became Fanie, Hendrik became Hennie; it was an accepted form of club-bar baby-talk that everyone took for granted.

Pikkie Joubert had a brother called Frikkie, an uncle called Fonnie (for Francois), and cousins called Klasie, Bokkie, Boetie, and Jannie. His son, if he had one, was likely to be called Kokkie or Dame. Some historians maintained that the habit stemmed from the South African atavistic fear of being alone – as white men in an overwhelmingly black continent must always fear isolation: that such nicknames had the effect of drawing people together behind the encircling *laager*; and that chummy nicknames especially, like Ockie or Blinckie, beckoned one man to another irresistibly, and made them blood brothers, inherently good chaps, nuzzling their rifle stocks side by side ... But whatever the reason, Pieter Joubert called himself Pikkie, and felt himself a safer man for it, and everyone's pal – at least from the Vaal River to Table Bay, which was all that mattered.

He was calling Tulbach Browne 'Tullie' – to the latter's frigid astonishment – within two minutes.

Lastly (as Tulbach Browne looked round the bar), lastly there was the world's best-known photographic team, gossiping over giant gin-and-limes in one corner – the famed lens-women of five continents, Clandestine Lebourget and Noblesse O'Toole.

Miss Lebourget was a huge, bellowing, slatternly New Yorker whose generous form – two hundred and sixty pounds, give or take a four-course steak dinner – had heaved and puffed its way at least three times round the world. Her companion, Miss O'Toole, was a small, foul-mouthed, waspish Bostonian who did most of the work and made most of the enemies. Together, as they had been for the past thirty years, they were a formidable twosome whose output was the chief attraction of *Glimpse Magazine*, and whose rowdy lesbianism was tolerated (at a price) in every top class hotel from London to Tokio.

Whenever there was trouble – political, sexual, financial, or religious – Clandestine Lebourget and Noblesse O'Toole were to be found in attendance: lining up the subject, strewing flashbulbs like confetti, trampling the flowerbeds, blocking the side-walk, annoying the *élite* – and securing photographs of exemplary perfection, candid, absorbing, unbeatable. They had been at it for a very long time, with increasing success; they had been the delight of Hitler, the bane of Lindbergh, the scourge of Franco. When General Smuts scratched his hams at Lake Success, *Glimpse Magazine* had carried a full-page picture of it; when Queen Marie of Roumania pensively explored her nose at Bad Aussee in 1928, Lebourget and O'Toole had been on hand to chronicle the fact for posterity.

They had done features on war and peace, violence and tranquillity, love and hatred. Their series on the sex-life of a senior crooner had soured his career in mid-song; their candid sequence on King Farouk had done much to secure that monarch's downfall. At least one President of the United States owed his nomination to their warm-hearted, pet-infested photographs of his home life; at least one British general, caught giving the cold-eye treatment to a sleepy sentry, blamed them, legitimately, for his subsequent and speedy retirement.

They were everywhere – and now they were in Pharamaul, and that meant that Pharamaul was finally, irretrievably, on the map. Tulbach Browne could almost see the double-page spreads that would be adorning *Glimpse Magazine*, a few weeks from now. There would be a huge photograph of Dinamaula trying on the crown (if there was a Maula crown: otherwise the ceremonial robes); there would be a parade of Gamate 'beauties' – naked to the waist – doing some spurious tribal dance with empty water-pots on their heads.

There would be a shot of Andrew Macmillan looking exhausted and severe; another shot of Dinamaula gazing at a vague photograph of a white woman. There would be (perhaps in colour) the bottle stacked shelves of the Gamate Hotel bar, contrasted with some communal native drinking-place served by a single rusty tap. There would be very good scenes of the village itself, flanked by goats with enormous udders – the Lebourget–O'Toole speciality. There would be Father Schwemmer, soil-erosion, native bead work, a dusty tax office, and a very old man with a decorative pipe who didn't appreciate progress.

Lebourget and O'Toole would do it very well, thought Tulbach Browne sourly, calling for another round of drinks, and staring at John Raper of the *Globe*, who was showing Pikkie Joubert how to play shove-ha'penny – using Pharamaul half-dollars that slurred and skipped on the rough-hewn counter. They would do it very well – and he could scarcely complain, because the job that they would do would be the pictorial equivalent of what he himself had written about Pharamaul: selective, sharply focused, misleading, saleable. Indeed, he could not help being proud, at that moment; he had broken this story, and the rest of them were busy cashing in, and it still had a Tulbach Browne label on it, as concise and unmistakable as a Cole Porter tune or a Hapsburg nose.

Slightly hazy – it had been a long, drink-filled day – he watched them and listened to them. They were his hangers-on – almost his own creations.

John Raper was idly tossing a half-dollar, looking in the bar mirror at the cream-coloured girl who was collecting the empty glasses.

Clandestine Lebourget, her enormous bosom lunging and shuddering against the table, was roaring with laughter at something that Noblesse O'Toole – thin and unsmiling as a hotel credit-manager – had just said to her.

Axel Hallmarck, crew-cut hair at the alert, was showing the barman a new kind of fountain pen that wrote (unwillingly) in three different colours.

Pikkie Joubert, owlish and sweating, was nudging him and saying, 'It's like this, Axie …'

Tulbach Browne could not help being proud. He had virtually peopled this bar ... And there was much more to come, tomorrow.

III

It was a very unusual morning at the Secretariat. The customary sun-drenched, sleepy calm had given place to a bustling, almost raucous activity; voices and footsteps, never before heard in such profusion, filled the corridors, so that the whole crumbling building seemed to have become a whirlwind of banging doors, sudden conversations, telephones ringing, taxis swooping up with Cossack determination and grinding away again in low gear. The Governor pressed every bell on his desk; the Registry scattered files like ticker-tape; coffee was made four times in two hours; the Social Secretary's half-yearly migraine made its appearance at least six weeks ahead of schedule.

It was as if the twentieth century had suddenly dawned upon the nineteenth. Indeed, not within the memory of the oldest typist in the typing pool had office life at Government House been so disorganized and so enthralling.

Clandestine Lebourget and Noblesse O'Toole, seasoned campaigners who had routed so many competitors that they no longer recognized competition, had secured first crack at the Governor; and they made full use of their advantage. While Noblesse O'Toole – small, determined, blasphemous – was setting up a tall tripod to hold her battery of flashbulbs, Clandestine Lebourget stalked the Governor, first from one side, then from another, 'sighting' him through her arched fingers, trundling her enormous bulk on tiny, moccasined feet. She was looking for an angle

– several angles, in fact – and if the process meant treating the Governor of Pharamaul like an inanimate and none too promising exhibit at a county fair. that was just his bad luck. He wouldn't mind, in the end. He'd be the same as everyone else, from New York to Hong Kong. Everyone liked to have his photograph taken.

'Christ's boots!' said Noblesse O'Toole, breaking an uncertain silence. 'This damned tripod's spreading its legs like a Third Avenue whore.'

'Hush up, honey,' said Clandestine Lebourget, fondly and yet vaguely. She was staring at the Governor through a haze of smoke which drifted from the small Trichinopoly cheroot dangling at one corner of her mouth. 'You're worrying the Governor.'

'Please hurry,' said Sir Elliott, with all the determination he could muster at so unlikely a moment. 'I have important business ... Ten minutes, at the outside.'

'Why, you old sweetie!' said Clandestine. 'I believe you're shy!'

'My dear lady – ' began Sir Elliott.

'Don't you trouble your head,' said Clandestine. 'It's entirely painless. I want to get some *real* shots of you, looking cute and benevolent. No one goes for that phoney white-man's-burden stuff nowadays.'

'My dear lady – '

'Oh, let's relax, for Christ's sake!' said Noblesse O'Toole.

'Very important business,' repeated the Governor determinedly, though with less conviction.

Clandestine Lebourget set her cheroot down on one corner of the teak desk. Then she loomed over the Governor like a sloppy cliff, her eyes screwed up in intense concentration.

'Got any children?' she asked suddenly.

'A daughter, yes.'

'That's real sweet ... Try thinking of her.'

There was another pause.

'My God!' said Noblesse O'Toole. 'You'd better think of something else, right now!'

'Shut up, Tooley … Got any *other* children?'

'No,' answered the Governor. 'And I really think …' His eyes narrowed. 'Your cigar is burning my desk.'

Clandestine tossed the butt negligently into the paper-filled fireplace, where it continued to smoulder acridly. She was still stalking her target, the camera with its trailing flex poised for action.

'Just take my photograph,' snapped the Governor, finally losing patience. 'I'm really very busy this morning.'

'You old darling!' said Clandestine. 'You know you haven't a damned thing to do.' The bulbs flashed suddenly, and she lowered her camera. 'That will do for a start,' she said. 'We'd better call it "Governor in Stern Mood" … Set 'em up in the other alley, Tooley.'

'Roger!' said Noblesse O'Toole. 'Coming right up.'

'Surely one photograph will be enough,' suggested Sir Elliott, mollified by this evidence of action.

'No, sir,' said Clandestine Lebourget. 'It sure won't … What do you do for laughs?'

'Laughs?' repeated Sir Elliott.

'I mean, do you have any hobbies?'

'Certainly,' answered Sir Elliott, after a pause. 'I collect stamps.'

'Jesus!' said Noblesse O'Toole.

'No, it's kinda cute,' said Clandestine. 'I can see it photographically. Rare specimens. The finger poised. Maybe a magnifying glass.'

'I'm terribly busy,' said the Governor. 'I really thought this would be just one photograph.'

'Governor,' said Noblesse O'Toole tartly, dropping three expended flashbulbs on the carpet, and reaching for another set, 'you'd better face it – we're here for an hour. This old bitch is a *genius*.'

Pikkie Joubert of the South African News Service was making heavy weather of his interview with Aidan Purves-Brownrigg. Indeed, there were very few reasons why that should *not* be so. Joubert was a big man, blond and tough, slow-moving, slow-thinking; Aidan Purves-Brownrigg was the precise opposite of all those things, and was patently disinclined to regret the fact. His quicksilver speech and *dégagé* air struck no answering chord, and aroused only scepticism and ponderous mistrust. There were many reasons, well-grounded in history, why Boer and Briton should fail to charm each other, particularly when the Boer was a heavy-stepping ex-athlete and the Briton was Aidan; but whatever the basis of their conflict, it was certainly as strong now as it had been a half-century earlier.

To Joubert, Aidan Purves-Brownrigg was a slim, cunning *rooinek*; to Aidan, Pikkie Joubert was a rustic joke. They both took it from there, and the process could hardly carry them very far in any direction.

'What will be the outcome,' asked Joubert, laboriously, after they had talked without profit for some minutes, 'of a mixed marriage such as this?'

'Coffee-coloured triplets, I shouldn't be in the *least* surprised,' answered Aidan. He smiled winningly. 'The Maulas are a very fertile race, you know.'

Pikkie Joubert shook his head. 'I did not mean that, understand me. What will be the effect on the country?'

'Distinctly odd,' said Aidan. 'I should think the Maulas themselves would be shocked to ribbons. It means the lowering of all their standards.'

'Lowering?' said Joubert. 'What the hell do you mean, man? He's marrying a white girl, isn't he?'

'I mean that the older Maulas, who control things, have very exaggerated ideas of racial purity. The tribe is sacrosanct. They don't want any outsiders. A thing like this cuts right across all their established rules.'

'Hell, I don't mind about the bloody *kaffirs!*' exclaimed Joubert disgustedly. 'What about *our* standards?'

'It's contrary to tradition there, too, of course.'

'So what?'

Aidan raised his eyebrows. ' "So what?" ' he repeated.

'What are you doing about it?'

'Directly, at the moment, nothing. There are lots of reasons. Firstly, I doubt if the story is true. Secondly, we couldn't forbid such a marriage, though naturally we would do all we could to discourage it – '

'Of course you can forbid it! It's mixed, man – *mixed!*'

Aidan shook his head. 'But it's not *illegal*. I agree with you that it would be a bad idea, although – ' he smiled, ' – my reasons for saying that might not be the same as yours. From our point of view, it would be bad because it topples over – ' he gestured with elegant, slim hands, ' – it simply *topples* over every basic custom of this country, all the traditions that have worked very well for hundreds of years. *We* wouldn't like it. The Maulas wouldn't like it. That *may* be enough to discourage it. But we can't forbid it, in so many words.'

Joubert hunched his shoulders contemptuously. 'We do things better, where I come from.'

'You do them differently,' answered Aidan briefly. He did not want a direct clash with this uncouth young man; in fact, he did not want any dealings with him at all. The standard of foreign correspondent must have been lowered a good deal since the days of Russell and Nevinson, Duranty and Shirer ... He caught himself up at that point, aware of an irritated snobbery that was sterile and useless. This *footballer* had come out for the Pharamaul story. He had better be given it in palatable form, even if the palate concerned were already morbidly tempered to South African racial cooking. 'We've always held the view,' he began again, 'that if a thing is made illegal, it automatically becomes more attractive. That's especially true of sexual intercourse. No wife, after the first few years, can be half as attractive as a casual amateur who wanders into the wrong bedroom in a brassiere and a winning smile. Don't you think so?' he added, as he saw that Pikkie Joubert, so far from being amused, was looking somewhat grim.

'I'm a married man,' said Joubert.

You're a *clot*, said Aidan Purves-Brownrigg to himself, and I hope your wife has half a dozen randy *kaffirs* to take the taste of you away ... He sighed wearily. He had a hangover, a fit of depression, and a conviction that he was wasting his time. He longed for Paris, London, Rome, New York; for delicate, close-coupled interchange of thought; for the fencing of conversation, the balm of silence; for opera, *belle cuisine*, Arrau playing Chopin, Armagnac, *Cosi Fan Tutte*, the drolleries of Dior. Instead he had Port Victoria and Pikkie Joubert ... He squared his shoulders, and leant forward again. He had, also, a job to do, and he would fill his quota, come what may, like any sweating miner.

'That answer does you credit,' he said, with severely controlled irony. 'So few of us have *any* moral standards ... Now let's get back to the Maulas.'

Full twenty years divided Captain Simpson, the naval aide-de-camp, and Axel Hallmarck of *Clang*; twenty years, two wars, a lifetime of discipline, and a fathomless diversity of accent. They got on extremely well.

They discussed Nelson, the maritime history of Britain during the nineteenth century, the Boer War, Pearl Harbour, Senator McCarthy, communism, television, and the colour bar. Captain Simpson mentioned his possible promotion to admiral; Axel Hallmarck asked sympathetic questions about life in Port Victoria, home leave in England, current social obligations, and the duty-free importation of liquor. Captain Simpson confided that his wife was 'not really terribly keen about' Pharamaul. Axel Hallmarck agreed that it must have a good many drawbacks, and then asked if there was likely to be trouble over Dinamaula.

Captain Simpson said that whatever trouble there was would be taken care of, without the least difficulty. Dinamaula was 'just feeling his oats'.

Axel Hallmarck asked if the use of force was contemplated.

Captain Simpson said: 'I suppose so, old boy – if necessary.'

Axel Hallmarck, laughing, said that in that case it would probably come as quite a relief, to see a bit of action.

Captain Simpson said: 'You're telling me, old boy! This place is like a bloody mausoleum ... Now, how about a gin?'

They got on extremely well. People always got on extremely well with *Clang* correspondents, until later, when they read the current issue.

David Bracken was talking, without enthusiasm, to John Raper of the *Globe*, when Nicole Steuart came into his room. She would have been dearly welcome, at any other hour of the day or night; but just at that precise moment, when John Raper – paunchy, red veined, unbuttoned in dress and mood – was concluding a story of complex and startling crudity with a dig in the ribs and a burst of laughter – just at that moment, he could have wished that Nicole was a very long way away from them both.

John Raper lumbered to his feet as she entered. 'What ho!' he exclaimed. 'A bit of talent, for a change!' His eyes roved over Nicole's figure, frankly displayed in a yellow dress of cool brevity. 'Little one, you're a sight for sore eyes. In fact, you're a sight for sore anything.' He was already rather drunk. 'Introduce me,' he said to David, 'before I burst a blood vessel and ruin the carpet.'

David, torn ineptly between love, shame, and anger, mumbled the appropriate sentence. It was swiftly caught up.

'Nicole, eh?' said John Raper. 'Pretty name for a *very* pretty girl.' It seemed that he must already know every line of her body by heart. 'And what do *you* do? – in office hours, that is.' He guffawed. 'I don't want any true confessions – not while young David is here anyway.'

'You won't get any,' said Nicole briefly. She was in love with David that morning, and perhaps for every morning thereafter; she was in love with David, after a meeting wonderfully indecorous, wonderfully new, in her apartment the previous night. They were not *quite* lovers. Soon they would be. Let it be soon, the moment when they were *quite* lovers ... But at *this* moment, there was this horrid man. 'I'm one of the secretaries,' she said. And then, quickly, 'See you later, David,' she went on, without looking higher than his tie. 'It was nothing special.' Then she was gone.

'One of the secretaries, eh?' said John Raper, not at all abashed. 'What are the others like?'

'She's the only one,' answered David awkwardly.

'She'll do to go on with,' said John Raper of the *Globe*. 'What are my chances of taking her out?'

'You'll have to ask her.'

'Try and stop me. I feel twenty years younger already, even in this heat ... Now, what were we talking about?'

263

'Dinamaula,' said David readily. 'And the question of the succession.'

'Sounds bloody dull,' said John Raper. 'That girl's taken my mind off things – things like that, anyway.'

David, standing near the window, was attracted by a movement in the courtyard outside. He turned to look. It was Anthea Vere-Toombs, getting out of her car, and displaying a cornucopia of leg and thigh in the process. She glanced up at his window, as if from force of habit, and waved as soon as she caught sight of him. Then she started to walk, not towards Government House but towards the Secretariat. She kept her eyes on him all the time. She was smiling widely.

David turned without delay. 'If you really want to make a date,' he said, 'I've got a much better suggestion. There's a girl coming into the office now. The Governor's daughter. You'll like her.'

'Not my type,' said John Raper, leaning back in his chair. 'I'm a Socialist.'

'She's very attractive,' said David desperately.

'How old?'

'About thirty.'

'Name?'

'Anthea.'

'H'm … What's the form?'

'She's very attractive,' repeated David.

'No – the *form*. I've only got a day or so here.'

'That ought to be enough.'

John Raper raised his eyebrows. 'Sounds promising. I suppose all you bastards have had a crack at her already.'

'Well,' said David.

'Not that that matters much … Recommended, eh?'

'Highly.'

'Anthea's a pretty name,' observed John Raper, starting to lever himself up. 'I might give her a whirl.'

'A whirl,' said David, 'is just what it would be.'

'But I liked the look of that Nicole Steuart lass.'

'Anthea is much more your type ... I just know ... Try her, anyway.'

'Remind me,' said John Raper, as the door began to open, 'to offer you a good steady job in a brothel.'

'Don't go up to Gamate,' said Anthea Vere-Toombs, later that night. 'It's hot and dusty and dirty. It's like Cairo, only duller, without Farouk. There are *much* nicer things to do here.'

'I wouldn't deny that,' said John Raper of the *Globe*. He was lying back on the tumbled hotel bed, a towel draped round his middle, a glass of whisky in one hand, a cigar in the other. In his specialized world, there could be no finer moment. 'But I've got to earn my living. There's a story to write – a hell of a story.'

'There's a story here,' answered Anthea, stroking his shoulder. 'That was only chapter one.'

'You're quite a performer,' said John Raper appreciatively. 'Why don't you come up to Gamate with me?'

'It's a small town,' said Anthea. 'People notice these things.'

'It *would* stick out a bit.'

'Like you,' said Anthea. 'So rewarding.'

'My paper's really interested in Dinamaula,' said John Raper, after a pause. 'Who he's going to marry, why he's going to marry, what sort of a girl she is, what sort of a life they'll have. It's a *Globe* story.'

'You ought to run a competition,' said Anthea hazily, staring at the flaked plaster of the ceiling.

'Huh?'

'Choose a bride for Dinamaula. You know. The *Globe* is always running that kind of competition. The perfect man.

The perfect engaged girl. The perfect kitchen, or car, or poodle, or wedding dress. Who's the next prime minister, who's the nakedest film star, who has the smallest waist in northern Scotland. You ought to run a *competition*.'

'Go on,' said John Raper. 'You have other talents. I should have known.'

'Choose a bride for Dinamaula,' said Anthea readily. 'Who would YOU like him to marry? Big girl, little girl, blonde, brunette? How much round the bosom, how long in the leg, how big –' she elaborated freely, drawing on a copious imagination, while John Raper smiled and listened. 'Choose a bride for Dinamaula,' said Anthea, summing up. 'HE wants a white girl. YOU give him one. Only DON'T forget to fill in the coupon.'

John Raper set down his whisky glass, and rolled over. 'You're a genius, sweetie. Your father ought to be very proud of you.'

'I'm not a genius, but I *am* a sweetie.' She looked at him fondly – the new-found cure for her *malaise*, the ready fountain of satiety and calm. 'Don't go up to Gamate. Stay here and work it all out.'

'You're a genius,' repeated John Raper. 'I'll stay as long as I can. We'll work it out together.'

'How long *can* you stay?'

'Day after tomorrow,' said John Raper. 'Say, thirty hours. Then I must take a look at Gamate. For one thing, I want to ask Dinamaula about his prospective bride. We'll make him one of the judges. Only fair.'

'Thirty hours,' repeated Anthea. 'OK ...' She inched her slim, angular, complaisant body towards him. 'I love the *Globe*,' she said. 'So well-informed ... Can we get some more whisky? Let's stay in this lousy room *all* the time. Thirty hours is *sixty* half-hours.'

'You keep the score,' said John Raper. 'I'll stay in the clouds.'

'You'll stay with me,' said Anthea. 'It's the very least you can do, you … old … newspaper … man …'

IV

If the Press contingent had a disturbing effect upon Port Victoria, it was nothing to the confusion and uncertainty that they brought to Gamate.

It could hardly have been otherwise. Out of a hot blue sky they descended upon the town, avid for a story – eager to probe, to question, to promote controversy, if controversy and probing would produce the desired effect. In an old pattern, they were the new messengers of doubtful rumour; subtly they acted as a dissolvent of grace and order, bringing to this delicate balance a greedy expedience and a ruthless incomprehension of what such a balance involved.

It did not matter to them what degree of chaos they left in their wake; they would not be there to reckon the price, much less to pay it. Only the story mattered, and the story sprouted like a gory weed under their able hand.

They came to this ancient, orderly, and simple town as new minted human beings from the vast outside world, supposedly authentic, accidentally godlike; they made an extreme mark, as men and women must who talked differently, greeted strangers in a novel way, spent their money carelessly, laughed and walked and looked round them with a flattering blandishment such as no one else had used within living memory. They did all these things to Gamate, descending upon the modest community like gamblers and harlots upon a gathering of innocents. Their strength was the careless strength of men who would shortly disappear, leaving the bill for someone else; leaving the scattered fragment to be picked up again, and the tangled ends retied, by anyone who was stupid enough or unlucky enough to be left upon the field.

They came as fortune-seekers, stayed briefly as exploiters, left as conquerors. They sucked up from Gamate, and from the whole of Pharamaul, a tribute of hatred, bloodshed, and confusion wonderfully calculated to edify the outside world; and thereafter they took flight again, leaving behind them all the scars to be healed, all the dead to be counted, every penny of the price still to be paid.

But on the day that they arrived in Gamate, the blessed day of their departure was still far distant.

Press headquarters was the Gamate Hotel; and from there (like Tulbach Browne, a few weeks previously) the new arrivals foraged with diligence and cunning, looking for trouble, and returning at nightfall to refresh themselves, exchange stories, show off to the village clodhoppers, and plot tomorrow's excursion. Fellows, the landlord, loathed them and everything about them – Fellows, tough, strong, competent, who remembered vividly the Tulbach Browne–Dinamaula incident, and the complex, continuing trouble it had caused. He knew that it might all happen again, because these were the sort of people who made these things happen. If Tulbach Browne could fake a colour bar incident (and it *had* been faked, no question about that), then the rest of them might try the same trick. If not the same trick, then something worse.

Fellows' brow grew black, and his bald head shiny with sweat, as he swabbed down the bar counter. Bloody idiots, playing with something they knew nothing about … He hated them, in spite of the money they spent, the good-humoured camaraderie they spread (though that could easily turn to quarrelling, the way they talked about Gamate and Pharamaul), the brittle liveliness which their presence inevitably brought. He hated them because they were here to make trouble, all the trouble they could promote; and a few laughs and an extra pound or two in the till each evening could never compensate for that sort of thing.

He hated Clandestine Lebourget and Noblesse O'Toole – bloody disgusting old bags, he called them – because they had said: 'We want a colour shot of you behind the bar, with all those bottles and glasses, saying "No" to Dinamaula. Can you fix it?'

He hated Pikkie Joubert of the South African News Service, who said: 'Hear you had a bit of *kaffir* trouble the other day. Man, you've got to keep stamping on them all the time!'

He hated Axel Hallmarck of *Clang*, partly because of his crew-cut hair and outlandish bow tie, partly because of the two questions, warily spaced with at least an hour between them, which he asked. The first was: 'What sort of profit do you make here?' and the second: 'How much do you pay the Maula boy who washes up the glasses?'

He hated John Raper of the *Globe*, who arrived forty-eight hours behind the rest of the party, to be greeted by knowing cries of 'You've certainly earned your OBE!' and who got raucously drunk on the night of his arrival, and had to be put to bed by friendly hands, in full sight of the hotel servants.

He hated, especially, Tulbach Browne, who, brazenly cheerful, leant on one corner of the bar with the air of a man who doesn't need to work for some time to come, and said: 'I told you I'd make you famous, didn't I?'

Fellows hated them all. They were living in the hotel, taking up all the available rooms, crowding the bar, complaining about the service, spoiling everything. They were strident in their dislike of every single aspect of Gamate – the heat, the flies, the tepid drinks, the dust, the greasy food, the lumpy mattresses, the dull menus, the fact that they had to share rooms. it was as if they had burst into the hotel – the hotel he was reasonably proud of – determined to sneer and bitch about everything. He hated them all. He was always glad when, at ten a.m., they took themselves off for the day. At least, he *would* have been glad, if he had not known and cared what they were doing and trying to do.

Pikkie Joubert talked to the two senior Regents, old Seralo, and Katsaula the historian of the tribe. It was not an easy meeting, on either side. Joubert had to hold in check, all the time, his natural, ingrained contempt for negroes, whatever fancy ideas they dreamt up for themselves. The Regents on their part did not understand why Joubert, or any of the others, had come to Gamate in the first place; they could not comprehend their behaviour; they could not forgive the strange tales they heard.

But they would have felt guilty of gross discourtesy if they had hinted at this lack of understanding, this disapproval, when talking to a guest.

'We greet you,' said old Seralo, sitting upright in the tall chair of state, formally placed at the head of the long table in the council room. Katsaula sat at his side, worried and uncertain. He knew nothing except that new men had come into Gamate, talking of strange things, writing all words down, laughing like foolish girls, chattering like *katlagter* birds. It could only forebode ill for the tribe.

'We greet you,' echoed Katsaula none the less. '*Ahsula!* We are glad to see you in Gamate. You come from England?'

'No,' answered Pikkie Joubert brusquely. 'From South Africa.'

'We have heard many things of your country,' said Seralo after a pause.

'It's on the map,' said Joubert ironically. 'Now let's get a few facts … What's all this about Dinamaula marrying a white girl?'

'We know nothing,' answered Katsaula. 'That is a hidden matter.'

'Don't give me that!' said Joubert immediately.

'We know nothing,' repeated Seralo, with tremendous, quavering dignity. 'We are the Regents of the tribe. We have no lies in our mouth.'

'Who are you covering up, for Christ's sake?' asked Joubert. 'You know he told one of the newspapers he was going to marry a white girl.'

'The marriage of the chief,' said Katsaula, 'is a matter for him, and for the tribe. It is a great matter. Until it is settled, silence is best.'

'That's just double-talk,' said Joubert contemptuously. 'But I'll play it your way, if you like. Let's see … *If* he chose to marry a white girl, what would the tribe think about it?'

'That is a difficult question,' said Seralo, after a long moment of silence. 'It is not a question to be answered in a few minutes of talking.'

'I'm in no hurry,' said Joubert.

'It is a question we cannot answer,' said Katsaula finally.

'You'd better find an answer,' said Joubert, on a hard note, 'before it's too late. The world wants to know about this. So does South Africa.'

'It is a matter for the chief and the tribe.'

'Bull!' said Joubert rudely. 'There's a hell of a lot more to it than that, and you know it – or if you don't know it, you bloody well ought to!'

'Sir,' said Seralo, with formal dignity, 'we cannot answer such questions.'

'In my country,' Joubert persisted, 'a marriage like that is against the law.'

'In our country,' said Katsaula, 'it is against the custom.'

271

'What are you going to do about it, then?'

Katsaula shook his head. 'It is a matter for the chief and the tribe.'

'If you mean,' said Joubert, 'that you're going to let him get away with it, then you'd better think again, and think differently. South Africa is very interested in this marriage.'

'This is not South Africa,' answered Seralo simply. 'We are the children of the Queen.'

'What the hell difference does that make?'

Seralo, suddenly intent, suddenly ironic, looked at Pikkie Joubert for a long moment. 'There has been a difference in our minds,' he said finally, 'for more than a hundred years. I think it is in your mind also.'

Baffled, brought up short against a wall of dignity and deep feeling, Joubert cast about him for another approach. He did his best to make it sound effective.

'If you won't talk,' he said, 'I'll find someone that will. I'll go direct to the chief.'

'We understand,' countered Katsaula smoothly, 'that Dinamaula will see no one – no friends, no strangers – at this time.'

'I'm not surprised. He's certainly blotted his copybook in a big way. But I'm still hoping …' Joubert stood up. 'Well, that's that. I'll get going.'

'Sir,' said old Seralo, also rising, 'we are glad to have met you. Please take back our greetings to South Africa.'

'For Christ's sake!' muttered Pikkie Joubert.

'*Ahsula!*' said Katsaula, raising a formal hand. 'Peace to you and to your country, of which we have heard so much.'

Miera Katsaula, the forlorn bride who was no bride, sat sullen and silent on the clay-daubed *stoep* of her hut. She was not alone, though she would have wished to be – alone with the sunlight and the dusty air, alone with the bare mud floor, and the goats who had no thoughts, and therefore no sly contempt. She was not alone. Within reach of her hand and her voice was the fat white man who wanted to ask certain questions, and the interpreter – Voice Tula, so-called – who was there to help them both. Within call was her mother, pretending to be busy, listening from the guarded silence of the hut. Within sight were many neighbours, passing and repassing, not looking, not watching, yet consumed with curiosity, wearing their ears like the fronds of the reeds on the edge of the dam, when the spring pricked them to fullness.

Within sight also were the children, the hated children, moving always, laughing always, looking sideways and whispering 'No Bride Miera' without moving their mouths, giggling and chattering and running away before even anger could hope to catch up with them.

Miera sat without movement, without pleasure, her eyes downcast, her hands passive. The rough grey blankets hid her body, her eyelids hid her eyes. The sun laid a slatted pattern upon the contours of her face, outlining the broad black nose and the gross mouth with a curious weave of intermittent light and warmth. In between, dullness and shame and hatred burned like forgotten fires ... Miera sat without movement, not looking at the fat white man who had dismissed her body with contemptuous eyes, and who now threw words in her direction like small bones to a smaller dog – words caught up and smoothly offered to her by Voice Tula, a bought man of no pride, a hired dog himself.

'Ask her,' said John Raper to the interpreter, 'what she thought when she heard that Dinamaula was going to marry a white girl?'

Voice Tula spoke obediently in the slipshod Maula tongue, using equally his hands and his voice, looking at the ground. He was a small man, a bespectacled clerkly man of twenty-five, an interpreter on Forsdick's staff. Mostly he worked in the tax office, sometimes he worked in court, standing between the wrath of the law (as expressed by George Forsdick's breezy inconsequence) and the cowed malefactors on the other side – usually exuberant drunks or righteous wife-beaters. Only rarely did something of true interest come his way; and never before had he assisted at such a scene as this, a scene in which history, drama, and scandal were so royally blended.

Voice Tula glowed inwardly, listening and talking by turns, aware of power, aware of his own essential role in a legendary exchange. There would be much to tell his wife, later that evening, and much to tell his friends.

When he had finished speaking, there was silence. Then Miera answered briefly, looking also at the ground, as if their words did not travel from person to person, but were part of a vague ambiguous pattern which was spread like a rug at their feet, a pattern to which each of them could contribute a long or a short thread, as they willed.

Voice Tula translated, now using a different speech. When he spoke in English, his voice took on a precise, out-moded punctilio, like a Victorian floorwalker in one of London's oldest department stores.

'She answers, sir,' he now said evenly, without expression, 'that she has heard nothing of such matters.'

'Well, I'm telling her now,' countered John Raper, who was somewhat less than sober, and irritable from the combined heat and smells of Gamate's lowering noontime. 'Dinamaula is going to marry some white girl he met in England. He's definitely said so. What does Miera think about that?'

The voices murmured again, quiet, impersonal, adding to the pattern that lay between them.

'She says,' answered Voice Tula presently, 'that she does not believe this thing.'

'Has she seen Dinamaula recently?'

'No,' – after a pause – 'Dinamaula is absent, visiting a cattle post to the south. He cannot be reached.'

'Smart guy,' commented John Raper. 'If I were him, I'd keep it that way.'

'Sir?' asked Voice Tula, 'I am to translate?'

'No,' said John Raper, 'that was just one for you and me.' He dabbed at his brow with a large khaki handkerchief. He was getting nowhere, but it did not matter. This girl was a squalid sort of cow, in any case – far from the coffee-coloured, honey-voiced charmer that the *Globe's* readers demanded. With the best will in the world, she was nothing like Rita Hayworth with a South Seas wiggle and a cocoa make-up. Interest must lie elsewhere – perhaps with the unknown white bride … He mused on this for a moment, recalling Anthea Vere-Toombs's idea for a 'Find-the-Bride' competition, recalling Anthea's other attributes, other inventions. It was a pity he had ever left Port Victoria.

'Ask her,' he said finally, carelessly, 'if she's a virgin.'

'Sir,' said Voice Tula, with rare dissent, 'that is not a suitable question.'

'Well, is she?'

Voice Tula smiled, raising his soft absorbent eyes for the first time. 'I understand,' he said, 'that such is the case. She was to have been the bride of the chief. These things are customary with my people.'

' "Was to have been"?'

'There is now a state of suspended animation.'

'Huh?' exclaimed John Raper. 'Where were you educated, for God's sake?'

'At Fort Hare College, in South Africa.'

'Must be quite a place … You mean the whole thing's definitely off?'

'Sir?'

'He's not going to marry this one?'

'Sir, I do not think so.'

'Is she sad about that?'

'She is a simple girl, sir. Probably she is sad.'

'Ask her if she is sad.'

Another pause, longer this time, while Voice Tula talked, and Miera Katsaula stared before her, her blanket covering her chin, her eyes downcast. Finally she spoke a single sentence, and Voice Tula spoke after her.

'She says, sir,' he translated, 'that she does not wish to answer any more questions. She has household work to do.'

'For Christ's sake!' exclaimed John Raper, rising to his feet. 'That's not the trick of the week! I could do with a drink myself.'

It was a drink which he was able to enjoy within a very few minutes, in the bar of the Gamate Hotel. There, the usual lunchtime session was in progress – both men and women, some drinking determinedly, some passing the time without urgency, some munching their sandwiches. Forsdick was there, and Oosthuizen the farmer, and one of the hospital nurses, and Pikkie Joubert, and the huge bulk of Clandestine Lebourget.

John Raper made a play for the nurse, and was repulsed with antiseptic skill; he took a look at Clandestine Lebourget, and shook his head – a man must have some pride; then he applied himself to whisky and water, drinking George Forsdick level with mutual appreciation. Pikkie Joubert started an argument with Fellows the landlord; Oosthuizen joined in, siding at first with his fellow South African, then veering round and hammering home his encroaching dislike. Their corner of the bar developed a flushed and argumentative air. Then it ebbed away again. Clandestine Lebourget withdrew to comfort Noblesse O'Toole, who was lying down with a headache. Oosthuizen said: '*Tot siens, kerels*,' and lumbered off to his car. At the twelfth whisky, Forsdick backed carefully away from the bar, and said: 'That's my score for now. How about coming home for a bite of lunch?'

'Are you sure it's all right?' asked John Raper. 'What about your wife?'

'She'll love it,' answered Forsdick largely, 'though she may not say so out loud. Difficult woman. *Shy* woman. Let's get going.'

They drove back erratically, Forsdick humming 'Roll Out the Barrel', John Raper beaming owlishly about him like a minor royalty on the loose. They only exchanged three sentences during the journey. Out of the blue, Forsdick asked: 'How was Anthea?' and John Raper answered: 'Terrific!' and Forsdick countered wistfully with: 'That's what they all say.' Then they were home, and Mrs Forsdick – grim, resentful, and cold sober – confronted them on the doorstep.

She remained none of those things for very long. There was something about John Raper's intrinsic, gamey sexuality which nicked all ice, solved all female problems. Within a few moments, he was in the kitchen, advising on the preparation of a sauce to go with the corned beef, pledging his hostess in a brew of whisky-sour which she was delighted to share. The two of them talked animatedly all through lunch, while Forsdick kept silence, amazed at his luck, glad to play along with it. John Raper was adroit at all the niceties of gallantry – standing up when Mrs Forsdick came into the room, drawing back her chair at table, making coffee, offering to wash up the dishes afterwards. When she lamented the fact that they were so far from Government House in Port Victoria, John Raper assured her that it was only a matter of time before she took over as *châtelaine*. When she brought out a photograph album, he maintained an unwinking interest in its contents. When she mourned the lack of companionship in Gamate, he said, 'What? – a pretty girl like you?'

When Forsdick went back to his office for the afternoon session, John Raper stayed behind. When Forsdick returned, John Raper was still there, feet on the sofa, drinking coffee with neat whisky on the side. Grace Forsdick – slightly flushed, indubitably relaxed – received her husband with rare affability, and presently cooked them both an excellent meal.

'You must come again,' said Forsdick to John Raper, when they said goodbye, much later, under the lambent Maula moon. 'Every night, as far as I'm concerned.'

Axel Hallmarck of *Clang*, sitting in his hotel room, filling an hour between lunch and his appointment with Andrew Macmillan, was playing his favourite game. It needed only three things – a typewriter, a good memory, and a wish to perfect his current style. He had all three.

> It was a hot day in the cemetery, [*he wrote, his fingers supple on the keys*]. Even the war graves seemed to wilt at the prospect of a routine presidential speech. The President, an ageing (54), awkward, and angular figure in hit-or-miss store-clothes, fidgeted as he faced his audience. He was ill-at-ease, though not (according to current reports) more so than usual. Behind him, his aides, much better dressed, fingered their carefully ghosted briefs, wishing audibly that the President would not talk off so frayed a cuff.
>
> The troops in the guard of honour yawned. When the President began to speak, the nasal twang was as prominent as his Adam's apple.
>
> 'Four score and seven years ago,' he began, hitting a pedantic stride, 'our fathers brought forth on this continent a new nation, conceived in liberty and

dedicated to the proposition that all men are created equal.'

The lines of soldiers, recognizing the old presidential malarcky, settled down to a bored indifference. The war, for them, had been mostly waiting in line. Now they were waiting in line for yet another politico to go through the motions of democracy.

'Now we are engaged in a great civil war,' ('Jesus!' muttered a disgruntled GI, 'who does he think he's telling?') 'testing whether that nation or any nation so conceived and so dedicated can long endure. We are met on a great battlefield of that war.'

The assembled aides smirked and looked brave, though it was safe to say that none of them had been near this, or any other, battlefield, until that morning. Perhaps aware of apathy among the fighting section of his audience, the President now played it for pathos.

'It is for us the living, rather, to be dedicated to the great task remaining before us – that from these honoured dead we take increased devotion to that cause for which they gave the last full measure of devotion.'

Up on the platform, a stage widow in militant mourning wiped away a tear, using elaborate care and a black-edged handkerchief. The aides looked sad. The soldiers looked at their boots.

'We here highly resolve … that government of the people, by the people, and for the people shall not perish from the earth.'

The aides raised their eyebrows ironically, and reached for their hats. The soldiers relaxed, recognizing a political peroration when they heard one – even if none of them could have spelt the word.

The President nodded glumly, and stepped off the platform.

No one cheered. No graves opened, since no one could have mistaken this flat unmusical occasion for the Last Trump. Without regret, Gettysburg Cemetery went back to sleep.

Axel Hallmarck grinned, pleased with his effort. He read it through, pencilled in a word here and there, and then deliberately tore it up. The day's game was played, the exercise was over. Here, in Gamate, were other battlefields, and other cemeteries, promising more elegant slaughter, deeper corruption, than any from the past.

With a curious, twilight sense of doom, Andrew Macmillan read over the last sentence he had written, the beginning of the account of the big tax troubles in his *History of Pharamaul.*

> The centre of unrest [*he had written*] was the town of Gamate itself, already uneasy owing to the prolonged absence of Chief Simaula, who was visiting the outlying tribes.

Andrew Macmillan raised his head from his manuscript book, suddenly wishing to write no more that day, nor to think of the troubled past. What he had just written was altogether too apt to the present, too much a part of the inevitable history of the Maulas. Five years ago there had been a sudden blaze of riot in Gamate, stemming from discontents as frivolous and as varied as the colour of a new tax form, and the rumour of restrictions on the practice-periods of the Gamate Town Band. Starting with senseless defiance, it had run a furious and bloody course, and ended with many dead men on either side, including four Maulas hanged for murder in Port Victoria jail.

Was the present to be another segment of the same murderous spectrum? Andrew Macmillan let his pen fall on the desk, and sat back, his hand rising automatically to cover his eyes. He was, as usual, desperately tired; he had a sense of defeat and inadequacy such as he had not felt in ten and twenty years – a sense of defeat even before the battle was joined … Certainly Gamate today was full of rumour, full of uneasiness; certainly Dinamaula, like his father Simaula, was absenting himself indefinitely somewhere outside the town, and the fact was causing all sorts of gossip and unrest. Certainly there were many things likely to set a spark to trouble – wild talk about the chief's marriage, vague surmise of 'new things' which the new chief was to bring with him, vivid speculation on the presence of strangers in the town. This was no time for the Resident Commissioner to loosen his grip. But that was what was happening.

He wished he had been able to see Dinamaula, and clear up at least one aspect of the problem – his marriage. But Dinamaula had first sent non-committal messages of delay. Then he had been ill. Then he had left town, ostensibly to visit some of his cattle posts in the surrounding ranchland. Until Macmillan could talk to Dinamaula, get the truth from him, persuade him (if necessary) to see reason, then he could make no start of any sort.

If it had been twenty years ago – if it had been ten years ago – he would have taken all this in his stride, dealt with it in a few sentences, a few brusque summonses to the tribal leaders, a quarter of an hour's forthright speaking on the *aboura*. Now, faced by shadowy difficulties, vague and grotesque fears, he felt powerless to cope with them. Perhaps he had been too long in the territory. Perhaps, at fifty-seven, he was too old and worn out. Perhaps history in Africa had moved on, leaving him bobbing foolishly in its wake, using old methods, mouthing old phrases, when the call was imperative for the new, the experimental, the bold and dramatic.

He wanted nothing more than to reach across the dusty cluttered desk, pick up the telephone, put through a priority call to Port Victoria, and say to the Governor: 'Sir, I resign.' Then he would stroll out into the Residency garden, enjoying the late afternoon sun, ignoring the ants. Then he would go back to his armchair, fill his pipe, ring the bell for Johannes (that other old has-been) and sip whisky and water until it was time for an early bed … Instead, he could do none of these things: not now, nor for two or three years to come. Instead, he had to cope with Dinamaula (as soon as he could get a grip on that elusive character); he had to curb the running riot of rumour that was filling the town; he had to watch a dozen other things – normal things, abnormal things, inexplicable things – that were reaching his eyes and ears from a dozen different sources.

Especially, he now had to talk to an American Pressman with the defeating name of Axel Hallmarck – and talk to him in the light of a truly preposterous directive which had just reached him from the Secretariat at Port Victoria. In paragraph one, it stressed the need for extreme caution in dealing with the Press. In paragraph two, it called for 'a demonstrated readiness to discuss all aspects of Maula affairs'.

It was a wonder, thought Andrew Macmillan sourly, that there wasn't a paragraph three, telling him to do the whole thing standing on his head under a full moon.

But when finally he met Axel Hallmarck, at teatime, with the sun lengthening all shadows in the garden as it dipped towards the west, Axel Hallmarck turned out to be one of the nicest young men he had ever encountered.

True, the spotted bow tie and the convict hairstyle were a little hard to endure, when first one caught sight of them; but Hallmarck himself was so pleasant, so patently sincere, so ready with deference towards a man many years his senior in age and experience, that Andrew Macmillan could not complain on any score.

He had been expecting a trying end to a trying day; instead, he found his new companion delightful, and their short meeting – for the young American was especially concerned lest he intrude too long on his host's privacy – their meeting was a refreshing tonic.

Axel Hallmarck's questions were few, and innocently concerned with the normalities of life in Gamate. He wanted to know about the tribal hierarchy; he was interested in the local system of control and organization – how much was delegated to the Maulas, how much rested in the hands of the Resident Commissioner and his staff. He asked a few questions about native diet, and housing, and the average wage of a black man – any black man, the first to be met on any street – compared with the wage of someone like Fellows, who presided over the bar of the Gamate Hotel. He showed an interest in the local crime rate, and the length of time that Andrew had been in the territory, and the feeling – the general feeling, nothing detailed or quotable – of the local white residents concerning a possible mixed marriage. Presently, unassumingly, he asked if he could have a quick word with Johannes, Andrew's old servant.

'Now why on earth should you want to talk to *him*?' asked Andrew, amused. He was feeling more relaxed than for many days past, sitting at ease in one corner of the *stoep*, sipping his tea, pulling at his pipe. Closing his eyes, he could almost imagine himself to have retired a few hours earlier ... 'I doubt if Johannes has ever met a reporter in his life. I'm certain he's never read a newspaper. He wouldn't know what to say.'

Axel Hallmarck smiled agreeably. 'You said he was an old man. I wanted to talk to one of the older Maulas. Just to get their point of view.'

'Johannes hasn't got a point of view,' answered Andrew. 'He's been my houseboy for over thirty-five years.'

Axel Hallmarck was still smiling, with the utmost goodwill. 'That, for me, is the interesting part. He must have a whole range of significant memories, just because of that long service record.'

'See him if you like,' agreed Andrew carelessly. 'But I warn you, there won't be any surprises for you. He's my houseboy. Hasn't got a thought beyond that. Thickest head in the territory. But have a word with him, if you care to.'

'I surely would.' Axel Hallmarck rose to his feet, and held out his hand. 'Thank you very much indeed, Commissioner, for a swell meeting. Just what I wanted. Just what I hoped for.' He looked round him, at the garden and the sunlight. 'You know, I envy you, living here … Now, if I can just go through to the kitchen or whatever it is, for a few moments.'

'I'll show you,' said Andrew, preparing to rise in his turn.

'Don't you bother,' said Axel Hallmarck, showing his only sign of true alacrity so far. 'I feel I've taken up far too much of your time, as it is … I reckon this is the way.'

He opened the swing door leading to the dining-room, and passed through, adroit and untraceable as quicksilver. Silence fell again, broken only by a vague murmur from the direction of the kitchen. Presently, lulled by its sound, Andrew Macmillan dozed off.

On the other side of the town, under the sad cypress trees and the shadows of the great rocks, among the chipped and weathered tombs of the Maulas, some of the older headmen were gathered. They stood, as befitted their rank, in attitudes of grave attention, their heads bent, their eyes resting on the largest tombstone, the tombstone of Maula the Great. One of them, the oldest man of all, whose trailing blanket covered a thin, wavering body, had placed one hand on top of the headstone, and with the other was pointing at the august name. The others watched him, their expressions masking a deep bewilderment.

The flashgun popped, and Noblesse O'Toole, observing from a distance, called out: 'Try it again, for God's sake! They look like act two of *Porgy and Bess*.'

Clandestine Lebourget, striding forward, took hold of the oldest man by his meagre shoulders, and moved him a half-pace nearer to the grave. Then she reached out a hand, and tucked his blanket neatly under his beard. The others watched her, wary and uncomprehending. She felt in the pocket of her huge corduroy slacks, brought out a handful of loose change, and gave each of the headmen a silver coin – either a sixpence or a shilling. Then she pointed at the tombstone, and commanded, 'Keep looking at that. And look sad.'

Nothing happened.

'They just don't speak the language,' said Noblesse O'Toole disgustedly.

Clandestine Lebourget took out a large coloured handkerchief, none too clean, and pretended to mop her eyes.

'*Sad!*' she repeated, at the top of her voice, and pointed to the tomb. 'Great chief dead! Wah! Wah! Make like with tears.'

The old men regarded her unwinkingly. They admired large women, who were traditionally fertile; but for the Maulas, women in trousers had long been a tribal symbol of venereal infection. Perhaps the box with the blinding light would prove to be some kind of safeguard.

'Got me an idea,' said Noblesse O'Toole, after an unprofitable pause. 'Get ready to take a picture …' She stooped down, picked up a stone, and flung it at the base of the tombstone of Maula the Great. The old men recoiled in horror and astonishment, then stared at the desecrated tomb with expressions of the utmost consternation. The flashgun went off.

'Perfect,' said Clandestine Lebourget happily. 'Never seen six old guys so depressed …'

She brought out another handful of coins, and distributed them to the headmen of the Maula tribe. To the oldest one, a distant cousin of Dinamaula, she gave a two-shilling piece, then shook him by the hand.

'You're just *darling!*' she said, as she turned away.

Presently, in his own tongue, the old man inquired of his neighbour: 'What is this dar-ling?'

The man he spoke to was the father of Voice Tula, the interpreter, and with him had talked much of the language of the white men.

'It means,' he answered gravely, 'that she loves you.'

The old man raised his hands. 'Are they all mad today?'

On their way back to the town again, Clandestine Lebourget and Noblesse O'Toole passed by the edge of the Gamate dam. Here, some groups of young girls were washing out their blankets, sitting by the margin of the water, sluicing the rough fabric and then pounding it with small flat stones. It was a scriptural scene, a scene as old as the dam itself.

Some sang as they worked, some sat in dreamy meditation. All the girls were naked from the waist upwards, and the sun made a dappled pattern on their breasts and shoulders. Many of their bodies, shyly flowering, were of exquisite grace and contour.

'Set 'em up again, Tooley,' said Clandestine Lebourget, coming to a dead stop. 'This is where we get a bit of art.'

V

Suddenly, Tulbach Browne, that enigmatic key man whom everyone liked to keep within their sights, was nowhere to be seen. One evening, he was drinking and gossiping at the bar of the Gamate Hotel; the next morning, he was gone, leaving a note for Fellows which read, curtly: 'Hold my room for me.' ('Like hell!' said Fellows to Oosthuizen, later. 'The next commercial that turns up can have it free.') It was rumoured that Tulbach Browne had gone north, up to Shebiya; or alternatively, that he was looking for Dinamaula, somewhere among the scattered cattle posts to the southwest. He left behind him an uneasy feeling that, good as Gamate was, there might be an even better story about to break somewhere else.

But to take his place, a new character altogether arrived at lunchtime the same day. Noblesse O'Toole was in the bar when the tall scraggy figure in white cassock, ornamental leather belt, and grey suede sandals made its appearance, striding through the swing door like a Texas ranger who had just had a row with the wardrobe department. She gulped her drink, muttered: 'My God! Christ comes to Unesco!' and signalled urgently for another gin-and-lime.

It was Father Hawthorne.

Perhaps it was inevitable that Father Hawthorne, famed champion of a hundred lost causes, should have arrived in Gamate; indeed, there were many who maintained that no cause could be regarded as truly lost, until Father Hawthorne had appeared on the scene. Tall, good-looking, dramatically poor, his fame had spread far beyond the London slum parish where, many years ago, he had held a curacy; from that humble and constricted beginning (which had not detained him long), Father Hawthorne had blossomed out into global fame.

He was perhaps the classic cause-embracer, gullible, erratic, and sly. Wherever injustice flowered, wherever tyranny held sway, Father Hawthorne was inevitably to be found – flaunting his white cassock like an old ballerina with a new lease of life, springing to arms in defence of the very latest martyr, trailing the headlines like a St Bernard dog with a keg of acid round its neck.

If a strike paralysed the New York waterfront, Father Hawthorne was there, conferring with the leaders in the nearest fogbound shack, tripping over the mooring ropes as he implored all concerned to seek the Lord's will in a just settlement. If some Indians, intent on passive resistance, went to prison in South Africa, Father Hawthorne was there too – not exactly going to prison, but at least showing the Indians where the prison was. If certain obscure tribesmen in the Belgian Congo ran amok at some fancied injustice, Father Hawthorne jumped the next plane for the United Nations Assembly, and made a plea – before the conscience of the whole world – for their instant reinstatement in positions of authority. If a Malayan terrorist was hanged in Selangor, Father Hawthorne spent three days with the widow, was photographed patting an unidentified child, and wrote a stirring call to democratic action which an equally gullible London Press always allowed to run riot on its front pages.

Whenever five Arabs got together and denounced British imperialism, Father Hawthorne flew in and made a sixth. If the ruling chief of Basutoland was deposed, for good and sufficient reasons, Father Hawthorne could not rest until he had sat under a thorn bush with the bereaved tribesmen, shared a highly publicized cup of tea with the current grass-widow, and broadcast the whole story over an American coast-to-coast network.

It was all very admirable. Students of affairs always maintained that the world needed someone like Father Hawthorne – a kind of rambling global conscience who could serve as a trigger for man's inalienable right to kick up a row. Indeed, if he had not existed (so the formula ran), the popular Press would have had to invent him. The trouble was that there was a flaw – as perhaps there must always be, even with the very best of men. It wasn't women, though certainly there were women – young, old, rich, vagrant, intermediate – who were ready to follow that buoyant cassock through hell and high water, and who trailed it from Lourenço Marques to San Francisco, scattering savings, virginity, and roneoed protests like ill-classified confetti in their wake.

The real trouble was that Father Hawthorne was never there when he was wanted.

He might make a great impression on the New York longshoremen, but when the time came for a showdown, Father Hawthorne was on a boat heading for South Africa, where frightful things were rumoured. He could not have been better disposed towards the Indians in Natal – indeed, he rallied their spirits tremendously – but when the need for action mounted to a crisis, he was somewhere in Saudi Arabia, denouncing a pipeline. He would then enthrall the entire world by addressing the United Nations Assembly on the subject of oil monopolies; but next year, when it was time for some intensive and rather dull spadework in committee, he was dimly to be heard of in Nyasaland, where (as everyone knew) disgusting cruelties were daily blotting the conscience of the world. He had once headed a semi-religious demonstration of depressed peasants in Ecuador – up till the very moment when they were crudely haled into the local police court on a charge of public violence. Then he sent them an encouraging telegram, while changing planes at Montreal.

Now he was in Gamate, which meant two things – that enough had been written about it to focus the world's attention satisfactorily, and that Father Hawthorne's sensitive nose had chosen it as the likeliest contemporary target. No one could doubt that he had wrestled long and fiercely in prayer, before accepting the call. But when the call was accepted, he went into action with a huckster's appetite.

On that morning of glaring heat in Gamate, Father Hawthorne did not remain long in the hotel bar – just long enough, in fact, to make everyone else, however abstemious, feel as if they were wallowing in swinish self-defilement. Then he nodded in a manly sort of way to Fellows, and his white-cassocked figure swished through the swing door again. He had a luncheon engagement with Father Schwemmer, and he knew the importance of punctuality to a simple household.

The two men were in sharp contrast; indeed, as they sat at table together, the small old priest and the tall youngish one might have served as the 'before and after' recommendation for some essential brand of Tonic. No one could have looked less dramatic than Father Schwemmer, whose meagre frame and grey lined face seemed to shrink almost to nothing when set close beside Father Hawthorne's virile and intrusive presence. No one could have failed to recognize the faith and calling of Father Hawthorne, whose Christlike humility was famous in five continents and could be detected at twenty paces across the most crowded room. No one, asked to choose between the two men (in any realm save simplicity) would have hesitated for a moment before stepping up to Father Hawthorne and exchanging a hearty Christian handshake.

Equally, there was no doubt which of them could make the most significant contribution to a modern world beset by modern problems.

Father Schwemmer, looking at the other man, felt almost apologetic. If this were truly a priest, then how could he himself deserve the title?

He was puzzled also as to what had brought this famous visitor, of whom he had heard so much, to the small backwater of Gamate. Nor did anything that Father Hawthorne now told him prove very enlightening.

The flies buzzed endlessly, the sun fell searchingly on the threadbare carpet, as the two men applied themselves, with varying degrees of enthusiasm, to the dish that was a staple item of diet with Father Schwemmer, and indeed with the rest of Gamate – a scraggy cut of beef, sinewy and tough, burnt brown and dry on an ancient oil stove. Father Schwemmer ate sparingly, as he had done for many years past: Father Hawthorne at first fell to with optimistic zest, and then, sighing an admirable sigh, abandoned the meat and helped himself to more mashed potatoes. They were served by a young Maula, one of Father Schwemmer's altar boys, a slow-moving, ragged youth whose heavy breathing emphasized the increasing silence and whose acrid sweat, falling from his brow and coursing down his arms, was not calculated to coax the appetite. To Father Schwemmer, he was Joseph, son of a respected parishioner, a good boy, slow but willing. To Father Hawthorne, he was an early and additional cross to be borne. But also, of course, one of God's creatures.

Having inquired his name: 'Thank you, Joseph,' said Father Hawthorne heartily, as his plate was removed. 'That was very good indeed. Did you cook it yourself?'

'*Barena?*' said Joseph, startled.

'Did you cook it?' He pointed to the meat, so much of which had clearly proved unpalatable. 'You make it hot, yes?'

'No, he did not cook it,' said Father Schwemmer gently, as Joseph disappeared through the kitchen door, intent only on taking refuge. 'There is a woman – Joseph's aunt, indeed – who cooks for me. And Joseph's father is one of my deacons.'

'Splendid,' said Father Hawthorne. 'A loyal, close-knit community ... But we must do something for them,' he went on, looking in the imagined direction of Joseph, for whom, clearly, much remained to be done. 'That is the message I have brought with me.'

'Message?' asked Father Schwemmer, uncertainly. He pushed towards his guest a wooden platter of cheese, conscious as never before of the shortcomings of his housekeeping. 'You will have some cheese?'

'Admirable!' exclaimed Father Hawthorne. 'A local peasant product, no doubt.' He took a generous cut of cheese, which was so clearly stencilled 'KRAFT' on three of its four sides that Father Schwemmer shrank within himself. 'Yes, a message,' Father Hawthorne continued, his mouth not entirely empty. 'We must bring these people the blessing of hope. We must place their problems uncompromisingly before the bar of world opinion, and let humanity be the judge.'

'Their problems?' inquired Father Schwemmer, increasingly puzzled. The noonday heat had tired him, the meal had proved, even by his limited standards, a domestic disaster, and he still had a long afternoon of visiting ahead of him. 'What problems are these?'

'Their *problems*,' insisted Father Hawthorne, chewing manfully on a piece of silver paper. 'Their racial problems, and their shocking state of servitude. The newspapers have been full of Pharamaul during the past few weeks – ' he smiled a bulging smile. 'I can assure you that your little parish of Gamate is very much in the limelight nowadays. I hope that this proposed marriage of Dinamaula, challenging as it does all the outworn concepts which are still the plague of this whole dark continent, will bring matters to a head.'

His voice went on, striking a rich and rounded note somewhere between a lecture, a television interview, and a prepared Press statement, while Father Schwemmer sank deep in confusion and doubt. He could make very little of this, and what he understood was far from the truth as he himself knew and lived it. The other man – so assured, so well-informed – was talking of the Maulas as if they were slaves, to be rescued from some degrading bondage. How could that be reconciled with the simple, uncomplicated life – primitive, yet happy – which was what he himself knew of Gamate? Which of them was right? He must have failed in his mission, he must indeed have failed in his life, if wise and good men from the outside world, weighing what had been done and what remained to be done, found the gap between them so wide, and so full of blame.

Presently, not far from despair, he took advantage of a pause.

'This marriage of Dinamaula's,' he said. 'You are in favour of it?'

'Naturally,' answered Father Hawthorne. 'In the sight of God, what could be more appropriate? This is a mixed community, black and white. What better point of fusion could there be than a marriage, hallowed by the Church, acclaimed by all but a few intransigents? What does the colour of a skin matter? We are all God's creatures, after all!'

'A horse and a cow are God's creatures,' said Father Schwemmer, gently chiding. 'Are they then to be mated?'

Father Hawthorne pushed back his chair, and gathered the skirts of his white cassock. 'Will you call a blessing?' he asked quietly.

After a moment of surprise, Father Schwemmer bent his head. '*Benedictus benedicat*,' he said.

'Amen to that,' rejoined Father Hawthorne, with deep feeling. 'And now, perhaps a little coffee, to round off that excellent meal?'

'You would like some coffee?' asked Father Schwemmer, rising. 'I am sure it can be arranged – ' his voice trailed off uncertainly as he went through into the kitchen. There was a pause, filled vaguely by speech from somewhere at the back of the house, and then Father Hawthorne, glancing out of the window, saw the figure of the boy Joseph setting out at a loping trot towards Gamate village. When his host rejoined him: 'I'm afraid I am putting you out,' said Father Hawthorne. 'I thought perhaps – er – that you would be taking coffee after the meal.'

Father Schwemmer smiled shyly. 'I fear my housekeeping arrangements are not of the best standard,' he said. 'It is good to be reminded of it sometimes. Now,' he went on, sitting down again, 'there is this question of the marriage.'

'Yes, indeed,' rejoined Father Hawthorne, with cheerful readiness. 'You mentioned a horse and a cow, I think, as an illustration of the incompatibility of black and white. Perhaps in an enclosed world such as you have here, that may seem to be a valid comparison. I can assure you that many people overseas would find such a prejudice strange, and even offensive. Possibly the longer perspective that comes with distance – ' he smiled indulgently. 'The wood for the trees, you know … Fresh ideas are stirring all over Africa, all over the world. We must not resist them. Indeed, we owe it to our conscience and our sense of justice to do all we can to aid them.'

'There are so many ways of aiding them,' said Father Schwemmer uncertainly.

'My dear fellow,' said Father Hawthorne, laying his hand on the other man's shoulder, 'I would be the last to deny that the labourer in the vineyard is doing God's work also. Your mission here doubtless does much to reconcile the Maulas to their humble station. But there must be changes, vast and far-reaching changes. No one with a grasp of world problems and world trends can doubt that.'

'This is not a world problem,' answered Father Schwemmer, with diffidence. 'It is Gamate, a small community with long traditions and a certain fixed pattern. They are not ready for "vast changes", as you say.'

Father Hawthorne raised a commanding hand. 'It is we who are not ready, we who must open our minds to new ideas, and be ready to take a step forward.' His voice assumed a sonorous note of prophecy. 'We must search our souls, we must cleanse the temple. If it is God's will that these poor folk be raised up, then who are we to blaspheme by standing in the way of that will?' He lifted his hand again, and brought his chin up to the cameras. 'I tell you, Father, that we can light such a lamp as will never be put out! Here in Gamate, we can bring the sunshine into their darkness, set bondsmen free – not tomorrow, not in the far future, but now!'

Father Schwemmer shook his head, but he said no more. He remembered arguing with Tulbach Browne on this very point, and being sure, then, of his faith and his work. Now he was less sure, and he felt older and more tired because of that uncertainty. He knew in his heart that there was a place for his mission in Gamate – a humble place, but a place none the less. But while he was striving for one thing, the world outside was apparently striving for another. Father Hawthorne was the revealed apostle of that world striving. How could Father Hawthorne, whose very name meant hope to millions, be wrong, and he himself be right – he, a poor German missionary who could not even have ready a cup of coffee for an honoured guest?

Later that evening, Father Hawthorne accompanied his host to a meeting in the village school, where Father Schwemmer held a weekly Bible class. When it was over, Father Hawthorne sat on, talking freely to whoever would listen to him, gathering round him a wondering circle who hung on his words and his fine gestures, while others, young and old, crept out of the shadows to hear and to marvel.

He talked of the future, when Gamate would be a free and happy place, having struck off the shackles of the past. At one point, indeed, he used the word 'liberation'. He told them that the Maulas had many friends in the outside world. He assured them especially that all men were equal, and that the time was near when this must be made manifest.

It was no wonder that, during all these days and nights, rumour ran through Gamate like a rabid dog, leaving in its train hysteria, convulsive fear, and fleeting unreasonable joy.

CHAPTER EIGHT

❖

Captain Crump of the Royal Pharamaul Police – jovial Irishman in khaki, happy man in love – sat at his desk in the drab living-room of his official quarters, rough-typing a report for Andrew Macmillan. Since they were of equal rank, his living-room was a replica of the living-room in the house of the District Commissioner, George Forsdick; that is to say, it contained the same number of square feet, calculated by some nameless actuary in the Ministry of Works as long ago as 1906; it had the same articles of furniture; it had an identical colour scheme (Government beige woodwork relieved by Government Floral Pattern Three wallpaper); and it had the same area of Space, Carpeted, balanced elsewhere by Space, Uncarpeted, and Space, Unroofed, Recreational.

To a man less contented, to a wife less loving, such dreary domestic algebra might have proved a fatal flaw to happiness. It did not worry the Crumps, who (like the Ronalds) would have been happy anywhere. Possibly, on this particular morning, a more cheerful room, a less rigidly dictated pattern, might have served to relieve Crump's air of worried preoccupation. But it was safe to say that no improvements, however fundamental or inspired, could have altered the facts he had to record, facts which were the only pattern that mattered, and the only thing that now concerned him.

Crump typed slowly: two fingers of the right hand, one finger of the left, with frequent pauses, frequent revision. He typed in accordance with his thoughts, which were slow, concise, and heavy with contrasting items of intelligence. He weighed here, he accepted there, he discarded or reserved elsewhere. The result was the distilled, succinct truth of a hundred reports, a thousand whispers, a score of hints and evasions. He took many chances in drawing up such a report, as he took many chances every day of his life.

A man unjustly disbelieved, a woman foolishly trusted, might be the single slender thread which could secure or snap the web of accuracy – and with it, in the long run, secure or snap the fabric of order in Pharamaul.

Crump was not daunted by such a possibility, nor by such ravelled tensions. He was not that sort of man. But on this morning, he typed slowly.

ONE, [*he wrote*] the Chief-Designate. Dinamaula has left Gamate to visit cattle posts to the southwest. He is alone, except for Mr Llewellyn (Agricultural Officer), who chanced to be touring in the same area, and is now accompanying him as adviser. There is nothing to suggest that Dinamaula is trying to gain support for his personal point of view, either in relation to his own future or the future of the chieftainship.

Under a yellow, low-hanging moon, the handful of men sat round the campfire – the fire that was a tiny prick of flame in a vast silent plain stretching many miles on either hand, until it was lost in the mist. Behind the men was a circle of confused and varied shadow – a clump of trees standing

sentinel beside the well and the small water-pan of Baraula:
a thatched reed hut for the herdboys; a darker shape that,
towards dawn, would resolve itself into two trucks placed
close together. Further beyond them was a vaguer, more
intangible, wider stretch of greyness – one of the royal
herds of Dinamaula. The cattle at long last were quiet;
round the campfire, the men talked in slow turn as the
embers settled, and the moon lifted above the rim of the
far horizon.

The scent of the night was the scent of cattle and cooling
earth – the burnt-out smell of Africa, no longer tortured by
the day's raw heat. The sounds of the night were tiny, and
quickly swallowed up in a huge stillness. The men alone
were restless, as if the small flame of the campfire warmed
their blood and stirred their tongues. But only three men
talked: Dinamaula, soon to be chief of the Maulas;
Llewellyn, the agricultural officer, present at the cattle-
well by the true working of chance; and old Paulus, chief
herdboy of this small part of the royal herd, as his father
had been chief herdboy before him, and his grandfather
(blood relation of the Great Maula) had also been in his
day.

Of the three men, one of them – Paulus – was
contented, because his chief had come to see the state of
the cattle, and the state of the cattle was good. Another –
Llewellyn – was uncomfortable, because he had blundered
by accident upon this meeting, and his orders now were to
stay where he was until it was ended. The third,
Dinamaula, was unhappy, puzzled, and angry.

The chance that had brought Llewellyn to the well of
Baraula seemed to him no chance at all, but a matter of
calculation – a continuation of the mistrustful, official
spying which had so enraged him during the last few
weeks.

He himself had come to this place – truly a pebble on the map of Pharamaul, a half-dried water-pan eighty miles from Gamate – to see old Paulus, honoured servant of his father, a man who could look at six head of cattle, chosen haphazard from the herd, and then name the sire and the grandsire of each. He had come, also, to be alone – alone and traceless under the sky of his own country, alone with simple people, alone as a chief might expect to be alone, if he wished it so.

But on the third day of his private wandering, Llewellyn the agricultural officer – the man, moreover, who had been a close witness of his shame in the bar of the Gamate Hotel – Llewellyn had driven up to the camp at the edge of the water-pan, and hailed him as a friend, and then talked secretly on the radio … It had meant the end of privacy, of the dignity of a chief visiting his royal herds; the end, indeed, of his freedom to talk and think as a chief.

Now, when he talked, he was conscious of the white man, the official, sitting cross-legged across the campfire, doubtless taking notes, doubtless listening, doubtless spying. Was there to be no end to this indignity? When was he to be chief, in fact as well as in name?

Paulus, the old man who had been an old man before Dinamaula was born, bent his head towards his chief, oblivious of tension, oblivious of any shadow on their meeting.

'Then there was the second year of the great drought,' he said, intent on his careful account. 'This water-pan of Baraula was nearly dry, even at the season of rain. A hundred and a hundred and a half hundred of cattle died that year. All their bones you will see, my chief, within a circle of a mile from the water-pan. But still the herd is good, the herd is good. It has increased – ' the old man held up four stick-like, trembling fingers, ' – fourfold since the days of your honoured father, whom God loved as we still love him.'

Llewellyn, a small dark figure across the fire, stirred and spoke: 'How big is the herd now, Paulus?' he asked.

The old man frowned, in deep concentration. 'This small herd,' he said formally, 'is seven hundreds.'

'And the others?' asked Llewellyn.

'*Barena?*'

'There are other royal herds besides the herd of Baraula,' said Llewellyn, slowly framing the laborious Maula words. 'There are five others, indeed. How big are they?'

The old man spread his hands, so that they caught the flickering firelight.

'They are of many sizes,' he answered slowly. 'At the Pula well, let us say six hundreds. At the Batwela, eight. At the Batwena, six. At the dry place, Espensa, four hundreds. At the Saksaula, best well of all, because of the great river, nine hundreds.'

Llewellyn felt his fingers moving childishly as he completed the sum. Seven hundred, six hundred, eight hundred, six hundred, four hundred, nine hundred. That meant four thousand head of cattle, in good condition, on grazing land that could well support them. Say that they would fetch, in open market, an average of twenty pounds a head. That was eighty thousand pounds – and all, by tradition and by law, belonging to the chief himself, to Dinamaula.

Across the campfire, a harsh voice interrupted him suddenly.

'I make it eighty thousand pounds, Mr Llewellyn,' said Dinamaula. 'Do you agree?'

Honesty was best in such an awkward moment; honesty, indeed, was inevitable. Llewellyn felt himself grinning in the darkness as he prepared to answer. There were no flies on this young fellow – and that, alone, could be good for the Maulas, if sharp wits could somehow be turned to proper account.

'You beat me to it, Chief,' he answered cheerfully. 'But then, you were last in school, by a good few years … Eighty thousand, I made it, yes.'

'I am no longer in school,' said Dinamaula gratingly. He longed to strike at the other man, good man though he was, friend though he might be. 'And I have eighty thousand pounds. Can you add *that* together, also?'

'I don't know what you mean, Chief,' said Llewellyn, taken aback.

'I mean that I am no longer a child, to be spied on and – and followed.' Dinamaula was suddenly enraged, as he stumbled over the words. It seemed that he could not even rebuke an agricultural officer, without being conscious of their dividing colour … 'This is my country,' he said hotly, gesturing with his hand in the half darkness. 'These are my herds, these are my subjects … If you had been here,' he went on, conscious even as he said it of a childish boastfulness, a barbarous pride, 'when I arrived at this well of Baraula, you would have seen how a chief is greeted in Pharamaul. That old man – ' he pointed, ' – fell on his knees and touched my feet with his forehead. That is how an old man greets his chief.'

After an uneasy pause, Llewellyn said: 'I know that you have loyal tribesmen. And there is no question of spying or following.'

'You were talking about me on the radio.' Again Dinamaula gestured, towards Llewellyn's big cross-country caboose, with its heavy-treaded tyres, its sleeping berth, its radio mast. 'You have all this equipment, and you used it.'

'I made a routine radio report on the police schedule,' answered Llewellyn, somewhat sharply. The Welsh accent was very prominent. 'I mentioned that I had met you here, at the Baraula well. I would naturally mention it. The Resident Commissioner would expect me to.'

Dinamaula smiled sourly. 'Oh, I know that he would expect it. What else does he expect?'

'He expects to see you as soon as you get back.'

At that there was a pause. They had been talking in English, and Paulus and the herdboys, content to be excluded from such company, had fallen back into the shadows of their exchange. But when the silence lengthened, and a faraway birdcall emphasized the unnatural stillness, one of the herdboys rose and threw a handful of dry sticks on to the fire. It blazed up, and showed their faces in sudden clarity. Dinamaula's was brooding and sullen. Llewellyn's was watchful, but ready to snap fire if need be. Opposite them, old Paulus, deaf to all overtones, seemed proud and content – proud to be with his chief, content that black man and white could talk in this fashion round a campfire, and find much to interest them. It had been so in the old days, in the days of the great hunters and great rulers; now it was so again.

Dinamaula asked suddenly: 'Why does he want to see me?'

'I think you know why,' answered Llewellyn.

'Why?'

'There is talk of your marriage. There is talk of certain changes for the tribe.' Unconsciously, Llewellyn lapsed into the Maula form of speech, even though he still spoke in English. 'You have said many things to the newspapers. Mr Macmillan wants to discuss all this with you.'

'Is he angry?' asked Dinamaula, in spite of himself.

Llewellyn shook his head. 'He is disturbed. He wants to talk to you … Chief,' he said suddenly, appealingly, 'when you talk about marriage in the way you did, it is not a good thing that you immediately go away from Gamate.'

'I am visiting my herds,' said Dinamaula.

'But even so.'

'I am visiting my herds,' repeated Dinamaula. 'I came here, and I am going to the other wells also, to talk of such things. I wish to discuss old matters, not new matters that bring trouble and insults.'

'Insults?'

'Yes, insults. If I wish to marry, that is my own affair. If I wish to choose a wife in England, that is my own affair also.'

After a moment, Llewellyn answered: 'You know that that is not so ... For God's sake, man!' he burst out, forgetting the formal pattern of their talk. 'Think what you're doing!'

'Paulus,' said Dinamaula, turning his head.

'Yes, my Chief?' said the old man.

'I will sleep now. Tomorrow we will talk of the herds, and the care of them.'

'Yes, my Chief.'

'It may be that we can increase the shelter from the sun, by planting fresh trees.'

'Yes, my Chief.'

Llewellyn stood up. 'I'll turn in,' he said curtly. 'I'm sorry that we don't agree.'

'You wish to talk on the radio?' asked Dinamaula ironically.

'No,' said Llewellyn. 'I want to think.'

'Whatever you *think*,' said Dinamaula, with insulting emphasis, 'I am not coming back until I choose to.'

TWO, [*wrote Crump, continuing his weekly report.*] Port Victoria. A meeting of the 'Maula Freedom Party' was addressed by Zuva Katsaula, Dinamaula's cousin. It was attended by about 220 persons, including Mr Tulbach Browne, *Daily Thresh* correspondent, who spoke very briefly and at one point told the meeting (verbatim quote): 'Whatever you decide to do, I can assure you that you have a lot of friends in England'. Zuva himself came near enough to advocating violent political changes in the Territory, to justify our close attention in the future. He is no longer at Port Victoria, and is at the moment untraceable.

The hall, a converted garage with boarded-up windows, a rickety platform set on trestles, and rows of wooden benches, was hot, and smelt acridly of sweat and tobacco. At the back of the platform was a faded United Nations flag, crudely stencilled with the outline of a fish at one corner. Overhead was a long paper streamer, which read: 'MAULA FREEDOM PARTY', the three words being divided also by the fish sign. Tulbach Browne, sitting in the front row, looked at it curiously, searching for clues as to the party's affiliations; but he soon found his attention wandering. The people pressing close round him, the dim smoky light, and the smell of Maula humanity, distracted one's attention from higher things ... There were no women present, and the men were a kaleidoscope of downtown Port Victoria; clerks in flashy suits and zoot ties, labourers in singlets and jeans, other men in blankets, their bare feet set solidly on the cracked concrete floor.

All of them, as they entered, had been greeted by a smartly dressed 'steward', wearing a wooden fish sign in his lapel, and using the same phrase: 'Welcome, brother.' To Tulbach Browne he had said somewhat slyly: 'Welcome, white brother,' and guided him to a conspicuous seat under the platform.

Tulbach Browne was there by arrangement with Zuva Katsaula, who had asked him to come along 'to see the democratic front in action'. So far there had been no surprises; it looked like the ordinary sort of independent political gathering, to be duplicated in hundreds of towns and cities all over the world – vague, earnest, and probably ineffective. When there was a stir at the door, and Zuva was announced, Tulbach Browne turned his head without a great deal of interest, to look at the newcomer.

The first surprise was Zuva's bodyguard, which preceded him into the hall and took up a position flanking the doorway as he entered. They stood staring at the crowd under lowered lids, their hands in their coat pockets, their whole bearing one of suggestive readiness. There were four of them, dressed almost identically in tightly cuffed black trousers, American-style check coats, and red bow ties. As they glared about them, and as Zuva, after a suitable pause, strutted into the hall, Tulbach Browne was reminded irresistibly of Sir Oswald Mosley, the British fascist leader, entering a gathering of the faithful in an East End pub, when he finally came out of prison after the war. There was the same self-conscious toughness, the same theatrical menace, the same air of semi-military, semi-gangster alertness. Among the audience too, the same down-at-heels dedication was apparent.

They stood up, they nudged each other, they clapped, they started to sing *Ekartha i Maula* – 'The Land of Maula is my Home' – in ragged discord, and then changed it to another song which Tulbach Browne could not identify. When Zuva strode towards the platform, his bodyguard lounging like lurcher dogs at his heels, many men on the aisle leant across to touch him on the shoulder.

The second surprise was Zuva's quality as a speaker – his quality, and his elusive skill. As he stood before them, good-looking, slick, self-assured, one could feel the audience settling back, prepared to allow this young man to do their thinking, talking, and acting for them, without reservation … There was no doubt that he was a spellbinder, though the spell by which he sought to bind them was relentlessly vague.

His theme was a 'new deal' for Pharamaul, a new deal that was to be won 'come what may', a new deal that was to include 'a fundamental change in Pharamaul's social structure'. So far, so good. But Tulbach Browne could not help noticing, as the spate of words multiplied and the phrases fell like warm misty rain, the infinite skill with which Zuva avoided the word or the phrase that might trip him.

He inferred that this 'new deal' would mean a struggle. What sort of struggle? Zuva never said. He warned them that they would meet with resistance. How would it be overcome? He did not elaborate. He promised 'all power to the Maula people'. What then would happen to the rest of Pharamaul – to white, non-Maulas? He offered no explanation.

If anyone in the hall had been hoping for a message of political encouragement, they got it in abundance. If anyone had been looking for sedition or the threat of force, they would have been disappointed. It was a performance so persuasive, so brilliant, and so studded with gaps, that Tulbach Browne found himself lost in speculation long before the end. Indeed, when Zuva Katsaula, pausing towards the close of the meeting, looked down at him and said: 'We have a special friend here tonight, a white friend from England. I am going to ask him to say a word to you,' it was some moments before Tulbach Browne awoke to the fact that he was expected to rise and speak.

Another man, less ready to seize an advantage, might have found it an awkward moment; Tulbach Browne showed no hesitation. He stood up, and turned towards the body of the hall. The audience craned their necks, whispering.

'I cannot make speeches,' he said, 'and with this man in the same room – ' he gestured towards Zuva Katsaula, ' – I would not try.' There was a stir of laughter, and some hand

307

clapping. 'All I want to say is that I have been very interested in all that I have heard tonight, and I will think about it a great deal. I would like to add that, whatever you decide to do, I can assure you that you have a lot of friends in England.'

He sat down to a full burst of clapping. Only the bodyguard, their faces professionally bare, their lidded eyes alert, did not join in. Zuva rose again. He was smiling broadly.

'You have all heard,' he said, 'this promise of active help, from a man who is a great power in his own country. We have many other friends who will also help us in our struggle for freedom. Soon I am going to talk with our brothers to the north.' ('What brothers?' thought Tulbach Browne, and felt his question shared by the whole audience. How far north did Zuva mean? The U-Maulas? The English comrades? The Russians? But what did it matter, so long as they were *brothers* ...) 'I would like to take with me,' continued Zuva Katsaula, 'a vote of confidence from this meeting. It will be a symbol of the vote which one day – perhaps very soon – we shall all possess. When we have that vote, we shall use it. That I can promise you, on my life.' With his two hands, he sketched the sign of the fish in the air, like a benediction. 'You know what that means,' he concluded. 'We are all sons of the fish. Give me your vote, and I will give you power in your own country.'

The applause that filled the hall was the hungriest, crudest, most whole-hearted that Tulbach Browne had ever heard.

Two men, one smartly dressed, the other blanketed and barefoot, smiled at each other on the way out.

'What is this vote?' asked the older man in the blanket. 'I do not know the word.'

'I have heard,' answered the other, 'that one puts a piece of paper into a box, and soon a man comes out, a leader.'

'But that is magic!'

'A sort of magic, yes.'

'Ow … Let us all use this vote.'

THREE, [*wrote Crump, squaring his shoulders for what he knew was the most diverse and complicated part of his report*:] Gamate. A tribal *aboura* was held to discuss various local matters, including recent rumours in Gamate. It was attended by nearly two thousand Maulas, men and women (four times the normal number), and was addressed at length by Seralo and Puero (first and third Regents). Discussion included such matters as the 'colour bar incident' at the hotel, the induction of the new chief, the possibility of changes in the territory, and the question of Dinamaula's marrying 'against the custom'. Seralo opposed the latter uncompromisingly. Puero, who seemed unusually confident, said that the Maulas should not be afraid of changes, and that the marriage of the chief, no matter to what woman, was the chief's own affair, and his choice should be backed up loyally.

There is a clear possibility of a tribal split over the marriage question. The greatest interest was shown when Puero hinted that if Dinamaula were opposed in any of his plans, he might leave the tribe. (No evidence of this.) No decision or show of hands was called for, but there was lively discussion afterwards.

The Press (who attended the *aboura*) have been very active, and seem to be concentrating on Puero, possibly advising him and suggesting various courses of action. Father Hawthorne (visiting priest, staying with Father Schwemmer) has also been active. At an informal meeting in the schoolhouse, he said (verbatim quote): 'Nearly everywhere else in the world, black men and white men are regarded as equals. If you are bold, and decide to strike off your chains, there are many people who will help you.'

The Dinamaula Regiment (young men of the chief's own age group) have been drilling outside the town, and practising the mock killing of some prisoners shut up in a hut.

Though it was high noon, the hottest and most humid hour of Gamate's lowering day, the throng on the *aboura* was vast. Lapping within a few feet of the shaded *stoep* which was the place of honour, it stretched far back under the thorn trees at the edge of the tribal meeting ground. It was an orderly throng, standing according to the custom in the ordained ranks: the old men in front, the younger behind them, the women in a wide circle on the outer edge. The sun, beating down fiercely, found little colour in the packed assembly: here and there a white handkerchief served as a protecting headdress, here and there among the brown or khaki blankets was one of a more elaborate weave – red or blue or yellow. But the general colour of the crowd was dark; black faces, black arms, drab clothing. It suited the traditional temper of the *aboura*. Words spoken on these occasions were not light words. A man with a joke to tell, a man with loose speech overflowing, did not come forward. This was a time and a place of spoken history, sometimes to become legend, always to be borne in mind.

Traditionally, the *aboura* was not an outlet for general discussion; the Maulas of Gamate assembled there to hear the words of their chief, or to listen to an official Government pronouncement, or to praise a man lately dead. Though, in theory, anyone who had something to say could walk forward and, after due ceremony, speak to the assembly, yet in practice only three or four men from the council of Regents, or from the headmen, or from the inner circle of older tribesmen, ever used this privilege. At the time of the tax troubles, a few young men had tried to gain the ear of the tribe in this fashion, and had for a while succeeded. But a new speaker had to prove his worth; he must be self-assured, and a man of a certain weight and standing in the tribe, and he must have something to say.

If any new man, trying to pass these customary portals, made a fool of himself in the *aboura*, it was a long time before he spoke again.

Proceedings at this hot noon-hour began decorously enough. Katsaula, the second Regent and the historian of the tribe, who usually opened the meetings, was ill and could not attend; in his place, old Seralo came forward to raise his hand in greeting, and to speak to the people, while Puero the third Regent, sat in the shade behind him, a fat watchful man with friends and enemies within reach on the *aboura*.

'*Ahsula!*' began Seralo, wavering, and yet impressive on account of his age and his great wisdom.

The old men, and the young behind them, called back '*Ahsula!*' in their turn. Some of the older faction bowed towards Seralo, some raised their grass-woven hats. It was a moment of formal ceremony; the people greeting their ruler, the ruler showing himself before all eyes. When – within a few weeks – Dinamaula himself assumed the mantle of chief, he would receive the same homage and courtesy, from young and old alike.

'*Ahsula!*' repeated Seralo, his wrinkled face and dimmed eyes turning this way and that as he surveyed the great crowd on the *aboura*. Then he continued the words of formal opening, long prescribed by custom. 'I am glad to see you, in the matter of the Regents of this tribe. I have some matters to speak of.'

He paused, while the throng settled itself to listen. Their number was much greater than usual, and there was an expectant air among them which no one could have missed. Yet Seralo, who knew that his task was difficult, faced them with the dignity and the settled wisdom of a ruler resting on the love and respect of his people. An old man who looked always to the law and the custom need fear nothing.

'First,' he began, when all was still, 'I would speak of our chief.'

'*Ahsula!*' came an answering shout from the crowd in front of him.

Seralo smiled. 'I see that you love him,' he said, 'as I love him. Soon there will come a day when my task is done, and Chief Dinamaula, grandson of the great Maula, will rule in my place. That day – ' he paused, ' – will be three weeks from this day.'

There was a murmur of agreement from the crowd. Three weeks was not too long a time to prepare all the ceremonies and the feasting. But it was noticed that, behind Seralo, fat Puero suddenly smirked and looked about him, catching here and there the eye of a friend on the *aboura*. There were many who felt that he must be waiting his turn to speak, and that he would speak strangely. Yet few could tell what form his speech would take, or why it should be strange. The words of a Regent of the tribe must always follow the path of custom.

Old Seralo, who could not see the face of his young brother Regent, went on smoothly enough: 'It will be a time of great rejoicing, which we will all share. But it is right for me to say that all things should have their proper measure. It will be a time for rejoicing, not a time for drunkenness. Let us take care that the honour of the tribe is not stained, on this great day. Let us set a curb to our drinking and our feasting.'

There was a mixed murmur from the *aboura*. From some of the older men, it was a sound of agreement. From those at the back, it came near to laughter. Old Seralo seldom missed his chance of pointing out the path of virtue to the tribe.

'I say these things,' went on Seralo, when all was still again, 'because I have witnessed with sorrow the growth of drunkenness among the tribe. It is not seemly to see, as we have seen in the past few weeks, men stumbling and falling, full of their beer, empty of their sense. Often it is not beer,' he went on sternly, 'but *bariaana*.' He used the Maula term for the vicious home-brew, of fermented bread and fruit, which was forbidden by the law. 'Let it be beer, and beer only,' said Seralo, with ancient authority, 'and not too much on any single day.'

Again there was a murmur, of mingled agreement and derision. Then suddenly there came a more crude interruption. From among the young men gathered in the middle of the *aboura*, a grinning youth called out, 'You say, let it be beer, and not too much beer. You say, let it never be *bariaana*. But you and the other Regents and the chief can get the white man's strong liquor, at the hotel, on any day that you choose.'

At that there was a hiss of disapproval from the older men, quickly drowned in a shout of laughter. The young man drew back, well pleased with himself. As Seralo was about to speak, in rebuke of this grave breach of custom, he heard a movement behind him. It was Puero, standing up and advancing to his side. Then Puero himself spoke, in a voice of anger and contempt, using a single sentence.

'The chief,' he said, '*cannot* get the white man's strong liquor at the hotel.'

There was now no division or doubt in the sound that came from the *aboura*. It was a growl of anger, long continued, rising from every heart. There was no man there who did not know what Puero was talking about; they all knew that their chief had been shamed before all eyes, when he went into the hotel. They knew it because it was common talk, because the new white men who wrote with the machines had repeated the story for every ear … Seralo was deeply astonished at Puero's words; for a moment he could say nothing. Then he took a step forward, in full authority, and called out to the still murmuring *aboura*: 'Let us not talk of foolish things. What was done in the hotel was done in accordance with the custom. I am surprised – ' he said, gazing in cold disdain at Puero, who was still standing at his side, ' – that Puero, a Regent, should make a complaint of such a thing. It is not the custom for any Maula man, even the chief himself, to drink with the white men. You know that. Let us not be led aside.'

'The day may come,' countered Puero, unhesitating, as if he had prepared his words for many hours, 'when the custom will be changed, and the hotel will be a meeting place for the tribe – and only for the tribe.'

Now there was stillness all over the *aboura*. Seralo had fallen back a pace, quivering and impotent in his anger. Puero's words filled the space before him.

'I have said that thing,' he went on, 'because it was in my heart. Now I will say other things. Just as the custom in the hotel may be changed, so many other customs may disappear. We have all heard talk of new matters. Let us not be afraid.' His voice was strong and bold; one forgot his fat body and gross mouth, and heard only the words of boldness. 'Why should we be afraid? This is our own country. If there is a law that we hate, let us change the law. If there is a custom that offends, let us do away with it. If – ' Puero paused, for effect and for breath, ' – if the chief wishes to do a certain thing, he is the chief and he may do it freely, while we support him. If the chief, Dinamaula, wishes a certain marriage – '

The rest was drowned in furious clamour and movement. Suddenly the younger men at the back were shouting and surging forward, as if they would invade the *aboura* and take possession of it. The older men stared at Puero in anger and astonishment; some called out curses, some spoke loudly to Seralo, telling him to bring order and decency back again. Seralo struggled to speak, while beside him Puero laughed suddenly, as if he had foreseen this tumult, and rejoiced in it. Finally, old Seralo was heard, above the lingering disorder: 'I am ashamed before the tribe,' he said, quavering, 'that such things should be said. The marriage of the chief is not a thing to be thrown from mouth to mouth. But since this man – ' he pointed to Puero, while on the *aboura* stillness fell again at the insulting word and gesture, ' – talks so freely of it, I will say this. A marriage such as we have heard spoken of, is against the custom. I do not say it is forbidden. I say it is not seemly.' The silence on the *aboura* was now deep and full of meaning, as Seralo talked of shameful, unheard-of things. 'The chief should marry one of his own race. Anything else would be an impurity. He should not wish to marry a woman – ' Seralo hesitated, and turned aside from what he was going to say. Old and full of years as he was, angry as he had become, he could not cross the threshold of tribal taboo, public modesty, and talk openly of white women or a mixed marriage. 'That is all I have to say,' said Seralo, his voice falling sadly, as was the way with old men overwhelmed by new things. 'The *aboura* is ended.'

But Puero seized the last word. Before Seralo could step back, before the men on the *aboura* made their first move to disperse, he called out: 'Hear this! If the chief is opposed in this marriage, or if he is opposed in any way, he may not wish to step up to his father's throne. A new chief who is ruled by the old men, or by Government, is no chief at all.

Indeed,' he said, on a last note of sly, mocking inquiry, 'where is our chief today?'

Then he turned and passed within the doorway at his back, while behind him on the *aboura* astonished voices broke out in violent speech, and Seralo put his hand up to his heart, and sat down as if he had taken a mortal blow.

FOUR, [*wrote Crump, squaring off his report on what seemed a satisfactory note of finality*:] Shebiya. There is nothing to report from this area.

In the deep fronded silence, among the dripping trees which made the clearing in the forest a cavern of secrecy, two men advanced to their meeting, preserving each his barbarous self-esteem. When Gotwela, chief of the U-Maulas, looked at Zuva Katsaula, the man from the south, he restrained with an effort his contempt for a black man who used the white man's clothes to assume a white man's skin. When Zuva looked at Gotwela, he saw a savage, still bound hand and foot to the jungle. It was from this black ape that his own race had sprung. When all things were settled, this black ape would disappear with the rest ... In the meanwhile, each had a service to seek from the other.

'*Ahsula!*' said Zuva formally, when the guards had withdrawn and there were only the two of them face to face, sitting within the shadow of the royal hut. 'I have made a long and secret journey to see you.'

'You are welcome,' growled Gotwela in answer. His huge sweating body, clad only in the *simbara*, the ceremonial lionskin, swayed backwards until it found the support of the reed wall of his home. His breath was beer-laden, reeking in the hot sunshine. 'Your messengers came before you, with much talk of new things. I am interested in these new things. Tell me of Gamate.'

Zuva told him of Gamate, and of Port Victoria also, while the sun, which had been high above the clearing in the forest, dipped towards the horizon, and the dank interlaced trees grew darker and more secret. The story he told was a many-sided story: it was the story of the men of the fish as he himself knew it, the new creed that was driving like a flame through many parts of Pharamaul. Of course, Gotwela already knew of the fish, said Zuva, looking at the great greasy body of the man who was to be his ally. Indeed, the story of the fish had started, in ancient days, in this very village of Shebiya ... But many others now thought the thoughts of the fish; others in Gamate, others in the white man's town of Port Victoria. There would come a moment when the fish-men of Port Victoria and Gamate and Shebiya would all join hands. When did Gotwela, chief of the U-Maulas, think that this moment would come?

'Certainly we know of the fish,' said Gotwela sarcastically, ignoring the direct question, his sweat coursing down his great shoulders till it was lost in the folds of his belly. 'Indeed, we take an oath on the fish – ' he grinned suddenly, and then laughed aloud, ' – we take an oath *through* the fish. Do you understand me?'

'I understand you,' said Zuva. His own messengers, men with keen eyes and furtive tongues, had spoken with certainty of this matter, though he himself scarcely believed it. 'I am told that you prove your manhood through the fish. I have not seen this thing.'

Gotwela grinned again, his contemptuous eyes watching the other man, the man from the Maula country, the despised south. 'It can be seen ... Indeed, if we are all to be men of the fish, then you from the south must be ready to prove your manhood in the same way.'

'My men are ready,' said Zuva grandly. 'But it may be that our fish is not the same as your fish.'

Gotwela shook his heavy head angrily, so that the sweat-drops showered round him. 'There is only one fish,' he answered roughly. 'It is the sign of freedom, the sign of bloodshed.'

Zuva nodded, warily. 'That may be so.'

'We are ready to strike,' said Gotwela. 'Are you ready?'

'Nearly ready,' answered Zuva. 'When next I come, that will be the moment to strike.'

'And Dinamaula?' asked Gotwela, coarse contempt in his voice as he spoke the name of his rival. 'That famous man? Is he perhaps ready?'

'Dinamaula is ready also,' said Zuva, casting down his eyes.

'I do not believe you,' said Gotwela crudely. 'Cowards are never ready.'

'If Dinamaula is not ready,' said Zuva, after a pause, 'then I swear that others are ready.'

'How can I believe that?'

'I swear it.'

Gotwela's heavy eyes narrowed. 'You will take the oath?'

'What oath is this?'

'The oath of the fish – *our* fish.'

Zuva swallowed. Truly, he was not ready to take such an oath, for he knew that his inner thoughts were not the thoughts of Gotwela the savage. But he needed allies, and the oath-taking might secure them. 'Let it be as you will,' he said finally. 'I am prepared.'

'You will take the oath, and prove your manhood through the fish?'

'Yes,' answered Zuva. He steeled his heart. He knew more than ever that his fish was not the same as Gotwela's fish, and yet perhaps it must become so, if the battle were to be won. He felt himself sinking back into a barbarous swamp, despised and yet welcomed. Perhaps, after all, it was not to be a brain-battle, but a blood-battle; and if that were so, then this crude man, wearing his lionskin in half-drunken splendour, was a natural ally. 'Yes,' he repeated. 'I will take that oath.'

Gotwela, his gross face gleaming, clapped his hands. From the hut behind him, an old man appeared, walking slowly on thin shanks, his eyes bitter and angry. He bowed to Gotwela. 'Chief,' he said, 'My Chief.'

'Make ready,' ordered Gotwela curtly, and rose to his feet.

Zuva rose also. Now it was as if he were moving in a dream, a dream that was a trap at the same time, a trap he dared not avoid. He knew something, by rumour, of the U-Maula initiation, the rite of the fish, by which the inner circle bound themselves and were thereby forever exiled beyond the pale of normal living, and doomed or dedicated to a path of hatred and violence. He watched, still in his dream, as the old bitter man struck a note upon a gong, and other men came out of the forest to gather round the royal hut, and a youth appeared with a huge fish-head laid out on a wooden gourd, followed by a naked comely girl who walked towards him with drugged and burning eyes, and without hesitation, as if following ritual, fastened her slim hands upon his secret parts.

Zuva, small man with ready tongue and keen brain, Zuva who thought, in a cloudy moment of self-disgust: A year ago he was in England, at the university, reading criminal law and the law of nations – Zuva now cast all this aside, and gave himself up to the rite of the fish. The comely girl, herself aroused either by some drug or by the pressing nearness of the men who crowded round, touched and stroked him with greedy hands.

She worked by rote, and he acknowledged her skill and her allure, and gave himself to it. It was as if, from the depth of the forest, an accomplished harlot had gently sidled forth, and there were no witnesses, and he was free to accept her compliance. He gave himself to her ministrations, loathing and lusting at the same time.

Presently, when all was prepared, the old man took the huge fish-head, a decaying hollow with a gaping mouth, and placed it over the secret parts of Zuva Katsaula, while the youth, lathered with excitement, lowered the gourd and held it under the mouth of the fish. The girl, her body shaking, continued to stroke and touch him. He heard, as in a fantastic dream, the far-off voice of Gotwela, thick and guttural with communicated lust.

'Say after me ...' The girl stroked and touched, the men who had come out of the forest watched, hard-breathing, equally roused, equally doomed. 'I, Zuva Katsaula, swear – '

Zuva repeated the words, his body arched over the head of the fish, and the waiting bowl.

' – that as I prove my manhood now – '

Zuva began to sweat, and to move rhythmically.

' – so will I kill every white man in my country – '

The girl was smiling at him, herself near to writhing crisis.

' – and so will I drive them out – '

The men pressed round him, the youth held the empty bowl, the girl grasped him with firm lascivious hands.

' – out, out, out – '

His head swam, as the sun smote hot on his loins. The girl's hands moved as he himself was moving, the fish-head enclosed him like a sheath.

' – out of my country, out of my body – '

As he stared downwards, the eyes of the fish met his own. Its jaws were widened, by the swelling of his secret parts. The girl, crouching by his side, was groaning as she worked.

' – till nothing is left – '

All was turning red before his eyes. This truly was the moment of triumph.

'– but the force of the spear – '

The spear, the spear.

'– and the seed – '

The seed, truly the seed.

'– the strong seed of our race – '

The girl screamed suddenly, the men bore down on his shuddering loins, the youth lifted the bowl. Zuva's body writhed, the fish-head gaped. Then it was over, and the bowl was swept high in the air like a holy offering, while all around the slackened body of Zuva Katsaula a barking clamour rose, shaking the very leaves of the forest.

II

David Bracken, roaring with laughter, paused long enough to ask: 'But what happens? We can't fill a whole afternoon, just by staring at each other and eating ice cream.'

'Well, it's a garden party,' answered Aidan Purves-Brownrigg. He sat back in his chair, immaculate and cool, pleased with his audience – David – and the happy choice of phrase which had set the latter laughing. 'They all arrive, bang on time, at four o'clock. Naturally, the Diplomatic Corps have the Private Entrée.'

'Huh?' queried David.

'They slip in by the side door, past that *sordid* lavatory. There aren't many of them, as you know: the South African consul, the French commercial counsellor – my dear, what he does with his duty-free champagne – that sweet man Lou Strogoff, and the honorary representative for Poland.'

'Which Poland is that?' asked David, interested.

'Impossible to say,' said Aidan. 'He's been here since 1906. He's a cousin of Paderewski … They're all dressed up, of course. You'll see one or two frock coats, *école de Edward the Seventh*. Then there's the town council, in a body. They wear chains, like slaves. Then there's everyone else, mostly in flannels and *blazers*.'

'How long does it go on for?'

'About three hours. The band play their ten tunes, including "A Life on the Ocean Wave" – so appropriate. People walk about, the old gentleman shakes hands, the local debs are presented. First the tea runs out, then the ice cream, then the lemonade, then the guests. H E used to have a bar operating after six o'clock, but it turned out to be a mistake.'

'How was that?'

'One year the nurse got paralytically drunk and started taking everyone's temperature with a cheese straw.'

'What nurse?'

'The *nurse*. There's always been a nurse in attendance, ever since 1925. *Not* a good year, 1925. One of the debs had a miscarriage.'

It was scarcely an appropriate moment for the Social Secretary, tremendous in flowered chiffon and a cartwheel hat, to poke her head round the door and say lugubriously: 'Mr Bracken, I'm in trouble.'

David, struggling with laughter, rose to his feet. 'I'm sorry to hear that. Can I help?'

'The first guests will be here in less than an hour,' said the Social Secretary. She made it sound like an imminent, catastrophic annunciation. 'Among them will be the *Press*. All those *new* names ... Of course, I sent them all cards, but I don't *know* them from Adam. Who is to introduce them to His Excellency?'

'Just let them filter through,' said Aidan flippantly. 'Like the tide coming in.'

'Mr Purves-Brownrigg!' said the Social Secretary. 'You *can't* be serious.

'I know most of them by sight,' said David. 'I'll lead them up, if you like.'

'Will you?' said the Social Secretary.

'I'll be glad to.'

'You do see my position, don't you?' said the Social Secretary earnestly. 'I sent them cards, because they all signed the Book. But I don't *know* them.'

'I'll introduce them,' David reassured her again.

'That will be very kind,' said the Social Secretary.

'As a matter of fact,' said Aidan, 'if we're having this Press conference afterwards, it doesn't really matter if they're actually introduced at the party. H E can meet them all later.'

'Mr Purves-Brownrigg,' said the Social Secretary, 'you know very well that that would not do at all. It would mean that they would be wandering about the grounds *without being introduced*. At the Garden Party! A Press conference – ' she sniffed, ' – is quite a different matter.'

'It's liable to be,' said Aidan caustically.

'All those new names,' said the Social Secretary, in unflattering despair. 'Such a difference from other years … And there's another thing.'

'What?' asked David.

'I drew a line under the names in the Book, yesterday. I always do. So that no one can sign at the last moment, and get an invitation to the Garden Party.'

'And?' prompted David.

'This morning,' said the Social Secretary impressively, 'underneath the line, someone drew something else.'

'Do tell,' said Aidan.

'Someone drew a fish!'

The Government House Garden Party pursued its well-established pattern. At one end of the lawn, under the oak trees, the band played mournful and patriotic airs – the

Port Victoria town band, nine black men resplendent in frogged hussars' uniforms, commanded by a spectacled conductor whose military shako and blazing epaulettes could not disguise a certain studious terror. Opposite them, the trestle tables, laden with lemonade, tea, ice cream, and wilting cucumber sandwiches, attracted an increasing throng. In the centre, under the pillared portico, the Governor, in dazzling white uniform topped by a helmet plumed with red and white cock's feathers, held his court. He was supported by Lady Vere-Toombs, whose huge hat, tasselled parasol, and *bouffant*, ankle-length lace dress, struck all hearts with intimations of social doom.

A receiving line formed automatically. First came the members of the Diplomatic Corps, who had already been greeted inside Government House, but who now returned for a second, more public accolade. At their head was the *doyen* of the Corps, the French commercial counsellor, a wizened cynical man with the look and pace of an ancient tortoise, followed by his wife, a deadpan blonde who affected the airs of Paris, but whose *chic* was the *chic* of off-season Biarritz. Next, treading lightly, smiling gently, came Lou Strogoff, the American consul – an old man at ease in an environment he trusted. Next, the Honorary Representative for Poland – courtly, trembling with ague, clad in an ancient frock coat, and borne down by the weight of a spreading white moustache which recalled (according to one's age and one's recollection of history) the Duke of Wellington, Marshal Pilsudsky, the old Kaiser Wilhelm, or a superannuated Battle of Britain pilot. Among the onlookers, it was freely forecast that he could not possibly last another year. There were some, indeed, who doubted if he could last this one.

Lastly – because he was newly appointed – came the South African consul, Mr Quintus de Kok. Mr de Kok, an ardent politician who was awaiting his turn to enter

Parliament, suffered from one considerable defect which might, in other circumstances, have prejudiced his chances of diplomatic preferment; he spoke an English so halting and so malformed that many people, confronted with its guttural chaos, further confused him by saying, apologetically: 'I'm terribly sorry – I only speak English.' He was followed by Mrs de Kok, a vast woman whose monumental bosom and fantastic flanks excited particular admiration in Pharamaul. Whenever she appeared in public, she was always followed by respectful Maula glances. Every Maula man knew, and admired, a bargain when he saw one. This one was certainly a bargain ... Whatever *lobola* the high-born white man had paid, whatever crushing tally of sheep and goats and cattle, this woman was worth it. A giant wife such as this promised endless pleasure, many fine sons, much hard work in kitchen and field. Ow ...

Hard on their heels came the twenty-four town councillors of Port Victoria – twenty-one white, three black – in robes of russet brown and chains of gold; the suspect Metropolitan Bishop, who sold dubious Ethiopian passports on the side, but was still (by a margin far thinner than his person) acceptable at Government House; and such notables as William Ewart O'Brien, the editor of the *Times of Pharamaul*, Mr Rogers, the bank manager, and his wife, Mr and Mrs Burlinghame, and Miss Cafferata. The line moved forward slowly, trying not to keep in step with the band, which presently abandoned 'Greensleeves' and embarked on 'Body and Soul' with crushing nonchalance. The Governor gently massaged his knuckles, pinched and sore from many handshakes. The Press correspondents were presented, led towards the Governor by David Bracken: Tulbach Browne, Axel Hallmarck, Pikkie Joubert, John Raper, and finally – trailing light meters and shedding flashbulbs – Noblesse O'Toole and Clandestine Lebourget.

The Social Secretary eyed them with cold disdain. Lady Vere-Toombs signalled for a fresh glass of lemonade. A man in an old, faded Royal Flying Corps blazer failed to see the edge of a flowerbed, and measured his length among the zinnias. Father Hawthorne made a theatrical appearance, staring about him like an eagle of executive rank, his white cassock swirling as he advanced, his suede sandals exciting a rustle of comment. The sun burned fiercely down, while under the wide shade trees a decorous conversational uproar broke out.

Then, at a sign and a ragged flourish of trumpets, the season's debutantes were presented – twelve girls in identical powder-blue dresses and long white gloves, coming forward to curtsey and pass on. Two of them were pretty, and were promptly seized on by assorted admirers; one made an over-ambitious curtsey, and spent the rest of the afternoon striving to conceal an ugly green patch on her hip; the rest were at that stage of doughy inelegance which only a mother could love. John Raper of the *Globe*, from a strategic position at one side of the dais, eyed them hopefully; his eyes gleamed when one of the girls, stumbling in her curtsey, displayed several inches of prime interior thigh; but presently he was cornered and borne off by Anthea Vere-Toombs, leaving the field to lesser connoisseurs.

There was over all the wide garden and the static throng a certain leisurely dignity. This was the Garden Party – formal, dictated by tradition and protocol, and yet appropriate to Pharamaul and the season of the year. The Governor, his cock's feathers nodding, moved among his guests, smiling easily, greeting a curtsey or a bow with a gracious inclination of his head. His staff, impeccably tail-coated, kept one eye on his beckoning finger, the other on guests who in past years had proved themselves awkward, or argumentative, or dull. The household servants, in their yellow robes, their scarlet tarbooshes, their tasselled sashes of office, moved about also from group to group, serving cooling drinks and sandwiches with deferent skill.

The band played 'Men of Harlech', and 'The British Grenadiers'. The sun bore down, piercing even the trees, while a myriad ants fought for lawn-space among the trampling feet. The pattern was the same as last year, and the year before. It was the Spring Garden Party. Next year it would be just as good, just the same as today.

Under a strategic tree, well shaded from the heat, within easy reach of the tea urn, the lemonade jugs, and the sandwich trays, the LADIES reviewed the proceedings. They were Miss Cafferata, Mrs Burlinghame, and Mrs Rogers; Mrs Simpson, the wife of the naval aide-de-camp, and Mrs Stevens, wife of the First Secretary. They all wore long dresses, picture hats, elbow-length gloves, and parasols. They were flushed with the heat, excited and intent on the scene around them. It was Miss Cafferata's twenty-seventh Garden Party; it was Mrs Simpson's third; it was Mrs Stevens's first. But they all shared the same appetite, the same avid nose for the unusual.

'Who was the girl who tripped up and showed her pinkie?' asked Mrs Simpson.

'Her *what?*' countered Mrs Rogers, prepared to be scandalized.

'American slang,' explained Mrs Simpson briefly. 'It means anything you don't want people to see.'

'Have you known many Americans?' asked Miss Cafferata.

'Enough,' answered Mrs Simpson, who had once been whistled at by a drunken and presumably desperate GI in Piccadilly.

'Her name is Thompson,' said Mrs Burlinghame authoritatively. 'Her father runs that big furniture shop on Albert Street.'

'Well, of course,' said Miss Cafferata, 'if they're allowing *tradespeople* into Government House ...'

'It's really a very nice shop,' interposed Mrs Stevens pacifically. Mrs Burlinghame's husband, who sold blankets on a large scale, was technically a tradesman; the topic was a delicate one. 'I always think that if a shop's big enough – ' she floundered, while an edged silence fell on the group. It was ended by Mrs Rogers, who sought to break new ground.

'The Governor looks so distinguished, doesn't he?' she said, glancing across the lawn to where Sir Elliott Vere-Toombs was talking to an attentive ring of guests. 'But where is Anthea? I haven't seen her at all.'

'It's a reasonable certainty,' answered Mrs Simpson, 'that she's somewhere with that awful reporter. The fat one with the roving eye.'

'Mr Raper,' said Mrs Burlinghame.

'*Such* a funny name,' said Miss Cafferata delicately. 'If I had a funny name like that, I think I'd change it.'

'Why don't you?' asked Mrs Simpson, with a loud laugh.

'I beg your pardon?' said Miss Cafferata. Her tone was frigid. 'I don't understand that remark at all.'

'Meant to be a joke,' explained Mrs Simpson. 'Sorry.'

'I am sorry,' said Miss Cafferata, with immense aplomb. She rose, her long dress swirling, her parasol at the ready. 'I think I will take a little walk.'

'Now, dear – ' began Mrs Rogers, but Miss Cafferata had already moved out of earshot.

'You shouldn't have said that,' said Mrs Burlinghame reprovingly. 'She's very sensitive, we can't all have *ordinary* names you know.'

'Meaning exactly what?' asked Mrs Simpson menacingly.

'Just what I say!' snapped Mrs Burlinghame.

Mrs Simpson rose and swept off in the direction of Government House. The diminished party – Mrs Rogers, Mrs Burlinghame, and Mrs Stevens – looked at each other uncertainly.

'It's the hot weather,' said Mrs Rogers presently. 'We're all friends *really*, aren't we?'

'I've never liked that woman,' said Mrs Burlinghame, still aroused.

'For some reason,' said Mrs Rogers, gazing round her, still searching valiantly for a neutral topic, 'it all seems rather different, this year.'

'There are an awful lot of Press people,' said Mrs Stevens.

'And more niggers,' said Mrs Burlinghame. '*Four* ... There were only two, last year.'

'It's the way things are going, I'm afraid,' said Mrs Rogers. She lowered her voice, her eye on the nearest Maula servant, a tall youth who was handing a tray of sandwiches with an air of enormous preoccupation. 'Do you think that Dinamaula will really marry a white girl?'

'Disgusting,' exclaimed Mrs Burlinghame.

'My husband says,' said Mrs Stevens, 'that it's all a newspaper story.'

'What decent girl could *dream* of such a thing?' asked Mrs Burlinghame.

'A lot of people *dream* all sorts of things,' said Mrs Rogers, with vulgar emphasis.

'I said "What *decent* girl",' said Mrs Burlinghame.

'I believe some women find them very attractive,' said Mrs Rogers, 'in certain ways.'

'Of course, if that's the way you feel – '

'I said "*Some* women",' said Mrs Rogers edgily, copying Mrs Burlinghame's own phrase.

'If you give an inch,' said Mrs Burlinghame, 'you give *everything*. Do you *want* to give everything?'

'Don't be ridiculous,' said Mrs Rogers.

'Don't be loose-minded,' said Mrs Burlinghame.

Mrs Rogers rose. She was a tall woman; her husband was a bank manager; the day was very hot. 'Just because your husband sells blankets,' she said, with concentrated spite, 'you mustn't take it for granted that *all* our thoughts are *all* about beds *all* the time.'

In the deep silence left by Mrs Rogers's departure, Mrs Stevens looked at Mrs Burlinghame. It was Mrs Stevens' first garden party, and she still hoped to enjoy it.

'I think I would like an ice,' she said tentatively.

'One of the boys will bring it.'

'Oh, I'll get it myself.' Mrs Stevens rose in her turn. 'Will you be all right?'

'Yes,' answered Mrs Burlinghame, aware of total victory – victory which she had not planned, and yet could not refuse. 'I shall certainly be all right.'

'I don't think that anybody *meant* anything,' said Mrs Stevens appeasingly.

'Whether they did or they didn't,' answered Mrs Burlinghame, 'we certainly don't want any unpleasantness. After all, this is the Spring Garden Party.'

The pattern was the same, and yet not quite the same. In one sense, it was just another Garden Party – possibly the sixtieth, possibly the sixty-fifth, since the function was first inaugurated at the turn of the century. In such a pattern, only the people could change. There would be new guests, as some died and others grew up; a new Governor (Sir Elliott Vere-Toombs was the seventh since 1882), new members of his staff, certainly new servants. But there could be nothing new about the *Party*, as such.

And yet, in another sense, this year's Garden Party was entirely and disturbingly new. First, there was the situation in Pharamaul, of which no single guest could be unaware. Everyone present had read the astounding news story in the *Times of Pharamaul*; and everyone present included the servants, who by now must surely be looking at the women guests with new and speculative eyes. If Dinamaula, chief-designate of the Maulas, were really going to marry a white woman, then any Maula must feel himself free to seek a bride from the same white race. That meant that the man who handed you a plate of sandwiches was possibly planning to propose, a little later in the day; it meant that he was looking at your body, not with the dead eyes of a native servant, but the live eyes of a man. That, in itself, was a change so degrading and so horrible that the very fabric of the Garden Party seemed threatened thereby with disaster.

But above all, there were this year's *new people*. There were too many new names – at least, so thought the Social Secretary, as she pursued diligently and yet forlornly her task of seeing that all went off without a hitch. For the first time in many years and many different countries, her heart was not in it ... The new people (apart from the Thompson girl, who had slipped in as a debutante by virtue of her father's bank balance, and promptly disgraced herself by that *revealing* curtsey) – the new people were chiefly the members of the Press; and everyone knew what they thought about Pharamaul, what they had said about it, what they were trying to stir up. It was a downright shame that they had to be invited. They didn't even know how to behave. They were laughing at everything. They would go away and write awful things about it. They would spoil it all. Indeed, they didn't even pretend to act like normal guests at all. Just look at them.

Clandestine Lebourget and Noblesse O'Toole, unusual figures in any surroundings, were really an extraordinary pair, when set against the formal background of a Government House Garden Party. In deference to this occasion, they had abandoned their corduroy slacks in favour of print dresses bought hurriedly and carelessly at one of the Port Victoria stores; they even wore hats, following a hint from the Social Secretary – hats of thick cream straw, decorated with false Michaelmas daisies, edged at the brim with scarlet piping. On Noblesse O'Toole, a small woman with a neat figure, the effect was tolerable; on Clandestine Lebourget, the print dress and the flowered hat sat like a child's toy *howdah* on a full-sized elephant.

Many who saw them thought that there was to be, this year, some departure from the normal, and that these two were performers, who would presently withdraw behind the scenes, and then, at a roll of drums, make a low-comedy entrance down the main steps, perhaps playing guitars, perhaps spinning ropes or juggling with coloured balls. They could scarcely be guests ... When Clandestine Lebourget and Noblesse O'Toole presently dropped their anonymity and started taking photographs, it still did not seem a sufficient explanation for all the wonder that had gone before.

They took a photograph of the Governor, his cock's feathers nodding, talking to the Honorary Representative for Poland. They took one of the debutantes curtseying, and two quick snaps of the luckless girl who subsided on the grass during her presentation. They took one of a line of Maula servants awaiting the signal to serve sandwiches; one of the perspiring band plugging its way through the

'Skaters' Waltz'; and one of the hinder end of Mrs de Kok, as she lowered herself in massive obeisance before the Governor. Then, looking about for further targets, Noblesse O'Toole nudged Clandestine Lebourget, and pointed.

'Get him,' she said, out of the side of her mouth. 'That one we can't miss!'

'That one' was Father Hawthorne, whose lean granite face and billowing white cassock were a focus of attention wherever he went. At the moment that Noblesse O'Toole pointed him out, Father Hawthorne was scornfully eating fruit salad and ice cream, and talking, scarcely less scornfully, to Lady Vere-Toombs. His suede-sandalled foot was going tap-tap-tap on the hard-baked lawn as he surveyed this idle woman, this worthless bird of paradise, clearly drunk with power and position, who queened it at her garden party in brutal disregard of poverty and discrimination. It seemed that, within a few moments, he must surely cast away his plate of ice cream and fruit salad, twin symbols of luxury and fascist reaction, and begin to cleanse the temple.

Clandestine, festooned with apparatus, edged forward, but Noblesse O'Toole checked her.

'Hold it,' she commanded. 'Plenty of time. He's sure to do something real crazy before long.'

'Such as?'

'Christ knows! Make a speech – climb a tree – free the slaves. I know this guy. He just is *not* Garden Party material. We've only got to wait.'

Father Hawthorne, leaving Lady Vere-Toombs with an ironic bow, strode obliquely across the lawn towards the nearest serving table. His tall figure, theatrically garbed, seemed to cut a swathe through the lesser human beings standing in his path. Whiter and more virginal than any garden-party dress, wider and more dramatic than any crinoline, his cassock clove a historic pathway through the mob ... The old Maula servant – the Governor's headboy Simeon, gnarled and grey as the tree trunk at his back – could hardly believe his eyes when Father Hawthorne stopped in front of him and said, with a wide smile: 'How are you, my brother?'

'*Barena*?' Simeon stepped back a pace before this strange onslaught. He had been about to take up a tray of lemonade, and as he stooped, his alarmed old eyes fixed themselves on Father Hawthorne. '*Barena*?'

'How are you enjoying yourself, on this fine afternoon?'

'Lemonade, *barena*?' Simeon, uncomprehending, offered the tray.

'Let me take that from you,' said Father Hawthorne. Simeon grew seriously frightened. He looked swiftly about him, aware of attentive eyes, aware also of Lady Vere-Toombs watching him across the heads of the crowd. Perhaps the *barenala* had said that the service was too slow, and had sent this man in the bedclothes to rebuke him.

'Sorry, *barena*,' he said humbly. 'Too many people ... You take lemonade?'

Father Hawthorne shook his head. 'I just wanted to ask you if you are happy.'

'*Barena*?'

'Are you well?'

'Yes, *barena*.'

'And your wife?'

'Wife dead ten years, *barena*.'

'I'm so very sorry,' said Father Hawthorne. 'You have children, perhaps?'

'Son and daughter,' said Simeon, still far from understanding but ready to follow the white man's lead. 'Son killed in war.'

'I'm so very sorry,' said Father Hawthorne again.

'Daughter no good.'

'Indeed?'

'In prison with baby.'

'Ah.'

'Lemonade, *barena*?' asked Simeon.

Father Hawthorne reached out his hands. 'Let me take that tray,' he said again.

Simeon surrendered it, unhappily obedient. The *barenala* must be very angry, if the white man was taking his tray.

'Sorry, *barena*,' he repeated. 'Too many people.'

'I will help you,' said Father Hawthorne. 'Our Lord did not disdain to serve at the feast of Cana in Galilee.'

Tray in hand, he turned, and made towards the nearest black guest in view – the Metropolitan Bishop of Port Victoria. When he reached the other man's side, he inclined his head, and offered the refreshments.

'Monseigneur,' he said courteously, 'will you partake?'

The bishop, his eyes rolling, stared at Father Hawthorne, wondering what this fantastic gesture could mean. His conscience jerked to an anguished attention. Perhaps the man in white was a policeman or an informer, perhaps the lemonade was drugged … Then he reached out an uncertain hand. From somewhere nearby, a flashgun exploded.

'I thought it only right,' said Father Hawthorne, with an understanding, infinitely compassionate smile, 'to share the burden of the heat of the day with the labourers in the vineyard.'

Tulbach Browne and Axel Hallmarck, natural allies in this benevolent climate, summoned all their talents as they talked to Lou Strogoff, the American consul. Word had spread among the overseas correspondents that here, amazingly, was a weak link in the chain of criticism and comment; that this was a man, an American, who had lived for twenty years in a British colony, and still retained a lively admiration for his surroundings. Axel Hallmarck had become accustomed to American officials who exhibited a curt impatience with all things British; Tulbach Browne had his own highly developed contempt for every aspect of colonial rule. Piqued by so unusual a tolerance, they sought to undermine and to deride it.

'Glad to see you, Mr Strogoff,' said Axel Hallmarck, by way of introduction. 'Heard a lot about you … You've been here a long time, I understand.'

'Twenty years,' answered Strogoff courteously.

'I've been here just six weeks,' said Axel Hallmarck.

'Yes,' agreed Strogoff. And added: 'I had hoped to meet you earlier.'

'I've been pretty busy.'

Strogoff inclined his head. 'I have no doubt of it. But as far as possible, we like all American visitors to check in at the Consulate, directly they arrive.'

Hallmarck grinned. 'All that protocol …'

'If you happened to get into any sort of trouble,' returned Strogoff equably, 'you might be glad of it.'

Tulbach Browne, aware of a budding antagonism, closed in. 'Well, it's a nice garden party, anyway … I see that you take it all pretty seriously.'

'Excuse me,' said Lou Strogoff formally. 'I don't understand you.'

'The tail coat,' said Tulbach Browne. 'You seem to have trotted out all the trimmings.'

Surprised, Lou Strogoff looked down at his clothes. He was indeed formally dressed, in tail coat, striped trousers, and tall hat; his dignified bearing made them seem the most natural garb in the world.

'It's the Spring Garden Party,' he said coolly, after a pause. 'This is what people wear.'

'They call that a claw-hammer coat, back home,' said Axel Hallmarck.

'I know,' answered Lou Strogoff. 'But I still can't think of a reasonable alternative, for a formal occasion.'

'Don't you think that that kind of striped-pants diplomacy is on its way out?'

'No,' said Lou Strogoff.

'We'll have to have you investigated!' said Axel Hallmarck, cheekily.

'Un-American activities,' explained Tulbach Browne.

Lou Strogoff said nothing. He had a glass of iced tea in his hand. He sipped it slowly, looking over the heads of these young men, so far removed from his own generation, so far from his own brand of thought and feeling. Inconsequently, he felt happy that this division was so wide. He had no sense of having been left behind. Indeed, it seemed that it was these young men, mocking, tough, and unattached, who had themselves been left behind, trapped in a lonely Limbo, a web spun from the most forlorn kind of human indiscipline. More than ever, he felt himself content with an old-fashioned label, an old-fashioned piety.

'Of course, all this sort of thing,' observed Tulbach Browne, 'is hopelessly out of date, even in England.'

'I'm sorry to hear that,' said Lou Strogoff.

'You're *sorry*?' queried Tulbach Browne, unbelieving.

'It's something that suits Pharamaul,' explained Lou Strogoff. 'I'm sorry if it doesn't suit other places.' He looked squarely at Tulbach Browne. 'But isn't there still a garden party, at your own Buckingham Palace, two or three times a year?'

Tulbach Browne shrugged. 'I believe so.'

'And that is out of date?'

'Completely.'

Lou Strogoff raised an inquiring eyebrow. 'You mean that it should be discontinued? I didn't know that your paper took such a radical standpoint.'

At that, Tulbach Browne paused. Strogoff's remark was an awkward one – as it was intended to be. The *Daily Thresh* did indeed stand for progress in all directions – it was traditionally anti-Colonial, anti-conservative, anti-House of Lords. But it was at the same time tremendously pro-monarchy; it always treated the Royal Family with horrible condescension, as if they were its favourite performers in some global variety show, of which the *Daily Thresh* had a majority percentage. It would never be true to say that the *Daily Thresh* took a stand against Buckingham Palace garden parties (to which the aged peer who owned the paper was inevitably bidden). It might dislike every other aspect of tradition. But it certainly liked Royalty. As Tulbach Browne paused, Lou Strogoff pursued his advantage.

'Today we are the guests,' he said, 'of the Governor of Pharamaul. He is the Queen's personal representative in this part of the world. If you accept his hospitality, then you should be prepared to dress according to protocol.'

'I meant,' said Tulbach Browne, somewhat weakly, 'that all the stuffed shirt side of it is out of date.'

Lou Strogoff smiled bleakly. 'You use these easy phrases, but you do not follow them through. To you, "stuffed shirt" presumably means formality and old-fashioned tradition. You don't like them. But you would be completely shocked if, at a Buckingham Palace garden party, the Queen appeared in blue jeans, or the Duke in corduroy slacks.'

'This isn't Buckingham Palace.'

'It's an extension of Buckingham Palace. It is part of the Queen's own hospitality.'

After a long pause: 'I never thought,' said Axel Hallmarck austerely, 'that I'd hear an American citizen talking that way.'

'Young man,' answered Lou Strogoff, 'it is sometimes a matter of courtesy to be un-American.'

'But all these servants,' insisted Tulbach Browne. 'The world just isn't like that any more.'

'How many servants have you?'

'None, of course.'

Lou Strogoff shook his head. 'Nonsense. You employ at least twenty, every day of your life. The woman who makes your bed in the morning. The waitress who brings you your meals. The bus conductor who gives you a ticket. The driver who takes you to work. The doorman who says good morning. The elevator man who takes you up to the sixth floor. The stenographer who types out your letters. The boy who collects your copy. The girl who brings your coffee. The waiter in the restaurant who serves you lunch. The man behind the bar. The hat-check girl. The sub who works on your daily column. The compositor. The Linotype operator. The distributor. The man who drives the truck that delivers the paper. The man who sells it. The taxi driver who takes you home. The telephone girl who wakes you up next morning ...' He paused, somewhat out of breath. For him, it was a considerable speech. 'All these, and dozens of others – barbers, salesmen, shop assistants, radio announcers – are technically your servants. You couldn't last a single hour without them. They all live and work, so that you can write something every day in the *Daily Thresh*. All these people – ' he gestured round him, ' – live and work so that the Governor of Pharamaul can run this country, as the Queen's own representative.' He smiled wryly. 'If I had the choice, I know whose servant I would be.' His tall figure, formally clad, suddenly commanding, straightened as he put down his glass and prepared to move. 'In fact, I am a servant,' he said, 'the servant of the American people. You are a servant, the servant of an editor, and a newspaper owner, and four million readers. Even you – ' he turned unexpectedly to Axel Hallmarck, ' – are a servant, a servant of *Clang* magazine. And if you do not write exactly what *Clang* wants you to write, you would be an out-of-work servant. You must have thought of that,' he concluded acidly, 'otherwise you would not write the way you do.' Then he turned, and was gone, a formidable victor in a field that had seemed, earlier, to promise quite another outcome.

Mrs de Kok, mountainous in blue satin, every inch – indeed, every foot – the wife of the South African consul, talked to her fellow countryman, Pikkie Joubert. They talked in Afrikaans, because that was for both of them their natural tongue. It was not the only thing that they shared. Inevitably, they talked of Dinamaula's rumoured marriage. They spoke of it in the same sense as ninety per cent of the other white inhabitants of Pharamaul. Only the phrasing was different, because the feeling behind it was different also.

'Damned *kaffirs!*' said Mrs de Kok malevolently. 'They want shooting, that's what they want!'

'Do you think the marriage will go through?' asked Pikkie Joubert.

'Yes,' answered Mrs de Kok. 'I wouldn't be surprised if it did. Nothing would surprise me, the way this country is run.'

'But people here don't like the marriage, either.'

'Of course they don't like it,' sneered Mrs de Kok. 'But they do nothing about it. It's not even illegal! Man, they don't deserve to have a colony here!'

'It's the British way of life,' said Joubert sarcastically.

'Don't tell me about the British,' returned Mrs de Kok, with tremendous violence. 'My own mother was in a British concentration camp. They tried to poison her with fish-hooks – fish-hooks in the bloody corned beef, man! And they put ground glass in the sugar – I've seen it myself, in the museum at Bloemfontein. They hired the British Red Cross to do it. But my mother was too smart for them.'

'What happened?'

'She refused to eat any of it. She ate nothing for six whole weeks. In the end they had to let her go. The commandant himself came up and said: "You can go home, *Mevrouw*. You're too smart for us." That shows you how the British rule a country. I heard,' she added, 'that they all ran away during the war, too.'

'Where was that?'

'Ach, some place up north in the desert. They had a lot of nigger soldiers fighting for them, and the nigger soldiers threw their guns in the ditch and ran off, and the British ran away too, and by God they got back home before the niggers did!'

'I hadn't heard that,' said Pikkie Joubert.

'Man, it was all over Pretoria …'

A Maula servant approached them, with a loaded tray. As he offered it, he bent a respectful glance upon Mrs de Kok. Among the Government House servants, she was always a focal point of interest; today, as usual, she was by far the largest woman at the garden party, costing – they said – seven hundred head of cattle and a thousand goats, and shouting curses whenever she was angry … Mrs de Kok inadvertently caught his eye.

'Boy!' she said loudly.

'*Barenala*?'

'Take that God-damned tray away! I don't want it.'

The Maula servant, startled and yet gratified, withdrew. He was not at all put out. A woman so highly priced could well afford to talk in this fashion.

'Bloody *kaffirs!*' said Mrs de Kok. 'They're everywhere, man, everywhere!'

Aidan Purves-Brownrigg, David Bracken, and Nicole Steuart met almost guiltily under a tree at the further side of the main lawn. They felt guilty because such a respite was something that they were specifically not entitled to enjoy; their orders, implicit or official, were to watch the Governor at all times, in case he might need help or relief, and otherwise to Mix with the Guests. But after an hour, both these things had palled; they found themselves under the same tree as if drawn there by a beckoning thread. Together, the three of them were by far the most distinguished group. David wore a black morning coat, Aidan a pearl-grey one with a high stock; Nicole looked completely ravishing in a formal dress of pale blue.

'So nice of you to come,' said Aidan, ridiculously, as the three of them drew furtively together. 'I *know* how busy you are ... Don't you think the lemonade is absolutely stunning?'

Nicole giggled, then looked about her nervously. 'We really shouldn't be doing this,' she said. 'You know we're not meant to talk to each other.'

'If that's the worst thing you children have on your conscience,' said Aidan cheerfully, 'then you needn't worry.'

It seemed natural for Nicole and David to catch each other's eye at that moment, and then look swiftly away.

'Our consciences are clear,' said David, after a moment's silence.

'Crystal clear,' said Nicole.

'Crystal,' said Aidan, 'is being worn a trifle *cloudy* this year.'

But it was true, thought David, as he looked again at Nicole, admiring frankly her face and her figure, recalling (as he easily could) the warm texture of the one, the candid shapeliness of the other; their consciences were clear, because they were past the edge of love, and already felt themselves to be deeply bound to each other. But perhaps it was time for that feeling to be declared. He remembered, with a kind of tender astonishment, their last meeting, a little more than twenty-four hours earlier. Then, they had had lunch with the Stevens' – a sketchy meal made nearly intolerable by the demands of the four Stevens children.

The grimy, tattered, and ill-organized appearance of these had seemed to sound the knell of family life, though Nicole seemed unaffected by it, and by all that went with it. One of the children had turned sulky, and had refused to come to the table at all; one of them had all the unlovely symptoms of a heavy cold; the third, having spent the first course resolutely patting its mashed potatoes into the shape of a house, had screamed with rage when refused a third helping of fruit salad; and the fourth – the youngest, a few months old – had positively beamed as it rounded off the meal by 'having an accident' of copious proportions.

When this happened, Mrs Stevens had said fondly: 'T'ch! T'ch! All down your wooden leg!' Nor was Nicole in the least put out by this domestic lapse. Perhaps women – even the prettiest women – really didn't mind these things. Perhaps one had better marry them after all …

David was interrupted in his daydream by Aidan's remarking: 'Have you seen that *splendid* Mrs de Kok? She must have put on at least fifty pounds since last year. What a *monster!*'

'I believe she's very kind-hearted,' said Nicole.

'Don't you believe it!' answered Aidan. 'She'd drive us all into the sea, if she had the chance. And *what* she'd do to those wretched blacks!'

'H E is in good form,' commented David presently.

'I wish he'd conserve his strength,' said Aidan. 'He's going to need it, at the Press conference.'

'Do you think it will be difficult?' asked Nicole.

'Yes,' answered Aidan. 'I think it will be *crucial*. And it's much too important to make a mess of.'

'But he's got all the answers,' said David. He and Aidan had been working hard on a Press brief for the Governor, during the last few days. 'You know that.'

'He's got all the answers,' agreed Aidan, 'but he may not have all the questions.' He sighed. 'One can't think of everything, particularly where the Press are concerned. Some of these people could tie him up in knots, if they really got going ... Oh well,' he said, his hand going up to his stock, his slim shoulders squaring, 'we'll know the worst in about an hour ... I must start prowling again.'

Nicole looked about her. 'So must all of us. I just caught Lady Vere-Toombs's eye, from over there.'

'But she's about fifty yards away,' protested David.

'It's her favourite range,' said Aidan, 'and still one-hundred-percent lethal.' He began to sidle away, out from the shade into the sun, calling over his shoulder: 'Bless you, children! Behave yourselves.'

Alone, happy in isolation, Nicole and David looked at each other.

'Hallo,' said David. 'You're looking really lovely.'

'You're looking very smart, too.'

'Blue suits you.'

'Black suits *you*.'

'Will you marry me?'

After all, it was as easy as that.

William Ewart O'Brien, editor of the *Times of Pharamaul*, sprightly old gentleman in a wonderful frock coat with watered silk lapels, talked to his social editress, Miss Sproule. Miss Sproule, a tall angular woman who had been his mistress for thirty years but was now (as he was) finally let out to pasture, was busy taking notes as they talked. She attended, and reported, the Garden Party every year. The *Times of Pharamaul*'s account hardly varied by a paragraph from decade to decade. But still she managed to write her annual version of it as if from a breathless, dewy enthusiasm.

'Strolling on the spacious lawns,' scribbled Miss Sproule, 'the guests partook of the ample refreshments hospitably offered by their affable host, His Excellency Sir Elliott Vere-Toombs. The extensive grounds, as usual, were at their very best. Splendid displays of massed zinnias – '

William Ewart O'Brien was far from happy. He was almost certain that he had been directly slighted – not by the Governor, whose manners were impeccable, but by several of the guests. They had seemed to avoid his eye – even to turn away and whisper at his approach. It must be that damned article of Tulbach Browne's. True though it had turned out to be, and backed up by independent evidence from many other sources, yet it had been a mistake to feature it so prominently in the Times of Pharamaul. At the club, they were even saying that he had come out in favour of the marriage ... He turned to Miss Sproule.

'Tilly,' he said, unhappily.

'Yes, Mr O'Brien?' In public, their relationship was still rigidly formal.

'Don't mention the Bishop of Port Victoria.'

'All right,' said Miss Sproule, abstractedly.

'Or the coloured town councillors.'

'Good heavens!' said Miss Sproule. 'What do you take me for?'

'Concentrate on the debutantes.'

Miss Sproule nodded vaguely, her pencil busy. 'The bevy of charming young girls,' she wrote, 'who had the honour of being presented to His Excellency, struck all beholders with their rare grace and beauty. They seemed like a veritable bouquet of perfumed blooms. As the band played a stirring fanfare – '

'Tilly,' said William Ewart O'Brien again.

'Yes?'

'Better leave out Father Hawthorne, too.'

High above the Garden Party, on the third floor of Government House, two figures, intimately entwined, looked down on the proceedings below. They looked down on top hats, panamas, bald heads, wide-brimmed confections of lace and straw; they looked down on black men in flowing robes, fat men in blazers, tall women in long dresses, dumpy girls in bulging satin gowns. They watched groups coming together, other groups separating and going their ways; they watched lonely men repairing forlornly to the tea table, unassimilated women staring at space, debutantes valiantly pretending that they did not mind an hour-long isolation. They watched the progress of the Governor, as his nodding cock's feathers clove a gentle, swaying path through the throng. They watched a crisis at the lemonade table, and some sort of scuffle at the side door of Government House. They watched from their high vantage point, their bodies closely linked, their elbows resting on the rough stone windowsill. They watched in companionable silence, while the sun drew slowly westwards, and the crowds below them perceptibly thinned.

'I ought to go down,' said John Raper presently. 'Looks like the end. You know there's a Press conference.'

'Yes,' said Anthea. 'Poor Daddy ...'

'Oh, he'll be all right.'

'Do you think so?'

'No,' answered John Raper. 'I don't. It was just an expression.'

'Like "women and children first".'

'Just like that.'

Mrs de Kok lumbered into view, her vast blue dress billowing round her like an ill-anchored tent.

'What a big girl,' commented John Raper.

'Have you ever had one like that?'

'Yes,' answered John Raper readily. 'In Singapore, in 1932. There was the damnedest woman singing in a nightclub. Must have weighed over three hundred pounds, all done up in ostrich feathers and sequins. She used to sing *"All of me, why not take all of me?"* We did that.'

'You bastard,' said Anthea fondly.

'Then there was another very big woman in Berlin, just before the *Anschluss*. She – '

'All right,' interrupted Anthea. 'I don't really want to know.' She looked down, at the burnt lawn and the melting crowds, the Maula servants who were beginning to collect glasses and cups and plates. 'This is nearly the end, I think ... How long will the Press conference last?'

'Depends,' said John Raper. 'If there's a row, a couple of hours. If nothing happens, about twenty minutes.'

'Can we have dinner afterwards?'

'Maybe.'

'Did you miss me when you were in Gamate?'

'All the time,' answered John Raper, turning. 'You too?'

'All the time.'

They kissed and embraced, briefly and professionally.

'I like your bedroom,' said John Raper. 'Such a wonderful view of the grounds.'

'Have we got time?' asked Anthea.

'Yes,' said John Raper. 'If you don't dawdle.'

'I'll be quick as a flash … And then we'll have dinner?'

'Yes.'

'And then do this again?'

'Yes.'

'Darling, why are you such a good lover?'

'I work for such a good newspaper.'

The last guests caught the Governor's eye, bade him farewell, and made for the main gates. The staff rallied and came together, under a deserted elm tree that sheltered a table spread with derelict coffee cups and plates of biscuits. Under another tree, the Pressmen also drew together, waiting for their private audience. Under a third, Father Hawthorne, magnificently isolated, stared at space as if it were a heathen congregation. Nothing was going to keep him from attending this Press conference … The trampled lawn started to breathe again, the flowerbeds could at last be seen. The very last guest of all, Mrs Burlinghame, noticed a curious fact as she got into her car; on the main gateposts, under the Royal coat of arms, some child or vandal had chalked a criss-cross pattern vaguely resembling a fish.

Sir Elliott Vere-Toombs, approaching his staff with a gallant smile, took off his plumed helmet and smoothed his hair.

'I think it all went off very well, don't you?' he said cheerfully. 'It's always a dreadful bore, of course, but people *do* appreciate it. Now I suppose we'll have to have our wretched Press conference.'

III

There were many different versions of that Press conference, in many different newspapers; indeed, much of it passed into journalistic legend, with yearly, increasingly ribald accretions, so that later, if a man remarked: 'I was at that first Pharamaul Press conference,' he was likely to be asked: 'Is it true that the Governor said "I would rather see my daughter dead at my feet than marry a black man", and John Raper leant out of her bedroom window and started applauding?' There were many different versions, some written by the same man for different newspapers; Pikkie Joubert, for example, called the situation 'a challenge to white supremacy' when filing copy for the South African News Service, but he used the phrase 'reactionary colour-bar tactics' when cabling his story to the liberal newspaper for which he also served as African correspondent. There were many different versions; it would be wrong to say that, from their synthesis, an accurate picture emerged, but at least it was a picture that delighted many a spiteful heart, scandalized many a grim breakfast table.

The *Daily Thresh* (Tulbach Browne reporting) made it the high-water mark of its 'Spotlight on Pharamaul' series. This, it said, was what happened when reaction was allowed to flourish in a concealed corner of the Commonwealth. Pharamaul, struggling towards the freedom it had earned, found itself blocked by aged nincompoops and youthful official flunkeys. It recommended three cures; one, the immediate granting of independent status to Pharamaul; two, a declaration that mixed marriages such as Dinamaula's would receive automatic approval from Her Majesty's Government; and three, the compulsory retirement of Colonial civil servants, whatever their rank, at the age of fifty-five.

Glimpse Magazine (Clandestine Lebourget and Noblesse O'Toole contributing) produced a special eight-page feature on the garden party and the Press conference. The focal point of this was a full page picture of Father Hawthorne offering a tray of lemonade to the black bishop of Port Victoria. The caption read: 'Good Samaritan to the Rescue', and underneath: 'But for the kindly intervention of Father Hawthorne, this man would have gone without refreshment for over three hours. Reason? He was a black man at a white man's party.'

Father Hawthorne, returning hotfoot to his hotel, forthwith made and despatched a tape-recording of his impressions – a recording put out, within forty-eight hours, by 117 North American stations. He was deeply shocked, he said, by conditions in Pharamaul. He would not rest until these glaring social wrongs had been righted. It reminded him of South Africa, British Guiana, and certain parts of Ceylon. It cried to Heaven. He stood aghast. The imagination sickened. Men of good will could not stand idly by. The bar of history would decide. The Great Governor of us all ... This was Father Hawthorne, reporting for the Lord from Pharamaul.

John Raper of the *Globe* (who appeared to have missed most of the conference, and to have misunderstood the rest), said that it pointed up the timeliness and the urgency of the *Globe*'s 'Find a Bride for Dinamaula' competition. The whole country, he said, was behind the *Globe* in its search for the ideal candidate.

But it was *Clang*, as usual, that produced the most readable version, trimmed down to a diamond pattern, pre-digested to the very last adjective.

'The gardens of Government House,' wrote Axel Hallmarck, 'were at their plutocratic best. Garden boys (aged fifteen to sixty-five), disciplined by a hard-riding major-domo, scurried to and fro, putting the finishing touches to the heat-loaded borders. Sweating black servants (paid, in accordance with Pharamaul's strait-jacket economy, at one-third the rate of their poor white competitors), tended the mounds of sandwiches, the jorums of lemonade and ice cream. Dowagers beamed or glared. Debutantes curtseyed. Pharamaul society perspired and chattered. Newspapermen (allowed in as a democratic concession to British protocol) lurked in the bushes.

'When the formal fun had dragged to a close, reality returned (for a brief spell) to Government House, while the Governor, Sir Elliott Vere-Toombs, KBE, etc., his scarlet cock's feathers a-droop, held a Press conference. There were many who saw, in those drooping cock's feathers, a drooping hold on this long-subjugated corner of the British Empire. After the washy lemonade and the lumbering debutantes, it was a comforting thought – for those who recognized comfort when they saw it.

'The Governor, surrounded by top-hatted aides, did his best on what he would undoubtedly have called a sticky wicket, what? At times sidestepping, at times disastrously frank, he may not have known that he was giving the assembled company a blueprint of the colonial mind.

'Everything in Pharamaul was going jolly well, insisted the Governor. There were one or two agitating fellows about, of course. But nothing serious. A colour bar? Nothing of the sort. But naturally a black man couldn't drink with a white chap, eh? That was going a bit too far.

'Progress? Of course there would be progress. Jolly good thing, progress. Not too much of it at a time, though. That would be a jolly *bad* thing.

'What about Dinamaula's ideas for social development? They would be taken under consideration.

'Communism? Never heard of it. Outside interest in Pharamaul? Always glad to see visitors, of course, provided they signed the book. But there was no good stirring things up, what?

'What about Dinamaula's marriage? The Governor hadn't heard anything definite.

'What if he did? The Governor smiled toothily. That, too, would be taken under consideration.

'The aides, top hats at the ready, eyed the Governor admiringly as he produced, with antique faded charm, his answers. At a decent distance, the servants cleaned up the tables, collected the lemonade glasses, chattered covertly among themselves. Taller than the rest, Captain Simpson, the naval aide-de-camp (*Clang*, October 28th) beamed vacantly round him, smoothing his elegant white uniform, glancing fondly down at his liberal fruit-salad of medals.

' "Pharamaul?" he had said earlier. "Haw! All right, don't you know, in small doses. Good chance of a scrap, if the niggers get uppish. But my wife doesn't really care for it, what? Haw!"

'The Press conference petered out. The aides bowed low as the Governor withdrew. Reality, which had peeped through here and there, retreated as if ashamed. Pharamaul slept – until tomorrow.

'Tomorrow might come very soon for Pharamaul, lotus-eating British colony on the verge of a headlong collision with history.'

CHAPTER NINE

❖

When old Seralo, after hasty and doubtful conference with his fellow Regents, decided to call the tribe once more to the *aboura*, he did so with the words of a ruler, but the quaking heart of a child. There were three things he knew. First, that there was great trouble in the tribe. Second, that at the heart of the trouble lay the chief, and the marriage of the chief. Third, that though Dinamaula was to assume the chair of rule within a few days, those few days could not be left to the idle passage of time. He himself was still the first man in the Council of Regents, and the troubled tribe had need of his counsel and his hard words of admonishment.

There was a fourth thing that he guessed at, and a fourth thing that he came to know in full certainty, as soon as he stood up to face the restless, murmuring crowd on the *aboura*. The fourth thing was that his power was ebbing away from him like the rattling breath of a lion torn by spears, and that in its place was an ugly emptiness. Into that emptiness might step a single strong man – Puero, the third Regent, or Dinamaula himself; or else white Government, intent on re-establishing the pattern of order; or chaos itself, wearing the bloody mask of mob rule.

He wished in his old heart that there was a fifth thing that he knew. The fifth thing would be that peace and decency would return again, at a word from himself, a magic and binding word which would be taken up and acclaimed by all the assembled tribe. But he no longer had that authority, nor that magic. At his back sat Katsaula, an ill man still, and troubled by conflicting thoughts; and Puero, who might seize the moment and turn it to gross advantage. Before his eyes, restless like the waters of the dam at the time of flood, was the whole concourse of the Maulas. The burning sun was not less hot than their temper. Caught between these two forces, the one uncertain, the other violent, his ancient body trembled and his old head grew pinched and of no account.

But even he, on whom wisdom and authority still sat, was not to know that within the space of a short hour, the flood waters would turn to a muddy raging torrent, no longer to be controlled by a single man or a single thought.

At the end of that short hour, he knew. By then, his astonished eyes and ears had witnessed shameful things that should never fall to the lot of an old man near the end of his rule and his life.

Even as he spoke the accustomed words of greeting, he heard the young men in the middle of the *aboura* chanting in chorus: 'Where is our chief? Where is our chief?'

He heard the scream of the women, in unheard-of interruption, taking up the chant.

He heard an older man, a man of the first rank, not given to foolishness, propose that no taxes should be paid until Dinamaula was installed as chief, and his rule accepted by white Government.

He heard Puero at his side making a long speech on the marriage of the chief, saying that whatever woman Dinamaula chose should be accepted by the tribe, without question.

He heard the utmost divided confusion break out when those on the *aboura* understood what was being said.

He heard himself say, in a voice not strong, that such a marriage was against the custom.

He saw Puero's contemptuous smile, and the answering laughter from the young men.

He heard another headman, from a nearby village, saying that such talk was not seemly, and should be ended.

He heard the uncle of Miera, the former chosen bride of Dinamaula, say that all Maulas would be shamed unless the chief married one of his own race.

He heard a further wave of coarse laughter from the young men, and silence from the women, and yet another headman declare that his people would rather leave the tribe than countenance such a marriage, which was impure.

He saw fighting break out at the edge of the *aboura*, between some of the young men and some of the men not so young. He heard his own reedy voice call for peace and order, and knew that his voice was powerless.

He saw Katsaula, the second Regent, rise with a face of innermost sorrow, and heard him declare that tribal custom made it necessary for them all to accept whatever the chief did, without question, and without further discussion.

When a young man called out: 'Even a white woman?' Katsaula answered: 'Even so.'

He heard another young man ask, in the deep ensuing silence: 'What shall we do if Government forbids such a marriage?' and he stood aghast as the whole middle ground of the *aboura* broke into angry, sustained cursing and shouting, and the older men in the foreground stood sullen and muted, shaking their heads.

He heard vile laughter as a small child on the edge of the *aboura* called out, mimicking: 'No white woman, no taxes.'

There had never been a more shameful moment, in all the seventy years of his life.

He heard himself calling for silence and order, and then say: 'It is not seemly to decide these matters in open *aboura*. I and the other Regents will take counsel.'

He heard Puero say, insultingly: 'I have given my counsel.'

He heard Katsaula say, with sorrow and grim duty in his voice: 'I have given my counsel.'

He saw a movement at his side, and turned, and watched in terrified amazement as Dinamaula himself appeared on the balcony at the front of the *aboura*, while the whole huge crowd burst into a scream of welcome and homage. Even though the young chief said nothing, simply standing there under the fierce sun in grave stillness, yet Seralo knew that he was accepting this moment, and the confused salute of the *aboura*, and that from this tempest could come nothing but bloodshed and sorrow and shame.

Yet when Seralo strove to speak and voice these thoughts, his words died in his dry throat, while at his side Dinamaula stood nobly presented, and before them the Maulas of Gamate, in full *aboura*, roared their acclaim in wave after wave of thunderous tumult.

Andrew Macmillan was dozing in his chair when the telephone rang. Caught between sleeping and waking, his heart gave an uneasy leap at the harsh sound. He looked at the clock on the mantelpiece. It was ten o'clock, and through the undrawn curtains he could see that full darkness had come to the Residency garden. The phone rang again, and he reached out for it.

'RC,' he said.

He heard a voice say: 'Andrew? – Keith Crump here.' Without the label, he might not have recognized it; Crump's voice was taut, and he seemed to be breathing fast. Behind the voice was the staccato tapping of a typewriter, and behind that a vague murmuring, like the sound of a crowd over the rim of a hill.

'What is it, Keith? Where are you?'

'Down at the tax office. I'd have called you earlier, but things blew up suddenly.'

'What things?' asked Macmillan harshly.

Crump reacted to the harshness. His voice became more controlled, measurably more formal. 'There's been a bit of a riot down here, sir. I think it's OK now, but we had a sticky session for a time.'

'What happened?'

'They got hold of some waggons down on the *aboura*, and overturned them, and set alight to a couple of them.'

'Who is "they"?'

'The young chaps. The Dinamaula Regiment. The waggons belonged to the headmen who spoke against the marriage, this afternoon.'

'What happened then?'

'A lot of fighting. One of the headmen was knifed in the groin. He's in poor shape. And one of my chaps got beaten up pretty badly. We had to make two baton-charges.'

'Why the hell didn't you call me?'

'Sir, it blew up so suddenly. And – ' Crump's voice took on a small edge of pride, ' – we got it under control again, after a bit.'

'What's the position now?'

'They're drifting away. There's still a lot of noise, but my chaps are keeping them moving. The waggons are burnt out. I'm having a report typed.'

There was silence between them, while the telephone wire hummed, and in the background the noise of the crowd was heard on a low note of discord.

'Was Dinamaula there?' asked Macmillan.

'No. None of the Regents were showing themselves. It just started with some drinking at the back of the tax office, and then they made a rush for the waggons. But one or two of our Press friends were on hand, *very* punctually.'

'Taking any part?'

'No,' answered Crump again. 'Just watching. Enjoying it, obviously. Father Hawthorne did a bit of first aid.'

'Is it really quiet now?' asked Macmillan after a pause. 'Do you want me to come down?'

'There's no need for that, Andrew.' They were back on a normal plane once more, after the disquieting moment of anger. 'But I think you'll have to give them a pep talk, fairly soon. Otherwise it's going to happen again.'

'You couldn't pick out any actual ringleaders?'

'No. I've got about a dozen of them in the cooler, but they were no worse than the rest. I've booked them all on riotous assembly. We might be able to pin the knifing charge tomorrow, if the headman recognized anyone – and if he recovers.' Crump paused. '*Will* you talk to them, Andrew?'

'Yes, I'll talk to them,' answered Andrew Macmillan grimly. He leant back in his chair, no longer sleepy, no longer rendered indecisive by doubt of his own capacity. This was something he could surely deal with … 'Get on to George Forsdick, first thing in the morning – or now, if he's still awake. I want Seralo to call an *aboura* – my official *aboura* – for tomorrow afternoon. Five o'clock. All the Regents are to be there, and the headmen. Can you rig up the public address system?'

'Yes, we'll lay all that on.' Now Crump sounded cheerful and confident, catching Macmillan's forceful change of mood. 'What about Dinamaula?'

'He is officially invited to attend.'

'I doubt if he'll come,' returned Crump. 'There's a lot of talk that he's not going to say anything, or do anything, until he's confirmed as chief. Then he'll really go into action.'

'What action?'

'Marriage. Reforms. Taking things over generally.' Crump hesitated. 'It's a bit vague at the edges, and I wouldn't like to swear to it on paper. But I get the impression of a plan of campaign, something a bit more subtle than the usual Maula shennanigans. It could be something that Dinamaula has worked out for himself. Or it could be those Press chaps, telling him how to go about it.'

'Dinamaula's no fool, on his own.'

'Educated in England,' answered Crump sourly. '*My* income tax.'

'I'll fix Dinamaula,' said Macmillan brusquely. '*And* the Press, if I have to. A few deportation orders would work wonders. The first one of those lads I hear talking out of turn will end up on the plane for Windhoek. And that goes for Dinamaula, too.'

There was a vague noise at the other end of the telephone, and a third voice was faintly heard.

'That's my sergeant,' said Crump after a moment. 'The *aboura* is pretty well clear. They've called it a day.'

'Suits me,' said Macmillan. 'I'll see you tomorrow, Keith. Fix up that *aboura*, as I said. And come down to my office about midday. There are one or two other things I want to work out.'

'All right,' said Crump. He paused. 'There's just one thing, Andrew.'

'What's that?'

'They're in a funny mood.' Crump's voice was careful. 'So are the Regents. So is Dinamaula. It might be a mistake to get too tough.'

'The mistake so far,' said Andrew Macmillan coldly, 'is that we haven't been tough enough. We'll change all that tomorrow. And Master Dinamaula and I are going to have a very instructive meeting, if things don't go exactly as I want them.'

II

A silence altogether too decorous, too perfect, greeted Andrew Macmillan as he stepped forward from the shadow of the balcony overlooking the *aboura*, and showed himself to the assembly. This formal appearance was something which he organized very rarely – once a year at Christmas time, and occasionally when there was some special proclamation to be made, like the King's death or the birth of an heir to the throne; and it should have been a moment of dignity and solemn ceremony. All the stage dressing was correct. Behind him, on one line of chairs, sat the three Regents – Seralo, Katsaula, and Puero – and the chosen headmen of the Maulas; level with them on the other side were George Forsdick, his District Commissioner, and Llewellyn the agricultural officer, and Captain Crump, resplendent in freshly-pressed khaki uniform, the butt of his revolver gleaming in the sunshine.

Below them, too, the setting was authentic. There was a huge crowd on the *aboura*, ranged in rank according to the custom; the older men in front, the young men behind them, the women and children on the outskirts. There were many policemen, posted like sentinels at the rim of the *aboura*. There was a small knot of Press correspondents, including a movie-camera crew which had driven in from Port Victoria the previous night.

There was, in fact, everything that the Resident Commissioner was entitled to see, when he summoned the chiefs and the tribesmen to his official *aboura*. There were all the trappings of authority, there was an assembled crowd, there an air of expectancy. The pedestal microphone of the public address system stood waiting for him. He had only to raise his hand for a police orderly to come running. He had only to speak, and many hundreds of men and women would listen attentively. But Andrew Macmillan knew, as soon as he stepped forward, that he had suddenly become a hated man.

He had seen it happen so many times, in small gatherings and in large ones, and had met it so often himself, that there could be no mistaking. He did not need, for proof, the total, mutinous silence which met him as he stepped forward. He did not need the eyes of the headman Amtauro, a firm friend, turning aside from his own. He felt the sullen, rocklike wall of dislike, as soon as he came into full view, and it was enough for him.

It was enough for him in many ways. He had certain things to say that afternoon, and he was going to say them. The people he had to say them to were Maulas – Maulas in a bad mood, but Maulas none the less: Maulas whom he had known and loved for thirty years, Maulas whom he distrusted profoundly, Maulas whom he laughed at, Maulas who, a few hours ago, had been engaged, many of them, in a bloody riot on this very *aboura*. (The stabbed headman had died during the night; that meant that there was a murderer loose among the crowd as well.)

He had these things to say, as part of his duty as Resident Commissioner, and as part of his conviction as a man; and the mood of the people he was addressing counted for nothing with him. He was not preparing to argue with adults, or to wheedle with children, or to bribe malcontents. He was going to tell the assembled Maulas of Gamate what they were going to do next, without alternatives and without equivocation.

If, divining this, they had already turned sullen or sulky, that was no surprise and no bar to plain speaking.

'*Ahsula!*' began Andrew Macmillan formally, his hand touching the pedestal of the microphone, his tall tough body standing trim and erect before the crowd. His deep voice, magnified many times, rolled across the width of the *aboura*, while the absolute stillness continued. '*Ahsula!* ... I bring you loving greetings from your mother the Queen.'

He spoke in the Maula tongue, and the opening phrase was ceremonial and trite; nevertheless, a murmur of respect greeted his words. To most of the vast throng who heard his greeting, 'your mother the Queen' meant Queen Victoria, their true mother, enshrined perpetually in love and honour. Even the smallest Maula child knew that this was the far-off queen whom the Great Maula had visited long ago, exchanging gifts, swearing loyalty, making safe their lives for ever. Maula the Great was dead, but the old Queen still lived on (it was said), and still loved them, and still bore children who sometimes visited them as a pledge of protection.

The murmur of homage for the name of the great Queen was the last sound that greeted Macmillan. Thereafter his words – heavy, cold, and grim – fell like stones upon a vast silence, the stillness of hatred.

'I have some matters to speak of,' he began formally. 'Listen, and take heed ... There is great unrest in Gamate. Last night there was fighting against the forces of Government, and a headman was killed. He was a man of honour, who had spoken his thoughts freely before the *aboura*, as he was entitled to do. His killing shames the whole tribe ... Those taking part in the fighting will be punished. If the man who did the killing is caught, he will be hanged.'

The silence grew in intensity as he spoke, drawing coldness from his cold tones. Behind him, the Regents and headmen sat with faces of stone. Crump was frowning, looking straight ahead of him. Forsdick, his red face flushed, stared across the *aboura* to the small crowd of Pressmen gathered under the camel-thorn tree. He saw that Voice Tula, the interpreter, stood at the centre of the knot, and that they were all writing busily, and the movie cameras were turning. To hell with the lot of them!

'There are many other heavy matters,' continued Macmillan. 'Taxes are being paid too slowly. Cattle are being withheld from Inspection. There is too much foolish talk, too much rumour. The tribe is divided.'

'I say this!' he declared, raising his voice, looking about him. 'If you have complaints to make against any man or any law, state them according to the custom. Tell your chiefs and headmen. They will tell the Regents in council. The Regents will tell me. I will listen, and deal justly.'

He spread his feet slightly, and put his hands on his hips. His tall body seemed to grow in stature and toughness. 'But I will not listen to foolishness,' he said harshly, 'and I will not tolerate disorder! There is to be no more violence in Gamate, no more foolish talk, no more bearing of rumours from hut to hut. That is the way of women! You are men. Behave like men.'

Now his whole bearing took on an air of forceful contempt. 'Soon you will have a new chief at the head of the tribe. He is not here today –' Macmillan's tone was ironical, ' – but he knows well what is in my mind ... It may be that the idea of a new chief, and what he will do, is unsettling to the tribe. But a new chief in Gamate does not mean new things, nor any great changes. There will be no great changes in the tribe, and nothing will be done that is against the custom ... That I tell you plainly, so that there may be no more doubt.'

A thousand pairs of eyes gazed back at him as he spoke the last few phrases. All knew that he talked of the chief's marriage, and that his words were very heavy. But the heaviest were still to come.

'It may be,' he went on, slowly and weightily, 'that the idea of a new chief, and new prospects, is too unsettling, and divides the tribe. I will consider that matter ... If it seems to me that the tribe is deeply divided, and the moment for change is not yet come, I will ask your mother the Queen to wait some time before the new chief is proclaimed.'

He paused for a long moment, hands still on hips, his bleak face stern and unbending. Then he said. 'That is all. The *aboura* is ended.'

Behind him the Regents and the headmen rose to their feet, their faces impassive, their eyes downcast. Flanked by Crump and Forsdick, Macmillan turned, and walked through the first few rows of the older men, towards his car. A few of them raised their woven beehive hats as he passed, but not a sound could be heard, nor any other movement. When he reached the edge of the *aboura*, he saw the Pressmen breaking ranks, as if at a signal, and begin weaving swiftly through the crowd towards the Regents, while all round them the whole concourse came to sullen, murmuring life again.

That night it was George Forsdick who telephoned him, towards midnight. Macmillan had been waiting for the call, ready dressed, his car and driver alerted; none the less, the sound of the telephone shrilling through the silent house startled him painfully. He put his hand on his hammering heart, glad that there was no one to witness his weakness. He must be getting really old ... Then he lifted the receiver.

'RC,' he said, as before.

'It's me,' said Forsdick immediately. His voice was urgent, clear of alcohol, tense with feeling. 'I'm at the tax office. I think you'd better come down, Andrew.'

'What is it this time?'

'They've fired some huts at the back of the *aboura*. It's all under control now. But the police are having a tough time, breaking up the fighting.'

'Where's Crump?'

'Outside somewhere.'

'Hasn't he got enough men?'

'Yes. He had them all standing-to, like you said. But part of the Regiment made a diversion, somewhere up by the hospital, and then another gang started setting light to the huts. There were about a dozen of them burning before the police could get back on the job.' Macmillan heard an odd fading note in Forsdick's voice, as if he had turned his head away. Then it came back again, in full strength. 'Now that's funny,' said Forsdick, puzzled. 'It's suddenly gone absolutely quiet outside.'

'I thought I heard a shot,' said Macmillan, with foreboding.

'So did I,' said Forsdick. 'But there was such a hell of a noise across there ...' They both waited, in the charged silence. 'I was right,' said Forsdick presently. 'It's all gone as dead as a doornail.'

'I'll come down,' said Macmillan. 'Wait for me by the tax office door.'

'Better bring a gun, Andrew,' said Forsdick. 'Just to be on the safe side.'

'No,' said Andrew Macmillan curtly. 'I haven't had a gun in my hand for twenty-five years, and I'm not going to start tonight.'

It took him a minute to get to his car, five minutes to drive downtown, another minute to cross the *aboura* – but already an unearthly stillness had settled over Gamate. His headlights picked out a few shadowy figures here and there, but they melted soundlessly into the cover of the grey trees and the huts, as he passed. Near the tax office a hut was still burning fiercely, and there was an acrid smell of smoke in the air. All else was profoundly still.

Forsdick ran out as his car drew up at the tax office.

'Someone's been shot,' he said, his voice queerly constrained. 'A Maula kid of about ten. Back there by the burning hut. Then they all ran away. That's what the sudden silence was.'

'Who did the shooting?'

'Only Crump has a gun,' said Forsdick.

Macmillan called out to his driver: 'Turn the car. Point the lights *there*.' As the man obeyed, and the car's headlights swivelled, he walked forward towards the knot of men, standing and kneeling, who had suddenly come into view.

The headlights, and the flickering fire from the burning hut, showed him a scene full of menace and ill omen. A Maula child, half-naked, lay on the ground, in the ungainly stillness of death, the blood already drying on the deep wound in his throat. Crump and a policeman were looking down at him. By their side was Tulbach Browne, and Clandestine Lebourget who, even as Macmillan approached, took a flashlight photograph of the scene and then walked away while his eyes were still blinded. Kneeling beside the dead child, murmuring gently, was a white-cassocked figure – Father Hawthorne.

'Keith,' called out Macmillan as he drew near.

Crump turned slowly. In the lamplight, his face was stricken. There was blood on his tunic, sweat on his overwrought face. It was the first time that Macmillan had ever seen him less than cheerful, less than lively, and the change was mortal.

'He did it himself ...' Crump's voice was constricted, and he cleared his throat. 'He was in the crowd when we charged. He must have reached up and tried to take the gun from my holster. It went off as he pulled it out.'

'Are you sure?' asked Macmillan harshly.

'Certain,' said Crump, a little more strongly. He raised his arm, and wiped some of the blood off his chest. 'I had a cane in my right hand. This cane. I never went near the gun. There wasn't any need.'

There was a sudden movement nearby, and they all turned. A woman on the edge of the clearing, silhouetted by the burning hut, was shouting and wrestling with one of the policemen, seeking to evade his grasp. Macmillan called out: 'Let her through,' and she shambled forward at an unsteady run, her voice breaking into piercing screams as she saw the body of the child on the ground. Then she threw herself down, in whimpering agony, by the side of the corpse.

Father Hawthorne raised his head. 'May God forgive you all,' he intoned.

In the deep foreboding silence, there came Tulbach Browne's stony voice, 'It does seem a curious way to run a country.'

III

Waiting for Dinamaula to arrive at the Residency, Andrew Macmillan found that he could concentrate on nothing – not even drinking coffee, or smoking a pipe. He knew what he wanted to say to the chief-designate, he knew how he wanted the interview to develop; but the events of the previous night, and the woman's screams, and Crump's stricken face, and the general sense of guilt which, however unfairly, affected every white man in Gamate on that morning – all these things were working fatally against composure and control.

He believed Crump's story implicitly; indeed, there could be no other feasible explanation of the chance pistol-shot which had killed the Maula boy. But it was the second death that had visited the tribe in two days, and it was the sign manual of total confusion in his own area of rule. There could be no gainsaying the ugly fact of disorder.

When the police jeep stopped at the front gate, and Dinamaula, unattended, climbed down and walked across the lawn towards him, he still did not know how best to treat this young man who was now divided from him by so many thoughts, and so much blood.

Dinamaula spoke first. He came to a stop at the foot of the steps leading up to the *stoep*; a young man withdrawn and self-contained, his eyes showing nothing, his face a mask of aloof inexpression. He looked up at Andrew, and said, 'You sent for me, Mr Macmillan.'

'Yes.' Andrew Macmillan nodded. 'I wanted to talk to you, Chief ... I don't like the way things are going.'

Confronted by so swift a declaration, Dinamaula said nothing. His face continued expressionless and controlled. It was as if, having fulfilled a dutiful formality by speaking first, he need make no more contribution.

After a moment of silence: 'Come in,' said Macmillan heavily. He opened the door of the *stoep*, and motioned Dinamaula forward. 'We can talk better in here.'

Macmillan, vilely depressed by the previous night, had hoped for a smoother beginning to their meeting. But when they were indoors, sitting opposite each other in the worn armchairs, it was no easier; Dinamaula refused coffee, and a cigarette, and appeared to be reconciled to unpleasant duty. He had no choice – so his whole bearing proclaimed; he was waiting, in formal resignation, for what the Resident Commissioner had to say.

'I hoped to see you at my *aboura*,' said Andrew after a moment.

'I was unable to be present,' returned Dinamaula formally. 'I am sorry.'

'You know what I said to the tribe?'

Dinamaula inclined his head. 'I have been informed.'

'Did you agree with it?'

Dinamaula looked almost theatrically surprised. 'It is not for me to agree or disagree. I am not yet the chief. I have no position at the moment. What the Resident Commissioner says in his *aboura* is not my affair.'

'What are you getting at?' asked Macmillan roughly. 'What's it all about?'

'I do not understand.'

'Chief,' said Macmillan, leaning forward, 'I knew your father, and two of your uncles who were senior headmen. They were all fine men, as everyone in Gamate remembers. We were able to work together for the good of the tribe, I hope to be able to work the same way with you.'

'I hope so too.'

'Then what's it all about?' asked Macmillan, striving for a smile.

'I do not understand,' said Dinamaula again. His eyes gave nothing away, and his face still wore the mask of wary, expressionless disinterest. 'What is *what* all about?'

Macmillan sighed. 'Let's begin at the beginning, then … There's a lot of unrest in the tribe. There have been two riots, and two deaths already. There are a lot of rumours flying about … When you first arrived here, you talked a lot of hot air – ' Dinamaula's eyes narrowed briefly at the words, and then grew coldly negative again, ' – a lot of hot air about reforms. Later on you talked to the Press about marrying a white girl … Those two things,' said Macmillan hardly, 'have led directly to all the trouble we're in now.'

'I do not agree,' said Dinamaula, with cool decision.

'But it's obvious. You can't deny it.'

'I do not agree.'

'Then what is the trouble?'

'I do not know. Perhaps the tribe is disturbed by these – deaths.'

'What caused the deaths?'

'A knife and a revolver,' answered Dinamaula succinctly.

Macmillan looked at him for a long moment. If Dinamaula would not even meet him halfway, it was going to be impossible to make any progress, any dent in the surface of their difference. At the moment, he had no other weapons save words – or none that he cared to use.

'I want you to answer some questions,' said Macmillan, after a moment.

Dinamaula inclined his head.

'What are these reforms that you have in mind?'

'Until I am proclaimed chief, I cannot say.'

'You said enough when you talked to the Press.'

'I am still considering the details.'

Macmillan swallowed. He was getting nowhere, and this cool young man was making the fact plain. Bloody Oxford double-talk, he thought, and gripped the arms of his chair. It was a mistake to teach these people to read and write … Then he took a fresh pull, aware of foolish thoughts which he did not really believe: aware also that he must take command now, or lose it altogether.

'Then there's the question of your marriage,' he said, as if they were progressing easily from subject to subject. '*Are* you planning to marry a white woman? Who is she?'

'I do not wish to discuss it.'

'You *must* discuss it!' said Macmillan roughly. 'You know it affects the whole tribe, the whole country.'

'When I am chief,' answered Dinamaula, 'I will announce my marriage plans, and the reforms I have in mind.'

Macmillan looked at him straightly. 'You will never be chief if you talk like that.'

Dinamaula smiled faintly. 'So you told my people. I understand that it was not well received.'

'I don't give a damn how it was received!' returned Macmillan angrily. 'I know what's best for this country. You are splitting the tribe from top to bottom.'

'I shall know how to bind them together again, when I am chief.'

Macmillan sighed, leaning back in his chair. Weariness assailed him, and a feeling that history was passing him by, and that his day was done. Perhaps Dinamaula and Gamate and all the Maulas would leave the old paths, and march off into the evil future, leaving him defeated, with all his years of work vanished, and his hopes in ruins.

Without looking at Dinamaula, he said, more gently: 'Chief, please understand that I'm asking you to help me. I don't want to quarrel, I don't want to use force ... The whole tribe is split, as we know. We haven't seen the last of this unrest – in fact we may only be at the beginning of it. I want you to come in on my side, and use your influence to smooth things out again.'

'What influence have I, Mr Macmillan?' Dinamaula's voice was faintly bitter – the first sign of his true thoughts. 'You know what they call me in Gamate? The Resident Commissioner's dog ... It will always be so, until I am proclaimed chief.'

'I'm asking you to help me,' said Macmillan again. 'Drop all this talk of reforms, drop the marriage ... Work with me, for the good of the tribe as a whole.'

'I *am* working for the good of the tribe.'

'Then what is it they want? What is it *you* want?'

They were staring at each other again. 'I would like to be able to tell my people,' answered Dinamaula slowly, 'that you have agreed to my plans, and that when I am chief I shall be free.'

'Free for what?'

'To rule as I wish. To marry as I choose.'

'A white woman?'

'I will discuss that when I am chief.'

Macmillan shook his head decisively. 'You know it's out of the question. This country has never been run like that. You'll destroy everything.'

'I will build everything afresh.'

They were making no inch of progress; their cleavage was absolute; the time had come for decision and plain speaking. Macmillan leant forward again, his heavy shoulders hunched and square.

'We're getting nowhere,' he said curtly. 'Perhaps I was a fool to hope that we would … You'd better understand this. I'm *not* giving you a free hand, either now or in the future. You can forget that idea, for a start … If there are to be any reforms, they'll be worked out by you and me together, and they *won't* come with a rush. The marriage, of course, is out of the question … Whatever you do or say, Gamate is my responsibility, and I have the last word. I'm going to run it *my* way.'

Dinamaula rose. His bearing was suddenly icy, his face set. 'I must ask you to excuse me,' he said, with glacial formality. 'I have to attend a funeral.'

IV

That night, and the night following, there was no more violence in Gamate. Macmillan was not sure why. It might be that the tribe was shocked into sullen compliance by the death of the headman and the small boy, whose funeral was witnessed by a vast silent throng, trooping in endless procession up the hill to the burial ground. It might have been due to Crump's well-advertised precautions, which brought in an extra squad of police from Port Victoria. Or it might have been the sunset curfew which he imposed, as a matter of urgent necessity.

Whatever the cause, forty-eight hours passed with no ripple breaking the surface of the troubled pool that was Gamate township. Then, on the third night, after a brooding, malevolent respite, rioting broke out again.

It started with a Maula girl-child, who was taken to hospital with acute pleurisy. She reached hospital too late, and died during the afternoon.

Word instantly spread (so Crump told Macmillan later) that the child had been poisoned, so cruelly that the whole corpse was blue, and that all Maula children would be so disposed of, one by one, till the entire tribe disappeared and the white man ruled a deserted village ... Windows were broken at the hospital; a car taking some nurses to work from their hostel was overturned and set on fire, and the girls themselves manhandled. A police charge produced a crop of broken skulls, two stabbings, and furious resentment throughout the tribe.

The child's body was stolen from the hospital and paraded through the huts, with screams and wailings from the women such as Gamate had never heard before. Thousands of people broke the curfew, and the police, powerless to enforce it, were taunted and mocked intolerably.

Andrew Macmillan rang the Governor at midnight, after a tour of the huts in his car, and a brave, fruitless appeal for order. He was calm, following a nerve-stretching half-hour during which anything might have happened; but his intense weariness induced a sense of doom which the sound of the telephone endlessly ringing and ringing, two hundred miles away in Port Victoria, seemed to crystallize. When finally he heard the answering voice at the other end of the wire, it was like a speck of light at the farthermost limit of an enormous gloomy tunnel – a speck of light which somehow had to be reached, if sanity and order were ever to be restored.

He had never before felt so feebly armed, so dependent on higher authority. A few months earlier he would have been appalled at such personal inadequacy: a few years earlier, it could never have happened. Now it was here, and it stemmed from four sources.

There was the silence at his *aboura*, which had sounded, for Macmillan, an initial private knell of defeat. There was the tribe, which continued mutinous and violent. There was Dinamaula, at once guarded and slippery, impossible to treat with, impossible to pin down. There was the death of the Maula boy, as sad and senseless as a child struck by lightning, a bride dying on her wedding night.

Taken in series, these things might have been negotiable. Taken together, at the low ebb of his fifty-eighth year, they were an avalanche of ill fortune whose repeated blows seemed to have brought him to his knees.

Sir Elliott Vere-Toombs awoke swiftly to crisis. He had been irritable, when first he was called from his bed to answer the telephone; during the past forty-eight hours the Scheduled Territories Office had been plaguing him with cabled excerpts from the London papers, coupled with requests for information to combat a totally adverse Press; and his staff – notably Aidan Purves-Brownrigg – had filled in the gaps with minutes, memoranda, draft cables, and the steady pressure of eager subordinates. But as Andrew Macmillan painted *his* picture, in a few brisk foreboding words, the Governor progressed quickly to energy and decision.

'I'm not surprised,' he said presently, when Macmillan reached the end of his recital. 'There's a good deal of unrest here, too, a decided undercurrent …' He paused. Then he asked: 'How is your telephone manned, Andrew?'

'I'm at the police post, sir,' answered Macmillan. 'I've got a policeman on the switchboard – one of Crump's sergeants. The line's clear at this end.'

The Governor nodded to himself. At his end also, the privacy of their exchange was assured; the call was routed by direct line through the Secretariat switchboard, which Aidan, on his own initiative, had now organized on a twenty-four-hour basis.

'That's all right then ... What do you suggest, Andrew? I can't let you have any more men, I'm afraid.'

'I've got enough men, sir,' said Macmillan. 'But we *must* somehow relieve the pressure locally. I'd like you to talk personally to Dinamaula. He's the key point in all this.'

'Is he active?'

'Not openly. But behind the scenes I think he's doing a lot of manoeuvring and organizing. So are the Press boys, though it's almost impossible to pin them down.'

'What about the Regents?'

'Seralo has virtually given up. Katsaula is talking about the divine right of kings to do exactly what they want, all of the time. Puero's working openly for a free hand for Dinamaula.'

'You must speak to them all, very strongly,' said the Governor, fussily.

'I'll try again, sir,' said Andrew. 'But I don't think it's the answer. Dinamaula himself needs to be taken out of this altogether.'

'How do you mean, "taken out"?'

'I'd like to send him down to you, sir. And I'd like him kept in Port Victoria, until things quieten down a bit.'

There was a long silence on the wire. Across two hundred miles of parched, arid scrub, now cooling after a day of fierce heat, both men were listening and thinking. The Governor was listening to the peaceful silence of Government House, and a radio playing far away in the kitchen quarters; he was thinking of what the reaction would be, another five thousand miles away in London, if Dinamaula were 'taken out' in the way that Macmillan had suggested.

Certainly, as Governor, he had the necessary emergency powers, and the necessary discretion as well; but the fierce light now beating upon Pharamaul called for an unassailable moral warrant as well.

Macmillan was also listening, to the confused, nearby sounds of a town in revolt. He was in the small bare office of Crump's police post. By his side was the sergeant on the switchboard, across the room were two other native policemen, their faces intent, their clubs swinging from leather thongs circling their wrists. Outside was shouting, and the drumming of feet on bare naked earth, and a battery of floodlights on the police jeep steadily sweeping from side to side across the *aboura*, and the occasional crash of broken glass from the schoolhouse.

Outside, somewhere, was Forsdick the District Commissioner, with one squad of policemen, and Crump with another, and a first-aid detachment from the hospital. Outside were other volunteers – Oosthuizen the farmer, and Fellows from the Gamate Hotel, and the postmaster, and one of the hospital doctors – all doing their best to bring calm and quiet to the violent night. Outside also were three Pressmen who demanded a statement, and Father Hawthorne who wanted permission to hold a solemn requiem mass (interdenominational) for the Maula boy and the stabbed headman; and Father Schwemmer – a deeply troubled Father Schwemmer – who simply wanted to help.

Macmillan was thinking of immediate security, safety measures, the delicate balance of an angry mob who must be outfaced by a few cool men. To the Governor must be left another kind of balance: the intricate balance of policy,

the weighing of the expedient against the desirable …
Even as Macmillan thought, and listened, there was a long
concerted howl from across the *aboura*, and the policemen
half turned, also listening, and gripped their thonged clubs
in supple readiness.

The Governor spoke, far away from this crude scene, but
blessedly aware of its menace.

'All right, Andrew,' he said briskly. 'Send Dinamaula
down to me. I'll keep him here until things have a chance
to cool off. We'll make out an Order-in-Council, if
necessary.'

'When shall I send him?'

'Now,' said the Governor.

'I can't spare Crump,' said Macmillan, relieved, but
already beset by yet another problem. 'Or Forsdick either.'

'Llewellyn will do,' said the Governor, while Macmillan
wondered at his decisive, knowledgeable control, and was
deeply grateful for it. 'He's got a car, hasn't he?'

'Yes, sir. He's got his own truck.'

It was almost as if the Governor knew of Macmillan's
defeat and fear, and was planning and working overtime in
order to cover them up.

'Write out a formal letter of instruction,' came the
Governor's voice. 'Signed by you, on my behalf. Dinamaula
is to come down to Port Victoria, *forthwith* – ' the unlikely
word crackled over the wire, ' – *forthwith*, for personal
consultation with me. He is to come by himself, with no
attendants of any kind. He is to be conducted by Mr
Llewellyn, agricultural adviser, who is nominated as my
personal representative.'

'Yes, sir,' said Andrew Macmillan again.

'See the Regents again tomorrow,' said the far-away
voice. 'Tell them there's to be no more nonsense. Tell them
that unless things quieten down again, there'll be *another*

Order-in-Council, imposing martial law on Gamate. Then they'll find themselves out of a job altogether.'

'Yes, sir.'

'Don't give anything at all to the Press.'

'No, sir.'

'Let me know tomorrow how you get on with the Regents.' The Governor's voice was fading. 'How soon will Dinamaula be in Port Victoria?'

'If he starts by one o'clock,' said Macmillan, 'he should be there by breakfast time.'

'The sooner the better,' said the Governor. 'Allow him twenty minutes to pack … Good night, Andrew.'

'Good night, sir.'

The line was already dead as Macmillan replaced the receiver. He leant back against the wall of the office, thinking of his next move, while outside the raging turmoil in the *aboura* continued unabated. The Maula sergeant at the switchboard pulled out the two plug cords, killing the connexion, and leant back also, easing one of the headphones away from his ear. He was an alert young man, keen on his work, already schooled in contrasting cultures. As he sat back he was smiling, patently pleased at the way things were going.

'Hot dog!' he said.

Llewellyn, the agricultural officer, was not the prototype of a brave man. But he was a small Welshman with a job to do, and that was enough to take the place of valour. Leaving the engine of his truck still running, he walked up the short path to the hut of Dinamaula, a single piece of paper in his hand. The hut stood well back from the *aboura*, but even here the tumult could be heard in angry waves of sound.

A hanger-on – perhaps a guard – moved to intercept him as he approached. He said: 'Get out of my way, damn you!' and then, calling more loudly: 'Chief!'

'Who is it?' came Dinamaula's voice from within.

'Mr Llewellyn,' answered Llewellyn.

'Come in, please,' said Dinamaula.

The hut was well lighted, with candles, and two flaring kerosene lamps. Inside were five people: Dinamaula, lying seemingly exhausted on his couch, Puero, lolling in a corner, and three Pressmen – Axel Hallmarck, Tulbach Browne, and Pikkie Joubert. Bottles of beer and whisky stood haphazard on a rush mat at their feet.

Llewellyn looked slowly round the hut. 'I would like to speak to you alone, Chief,' he said, after a pause.

'I am with my friends,' said Dinamaula coldly.

'I have a message from the Resident Commissioner.'

'I am with my friends,' said Dinamaula again.

'Very well …' Llewellyn proffered the piece of paper. 'This is an order from the Governor,' he said formally.

Dinamaula reached out his hand and took the piece of paper. Llewellyn was suddenly made aware of the vulgarity of the moment, as first Puero, then Tulbach Browne, then Hallmarck and Joubert, leant across to read what was on it.

After a long pause, Tulbach Browne said: 'This is completely unconstitutional.'

Llewellyn was looking at Dinamaula, and only at Dinamaula. He saw a deep shadow cross the other man's face, as if some sudden thought, too heavy for words, had reached his tired brain. Then Dinamaula raised his eyes.

'This comes as a surprise,' said Dinamaula. 'I am not prepared for travel.'

'I will give you time to pack,' said Llewellyn. It sounded a ridiculous phrase, absurdly westernized, totally inappropriate to the thatched reed hut and the flaring light of candles and oil lamps. After a moment he said, in the Maula tongue: 'Please make ready for the journey.'

'Do not go,' said Puero contemptuously. He was, as usual, somewhat affected by liquor. 'This man –' he gestured crudely, ' – can wait till morning.'

'We must start tonight,' said Llewellyn evenly.

'Who says so?' asked Tulbach Browne.

'Keep out of this,' said Llewellyn.

'Who says so?' repeated Tulbach Browne.

'It is an order from the Governor,' said Llewellyn.

A new voice now made itself heard. It was Axel Hallmarck, crisply inquisitive.

'But what's it mean, for God's sake?' he asked. 'Is he being deported?'

'He is going to Port Victoria for consultation with the Governor.'

'Do not go,' said Puero again.

'When will he come back?' asked Tulbach Browne.

Llewellyn said nothing.

Dinamaula rose to his feet. His face was tired, his slight body drooping. Instinctively Llewellyn knew that the other man had been thinking swiftly, and that his thinking had led him to a preordained conclusion.

Dinamaula asked: 'You have a car?'

'All is ready,' answered Llewellyn. 'But what about your packing?'

Dinamaula shook his head. 'I will pack nothing,' he said coldly.

'When will he come back?' asked Tulbach Browne again.

Llewellyn gave no answer.

'I never thought I'd see this, anywhere in the world today,' said Axel Hallmarck.

Pikkie Joubert, sweating and owlish with drink, spoke for the first time.

'Man!' he proclaimed. 'You can't do this sort of thing, not even to a native!'

Tulbach Browne said, looking at the piece of paper, which he had been careful to retain: 'Even if the chief goes, there's an implied undertaking that he'll come back to Gamate again, as soon as he's seen the Governor. Isn't that so?'

Llewellyn said nothing.

'Do not go, my Chief,' said Puero, for the third time. 'It is a trick.'

'I am ready,' said Dinamaula to Llewellyn. Then he paused, as if remembering something. 'But I make a formal protest,' he said, in a strange, almost theatrical voice, 'against being ordered to leave my home in this irregular way.' Then he brushed past Llewellyn, and with bent head walked through the door of the hut, and towards the waiting truck.

Llewellyn followed closely, aware of the thin knife-edge of his authority, and of the threatening scrutiny of the guard; alert for any new move. But none came, and within a few moments the two of them, settled in the truck, had set off down the bumpy road leading out of the town. The headlights dipped and wavered, the dust scattered as they passed; while behind them the din of shouting and violence rose and fell in ugly, senseless crescendo.

Behind them also, within a few moments, a second car fell into line, keeping pace and distance as they reached the open road to the south.

But if Dinamaula heard the noise, or noticed the second car, or was aware of any special significance in this farewell to Gamate, he gave no sign. Head sunk on chest, eyes closed, he seemed already to be sleeping.

V

'*Ahsula!*' said Macmillan crisply. 'I have called you here in order to help me to restore order to the tribe.'

The faces of the three men grouped in front of him were not reassuring; indeed, even as he spoke his greeting, Andrew Macmillan realized that he would have to work hard to gain even an inch of progress. He had chosen to summon the three Regents to the Residency, and to talk to them informally, because he wanted, if possible, to lift their meeting out of the poisoned atmosphere of Gamate itself. In the town, there was nothing that did not bear the imprint of violence, vengeful muttering, and the funereal trappings of death; here, half a mile away, on the quiet Residency *stoep*, he had hoped to establish reason and order, by an appeal to the only three men in the tribe who could co-operate effectively.

But when he looked at the three men, he was no longer hopeful; and his greeting '*Ahsula* – Peace!' left an ironic echo in the silence.

He remembered, years ago in England, hearing a detested politician salute his radio audience as 'My friends!' There had been, in that professional greeting, the same sour note of pretence and defeat.

They sat on their three chairs, against the inside wall of the *stoep*; Seralo, Katsaula, and Puero. Johannes, bowing low to the august company, had just served them coffee; and they had answered the formal, dutiful greetings of Johannes with a courtesy equally formal, a regal acquiescence. But now, when they turned their faces towards Macmillan, they did not allow him even such guarded admittance. They could greet Johannes, it seemed – a servant in the Residency – because he was a Maula, and an honest man. But Macmillan, the Resident Commissioner himself, they would not greet, because he was a white man, and had proved himself an enemy.

Macmillan read their thoughts, and they in turn read his, and the wall grew like a tall cliff between them, without a word being spoken.

Macmillan cleared his throat. He addressed Seralo, the senior Regent. 'What can we do together?' he asked.

But Seralo, for the first time in his long life, would not meet Macmillan's eye. 'I know nothing,' he answered, on a low note, his head shaking. 'I have no thoughts.'

'There is violence and unrest in the tribe,' prompted Macmillan hardly.

'Yes,' said old Seralo. 'Alas …'

Macmillan waited, but there was no more to come. Exasperated, he moved his head slightly. 'And you, Katsaula?'

Katsaula, the historian of the tribe, the formalist, also turned aside his eyes before he spoke. Macmillan, oddly, felt a moment of pity as he noted the movement. Neither Seralo nor Katsaula, deeply imbued with tribal feeling and tradition, could ever find it easy to avoid the eye of the Resident Commissioner; no man so proud and so honoured as a Regent should ever need to make this shameful evasion … On both sides, for many scores of years, the Maula rulers and the officials of white Government had always met each other's eyes, in honest dealing and mutual respect.

If an end had now been set to that level exchange, then truly it was the end of many other things in Pharamaul.

Katsaula said, faintly (for he was still sick, and the skin of his face was pinched and shrunken): 'I have no thoughts.'

Macmillan's glance moved again, without comment. He wished that his brain might move as readily as his glance, but his brain was lagging painfully, and the margin of his control and planning was already as thin as paper.

'And you, Puero?' he asked the third Regent. 'How can we bring peace to the troubled tribe?'

'I have no thoughts,' answered Puero in his turn. Though he did no more than repeat the formal Maula phrase, yet the inflexion of his voice, and the gross sneer on his lips, gave it an added force, and many overtones. His two old companions (so his eyes and his silent lips seemed to say) had used this foolish phrase: 'I have no thoughts.' He himself had used the same phrase, because he did not care to search for another; but what he really meant to say was: 'I have many thoughts, but I do not choose to share them with you, because you are an enemy – and a defeated enemy also.'

No man so proud as a young Regent of the Maulas need treat with an old, defeated Resident Commissioner, whose term of life and rule was drawing to a ridiculous close.

But from such a man Macmillan would not accept such a phrase. He frowned, and said, 'You must have many thoughts, Puero. Let me hear them.'

Puero turned his gross body and heavy face, unwillingly, towards Macmillan. His black brows drew together, in harsh concentration. He said: 'Very well, then … My first strong thought is: where is our chief?'

In spite of himself, Katsaula sucked in his breath sharply as he heard Puero's words, while Seralo shook his old head in sorrowful disclaimer. Andrew Macmillan knew well enough why. The words 'strong thought' had, in the Maula tongue, a special significance, a significance contemptuously tough; they meant, by implication, that the speaker declared that his own thoughts were true thoughts, and that any others were wasted breath. Neither Seralo nor Katsaula had ever heard such a phrase used in conversation with a white man; and to hear it addressed to the Resident

Commissioner was something like blasphemy. But Puero only sat on, with lowering head, as if unconscious of any lapse.

After a moment, Macmillan said with cold emphasis: 'Your strong thought is a foolish thought ... You know very well where Chief Dinamaula is. He is in Port Victoria, meeting with the Governor.'

'There has been no proclamation,' said Puero sullenly.

'Proclamation? Since when has there been a need for a proclamation when a man makes a journey from Gamate to Port Victoria?'

'But the man is our chief,' interposed Katsaula, with firmness.

'He was summoned openly,' answered Macmillan, 'by letter of instruction from the Governor. There was no secret. Such a summons is nothing new. There was no need of a proclamation.'

Seralo swallowed. 'He went without warning,' he said waveringly, 'between sunset and sunrise, like a thief led away. We should have been informed.'

Macmillan took a grip on his temper. 'Very well. You are informed now. The chief-designate has been summoned to Port Victoria, for consultation with the Governor, in accordance with the custom.'

'What custom is this?' asked Katsaula coldly.

'There have been many such meetings. It is nothing new in the tribe ... Now let us think of Gamate. How can we put an end to this unrest?'

Puero looked round at the other two Regents. Neither of them seemed to be preparing to speak. He said boldly: 'Our own chief can put an end to it, when he returns to Gamate.'

'That may not be for some time. I am speaking of today and tomorrow.'

'Only our chief can speak of such matters.'

So that was it, thought Macmillan, as he looked round from one to another, and saw Puero's thick mouth harden into a sullen mutinous line, and Seralo and Katsaula nodding agreement to his words. The Regents were virtually going on strike, because Dinamaula had left Gamate; they would do nothing to help until the chief-designate returned. And since Dinamaula was going to be kept away until order returned to the town, that meant a complete deadlock ... Suddenly, as he realized this, he felt a new onset of tiredness, and a pain rose sharply behind his eyes, and hovered there, throbbing like a steady drumbeat.

There were too many things to think about in this business, too many loose ends, too much danger, too much disappointment. His rule, which had seemed so settled and so secure a few months ago, had now grown utterly confused; the tribe was in revolt, and the Regents would not help him – they were only trying to blackmail him in order to bring back Dinamaula, the very head and crown of the disturbance in Gamate.

There could be no solution that way ... But when he summoned his thoughts again, and set to work to persuade them, it was like beating the air. First politely, then crudely, the three Regents continued to defy him. They repeated the same set of phrases. with dogged Maula persistence. They faced and outfaced him, united in disobedience, sounding a close-linked counterpoint of refusal.

They would do nothing (they said) without their chief.

Why had he been spirited away in the night?

When would he return?

Would he be declared chief on the appointed day?

How could they hope to reassert the law, when Dinamaula was not at hand to lend them his authority?

And again: They would do nothing without their chief.

Once they spoke of the violence in Gamate. 'You have killed two of our people!' proclaimed Puero, in throaty anger, 'and wounded many others. How can we hope to restore order, when such things are done?'

'You know well,' said Macmillan, with impatience, 'that the killing was not the work of Government. One man was killed in a fight. Another – the boy – died by an accident. It was the result of tribal lawlessness, it was not a Government killing.'

'Well, they are dead,' answered Puero contemptuously, 'whatever the RC chooses to call it.'

Macmillan glared at him. 'Do not speak of me as the RC,' he snapped.

Puero's eyes flickered under lowered lids. His voice was ironic and insolent. 'Whatever His Honour the Resident Commissioner chooses to call it,' he amended, as if it were no great matter, 'the man and the boy are dead.'

'Because of rioting among the tribe, which you will not help me to stop.'

'How can we help when our chief is taken from us?'

Once they spoke, briefly, towards the end of their meeting, of the marriage of the chief.

'Dinamaula has divided the tribe,' said Macmillan, 'with all this foolish talk of marriage, and of new things. He cannot return until matters are quiet again.'

'The chief's marriage is his own affair,' said Katsaula. 'It does not divide the tribe.'

'Nonsense!' exclaimed Macmillan. 'You saw how it was in the *aboura*. Many of the tribe are ashamed of such a marriage. That was why the headman was killed, because he spoke out against it.'

'Perhaps,' said Puero carelessly. 'But the tribe is not divided now.'

'What do you mean?'

'If the tribe has to choose between condemning a marriage such as this, and the chief, then they will agree to the marriage, and keep their chief.'

'It divides the tribe.'

'It divides the tribe no longer, if it means they will lose the chief.'

'Such a marriage is impossible.'

'For our chief to leave us is also impossible.'

It was then that Macmillan suddenly lost his patience. 'Let's get this straight!' he said crisply. 'Dinamaula is *not* coming back! Make up your minds to that.'

The three Regents looked at him, startled and taken aback. Seralo was the first to speak. 'Do you mean he will never return to Gamate?'

Macmillan, angered, longed to answer 'Yes' to that question, but he could not be so definite. He stood up.

'Now hear this,' he said, speaking slowly. 'It is my last word. The chief will not return, and he will not be proclaimed, until I am satisfied that order has been restored in Gamate ... I have asked you to help me in that task. You have refused ...' He stared down at them all in turn, frowning. 'If you will not rule for me, then I shall rule for myself. If you do not like the way I rule, if it means the bringing of policemen, perhaps even of soldiers, then you have only yourselves to blame. But I *will* rule!'

'You would bring soldiers?' asked Katsaula incredulously.

'I will bring order,' answered Macmillan, 'whatever kind of man is needed to help me ... The meeting is ended.'

He turned briskly on his heel, and left the *stoep* by the house door, while the three Regents, after a moment of silence and hesitation, filed out into the garden, and made for the front gate. But within the house, Macmillan grew suddenly weak, and found that his legs were trembling. He sat down heavily in the nearest armchair, and put his head in his hands.

He knew that the meeting had failed, and that he himself had failed with it. He had talked of soldiers, but soldiers could never be the answer, in a country like Pharamaul. Soldiers were failure in themselves, the defeat of reason and the rule of law. Soldiers were only another aspect of disorder, equally shaming to the civil arm.

Macmillan's heart fluttered uncertainly, and the pain behind his eyes stabbed him, as he surveyed the ruin of his hopes. Fancifully, he felt that within the last few minutes he had lost a tug-of-war for the soul of the Maula tribe. There had once been a happy time when there was no tug-of-war, a time when black men and white men all wanted the same thing, and strove side by side to win it. Now it was to be done with soldiers …

No just man ever governed in such a fashion, save in dire urgency. And the urgency itself was the brand of failure. To use the threat of military force, in his own town of Gamate, had sounded the defeat of his whole life.

The worst thing of all was that it had to be done. Within a little while, unless all roles were reversed, he must be his own executioner.

VI

Two hundred miles away in Port Victoria, the Governor and Commander-in-Chief of Pharamaul was also speaking his mind. But he, at least, had no hostile audience. He was briefing his staff, at the beginning of what might well be a new and critical phase in the affairs of Pharamaul; and his staff, all five of them, were (with only a stray reservation here and there) united in his support.

Lucky was the man, thought Aidan Purves-Brownrigg, fanning himself with a draft Order-in-Council, who could command such a dutifully captive audience. Apart from successful whoreshops and schools for very small boys, there must be very few of them left, *anywhere* in the world.

Idly, watching the staff assemble, greet the Governor, and settle down in their armchairs, Aidan wondered which of those two categories best suited the present company. It was a point verging on the moot … But for good or ill, this was the team which had to run Pharamaul. At the top there was the old gentleman, and himself. They both did their best, thought Aidan wryly, but it didn't seem terribly good … There was Captain Simpson, Royal Navy, a four-striper fish out of water among these land-borne dilemmas. There was David Bracken, in love with Nicole Steuart; and Nicole, in love with David. If they could just detach their *naughty* little minds from that particular subject, their contribution was not ineffective. Finally, there was Stevens, who was ineffective.

That was all there was, to deal with a hundred thousand *revolting* Maulas – except for a handful of outlying players up at Gamate, who were making (at the moment) a monumental balls-up of the whole thing.

His sombre thoughts were interrupted by the Governor, sitting trim and birdlike behind his desk, seemingly unaware of the sticky heat which neither drawn blinds nor whirring fans could relieve.

'Everyone comfortable?' asked Sir Elliott, looking round him. 'Let's make a start, then …'

Aidan sat back in his chair. Captain Simpson allowed his mouth to drop open slightly. David winked at Nicole, and Nicole bent her head, a slight smile on her lips. Stevens took out a notebook and a ballpoint pen.

'I've asked you to come along,' said Sir Elliott, elbows on desk, palms gently placed together, 'because I want us all to be up-to-date about what's going on in Gamate. Not much good not knowing what's going on, what? We don't want to get the wires crossed …'

He looked down at the memorandum pad tucked into one corner of his blotter. On it was written:

Press in London, critical
Dinamaula here, unco-op
Macmillan report, very bad
Order-in-Council
To Gamate

The Governor cleared his throat.

'Some of you,' he began again, 'will have seen the telegrams we've had, containing excerpts from the London Press, dealing with what's going on in Gamate. They are highly critical, most of them – unfair, of course – and – er – highly critical ... This is the sort of thing.' His voice rising several tones higher, he read from a selection of headlines contained in one of the previous night's telegrams. ' "Chief Spirited Away from Gamate". "Dinamaula Hi-jacked, Leaves Under Protest". "No Time to Pack". "Dinamaula To Be Sacked". "Tribe Robbed of Chief on Eve of Coronation".'

Sir Elliott paused, while his staff waited in varying degrees of expectancy. I don't think much of those headlines, thought Aidan, examining his nails. I could produce much better ones, given this *shoddy* situation ... The RAPE of Gamate. Chief Dinamaula Absolutely KIDNAPPED by Government Gangsters. Official BEASTS At Work ...

'The Secretary of State is naturally disturbed,' went on the Governor, reasonably, 'though I hope to be able to reassure him. The facts are, of course, that Dinamaula wasn't "spirited away", or any nonsense like that. He was invited to come down here for talks with me. In view of the disturbances in Gamate, that was entirely justified ... As for "No Time to Pack" – ' he smiled briefly, ' – the phrase is quite inaccurate. He actually *refused* to pack anything ... Very important point, that.'

391

For Christ's sake, thought David Bracken, suddenly jerking to attention, abandoning the sensual contemplation of the curve of Nicole Steuart's shoulder – for Christ's sake, if he *really* thinks that that's important, we might as well be walking up and down the Residency garden playing the bagpipes, for all the progress we're making in Pharamaul ... Not for the first time during the past few weeks, David was conscious of the ineffectiveness, the basic ineptitude, of what the Government team was doing in Pharamaul, when contrasted with what the situation demanded. They had right on their side, but they never bothered to explain how and why, in clear and explicit terms. They were getting an atrocious press all over the world, and somehow they never caught up with it, never fought back at all.

They were trailing the headlines all the time, and the headlines, brutally one-sided, were steadily widening their divorce from the facts. There was an official version of what was going on in Gamate, and it *could* be made convincing. The Governor, when put to it, was efficient and capable. He was also, at all times, scrupulously just. But if they were going to worry about such pinpoints of truth as whether Dinamaula had packed or had not packed – worse still, if they were going to waste time kicking these minute cloudy bubbles around in closed session, instead of producing their own daily, definitive account of what they were doing and trying to do in Pharamaul – then they would be sunk, and they would deserve to be sunk; sunk in general infamy, sunk under a flowing tide of prejudice.

He awoke, despairingly, to the Governor's next sub-heading.

'I saw Dinamaula yesterday, as you know,' continued Sir Elliott. 'He was very unco-operative ... I hoped that he would play, but he won't play. Not at the moment, anyway.'

Play, thought Nicole Steuart. Now there's a funny word ... She had a sudden, irreverent vision of Dinamaula, in a loincloth, playing leapfrog with Sir Elliott Vere-Toombs, in cocked hat and spurs; they gambolled together under bright sunlight, while a crowd of loyal Maulas stood around, smiling and clapping their hands. From there, they would go on to skipping, while the Maulas chorused 'Salt – pepper – mustard – vinegar!' in benevolent glee. But Dinamaula, alas, wouldn't play ... I mustn't be unfair, thought Nicole contritely. It was just an Old Boy's expression, after all. He's doing his best, and his best can be first-class. I love David Bracken, anyway.

'Dinamaula won't play at all,' repeated the Governor, as if he could scarcely believe what he was called upon to tell them. 'I can't understand what's got into him ... You know the background, of course. He's been talking a lot of guff about reforms in the Territory, and that sort of thing, and he's also said – ' he paused, glancing momentarily at Nicole Steuart, ' – that he intends to get married, and that he's going to marry a white girl ... All of which adds up to a very confused situation in Gamate, with a lot of violence and rioting on the surface, and an undercurrent of continuous passive resistance to authority ... Macmillan tells me that, as far as he can judge, the majority of the tribe are pretty solidly behind Dinamaula, and that they'd even accept a mixed marriage, if otherwise it meant losing him as chief ... I must say that Dinamaula himself seemed pretty set on it.'

But was that strictly true, the Governor wondered privately, as he paused in his recital. Certainly Dinamaula, in their interview the day before, had preserved an unbroken front of non-co-operation. But he had not taken a firm stand on any particular aspect of policy or action. The most he had done was to produce one phrase, which he had repeated over and over again. 'I do not understand,'

Dinamaula had said, 'why I have been taken away from my people.'

Sir Elliott had done his best to explain the official point of view to him, with statement, question, restatement, and challenge. Was it not true (he had asked) that the chief intended far-reaching reforms, irrespective of what Government planned? Dinamaula did not wish to answer that question. Was it not true that the chief planned to marry a white woman? That was his (Dinamaula's) private affair. Surely the chief must see that his present attitude was disrupting the tribe? Dinamaula did not agree. How could he be allowed to return to Gamate when his presence obviously increased the threat of disorder? Dinamaula did not recognize the problem, and wished to be restored to his people. But how could he be proclaimed chief, in the present circumstances? That was a matter for the tribe, and the strict laws of inheritance.

It had been a very difficult interview, with a young man who disdained to gain a single inch of ground, and yet, by refusing argument on all matters of disagreement, had presented the Governor with an impenetrable opposition. It had been like talking to a brick wall.

Dinamaula was not bitter, he was not directly mutinous. He was simply *there* – an enigma, a blank denial, an undoubted focus of strength. Towards the end, the Governor was left with the conviction that he no longer understood the Maulas – or the younger generation.

When at last he had said, prepared to bargain, stepping down in tone and approach: 'We don't want any sort of crisis, Chief. Will you undertake to leave all these questions to negotiation, later on?' Dinamaula had answered: 'I will promise nothing. I will undertake nothing. I wish to return to Gamate.'

'But he *won't* return to Gamate,' said the Governor suddenly, ending his reverie, answering his own thoughts with such conviction that all his staff looked up with new attention. 'Not under the present circumstances, at least. And that brings me to my next point ... Andrew Macmillan rang me up late last night, and again this morning, just a few minutes ago. Gamate is full of rumours about Dinamaula – that he's imprisoned, or going to be hanged – all sorts of things like that. There was some very bad rioting last night – the worst so far, in fact. I'm sorry to tell you that a policeman was killed.'

'Who?' asked Captain Simpson, jerking to sudden attention. 'Not Keith Crump?'

'No, no,' answered the Governor testily. 'A *policeman* – a Maula corporal.'

'Oh ...' said Simpson. 'But that's a pretty bad show, all the same.'

'Things are a great deal quieter this morning, I'm glad to say,' Sir Elliott continued, 'but there are still gangs of people roaming about, shouting for Dinamaula, and huts are still being burnt here and there. Macmillan has enrolled every available man as a special constable, and he thinks he can get things under control in a couple of days. But he is adamant – ' the Governor repeated and stressed the odd word, ' – *adamant* that Dinamaula cannot be allowed to return at present. And so am I.'

The Governor paused. He did not enjoy talking at such length and in such detail. Almost always, by now, he would have given himself a respite by asking a question, or by inviting someone else's point of view. But in the present case he was the only one who could submit this comprehensive account.

After a moment, he continued: 'It's quite obvious that, if he went back to Gamate, Dinamaula would continue to be the centre of revolt, either active or passive – he couldn't help it. He must therefore stay here in Port Victoria. With that in view, I am issuing this Order-in-Council.' He looked round his desk, riffled through some papers. 'Now where is it?'

Aidan stood up. 'Here, sir. I was having it retyped.'

'Oh, yes …' The Governor took the sheet of stiff blue foolscap. 'This is modelled on an Order-in-Council which we had to use about fifty years ago, and another which was prepared – though we *didn't* have to use it – at the time of the tax troubles in 1951.' He adjusted his spectacles. ' "In pursuance of the powers vested in me under Section Seventeen of – " well, that's just the usual preamble, " – Be it therefore enacted as follows. ONE. A State of Emergency is declared within the Township of Gamate, and within a prescribed zone extending one hundred miles in any direction therefrom. TWO. This State of Emergency shall continue until the Governor in Council is satisfied that the necessity therefore no longer exists. THREE. Chief-designate Dinamaula, by reason of his refusal to co-operate with the Resident Commissioner, Gamate, in matters affecting the future of the Maula tribe, is hereby declared a Prohibited Person under Section Eighteen of the foregoing, and is prohibited from entering the prescribed zone affected by the State of Emergency. FOUR. Chief-designate Dinamaula is hereby directed to reside within the metropolitan limits of Port Victoria, until the Governor in Council shall decree otherwise. FIVE. The Native Authority in the Township of Gamate shall continue to be the Council of Regents." That's all.'

'Sir,' said an unexpected voice, after a brief pause. It was Stevens.

'Yes?'

'Hadn't we better give him his full name? I think it ought to be "Chief-designate Dinamaula *Maula*".'

'True,' said the Governor. He made two careful corrections to the Order-in-Council. 'Thank you, Leonard.

We can't afford any procedural mistakes ... Has anyone else got any questions or suggestions?'

There was another pause, which lengthened gradually to a receptive silence; it was as if no one in the room cared to add anything to so well-rounded a chapter. Once again, David Bracken was aware of a prickling uneasiness. There was a gap here – the same gap as before; the Government side were planning to do something, something pretty clear-cut and decisive, and they weren't bothering to explain why. Once again, they were bound to make more enemies than friends in the process.

'Sir,' he said tentatively.

'Yes, David?' said the Governor, turning.

'Couldn't we issue a statement to the Press about this? They've been very active, as you know – '

'I know that,' answered the Governor fussily. 'Two of them actually followed Dinamaula down from Gamate. Extraordinary. They interviewed him immediately after he'd seen me – badgered the poor chap into telling them all sorts of things that were really confidential.'

'That's why, sir,' pursued David, 'I think we ought to try to put our side of the thing across.'

'Put it across?' repeated the Governor fastidiously. 'What an odd notion ... Why should we do that? Our business is to restore order in Gamate. This – ' he tapped the Order-in-Council, ' – is how we are going about it.'

'But we're lagging behind all the time, sir.' David was aware of the others watching him, and especially of Nicole's face, gravely speculative, hearteningly lovely. He drew a deep breath. 'We really *must* explain why Dinamaula is being barred from Gamate. Otherwise the newspapers will automatically take his side, as they have done all the time, without bothering to find out our reasons, or give them any space.'

'But we've stated our reasons,' countered the Governor. He peered down at the Order-in-Council, and read out: ' "By reason of his refusal to co-operate with the Resident Commissioner" ... There you have it, in black and white.'

'Sir, that's a single sentence – not very explicit – in a fairly long document. It makes us sound so – so inhuman ... The Press have already said that we tricked Dinamaula into leaving Gamate. Now they'll say that we never had any intention of allowing him to come back. He's banned from Gamate, he's directed to live in a specific place, he'll be under police surveillance here. Unless we explain why, in much more detail, it will look as if he's being bullied and badgered by the officials, just because he won't obey orders.'

'Ridiculous!' exclaimed the Governor. His blue eyes, a trifle frosty, formidably direct, regarded David steadily. 'How could anyone in their right senses formulate such a view? I hope no member of my staff – ' his voice tailed off; though he continued to stare at David with level persistence. Suddenly he said: 'What sort of statement have you in mind?'

David gulped. 'Nothing elaborate, sir. It would need to cover three things – ' he thought rapidly, ' – the explosive situation in Gamate, the fact that we think it's due to Dinamaula talking too freely about reforms, and the obvious necessity of removing him, as a disturbing element, at least temporarily ...' He smiled, aware of an inner relief. 'It could be made quite convincing, sir.'

Across the room, Aidan spoke: 'I think David's right, sir. We've got a case. We ought to state it more clearly.'

'But will anyone print it?' asked the Governor dubiously. 'Last time we tried to put our side of the case, as you call it – at my Press conference – it seemed to make things worse than they were before.'

After a reflective silence, Aidan said: 'I still think it's worth trying, sir. Shall I put up a draft?'

The Governor sighed, unconvinced. But a draft was something he understood, something manageable. 'Very well,' he said. 'Let me have it as soon as you can.'

Nicole Steuart spoke suddenly, a rewarding enthusiasm in her voice. 'Perhaps we could issue it simultaneously with the Order-in-Council.'

'The Order-in-Council is an administrative legal instrument,' replied the Governor precisely. 'It would be very unusual to accompany it by a – a statement of any kind.'

'It would give us the initiative, sir,' said David.

'I don't think,' said Aidan, joining in the delicate task of tipping the Old Gentleman off balance, 'that there would be any harm in issuing an *interpretive* statement at the same time. In fact,' he said, ad-libbing freely, 'the papers might appreciate it.'

'Very well,' conceded the Governor again. 'Perhaps, considered in that light …' He glanced down at the slip of paper on his blotter. There remained one more item. 'That takes care of Dinamaula. It still leaves Gamate. I'm not quite satisfied – ' he spoke carefully, ' – that we're doing all we can to impress on the tribe the necessity of returning to normal again. Andrew, of course, is very overworked … But if the Regents won't co-operate, it's possible that their powers will have to be suspended, and Andrew declared the sole Native Authority … I propose to go up to Gamate myself, in two days' time, and hold an *aboura* to explain matters to the tribe.'

He looked round the room. Only Aidan had known in advance of this move; the faces of the others reflected their surprise.

'It will be a full-dress affair,' said the Governor. 'I shall want *you* to come up with me – ' he looked at Captain

Simpson, indubitably a full-dress individual, ' – and you too, David. Uniforms, of course, and – er – swords. We'll leave by train tomorrow night … I think that's all,' he said, looking round him, relaxing somewhat. 'Thank you for coming along.'

'Well done,' said Aidan unexpectedly, outside the Governor's room. 'It was about time we struck a blow for our side.'

'Thanks for your help,' said David. 'I didn't think he'd fall for it.'

'Oh, the old gentleman's doing all right,' answered Aidan. 'Much better than I expected.'

'Have you got a sword?' asked Nicole.

'No,' said David.

'*I* have,' said Stevens. 'It belonged to my father. He was a District Officer in Basutoland. I'd be glad to lend it to you.' Noting David's hesitant expression, he added reassuringly: 'You'll find that the pattern hasn't changed at all.'

CHAPTER TEN

❖

For the Governor of Pharamaul to hold a personal *aboura*, with full ceremony, was a very rare happening indeed. Even the oldest of the Maulas of Gamate could only remember three other occasions, in seventy or eighty years; the most ancient memory was a cloudy legend, almost lost in the mists, when the Great Maula himself had returned from a visit to their mother the Queen, bearing gifts, and had joined with the Governor at an *aboura* full of splendour, to mark the sixtieth year of the old Queen's reign. Now, it was freely said, the old Queen had turned angry, and had taken away their chief; and her special emissary the Governor was coming with soldiers to kill all who resisted, and to put on new taxes … It was no wonder that, all over the town, the old men talked with lowered voices, and the young men made secret plans, and the children played games that started with processions and speeches, and finished with cruel hangings, and wild running away.

On the *aboura* itself, there was much to see, much to enjoy and comment upon. Men came to decorate the balcony, putting up banners and coloured emblems, setting out chairs and tables. Other men – policemen – went through curious actions, marching towards the *aboura*, flourishing their clubs, halting at a shouted word of command, making a ceremonial circle round a spot marked with a large white cross. There, it was said, the Governor himself (a man ten feet tall, dressed in feathers) would stand holding a golden spear in his hand, and the policemen would close round him, ready for secret tortures … Yet other men came out with broad brushes made of thorn twigs, and pots of white paint, and drew marks on the dusty earth of the *aboura*.

'What are these marks?' they were asked, many times.

'They are for the *aboura*.'

'What do they mean?'

'They are to show where to walk, and where to stand.'

'Cannot men walk and stand without white marks?'

'There will be many men, many policemen. This is to show them how to form a pattern of honour.'

'Are they children then, that they cannot form a pattern of honour without white marks to guide them?'

'Do not mock.'

'You there – put some white paint on your face, and be a white man forming a pattern of honour!'

'Or be a white woman, ready to marry the chief!'

'Do not mock. Go away from here.'

'Since when has the *aboura* been a private place for making white marks?'

'Take your white paint, and leave us in peace.'

'They say no one will come to this *aboura*. It is an *aboura* only for white men.'

'For white men, and for Maulas with white paint on their faces.'

'There are to be no such Maulas. It is an order.'

The long white lines were drawn, with crosses to mark certain places. The coloured decorations were raised up; chairs and stools were ranged in careful ranks; the policemen drilled and marched, time and time again, while the children watched, and the bystanders talked among themselves.

Out of sight, over the hill towards the burial place, other men also drilled and marched. They had no uniforms, no white lines, no chairs and stools; but their drilling and marching were not less orderly and determined.

'I don't like it,' said Crump decisively. 'It's not just gossip and rumour – it's something more definite. I don't like it at all.'

'Cheer up, Keith!' said Forsdick. 'Even if some of them do stay away from the *aboura*, there'll still be enough Maulas to make a show. That's all the old boy wants.'

Crump shook his head. 'I wish I could agree with you.'

Forsdick, red-faced and sweating, rose with ponderous determination and made his way to the sideboard. 'What you want,' he said over his shoulder, 'is another beer.'

It was high noon in Gamate, twenty-four hours before the Governor's *aboura*; Crump and George Forsdick, meeting in the latter's house, were running over the final plans for the morrow's ceremony. That, at least, had been their original intention, but they had not progressed very far; the day was too hot, Forsdick too hospitable, and the omens (as Crump saw them) much less than favourable. Crump, waiting for Forsdick to return from the sideboard, was well aware that some of his doubts might stem from within himself; the last week had been the most trying seven days of his life, and the three futile deaths that had marred it – the stabbing of the headman, the shooting of the Maula child, and the killing of one of his own men – had depressed him vilely.

But even allowing for personal misgivings, he could not join in Forsdick's easy optimism. Within his professional world, there was too much evidence against it.

'Cheers,' said Forsdick, proffering a newly filled tankard of beer.

'Cheers!' replied Crump automatically.

Forsdick, subsiding in his chair with the careful economy of a heavily built man nursing a freshly poured drink, surveyed his preoccupied guest.

'All right,' he said. 'Let's have it. What's on your mind?'

'It's talk, mostly,' admitted Crump, staring at his tankard. 'But it's pretty definite talk. My chaps have been drilling down on the *aboura*, as you know; practising the guard-of-honour ceremony. They've heard a lot of funny things while they've been there. And then my *other* chaps – ' he jerked his head as if to mark a special category, and Forsdick nodded, ' – my other chaps have brought in a whole batch of stories. The talk downtown is that this is a special *aboura*, for white Government only, and no Maulas are to attend. If they do attend, there'll be trouble.'

'But that's just another rumour!' said Forsdick. 'You know how many of *them* there've been lately.'

'Maybe. But it is a fact that the Dinamaula Regiment have been drilling and practising, up on the hill, and the thing they've been practising is, putting a cordon round the *aboura*. Or at least, that's what it looks like. They've marked out a space the same shape and size as the *aboura*; they run out and surround it, just like my policemen, as soon as the signal's given; and then they all turn *outwards*.'

'Odd,' said Forsdick carelessly.

'It's bloody odd,' replied Crump. 'And if you put the two things together – the talk of a boycott, and the drill to keep people away from the *aboura* – then it adds up to a fair-sized flop, tomorrow afternoon.'

'Could be,' agreed Forsdick, still unimpressed. 'Certainly it fits in with what one of those bloody Pressmen said to me in the bar last night. It was that bastard Tulbach Browne – he's just back from Port Victoria. He said: "I'll give you three to one there won't be an *aboura*." I took him in pounds.'

'You'll lose,' said Crump morosely. 'The fact that he's back in Gamate is just about all we needed.'

'*But*,' continued Forsdick, after a deep draught of beer, 'I honestly don't think it will work. You know what the Maulas are. They'll walk twenty miles, just to watch Andrew laying the first stone of a new wash-house. They'll ride *fifty* miles for a firework display on Guy Fawkes night. Anything for a free show ... I'll bet you they won't be able to resist the idea of a full-scale Governor's *aboura*. They'll turn up in their thousands, whatever the talk is beforehand. They always do. The town's absolutely bursting with people already.'

'But if they're kept away,' said Crump doubtfully. 'What then?'

'How can they be kept away? There are a hundred thousand of them.'

'It could happen ... To start with, the word seems to have got around that there's to be a boycott. Some Maula herdsmen from one of the outlying villages were seen trekking *away* from Gamate, this morning. When they were asked why they were leaving before the *aboura*, they all said: "A man told us there could be no *aboura* without the chief." When there's that sort of uncertainty, it wouldn't take many people – if they were really tough and determined – to block off the *aboura* ground, and keep it blocked off ... There may be a hundred thousand Maulas in Gamate, but they're mostly sheep, as you know.'

'They haven't been behaving like sheep, during the last few days.'

Crump shook his head. 'That's exactly what they have been behaving like – sheep on a stampede. They've been persuaded that they're being ill-treated, and that Dinamaula has been railroaded out of Gamate. Result –

the whole place is in an uproar, and a hundred thousand Maulas, normally as sweet as a nut, have become completely unmanageable.'

'Who's behind it all?'

'Puero, chiefly.' Crump brooded. 'Now there's a character who is high on my list for exile, when the time comes for a showdown ... But the whole resistance idea has caught on amazingly, in the last few days. It hardly needs a single leader now. In so far as there's ever been a co-ordinated tribal movement, with definite aims, this is it.'

'I wish to God Andrew would do something constructive about it,' grumbled Forsdick.

Crump remained silent. Forsdick's position as District Commissioner was less delicate than his own. Forsdick, near the throne, might comment freely. Crump – the security arm – could only do what he was told. He also liked Andrew Macmillan a great deal better than he did Forsdick, whose partiality for Molly Crump continued to be notorious.

'I suppose I shouldn't say this,' continued Forsdick, closely regarding his beer, 'but the old boy rather seems to have lost his grip lately.'

'It's been a very difficult situation altogether,' said Crump noncommittally.

'For God's sake, all it needs is a bit of organization! Just work it out. Our side can't really function, with so few chaps, unless we nail down the people who are behind the resistance. That means the Press, and the Regents.' He gestured expansively. 'We've got to clear the Press out of Gamate, and then tell the Regents that they'll be out of a job unless they toe the line. Simple.'

Crump smiled in spite of himself. 'Simple! I'd like to hear something complicated. First, the Press won't go. Why should they? Second, the Regents won't co-operate. Why should *they*? Thirdly, even if by a miracle both these things happened, you've still got a tribe in a state of continuous revolt, refusing to obey any sort of order unless Dinamaula comes back.'

'And fourthly,' said Forsdick obstinately, 'we've got to give Dinamaula the sack, once and for all, and find a chief who will co-operate properly.'

After a pause, Crump said: 'I'm beginning to see why Andrew's job is so complicated.'

Presently there was an interruption. Mrs Forsdick, in a faded cotton housecoat, her expression one of long-continued, acid discontent, put her head round the door. She noted the beer, and the air of masculine relaxation. She noted her husband, flushed and pontifical, raising a glass to his lips.

'Still hard at it?' she inquired, with practised domestic irony.

'Yes,' answered Forsdick shortly, not turning round.

Mrs Forsdick sighed. 'All this,' she said, 'just for a visit from the Governor.'

Crump smiled a conciliatory Irish smile. 'Just you wait till George is Governor himself. Then you'll appreciate all the planning.'

'I'm still waiting,' said Mrs Forsdick sourly, and withdrew.

Forsdick pursed his lips, and then, with an edge of guilt in his manner, reached out for the file of papers on the table at his side.

'Well,' he said heavily, 'let's get down to details ... First there's the timing tomorrow. If the Governor leaves the Residency sharp at eleven-forty ...'

Waiting on his *stoep* for the three Regents, whom he had summoned for a final appeal for co-operation, Andrew Macmillan talked to his headboy Johannes. It was the cool of the evening, the most grateful moment of Gamate's heat-oppressed day; the sun, low in the west, was screened and softened by the smoke from tens of thousands of Maula cooking fires, the air in the shaded garden was benign. Macmillan's life had held many such moments, when the end of the working day brought him ease and peace; but on this evening there was hardly a memory of the old contentment – for the peace of the Residency garden was a deceptive peace, and the smoke cloud drifting over the enclosed valley of Gamate was a cloak for plotting and secret hatred.

When he talked to Johannes, he had the same sense of doom. It sometimes seemed that Johannes was now the only man in Gamate to whom he could speak freely and easily; they had shared much of the past, they agreed on many things, they were both old men of Gamate, with a sense of tradition and order ... If all the Maulas were like Johannes, thought Macmillan morosely, then Gamate would be a happy place. But every hour of every day showed clearly that Gamate was not a happy place, and might never be so again; that men like Johannes were rare men; and that their place in the tribe had been usurped and taken over by tough and truculent youngsters.

It might be that the day of himself and of Johannes was now over. History might have left them behind; history, and change, and a hungry search for freedom. None of those things was a bad thing, but they were things to be controlled, not allowed to run riot; explosive things that must be guarded from the malignant spark. Gamate was old and backward; the world outside was new and sophisticated; the two could only come together, and mix, under a formal pattern and a parent eye.

It was true that some day Gamate itself would catch up with the rest of the world, and would be new and sophisticated in its turn; but that day was not tomorrow, nor the next. It could not be, without disaster. Macmillan knew his Maulas; he knew what they could naturally learn, what they could not digest, what would intoxicate them beyond bearing. It had long been his task to act as a pacemaker for the tribe – just as thousands of other devoted men, in thousands of other parts of Africa, were striving to preserve a balance between the somnolent old world and the forceful and garish new.

It could be that this very country of Pharamaul was next in line for the disaster of sudden emancipation. It might be their turn for the fiercely coloured spotlight, the nakedness of prematurity … All Macmillan's instinct, all his long training, told him that Pharamaul was not ready for it; it would be like a heady and burning draught which, after uneasy gulping and choking, the patient would spew out, with disgusting violence.

Meanwhile, Macmillan talked to Johannes, the other old man of Gamate; talked to him, listened to his slow answers, and feared for the future. It had not surprised him when Johannes, two days earlier, had said: 'Governor come, hold big *aboura*', at least an hour before he himself got the telegram of instruction. Pharamaul was like that. Now, chatting with his old servant, his old friend, he wished he might borrow a like prescience, where the near future was concerned.

'What do they say about the *aboura* tomorrow, Johannes?'

Johannes considered carefully before replying. He was shuffling up and down the *stoep*, tidying, dusting, rearranging. His bare black feet slurred on the rough boards, his white coat hung in folds round a body which seemed to be slowly shrinking inwards to ancient skin and bone.

'They say, many people coming in to Gamate, *barena*,' he answered after a long pause. 'Coming in from all around …' He gestured. 'But they say, can they pass through to the *aboura*?'

'Pass through what?'

Johannes scratched his head. 'Pass through other people,' he answered finally.

'What other people? Do you mean other people who will stop them coming to the *aboura*? Who are these people?'

'Young men,' said Johannes.

'How many young men?'

'Not many,' answered Johannes. 'But very strong. They say they are ready to kill, to stop the *aboura*. Some people go back to their village already.'

Macmillan sighed. It confirmed all that Crump had been telling him; there was to be a boycott, and it would be tightly and toughly organized.

'Have we no friends in Gamate?' he asked after a moment.

Johannes paused in his task of cleaning an ashtray. 'Some friends, *barena*,' he said gently. 'But they have been led away by clever men.'

'What clever men? Maula men?'

'Some Maula men. Some white men. They say, how can there be an *aboura* without the chief? They say, where is our chief?' Intent and serious, his old face changing expression with swift and deadly clarity, Johannes was suddenly acting the dilemma of the tribe: the clever men asking their questions and pushing their argument, the others listening and being persuaded. 'They say, is he in prison? Is he dead by hanging? They say, how can we trust Government, since our chief is stolen away when he should be declared chief before all the tribe?' Johannes shook his head, returning to his own thoughts. 'The tribe is not happy, *barena*. Clever men know this.'

'But that is what the *aboura* is for,' said Macmillan curtly. 'So that the Governor can explain why Dinamaula has been taken away, and what will happen in the future.'

Johannes, polishing slowly, said: 'Perhaps too late to explain those things.'

'It's not too late!' exclaimed Macmillan. 'There will be an *aboura*.'

'Yes, *barena*,' said Johannes. 'White suit all ready.'

'The Governor will speak to the tribe. At twelve o'clock tomorrow morning.'

'Yes, *barena*.' Johannes put his head on one side, and turned towards the garden and the road leading down to Gamate. 'Car coming now,' he said.

Macmillan turned, looking over his shoulder. The yellow dust cloud which signalled an approaching car was slowly mounting, between Gamate and the Residency, catching the last sun as it billowed and spread.

'That's the Regents,' he said. 'Bring coffee in five minutes.'

'Yes, *barena*.'

'And tell your friends, there will be an *aboura* tomorrow.'

'I tell them, *barena*.'

'Tell them again.'

'Yes, *barena* … You keep many policemen here in Gamate?'

Macmillan stared. 'I shall keep enough. Why, Johannes?'

'My friends say they like *plenty* policemen, tomorrow and the next day.'

But the car did not bear the Regents, coming for their instructions; the car bore Captain Crump, bringing an odd and disgraceful piece of news.

Crump stood before Andrew at the open door of the *stoep*; trim and taut in his freshly-pressed khaki uniform, his belt and holster polished to a brilliant sheen. He looked at Andrew, and said laconically: 'The Regents are all ill.'

It took a few moments for Macmillan to realize what the other man was talking about.

'Ill? What the hell do you mean, *ill*? I sent for them. Aren't they coming?'

'No.' His principal communication made, Crump relaxed somewhat, like a herald who has delivered, against his will and prudent judgement, an insulting answer to an offer of parley. 'I tried Katsaula first. He really is ill, as you know. Then I went to Seralo's hut. He sent his best respects to the Resident Commissioner – ' Crump's voice was ironic, ' – but he is too ill to come to the Residency this evening. Then I called on Puero.' Crump paused.

'Well?' asked Andrew, near to violent anger.

'He made *me* ill,' said Crump contemptuously. 'He was drunk. There were a couple of Pressmen there. He said he couldn't come. I asked why not, and he lurched forward and was sick all over my boots … Then he said: "You see now that I am ill", and lay down again. I damned nearly hit him.'

Suddenly Andrew Macmillan felt very old. He was glad that he was sitting down, in a wide chair that offered him total support. At that moment of feebleness and defeat, he could not have raised a hand in greeting.

'Well, I can't *make* them come,' he said, on a low note, after a long silence. 'All I wanted to do was to ask them to meet the Governor at the *aboura*, and to persuade the tribe to listen …' It was a pathetic scaling-down of his earlier hopes and intentions; Crump felt as if he were listening to some lachrymose apology from a publicly convicted liar. 'If they won't come, they won't … Is there anything else we can do?'

Crump thought: it's too late to do a damned thing – we should have handled this differently, from the very beginning he knew in his heart that he had disagreed entirely with every phase of Andrew Macmillan's tactics; the latter had been tough with Dinamaula at that delicate moment when he should have been persuasive and friendly; then he had relented and cajoled, when the only course was a steady disciplinary pressure. But Crump could not say these things now, in this hour of inner decay; for now it was a salvage job – salvage of the *aboura* tomorrow, salvage of Macmillan himself.

'I don't think there's much to be done at the moment,' he answered slowly. 'As far as the *aboura* is concerned, we must take all the precautions that we can. I'll be posting a sharp lookout for intimidation, and of course we'll make our own arrangements, to keep the *aboura* as free and open as possible. It ought to be all right, even if we don't get as many people as we expected.'

'Perhaps the *aboura* doesn't really matter,' said Andrew. Again he was scaling down his plans, fatally cheapening his price. 'If it's a flop, it just can't be helped. But as soon as it's over, we've really got to get a grip on Gamate.' The word 'grip' made him look at his hand, lying open on the arm of his chair; the fingers, loose and flaccid, were trembling perceptibly. Not much grip there, he thought in forlorn humour, and let his hand drop on his lap. 'Even if the Regents won't co-operate, somehow we've got to persuade the tribe to settle down again.'

'But that's the whole idea of the *aboura*,' said Crump doubtfully. In his heart he was appalled by this progressive surrender of their few remaining strong points. 'Surely it's got to be our first consideration, to make it work. The Governor's visit could do a lot of good. We've got to back him up, haven't we? – lay on the best show we can?'

'Certainly,' agreed Macmillan. 'But if it doesn't work, if there is a boycott ...' His voice tailed off. 'We must just hope for the best.'

'We must just *do* our best,' corrected Crump, made bold by his own impatience, his still-confident determination.

'Yes,' said Macmillan, nodding, as if it were the same thing either way. 'We must just do our best.'

II

It was David Bracken's second dawn in Pharamaul; the second sunrise that he had spent on the train winding its slow way north from Port Victoria to Gamate. Much of that second journey was like the first, because an African dawn did not change in a thousand years; the ants still crawled, the burnt-grass smell of the desert still rose inexorably to the day, the sun still set the eastern sky on fire. What was different was the occasion. A few weeks before, he had travelled to Gamate as a pilgrim, on a new journey involving a personal quest. Now he was part of the Governor's formal entourage, part of the baggage train of officialdom; and the excursion had nothing personal about it – it was undertaken in accordance with a set of rules which, like the African dawn, had not changed within the memory of man.

They had been seen off in Port Victoria by the whole Secretariat staff, a police guard of honour, twenty-four town councillors, a troop of boy scouts, and the fire brigade band. The Governor had inspected the guard of honour, shaken hands with the town councillors, nodded encouragement to the boy scouts, and taken formal farewell of his staff. The band had played 'God Save the Queen', and 'Will Ye No' Come Back Again'. Then there had been a mortifying pause; the stationmaster signalled furiously to the engine driver, and the engine driver wrestled with a recalcitrant valve, while the staff, the scouts, the guard of honour, and the town councillors, frozen into a static tableau of farewell, waited for release.

The band performed a hesitant *reprise* of 'Will Ye No' Come Back Again'. Then the train started, with a teeth-rattling jerk, and their mission became part of the assembly line of history.

David shared a compartment with Captain Simpson, the naval aide; and no two men, on a simple overnight journey of two hundred miles, could conceivably have taken more personal luggage with them. Captain Simpson, it seemed, intended to be ready for anything, on this venture into the dark interior. He had a large suitcase full of clothes. He had a tin box, teak-lined, containing his tropical uniform. He had a swordcase housing his sword, a gun case with a matched pair of twelve-bore shotguns, and a velvet lined casket for his medals. He had a bedroll, a portable canvas washstand, and a wicker basket (made by Aspreys of Bond Street) fitted up as a six-person travelling bar.

David could not fully match this paraphernalia; but he himself had four cases, one of them a curiously shaped aluminium box containing the white doeskin helmet that went with his uniform. Altogether, their compartment was crowded to the roof. They were late to bed, on that first evening. Captain Simpson's wickerwork bar had been in full operation. David's portable wireless (a parting present from Nicole Steuart) had given them a series of soporific airs from Radio Port Victoria. The Governor, indubitably relaxed in tartan carpet slippers and a velvet smoking jacket, had paid them a visit from his private coach next door, and had talked long and learnedly of Pharamaul's lesser-known airmail stamps, and the curious bird life which (with luck) they might be able to see the following day ... When he had gone, Captain Simpson poured them both another monumental pink gin, and said, with massive deliberation: 'Remarkable man, that ... Of course, he's wasted in Pharamaul.'

In the morning, it was the same as David remembered from his last journey. Their train stopped at a nearly deserted siding, where the single-track railway line split briefly into two, in order to take on water and allow the southbound train to pass them. Once again, it was a moment of magic; a fiery dawn in Africa, in the middle of a limitless plain of burnt grass, withered scrub, occasional grey reed huts, and cattle standing immobile, caught in the trance of centuries. As David prepared to leave the compartment, eager to tread an earth so strange, Captain Simpson opened a bloodshot eye and peered down from the upper berth.

'Up pretty early,' he remarked gruffly.

'I'm just hopping out to take a look around. I can probably get us some coffee.'

Captain Simpson brightened. 'Can you, by Jove? Have they tacked on a dining car?'

'No. I'll scrounge a couple of mugs from the engine driver.'

'I beg your pardon?'

'They make their own coffee in the cabin. It's pretty good.'

Captain Simpson closed his eyes. 'Thank you,' he said austerely. 'I would prefer to wait till Gamate.'

Two hours later their party was welcomed with an equal formality at Gamate station. The band played, the baggage boys stared, the policemen formed a guard of honour; Crump's tremendous salute was matched by Andrew Macmillan's grimly ceremonial greeting, while the cameras flashed and a handful of white bystanders clapped and smiled. But presently, driving through the town towards the Residency, where they were all to have breakfast before going over the details of the *aboura*, David was struck by its wholly dead air. Remembering the telegrams and the police reports and Crump's ominous assessments, he had prepared himself for many things: threatening crowds, police charges, stray rifle shots, bodies lying prone on the dusty earth.

He had been ready for anything save what he now saw – a lifeless town turned inwards upon itself, and confined within its own huts. He was reminded of Shebiya, the U-Maula capital to the northwards, when he had visited it a few weeks earlier. On the surface, there was nothing to remark, nothing to catch the eye; behind the nothing was an atmosphere of close-pressing sullen menace. The *aboura* ground itself, as they crossed it in the wake of the police jeep, and the Governor's car with the standard bravely flying, and Forsdick and Captain Simpson in an old-fashioned shooting brake, was absolutely deserted, as if it were a special part of the earth's surface utterly damned, utterly taboo.

When he mentioned his thoughts to Llewellyn, who was driving him, the latter shook his head grimly.

'Aye, it's quiet,' he agreed. 'Much too quiet … The town's stiff with people, but they're all keeping indoors.' He looked at the dashboard clock. 'Seven o'clock – that means five hours to the opening of the *aboura*. At any other time, the whole *aboura* ground would have been jam-packed with people already – in fact, half of them would have spent the whole night there, to make sure of a good place.'

'What's it mean?'

'A fiasco,' said Llewellyn laconically. 'You can see it coming a mile off.'

'You mean, they're not going to attend.'

'No,' said Llewellyn, 'they're not.'

'I noticed something from the train, during the last few miles,' remarked David. 'There seemed to be a lot of people, and waggons, moving away from Gamate.'

Llewellyn nodded. They were clear of the main town now, and climbing the hill towards the Residency. The sun was melting the last of the dew, the day was new and bright; but the only things moving were goats, and the small naked children that herded them. All else was blank. The hut doors were shut, the road deserted; no single salute greeted their four-car cavalcade. The police jeep, the Governor's standard, Forsdick's shooting brake, Llewellyn's car – all might have been invisible.

'There's been quite an exodus,' agreed Llewellyn. 'I don't blame them, mind you – things have been pretty rough here, the last few days, and the ordinary Maulas, particularly the ones who come trekking in from the villages, are very respectable and law-abiding. But there are still thousands of people here, and not a shadow to show for it.' He laughed. 'I hope H E won't be too disappointed.'

David, aware of subtle overtones, asked suddenly: 'Didn't you want the Governor to come?'

Llewellyn, turning sideways, gave him a sardonic look. 'We can always use a good man,' he said. 'But it may not be *quite* what H E is accustomed to.'

At the same moment, two cars ahead of them, the Governor was looking round him, with puzzled eyes.

'Seems extraordinarily quiet,' he observed after a moment. 'I suppose it's still a bit early in the day, what?'

Andrew Macmillan, beside him on the back seat of the ancient Residency limousine, stared steadfastly at the back of his chauffeur's cropped head.

'It is quiet,' he agreed. His hands, sweating in their white cotton gloves, were gripping the knees of his immaculate white dress trousers. His tall helmet pressed heavily on his head; his sword, caught at an angle, irked his leg. It was the very first time, in thirty years of official life, when he felt his uniform to be ridiculous and futile.

'But plenty of crowds later on, eh?' pursued the Governor.

'Sir,' said Andrew, with difficulty, 'there have been some developments ... It's possible that most of the tribe will refuse to attend the *aboura*, unless Dinamaula is allowed back to Gamate.'

'Oh come!' said the Governor, stiffly. 'That can scarcely be so, when my sole purpose in being here today is to explain why he must be kept away.'

III

'Stand still!' commanded Mrs Forsdick, her mouth full of pins, her expression one of roguish servitude. 'How can I get you ready, if you fidget so?'

'You're tickling me,' said David Bracken, squirming. There was something about Mrs Forsdick's manner which was contagious. 'When this uniform was made for me in London, I swear that the collar was all right.'

'Well, it's not all right now.' Mrs Forsdick gave a sharp tug at David's shoulder. 'And your medals are all crooked, too. Pity the poor girl who marries you!'

'What poor girl is that?' asked David.

'Oh, I've heard lots of stories ...' Breathing heavily, obviously enjoying herself, Mrs Forsdick began to sew up the blue-and-gold collar that topped David's uniform, while David, standing like an old-fashioned tailor's dummy in the middle of the Forsdick sitting-room, wondered how long the session would be prolonged. There were quite enough accommodational hazards in being quartered on the Forsdicks, during his visit to Gamate, without becoming involved in a domestic melodrama as well. 'I suppose,' said Mrs Forsdick, turning more thoughtful as she completed a difficult corner, 'that you think you're going to set everything to rights, just by putting on full-dress uniform and holding an *aboura*.'

'Yes,' said David, amused. 'I think that's a very fair statement.'

From the room beyond, George Forsdick, who was sipping a mid-morning whisky and reading a week-old copy of the *Times of Pharamaul*, broke in: 'They've got as good a chance,' he called out, 'as anyone else in this bloody place!'

'George!' said Mrs Forsdick, sewing busily and automatically, 'watch that language!'

'How am I looking?' asked David, covertly squeezing her hand.

'Wonderful,' answered Mrs Forsdick. 'Perhaps she's a lucky girl, after all.'

'If there *was* a girl,' said David, 'I'd agree with you.' He gave Mrs Forsdick's sandpaper palm another squeeze, mentally apologizing at the same time. Sorry, Nicole, he thought, almost aloud; you know how it is, you know it doesn't mean a thing … Mrs Forsdick's emotional imbalance was really highly infectious, and for a few hours at least he had to live with it.

'I suppose all the Press people have come back to Gamate?' said Mrs Forsdick, preparing to bite off a thread.

'Yes,' answered David. 'Those jet-propelled vultures are back at work.'

'Have you met one called John Raper?'

'Oh, yes!' said David. 'He's quite a well-known performer.'

Mrs Forsdick's hand hovered over his collar. 'Performer?' she repeated.

'Well,' said David, retrieving from the cobwebs of his mind the faint shadow of a piece of gossip. 'I mean, he's a pretty good Pressman.'

'Is he back here?' asked Mrs Forsdick.

'I don't think so.'

'I thought you said they were all here.'

'John Raper,' said David, 'is something of an exception.'

'I'll say he is!' came Forsdick's booming voice from the next room.

'But why should he want to stay in Port Victoria?' insisted Mrs Forsdick.

'It's a long and dirty story!' called out George Forsdick, with unnecessary relish. 'And I speak as an expert.'

'George!' warned Mrs Forsdick.

'Sorry, dear,' said Forsdick, unrepentant. 'Just a spot of *lèse majesté*.'

The telephone rang in the narrow hallway, seeming to rescue the household from incipient crisis.

George Forsdick took the call; they heard him saying first, 'Forsdick,' then 'Yes,' then 'Yes, sir,' the latter many times, with increasing formality. It was a one-sided conversation, which the other two listened to with conventionally disguised, secretly avid curiosity. Mrs Forsdick continued to sew, David continued to stand in an attitude of constrained availability; but on this morning in Gamate, with the dubious *aboura* in the forefront of all their minds, any telephone call was part of a pattern of speculation, of which no segment could be disregarded. When Forsdick, with a final: 'I'll tell Bracken straight away, sir,' put down the receiver and walked through into the living-room, he found waiting a readily attentive audience.

He looked at David. 'That was the Governor,' he said importantly. 'There's a job for you.'

'For me?' David straightened his collar, adjusted his helmet, all with the uncomfortable feeling that he was exhibiting a childish, do-or-die reaction. 'What is it?'

'According to Crump,' continued Forsdick, 'the boycott is working, and it may not be worthwhile holding the *aboura*.' He looked at his wristwatch. 'It's half past ten already – an hour and a half to go. There still isn't a single soul down on the *aboura* ground. The Governor wants you to go down now, scout around to see what's happening, and report back to the Residency on the tax office telephone.'

'All right,' said David, feeling heroic and inadequate at the same time. 'How do I get there? Do I go now?'

'Crump is driving by in the jeep,' answered Forsdick. 'He'll leave you at the tax office, while he takes a look round himself. All you have to do is keep in touch on the phone.'

'But what happens if no one comes to the *aboura*?' asked Mrs Forsdick.

'Among other things,' said Forsdick grimly, 'Andrew Macmillan will be out of a job.'

Equity struggled briefly with ambition, in Grace Forsdick's mind. Equity won.

'But it isn't his fault,' she said.

'It's going to be someone's fault,' said her husband. 'And it's not going to be mine.'

'How many people will there have to be,' asked David, wrestling with the outlines of his task, 'before it's worth while holding the *aboura*?'

'The Governor is leaving that to you,' answered Forsdick, somewhat dauntingly. 'He's got to have some sort of a crowd to talk to. If there isn't a crowd, he won't come down.'

'What a terrible thing!' said Mrs Forsdick, lost in some interior speculation.

'You wait,' said Forsdick grimly. 'This is just the beginning of chapter two.'

'I'll drop you off here,' said Crump, braking the jeep sharply as it drew level with the tax office. 'You know where the phone is. If I were you, I should ring up the Residency every quarter of an hour.'

'Where will you be?' asked David, preparing to step down.

Crump waved his hand vaguely. 'Around ... I want to see how my chaps are doing, and if there's any open picketing or intimidation that's keeping people away from the *aboura*. I'll come back here in about half an hour.'

The sun burned suddenly hot as David, stepping down, stood between the jeep and the ramshackle, forlorn tax office. He grinned nervously at Keith Crump.

'It's just like Shebiya,' he said, 'with all those tough customers keeping well out of sight.'

Crump put the jeep into gear. 'Good luck,' he said, with no answering grin. And then, surprisingly: 'Lock yourself into the inner office if things get tough. I'll bail you out myself, for certain.' Then he was gone.

David Bracken looked cautiously about him. He stood in isolation at the top end of the *aboura*; before him was a space three hundred feet square, of bare brown earth beaten level by countless generations of Maulas, and now entirely deserted. The pattern of white lines, the carefully calculated crosses and squares, the fluttering decorations, all were mocked into futility by the deep brooding silence that enclosed the whole scene. It had other containing outlines, but they were not the outlines that could bring him any comfort or hope.

Directly across from him, under the arid thorn trees, was a group of people; he could make out several Pressmen – Tulbach Browne and Pikkie Joubert among them. There was the prominent white cassock of Father Hawthorne, the small brown figure of Father Schwemmer; and Oosthuizen's enormous bulk towering over them all. There was a handful of other white spectators – Fellows from the Gamate Hotel, one of the doctors from the hospital, a couple of nurses in trim blue uniforms. But in the whole circle, only three black faces were visible: Voice Tula, the tribal interpreter, and two of Crump's native policemen.

They were all looking towards him, as he stood on the balcony of the tax office, and listened to the diminishing sound of the police jeep as it moved out of sight between the huts. Under the hot sun, he was aware of three elements: the silent, watchful players, the frieze of goats and dogs and flies and heat and dust that was a normal part of any Gamate morning; and the cruel solitude of the *aboura*, on which no foot save his own had yet trodden, or was likely to tread. At his back, the paper decorations rustled in the faint breeze, making a dry noise like the stirring of ancient bones.

In front of him was the loudspeaker and the control panel of the public address system. At a loss for his next move, David stepped up to it, switched it on, and blew through the microphone. A subdued roar answered him. Then he said, on a low note: 'Testing, testing, testing ...' and his words were carried to the farthest limits of the *aboura*. The people under the thorn trees all stared afresh in his direction; the goats and dogs raised their heads momentarily. He longed to say: 'Come to the *aboura* now, or I will burn your whole village ...' He switched off the microphone, and retreated into the shadows of the tax office. His immaculate white uniform, clinking medals, obtrusive sword, all seemed part of some ridiculous, fatuous charade. He closed the screen door behind him, and picked up the telephone.

Unexpectedly, Captain Simpson answered his call, with a bare moment's delay; David could imagine them all waiting up at the Residency, with the Governor and Andrew Macmillan talking weightily in one room, and Simpson (whose views were not essential) detailed to man the telephone. Momentarily, David was conscious of a great gulf, between the bare *aboura* and the naval aide-de-camp: between black Gamate and white officialdom.

There was this vast empty space, hot and deserted, which he could just see out of the corner of his eye, through the tax office window; and then there was the Residency, with the Governor, the Resident Commissioner, and the naval aide-de-camp, all three of them tremendously starched and white, sharing between them at least twenty assorted orders and decorations of undoubted merit, and waiting – waiting like tormented virgins for the invitation to the dance.

It was his sad duty to tell them that, so far from their being the belles of the ball, the ball itself might never be held. He wished he could feel like a mother – jealous, protective, and solacing. As it was, he felt like a fool.

'Hallo,' he said. 'I just rang up to say that I'm here.'

'That's good,' came Captain Simpson's booming voice. 'We were hoping you'd keep in touch. What's the form, old boy?'

'Not too encouraging,' answered David. He looked once more beyond the dusty room to the *aboura*. The sunlight was fatally revealing. Not a single human being stirred. 'In fact, there's no one here at all, at the moment.'

'I say!' said Captain Simpson. 'That's a pretty bad show, isn't it? I must tell H E.'

'Do that …' David looked at his watch. It was eleven o'clock. 'I'll ring again in a quarter of an hour.'

'Good show!' said Captain Simpson. 'Anything else? Where's that policeman fellow?'

'Driving about. Trying to find out what's going on. He'll be back before very long.'

'Good show,' said Captain Simpson again. 'I'll tell H E.'

David felt a sudden wish to draw aside the curtain and lay bare the facts. 'I don't think this is any good,' he said.

'How do you mean, exactly?' asked Simpson.

'They're not going to turn up. No one is.'

'Oh … I'd better tell H E.'

'I'll ring again,' said David, depressed, 'at eleven-fifteen.'

He replaced the receiver, opened the screen door, and went out into the sunlight again. The heat smote him, and the scorched, dusty smell of the *aboura*. Just in front of him, a scrawny goat was licking at the white-painted cross where the Governor was to stand. After a moment David set out, determinedly, to traverse the empty ground towards the Press correspondents.

It was a long walk; his uniform was tight and stiff, his sword bumped foolishly against his thigh. He felt that there must be many intent eyes watching him – not just the eyes of the Pressmen, whose curiosity was obvious, or the handful of white spectators, but thousands of other eyes, Maula eyes beyond the fringe of thorn trees and the grey ranks of the huts. They must be watching, and hating, and mocking, and thinking: 'At last a man enters the *aboura*.' But he was a white man, a very white man with medals and a sword. One such man, they would say, does not make an *aboura*.

The group of Pressmen opened outwards as he approached. Tulbach Browne smiled a thin smile of welcome. Clandestine Lebourget and a news cameraman took a few quick shots. Pikkie Joubert nodded, Axel Hallmarck regarded him with sharp, weasel attention. Father Hawthorne stared with burning eyes at a point two feet above his head. David did not know what to say, and therefore said the first thing that came into his mind.

'*Ahsula!*' he said, and raised his hand in the formal Maula salute. There was a vague murmur in reply. One single man answered him directly. It was Voice Tula, standing dutifully at one side, ready to help. '*Ahsula,*' said Voice Tula, and bowed.

After a pause, Tulbach Browne asked, ironically: 'What time is the meeting?'

'Twelve o'clock,' answered David.

'Is it still on?' asked Axel Hallmarck.

'Yes,' said David.

'Man!' said Pikkie Joubert, 'those niggers had better hurry up!'

'When is the Governor coming down?' asked Noblesse O'Toole, throwing away one flashbulb and substituting another.

'At eleven-forty-five,' answered David.

'How will he be dressed?'

'The same as me, roughly.'

'Only wearing more medals, one supposes,' said Tulbach Browne blandly.

'He's older,' said David flippantly. He felt in a curious mood, of mixed anxiety and carelessness. He knew it was wrong to give any save the most guarded answers, but he could not bring himself to the necessary point of watchfulness. The *aboura* was going to be a complete disaster. He did not like these people, who were partly responsible. He tried, and failed, to feel that the thing mattered at all.

Pikkie Joubert was surveying him with inquisitive eyes.

'Excuse me,' he said presently. 'What's that first ribbon, eh?'

'The Military Cross,' answered David briefly.

After a long pause, Tulbach Browne jerked his thumb towards the empty *aboura*. 'You must be finding this a very different sort of war.'

'It is a war of ideas!' proclaimed Father Hawthorne, with holy fervour. 'Here there are no medals – only wounds.'

David Bracken turned aside, looking out across the *aboura*. It was no good being angry, or becoming provoked in any way. The day was too hot, the whole occasion too ridiculous. He found himself gazing into the eyes of Voice Tula.

'Where are all the people?' he asked, on the spur of the moment.

'*Barena*?' said Voice Tula.

'It is nearly time for the *aboura*. Where are the people?'

'They do not come, I think.'

The others were listening closely; Axel Hallmarck was scribbling on the back of an envelope.

'But this is a special day,' said David, persevering.

'Oh yes, sir,' answered Voice Tula. His voice had a musically ironic lilt. 'It is the day when Dinamaula was to be proclaimed chief.'

'It is the day that the Governor holds his *aboura*,' corrected David sharply.

'Yes,' agreed Voice Tula. 'The very same day.'

Their eyes met briefly before David turned away again. He tried to make allowances for the other man's situation, the delicate balance of an interpreter, with one foot in the tribal camp, the other among the white men – and an audience of yet a third group, dubious in their allegiance, flatteringly attentive. If he himself had been Voice Tula, he might well have tried to show off in the same way … He raised his head as a new sound made itself heard, among the huts at the upper end of the *aboura*.

It was the police jeep returning, grinding in low gear with the engine revving at near-maximum speed. It came into view between the tax office and a nearby clump of thorn bushes, with Crump at the wheel, square and trim in his full-dress whites, and a policeman by his side. They all watched it as, after pausing at the tax office, it circled the *aboura*, making for David's easily recognizable figure at the other side of the open space. It flew a small Union Jack from a metal staff welded to the top of the radiator; it seemed the only sensible and dependable thing within many miles ... *Enter a messenger*, thought David, unreasonably glad of the khaki jeep, the white of Crump's uniform, the fluttering red-white-and-blue of the flag; enter a messenger, bearing tidings of magnificent victory from Agincourt, Waterloo, Alamein. But he knew well enough that, for all its brave air of competence, the jeep bore news of shoddy defeat.

Once more the circle of correspondents opened outwards as Crump, stepping briskly from the driving seat, strode towards them. Watching him, David remembered his Maula nickname – 'The Shining Soldier'. It seemed especially appropriate now, as he drew near to them; on this day of the Governor's formal *aboura* in Gamate, Crump seemed to embody all the soldierly virtues of smartness, cleanliness, and discipline. It might be that, in the present circumstances, these virtues were making no inch of headway in any direction; but that did not mean that they would be abandoned – rather that they would be maintained with special determination.

Crump saluted David as he drew near – to the latter's surprise. He suddenly realized that Crump was indicating the necessity for putting on a show, and that he himself, as the Governor's personal envoy, could be accorded full ceremonial treatment. He returned the salute, with equal gravity and ceremony. If they were starting to retreat – as he already guessed and feared – then they would retreat in good order.

'Any news?' he asked.

'Yes,' answered Crump, in crisp tones. 'The tribe is being prevented from reaching the *aboura*.' He was speaking half to David, half to the ring of correspondents who stood within earshot. 'The opposition have managed to put a pretty effective cordon round the *aboura* ground. No one can get through.'

'That means,' said David, conscious also of a public audience, 'that the *aboura* can't be held.'

'No,' answered Crump. 'Not in the present circumstances.'

The Pressmen drew closer, surrounding the two of them.

'What "opposition"?' asked Tulbach Browne. 'What kind of an effective cordon do you mean?'

Crump looked at him, his glance cold, his bearing stiff. 'There's a sort of noose round the whole *aboura*,' he answered, after a pause. 'All the paths and approaches are guarded. There's a rough element at work as well. It's impossible to break through.'

'Does anyone *want* to break through?' asked Axel Hallmarck.

'Of course they do,' answered Crump brusquely. 'There's a meeting. There should be a lot of people here. They're being kept away, sometimes forcibly.'

'Have you any evidence of that?' asked Tulbach Browne.

'Yes,' said Crump, without hesitation. 'I've already arrested two people for using threats and intimidation.'

'Two,' repeated Axel Hallmarck, with careful emphasis.

'There are lots of others,' said Crump, persevering. 'But it's almost impossible to put them down.'

David became aware that other people were joining their group: Oosthuizen and Fellows walked towards them, and then some of the nurses from the hospital. There was a general murmur of comment. He raised his voice.

'It's obvious,' he said, 'that there's an organized boycott of the *aboura*. But apart from that, the people who actually want to attend are being kept away.'

'Who by?' asked Pikkie Joubert.

'The gangster element in the tribe.'

'Can we quote you on "gangster element"?' asked Tulbach Browne, faintly menacing.

'Yes,' said David hardily. 'There's a definite strong-arm organization – you can call them gangsters – who are keeping people away from the *aboura*.'

Pencils were busy as he finished his sentence. Bang goes my career, he thought, nervous and reckless at the same time. But something in Crump's confident bearing made him totally unwilling to retract what he had said.

A new ally raised his voice nearby. 'It's a bloody disgrace!' said Oosthuizen, solid fury in his voice. 'This is the Governor's *aboura*. It happens once in ten years – in twenty years! Now they're staying away from it, just because some bloody agitators tell them to.'

'They could be staying away from it because they want to,' said Tulbach Browne.

Father Hawthorne raised a white-cassocked arm. 'Blessed are the meek,' he said. 'I say unto you – '

'Bunk!' interrupted Oosthuizen roughly. 'They're not meek at all! They're bloody mutineers! They've been put up to every bloody trick in the book! And we've got to go on living here, when all you half-baked bastards are safe back in England!'

In the pause that followed this, Father Schwemmer's gentle voice was heard. 'If only I could talk to them,' he said. 'The true Maulas are not such people. They are always lawful ... Can we not hold a meeting of both sides?'

David detached himself from the group, and spoke privately to Crump.

'It's about time I reported again,' he said. 'Will you take me back to the tax office?'

'Yes,' answered Crump readily. 'I'm getting a bit tired of your friends, anyway.'

As the two of them drew aside, making for the jeep, Axel Hallmarck raised his voice.

'Has the *aboura* been cancelled?'

'No,' said David, half turning his head.

'Will it be?'

'Perhaps.'

'Honey lamb,' said Clandestine Lebourget, with heavyweight archness, 'I came here to photograph thousands of enthusiastic people, and there's not a darned soul in sight. Do the British give out with rainchecks?'

David found it impossible not to join in the laughter, as he took his place in the jeep. The trouble about this assignment was that it had at least seventy-seven different sides, and no intelligent human being could choose one of them, and disregard the other seventy-six.

Back in the uncertain, heat-hammered shelter of the tax office, David conferred briefly with Crump, seeking any new facts that might be worth reporting. But there was virtually nothing save what Crump had already told himself and the correspondents, nothing beyond the bare outline of their defeat; the boycott was on, and it was too late to do anything about it, or to salvage the official face in any way. The clock showed 11.25, as once more David dialled the private line to the Residency.

This time Andrew Macmillan himself answered; David could imagine the other man, nervous and harassed, glad of any sort of physical action that would take him out of the bitter cage of his thoughts. Andrew's voice was severely controlled, and totally revealing; he sounded all that he was, at this moment of Maula history – grim, intent, and powerless.

'The situation's the same,' David told him, in answer to his query. 'There's nobody here at all. There *is* a cordon round the *aboura*, though it doesn't show on the surface, except here and there. Keith Crump has just got back. He's had two people arrested for intimidation, but he says it won't make any difference.'

'Why not?'

'The police are hopelessly outnumbered.' David looked at Crump, sitting across on the other side of the tax office desk, and Crump nodded his agreement. 'It wouldn't be possible to break the cordon without an equal number of men – which would make it a full-scale operation. At the moment, no one can get through, and nobody really wants to try.'

'Is Crump there with you?'

'Yes.'

'Ask him if it would be possible to open up one end of the *aboura*, using whatever force is necessary, and let a small number of people through.'

David repeated the question; Crump gave his answer, in a few short phrases.

'He says,' relayed David, 'that he *could* make a passage into the *aboura*, concentrating all his men, but that no one would use it. Most of them don't want to, the rest are scared.' He paused. 'I think we'll have to call it off.'

'Not until twelve o'clock,' answered Andrew harshly.

'That's half an hour,' said David, glancing at his wristwatch. 'We'll have to say something to the Press, too.'

'To hell with the Press!' said Andrew.

'Hear, hear,' said David. 'But they do exist … There's just one thing we might still try,' he went on. 'I don't know whether it would work.'

'What's that?' asked Andrew.

'Round up the Regents. Say what a disgrace it is to the tribe, not to attend the Governor's *aboura*. Ask them to use their influence, and bring a few of their people to the meeting.'

'What does Keith think?' asked Andrew, after a moment.

David raised his eyebrows in Crump's direction. 'What about it?'

'It won't work,' said Crump glumly. 'But I don't mind trying it.'

'He says yes,' said David.

'All right,' answered Andrew Macmillan, after a second of hesitation. 'I don't think it will work, but we'd better try everything. Tell him to go off now, and report the result as soon as you can.'

'He's on his way already,' answered David. It was true. Crump was even now pushing his way through the screen door, and a moment later the jeep's engine started up with a decisive roar.

Left to himself, David stood uncertainly at the tax office door, looking out across the *aboura*. The scene was the same; the sun still bore down on a deserted space, with the figures of the Press correspondents, and of the white spectators, the only living things within sight. He had a feeling now that he was watching history – morbid and regrettable history, history that would earn a disdainful paragraph in all the books for the next five hundred years. Here in Gamate something died, he thought – and the death wasn't a good thing, because something worse was inevitably going to take its place.

The correspondents were talking among themselves. Father Hawthorne was gesticulating; Oosthuizen was leaning back against the trunk of a thorn tree, in brooding ill-humour. The same yellow goat was still at work on the white-painted cross. The rest of Gamate waited somewhere out of sight, fearful and exultant at the same time. It was twenty minutes before the time appointed for the Governor's great *aboura*, and still no single Maula was to be seen.

The deserted ground had an air of triumphant decay, like a town in the grip of a plague which no one would acknowledge, and no one dared to fight.

David's sombre thoughts persisted, while the hands of the clock crept round, and the fierce angle of the sun drew close to its fatal station overhead, the appointed hour of noon. Unconsciously, while he waited in the hot silence, playing out the last few moments before their official bankruptcy, he was seeking some means to salve their embarrassment. It was too late to do it now, but it must surely be done in the future. His line of search grew impatient, degenerating into an arid violence. Either they should all of them quit Gamate and Pharamaul, thought David – withdrawing their patronage, leaving the Maulas to sink back into a stinking savagery, teaching them a cruel and remorseless lesson; or they should attack them out of hand, beat them down, subjugate and enslave them; while he himself, David Bracken, plumes waving, sword plunging and swinging, formed the avenging spearhead of a final punitive column.

There could be no half measures. One should either rule, or consign to the scrap heap – the noise of the returning jeep broke in on his thoughts, and guiltily he shook them off, and went out to meet Keith Crump.

Crump himself offered a minor object lesson in colonial patience. The policeman, whose authority was being directly challenged, and who had, during the last few days, endured rare ordeal of danger and provocation, might well have matched the anger and violence of David's thoughts; instead, his short absence seemed, if anything, to have improved his humour. He approached the *stoep*, his uniform still immaculate, his swagger-stick swinging; when he caught sight of David, he remarked: 'That was a waste of time,' as if time today were of no account, and all his years spent in the territory had conditioned him for just such a moment as this.

'What happened?' asked David. 'Did you see the Regents?'

'They sent a message,' answered Crump ironically. 'They're still ill. They can't come. In fact, they had almost forgotten there was such a thing as an *aboura* today …'

'Bastards!' said David angrily.

'Oh, I don't know,' said Crump, without rancour. 'If you get an idea, you might as well stick to it … But that puts the stopper on our plans. You'd better tell Andrew.'

Once more David looked at his watch. it was five minutes to twelve. He was still unwilling to concede defeat, and especially to be the herald of it.

'Is there any more news, otherwise?'

'Another of my chaps was beaten up, down by the post office. He was trying to lead a couple of old people through to the *aboura*, but he was chased away.' Crump sighed, laying his helmet down on the table. 'It's just not our day.'

'When will it be "our day"?' asked David, with an edge to his voice.

Crump looked at him. 'Don't let it get you down,' he said reassuringly. 'It'll come again. These things go in cycles … But it's not today.'

This time, when David dialled the Residency, the Governor himself answered the telephone. Momentarily, David was sorry that he was not up at the Residency himself, for there, it seemed, the most consequential drama of all was being played.

'Ah, David!' said the Governor, on a confident note. 'What news have you for us?'

'There's no one here, sir,' answered David unwillingly. 'The situation's the same as before. Crump tried to get the Regents to come to the *aboura*, and bring some of their people, but they refused. I'm afraid it's no good.'

'No good?' repeated the Governor, as if he could scarcely believe his ears.

'No, sir. It's a complete boycott.'

The wires fell silent between them, for so long an interval that David had an idea that the Governor might have fainted dead away. But presently his voice came through again, as stiff and precise as ever.

'Extraordinary business,' said the Governor. 'I suppose we should make an announcement.'

'Yes, sir,' said David.

'*You* make it, there's a good fellow,' said the Governor, as though struck with a thoroughly constructive idea. 'Wait until twelve o'clock. Then just say that the *aboura* is cancelled.'

'Very well, sir. What about the Press?'

'The Press?'

'Won't you be holding a Press conference, sir?'

'Good heavens, no!'

'I think we ought to say something, sir.'

'Why?'

'To explain what's happened.'

'Anyone can see what's happened.'

'All the same, sir,' David persisted, 'I'd like to put our side of it. Explain about the boycott, and the cordon round the *aboura*, and what it was you wanted to tell the tribe.'

'I wanted to tell the tribe,' said Sir Elliott aloofly, 'that Dinamaula won't be coming back to Gamate, until things have quietened down.'

'I think we should put that on record, sir. Officially.'

'Very well,' said the Governor, with one of his baffling reversals of mood. 'You "put that on record", as you say …'

From somewhere near at hand, a clock – the schoolhouse clock – started to chime midday, in tinny, unmistakable accents.

'When will you be leaving Gamate, sir?'

'Tonight,' answered the Governor. 'Informally.'

'It's just about twelve o'clock,' said David awkwardly. 'I'd better make that announcement.'

'Very well,' said the Governor. 'And thank you, David. You've really been awfully useful.'

437

David turned away from the telephone. He looked at Keith Crump, now comfortably settled in an armchair.

'Poor old boy,' said Crump, without a great deal of feeling. 'Was he very depressed?'

'Difficult to tell,' answered David. He felt in a sudden mood of formal, heroic determination. Someone had to make a good end to this fiasco. That someone had better be himself. 'What's the Maula phrase,' he asked, 'for "the *aboura* is cancelled"?'

'That's easy,' answered Crump, grinning widely. '*Aboura i faanga.*'

'*Aboura i fanga,*' repeated David inexpertly.

'Longer vowels,' corrected Crump. '*Faanga … Faanga..*'

'*Aboura i faanga,*' said David.

'Fine,' said Crump. 'That's one you'd better memorize …'

The school clock had long ceased to strike the hour. It must be, thought David, at least two minutes after twelve. He pushed his way through the screen door, and out into the bright, the midday sun.

The *aboura* ground was still defiantly empty. At the lower end, the correspondents were all watching him. He switched on the microphone. There was no reason for delay.

'I have an official announcement to make,' he intoned. His echoing voice swept the deserted space in front of him. 'The *aboura* is cancelled … The *aboura* is cancelled …' Then he braced himself, enunciating with Parisian delicacy: '*Aboura i faanga … Aboura i faanga.*'

As the echo of his voice faded, the Press correspondents swiftly broke their ranks, and started to hurry towards him. For some few seconds, that was the only visible movement. But then, with deliberative unconcern, other men and women – Maula men, Maula women – began to appear in twos and threes between the grey huts, and presently, without intent and yet without hesitation, to move on to the *aboura* ground, in a steady black encroachment, shamefully free, shamefully released from care.

IV

On that night in Pharamaul, the focus of violence was naturally the town of Gamate. There, men had something to celebrate, and celebrate they did, with a wicked edge to their rejoicing which no sober thought could curb. The whole *aboura* was given over to riot; riot by torchlight, with shrieks, and savage dancing, and the burning of huts and buildings in a wild circle of flame. Some oxen which had been outspanned at the lower end of the *aboura* were stampeded out into the open, and driven to and fro with cruel goading, and finally slaughtered. Men and women tore off strips of flesh, and crammed them into their bloody mouths; other men, and other women too, smeared themselves with the smoking entrails, and advanced prancing and screaming on the police post (the tax office having been burned to the ground), and were only driven off with fearful effort.

Long past midnight, the crowds danced and stamped among the corpses, of men and animals, on the *aboura*. When at last dawn came up, something else had been added to the scene. Some of the white lines, drawn with care and good faith in the forgotten era of order, had been incorporated into a gigantic, crudely fashioned emblem of a fish.

On that night, the Pressmen in Gamate worked late, and then ventured out in a body to see what was to be seen, and then returned to their hotel, eager to commit further morsels of public information to thirsty type. On that night, Katsaula lay deep in fever, and Seralo, the oldest of the Regents, turned his face to the wall, wishing to shut out for ever the evil sounds that smote his old ears; and Puero, in drunken exultation, led the wildest of the young men in a roaring foray against the hut of a headman who had refused to join in the boycott, and burned him and his wife and his two children alive.

On that night, Miera, the shamed and abandoned bride-to-be of Dinamaula, Miera the laughing stock, took secret counsel with the old women of the tribe, in a hut far from the bloody riot on the *aboura*; seeking to know how she could improve her fortune, and obtain her will. The ceremony was solemn, holy, and deeply hallowed. She was first given a purging mixture to eat, the newly-cut comb of a young cock, pounded and rolled into a ball with goat's dung and mealie husks; then she was stretched out on the floor of the hut, stark naked, and a rat's pelt was laid upon her like a knitted covering. Seven hags danced slowly round her body, crooning an ancient spell, jumping over her loins at the end of each measure; then the oldest of the hags plucked away the rat's pelt, and urinated in its place, and cried out, jerking and mouthing: 'All is well, daughter of kings! Dinamaula, grandson of Maula, will be restored to his people, and you will wed him seven days from this day!' And Miera, the laughing stock, the disregarded, was at last made content and confident.

On that night, six white men barricaded themselves into the bar of the Gamate Hotel, and drank themselves into a fearful stupor, hardly hearing the cries and the vicious rioting outside. They recalled the fiasco of the *aboura*, they pledged themselves to do something about it. They drank deep; two of them quarrelled and fought; one of them, heartsick, cried bitterly for a lost love. Then they all came together again, to sing choruses of 'Roll Out the Barrel' and 'Auld Lang Syne'. They drank a fresh round of whiskies and beers, and swore to take action the very next morning.

They put their arms round each other's shoulders, and said, loudly and repeatedly: 'Things can't go on like this.'

On that night in Pharamaul, the calmest and coolest man was probably the Governor and Commander-in-Chief, Sir Elliott Vere-Toombs, as he sat in his private railway carriage, rumbling its way southwards on the return journey to Port Victoria. He sat alone, in relaxed ease, his slippered feet stretched out on the seat opposite; he sipped weak whisky-and-water, and leafed through a pile of telegrams and minutes, while the train made its slow advance across the flat, interminable countryside. When the train stopped, the Governor stared out into the darkness, sometimes meeting a surprised black face peering inwards, as close to the dividing window glass as was his own. When it made steady progress, he read with swift concentration, and sometimes made marginal annotations with a slim gold pencil. When it gathered speed, and swayed and bumped over the rough-laid permanent way, he sat back, hands behind his head, and gave himself over to thought.

On that night, he had much to think about, but his thoughts were not especially troubled, and certainly not angry. He had no hard feelings about the day's events; the deliberate affront to his dignity was not really important, except in so far as it gave a clue to the grave state of affairs in Gamate. There were no scapegoats to be found, there would be no root-and-branch probing of whom to blame and whom to absolve. But there *must* be a concise assessment of what the boycott meant, in terms of Maula politics, and what it portended for the future.

He had left Andrew Macmillan, his Resident Commissioner, depressed and grimly apologetic. There, for example, was a prime focus of doubt. The Governor was not at all sure about Macmillan, who had proved himself,

441

in the past, a strong and capable man. But a strong man in decay was worse than any other sort of man, because his reputation promised something which he could not now deliver. The Governor had seen many strong men in decay, in very many different parts of the world; almost invariably, they turned out to be, in relation to their jobs, too expensive to retain.

He still could not quite make up his mind about Andrew, though he was glad that he had left David Bracken behind in Gamate, under the general heading of 'liaison'.

On that night in Pharamaul, the Governor took out his gold pencil once more, and jotted down four short phrases on the edge of a telegram dealing with water conservation. He wrote:

Dinamaula to remain out
Martial law? If necessary
More police? Bring in troops?
Macmillan, sick leave?

He noted, wryly, the number of question marks. But one thing was now beyond doubt. Things couldn't go on like this.

On that night in Pharamaul – but far to the north in the U-Maula country, far from private railway carriages, far even from the foreseeable violence of Gamate – on that night in Shebiya, Tom Ronald the District Officer, and Cynthia his wife, were washing up the dishes after supper. It was the one night in the week that they had to do this, the night that their houseboy Samson took off about four o'clock in the afternoon, and did not reappear until next morning. No hardship was involved thereby. Tom and Cynthia Ronald liked washing up. They liked anything that they did together.

Cynthia Ronald soaped and rinsed, Tom Ronald dried. For so tough and muscular a man, he handled the towel deftly. It was hot and steamy in the kitchen, hot and steamy outside; their small house, which always seemed to be on the very edge of the jungle, was silent all around them, and the only sounds were from the garden – sounds of frogs in the weed-covered pond at the lower end, sounds of crickets in the bushes, sounds of innumerable insects beating their hearts out against the screen door. Even though, a hundred yards away, the huts of Shebiya huddled close together, and a thousand U-Maulas talked or drank or slept, yet the Ronalds' house seemed entirely isolated, a pinpoint of order and life in the middle of a vast malevolent wilderness.

But once again, they did not mind. They had love, mutual pleasure, and now a special hope to sustain them.

'How are you feeling, old girl?' asked Tom Ronald, not for the first time that evening.

'Perfect,' answered Cynthia. She was looking unusually pretty, with an inner glow of contentment and happiness. 'Don't fuss, darling.'

'You've got to take care of yourself, you know.'

'Darling,' said Cynthia, 'I love you.'

There was an agreeable silence between them. The stack of dried plates grew higher; presently it was time for the grease-encrusted frying pan, and then for the saucepan that had held the mashed potatoes. Tom Ronald turned to the stove, and switched on the heater under the coffee. Then he walked to the screen door, and looked out into the darkness of the garden. A few fires flickered in the trees beyond it; for the rest, Shebiya was invisibly curtained by the night. It might be doing anything, out there in the darkness. It might be muttering spells, it might be preparing to rush them, it might be groaning in its sleep. It was Shebiya – unknown, blank-faced, ill-omened … From the doorway, he said over his shoulder: 'We ought really to take some leave. Get away from here for a bit.'

'It's not a very good moment, is it?'

'No. We'll have to wait, I'm afraid.'

'How was Gotwela, this afternoon?'

'Bloody-minded, as usual.' Tom Ronald sighed. 'In fact, even more bloody-minded than usual. He actually had the sauce to ask me if I'd heard about the *aboura* in Gamate.'

'How on earth did he know?'

'God knows. Maybe one of the police boys got it on the radio, and talked.'

'What did you say?'

'Told him to shut up.'

'Darling,' said Cynthia, turning as she laid down the last dripping pan on the draining board, 'Gotwela's not going to be difficult, is he?'

'He is difficult,' said Tom Ronald. 'They all are, at the moment. Probably it'll all pass off; it usually does. But there's an undercurrent, all the time.'

'When does Father Schwemmer get here?'

'Some time next week. Why?'

'Perhaps they need a pep talk. He's so good with them, and you know how they love him.'

'What they need,' said Tom Ronald curtly, 'is a bloody good boot up the arse.'

'Mr Ronald,' said Cynthia, 'steady with that language.'

'Mrs Ronald,' said Tom, 'coffee is served.'

'And then we'll go to bed?'

'I shouldn't wonder. I'm dead tired.'

'Now, that's not very encouraging.'

'Reckon my job's done, old girl,' answered Tom Ronald, grinning. 'But I don't mind making absolutely sure, now and again.'

On that night in Pharamaul, not all lovers were together. Tom and Cynthia Ronald might pass an evening of happy domesticity; John Raper and Anthea Vere-Toombs, coiled up like a nest of snakes, alternately drank and made love behind the closed door of Room 16 of the Hotel Bristol; but in a flat in the trim residential suburb of Port Victoria, a forlorn Nicole Steuart prepared to go to bed alone.

This was certainly not her choice; she and David Bracken had already established the fact that, with one eye on marriage and the other more soberly fixed on his salary scale, they would rather be lovers than anything else in the world. It was not an ideal arrangement; it had the furtive expedience of any smalltown love affair; but it would have to do, until better times came along.

On that night, she missed David very much, even though he was away, according to plan, for less than forty-eight hours. She was comforted by the fact that, this time tomorrow, he would be back in Port Victoria again, back in her arms, back in her bed. But that was not a total comfort – no anticipation falling short of reality could ever be.

Hurry back! she thought, as she shed her light silk robe, and climbed into a bed that now seemed less welcoming than it had ever been, in all her twenty-three years; hurry back, she thought, her long legs sliding to the foot of the bed, her hand on the switch of the bedside lamp as she debated whether to read, to lie awake, or to turn over and go to sleep; hurry back, and make it all come right again.

Like many another healthy young woman, with a normal awareness of sex, Nicole considered briefly an alternative whereby, somewhere between waking and sleeping, she might counterfeit the presence of her lover. So far, only in dreams had she achieved such vicarious ardours; only in dreams, and only in waking, with David in her arms, David her first love. But she did not dwell long on this idea, though her secret smile and a delicate tremor

445

pervading her flanks and thighs gave evidence of its soft clamour. That was one way to behave; but the other way was the grown-up way – to wait a little longer for a true invasion.

That true invasion should already be halfway towards her, on the long dreary railway journey from Gamate to Port Victoria ... When the telephone rang, and she heard David's voice from far away, she thought for a moment that she must have already fallen asleep, and that this was a tantalizing dream.

'But darling!' she said, aghast, when she realized fully that it was David who was speaking. 'Where are you? Why aren't you in the train?'

'I've got to stay here,' David told her glumly. He was sitting in a narrow passageway between the Residency sitting-room and the kitchen, trying not to disturb the household. Andrew had just shuffled wearily off to bed; Johannes had long ago shut the kitchen door behind him as he made for his quarters across the rear courtyard. David's voice sounded, to himself, unnaturally loud in the stillness. 'H E wanted one of the staff to keep in direct touch with things in Gamate. So I'm staying on.'

'But how long for?'

'I don't know, darling. Until things settle down again, I suppose.'

'Settle down?' Nicole, lying back, the telephone receiver balanced in the curve of her neck, felt the onset of a maternal alarm. 'What's been happening? How did the *aboura* go?'

'It didn't,' answered David. 'No one turned up. It was a complete boycott.'

'Oh,' said Nicole, inadequately.

'H E's on the train now,' pursued David. 'He'll be in at the usual time in the morning.'

'Where are you?'

'At the Residency, with Andrew Macmillan. Where are *you*?'

'I'm where you ought to be,' said Nicole sadly, 'and it's extremely lonely.'

'Darling,' said David, warming, 'I'll be there, one of these days.'

'Nights,' corrected Nicole.

'Nights.'

'How were the Press boys?'

'Same as usual. They had a real field day.'

'I can imagine ...' Disappointed for many reasons, feeling lost and lonely, Nicole returned to what was uppermost in her mind. 'I was counting the hours, darling. I was counting the *miles*. You should have been more than halfway here, by now.'

'Well, it proves one thing,' said David, his voice lower still, for fear of being overheard.

'What?' asked Nicole.

'It's time we were married.'

'Yes,' said Nicole, 'it certainly proves that ... Darling,' she said, relaxing, 'don't go away for a long, long time. Tell me *everything* that's happened.'

On that night in Pharamaul, in the same town of Port Victoria, four men slipped furtively into the hallway of a house down by the dock area. In the semi-darkness, they were challenged by a man who stood sentinel at the foot of the stairs. When he saw how many figures had crowded into the hallway, he said, curtly, in the Maula tongue: 'The chief will see one man only,' and Zuva Katsaula detached himself from his bodyguard, and walked forward. Over his shoulder, he called out: 'Wait there.'

'OK, Fingers,' answered one of the bodyguard, a tough, bunchy young negro in a black turtleneck sweater. 'But what if the cops come?'

'Just watch out, that's all.'

'OK, Fingers.'

Zuva Katsaula climbed the stairs swiftly, and knocked at the only door on the darkened landing above. A voice called: 'Come in,' and Dinamaula, his cousin, stood up as he entered.

'*Ahsula*,' said Dinamaula formally.

'*Ahsula*,' returned Zuva, on a conspiratorial note, as he came forward. He jerked his head behind him. 'I've left the boys downstairs. OK?'

'What boys are these?' asked Dinamaula.

'My boys,' answered Zuva, with meaning. 'We don't want any damned cops interrupting.'

'But I am free to receive visitors,' said Dinamaula. 'There are no restrictions at all.'

'All the same,' said Zuva, suppressing his irritation, 'I'd rather have them there.'

'As you will,' said Dinamaula. 'But there are no restrictions.'

Zuva, coming further forward, looked round the room, the room of the hereditary chieftain of Pharamaul. It was shabby and bare, mean as only a room in a dockside rooming house could be; the bed was narrow and iron-framed, the tables and chairs were fashioned of rickety, split bamboo. Drab curtains hid the view, but the view, seen or unseen, could have nothing to commend it; outside were the lights, shadows, noises, and smells of a thousand small waterfronts, in a thousand run-down ports, all the way round the world.

Zuva looked again at Dinamaula his cousin, Dinamaula whose title was Prince of Gamate, Ruler and Kingbreaker … It was some little time since he had seen Dinamaula, and it was hard to recognize him in the weary dispirited young man who now stood before him. A few weeks before, the two of them had driven up to Gamate, full of hope, full of cheerful confidence; now something had happened to Dinamaula, as if a spring had broken, a mantle fallen away. He was like (Zuva recognized it bitterly) like any other unemployed negro, in the dock area of Bristol or Swansea or Liverpool; he looked threadbare, defeated, and beyond rescue.

But Zuva was not the man to acknowledge defeat, when the situation called for something else. He held out his hand.

'Cheer up!' he said, with all the confidence he could muster. 'Things are really happening! From now on, you don't have to worry at all.'

'What things?' asked Dinamaula. His natural dignity was undiminished, but it had been overlaid by a pathetic and fatal hesitation. It was as if he did not know friend from foe, and would never again trust either.

'The *aboura* in Gamate was the hell of a flop!' Zuva told him gleefully. 'The poor old Governor went up there, swords and feathers and everything, and no one turned up at all! Man, that must have been really something!'

Dinamaula sat down, and motioned Zuva into the opposite chair. His hand as he lit a cigarette from the stub of another one was unsteady, and his expression had not altered from its air of guarded desolation. He seemed to have made up his mind that no news of any kind, however surprising, however fortunate, could cure the *malaise* that had eaten deep into his spirit.

'Tell me what took place,' said Dinamaula, using the formal Maula phrases, 'today in the town of Gamate.'

Zuva set to work to tell him, drawing freely on his imagination, painting a derisive picture of authority mocked, tribal solidarity triumphant, mutiny in the ascendant. For many a young man in Dinamaula's place, it would have made a happy picture, promising great hopes and great changes; for Dinamaula, it seemed to come as a confirmation of the worst of his fears.

His only comment at the end was: 'I wonder what Mr Macmillan thinks of all this.'

'You don't have to worry about Macmillan, or anyone else,' said Zuva. 'I tell you, the whole tribe's behind you. All they want is a lead.'

'What lead?' asked Dinamaula.

'A lead towards the next step,' answered Zuva, with a confidence he did not fully feel.

'What lead?' repeated Dinamaula. He motioned with his hand round the room. His expression was not even bitter. It was blankly resigned. 'I live in this room. I cannot talk to my people, I cannot succeed as chief. I have to report to the police, once every day. If I travel, Mr Bracken or Mr Llewellyn or Mr Brownrigg – ' his intonation was savage, ' – will accompany me. I await orders from the Governor, as to what I may do next. What lead can I give?'

Zuva looked at him. The aura of defeat was overwhelming, but still he persevered.

'All the people are ready,' he maintained stoutly. 'They are ready here in Port Victoria. They are waiting for you, in your own town of Gamate. And in Shebiya – ' he paused, ' – in Shebiya, they have taken an oath to drive out the white man, and make you chief of all Pharamaul.'

For the first time, Dinamaula looked at him with full attention. 'I have heard of such an oath,' he said quietly. 'Gotwela may well wish to drive out the white man. He does *not* wish to see me chief of Pharamaul.'

'That will follow,' said Zuva, uncertainly.

'It will not follow,' said Dinamaula. 'And the oath?' His eyes were steady and searching. 'You have taken that oath?'

'Yes,' answered Zuva.

'I have heard,' said Dinamaula, 'that the oath is disgusting.'

'It is a strong oath,' agreed Zuva.

'I have heard it is an oath for animals and savages,' said Dinamaula.

After an uneasy pause, Zuva answered: 'It is an oath to bind friends. You need friends. Gotwela could be a friend. When you are back in the chair of rule in Gamate, we can decide such small details.'

'I will never return to the chair of rule with such friends. I would not wish to do so. Above all,' said Dinamaula, 'I do not want to drive out the white man. Such talk is nonsense.'

'But they are our enemies,' said Zuva.

'You cannot drive out the white man,' said Dinamaula, as if he had not heard him. 'Part of this country belongs by right to the white man, and to white Government. There would be no Pharamaul today without the white man.'

'Or the black man.'

'Or the black man … But the one does not drive out the other. They work together. There is no need for the oaths of animals, or talk of driving out.'

Zuva stood up. 'I do not agree,' he said hardly. He could not gauge what it was that had changed Dinamaula so greatly; a few days in solitude seemed to have destroyed his true spirit, and turned him (in the Maula phrase) into a man with a white heart. Such a man was useless … Zuva thought of his bodyguard downstairs, and was comforted. There were other kinds of Maula men, and they were the true heirs of Pharamaul. 'This is a class struggle,' he declared, relapsing into an easier jargon. 'The forces of reaction cannot stand in the way of progress.'

'I also want progress,' said Dinamaula. His tiredness and lack of spirit were flooding into full possession again. 'Progress for my people, progress for this country. This black and white country.'

'You have been thinking strange thoughts,' said Zuva, 'in your strange room.'

'They are not new thoughts,' said Dinamaula. 'I never wanted to drive out the white man. I wanted quicker progress in Pharamaul. I wanted to prepare my people for the time when the white men would shake our hands, and wish us well in our ruling.'

'While you have been thinking these strange thoughts,' said Zuva, contemptuously, 'your friends have been acting and fighting. In Shebiya, they have taken the solemn oath. In Gamate, they have refused to greet the Governor. And here in Port Victoria – ' he smiled, as if conscious of playing a trump card, ' – here, there is actually, on this very evening, a strike.'

'A strike?' repeated Dinamaula, surprised. 'What strike is this? Where is the strike?'

'Where else,' said Zuva ironically, 'but in the Pharamaul Club itself?'

On that night, in the Pharamaul Club in Port Victoria, things were going splendidly. It was Friday, and the occasion was the fortnightly club dance; everyone was there, as they always were, and everything was going with a swing, as it always did, fortnight after fortnight. The bar did a tremendous trade, especially among those older members who were a bit past the dancing stage; the dance floor itself was crowded, with everyone ranging from Mrs Burlinghame – a simply wizard waltzer – to the sixteen-year-old daughter of the French commercial counsellor, who was reputedly very hot stuff indeed.

The band – the Port Victoria Moonbeam Downbeats – played manfully, for hour after hour. They were colloquially known as the 'Deadbeats', but it was generally conceded that, for nigs, they didn't play too badly.

Now and then, couples drifted away from the dance floor and made their way, elaborately unconcerned, out on to the shadowy balcony or the dimly lit club gardens. Keen eyes always watched their departure; their absences were timed; when they returned, it was to meet cheerful accusations from the rest of their party, and loud cries of 'You two ought to be ashamed of yourselves!' But sometimes, when the delinquents were married (though not to each other) they were greeted on their return with the stoniest of silences, and a red-faced husband or a vinegar-eyed wife would rise and stalk from the table, *en route* for the cloakroom or the bar.

Such moments were few, of course, because after all this was a club show, where everyone knew everyone else, and you couldn't exactly kick over the traces. But when they did happen, they spiced an evening already hilariously gay. They also gave the LADIES fresh fuel for their exchanges.

'Just look at that girl's dress! If I were her mother, I'd send her straight home.'

'My dear, take a look at *mother's* dress. There's nothing above the waist at all!'

'And precious little below.'

'Where's Mrs Clark-Gibson? Haven't seen her for a long time.'

'She'll be back, when the music starts. Just you wait. She'll come sneaking in, minus most of her lipstick.'

'Poor Mr Clark-Gibson.'

'Oh, I dare say he's consoling himself.'

'Why, have you heard anything?'

'Well, I haven't seen Molly Merriweather for a long time, either.'

'Really, the way people behave nowadays.'

'Jealous, darling? You were gone quite a long time, during the last dance, weren't you?'

'I had to sew up my shoulder-strap.'

'I'm not at all surprised, dear.'

'You and Captain Simpson!'

'I wish they'd stop playing this awful tune. Honestly, the Deadbeats get worse and worse!'

'What can you expect? They don't really *want* us to enjoy ourselves. Not since Dinamaula started all his nonsense.'

'If I had my way, that man would be shot.'

'Just wait, dear. Twotty Wotherspoon says they're going to run him out of Pharamaul, any day now.'

'Jolly good riddance.'

'Heavens, don't let's start on Dinamaula *again!*'

'But just look at that girl's dress! It's practically falling off!'

The Moonbeam Downbeats played a jaunty version of 'Miss Annabel Lee', while on the dance floor the couples circled sedately, waving to their friends, occasionally pausing to talk to other couples making the same steady tour. At one end of the room, near the band, a cheerful hilarity had broken out; Twotty Wotherspoon, veteran of hundreds of club dances, grew tired of foxtrotting and broke into a solo Highland Fling, while his partner – the Government House Social Secretary – looked at him with enraptured eyes. Presently he tripped, and fell heavily against the nearest table, breaking several plates and glasses. Shrieks and applause greeted him as he picked himself up.

'Good old Twotty!'

'He's in terrific form.'

'As usual!'

'Boy! Clean all this up!'

But some of the younger members did not share this admiration. The sixteen-year-old daughter of the French commercial counsellor, whose modest off-the-shoulder *décolletage* had occasioned so much comment, frowned up

at her partner, one of the secretaries from the South
African consulate.

'Is that man drunk?' she asked primly.

'Hell, no!' answered the South African, a large,
cheerfully sweating young man who was encircling her in
a respectful grip, as if he were clasping a sackful of electric
light bulbs; 'he's just a bit happy, that's all.'

'*I* am happy,' said the girl coldly.

'Are you really? Would you like to see the garden?'

'I have seen the garden.'

'It's very pretty, isn't it?'

'Yes.'

'Do you like Port Victoria?'

'Oh, yes.'

'But not as much as Paris, eh?'

The music stopped, on an uncertain windy climax. The
couples clapped. Twotty Wotherspoon picked up a flower-
vase and balanced it on his head, shouting: 'Gangway for
the Queen of Sheba!'

'I find such behaviour extraordinary,' said the girl.

'Cheer up!' said the South African. 'I like your dress, eh?
How about a walk on the balcony?'

'I have seen the balcony,' answered the girl.

'What about a drink, then?'

'No, thank you,' said the girl disdainfully.

'Aren't you enjoying yourself?'

'Oh yes ... Now I think my mother wishes me to return.'

The club bar was the habitual focus of all these
fortnightly dances, and tonight the club bar was well in the
picture. Gin, which had long been the essential fuel in
Pharamaul, now flowed across the counter in an
uninterrupted spate; gin-and-tonic, gin-and-lime, gin-and-
vermouth, gin-sling, gin-rickey, pink gin, gin-and-soda, gin-
and-water, gin-on-the-rocks, gin scarcely diluted, gin
straight. London gin, Canadian gin, Hiram Walker's gin,

South African gin; Gordon's gin and Gilbey's, Booth's and Bols Very Old Genever – in a score of forms it made its steady voyage, cased in wine glasses, sherry glasses, tumblers, liqueur glasses, tot measures, tankards, and jars like vases of flowers.

At the receiving end of this cataract were the *élite* of the Pharamaul Club, alcoholic section; men unmarried, men bored with their wives, men fugitive from social intercourse, men successful, men just making their way in the world, men avoiding other men who did not drink, men taking time out for a quick one, men warming and flooding their egos in the only agreeable way they had ever discovered. They drank, talked, shouted, argued, reordered drinks, disagreed about paying, tossed coins, played matches, shook dice, fell silent, broke glasses, spilt their drinks, and sang merry songs. They sang 'Tipperary', 'Mademoiselle from Armentières', 'Pack Up Your Troubles', and 'Good Night Sweetheart'. They talked about England, Dinamaula, women, football, business, golf, and sex. They told jokes about shy virgins, and bold whores. They frequently excused themselves.

'Back in a minute, old boy. Got to see a man about a dog.'

'Wait for me. Got to take a little time out myself.'

'Me for the boys' room.'

'Me for the gents.'

Sometimes there was a false note. 'Excuse me, old man. Got to go and splash my boots.'

'Who on earth's that chap?'

'Don't know him from a bar of soap.'

'Is he a member here?'

'Good God, no! He must be one of the airline pilots, or something.'

'Bit of a tick, what?'

'Definitely.'

And then, turning outwards again: 'What's that bloody awful tune the Deadbeats are playing?'

'Sounds like the "Refrain from Sexual Intercourse". Ha! ha!'

'I don't exactly get it, old boy.'

'You know! Like playing the "Refrain from Smoking".'

'I still don't get it, old boy. Terribly sorry.'

'Oh, forget it! Let's have a song ... "*Oh dear, what can the matter be?*" '

' "*Three old ladies locked in the lavatory*".'

'Good old Binkie!'

'Terrific form.'

But that night – so cheerful, so secure, so traditional – was not, after all, to be like other nights. It was difficult to say where the chill began, or from what direction it spread. But there came a moment – suddenly for some members, imperceptibly for others – when the bar seemed to dry up. At one moment there were two barmen and three aides, sweating as all Maulas sweated when they worked hard and continuously, ready and adroit behind the bar; and then, almost before anyone noticed, there was no one behind the bar at all – no one serving, no one collecting dirty glasses, no one washing up, no one taking the orders or spearing the bar chits on the spike.

Men hammered on the counter for quite a long time before they realized that there was nobody to hammer at. The counter before them had become fatally bare; the latticework grille in front of the stacked bottles had been clicked shut, and innocently locked; the space behind the bar was deserted. All along the counter rose the angry wail of men in the prime of life not only denied one for the road, but even the one before that – the one for the swing of the door. It was scarcely ten minutes to twelve.

Bells began to ring. Men began to crowd into the secretary's office, which was also empty. Other men sang, and thumped out: 'We want a drink!' to the tune of the *Lohengrin* Wedding March. Nothing happened. No one came running. No head peered round any door. Presently, bereft, they straggled back to their tables on the dance floor, to their wives, daughters, business associates, enemies; only to be greeted by matching cries of woe.

For here also the tide had gone out, disgracefully, unbelievably. The bandstand was empty. The piano was shut, the 'cello leant coldly against the tenor saxophone. Threadbare banners proclaimed 'The Port Victoria Moonbeam Downbeats', but the banners (silver lettered on black velvet) were the sole evidence of a vanished culture. Further out, extending the glacial ring, the tables were unattended. Not a waiter was in sight, not a Maula boy, not a black face.

Uproar renewed itself, confused, angry, indignant, and futile. It broke in waves, but it broke only against the shut bar, the deserted bandstand, the derelict tables, and the blank service doors.

The wife of the South African consul, Mrs de Kok, huge in navy blue lace, squared her massive arms and marched through into the kitchen. Scurrying feet preceded her, the slam of an outer door mocked her last advance. She found, in the back quarters, only a single Maula kitchen hand, a cripple, half-blind, softly crooning as he dried a plate.

'What the hell's going on?'

'*Barenala?*'

'Where are the others?'

'*Barenala?*'

'Where's that bloody head waiter?'

'Don't know, *barenala.*'

'You'll be sacked, *kaffir!* I'm warning you, eh?'

'Jah, *barenala!*'

The wife of the South African consul walked back into the ballroom. She was livid with anger, and fully prepared for action, but already the public tempo had faltered. People now sat at their tables, forlornly regarding the astonishment of reality. Tonight's club dance was over, at least an hour before schedule. There was no more to drink, no music to dance to, no waiters to bring sandwiches, bacon and eggs, hot coffee. The members sat close together, *laagered* within a fenced ring of frustration. Beyond that ring, beyond the bar counter and the service doors, not a man stirred and not a voice was to be heard.

'But it's incredible!'

'Something's gone wrong.'

'They must have mistaken the time.'

'Bloody Dinamaula!'

'Where's that — secretary?'

'Never here when he's wanted.'

'But what I can't understand is, how they could *dare* ...'

'Are you *sure* it's only twelve o'clock?'

'I'd just ordered six pink gins. Doubles, too.'

'The Deadbeats *promised* to play "Little White Lies"!'

'One thing I do know, old boy – things can't go on like this.'

CHAPTER ELEVEN

❖

Inside the gloomy, desiccated citadel of the Scheduled Territories Office, they were already beginning to think about Christmas. The messengers and office keepers were taking out, from a score of forgotten filing cabinets, the tinsel streamers and paper decorations, which, having already done annual duty since the end of the war, were good (they claimed) for many years yet. The typing pool was organizing a penny-a-week collection, towards a Christmas Eve party, and the biscuits, salted peanuts, fishpaste sandwiches, and South African sherry that traditionally went with it. There was one raffle for a prime turkey, another for a goose, and yet a third (restricted to Higher Executive Officers and above) for two bottles of port.

There was even a rumour that Establishments Branch were going to organize a Christmas tree, with envelopes for presents, and inside certain of the envelopes – a promotion, or even a bonus! The latter idea was heavily discounted by anyone who had put in more than a couple of years' service with the Scheduled Territories Office, and had thus been able to observe Establishments Branch at work; but at least the rumour of it was appropriate to Christmastime – the time of wishing, fantasy, miracles, and overwhelming surprise. If you could believe in Father Christmas, then you could conceivably believe in Establishments Branch and their fabled Christmas tree.

Within his citadel – not so gloomy, nor so desiccated – the Permanent Under-Secretary, Sir Hubert Godbold, was not thinking about Christmas, nor miracles, nor anything save hard fact. He was thinking about Pharamaul, as he had thought on very many occasions during the past weeks: thinking about the telegrams that spoke daily of violence and danger, thinking of the way that things in the Territory seemed to be grinding to a standstill; thinking above all of the next move.

When he summoned Crossley, his Assistant Under-Secretary, to talk about Pharamaul, he no longer had any need to say to him: 'Refresh my memory …' Pharamaul had been in the forefront of Godbold's mind, for many days and nights. Now, with the Press still ravening, the Secretary of State, Lord Lorde, yawing about like a ship without a rudder, and a fresh spate of Parliamentary Questions (and even a full-dress debate) coming up over the horizon, the time was at hand for the Scheduled Territories Office to confirm, limit, or extend its policy line.

Crossley, small, alert, his ear ever cocked for the faint hint of a far-off stratagem, his nose lifted to catch the cross-wind of rumour and advantage – Crossley stood opposite him beyond the broad, scarlet-topped desk, reading from some notes clipped to the outside of a massive file.

'There are three more PQs on Pharamaul, sir,' he began, with just the right touch of deferential sympathy. *I'm right here at your elbow,* his tone seemed to say. *Pray lean on me – I only want to help* … 'Nothing special, except that they advance the thing a stage further. They're set down for the day after tomorrow.' Crossley glanced at his notes again. 'They boil down to this: first, how long are we going to keep Dinamaula away from Gamate? Second, when will he be proclaimed chief? Third, how long will the present state of emergency continue?'

'M'm …' Godbold ruminated, his eyes level with the middle button of Crossley's waistcoat. 'Who's asking them, this time?'

'As usual, sir, the first two are Price-Canning's. But the third one is from George Bellows – ' he named a sedate Conservative backbencher.

Godbold raised his eyebrows. 'Bellows? I'm surprised … What's he getting interested in this for?'

Crossley pursed his lips somewhat primly. 'Pharamaul has gone beyond the usual crackpot stage, sir. I think we all recognize that … All sorts of people are involving themselves in it. The fact that it's spread to someone like George Bellows is indicative, I think.'

'Indicative,' repeated Godbold, with slight distasteful emphasis. He was not above catching the precise Crossley out in a slipshod expression.

'Indicative of the widespread interest in Pharamaul,' said Crossley, correcting himself smoothly. 'It's not just one party, or one sort of man, who is worried about this. It's nearly everyone. We've got to be very careful.'

'How do you mean, careful?'

Crossley sighed a very small, imperceptibly mutinous sigh. He recognized the Permanent Under-Secretary's mood, which was one of critical irritation. As far as Pharamaul was concerned, things were patently running against the Scheduled Territories Office; Godbold recognized this and, while he did not exactly take it out on his staff (he had never been that sort of man), he was still liable to communicate the resulting personal tension over a wide area. In a way, of course (Crossley realized), that was what his staff were there for – to share the burden of events, good and bad. But it made, occasionally, for missed heartbeats among those nearest the throne.

'We're not on strong ground, sir,' he answered, after a suitable pause. The solid room round him, the thick pile carpet, the high vaulted ceiling, all seemed to give the lie to his words, but he pressed on with his thesis. 'People generally don't like the ban on Dinamaula's movements. The Press is dead against it, of course. They still maintain that we tricked him into leaving Gamate ... I think that fairly soon we've got to say, at least, how long he's going to be kept away.'

Godbold set his jaw. His eyes rose, above the level of Crossley's watch chain to the level of his chin. 'He'll be kept away until things calm down. If they don't calm down, he'll be kept away – full stop. That's our policy, in two sentences. And we *didn't* "trick" him into leaving.'

'I still think we're vulnerable, sir.'

Godbold, instead of answering, maintained – even seemed to impose – a lengthy interval of silence. It was, for his staff, the Permanent Under-Secretary's most disconcerting reaction, but it was not a studied one; if, at any moment of discussion, negotiation, or judgement, he wanted to think, he invariably clamped down on words until the need for thought was fulfilled. Talkative members of the office, high and low, learned not to tamper with these charged silences ... In the present case, it was the word 'vulnerable' which had sparked the need for thought.

Truly, Godbold did not think that his policy over Dinamaula, so far, was in the least 'vulnerable' – that was, susceptible of defeat on valid grounds. But Crossley's 'vulnerable' meant something quite different; it meant untenable in the face of determined criticism, unpopular, liable to lose friends – of whatever quality these friends might be. Crossley meant that the Scheduled Territories Office, having taken a hard decision, were going to have a rough time if they stuck to it. He meant that the rough time was not worth it. He meant that heads might roll, careers falter, strong men trip and fall – bringing lesser men, who chanced to be near them, crashing to the ground at the same time.

Crossley, who wore his future like a precious gem tucked into his navel, was highly sensitive to such tickling draughts of fate. He was near enough to the top slopes of the Scheduled Territories Office to be affected, if their policy became too exposed a target, too unpopular. The taint of unpopularity might prove to be mortally expensive, in the subterranean world of advancement – costing ladder-rungs, costing a decoration in five years' time, a High Commissionership in ten.

Godbold came suddenly out of his trance, and asked, as Crossley had expected he might, 'How exactly do you mean, *vulnerable?*'

'I mean, there's been a certain amount of indecision and weak handling, at various levels … For instance, sir, I don't think Andrew Macmillan has put up a terribly good show.'

Godbold, recognizing the remark at its appropriate value, frowned, preparing to withdraw into silence again. It was one of any number of such remarks which he suspected were being made, at this moment; it was a remark slipped in, in fine print, contributing to a general trend of thought which would seep downwards through the office, adding up eventually to a possible series of demotions, a related shifting of jobs and levels, a KCMG for someone as yet unspecified, in two years instead of three. It was part – a tiny part – of the constant undercurrent of malignant opportunism, which infected many areas of the Scheduled Territories Office – in common with half a dozen other ministries, up and down Whitehall.

In moments of harsher criticism, it sometimes seemed to Godbold that his entire staff were either scheming to usurp his place in ten years' time, or else wetting their beds nightly about their chances of promotion. The Scheduled Territories Office, with all its manifold responsibilities all over the world, needed every ounce of guts and vision it could command; instead, what it got was the second-raters, the preoccupied careerists, the leftovers from the Foreign Office – and these were the future administrators, Governors, even High Commissioners, of Britain's overseas possessions! (They were as nothing compared to the wives, he recalled, in morbid parenthesis: the wives who clustered round him like rioting chickens at office parties: the wives who, during his recent tour of overseas posts, had practically sat on his knee at dinner, whispered his ear off, shaved him with their eyelashes, knocked him down in the rush. Those subtle, such-an-asset-to-husband wives ...)

But, as Godbold knew well by this time, if he ever tried to recruit from outside the office, in order to fill some crucial post, the STO banded itself together into one united, highly vocal trade union, and its screams of protest echoed and clashed the length and breadth of the Civil Service. There was even some evidence of a trade union within the trade union – a tight-knit Roman Catholic clique, busy, subtle, and exclusive, holding the fort against all unbelievers and assisting each other with extreme unction ... They would bear watching – just as, for another reason, Crossley would bear watching.

For here was Crossley, the human windsock, trying to do a delicate initial hatchet job on Andrew Macmillan ... He turned abruptly from the general back to the particular: back to Pharamaul.

For the first time he looked directly at Crossley. 'I think,' he said, coldly, 'that it's much too early to form a considered judgement about Macmillan, or about affairs in

Pharamaul generally. We should rather await developments … Personally, at this stage, I should say that Andrew has done pretty well, in extremely trying circumstances.'

Crossley, feeling the cold draught playing round his exposed flank, covered up with an expert twist. 'Things are certainly difficult enough,' he agreed deferentially.

'They're much more difficult than either Parliament or the Press realizes.' Godbold, having administered what was, for him, a considerable rocket, relaxed, placing his hands together, staring straight at the problem instead of at Crossley. '*We* know that things are serious, but they don't look particularly serious from England – scarcely serious enough to warrant our keeping Dinamaula out of Gamate, certainly not serious enough for what we might have to do, in the future. But that is *not* going to prevent us taking appropriate measures.'

Crossley, in spite of a well-developed self-control, swallowed uncertainly. He did not like the prospect before him, with its developing hazards; but this was not the moment to say so. Indeed, with Godbold in his present mood, such a moment might never come again … After a pause, he asked: 'What have you in mind, sir?'

Godbold knew exactly what Crossley was thinking, at that instant, and the extent of his professional terror. Firmly he withstood the temptation of piling it on too thick.

'If things get much worse in Pharamaul,' he answered judiciously, 'we may have to do one, or all, of three things. We may have to proclaim martial law. We may have to bring in troops from East Africa. And we may have to remove Dinamaula altogether.'

'Remove?'

'Into exile,' said Godbold curtly. 'If Dinamaula is the centre of disturbance and revolt in Pharamaul, then Dinamaula himself must go.'

'Sir,' said Crossley, stoutly, 'that would have a terribly bad effect.'

'Undoubtedly,' agreed the Permanent Under-Secretary. 'It would make us very unpopular indeed, nearly all the way round the world ...' He sat up suddenly, put his elbows on the leather-topped desk, and looked up at Crossley under massive lowered brows. He wanted to say '*Now hear this!*' on the American naval model ... 'I think we'd better take it as axiomatic that, until the rules are changed, it's our job to maintain order in Pharamaul. That means that we have a clear duty of *government*, however unpopular we become in the process. Very well, then – we'll govern!'

He waited for comment from Crossley, but there was none.

'That being so,' Godbold went on after a moment, 'I think we'll give pretty short answers to those three Parliamentary questions.' He held out his hand, and Crossley passed him the single sheet of notes. ' "How long are we going to keep Dinamaula away from Gamate?" ' he read out briskly. 'As long as is considered necessary, for the maintenance of public order ... "When will he be proclaimed chief?" This is not an appropriate moment to forecast the date of such a development ... "How long will the state of emergency continue?" I would refer the hon. member to my answer to the first question.'

Crossley, who had been noting down, in shorthand, the replies, looked up as Godbold finished speaking. He was secretly appalled by the curtness of the replies, but this was one tide which he was not, at that moment, prepared to stem. 'Sir,' he said, 'there are bound to be a lot of supplementaries.'

Godbold smiled, suddenly in firm good humour. '*You* ask the supplementaries,' he said jovially. 'I'll answer anything you like.'

But when Crossley had gone, with a markedly harassed expression and three pages of close-packed notes, Godbold found his cheerful mood melting into anxiety again. He had many other preoccupations that evening, as he had on every other evening of his life; but Pharamaul was the most complex of all, and the most threatening, and it affected him like a nerve pain, deep-seated and ominous. He was not daunted by the problem, in the sense that Crossley was daunted: he feared, not a blight on his career, but an inability to form a series of cast-iron, patently correct judgements, and to carry them through to the end.

Crossley had annoyed him, and Godbold in his turn had enjoyed administering a rebuke; but basically Crossley was quite right to be worried, fully entitled to oppose his view on this (and any other) policy matter, and eminently correct in his forecast of awkward supplementary questions to come, forty-eight hours ahead, in Parliament.

Pharamaul, as public and private reaction had already shown, held all the seeds of a furious Parliamentary row. The coming Question Time, and the curt, offhand answers he had dictated for his Minister, Lord Lorde, might well lead to an adjournment of the House, and a full-scale debate – unless Lord Lorde achieved an unusual level of firmness and competence. Godbold acknowledged to himself that the dictated replies were risky. But they were morally essential, and therefore had to be made. All that mattered was the *manner* of their delivery. Somehow he had to find a way, for the *nth* time, to stiffen the sinews of that forlorn old hop pole, the Secretary of State for the Scheduled Territories Office.

But even so, a debate, by itself, need not greatly matter: the Scheduled Territories Office had plenty of friends in the House of Commons, as well as such sniping critics as Emrys Price-Canning, and bumbling inquirers like Major the Hon. George Bellows. The outcome of such a debate, however, if it took a wrong turning, could be disastrous.

One possible outcome – the very worst – might be a reversal of policy in Pharamaul, with Dinamaula restored to the chieftainship, and red faces all round. That, he himself would fight to the last ditch, and would galvanize Lord Lorde to fight also. Another might be the usual feeble kind of self-inflicted stalemate: Dinamaula would be allowed to return (though hedged about with complex and unworkable safeguards), if within a certain time (say, six months) the level of crime, public violence, and provocation in Pharamaul (as calculated from police records) had not risen above an agreed percentage of an index figure to be determined by bi-partisan arbitration – October, 1947, for example.

That would be a compromise, straying near the lunatic fringe of administration. Across the margin of that fringe, there lay a third, horrific possibility – the despatch of a Parliamentary Commission of Inquiry to Pharamaul itself.

The Permanent Under-Secretary, with thirty-five years of public service behind him, could not fail to have the liveliest and most morbid memories of all Commissions of Inquiry. He had indeed, as a much younger man, served as *rapporteur* on two or three of them; he remembered them only as time-wasting, and wholly ineffective. Of others which he recalled, on the many occasions when Parliament, wishing to shirk an issue or postpone a decision, had used this shoddy weapon of disengagement, there had scarcely been one which did what it was presumably designed to do – observe the facts, hear the evidence, reach a conclusion, and present it in such a way that no body of honest men could avoid implementing it forthwith.

In the event, Commissions of Inquiry always deteriorated into a racket, an exercise of Olympian detachment, a high-level jaunt, or a farce. It depended on the people involved, and the people involved were usually of an identically dismal quality – busybodies, crusaders, pompous pro-consuls, men with so much time to spare that they should automatically have been suspect, on that account alone.

He remembered, in particular, a Parliamentary Commission of Inquiry which had gone out, under the aegis of the Scheduled Territories Office, a couple of years before. It had been a three-man commission, despatched to determine the rights and wrongs of an offshore fisheries dispute affecting various parts of British East Africa.

The three men involved had been a Conservative MP, an Oxford don of pronounced left-wing views, and a retired judge notorious for his erratic *obiter dicta* from the Bench. It would be an understatement to say that they made an ill-assorted trio; indeed, they were not on speaking terms, even before they sailed from Southampton.

On arrival, the judge, a greedy octogenarian, had succumbed almost immediately to ptomaine poisoning – from fish, naturally – and had been shipped home, never to be replaced. The Conservative MP, an old Etonian, spent much of his time deep in the interior – shooting big game, reading old copies of *Esquire*, and attending consular cocktail parties; subsequently he broke his arm playing squash rackets, lost all his notes in a sandstorm, and refused to greet the Oxford don, on the only public occasion when they were billed to appear together.

The latter, deeply concerned with the interior melancholy of the underdog, fraternized with the natives to such an explicit degree that the local authorities were plagued by real and fancied paternity suits for many months afterwards; he got drunk, made inflammatory speeches, and (as a climax) swept off his solar topee at a multiracial Government House reception and hurled it at his fellow Commissioner, when the latter, mounting the platform, turned his back upon him.

The missile had described a rare, triumphant arc before it knocked its quarry senseless, under a frieze of Union Jacks.

The Commissioners' report, after two years, was still awaited. It was safe to say that the only thing to emerge from that particular Commission of Inquiry was a conviction, in all the territories concerned, that the white man was entirely, entertainingly, and unquestionably mad.

The same sort of thing, in one degree or another, might happen in Pharamaul; it would bring, to a country and a people already distraught, a final ruinous touch of confusion. It must be avoided, at all costs.

It all depended, for good or ill, on the Secretary of State, Lord Lorde.

II

Hansard, once again, carried it thus:

23. *Mr Emrys Price-Canning* asked the Secretary of State for the Scheduled Territories Office if he can state how long Dinamaula Maula, chief-designate of the Maulas of Pharamaul, will be detained in Port Victoria, and when he will be permitted to return to Gamate.

The Secretary of State for the Scheduled Territories Office (Lord Lorde): Chief-designate Dinamaula will remain in Port Victoria as long as is considered necessary, in the interests of the maintenance of public order.

Mr Emrys Price-Canning: Cannot my right hon. Friend give us a more specific answer?

Lord Lorde: No, sir.

Mr Emrys Price-Canning: Can my right hon. Friend tell us what precisely is this threat to public order, and whether it really exists outside the minds of a certain clique of local civil servants?

Lord Lorde: I entirely repudiate the suggestion that there is a clique of any sort in Pharamaul. On the other hand, there is ample evidence that Dinamaula acts as a centre of disturbance, and must remain absent from Gamate.

An Hon. Member: Indefinitely?

Mr Emrys Price-Canning: Can the Minister give us some of this ample evidence?

Hon. Members: Answer.

Lord Lorde: I am satisfied with the facts as I have presented them from time to time in the House.

Mr Emrys Price-Canning: Never mind about from time to time. I'm talking about now, Thursday afternoon. Let's hear what sort of ample evidence –

Hon. Members: Order.

Mr Speaker: If the hon. Member has a supplementary question to put, he should cast it in the normal phraseology.

Mr Emrys Price-Canning: OK. What is the –

Hon. Members: Order.

Mr Emrys Price-Canning: Can the Minister communicate to the House the evidence of disturbance, or whatever it is, which is being used as a pretext to keep Dinamaula away from the capital?

Lord Lorde: I do not like the word pretext, but in the interests of general amity, I will let it pass. I can assure the hon. Member that our officials on the spot have produced ample evidence to justify the present ban on Dinamaula.

An Hon. Member: Let's hear it, then.

Hon. Members: Answer.

Lord Lorde: I have nothing to add to my statement of last Friday.

Mr C Merrivale: Do you mean that things are just the same, that they haven't got worse?

Lord Lorde: They certainly have not changed for the better.

24. *Mr Emrys Price-Canning* asked the Secretary of State for the Scheduled Territories Office if he can now state when Dinamaula Maula will be proclaimed chief of his tribe.

Lord Lorde: I regret that this is not an appropriate moment to forecast such a development.

Mr Emrys Price-Canning: What is the extraordinary veil of secrecy surrounding this matter? The Minister seems to have erected a sort of Gestapo barricade around Dinamaula. Is he, or is he not, going to be proclaimed chief? If so, when? If not, why not? It's as simple as that.

Lord Lorde: My hon. Friend knows very well that it is not as simple as that. For my part, I would like to say that I deplore the use of tendentious expressions such as "Gestapo" and "barricade".

Mr Emrys Price-Canning: Mr Speaker, sir, may I have an answer to my question, question number 24. When is Dinamaula going to be proclaimed chief of his tribe?

Hon. Members: Answer.

Lord Lorde: It really depends on what happens in the future.

Hon. Members: Oh.

Mr Sermon: Does my right hon. Friend mean, by that extraordinarily feeble reply, that the Government are so bankrupt of ideas that they are prepared to sit around and –

Hon. Members: Order.

Confused interruption.

Mr Speaker: Order. Question No. 25.

Mr Emrys Price-Canning: On a point of order. I am still waiting for number 24.

Mr Speaker: Number 24 has already been adequately answered.

Mr Emrys Price-Canning: What a racket.

Col. Meldrum: Sir, on a point of order. Is the expression "What a racket" a parliamentary expression?

Mr Speaker: I did not hear such an expression. If I had done so, I would have ruled it as unparliamentary. Let us proceed. Number 25.

25. *Major the Hon. George Bellows* asked the Secretary of State for the Scheduled Territories Office if he can state how long the state of emergency proclaimed in the Principality of Pharamaul will continue.

Lord Lorde: I would refer the hon. and gallant Member to my reply to the first question put by my hon. Friend, the Member for South Oxford.

Hon. Members: Oh.

Major the Hon. George Bellows: Seeing what we've already heard this afternoon, I honestly hoped for a better answer.

An Hon. Member: Order.

Major the Hon. George Bellows: Mr Speaker, sir, if I've said anything wrong, I'm sorry. I can't always find my way about –

An Hon. Member: Speech.

Mr Speaker: Has the hon. and gallant Member for Boddlecoombe East a supplementary question to put?

Major the Hon. George Bellows: Well, yes, I suppose I have. All I wanted to know was, how long is this sort of thing going on?

Lord Lorde: I am always glad to rescue the hon. and gallant Member from the intricacies of civilian thought –

An Hon. Member: Come off it.

Lord Lorde: But I really have nothing to add to my answer. The state of emergency in Pharamaul will last as long as our officials in the Territory feel that the maintenance of public order demands it.

Mr Emrys Price-Canning: Arising out of that, is the Minister aware that one of these so-called officials in the Territory, on whom he seems to place such reliance, saw fit to call the Maulas a bunch of gangsters, and does he honestly think –

Lord Lorde: I would like to correct my hon. Friend. The word "gangster" was, it is true, applied by a minor official to certain subversive elements in the tribe. Though it was used in a moment of stress, it is a word I deplore, and the official concerned has received a reprimand.

An Hon. Member: He should have been sacked.

Mr Emrys Price-Canning: How do you know that all the officials out there don't think the same way?

Lord Lorde: We are entirely satisfied, by and large, with our official representation in Pharamaul.

Mr Emrys Price-Canning: Well, I'm not.

Confused interruption.

I would like to ask the Minister –

Mr Speaker: Is this a supplementary question, within the normal terms of parliamentary usage?

Mr Emrys Price-Canning: Yes, sir.

Mr Speaker: Very well.

Mr Emrys Price-Canning: How long is the present Gestapo tyranny in Pharamaul going to continue?

Mr Sermon: On a point of order –

Major the Hon. George Bellows also rose.

Hon. Members: Answer.

Mr Emrys Price-Canning: I'm going to get to the bottom of this. You can't cover up any longer. I'm going to move the adjournment of the House to debate this thing as a matter of urgent public importance.

Confused interruption.

Mr Speaker rose.

Mr Speaker: Hon. Members will resume their seats.

III

Sir Hubert Godbold, Permanent Under-Secretary for the Scheduled Territories Office, listened to the debate, as he had listened to countless others, from the customary Civil Service vantage point: the modest cubbyhole at the northwest corner of the Chamber, to the right of the Speaker's chair and directly underneath the Press Gallery. Crossley was with him, and another eager young man from the STO, who would serve as a runner in case of necessity; but Godbold was, in effect, isolated – isolated by his own concentration, and above all by his own sense of responsibility.

During his seven years at the head of the Scheduled Territories Office, Godbold had seen three successive Ministers come and go; before that, in thirty years of junior and medium posts, he had served under at least a dozen of them. His inoculation had thus been intensive and prolonged. But in spite of it, whenever he watched debates affecting the STO, he could never rid himself of the notion that the whole thing was his personal responsibility. Out there at the Despatch Box, his Minister might declaim, thunder, persuade, or give way – but the Minister was Godbold's own nominee, going through certain strictly defined motions of strategy, and emerging either as a credit or a forlorn disappointment to his trainer ... It was not, truly, a condescending viewpoint; the fact was that the Scheduled Territories Office, like all the other ministries, was run by its permanent head; and, whether Ministers triumphed or succumbed, the thread of policy persisted as the same enduring, personal responsibility.

None the less, full-dress debates were something which Godbold always enjoyed, whichever way they went, and however deep was his own involvement. There was really nothing like the House of Commons, the world's most civilized and most critical forum ... If you were a good House of Commons man, you made the fact plain; if you were a phoney, you were always exposed. Even the physical attributes of the Chamber contributed to the same sense of historic assessment; the splendid panelling, the unequalled acoustics, the opulent yet serviceable dark-green leather of the benches – these were the true trappings of consequence, the essential decor of the Mother of Parliaments.

Meanwhile, there was *this* particular debate ...

'I tell you, sir,' said the hon. Member for Hutton Baskerville, an earnest young Labour supporter who had once been told, by the *News Chronicle*, that he had the makings of a future Prime Minister – and was personally and politically doomed on that account: 'I tell you that unless we right the wicked wrong which we are doing in Pharamaul, unless we restore this gifted young chief to the throne of his forefathers, our name will go down to infamy, and – ' he concluded, somewhat lamely, ' – it'll be entirely our own fault.'

He sat down, beaming as if at his own reflection in his spectacles; while Godbold, his heavy face expressionless, his hand resting lightly on the pile of briefs in front of him, permitted himself a gentle interior sigh. So far, the debate had gone as he had known it would go; the right wing had made comforting noises, the left had thundered and wailed about the rights of man. But, gauging the mood of the House, Godbold was uneasy; the big guns were still to come, and it was almost impossible to say how they would acquit themselves.

Emrys Price-Canning had not yet spoken: with his usual excellent sense of timing, he had left it to one of his friends to raise the matter of Pharamaul on the adjournment, and was conserving his energies for the final assault. Then Lord Lorde would reply for the Government, and Lord Lorde, as usual, was at the heart of Godbold's misgivings.

At his side, Crossley leant over and whispered: 'Nothing much to worry about *there*,' and Godbold grunted in answer. It was true that the member for Hutton Baskerville had posed no new point and induced no new crisis; the Scheduled Territories Office, in the person of Godbold, was not called upon to plug any gaps or supply any emergency ammunition. But it was equally true that the last speaker had contributed his quota to the critical atmosphere of the House; thus, a Commission of Inquiry (which someone had already suggested) or even a reversal of Pharamaul policy, still hung in the balance.

Major the Hon. George Bellows, having caught the Speaker's eye, embarked on a rambling, rather hurt complaint about the Minister's 'cavalier treatment' of his earlier question, while Godbold mused further on Lord Lorde, and the chances that he would show up well or ill. The whole thing, of course, was Lorde's own fault; if he had not made such a futile mess of his questions, if he had been consistently and gently firm all the time, instead of teetering ignominiously between asperity and apology, there would never have been a debate at all. Not for the first time, Godbold wondered if the Scheduled Territories Office could ever truly prosper if it were presided over by such hereditary numskulls as the present incumbent.

Lord Lorde ... There must be better men, thought Godbold with rare crudity, *blowing up* balls for a living, instead of talking them ... And then there was his wife! God preserve us, thought Godbold, from schoolmasters' daughters who come up in the world. He had seen her, earlier, entering the small reserved gallery on the far right of the Chamber, and inevitably complaining of how she had been seated; a humourless brocaded bourgeoise, sixty-three years old, who had to be courted and wooed as if she were a *prima ballerina* of seventeen.

Lady Lorde had given the Scheduled Territories Office endless trouble during the last three years: professional trouble, social trouble, trouble dug out of holes in the regulations and served up hot on the Permanent Under-Secretary's desk. She had a genius for the infliction of discomfort; she combined the acid frankness of certain senior admirals' wives with the sulky inelegance of a noblewoman whose welcome, at all levels, was guaranteed by standing orders. In particular, whenever she went on tour with her husband, Second Secretaries had to dance till they drooped, talk till their tongues ran dry, listen till they lapsed into a coma. And it didn't do them a scrap of good, anyway, because as soon as the Secretary of State reached home, a formidable string of complaints, emanating from the same obvious source, would be on Godbold's desk within twenty-four hours; and it would be his task to inquire, to assess, and to explain courteously that –

'On a point of order – ' Godbold looked up suddenly, to see a member rising at the far end of the Chamber, ' – is the hon. Member in order in charging the Minister with twisting the facts to suit his own purposes?'

By God, thought Godbold, while the matter was being tediously resolved by protest, withdrawal, and apology, if that's the worst thing they charge the Minister with, I'll go to bed happy ... He suddenly became aware that the Chamber was filling up, responding to the odd potent grapevine that seemed to operate at any hour of the day or night, throughout the whole vast building. Members were starting to filter in, in twos and threes, making their way through from the lobbies and corridors, pausing to bow to the Speaker before they crossed the bar, smiling to their friends, settling down in their places, turning to whisper to their neighbours.

There had been no announcement or forewarning; the current orator, who had succeeded Major Bellows, was still drawing an uneasy parallel between the detainment of Dinamaula and the execution of Nurse Edith Cavell. There was just the feeling, inexplicable yet compelling, that in a few moments there would be something worth listening to.

In this case, it meant that Emrys Price-Canning would be the next member to catch the Speaker's eye.

Godbold looked closely at Emrys Price-Canning, as the latter rose from his customary position just below the Opposition gangway; not for the first time, he found himself wondering what on earth it was that impelled and confirmed a man in lifelong rebellion – rebellion against the formal pattern of society, against all conventions, against the acceptance of customary standards. Emrys Price-Canning looked exactly what he was – a fighting rebel. His appearance, familiarized by a thousand photographs, caricatures, pen-pictures, told almost the whole story: any MP with that lean look of disdain, that flamboyant manner, that arresting shock of grey hair, could only be one of the world's self-elected pinpricks.

Price-Canning had spent his entire public life of nearly forty years in uncompromising opposition; ever since the day, in fact, when, during a particularly bloody period of the First World War, he had risen from this same seat in the House of Commons and (in a maiden speech) denounced the slaughter at Passchendaele as 'the calculated bloodletting of a handful of mad military surgeons'.

Since that electric occasion, he had been in and out of the headlines, in and out of favour, in and out of prison. As the Independent member for South Oxford for the last thirty-eight years, he had long been accepted as a freelance firebrand, distrusted by all parties, inexplicably adored by his constituents; one of the same fantastic, inevitable portrait gallery, bracketed with James Maxton, Clement Davies, Fenner Brockway – and, on the world scene (to give him his due), with Gandhi, Wendell Wilkie, Bustamente, and Tito. Indeed, some people, not lunatics, would have been prepared to add, Jesus Christ and Oliver Cromwell.

You couldn't ignore Price-Canning, because he stuck out like a professional sore thumb. You could call him anything you liked – publicity-seeker, crackpot, fake Messiah, bloody nuisance. But you couldn't discount him, because when he got hold of something – a thread of scandal, a hint of injustice, a real or fancied racket – he hung on to it, with the iron jaws of righteousness, until it was picked as dry and as clean as a bone under a hot desert sun. You might outshout him, laugh at him, cut him at parties, fail to invite him – but the one great mistake, proved over the course of several gory decades, was to underrate him.

Whatever secret fuel it was that drove such men, Emrys Price-Canning had it by the ton … When he rose to speak, on that evening in the House of Commons, Godbold would have been the last man in that great assembly to take it for granted that this was just another exercise in wrong-headed dialectics.

Price-Canning started slowly, as he always did when he knew he was on to a good thing. Part of this slowness stemmed from basic House of Commons tactics – he wanted to give his fellow members plenty of time to drift in from the lobbies, the various bars, and the dining-rooms; part of it was a natural habit, a forty-year-old public strategy, which laid down that one should first lull with reason, then warm with sincere ardour, and finally explode into indignation – and still keep the best till the last.

You had to hand it to him, thought Godbold, as he listened with bent head, while at his side Crossley shuffled his files and made quick shorthand notes on the back of a yellow flimsy: you had to hand it to Emrys Price-Canning – he always rose to an occasion, even if the occasion were a purely induced crisis. There he stood, gesturing widely, tossing back his mane of hair, looking round him for the freely accorded applause, scoring points all over the place; while the House enjoyed the performance, the Front Bench looked trim, and Lord Lorde, who would shortly have to reply, affected so careful an unconcern that he must surely be writhing at the bleak prospect of responsibility.

'The House has listened,' said Emrys Price-Canning, 'with what I take leave to call cynical impatience, to those apologists for the Government who have tried to excuse what we are doing in Pharamaul. As to their motives, I don't propose to inquire or to speculate – ' ('Order, order!' came from several members, and Price-Canning inclined his head as if to acknowledge the justice of the interruption.) 'In this House, Mr Speaker, we always assume that everyone is acting from the very best of motives, even though I'm sometimes reminded of the story of that ancient Greek optimist – can't remember his name – who picked up a candle and went out looking for an honest man.'

A gentle growl of dissent gave him fresh warning, and he switched briskly and adroitly back to his main subject. 'But be that as it may, I can't for the life of me see how the Government can justify their policy. *They* say, there's a crisis in Pharamaul, and they have to take emergency measures and emergency powers. *They* say, Dinamaula is the cause of all this, and so Dinamaula has to be kept out of the way, indefinitely. *They* say, just leave it to us, and to our lads on the spot, and everything will be all right.' He drew an impatient breath, and gestured with a wide, sweeping, satirical motion. '*I* say, and I hope the House will follow me, that there's not a tittle of evidence to justify all this strong-arm stuff, and that if we *do* leave it to the lads on the spot – and we've heard quite a bit about them already – we are automatically abdicating our right of directing Britain's colonial policy. There's another word for abdication, an ugly word, and that word is – *cowardice!*'

In the slight pause that followed, the stir of reaction to the strong staccato thrust of 'cowardice', Godbold pulled a pad towards him and scribbled three sentences. '*Plenty of evidence of threats and violence affecting public order,*' he wrote. '*Nine murders and countless riots already. Quite enough to justify emergency measures.*' Then he initialled it and, folding it over, passed it to a messenger to give to Lord Lorde.

He was aware that the House was unusually attentive, and somewhat grim; it was as if they were now, at last, becoming persuaded that the things that were being done on their behalf, at the end of the enormously long tentacle of command that stretched from Westminster to Gamate, were bad things, unworthy of their parentage, and due for brisk reform.

You had to hand it to Price-Canning, thought Godbold afresh, as he watched Lord Lorde unwind his long bony frame to read the note. Price-Canning, as usual, made it all sound so simple. All the villains were on one side of the fence, all the good chaps on the other side – *his* side. So why look for two answers, when there was only one …

'Cowardice!' cried Emrys Price-Canning, with a theatricality which would have been inexcusable in a man who lived less near the footlights of history. 'What crimes are committed in thy name! … Are we in this House – whatever our party allegiance – really going to sit back and let nature take its course in Pharamaul? – nature, I might remind you, as dictated and organized by petty officials who do not scruple to describe their charges as gangsters?' He smoothed over an interruption with a careless hand, as if quelling a small disorder in the nursery. 'Cannot we have the guts to say, here and now: all right – we've made a mistake – we'll turn the page and try a fresh start – we'll bring back Dinamaula, and make him chief, and see how the thing works out? Can't we make an *honest* effort at reconstruction in Pharamaul – forget the past, look to the future?'

He was nearing his peroration. The House was deadly quiet. Lord Lorde was still staring fixedly at Godbold's note, as if it were a charm. It would have been far better, thought Godbold, if he had been listening very carefully and undisguisedly to Emrys Price-Canning.

'Sir,' said Price-Canning, with a quick bob towards the Speaker, 'I have only a little more to add. I believe we're making a tragic mistake in Pharamaul, and I believe that this is the moment to admit it. I actually had a communication from one of the Council of Regents today – ' Godbold pricked up his ears, as did many members of the House, ' – assuring me that the reports of unrest were much exaggerated, and that if Dinamaula could only be allowed back to Gamate, and proclaimed chief, all would be well. I believe that.' He pounded one clenched hand upon the other, in solemn emphasis. 'I believe that, because I still haven't heard or read a single word to the contrary. There may have been a few minor disturbances in Pharamaul – but who is to say what gross provocation led to them? What do you think happens to a tribe, when its leader is spirited away? What iron enters into their soul? Would not you or I behave in exactly the same way, if we were a simple, pastoral people provoked in this brutal and cynical fashion?

'The reasons for keeping Dinamaula from the throne of his forefathers are manufactured reasons. They will disappear, melt away, as soon as he is allowed back. And when that happens – ' he looked round him, and then directly at Lord Lorde, ' – when that happens, I hope the right honourable gentleman opposite will have the grace to admit that he has been stampeded into hasty action, by three things – bad advice, rumours of disturbance, and rumours of a marriage which, if it reflects anything at all, reflects great credit on the womanhood of Britain.

'I say, I *hope* he will admit that, in all honesty. If he does so, I don't think he will find the House, or the country, vindictive or unforgiving. If he does *not*, he will learn to his cost that the price of stiff-necked pride is the price which we in this very House once exacted from an even more illustrious transgressor, Charles the First – and that is, a permanently stiff neck!'

It was a typical Price-Canning peroration – colloquial, gross, and infinitely effective. True to the textbook, he had left his audience laughing, but the laughter held a sourly critical note. It was as if a man of authority had told a genuinely funny story about a whorehouse, a story whose inescapable conclusion was that all whorehouses must be padlocked and put out of business forthwith – whether one continued to laugh throughout such disciplinary action, or not ... When Price-Canning sat down, flushed and trembling as he always was after making an all-out, public effort of persuasion, the ground-swell of 'Hear! Hear!' and the roar of damaging laughter seemed to sound, for the Government side, the knell of their policy.

Price-Canning, it appeared to the House, had been unduly generous. He had actually gone out of his way to concede a joke about Pharamaul. But Pharamaul, in spite of this graceful favour, was deadly serious, and Pharamaul must be solved, on a basis (if necessary) of fundamental moral rehabilitation. That was their next and their most urgent task.

In the continuing pause, Godbold frowned deeply, in concentration and in dislike. From long experience, he saw and felt the thing as a matter of balance, a battle of X against Y. 'X' was policy – a semi-sacred element, never formulated without deep and searching analysis, never advanced without profound professional conviction. 'Y' was opposition to policy; it might be uninformed, ignorant, prejudiced, spiteful, corrupt, or lunatic. But whatever the contrast of motives and urges, X always had to outweigh Y, by sheer, demonstrable merit. Otherwise it was futile to be a senior civil servant – a thing that was the heart and core of his being.

He knew, at that moment, that Emrys Price-Canning had by fair and foul means brought the Scheduled Territories Office, and himself, to the verge of disgraceful retreat.

Other people knew it also. Godbold, well equipped to gauge the mood of the House, appraised the symptoms, and found them disquieting. There was now an atmosphere of extreme tension and discomfort; as yet another speaker rose, determined to contribute his quota of criticism before Lord Lorde replied for the Government, the undercurrent of private conversation, and the ant-like to-and-fro of members in urgent conference, rose to such a pitch that the Speaker had twice to call for order.

Nearly all the Cabinet were in their places; nearly every seat in the House was occupied. Price-Canning, having bowed and withdrawn beyond the bar of the Chamber, was the centre of a tight knot of people, whispering and conferring. It was, patently, a moment of balance.

Godbold, not less clear-minded than if he had been behind his own desk at ten o'clock in the morning, ready to bring his massive gift of concentration to bear on the day's problems – Godbold was aware of a sense of personal guilt. He blamed himself for not having anticipated this crisis, and for having given Lord Lorde, at Question Time, such a bleak brief to speak from. If the Minister had been consistently firm, this debate might have been avoided; as it was, he had annoyed the House by wavering, and he was paying the price for it now. That should have been foreseen, at the outset.

On this day, in this place, it was not enough to be right, not enough to be coldly accurate, not enough to brush aside the vulgar intrusion of criticism. Something else was called for, some intimate quality of persuasion. This was not the climate of Pharamaul, prostrate and torn under a hot sun. This was England, the only decisive land – five thousand miles, and fifty million people, away from Pharamaul. However far removed, however sentimental and ill tuned to reality, it was the only climate that mattered.

Godbold was deeply worried, and he was not the only one to be so. As the stopgap speaker droned on, he noticed a single, silent, withdrawn figure, standing in the artificial twilight behind the Speaker's chair, listening with extreme concentration to the course of the debate. There could have been no better illustration of its crucial importance than that one attentive man. It was the Prime Minister.

It happened that the two of them were friends of long standing; and such was the compulsive power of personality, that Godbold realized, instantly, three things: firstly, that the Prime Minister – that admirable man, of infinite talent and resource – was now officially on deck; secondly, that he would proceed to do exactly the right thing, aided by an ear so delicately tuned to shades of triumph or disaster that he could distinguish wild applause from an ovation, or a brutal setback from a total defeat; and lastly, that the PM would walk across and speak to him, within a very few minutes.

They were old friends; indeed, they had been up at Oxford together, nearly forty years earlier – Godbold the most distinguished classical scholar of his year, the Prime Minister a glittering, somewhat bumptious orator, and a host of some notoriety. Thereafter, their paths had diverged widely. Civil servants belonged to the back room, the room of anonymity and sober calculation; politicians belonged to the front, and felt a sense of material degradation if as much as a single limb fell outside the circle of limelight. Godbold had risen by merit and application, the Prime Minister by luck, nerve, and aggressive political skill.

Both at the peak of their respective professions, they could afford to relax, and admire each other's uncompeting qualities ... They dined in company approximately once a month, alternating between the Atheneum and the Travellers'.

Now, inwardly amused, Godbold watched the Prime Minister make his expected move. The latter suddenly raised his head, looked round him as if surprised to find himself in the House of Commons, and then, with almost excessive unconcern, crossed the few paces that separated them.

'Well, Hubert,' said the PM.

'Good evening, Prime Minister,' returned Godbold. Save in private, he never strayed an inch outside the appropriate formality. 'An interesting debate.'

'Fascinating …' The Prime Minister nodded to Crossley, whom he knew by sight, and Crossley, almost rosy from the august contact, bridled and bowed. Then he drew back discreetly as the Prime Minister, with a side glance of crystal-clear import, started to talk.

Since they knew each other so well, and trusted each other, there was an atmosphere of absolute truth and reality in their exchanges.

'This is going badly,' said the Prime Minister. 'Damned badly. We might have to yield a point or two.'

'I hope not, sir.'

'You're absolutely sure of your facts?'

'Yes, sir. There's deep unrest in the tribe, and the possibility of more bloodshed. Dinamaula focuses it, whether innocently or not. He must be kept out.'

The Prime Minister stared ahead of him, into the lighted body of the Chamber.

'How long for?'

'Till things quieten down.'

'You can't be more definite?'

'No, Prime Minister.'

'I doubt if they'll take your word for it, here … What about a Commission of Inquiry?'

'It's the very last thing we want. It would unsettle everything, and produce nothing.'

'It might satisfy the House tonight.'

'That's not the point, sir.'

The PM smiled. 'It's not *your* point … I thought your replies were a little on the brusque side.'

'Yes,' conceded Godbold, honestly. 'We might have wrapped them up a bit. Or used a better tone. I left that to the Minister. It didn't work.'

'What do you want him to say now?'

'Just to stick to the brief. Be consistent and firm. He might even say – ' Godbold paused, knowing that what he suggested now was almost certain to be passed on to Lord Lorde, ' – he might even start by saying he's sorry.'

'Weak,' said the PM. 'Dangerous.'

'Worth taking a chance, though. If he could just – ' Godbold gestured, ' – just sound perfectly frank, perfectly reasonable, but convinced that we *have* to do what we're doing, in the interests of public order. Ask for a chance to prove that he's right.'

'It might buy us a breathing space. But is time on our side? In Pharamaul?'

'We need a breathing space there, too.'

The Prime Minister nodded, and straightened up. 'All right. I'll tell him … Come and see me tomorrow morning.'

He walked, with a firm step, towards his place on the Front Bench, and then, passing his accustomed seat, sat down beside Lord Lorde, and fell into deep and earnest conversation with the Secretary of State.

There were many members of the House of Commons prepared to swear that Lord Lorde's speech – in reply, that night, was the best thing he had ever done, the persuasive peak of his career. Even those who did not like him (probably, man for man, a marked majority) were ready to admit that it was a speech so good that it transcended the margins of the Minister's normal performance, and came within touching distance of sincerity.

In any case, it was a big surprise, the biggest of that evening, which had already seen the Pharamaul affair ebb and flow in discussion, and finally hang high in the balance of failure. To Godbold especially, deeply committed as he was to success or defeat in this debate, it came as an astonishing relief. Evidently the Prime Minister must have spoken to some purpose …

Lord Lorde, demonstrably less remote and authoritarian than was his normal aspect, adopted at the outset a role which the House always found it hard to resist – the role of the penitent. He began by apologizing for the apparent brusqueness of his earlier answers, at Question Time, on the subject of Pharamaul. He asked hon. Members to be generous enough to ascribe it, not to rudeness, but to the strength of his personal convictions about Pharamaul.

'I am so certain – ' thus he concluded his opening phrases, ' – that we are doing right, that I find it difficult to entertain, with patience, anything to the contrary. That is always an error, of taste if not of judgement. I can only ask the House to accept this apology – it is nothing less – in the spirit in which it is offered.'

This opening was so well done, with so genuine an air of contrition, that it had a remarkable effect on the House. They had been expecting many other things from the Minister, ranging from the 'stiff-necked pride' forecast by Emrys Price-Canning, to an abject retreat which the course of the debate had seemed to render inevitable. What they had not expected – after watching Lord Lorde for scores of years in scores of different roles – was an honest admission of guilt, paving the way for an honest stand on principle.

For the determined cynics, it simply demonstrated, with particular precision, how and why Lord Lorde had survived in public life for nearly half a century. For the majority, it reopened a question on which they had already made up their minds. That, for the Government, was the first major gain of the evening.

There were many others, though it was not a long speech, nor as detailed and laboured in rebuttal as most

Ministerial efforts tended to be. It was simply an exercise in the art of persuasion. Lord Lorde dealt first with Price-Canning's own plea for a reversal of policy in Pharamaul. He did not, he said, wish to question the sincerity of the hon. Member's own reports from the territory. Perhaps it was a matter of interpretation, difficult to appraise at this distance. For his own part, the best available sources seemed to confirm that the situation in Pharamaul was not normal, nor likely to be so for some considerable time.

'There is,' he said, quoting almost *verbatim* the note which Godbold had passed on to him earlier, 'ample evidence of threats and violence affecting public order. I need not remind the House that there have been nine murders, and countless riots, already. We must, on our side, regard this as quite enough to justify the emergency measures we have taken. In such an explosive situation, we have a dear duty to safeguard life and property. Part of that duty, regrettable though it may seem, has necessitated the detention of Dinamaula in Port Victoria, some distance from the immediate danger area.

It said much for the effect of Lord Lorde's opening remarks, that not even now was he interrupted. The House, once again, was attentive. Suddenly, it seemed, they wanted to hear to and judge the other side of the medal, fairly and honestly presented. The Minister was giving them just that. He deserved, if only on this one occasion, the tribute of silence.

Emboldened, Lord Lorde continued: 'Whether accidentally or not, Dinamaula is the centre of unrest. You may not agree with our view that he has been unwise in his expressions of opinion; but you can hardly deny that they have led to grave disturbances within the tribe. I should perhaps add that he is not being kept away because of the rumours of his intended marriage to a white girl, though it is perfectly true that the prospect of such a mixed marriage has shocked and divided the tribe.'

At that point, there came the only interruption – an anonymous voice calling out: 'They seem to like it all right now!'

Lord Lorde shook his head, eminently reasonable, eminently firm. 'I can assure the hon. Member that it is still a point of division and doubt, particularly among the conservative element ... But basically, Dinamaula has been removed, not because of this rumoured marriage, but because his expressed opinions, and some of his actions, and some of the actions of his immediate followers, have contributed directly to tribal unrest. The Maulas are split. Their minds and loyalties are confused. It is our task now to compose and heal these differences, these confusions.'

Godbold listened in honest amazement as Lord Lorde embarked on his peroration. It was, for him, a moment of somewhat absurd remorse. *All is forgiven*, he wanted to say to Lord Lorde. *Don't leave the Scheduled Territories Office. We need you* ... He had never been more surprised, or more relieved, in his life. The man was purging a whole lifetime of futility.

'Sir,' said Lord Lorde, 'I do not wish to detain the House further, because it is late, and perhaps it would be better now to *think* about this problem, not to talk about it. I can truly say that I am grateful to the hon. Member for South Oxford for deciding to raise this matter, since it has given me the opportunity of restating my convictions.' He smiled towards Emrys Price-Canning, who now seemed not less thoughtful than the rest of the House. 'I hope the hon. Member will not object to such an expression of gratitude. We do not often agree, but there is a first time for everything.'

The House accorded him a murmur of laughter. 'In this matter of Pharamaul, I would ask the House to reserve judgement, and give us a chance to prove we are right. I would ask them to help us by watching the position carefully, as we ourselves shall watch it.

'At one point in this debate,' he concluded, 'a Commission of Inquiry was suggested. I do *not* agree – I must be firm on this point – that now is the moment for it. But I can assure the House that if things *do* deteriorate, we shall not refuse the fullest public examination. Indeed,' he ended, with a wonderful air of frankness and sincerity, 'my own political honour would be involved, if we did *not* take such a course.'

It was at that point that the debate faded out, like a brief summer storm, on an astonishing note of anticlimax. It might be, thought Godbold, as he gathered up his papers and passed them to Crossley – it might be a Ministerial confidence trick of an especially gross kind; or it might be the House of Commons at its best, responding to truth, honesty, and conviction. But whichever it was, the blessed facts were there.

Though earlier it had seemed a very near thing, at the end there was, throughout the Chamber, a patent willingness to suspend judgement, to wait and see. That was all Godbold had wanted – the breathing space he had prayed for.

IV

Long afterwards, when it no longer mattered, Godbold asked the Prime Minister, over one of their dinners, how he had managed thus to galvanize Lord Lorde; and the PM, grinning reminiscently, had answered: 'I did something that perhaps I should have done more often with more of my Ministers – I put a time bomb under him. I told him – looking very friendly all the time, for the benefit of the

House – that he had got us into this mess, and it was his job to get us out. In fact, I said it would be his job, if he *didn't* get us out … Rather unfair, I'll admit. However – ' the Prime Minister gestured expressively, ' – it certainly worked wonders, didn't it?'

Godbold nodded. 'Yes … That was one evening when I really loved the House of Commons.'

But the Press, on the morrow of that debate, had been less impressed, less charitable; indeed, it seemed that, robbed of their legitimate prey, they were inclined to vent their spleen upon the whole body politic.

The *Daily Thresh*, of course, led the van; it was furious.

'Treachery in high places!' it roared. 'Smooth talk and false promises! The Maulas ask for justice, and what do they get? – soft soap and wait-and-see! The whole country will be well advised, etc, etc.'

The left-wing papers also took it out on the Government. 'Double-talk and double-cross!' they cried. 'The stuffed shirts will cheat you yet! Rally to Dinamaula! Let the electorate decide! Vote for HIM! Whose finger on the colour bar trigger?'

Even the Government side were worried. 'By all accounts,' said the *Morning Telegram*, 'the Maulas, a carefree and lovable people, are being systematically robbed of their sacred rights. Let us think long and hard of what we are doing to this simple, trusting tribe.'

'It is a tug of war,' said the *Winchester Guardian*, 'for the soul of a small country, with threats on one side, hopes on the other. Shamefully, we are on the side of threats.'

'Kaffirs are lively!' said the *Encomium*. 'Beware the Hides of Starch!'

'Victimized for marriage plans,' whined the *New Nation*. 'Black brides and whited sepulchres … See page 80, for this week's competition – "A Sonnet on Sexual Discrimination".'

The *Globe*, intent upon the same tack (as it had been for many weeks), published the winning essay in its '*Choose a Bride for Dinamaula*' competition – and ran headlong into trouble. For once, its captive audience showed that they were ready to wrestle with their masters. It seemed that the declared winner, an eighteen-year-old physical culture addict from Croydon, had stipulated (among other things) that Dinamaula's prospective bride should measure 35-25-36, and should have a skin 'roughly the colour of chocolate cream blancmange'. The answering howl from eight million readers rocked the very sinews of the *Globe*.

Letters poured in, whole editions were boycotted, windows were broken, compositors struck for an increased differential. Surely the *Globe* knew (so ran the tenor of infuriated complaint) that America had now standardized the ideal figure as a global 38-25-36 – that is, a 38-inch bust overhanging 36-inch 'hips'? Why was not Dinamaula entitled to this transatlantic titbit? Why such snobbery, why such barefaced prejudice?

And, in heaven's name, why chocolate cream blancmange, as a skin colour? Why not pure ivory, or succulent Cornish cream? Was this another subtle example of racial discrimination? Was the *Globe* really on the side of the colour bar prudes, who notoriously wanted a coal-black bride with monstrous hips and scarcely any bosom at all?

'Unfair to Dinamaula!' proclaimed the placards carried by the pickets. 'Give him a proper armful! Justice or bust! Keep a-breast of the times!' Though the police speedily intervened, the uproar was effective and the point was made; the *Globe*, on the following week, published a retraction, uncovered a fresh batch of entries ('delayed in transit'), and announced that the real winner was an unemployed glassblower from Liverpool, who said, simply: 'Let him marry Mae West (40-27-38).'

It came almost as an intrusion to read, a few days later, on a number of inside pages, the same small item: 'Further Riots at Gamate.'

CHAPTER TWELVE

❖

The weather did not help much. Often, at this time of the year, it grew oppressive, discouraging all personal enterprise, from lovemaking to petty larceny. But now, as if to demonstrate which side was the side of the angels, it turned a little cooler; and Pharamaul, freed from a ninety-five-degree noon temperature and a brutal humidity, gave itself afresh to the delights of popular demonstration. Throughout the length and breadth of the land, men stirred, and looked about them, and rose early to raise hell.

In Port Victoria, they were much heartened by the success of the strike at the club – and especially by its aftermath. On the morrow of the abortive club dance, and the shameful early closing of the bar, the Committee girded its ample loins and – impelled by the furious resentment of ninety per cent of its members – sacked the entire club staff from the major-domo who allocated the seating in the dining-room, to the diminutive youth who brought the cold drinks for the adolescents who hung up the tea-towels after the dishes had been dried.

The Committee then sent out an appeal – by Press, radio, proclamation, broadsheet, word of mouth, and police grapevine – for one hundred and forty Maulas of either sex, aged between ten and sixty, to undertake remunerative employment at the Pharamaul Club. Within half a day, the results of that appeal, and their full implication, were known in every home in Port Victoria. For not a man, not a boy, not a washgirl or sweeper, came forward to offer their services.

The consequences were immediate, and catastrophic. For the first time in sixty-five years, the Pharamaul Club failed to open its doors at sundown.

There were some who blamed the Committee, some who blamed the Press; some who blamed Dinamaula, or William Ewart O'Brien, editor of the *Times of Pharamaul*, or even Sir Elliott Vere-Toombs – who was, *ex officio*, Honorary President of the club. There were others who just could not make up their minds, and blamed democracy, or communism, or South Africa. The only zone of agreement concerned the extent of disaster and affront. If this could happen, *anything* could happen.

The trouble was, of course, that the Maulas were demonstrably in a far stronger position than were the club members. It was notorious that Maulas could live on nothing a day; the local equivalent of the Asiatic handful of rice was a couple of mealie-cobs and a swig of *kaffir*-beer. They could always stay alive, somehow; and they all had hordes of relatives, anyway ... On the other hand, the members *had* to have their club; in the entire course of their adult lives, they had never had to do without it, and it was too late to start now.

Various expedients were tried. An appeal to the Governor for police action to break the strike was politely dismissed, on formal grounds – there was no evidence of intimidation, only of passive resistance to employment. An attempt was made to draft in servants from private houses; but after an evening given over exclusively to acid comment on how terribly badly everyone else's servants were trained, this was abandoned. An emissary was even

sent to Dinamaula, at his lodgings in Port Victoria, asking
him to use his influence to persuade recruits to come
forward; the messenger returned with the unheard-of,
dusty answer: 'The chief-designate is not running an
employment agency.'

Then the LADIES themselves tried, toiling in eight-hour
shifts and running the club on a canteen basis. This worked
for two nights, and was then likewise abandoned. The
trouble was social rather than organizational. Everyone
wanted to preside behind the bar, and sometimes to sit on
it; no one volunteered to cook or to wash up. The
cloakrooms degenerated into a sordid maze of stopped-up
toilets and dirty towels; the kitchens were stacked waist-
high with greasy crockery. One entire collection of signed
bar chits, covering forty-eight hours, was inadvertently put
into the incinerator. The bar itself lost a fortune.

The Committee met again, for the eighth time in five
days. The meeting was brief, the discussion simple and
pointed. They needed the club. The Maulas didn't need it.
The Maulas would thus have to be reinstated.

But now a further difficulty arose. The spokesman for
the dismissed staff trained in heaven-knew-what school of
trade-union dialectics, suddenly confronted the committee
with an unprecedented demand for an increase in wages.

'What?' It was the Chairman himself, Twotty
Wotherspoon, who was the first to explode. 'Good God,
you must be round the bend! What the hell do you mean,
an increase?'

The spokesman, a smiling young Maula whom hitherto
they had only known as the quickest and best of the dining
room stewards, was smiling still. He stood before the five-
man committee in the Secretary's office – the first time in
his life that he had penetrated thus far.

'An increase, sir,' he answered. 'Ten shilling increase.'

'I don't think you quite understand,' said Wotherspoon, a strong and florid man with a tendency to high blood pressure. 'We're actually offering you your jobs back. All of you. We're prepared to forget the rotten way you behaved, the other night. Walking off the job like that ...' He drew a heavy breath. 'Well, never mind. We want you to get back to work, straight away. What about it?'

'Increase, sir,' said the young Maula. 'Cost of living increase. Ten shillings.'

'Bloody sauce!' said Splinter Woodcock.

'Get to hell out of here!' said the Chairman.

The young and smiling Maula withdrew.

The very long silence that followed was finally broken.

'You know, we're wasting our time,' said McCarthy, the youngest committee member present. 'We've been wasting our time for a week. They've got us by the short and curly ones. Can't you see that?'

'But it's bloody blackmail!' said Binkie Buchanan.

'Of course, if you want to side with those bolshy bastards ...'

'Call it what you like. It's time we faced facts. We need them on the job, and they know it. They're putting on a squeeze. We either give in, or close up the club.'

'Bastards!'

'What do you suggest, then?'

'He says he wants a ten-bob raise. Offer him five. Five shillings a month, all-round increase.'

'We can't afford it.'

'You know bloody well that we can. And even if we can't, we'll have to.'

It was on such ignoble terms, only concluded after a further full half-day of negotiation, that the Pharamaul Club got under way again.

As a strike, it had perceptible elements of humour; but in another part of the town – the dock area – there was a strike of another sort, with very different implications.

It started with a tavern brawl, involving some sailors off a small South African coastal freighter, and a Maula waiter who had been serving them. Either he was not quick enough for their liking, or he answered back, or he brought the wrong change, or he spilt some beer on a sleeve or a trouser-leg – versions differed widely, and lost nothing in the telling. But whatever it was, it sparked a murderous riot.

The unsatisfactory Maula servant was first sworn at, and then roughly assaulted; some of his friends joined in, with ugly intent: the South African sailors were forced to retreat, one with a torn scalp, another with a knife-wound in the shoulder. Ill-contented with this, they marched swaggering down the main dock street, shouting and shoving people off the pavement, followed by a crowd which presently hemmed them into a corner and seemed ripe to give them a bloody manhandling, if nothing worse.

The pushing and jostling, the catcalls, the wild black faces, the steady drone of anger and threat, proved too much for their nerves. One of them drew a gun, and shot a Maula through the head. Then they made good their retreat and, backed by the threat of the gun, fought their way back to their ship.

It sailed inconspicuously with the tide that night. It was the last ship to do so, for a very long time.

The dead Maula was a stevedore, a man famous for his strength and endurance, a shift boss who had many friends. At dawn the following day, after a mass meeting at the dockside, every single Maula employed in the dock area – stevedores, cranemen, winchmen, firemen, checkers, oilers, messengers, berthing parties, pilots' boatmen – walked off the job and vanished without trace into the town.

It all seemed to happen naturally and inevitably, the direct result of murder and mob anger; but it was also so well organized that it seemed to fit, even more naturally, into the current mutinous pattern of Pharamaul. It was something for the police, something for the town council, above all something for the Governor.

While the authorities investigated, and dug up what witnesses they could, the docks and the harbour seemed to fall dead, at a single stroke. Ships could not sail, ships could not enter, cargoes could not be moved; many of the new arrivals had to anchor in the long ground-swell offshore, unable to establish contact, or to find a vacant berth for themselves, or even discover what was happening. It was as if that particular corner of the island were tainted by plague; no one could enter, no one had the strength to leave.

After an emergency meeting with his advisers, at several levels, the Governor, as a first step, tried to find out who was behind it all, the particular and patently efficient organizer who must be approached in order to find a solution. He failed utterly in this search; so did the police. Dinamaula disclaimed all knowledge; his cousin Zuva, who was staying with him, returned a blank, impertinent negative to all inquiries, while his 'bodyguard' smirked and rolled their eyes. At the end, Zuva said, as if contributing something of value: 'Perhaps they do not choose to work for murderers.'

And one of the bodyguard, a short scarred man with a look of inward violence, said: 'Perhaps they want their chief.'

The harbour continued dead and forlorn, while the city merchants fumed, perishable cargo rotted on the quayside, and ships' captains sent messages, scrawled on signal pads, asking what the hell was going on. No one could tell them, because no one knew.

The Governor, back at his desk in the Secretariat after abortive conference with the police, decided that for his part also there was nothing to be done. It must surely be better to wait, and see if the thing would blow over, rather than to make himself, and the police, and the town councillors, ridiculous, by searching for a man, or men, who did not seem to be there at all ... In any case, there was no further violence in the town, simply a denial of activity. And what he had to deal with was only a shadow of what now began to happen, two hundred miles to the northwards, in Gamate.

II

'They are killing our own brothers, in the town beside the sea' – so ran the message that sped from mouth to mouth, and from hut to hut in Gamate, an hour or so before Forsdick, the District Commissioner, read an urgent telegram beginning: '*Disturbances in the dock area have led to a strike affecting port facilities.*' To Forsdick, a dock strike in Port Victoria seemed of precious little account; if that were the only thing they had to worry about, he thought sourly, then those superior bastards down in Government House could count themselves pretty well off. But to Gamate itself, already stretched to a fearful tension, plagued by rumours and strange visitors, consumed by the violent joys of intrigue and mutiny, the news from the south, presented as it was in terms of bloodshed and oppression, made glorious all that they dared to do.

For they were no longer alone – so the fresh rumours ran. The men who wrote on the machines, the priest who talked of freedom and the striking-off of chains, now seemed wonderfully vindicated. Earlier, there had been some who held back, doubting the wisdom of opposing their will to white Government. But now, it seemed, all

Pharamaul was in flames, and ready to throw aside its hated yoke. Any man could now strike any blow, provided it was a strong blow against tyranny. Had they not been told that the whole world was watching them? Had they not been assured that the time had come to prove their manhood?

David Bracken, once he had overcome the slight embarrassment of his position, found all that he did at this time, and all he watched, and all he recorded, more worthwhile than anything in his life so far. He had been left behind in Gamate, to act as the Governor's personal observer, and to report back directly to Government House. 'Seconded for temporary duty with the Resident Commissioner' had been the vague official delineation of his new assignment; but he felt it must be obvious to everyone in Gamate, and particularly to Andrew Macmillan, that he was nothing more than a Government House spy, detailed to keep an eye on the floundering yokels who were making such a mess of things, up there in the native capital …

However, it had all worked out on a simpler, less contentious plane. He lived at the Residency, and his relationship with Macmillan was cordial and uncomplicated. Resolutely he had put aside all conviction of spying, all implications that his very presence meant that the Governor was near to losing confidence in what Macmillan was doing and trying to do. As David Bracken, First Secretary, he was there to help. That was all that mattered.

Just as had happened at the time of the abandoned *aboura*, and the murderous confusion that followed it, his natural ally was Keith Crump, the policeman. Crump himself, grossly overworked, dealing hourly with a score of crises and a hundred conflicting rumours, seemed glad of his presence; though he was, at the same time, a man honest enough to make his own position clear at the outset. He had done this in a singularly direct manner, when he and David, touring one of the outlying circles of huts, had by chance come upon a wasted and putrefying Maula corpse, lying, half-eaten by jackals, beside its own grave.

'For once, that's natural causes,' observed Crump. They were seated side by side in the jeep, surveying the disgusting cameo of death. Crump pointed. 'You see what happened? That's an old man called Tembula – he died of pneumonia a couple of days ago. He was buried there – ' Crump pointed again, ' – and they put that big pile of stones on top of the grave. Along comes a pack of jackals, and they scrape away the soil, and burrow downwards, from the outside edge of the stones down to the corpse, until they've made an exit tunnel of the right size and at the right angle, and then they drag the corpse up, and sit down to dinner. Damned clever, these Chinese jackals ... Don't forget to put that in your report.'

'What report?' asked David, not sure, under the impact of such gruesome mortal decay, whether to laugh or to be sick.

'The one you'll be writing tonight.' Crump faced him, cheerful, unresenting, friendly. 'As a simple policeman, I deduce that you're here to see how we're handling things in Gamate, and to report back to H E. In fact, I'd be a bloody fool if I *didn't* deduce that.'

'I'm just here to help,' said David, with appropriate care.

'Fair enough,' answered Crump. 'We can always use a good man.'

'And also to report,' said David. He liked Crump, but this was not the moment to be patronized.

Crump nodded again, sure of himself as he always was. 'All I say is, give us the credit, along with the black

marks ... Now let's take a look at some of the people who
are still alive.'

That had seemed then, and at all other later times, a
most reasonable proposition ... Together they covered
many miles each day, improvising, snatching meals,
weaving new plans of action out of the confused air,
plugging the gaps in the fabric of security. Together they
struck many blows, held many conferences, looked down
on many dead men, watched much blood flow, and dodged
many weapons.

They were two white men, whose authority was no
longer invincible, in a black town – the lowering black
town of Gamate.

For now, the pause in violence broke by sheer weight of
ill-will, and was quickly left behind. All that had recently
happened in Gamate, and had escaped without notable
punishment, now served as a pattern; men who had
prudently held back grew bold, men who had been leaders
became wild prophets of revolt. By day, a brooding silence
overlay the town, while fires were put out, smashed
windows were boarded up, the wounded were cared for,
the dead were buried, and the police searched for known
malefactors; by night, the curtain came down on the rule
of law, and blood thickened and boiled until it spewed
over, once again, into disgusting violence.

For David Bracken, watching in fear and tension, the
focus of all those evil days was Keith Crump. Macmillan
seemed to have retreated into the shadows, from whence
he witnessed, mutely impotent, the destruction of his
whole working life; Forsdick also remained behind the
scenes, shouldering a burden of administration which had
now become unmanageable. Tribal affairs were at a
standstill; to take their place, a senseless destruction
possessed all but a few Maulas. Stemming this,
spearheading the counter-thrust of order and discipline,

Captain Crump of the Royal Pharamaul Police seemed like a lone heroic figure, moulded for this single purpose from some indestructible fibre.

Crump had always had a cheerful way with evildoers; basically, he always knew what was going on, all the crooks, all the smart boys, all the weaker vessels; and he had been able to deal with them from an all-embracing efficiency, with time to spare for paternal benevolence. But now it had become too tough for cheerfulness. Nothing was funny, any more in Gamate. There was no place for laughter; because between laughter and a grave look, a man might be murdered, a woman raped, a hut set on fire, a house torn down.

Fear ruled all their lives; fear, and a grim sense of execution. A dozen times each night, Crump, at the head of his police patrol, had to break up a riot, rescue hostages, defend a threatened strongpoint, give safe conduct to a doctor or a nurse or a Government official. His diary, and his subsequent reports, recorded a steady deterioration and a ruthless pressure from either side. The jail was hopelessly overcrowded; extra police were drafted in, living in tents behind a barbed wire enclave; convicted rioters or looters were sent down to the coast, to relieve the inroads on confinement; certain men were rounded up and cautioned, tough areas patrolled, appeals made to put an end to this murderous chaos.

But still the body of violence and disorder grew, fattening upon a profitable immunity. For the total of wrongdoing was more than could be dealt with, in any single working day. There came a time when, in one period of twenty-four hours, five huts were burned; every single window on the ground floor of the hospital was smashed; Father Schwemmer's mission church was broken into, stripped, and defiled; some cattle, seized for unpaid taxes, were maimed and had to be destroyed; two men were shot by a sentry while trying to steal the key of the jail; a police raid on an illicit brewing of *bariaana* was beaten off, with wild excess of celebration; a gang of simpleminded thugs breached the retaining walls of the Gamate dam, and let two months' rainfall escape in muddy chaos; and a waggon, overturned in reprisal for some faint-hearted support from its owner, crushed to death the four children sleeping in its shadow.

It was no wonder, thought David, that Keith Crump, charged with the care and solution of all such crises, grew taut and lean as a spear. His tribal nickname, 'The Shining Soldier', now seemed part of a remote, ridiculously benevolent past. Now, seeing a score of painstaking years evaporate like the precious water in the dam, knowing above all that he and his men had lost all tribal repute, and become the target for general hatred, he was grim, unsmiling, and resentful. So, indeed, were a lot of other people.

III

The bar of the Gamate Hotel had always been a refuge, of one sort or another – a refuge from wives or husbands, or from work which had become too dull or too demanding, or from the heat, or from boredom, or from the gruesome pressure of reality. But now, it seemed, it had become a refuge of a different sort; an actual encampment, with broken windows boarded up, strict precautions as to who could come in, and who must stay out – the latter being any Maula not directly employed in the bar – and a general air of encirclement.

When, after a night of terror and burning, Fellows, the hotelkeeper, unlocked the entrance door and prepared for another day's work, it was as if he were lowering a small, heavily guarded drawbridge, which under his direct supervision could admit a few chosen entrants to the inner citadel … The fact that, for the first time in his life, he had a loaded revolver secreted behind the till, was final proof that this was the focal ring of an armed camp.

Fellows polished the worn surface of the bar-counter, rearranged some glasses, swore at one of his Maula helpers who was being slow about bringing in the fresh stocks of soda and tonic water. Then the screen door of the *stoep* creaked open, and slammed shut again – a familiar sound, a sound he had heard a hundred times a day for the past ten years. He looked warily at the figure which shouldered its way in, and then relaxed. It was Oosthuizen, the Afrikaner farmer, huge and ponderous, his khaki shirt and slacks straining over giant muscles, his face and forearms bronzed to a deep mahogany hue.

Automatically, even as the other man advanced towards the bar, Fellows reached behind him for the bottle of pungent Commando brandy, and poured a generous tot into a thick tumbler.

'Good morning, Mr Oosthuizen,' he said, adding a dash of water and pushing the glass across the counter.

'*Gooie moré*, Ted.' Oosthuizen, already sweating in the hot midday air, came to a stop, and leant one elbow on the edge of the bar. With his other hand he swept up the tumbler, and swallowed lustily. The noise he made as he put the glass down again was like a pistol shot, shattering the peace of the empty bar. Oosthuizen grinned as he caught Fellows's eye. 'What's new, eh?' he asked. 'What did those bloody *bobijaans* do, last night?'

'Same as the night before,' said Fellows morosely. His busy hands swabbed down the bar, sponging out the spilt drops of brandy. 'Broke a lot more windows down at the hospital, burnt a couple of huts, tried to murder a policeman.' His polishing arm worked quicker and quicker as he added: 'You'll read all about it in the newspapers. Maybe before some of it happens, for all I know.'

'Those *pampoens* are still writing, eh?'

'Still writing.'

The screen door creaked again, and slammed to. The inner door opened in its turn. They both looked round. This time it was two people – Llewellyn, the agricultural officer, and one of the doctors from the hospital.

They greeted each other like men in a desert, come at last to an oasis. It was almost as if they were surprised to see each other alive, on yet another new morning. They sipped their drinks, and compared notes. The hospital had been kept busy most of the night, said the doctor – a pale young man called Templegate, not long out of Liverpool Northern Hospital and the sober role of junior house surgeon. Two split heads, a policeman with a deep stab wound, a woman frightened into a miscarriage, a child which, in flight from some juvenile gang warfare, had swallowed a forked twig – been the same as usual, only a bit more so.

'You'd be glad to get back to the Northern, I'd say,' said Fellows, who had himself worked in Liverpool. 'Sounds like a rough night in Scotland Road.'

'Scotland Road was never like this,' answered Templegate, brushing back his sparse hair. 'Then, it was just the Liverpool-Irish cutting up, and working off a bit of excess blood pressure. Now you don't know what to expect.'

Llewellyn stared down at his drink, his dark face seeming to brood on an inner sorrow. 'By God, that's true! I've been thirty years in this territory, and I'll admit it's got me beat. You don't know who to trust. The boy who brings you your coffee in the morning might just as easily whip out a knife instead of a teaspoon.'

More regulars drifted in, taking up their accustomed places at the bar, contributing their quota of news. Two men from the logging camp arrived, reporting all quiet after a tribal clash – Maulas against imported Basutu – and a threatened strike. Captain Crump put his head round the door, nodded in recognition once or twice, and withdrew again, intent on some private quest.

Then Forsdick, the District Commissioner, arrived, punctually on the stroke of twelve-fifteen, bringing a curious story of theft from his office – a theft involving nothing more valuable nor more lethal than two cartons of officially embossed envelopes. 'Perhaps they're going to write two thousand letters to the newspapers,' he commented savagely – and as if to point the remark, a knot of Press correspondents entered, and settled themselves (as they now always did) at one of the far tables, well away from the bar.

They made an uncomfortable, alien element in the room, notwithstanding that they were already as familiar as characters in some minor classic – Tulbach Browne exuding an air of paternal pride in the Gamate story, Pikkie Joubert arguing about South African politics, Axel Hallmarck massaging his crew-cut hair, Clandestine Lebourget and Noblesse O'Toole looking over some tear sheets of photographs which had arrived by that morning's mail.

Though they were now an essential part of the Gamate scene, there was no one who would not have rejoiced to see them go; and their physical distance from the fellowship of the bar indicated the fact, like a pointing arrow.

Fellows, returning red-faced from serving them, jerked back his head contemptuously. 'Wish it was poison, instead of beer,' he said, low-voiced. 'I'd cheerfully swing for that lot, tomorrow morning.'

'To hell with them!' said Oosthuizen, whose capacity for alcohol (following a recent switch of allegiance from beer to brandy) was uncertain. 'They're not worth spitting on, man!'

'They're causing a lot of trouble, all the same,' said Fellows. 'You know that.'

'The trouble's here, anyway,' countered Oosthuizen roughly. 'If all that lot over there – ' he turned and gestured, not bothering to lower his voice, ' – ran off home tomorrow, we'd still have trouble.'

Pikkie Joubert, who had looked up with the rest of the Pressmen as Oosthuizen spoke, called out in salutation: '*Gooie moré, kerel!*'

'Bugger you!' said Osthuizen, and turned back to the bar.

As he did so, a furious altercation broke out between Fellows and a Maula who had just entered by the service door. The latter was a post office messenger, a thick-browed, heavy-set youth with a telegram for one of the Press correspondents; he had come in, in all innocence, and started to walk from the bar to the corner table, before Fellows seized his arm and shoulder in a crude half-nelson and halted him. There was a brief struggle, an exchange of shouts and curses, and the young Maula left again, muttering, and nursing his wrist. Two of the Pressmen, who had been watching, simultaneously dodged out of the bar by the door nearest their table, hot-foot for an interview.

'For God's sake!' said Llewellyn, shaking his head in dismay. 'That was just one of the post office kids. He had a telegram. Didn't you see it?'

'I don't care if he had a medal for the District Commissioner,' said Fellows, breathing heavily. 'No one comes into this bar, unless I say so. I'm only protecting you.'

'He's right,' said Oosthuizen, nodding ponderously. 'You can't trust a single mother's son, these days.'

'If anyone *does* come in with a medal for me,' observed Forsdick pacifyingly, 'let them past, will you? I've been waiting a hell of a long time for it.'

The laughter dispersed the quarrelsome moment, but Llewellyn still brooded on it.

'There you have Gamate, in a bloody nutshell,' he said morosely. 'A kid comes in with a telegram, and we all think we're going to be murdered ... When you remember what it used to be like, in the old days ... Give me another pint, Ted – and anyone else who wants it.'

'I agree that we can't take any chances,' said Forsdick, in his fruity official voice. 'But it's bloody difficult to know what to do.'

'I know what *I'm* going to do,' said Oosthuizen. He slapped the side pocket of his trousers, and they all heard the solid, metallic sound that met his hand. 'No one is going to take *me* by surprise.'

'You've got a gun?' asked Fellows, looking up as he drew the beer.

'*Jah!*' answered Oosthuizen, with emphasis. 'I've got a gun, and a bloody good one too, and I don't mind who knows it!'

'You want to be careful of that sort of thing,' said Llewellyn warningly.

'*They* want to be careful, man!' said Oosthuizen. 'Why should I be careful? I've got nothing on my conscience.'

It was the same all over the town – every man's hand was against his neighbour's, every white skin was a lordly enemy, every black skin was suspect, for the first time within living memory. The careful cherishing, of black by white, that had been the rule for many generations, was abandoned as too dangerous and too undeserved; in its place, a poisonous mistrust flourished, reaching its extreme form in many normal homes, where, when men and women sat down at table, they added, to the knives and forks and spoons, a new essential for the peaceful enjoyment of food – a revolver.

Now, when rioting spilled over into bloodshed, there were no truce lines, no margins of brotherhood, no pity. Men bled to death because to bend over a wounded man on the ground only invited a knife in one's own back; corpses lay where they fell until daylight, and were then borne away, in savage resentment, or in contemptuous irritation at so menial a chore.

At the hospital, they worked as usual on the casualties, but it had become a half-hearted, cynical devotion; a Maula whose life one saved, after extreme effort, with great expense of drugs and stimulants and blood plasma, might well turn out to be one's own executioner, a short week from the day of his deliverance.

Tribal management became a farce; there was no 'management' in any ordinary sense, simply a deadlock, with impotence on one side, mute indiscipline on the other.

For the Press, there was much to report; and it was all bad news, when honestly measured against the past. For white Government, there was nothing but frustration and peril. For the Maulas, whether good or bad, whether fearful or pricked to wild defiance, there was uncertainty, a pause on the brink of their allotted history.

Both sides – for now the division was mortally apparent – knew well that things could not go on like this; black and white alike, they were condemned to the grinding wheel of chance – its blind axis unknown, its spokes as long as dreams or death, its rim already dipped in blood.

It was against such a background that Andrew Macmillan, the Resident Commissioner, made his last appeal to the three Regents of the Maulas.

IV

It seemed to Andrew Macmillan that he had waited a thousand times on this same *stoep* of the Residency, with lessening hope, with failing strength, for the appointed emissaries of the Maulas to talk with him and to hear his words. First it had been Simaula, the last chief of the Maulas – a difficult man, gaunt, nervous, and withdrawn, a man (it sometimes seemed) who was permanently astonished to be alive. Then it had been the three Regents, Seralo, Katsaula, and Puero, feeling their way in an interim period, pulling in this direction and in that, imperceptibly shrugging off the controlling hand of white Government. Then, briefly, it had been Dinamaula, the chief-designate, the debatable newcomer, withdrawing still further from the known paths of co-operation. Now, at this moment of crisis, it was the three Regents again, unwillingly come to talk and to listen.

There must have been a time (so he thought, as he stared at the darkening Residency garden, and the shadows which marked the accustomed margins of his life, and listened to the hum of insects, and smelt the coarse savoury smells of burnt grass and old, heat laden trees) – there must have been a time, in the distant, longed-for past, when he had looked forward to such a meeting, confident in its outcome, sure of its essential rightness ... But if there had indeed been such a time, it was now forgotten. It was sunk below the edge of hope, submerged by old quarrels and new ideas, fatally stained by blood.

As he waited now in the dusk – it was always dusk, there was no more true sunlight for him in Gamate – with a cup of coffee at his elbow, and David Bracken, ill at ease, in a chair opposite him, Macmillan knew the depth of his personal defeat. He was old, and tired, and unequal to the task. He no longer believed in what he was doing, since whatever he did turned sour and lapsed into failure. He was no longer in charge; he was going through the mere motions of command, because (a shameful thought) he was paid to do so, and, come hell or high water, he must play out time for his pension.

Remote and lonely, he knew now that he had failed both his sides. His own men feared (or perhaps laughed at) the inept grasp of his hand on the helm; the Maulas mocked the man he had become. Now, the main burden of his life (and this was another, infinitely more shameful thought) was not that he should acquit himself well, but that troops – men with guns instead of words – must be brought in, to bale him out, and set his rule to rights.

There could be no more desolate end to any reign. It was the ultimate disgrace, the overthrow of a man's professional striving. But it was imminently at hand.

He said, turning awkwardly and heavily in his chair: 'More coffee, David?'

'No, thanks, Andrew.' David, oppressed by the moment, summoned a warm response. 'But that was very good coffee … I suppose these chaps should be here, any minute now.'

'If they come at all.'

'Oh, surely …'

'Last time, if you remember, they were all ill …' Andrew lay back again, exhausted and spent. In the twilight, his face looked terribly old; the deep lines seemed to be carved by a most cruel, eroding hand. 'When you get back,' he said, his voice matching his defeated face, 'tell H E something from me, will you?'

'Whatever you say, Andrew.' David reacted sharply and forebodingly to the fateful tone of voice. 'But I hope you'll be telling him, yourself.'

'*You* tell him … Tell him two things, three things … When it's all over … Tell him that *originally* I was right about Dinamaula – he was trying to move too fast … Tell him to keep Seralo where he is, as Senior Regent – the tribe will trust him …'

There was a long pause; it was if the other man had only so much breath to spend, only so much strength to squander, and that he had outrun both those limits. But presently he stirred again, and continued: 'Tell him – after it's all over – that Dinamaula *could* come back as chief. In due course. With appropriate safeguards.' He seemed to be quoting from some carefully worded, interior memo-randum, which he had been keeping in reserve but now wished to release. 'I don't like him, and he doesn't like me. But that's not the last word on the subject. It isn't even important, when you look at this thing in its proper perspective … At the moment, he's pure poison, from our point of view. But later on, he should make a perfectly good chief. *If* he doesn't go through with the marriage, of course.'

Out of a deep disquiet, David said, 'But couldn't you say something of the sort, now? Couldn't you tell the Regents what you think, hold out some sort of hope? It might help to relax the tension.'

Andrew shook his head. For the first time in a full hour, he was smiling, though faintly. 'No … There are things to be gone through … It would be too early.'

'How do you mean, things to be gone through?'

'There's a pattern.' Though exhausted still, Andrew Macmillan's voice seemed to be gaining strength. 'This would look remarkably silly in a despatch, but it's something I believe in. Even if I can't quite understand it myself ... I know, as clearly and strongly as anything in my life, that it would be fatal to reverse our policy at this moment, and bring Dinamaula back. Even apart from the marriage, he doesn't deserve it. He's not ready for it. Before that happens, all sorts of other things have to happen. More people have to be disciplined. More lessons have to be taught. Perhaps more people have to die.' He was staring again at the shadowed garden, the loaded dusk of Gamate. 'I don't know why I'm talking like this to you,' Andrew said, his voice far removed from normal, 'except that I trust you – trust you to sort it all out – and I don't think you'll take advantage of it ...'

'I still think you should tell the Regents now,' said David. 'Even if you only hint at it. They don't even know,' he went on, emboldened, 'that you could ever think like this.'

'Did *you* know?'

'No, frankly.'

Andrew Macmillan smiled again. 'Then my reputation is secure. These things,' he said, with latent energy, 'are all for the future. They're not for tonight, and not for tomorrow. Tonight, and tomorrow, we have to play it out as it lies at the moment.'

'But what about you?' asked David, appalled and oppressed. 'It makes you out to be such a – such a dictator. You're not like that at all.'

'I'm the Resident Commissioner,' answered Macmillan levelly. 'I've done the best I can, for nearly forty years ... What the hell –' his voice was suddenly savage and forceful, ' – is that American expression? Expendable – that's it! Think of me as expendable.'

There was a noise behind them, and Johannes, Andrew's old servant, shuffled in on bare feet, padding and scraping across the worn boards of the *stoep*. His voice when he spoke was full of suppressed importance.

'*Barena,*' he said.

'Yes, Johannes?' said Macmillan.

'Three men come to see you, *barena*.'

'Three *men*?' repeated Macmillan, reprovingly.

'The Regents of the tribe, *barena*,' said Johannes.

'That's better ... Show them in.' Macmillan sat back in his chair, watching the dusk, watching the stars. 'Now,' he said, crisply, determinedly, seeming to regain, for a single instant, all his fabled strength and toughness, 'let's fill in our part of the pattern. The part – ' his voice was ironical, so that David already knew that there was nothing to be salvaged from this moment, ' – the part that comes before the important part.'

It was not a short meeting; to David, the watcher and recorder, it seemed at one point as if Andrew Macmillan were releasing his phrases and his words one by one, pausing overlong to hear the answers, regretfully letting slip the last moments of his authority. The Regents themselves, accustomed to prolonged and often tortuous discussion upon the simplest points of tribal procedure, found nothing unusual in this; indeed, they seemed relieved that the Resident Commissioner, a man famous for his crisp incursions into executive administration, seemed content on this occasion to allow time for the decency of discussion. As he watched the three Regents, David became suddenly aware of the defeating variety of the native mind.

Seralo, the senior Regent, was very like Andrew Macmillan; he was too old, too tired, too conservative, and too puzzled to make any worthwhile contribution. Katsaula, the formalist, was (in the poker players' phrase) playing it very close to his chest; he was a proud man, with a profound sense of history and decorum, and in these deeply troubled times he did the only thing he knew – he clung single-mindedly to the razor's edge of tribal custom.

Puero, as fat and gross as ever, was clearly the man of the moment. He had nothing to lose, everything to gain, by a display of tough independence. The deepest discomfort, the most definitive rejection of authority, came from his thick lips and coarsely supercilious features.

It was not a short meeting; but its outcome was as short as a single word – the word 'No'. From the Regents, it was made clear, the Resident Commissioner could expect no further help. The present chaos was of his own making. Let him then resolve it, or leave the field forever.

Seralo conveyed this answer by a feeble indecision of manner; Katsaula, by a blank refusal to act at all in circumstances so unorthodox. It was left to Puero to phrase the tribe's rejection of the rule of law; and this he did with such insolence, and with so crude a relish, that David was betrayed into wild thoughts of violence and punishment ... But such thoughts, he knew, were futile. White Government was looking for a solution, not for the sweetness and pleasure of retaliation.

Their conversation was drearily dialectic, demonstrating nothing but the vacuum which had usurped the place where agreement ought to be.

'You've got to help me,' declared Andrew, not for the first time. 'Good God, the whole tribe's getting out of hand! We've had a dozen murders already! Surely none of you can be pleased at the riots and disturbances that are breaking out, day after day and night after night?'

'Of course we are not pleased,' replied Katsaula primly. 'Such things are a disgrace to the whole tribe.'

'Well, then ...'

'Unfortunately, they cannot be controlled by any words of ours.'

'But you can use your authority,' insisted Andrew. 'You can show them that you are on my side.'

'Perhaps we are not on your side,' said Puero, his eyelids drooping momentarily.

'You *must* be on my side. All I want to do is to restore order.'

'We also,' quavered Seralo, 'wish to restore order. But the people will not listen. They want to see their chief again. Then they will listen.'

'Dinamaula is not yet their chief. You are the Regents, and *you* – ' he pointed directly at Seralo, ' – are still in the chair of rule. You must help me to bring back peace to Gamate. It is your duty.'

'I can do nothing,' mumbled Seralo. 'This man – ' he gestured to Puero, ' – has the ear of the people.'

'And what does *this man* say?'

Puero smirked, as if he could well afford to ignore Macmillan's tone. 'We want our chief to return. After that, I will talk.'

'Dinamaula is not coming back.'

'Then there will be no talk, and no peace either.'

'There would be no peace if he did come back.'

'Who can tell the future?' Katsaula broke in. 'If you bring him back, perhaps all will be well. He is to be our anointed chief. He should rule the tribe.'

'With a white woman by his side?' asked Macmillan suddenly. 'Does the tribe really want such a marriage?'

'The tribe wants Dinamaula,' said Puero roughly. 'The woman is another matter.'

'The tribe is disturbed *because* of the white woman, and because of what Dinamaula has said. For that reason, he will not return. I told you that, on the *aboura*, and I say it again now.' Andrew turned once more to Seralo, sitting shrunken and forlorn by his side. 'You know well what is in my mind, old man,' he said, his tone somewhat gentler. 'Will you not help me to bring back order?'

'I cannot,' answered Seralo, on a feeble and querulous note. 'The tribe will not listen to me.'

'Will you not help me, Katsaula?' asked Andrew again.

'I will help you,' answered Katsaula, with dignity, 'on the day that Dinamaula, our chief, is anointed and enthroned, in accordance with the custom.'

'That will not happen, for a long time … What about you, Puero?'

'My answer is the same, but also different,' said Puero, with uncouth emphasis. 'There can be no order without the chief. He must return – that is the price of our help. But when Dinamaula returns, *he* will rule, not you. Therefore you will not need help. You will not be here.'

David, who sat a little apart, was watching Andrew Macmillan at that moment; he saw a strange and pitiful shadow come down on the other man's face, robbing it of everything save a dull acceptance of Puero's insolence. It would have been something, thought David, if Andrew had appeared to be making a supreme effort to control himself, in the face of this infamous goading. But even that, appallingly, was not true. He was no longer resisting. He was allowing it all to happen to him, sunk in some spiritless hollow, the shameful waves breaking over him … In a flash of intuition, David Bracken realized that it was he himself who must bring this wretched interview to an end. Andrew Macmillan might never do it. He had forgotten the feeling and taste of authority … David stood up, his chair scraping loudly on the floor of the *stoep*. As the others turned towards him: 'I think that's about as far as we can go,' he said, with a determination he was scarcely feeling. 'The Resident Commissioner has other matters to attend to.'

'I – ' began Andrew, and then stopped.

'But what is going to happen?' asked Puero, puzzled.

'You will be informed,' answered David dismissively. His eyes were on Andrew Macmillan, whose head had now sunk so that his face could no longer be seen. 'The meeting is ended.'

The others had all risen. 'But suppose,' said Seralo uncertainly, 'that there are more disturbances in Gamate?'

'We will bring order,' answered David. 'With or without your help … The meeting is ended.'

Katsaula said: 'I do not understand. Will you then rule without us, the Regents?'

'We will rule,' replied David. He felt now an absurd sense of sureness and authority, like an Old Testament prophet emancipated to sudden infallibility. 'You can be certain of that.'

Puero, shifting on one leg, essayed a last contemptuous barb. 'Then what was the purpose of this meeting?' he asked. 'If you do not need us?'

'The meeting,' answered David, curtly, *'which is now ended*, was to give you a last chance to co-operate with us. It seems that you have refused.' He searched his brain, fearful of an anticlimax. 'The purpose of the meeting was to find that out. We will know what to do next.'

'What will you do next?' asked Puero.

'The meeting is ended,' David repeated, and sat down next to Andrew Macmillan again. Then he watched, with singular, childish pleasure, as the three Regents, after an uncertain pause, passed in procession through the door of the *stoep*, and out into the Residency garden.

Presently, the lonely, withdrawn figure by his side stirred to life again, breaking the charged silence.

'Thanks, David,' said Andrew Macmillan. 'I don't know what the hell's the matter with me tonight … Thanks for helping me out.'

'I thought you'd probably had enough of them,' answered David, offhandedly. He wished, above all things, to minimize his own contribution. 'I know I had ... Hope you didn't mind.'

'Far from it ... I suppose they'll rush straight off to those bloody newspaper people, and say they've been bullied and insulted ... Nothing much we can do about that, either.'

He sounded so spiritless, so utterly defeated, that David asked: 'Are you feeling all right, Andrew?'

'I don't know what' the matter with me tonight,' Andrew repeated. 'Too much paperwork, I suppose.' His face was in the shadow, but his right hand caught the lamplight, in a curious foreboding manner; it was pressed under his heart, coaxing and nursing it, as if a sudden pain had struck. His voice when he spoke again was taut and over-careful. 'You know yourself what the last few weeks have been like. No breathing space at all. No sign of a let-up.'

'You ought to get some sleep,' said David, anxiously. 'How about it?'

'You go off, if you like,' answered Andrew, in the same measured, economical voice. 'I've got some papers to look at. I won't be long ... Do you want a nightcap?'

David, rising from his chair, shook his head. 'I don't think so ... Can I get you anything?'

'No, thanks. A bit later, maybe. Good night.'

When David Bracken had gone through to his room, Macmillan also rose, and walked slowly into his study. On his desk – just as it had been for weeks and indeed years – was the loose-leaf manuscript of his book about Pharamaul; he had been unable to work on it, or add anything to it, for more than a month. Now he took it up, and walked out on to the *stoep* again. All his movements were slow and full of effort. He sat down in his chair like an old man, with care and laboured precision. His head was swimming, his heart still constricted by pain.

There was light enough, behind his shoulder, for him to read the typescript; and, opening the tattered, thumbed-over pages at random, he read thus: 'The Governor of Pharamaul was much assailed by contemporary critics, in and out of Parliament, for his action in summoning troops to back up his authority; but at this distance of time, it is safe to say that the move was fully justified. Indeed, if he had not taken such action, and with promptitude, it is probable that further bloodshed would have resulted, and the conduct of Maula affairs would have sustained a serious and possibly permanent setback. We can see now that, in its task of maintaining order, the civil arm had failed, and had to be reinforced.'

Andrew Macmillan sighed, deeply and painfully. His eye, searching for the relevant date, found it in the preceding paragraph; it had been July, 1913 ... Uncontrollably restless and disturbed, he got up again, and walked back to his study. Also on his desk was the red-tabbed file of the day's telegrams from Government House. The one on top – the latest to be received – was the one he was looking for.

'Unless you have any objection,' he read, 'I propose to proceed with plan for moving in troops at battalion strength from existing forces in Kenya. They should be in territory within four or five days. Dispositions will be discussed by commanding officer with you and Crump on arrival. Acknowledge.'

Andrew Macmillan looked at the date of that, and the date was that same morning.

He reached down, and opened the top drawer of his desk, and took out his revolver. He said, aloud: 'I'm just going for a walk.' The sentence, defiantly spoken, explained and excused the revolver, though it excused it only in a shameful context – the Resident Commissioner was going for an after-dinner stroll in his own territory of Gamate, and he had to take his revolver with him.

His steps across the room, and across the *stoep*, were slow. The door banging behind him was very loud in the silence.

David, lying back on his bed, not yet undressed, heard it, and he snapped to attention on the instant. Moving swiftly, with an illogical sense of fear and foreboding, he walked through first to the study, then to the *stoep*. Both were empty. He hastened, almost ran, to the kitchen. Johannes, drying dishes at the sink, looked round as he entered.

'*Barena?*' he said, startled.

'Where's the Resident Commissioner?' asked David.

'*Barena?*' repeated Johannes.

'He went out …' David was conscious of dramatic, probably foolish tension. 'Where did he go?'

'Don't know, *barena*.' Johannes smoothed his wrinkled hands over the dish towel, and came forward a step or two. 'Sometimes go for walk at night.'

'He's not well,' said David. 'He ought to stay in.'

'*Barena?*' repeated Johannes. His old black face was puzzled, his eyes meeting David's in communicated fear.

'He should be in bed,' said David, persevering. 'He's been working too hard.'

'Much work,' said Johannes, repeating a word he readily recognized.

David opened his mouth to speak again, realized the limits of Johannes's strained attention, and changed his mind. Instead, he walked through to the study again, and picked up the telephone.

It was some unhappy moments before he was talking to Templegate, the hospital doctor.

'I'm worried about Macmillan,' said David straight away. 'He's terribly tired and overworked. Now he's gone out, without saying anything.'

'Not much harm in that.' The Lancashire voice, pinched and nasal, was patently unimpressed. 'Though I'd rather he was tucked up in bed.'

'By God, so would I! … Look, I wish you'd tell me. I've noticed one or two things, the last few days. Is he ill? *Has* he been ill?'

After a pause, a professional hesitation, Templegate answered: 'Right between you and me, yes, he has. He had a minor heart attack, about three weeks ago. I warned him to go slow.'

'Anything else?'

'How do you mean?'

'You know – depression? Mental strain? Too much worrying about things?'

After another, much longer pause, Templegate asked: 'What exactly are you getting at?'

'Christ, I don't know!' Suddenly irritable, David grew conscious that he might be making an arrant fool of himself. 'But he's been looking like hell, the last few days. He's just had a very difficult session with those bloody Regents. Now he's walked out, without a word to anyone.'

'Take it easy, lad.' Templegate's voice was back to its normal level. 'I expect he wanted a breath of fresh air.'

Behind his back, David heard a closer, more urgent sound – the sound of a second door banging. He said quickly: 'That's probably him now – sorry to bother you,' and replaced the receiver even as Templegate started to question him. He stood up, and listened in the silent house; but there was no further movement or noise. In prickling fear, he walked from room to empty room, and finally into the kitchen again. Even this was now empty and deserted. The banging door must have been Johannes himself going out.

At the top of the steps leading into the dark garden, he called loudly: 'Johannes!' but there was no answer. He was alone in the Residency, and he still could not guess why he was alone.

What had started as a nearly innocent stroll, with only slight undertones of desolation and despair, quickly became a nightmare. The Residency garden was now wholly dark; beyond it, the rough bushland that sloped gently down towards the town of Gamate was unknown territory, full of traps and snares, dangerous and unyielding. As he buffeted his way onwards, tripping, pausing, sometimes brought up short by an unseen thorn bush or a waist-high patch of *tambuki*-grass, yet always plunging sightlessly towards a dim horizon, Andrew Macmillan fell deeper into a desperate and futile expense of energy.

This was his evening walk, the reasonable man's respite from the cares of office; he was going to take his evening walk, even if he killed himself in the process ... He forced his way on, panting, knowing that he had lost the path, and that the course he was insisting on would in the end bring him to a shaking stop, defeated by man's oldest and vilest enemy – his loss of strength before the limitless resistance of the jungle.

He still had something to steer by, even if the going was painful; he bore in view the myriad twinkling lights of the hut-town of Gamate, a mile or so below him – the fires and hearthlamps of his own homeland, now as rebellious and poisonous as the grass and scrub that persistently denied him progress ... Andrew came suddenly to a stop, this time not because of the rough impassable country he was battling, but because of a thought which had struck and troubled him.

He had wrestled a long time with Pharamaul, and with the Maulas – first as a young man, full of hope and high resolve; then in his maturity, when his long efforts seemed to be returning a sober profit; and then as a man old in years and in responsibility, entitled to rest upon the slim laurels of colonial achievement.

But the cutting truth was that, though he had wrestled, he had lost; Gamate, now become a murderous jungle like the jungle that hedged him in, had made no inch of progress under his rule, had returned no profit at all. Instead, it had swallowed him alive; and indeed, it was completing this gorging process even now, during these few moments of despair.

The bleak thought stopped him, but he would have had to stop anyway; for he now stood exhausted and embattled in a stockade of tall coarse grass and impenetrable thorn bush, mocked by the twinkling lights, totally rebuffed by Pharamaul. Presently, hard-breathing, he heard a sound behind him, a furtive rustling, an alien intrusion on his shame; and he turned with difficulty, and dropped his hand into his side pocket, and drew out his revolver. Against a low-hanging, blood-red moon, a shadowy figure suddenly confronted him. It might be anyone. At this late and tragic stage, it was more likely to be an enemy than a friend. He raised and aimed his revolver, calling out: 'Who's there?'

After a pause, he heard: 'Me, *barena*.' It was the voice he knew best, in all Pharamaul.

'Johannes … What the hell are you doing here?'

'I follow you, *barena*. You lost. I help you?'

It was too dark to see Johannes's face, but his tone – kindly, concerned, anxious – mocked in a single moment the whole concept of leadership and authority. By God! thought Andrew, angry and at bay, is this what I've finally come to? – I go for a walk, and my houseboy tags along behind, to see that I don't get into trouble.

His revolver was still raised and sighted. With his free hand he pushed aside a tuft of *tambuki*-grass, and the prickling edge of a low thorn bush. The shadowy figure became clear – clearer and more infuriating. His hand trembled, his trigger-finger came within an ace of flexing and tightening. He cried aloud: 'Get to hell out of here! You stupid old bastard! What the hell are you following me for?'

He could imagine, if he could not see, the dropped head, the penitent look. 'I follow you, *barena*,' said Johannes humbly from the darkness. 'Time to go to sleep.'

'Get to hell out of here!'

'Jah, *barena*.'

'I'm all right, you old fool!'

'Jah, *barena*.'

'I'll be back in a few minutes ... I'm just going for a walk. Get back to the house.'

There was no answer, and when he brushed the sweat from his eyes, and peered into the gloom, there was no Johannes either. The other man – his friend, his servant, his brother in the land of Pharamaul – had left him once again.

Suddenly it was overwhelmingly hot, though the night air was clear and cool. Andrew Macmillan still stood in his small stockade of grass and bush, surrounded by a hundred smells, a thousand secret murmurs of insects, birds, snakes, reptiles. He stood on his own two feet in the land of Pharamaul, within sight of the lights of Gamate, his revolver in his hand.

His head began to swim and to pound, more seriously, more painfully. It was the old onset of death, the thing the doctor had talked about. Breathe deeply, the Lancashire doctor had said. Breathe deeply, and lie down till it passes.

He could not lie down, nor sit down; in sober fact, he could not breathe either. Whatever it was, he must meet it standing up, on his own two feet, in the land of Pharamaul. The whole upper part of his body was leaden. Especially his right hand weighed heavy. It was the revolver.

He knew that the revolver, so heavy, so burdensome, belonged in his right-hand pocket, the old pocket of the old coat, lined with leather, ready and waiting for this trusted weapon. He flexed his elbow, trying to put the revolver back in its natural resting-place.

The trigger-guard caught on the edge of the pocket, and there remained, immovable. He wrestled briefly, trying to force the gun down into his pocket. It would not do what he wanted it to do – like many other things in the land of Pharamaul, many other men and things. He pressed down, harder, more angrily and determinedly.

The red rim of his pounding heart lifted before his eyes, like a containing wall. A small spear of grass pricked his thigh; a bird rose almost at his feet, with a furious whir-r-r of wings, screaming in wild alarm. All these things were real and serious. But there was one thing, even more serious, that he *must* do – put the revolver back into his side pocket. That was where it properly belonged. And if there was only one way to get it back, then he must follow that one way.

Knowing that he was doing wrong, sinning against instinct, not caring any more, deep in pain and defeat, he pushed down and pressed the trigger, once and then again, blasting a way into his coat pocket. *There*, he thought foolishly, as the warm blood began to flow, to gush out from his stomach, that was where I wanted to put the bloody thing … That was where it belonged, and I don't care who knows it. I had my wish, I had my will. It belonged in my coat pocket, the Resident Commissioner's coat pocket, the old RC now kneeling in the tall cutting grass within sight of Gamate, in the land of Pharamaul. I put it there … I knew nothing could stop me … There are some things I can still do … And having done them, I remain, Sir, With every Truth and Regard, Your Obedient Servant, Andrew Macmillan.

It was Johannes who, as dawn broke, discovered the body – for a body it had now become. Andrew Macmillan, sometime Resident Commissioner in the Principality of Pharamaul, had bled to death from two cavernous and fearful wounds in the stomach and groin. With the world's best care, instantly available, he could never have lived beyond a short, agonizing hour.

The discovery was delayed till first light, since Johannes, the only searcher, driven off by harsh words and the threat of a revolver, had returned at midnight to the Residency. Once there, secretive and ashamed, he told a disturbed David Bracken that Macmillan had gone for a walk, and that there was no cause for alarm; but thereafter he had been unable to retrace his steps in the darkness, or to pick up the trail again. He slept uneasily till a faint pale light to the eastwards foretold yet another incomparable Pharamaul dawn. Then he had gone out again, in search of his master.

Now, with a pearly grey light seeping in from the eastern horizon, falling on low-lying mists, spiders' webs, trees heavy and sleepy with dew – now the spoor was tragically easy to follow. It led from the edge of the lawn to a stubbly, sloping field, planted every second year with *kaffir*-corn, and roughly fenced at the lower end; then to a further slope of thickening scrub, and finally to a wilderness of tall *tambuki*-grass and thorn bush. The faint light, growing stronger, revealed with desolate clarity the last walk of the Resident Commissioner. Old Johannes, his face a brooding mask of pain and fear, followed it at a steady determined shuffle.

Here had the wandering *barena* stopped, and then walked with care round a tough thorn bush. Here, waist-high in *tambuki*-grass, he had forced a pathway; and here a six-foot circle of trodden, trampled earth and bush showed where he had desperately sought a way onwards. The way he had forced grew more cruel, the light more revealing. Here the *barena* had stopped again, then plunged headlong into impenetrable bush – bush that a simple child, granted full sight, would never have attempted. Here the light fell on a wide swathe cut through the undergrowth, at terrible cost of effort and pain. Here was a kind of slashed clearing, heavy with ill-omen. And here was the *barena*.

He lay where he had fallen, crouched over his gun, decently shielding his torn body from sight. Dew was on his back, and a misty shroud of cobweb; close to, the trampled grass was stained black with free-flowing blood, and the greedy ants in their battalions and armies had already arrived … Shaking, still swallowing his wailing prayers, Johannes stooped, and touched the *barena*'s hand, the hand that held the dew-moistened revolver. It was stiff and cold, as he had known it must be.

The face he could not bear to touch, nor any other part of the *barena*'s crumpled body. Indeed, after a moment, he sat down, near to but turned away from the dead man. Sitting thus, lost in the *tambuki*-grass, concealed below the surface of the wicked earth, he could see nothing, and no one could see him. His face began to work, and his ice-cold body to tremble.

At his back, in the circle of trampled and stained grass, the dead man lay in hard-won peace, while the dew of dawn started to melt and run together, and the drunken, ecstatic ants marched to and fro.

Johannes said, aloud: 'Oh, *barena*, hear me now,' and abandoned himself to bitter weeping.

'Macmillan died as he lived,' tapped out Tulbach Browne later, 'beating about the bush.' But having written it, somewhat gaily, with frequent pauses for refreshment, he did not send it. The old baron who owned the *Daily Thresh*, and therefore owned Tulbach Browne, was against death; he had had two strokes already, and the subject had to be treated seriously.

Instead: '*De moriuis*, etc,' said the *Daily Thresh* leader, a day later – and added, for the benefit of the second, third, and fourth million of its readership: 'Let us not speak ill of the dead. But let us not glorify the legacy they leave behind them, either, if that legacy is an embarrassment and a disgrace to us.

'The death of Mr Macmillan, Resident Commissioner in Pharamaula, affords an excellent opportunity to reverse the poisonous policy, pursued under the shoddy banner of colonialism, which will for all time be associated with his name.

'Today, a new page can start in the history of Gamate, long-time disgraceful trouble spot in our colonial empire. It is our Opportunity, NOW, to prove that we mean what we say, when we say: "Freedom and equality for all men, under the shining crown of the Commonwealth".'

V

It was the signal for disintegration. It was as if, with the death of Andrew Macmillan, a linchpin had been withdrawn from a wheel, or a span from a bridge. To many men, black and white alike, he had been a legendary figure, for two and three generations; indeed, there was no one in Gamate, young or old, whose life he had not touched. Now he was gone, in mysterious, perhaps shameful circumstances; his strength had departed with the quick ebb of his blood, leaving a void that no other man could fill.

During the two days between his death and his burial, in the dusty plot behind Father Schwemmer's mission house, an eerie stillness hung over Gamate. No one rioted, no one took advantage of the sorrow and perplexity of

Government; no one was killed. But it was the very last moment of such decent forbearance; for when Macmillan had been laid to rest, the dry tinder of revolt instantly caught ablaze again. Indeed, it was among the procession of mourners themselves, streaming down the hill after the burial service and the committal, that the signal for this was given.

They started singing, softly at first, as if they were still affected by the sombre occasion. But gradually the singing became louder, and somehow jovial; they seemed to be singing a song of freedom – freedom given to them by the death of a hated enemy. By nightfall, they were openly rejoicing, swaggering from hut to hut, drinking, boasting, shouting abuse at all who opposed them, and at all white men wherever they might be. There was no more need to obey, no more law – so the songs and the shouting proclaimed. Law had died with the Resident Commissioner, the Old Judge, whom all knew to have been struck by God for his wickedness and harshness.

It developed, day by day and night by night, into a raging turmoil, which spread swiftly as a bush fire. It was like nothing hitherto known or dreamed of. Forsdick, stepping into Macmillan's shoes, did his best, struggling manfully and hopelessly against the tide of ruin; Crump wore himself and his men to exhaustion. But the only effective answer to what was happening in Gamate was troops; and the troops, delayed by lack of transport, were still a full two days away from Gamate, when the first white man was killed.

Oosthuizen, packing his wife and seven of their nine children into the cumbersome old station wagon, had no special foreboding as he bade them goodbye. His family were taking their annual holiday, to be spent in his sister's house on the coast near Port Victoria. He himself, and his two elder sons, would stay on as usual to manage the farm. Later, it would be their turn to make the journey. It was a divided exodus which took place at about the same time every year; and if, this year, it seemed a good idea to despatch them to a safer, quieter corner of Pharamaul, with orders not to loiter on the way, yet there was no special urgency in their going.

He and his father and his grandfather had farmed *Morgenzon* for nearly a hundred and fifty years. Nothing ever happened at *Morgenzon*, save things pleasant and profitable and long-foreseen.

The last day of Oosthuizen's life started badly. It was a Saturday, the day when by tradition his servants and farm-labourers ceased work at midday, and gave themselves over to formal visiting and talk and beer-drinking. But early on Saturday morning, before dawn, one of the farm's outhouses was broken into, and four full cases of brandy were stolen and spirited away.

It would have been serious on any occasion; but with Gamate in the state it was, and the surrounding countryside full of wandering Maulas on the lookout for trouble, it could mean a disaster. He summoned his headman, and after inquiry went down to the main compound to question his farmhands. They were silent and respectful, but there seemed to be strangled laughter among some of the younger men, as if the secret of the stolen brandy were known, and shared, and would soon be enjoyed to the full.

Angry at the insubordination, Oosthuizen gave orders that work was to continue during all that Saturday afternoon; there was to be no customary holiday, no visiting from hut to hut, and no brewing of beer that night.

It was four o'clock on the same hot afternoon when Kleinbooi, the headman, woke Oosthuizen from his customary Saturday siesta. Kleinbooi, as his Afrikaans name implied, was a small man, wizened, shrewd, and energetic; he had been born on the Oosthuizen farm, like his father before him, and had risen from a barefoot, ragged child helping to herd the flocks, to a position of trust and considerable influence. Oosthuizen left a great deal of the day-to-day management of the farm to him, and had long been satisfied with the result.

But now, at this unheard-of moment, Kleinbooi was worried and unhappy. He had hesitated to wake his master, for the Saturday afternoon sleep was a ritual pause, never to be interrupted. But perhaps, since the *barenala* was away on holiday, the *barena* would not mind so much … Hesitant still, shaking his thin black head, he knocked on the door of Oosthuizen's bedroom.

The response was all that he had expected.

'What the hell do you want?' shouted Oosthuizen through the thick oak door, as soon as he had summoned his drugged wits. He was tired, at the end of the long working week, and the lunchtime brandies had been strong and many. 'Who is it? Christ, it's Saturday! Don't you know I'm asleep?'

'It's me, *barena*,' answered Kleinbooi fearfully. 'Something to tell you.'

'Come in!' roared Oosthuizen. It was not a reassuring invitation. 'What the hell are you talking about?' he demanded, rolling over heavily, as the door opened and Kleinbooi stepped within the room.

Behind the thick mosquito net, Kleinbooi could see his master's red face glaring at him from a tumbled mountain of sheets and pillows. Bravely he came a step nearer.

'*Barena*,' he began, 'boys stop work, go back to compound.'

'What!' shouted Oosthuizen. It was the hottest, least bearable time of the day, and he wiped the sweat from his face and neck with an angry hand. 'What do you mean, they've stopped work? Just you tell them to get cracking again, or I'll come down with a *sjambok* and tell them myself.'

Kleinbooi shook his head. 'I tell them already, *barena*. They laugh at me.' After a pause, he added: 'They drink the brandy.'

'What brandy?' asked Oosthuizen, whose memory, like his anger, was short. 'What the hell are you talking about?'

'The brandy they took last night, *barena*,' answered Kleinbooi. 'They open cases in the compound, make share of the bottles. Now they drunk.'

Behind Kleinbooi, two other figures now appeared, attracted by the noise – Oosthuizen's two sons, Koos and Danie, seventeen and sixteen years old. They were both tow-haired, sun-bleached, barefooted, dressed alike in the faded khaki shorts and shirts that almost matched their tan.

'What's the matter, pa?' asked Koos, the elder. 'Why did Kleinbooi wake you, eh?'

'Some bloody nonsense,' grumbled Oosthuizen. But he was alerted now. Sweating, cursing under his breath, he pushed aside the mosquito net and rolled sideways off the huge double bed. He looked suddenly and thunderously at the younger boy. 'What the hell are you eating, *jong*?' he demanded.

'Cake,' answered Danie briefly.

'Your ma will wallop you if she finds out,' said Oosthuizen. He felt beneath the bed for his heavy laced bush boots, looking now at Kleinbooi. 'When did they start this drinking?' he growled. 'Why didn't you tell me earlier?'

Kleinbooi kept a forlorn silence. The truth was that he had thought he could handle the matter himself, and had feared to wake his master from his sacred Saturday afternoon sleep. He had been wrong on the first count, and had delayed too long on the second. Now many men, Maulas young and old, bound to the farm of *Morgenzon* by ties of blood and fealty – now many of these men were shamefully drunk, and the things that had been said and shouted at him, as he tried to restore order in the compound, were still loud and ugly in his ears.

Oosthuizen stood up, huge and burly, buttoning his rumpled trousers. He had already guessed why Kleinbooi was silent, and did not wish to shame him before the boys.

'What are you going to do, pa?' asked Koos. He admired his father unstintingly; he knew that whatever he did would be utterly right, and also invincible. 'Can we come with you?'

'No,' answered Oosthuizen automatically.

'Oh, pa!' protested the younger, Danie, immediately. 'Go on – let us! We'll help you, eh?'

'All right,' said his father. Soft heart, soft head, he thought to himself; their mother would never have let them out of the house, at a time like this … But it's just a bit of bloody nonsense, anyway. I'll say two words, down at the compound, and they'll all go back to work. 'But just you keep quiet,' he cautioned. 'Stay with Kleinbooi, eh? – and don't get in my light.'

As an afterthought, he reached across to the polished, yellow-pine bedside table, and picked up his revolver. Then: 'Trek!' he commanded gruffly, still yawning, swallowing at the thick brandy taste in his mouth. 'I want to get back to sleep.'

He led the way towards the front door. Behind him, in the dark hall of the old rustling house, he heard Kleinbooi say: 'Be careful, *barena*. Much brandy. Boys very drunk.'

They made an odd, almost patriarchal procession as they left the house. Oosthuizen was in the lead, huge and lumbering, his heavy boots stirring the dust as he strode determinedly down the garden path; his two sons followed, excited and awed, picking their way barefooted over the rough gravel; his servant Kleinbooi completed the Indian-file of figures, padding along on calloused black feet, his face brooding and disturbed.

Their advance took them through a fair pathway, one that they all knew by heart, and loved by heart also; past whitewashed farm buildings that had been there for two and three generations, past oaks and cypresses, past vegetable patches and rough-fenced paddocks, and a creaking, rusty windmill that pumped water endlessly into the thirsty furrows.

The evening sun was still brilliant and fierce; it shone equally on white walls and black-thatched roofs, on humped cattle clustering near a gateway, on thorn bushes and late *kaffir*-corn, on the formal elegant gables of the old Dutch farmhouse. It fell on an ancient grey-muzzled dog, asleep on a pile of mealie sacks; and on a farm tractor, rusty-red with long weathering; and on the shimmering pond where, morning and evening, the whole family bathed and laughed and splashed each other.

It fell on the whole of *Morgenzon*, a known blessing, a rustic paradise. It fell, presently, on the outer wall of the main compound. But there the sun seemed to falter, and to lose its strength; for from within rose a confused and hideous sound, a roar made up of many odious notes – crude laughter, singing, stamping, the beat of drums, the banging of cooking pots, the cracked shouting of furious voices.

Oosthuizen did not falter. He gestured to the others to wait, and then he kicked open the heavy gate and entered the compound.

It was a wild and ugly scene, a synthesis of all the bad and evil things that had ever come to *Morgenzon*, in a full hundred years. The four cases of brandy, broken open and rifled, lay in the centre; round them, like worshippers or defilers, were fifty or sixty of his men, drinking, passing bottles from hand to hand, singing, dancing, vomiting, shouting in obscene chorus.

Oosthuizen still did not falter, even in the face of a menace which he could closely gauge. He was accustomed to command; he stood on his own land, a hard but just man among his own servants; they would do what he ordered, or take the consequences ... He strode forward towards the middle of the compound and the brandy cases, kicking out of his way two prone figures that seemed ready to impede him. A heavy quietness began to fall, as his tall figure was seen and recognized; the drums thudded into silence, the dancers shuffled to an awkward standstill. Behind his back, a man called out a warning. All eyes now turned towards him. When he came to a stop, he was surrounded by a hostile, graveyard stillness.

The hot sun beat down on his shoulders, and on the Maulas standing slack-handed near him, and on the fallen figures, and on the stinking remnants of debauch.

Oosthuizen, unhesitating, pointed to the brandy cases, and said loudly and roughly: 'Put those bottles back!'

No one moved. After a moment, he called over his shoulder: 'Kleinbooi!'

Kleinbooi shuffled forward till he reached Oosthuizen's side.

'*Barena?*'

'Collect all the bottles. Take them away from those that have them.' Oosthuizen suddenly turned, and pointed again, and shouted: 'To start with, take *that* bottle away from *that* man!'

He was pointing to a tall Maula, a sweating, swaying, near-naked young man who held a bottle of brandy poised at shoulder height. As Kleinbooi stepped forward, the young man rolled impudent eyes towards him, and then unclasped his hand. The bottle crashed on the hard-beaten floor of the compound, and splintered to fragments. The brandy gushed out, spread momentarily over the hot earth, and was lost.

A roar of laughter rose throughout the compound. There was a second splintering crash as another bottle was dropped; and then another scream of applause. Oosthuizen suddenly saw red. He jumped forward towards the laughing Maula nearest to him, drew back his fist, and clubbed him savagely behind the ear. The man went down with an earth-shaking crash, insensible even before he reached the ground. In the startled silence, Oosthuizen shouted again: 'I said, put back those bottles!'

As if in answer, a young, tough Maula shouldered his way through, his heavy chest gleaming, his reddened eyes fixed on Oosthuizen's face. He held in his hand, not a bottle, but a long-handled axe, raised already above the level of his neck. Advancing, he growled deep in his throat, something Oosthuizen could not make out. The axe rose higher, arching backwards; the man was now within six feet of him, intent on murder. Oosthuizen reached for his pocket, drew out his revolver, took careful aim, and shot him through the head.

The next few moments should have been full of noise and shouting, but after the initial gasp of anger and dismay they passed in deadly silence, full of a horrible concentrated violence. From the back of the crowd, now staring from Oosthuizen to the dead man bleeding on the ground, a single high voice was heard, as if intoning a signal: 'Come, brothers,' it said. 'Remember – the holy man said we should be free.'

Then there were no more voices, only panting movement and the daemonic onset of savagery. A press of black bodies suddenly bore in upon Oosthuizen, and when he raised his arm to fire again, the arm was broken by a brutal downward chopping blow from an iron-bound knobkerrie. Now the whole crowd set upon him with weapons suddenly conjured from the air or the ground – hatchets, sticks, spears, jagged stones. Here and there, a ribboned guitar flashed like a headsman's axe ... They fought each other to get within striking distance, and then stabbed and tore at their crippled prey with bare hands. Oosthuizen rose once above the mob, staggering from a fearful axe-blow at the base of his neck, and shouted wildly to his two sons: 'Run, Koosie!' he screamed. 'Run ... Both of you ...'

Then he went down again, under a torrent of blows. The two boys began to run and then, as if drawn back by a tightening cord, turned again, and started bravely towards their father. He was no longer in view, and when they drew near to the vile and gory centre of the compound, the crowd opened and received them with bloody claws.

It was all still done in deadly silence, under the hot sun, with the spilt blood smoking like the flavour of sacrifice. All three of the figures, one huge, two small and slight, were rhythmically beaten to pulp before being torn to pieces.

As an afterthought, the crowd, now beginning to talk and indeed to laugh, chased and caught Kleinbooi, and killed him ritually with a hundred steady spear-thrusts. Then they streamed and trampled their way across the fair face of *Morgenzon*, and entered the old house, driving before them the terrified servants, leaving red-rimmed footprints wherever they wandered. As night fell, they were still looting, and burning, and roaring out their triumph and their freedom.

Templegate, the hospital doctor, who twenty-four hours later went in, under heavy police guard, to recover the bodies, always started his account with the same set phrases.

'There's a stage direction in Shakespeare that I never really appreciated until then,' he would begin. 'It's somewhere in *Julius Caesar*. It says: "*The crowd fall on him and tear him to pieces*". By God, that's all you need to know about *Morgenzon!* ... There were four or five Pressmen with me when I arrived, and a couple of them were sick on the spot. Reckon it was our turn to do it to *them* ... You see, when we drove up to the farmhouse – '

VI

Far away in the secret northland, concealed in the forest which closed like a curtain behind their backs, three men met and conferred; Gotwela, chief of the U-Maulas, Puero, Third Regent of the Maulas of Gamate, and Zuva Katsaula, cousin and blood brother to Dinamaula himself.

Gotwela had been waiting for the other two, with contemptuous certainty, for many days; he knew in his gross heart that true revolt, true mutiny, centred only in himself and his outlawed tribe, and that all rebels, whatever their estate, would find their way to his side, sooner or later. Puero had slipped north as soon as Macmillan had died and the current of revolt began to flow so strongly and with so great an expense of blood; he had feared to stay in Gamate, where white Government would surely react to such indiscipline, and all men like himself must soon find themselves behind bars.

Zuva, the enigmatic Zuva, had made his longer journey by hidden trails, as soon as the two strikes in Port Victoria – the walkout at the club, and the more important strike down at the docks – had been safely engineered. He had come, not because of the shameful oath he had taken – indeed, that was, in his inner heart, a reason for staying away – but because he needed allies (Dinamaula being powerless and self-destroyed) and friends he could trust, to make the next advance – the very last advance.

He had come alone, to escape notice. He missed his bodyguard, every day and every hour, but that could not be helped. They would surely be at his back again, as soon as that last advance were made.

The three men met in secret, in the fronded clearing beside the chief's hut. There were things about each man that each man disliked and mistrusted. Gotwela was gross, and a little drunk, and purely savage in his bearing. Puero was gross also, with an eye for the women, and suspect also because of his years spent as a Regent, under the licence of white Government. Zuva was a dubious man, for all his oath-taking; he dressed as the white man dressed, he had travelled to their hated country, he talked of friends from outside, when no such friends were necessary …

Yet for all their dislike, their mistrust, their sly and brutish suspicion, they met by agreement, and talked for many hours. And what each man said was heartening, swelling music to the others.

Puero talked of matters in Gamate. There, their brothers had risen, he said. The RC, the Old Judge, had died – some said by his own hand, some by witchcraft. But he was dead, anyway, and his rule was over for ever. And another man hated by all, a known tyrant, a white farmer who used the whip, had been killed, together with his two sickly sons. Soon, others would die. It only needed a word.

'I have heard these things,' said Gotwela.

Zuva, small and energetic, took up the tale. In his own town, far to the south, the white man's town of Port Victoria, all was in ruins. Indeed, there was no town, now, because no one worked or went about their business. The merchants were at their wits' end; even the Governor himself walked in fear. It was the end of tyranny, brought about by Zuva himself and his strong army. It only needed a word, to drive the white man into the sea. Thus had he been driven out, from nearly all Africa. Why not from Pharamaul?

'I have heard some of these things also,' said Gotwela. His thick lips curled. 'But of Dinamaula, your great leader, I have heard nothing.'

'Dinamaula,' answered Zuva, 'is a man no more. We need only men.'

Now there was silence between them all, a bitter, loaded silence. The three men, unseen by anyone save the two sentries with their spears, squatted in close conclave at the edge of the clearing. Gotwela wore his *simbara*, the royal emblem, with a gross and rakish air; his huge body sweated out the beer-drinking of the past hour, his heavy flexed haunches rippled like the haunches of prime cattle. Puero, a man of the same cast, the same instinct, faced him; but he lolled with his back against a tree, for he had travelled swiftly, and was weary, and his grey blanket with the yellow trimming suited to his rank covered a body slack and overdone.

At their side was the smaller man, Zuva Katsaula, ill-dressed for the U-Maula country; a man of no consequence, save for his blood-kin to Dinamaula. He was suspect because he talked like a white man, because he had lived like a white man; a small man, a sly man – yet his talk had been the biggest talk of all, the most cunning, the most persuasive.

Typically, it was Zuva who now had no shame, who did not fear to break the silence.

'What now?' he said, as if prompting shy children. 'What more do we wait for? Let us strike, together. All three of us.' He looked at Gotwela. 'Do you agree?'

Gotwela spoke when he was ready to speak, at the end of a long, insolent minute of silence. He spoke as a ruler, and they accepted it.

'I am ready,' he declared. 'We will strike.'

Puero licked his lips. 'You have a plan?'

Gotwela eyed him with irony and contempt – the chief eyeing a man who was not a chief. 'I have a plan,' he acknowledged. His voice was like the jungle that pressed in on them, the lowering, sweating jungle; a voice deep and threatening. 'I have a plan, and I am ready.'

Zuva watched Gotwela as he made this declaration; he was disgusted, and touched by misgiving. This man is a savage, he thought. A crook, a fat mutinous criminal and murderer. A man of infinite evil power. A man whom I must use, even though he seems to use me. For the end excuses the means, even such means as this ...

Zuva shut his eyes, seeing a vision of Oxford, green lawns, girls, grave and friendly dons. He opened them, and saw Gotwela, sweating and swinish against the foetid, sun-drenched wilderness that was his kingdom.

Later, Zuva swore to himself, there must be a pause, a time for reconstruction, a sorting out of the civilized and the uncivilized. But later.

'Then we are all ready,' he said.

Gotwela eyed him from under heavy lowered lids. He had many thoughts about this Zuva, but they were not communicable thoughts. They were thoughts that would keep. His was the mindless power of the lion or the elephant: ponderous advance, ruthless strength, a wish to crush and to tear. No need to talk above a growl, no need to listen to a scream.

He looked down at the folds of his *simbara*, his royal lionskin. He looked at his sentries, and their brave polished spears. He looked at Puero, the white man's jackal, and Zuva, the sly blood-smelling hyena. Such company for a lion … Later, there must be a pause, a pause for the disposal of allies. But later.

He said, deep in his throat: 'We will make our beginning, here, tonight.'

CHAPTER THIRTEEN

❖

When the phone rang, David Bracken was standing, slightly muzzy from drink, in the middle of the forlorn Residency sitting-room, empty glass in hand, debating whether to refill it or to go to bed. In the silent, rustling old house, he was aware of ghosts – or rather, of one principal ghost, the poor ghost of Andrew Macmillan, who had lived and worked here for so long, and now was in his grave. There were other ghosts, but they were pale and faint by comparison.

Andrew was all around him still, implicit in the old armchairs, the dusty books, the pipes on the mantelpiece, the coats that hung shrunken in the hall cupboard, the overshoes, the dress sword, the shabby white helmet with the tarnished Royal cypher. Andrew was all over the bereaved house; his ghost was surely here, and he had left another one behind him to bear it company; the living ghost that was Johannes.

Johannes shuffled through his daily work like a forlorn old woman, scarcely attending when he was spoken to, scarcely lifting his head at all. David could hear him now, patiently padding to and fro between the kitchen and the dining room, tidying up for the night. It was like listening to a mourner's tread, wending homewards after a funeral.

There was one other ghost in the house – the ghost of Andrew Macmillan's working life. Sadly, it was summed up in the locked doors and windows, the police guard camping in the garden, the revolver that David felt heavy against his thigh. That ghost was a wretched failure … It was no wonder, thought David, as he crossed to the telephone, that he had taken a drink or two, to combat these wan surroundings.

The faraway voice, fading and then strengthening across the crackling wires, was Aidan Purves-Brownrigg, calling him from Port Victoria. It was wonderful to hear it.

'How are you, David?' began Aidan cheerfully.

'Not bad … It's nice to hear your voice … It's pretty bleak here.'

Aidan sounded immediately concerned. 'Are you all alone? Hasn't George Forsdick moved in yet?'

'Not till tomorrow.'

'My dear, it must be like a *morgue*.'

'Well …' The appropriate word was depressing, even frightening. 'How are things at PV?'

'The strike's still on.' There was a sudden crackle over the wire, as if to point the news. 'There's some kind of mass meeting going on at the moment, in fact … Nicole sent her love, before I forget. We're all pretty busy.'

'Stevens busy too?'

Aidan laughed. 'My dear, he's the *original* one-armed paperhanger.'

'How about our other friend?' asked David guardedly.

'The *noir*?'

'Yes.'

'Won't talk at all. Won't say yes to anything, won't say no. Just says he wants to go back home. It's driving the old gentleman completely mad … He asked me to ring you up, by the way.'

'What about?'

'The Press ... We've had pages of cabled reports from London, mostly editorial comment on the martial law proclamation. My dear, we haven't a friend in the world. They're *raving* at us!'

'For Christ's sake, what about?' David's voice was suddenly loud and truculent. 'By God, if they could just take a look at things here ... What about Oosthuizen and his kids? What more do they want? We're justified in imposing martial law, ten times over. Christ! I'd like to fly a few editors out to Gamate, and then see if they felt safe without it. And I'd like the plane to crash on the way back.'

'You sound a bit tight,' said Aidan.

The wires hummed between them. 'I suppose I am,' agreed David. He sighed deeply and resignedly. 'It was so damned sad about Andrew ... I feel as if he's still here. They killed him, blast them!'

'Indirectly, I suppose.'

'Indirectly my foot! It was all their fault. They stirred the whole thing up. Incidentally, talking about martial law, when do our khaki chums arrive?'

'In about twenty-four hours,' answered Aidan. His voice matched David's careful circumlocution. 'That's just been confirmed.'

'Good.' Then: 'What's this about the Press, Aidan?'

'The old gentleman's really worried at last. London are needling him all the time. He thinks we ought to hold another Press conference.'

'I agree.'

'But it's no good having it down here.' Aidan's far-away voice faded and then came strong again. 'Even if the poor old boy were any good at it ... All the Press are up at Gamate, aren't they?'

'Yes,' said David. 'The little loves.'

'You'd better hold it up there, then. And *you'd* better hold it yourself.'

'Me?' asked David, genuinely surprised. He groped behind him for the whisky decanter, poured out an impressive tot, added a modest splash of soda, and began to sip it. 'But what about George Forsdick? He's the obvious person, surely?'

'No. The old gentleman thinks it should be someone on his own personal staff speaking for him. George wouldn't be any good, any way. And he must be pretty busy, taking over as acting RC.'

'True,' agreed David. 'But hell – I don't want to be torn to bits!'

'That needn't happen, if you handle it right ... Just give them a list of things that have gone wrong, here and in Gamate. You can get all the details from our telegrams. Sum it all up, and then talk about the obvious dangers, which aren't getting any smaller, that lie in the future. Then say that the whole thing adds up to martial law, and nothing less. That's all we want you to do – just to put our side of the case.'

'Well,' said David, 'I'll have a crack at it, if you really think so. God knows what sort of questions they'll ask, though.'

'I honestly think we've got most of the answers.' Aidan chuckled. 'But try not to get into too many *sordid* arguments.'

'I don't mind a good argument.' The whisky had freshly emboldened him, within a few moments: he felt ready to take on a hundred sour-faced scribblers. 'In fact, I'd welcome the chance. It's about time our side went in to bat.'

Aidan gave a stage cough; across the wires, from two hundred miles away, it sounded like a chiding hen. 'You have been selected, my dear David,' he said, in a fair imitation of the Governor at his most pontifical, 'because of your singular discretion, imperturbable outlook, and iron self-control. Pray do *not* disappoint us.'

'You'll read all about it in the newspapers.' Suddenly, David wanted to stop talking, and to be by himself, and to think. 'Give my love to Nicole. How is she?'

'*Pining* ...' Aidan's voice was fading out, but the word was heartwarming, none the less. 'What's it like to be loved so boringly?'

II

When he hung up, David did not immediately sit down. Instead, he stood in the middle of the shabby sitting-room, cherishing his half-empty glass in his hand, enjoying his private stillness. He felt possessed by a secret exhilaration; it was partly whisky, as he well knew, partly the result of Aidan's telephone call. For the first time he had been given something important to do, not because he was the only available man, or because he was the next in line, the man at the near end of the bench – but because Authority had picked him out as the appropriate choice.

Once or twice, the same thing had happened during the war (he had won his MC on an identical basis of selection, for a daring, coast-hopping raid along the Italian shoreline near Salerno); but it was the first time it had happened to him on the dustier shoreline of civil life.

So they wanted him to run a Press conference in Gamate, at this crucial moment? By God, he'd run one fit to knock their eye out!

He tossed off the second half of the glass of whisky, and immediately poured himself a refill from the chipped decanter. He had a momentary qualm about the likelihood of a hangover next morning, but the thought passed swiftly. Nothing could stop him now; if necessary, he could run a Press conference from inside an iron lung.

He sat down, relaxed, happy, and gave himself to blossoming thought. Sometimes he spoke aloud, and when he did so, he spoke to Nicole.

On the telephone, he had said that it was time to strike a blow for their own side, and now the thought returned, strongly buttressed by the prospect of action on the morrow. He was to be given the chance, after weeks of frustration, and official inaction, and watching the Press outrun the best efforts of himself and his friends, by many a weary country mile. The thing couldn't be reversed at a single stroke, but it *could* be reversed, on a long-term basis. Tomorrow the foundation would be laid, the beginning of the long haul. And he had been chosen to make that beginning.

To hell with them all, anyway! (– now the whisky spoke, potent and rousing). Who were they, and why should he or anyone else be afraid of them? They weren't supermen, they weren't God Almighty, they couldn't *dictate* the course of events … They were just chaps with pencils and typewriters, who chanced to have the public ear. They'd made their mark on Pharamaul, because no one had dared to withstand them, no one had been smart enough to foresee their tactics, and forestall them. But tomorrow …

'Be with me, Nicole,' he said aloud. It was not a prayer, it was an invitation, formally proffered, to some notable entertainment. He tipped his glass, and the whisky flowed anew, crude and mellow at the same time. 'I want you to be proud of me, I want to deserve you … I *have* grown up a bit in the last few months … I *have* changed, and I think it's for the better.'

Whisky or no whisky, it seemed undeniably true at that moment. On the wavering edge of drunkenness, he surveyed the curious past and the crystal-clear present. He had come to the Island with nothing much to show for the vanished years – not much more than a Military Cross, a dislike of pansies, and a wish to liberate the blacks ... Where was he now? He still had the MC – honestly earned; but Aidan had shown him something new about homosexuals – their humorous, intuitive understanding, their devotion, their capacity to entertain – and already he realized that most blacks, in Pharamaul at least, were not nearly ready for liberation, and might indeed be destroyed by it.

'Must remember to say that tomorrow,' he muttered vaguely. He looked up at the tall grandfather clock at the other end of the room. 'Today, that is ... Be with me, Nicole. I've got a hell of a job to do.'

His thoughts strayed further, on this theme of work to be done. Andrew Macmillan was forever dead – the forlorn room round him echoed the recollection. Something precious in Pharamaul had died with him. Now there was a vacuum, crying out to be filled. Perhaps, in twenty years, he could come to fill it himself. He wanted nothing better than to be allowed to do that ... But already, today, the vacuum gaped in readiness for assuagement. On one small part of it, he could start to work himself: The Press part, the information part, the fair-dealing, honest-effort part. He could do it, because he felt so strongly about it. Indeed, what was he afraid of?

'I'm afraid of making a fool of myself,' he told the room, and Nicole. 'It boils down to that ... But that's not going to stop me. I've got some things to say, and I'll say them ... For you, and for Andrew ... Then I'll stay here, and work very hard, and be the District Commissioner, and then the Resident Commissioner ... As long as you'll be with me. Both of you. You and Andrew. You and Nicole.'

It was time to go to bed. The whisky was finished, and his thoughts were finished, and he had told Nicole enough, for one evening ... When, presently, David fell asleep in the armchair, he dreamed of Nicole; but it was an innocent dream, not like the dreams of other nights, the lovemaking, the warm and shaking congress of their bodies. He was addressing a crowd, and she was watching him, and smiling. He was acquitting himself well, and Nicole was pleased.

III

Once started, the ridiculous and deplorable wrangle was impossible to arrest, or even to divert to less hazardous pastures. It had to run its course, with sordid violence and ill humour; and the busy pencils and smirking glances showed how piquant and agreeable that course was. It stemmed from three things: whisky, the resultant headache, and a wish to impress.

Waking with a severe hangover and a corresponding sense of mission, David had taken a mid-morning drink to steady his nerves, and then another, to combat a queasy stomach, and then a third, on general principles of well-being. By the time the Pressmen arrived at the Residency, under a lowering midday sun, he was possessed by a careless and truculent irritation which was the least promising basis for any Press conference. In addition, he had the feeling, as soon as he started to speak, that they all knew he was wrestling with a hangover. That was possibly the worst irritant of all.

He was aware all the time of indifference, closed minds, the self-satisfied freemasonry which took it for granted that all Pressmen were the salt of the earth, and all officials low-paid dunderheads. But the thing that triggered the explosion (it could be labelled nothing less) was something relatively innocent.

They were all gathered in Andrew's sitting-room, now as on the previous night strongly recalling the dead man and his dedicated life. They had listened with reasonable attention while David made the points which Aidan had suggested over the telephone – the murders, the crisis in the territory, the clear need for martial law. Some of them asked questions, without much intensity of purpose; the rest lounged about, fanning themselves against the fierce heat, playing with the pens and ornaments on Andrew's desk, smoking his cigarettes. Then, when the session seemed virtually over, Pikkie Joubert, the South African, suddenly looked up and remarked, in his heavy accent: 'It certainly is a hell of a mess, eh? Seems like Macmillan picked the right moment to die.'

David stiffened. He could have let the remark pass, but he felt bound in honour to answer it. God damn it, the man was sitting in Andrew's own armchair … He said, with studied slowness of phrase: 'I agree that it's a mess. And it's liable to get worse, unless it's controlled. The rest of that remark doesn't seem to me to make much sense.'

Heads rose all round him. Tulbach Browne gave him a level stare; Axel Hallmarck, his crew-cut head on one side, seemed to be pondering a suitable contribution. John Raper looked at him as though his brassiere had slipped. The two photographers, Clandestine Lebourget and Noblesse O'Toole, watched his face as if certain that, during the next few seconds, it would produce some award-winning expression or movement. Pikkie Joubert himself, seemingly surprised at the answer, ground into guttural speech again.

'I meant that it's *his* mess, eh? Only he's not here to clear it up … It makes his career look a bit silly.'

'Silly?'

'Yes.' Joubert's bulbous blue eyes held his for a moment, before turning aside. 'That's what I said.'

'Andrew Macmillan,' answered David, conscious of anger, headache, sorrow, and crude contempt all tumbling over each other in the race for self-expression, 'was a hard-working and devoted public servant. He gave his whole life to this country. No career like that should ever be called silly.'

In the electric silence, Tulbach Browne's voice rose, annoyingly self-assured: 'Oh, come now!' he said, with infinitely reasonable calm. 'Don't let's lose our heads … Surely all he did in Gamate was to sit on the safety valve?'

Suddenly David was furious. Caution went to the winds, the need to impress was swept aside by the wish to punish. Bastards, ignorant clods! … Sweating in the close heat of the room, feeling the sticky shirt clinging to his back, the drops of perspiration coursing freely from his armpits down to his tight waistband, he cast swiftly about him for a fitting rejoinder. It came, with fatal readiness.

'He didn't sit on the safety valve. There wasn't such a thing as a safety valve in Gamate. There didn't have to be. Not until you people arrived.'

Now there was no doubt that he had thrown a rock into a virgin pool. Bang! Bang! Bang! he thought, with secret joy and terror; for the first time in the history of public relations, an official spokesman had proclaimed his own exact version of the truth … From all over the room, attention was now riveted on his face, just as it had jumped to startled life at his words; there were a few confederate and sidelong glances, and then a grand concentration upon a single focal point – himself. He felt twin threads, of carelessness and cunning, weaving fresh fabric for one corner of his brain.

It was hot. He had had three or four drinks. He hated these people. He had something worthwhile to say. He was speaking for many different people – for the correct Governor, the ideal official, the dead and dishonoured Andrew Macmillan. He had spoken once. Soon, someone would answer. Then he would speak again.

Tulbach Browne took up the challenge so directly offered to him. 'Let's get this thing straight,' he said, with formidable crispness. 'You say there's no need for a safety valve, in Gamate. Do you honestly mean they're all *happy*?'

'No, I don't.' David sought for an accurate and yet quotable phrase. 'There's no community in the world where everyone's happy. But the Maulas are not specially *unhappy*, either. We've done the best we can for them. We've nothing to be ashamed of, either now or in the past.'

'I should have thought it was obvious that we could have done a hell of a lot more for them. That's exactly why things have got out of hand.'

'We've done the very best we can for them,' repeated David, 'We haven't rushed things, and we haven't held things back, either. We've spent thousands of pounds in this territory – thousands of lives, too. In the last hundred years, living conditions have improved enormously.'

'Are you really taking credit for that?' Now it was Axel Hallmarck, satirical, eager to provoke, ready to join battle. 'Living conditions would have improved anyway – that's a world trend. I wouldn't say the British had any special medal coming to them, here or in Africa or in India ... Would you?'

His innocent blue eyes, his air of student research, were all intolerable.

'Yes, I would,' answered David roughly. 'In all those countries, we've made a bigger contribution than any other nation in the world.' Bigger than you, anyway, his eyes said, you creeping Yankee know-all ... 'Our contribution in the nineteenth century was the same as Greece, or Rome, or Spain, in the old days, hundreds of years ago. It's a definite, historic contribution to the world's progress and development.'

Covert smiles all round the room showed him how pompous and unreal his phrases must have sounded; his inner ear gave the same verdict. But he did not want to alter any of it. He was far gone already, in a fatalistic compulsion to give battle.

'The nineteenth century,' repeated Axel Hallmarck, ironically. 'That's just what we're complaining about. Things have moved on, old boy ... This isn't the nineteenth century any more. Don't you think that Gamate really deserves a breath of fresh air at last? Don't you think it's got a kind of musty smell about it?'

'No, I don't.'

'Far too much protocol?'

'No.'

'Rotten with colonialism?'

'No.'

'Colour bar stuff?'

'No.'

Hallmarck looked at him, expelling his breath. 'Well, I do. Trouble with you people is, you're centuries out of date. You're trying to settle modern problems with a horse-and-buggy mentality – and occasionally a whip. You're just plain *reactionary*.'

By God, thought David, in a fresh fury, here's another American newspaperman trying to solve the whole thing with adjectives. What would it be like if we applied your own brand of adjective to you ... I've never met a *Clang* correspondent who didn't look like a snide butler on the make ... 'Short-arsed, crew-cut *Clang*-man Hallmarck' ... His mind whirled, seeking how to strike and pin down.

'What the hell do you know about it?' he said, almost shouting. 'We've been running this sort of country, for over three hundred years. We don't need any smart outsiders telling us how to handle native problems. You won't solve things in Gamate on American lines – you won't bring peace and prosperity to Pharamaul by –' he paused, and then plunged swiftly, ' – by enrolling Dinamaula as a

561

Rotarian, and giving him a plastic ceremonial wagon wheel to wear on his watch chain … It needs patience, and determination, and a fixed plan. We've been working on it for generations, and we know what we're doing.'

Hallmarck was still looking at him closely. 'Tell us about Greece and Rome and Spain,' he said, with spiteful emphasis.

David swallowed. He knew he was being made a fool of, but he could not halt the process, nor run for cover. 'In their day,' he said, more moderately, 'each of those countries took their turn at organizing the whole world, as it then was. In our day, we did the same. Here and there, we're still doing it. If you people want to take over, as you're always saying you do, as you're always *trying* to do, you've got to deserve it. That means hard work, not just laughing at the British and edging them out of the sunshine … In the meantime, we're still in the ring. And we've got nothing to be ashamed of when it comes to adding up the past.'

'The past,' repeated Axel. It was the same tone of voice as he had used when he said: 'The nineteenth century' … 'The past is something we're all trying to grow out of,' he went on, dismissively. 'What's the good of quoting all that old stuff? You might as well go back to sailing-ships. The world doesn't need that sort of crap any more.'

'Do you sneer at your father, just because you've grown out of depending on him, just because his day is over?'

'Is your day over?' countered Axel swiftly.

'Maybe. I don't know. But we *still* have something to contribute, something to teach the world. We've still got lots of jobs to finish.'

'You can say that again,' said Axel Hallmarck, offhandedly. 'But I'd say you could use some help.'

Now there was a pause, a brief breathing space in the astonishing argument. It was as if they were all thinking: is this really an official Press conference? ... Then a new voice was heard. It was Pikkie Joubert.

Like all the others, he had been following the various exchanges with close, slightly incredulous attention. But earlier than the rest, he had started to lag behind; he was a slow man, of fixed ideas and channelled reactions, and historical analogies with the vanished past, whether in Spain or in Greece, surged over his head like froth over some ponderous rock. He raised his hand, as if asking to be excused.

'Just half a minute, eh?' he said. 'Isn't all this a bit far from the point? I thought we were talking about Gamate?'

'We are,' answered David shortly.

'Well, it doesn't sound like it to me.'

For the first time, John Raper of the *Globe*, florid and sweating in a rumpled, significantly stained Palm Beach suit, made his contribution.

'I couldn't agree more,' he said, with enormous menace in his voice. 'Honestly, I've never heard so much concentrated tripe in all my life ... I came up here for a Press conference, not a bloody history lesson. All I want to know is, when is Dinamaula coming back, when is he going to be allowed to marry this girl, and if not, why not?'

Raper was right, in a way, thought David Bracken, conscious of aching head, frayed temper, and imminent defeat; order and pattern were melting away, and with them all chance to impress and persuade. While he himself had been lunging wildly at a dozen targets, pursuing some sort of global truth with foolish zest, foolish anger, the others had merely been waiting for a definitive answer to one limited question – the exile of Dinamaula. He pulled himself together.

'I was trying to answer your questions,' he said, somewhat lamely.

'You sure were!' said Noblesse O'Toole suddenly. For her also, it was the first time she had spoken, but her thin waspish face was alert, critically attentive. 'And pitching a few of your own, too.'

'Well, just answer one or two more,' interjected Tulbach Browne, with equal suddenness, 'since you're in the mood …' He glanced down at his notebook: David had the feeling that he did not really need to do so. 'You said a little time ago, or rather – ' he smirked unpleasantly, ' – quite a *long* time ago, that there was never any need for a safety valve in Gamate, *before we arrived.*' His eyelids flickered upwards again. ' "We", I take it, means the newspaper correspondents?'

'Yes,' said David.

'The actual people here in this room?'

'Yes.'

Tulbach Browne nodded to himself, as if confirmed in some long-range, far-fetched diagnosis. 'Then will you please tell us,' he continued, with great care, 'what exactly the people in this room have done, to raise the temperature – or however you like to phrase it – in Gamate?'

It was the pay-off question, the crucial challenge; and the exact answer to it – the one that David believed with all his heart – could only be a frank and forceful arraignment. But could he possibly give such an answer? Truly, he believed that the arrival of the Pressmen in Gamate had sparked all their present troubles, that the main bloodstains were on their hands, and theirs alone; but could he say so? He was getting deeper and deeper in – with a kind of light-hearted anguish he recalled some of the things he had said that morning, and the probable consequences tomorrow, when they appeared in cold print. There would be no need to distort or isolate a single phrase, a single word … But he knew also that there was really no retreat for him; set on a grim path of self-justification, faced by questions of honour and conviction, he had scarcely any choice, and none that he cared to take.

The room – Andrew Macmillan's room – was silent and hot. They were all looking at him. He cleared his throat.

'It's difficult for me to be definite … It's the general effect, more than any special incident.' That sounded feeble, and not what he really believed either, and he tried again, facing their cold eyes. 'But I do think that there's one thing that you people have forgotten, or disregarded, and it's led to a lot of trouble. The Maulas aren't a sophisticated people at all. They just don't function like people in America and England, black or white … They're a simple, fairly backward lot, and that's the way they should be thought about, and written about, and organized and talked to.'

'You mean, talked *down* to?' interjected Tulbach Browne swiftly.

David shook his head. 'Not necessarily. But lots of them simply haven't reached the twentieth century yet. It shouldn't be taken for granted that they understand all the various issues involved, or are able to deal with them.'

Axel Hallmarck took the point, with raised eyebrows; his air of rueful puzzlement was very well done. 'I just don't get this at all. You mean, the Maulas are in an uproar because we've wandered outside the official pale, and started treating them like human beings?'

'I mean you've been treating them like sophisticated white men, when in fact they're very simple negroes.'

After a pause: 'Is that all?' inquired Tulbach Browne edgily.

'How do you mean?'

'Is that all we've done wrong?'

David stared back at him. The quality of menace in the other man's voice was something he wasn't going to take, from Tulbach Browne or anyone else. He decided to plunge, for good or ill.

'It's the general background,' he returned crisply, 'against which you've all been operating.' Pencils were again busy: he did not mind. 'Getting down to details, I'm absolutely certain in my own mind, though I can't prove it, that you've been advising Dinamaula and the Regents on what they should do, and how they should go about getting what they want.'

'What's wrong with that?' asked Hallmarck, and added: 'Even if we *have* advised them.'

'Because the direct result of that advice has been nine murders, a paralysing strike down at Port Victoria, and the whole Maula tribe in revolt ...' He turned his eyes now to Tulbach Browne. 'And there's one thing that *you* did, which certainly caused a lot of trouble and unrest. That time in the Gamate Hotel, when Dinamaula was refused a drink. You engineered the whole thing.'

'Did I now?' said Tulbach Browne quietly.

'Yes. And someone else, not a Pressman but not far from it – Father Hawthorne – also caused an enormous amount of trouble and disturbance, by telling the Maulas that the whole world would be on their side, if they decided to cast off their chains, or some bloody nonsense ...' David paused, though only for a second. 'That's all I can think of at the moment, but, by Christ, it's enough! Practically all the trouble in Gamate has been caused by the effect of the Press limelight on a very simple people. I'm not saying, because I can't, that it wouldn't have happened anyway, some time or other. But the one thing that's certain is that, without you, it wouldn't have happened *now*, and it wouldn't have been so cruel and so violent.'

Tulbach Browne took him up immediately; he was very angry.

'All that you're doing,' he said roughly, 'is shifting the blame. You've all made a thorough balls-up of running this country, and so you say it's our fault, when things get out of hand.'

David shook his head again. 'Not true. Things were going smoothly enough until you came along.'

Axel Hallmarck jumped in. 'What about Dinamaula, then? If it's all our fault, doesn't that let him out?'

'Of course not. He's the focus of the whole thing. He always has been. But – ' David held Tulbach Browne's eyes for a long moment, ' – we'll never know, will we, what persuaded him to get out of line in the first place.'

A new voice made itself heard – the voice, resonant yet arch, of Clandestine Lebourget. To his surprise, she was regarding him almost benevolently, like an elephant held in agreeable captivity.

'Honey,' she said, 'you don't seem to like us at all.'

But David was not to be turned aside. 'I like anybody,' he declared, 'who behaves themselves, and shows some kind of responsibility. But I think it's an unforgivable thing, to come in here and stir things up, just to get a newspaper story.'

The climax was obviously near.

'That's a hell of a thing to say,' remarked Axel Hallmarck.

'I think it's absolutely true, none the less. And as well as being unforgivable, it's terribly dangerous, too.'

'Dangerous for who?'

'For everyone here.'

'You talk,' rasped Tulbach Browne, 'as if the Maulas were apes or animals. They can think, can't they? Aren't they still human beings, even if they are the wrong colour, from your point of view?'

'Certainly they're human beings. But they've not yet reached a western level of civilization.'

'You mean, they're inferior?'

Now they were all hammering it home, and David was ready to meet them.

'Yes, I do. I think that, man for man, at this moment of evolution, a Maula native is inferior to a white man.'

'But that's not his fault, surely?'

'*Fault?* There's no fault. It's a historical accident, and it will be corrected in due course. But it is true *now.*'

'For Christ's sake! – ' this was Tulbach Browne again, ' – I thought people like you went out with the slave trade!'

'I'm trying to be honest and realistic. It's time we took another look at this idea of complete racial equality.'

'Then you don't think a black man can do a white man's job?'

'I think that may turn out to be the twentieth century's most fatuous illusion.'

David's answer – crude, arrogant, and deeply felt – might have been the last climax, the boiling-point of anger and counter-anger. It might indeed have been his last official utterance in Pharamaul. But suddenly, startling them all, demolishing the ugly tenseness of collision, there was a resounding crash nearby, out on the *stoep.* It was the noise of the screen door springing violently open, and then slamming shut again.

Everyone in the room came to wary, acute attention; some of them rose to their feet; a number of right hands dropped unobtrusively into coat pockets; through the hearts and minds of all, the idea of murderous surprise made an instant stab. There were four heavy footfalls, and then the sitting-room door swung open in its turn. But it was no ambush, no Maula assault with axe and knife and club. It was Keith Crump, of the Royal Pharamaul Police.

His appearance was disciplined and yet wild, at the same time. Parts of his uniform were neat and creased, others were tattered and bloodstained. His left arm was in a rough sling; he had a crudely fashioned bandage round his head. All down one side of his uniform tunic, a glistening trail of blackened blood led down his flank, down his bare thigh, and thence towards the floor. His eyes were red and inflamed, staring hugely out of a pinched unshaven face. He was far gone, in exhaustion and in wounds. But he could still hold himself erect, and stride like a soldier, and stand before them like a man.

David Bracken started forward. 'Keith ... What's happened? Are you all right?'

Crump smiled – a thin, tight smile in an exhausted face. 'I'm all right,' he answered. It was a croaking voice, but firm none the less. 'A bit ragged round the edges, that's all.'

Now they were all staring at him, staring at this evidence of something true, something critical and mortal. With sudden insight, with unworthy joy, David realized that for him this was rescue, total and undeniable; whatever the cost, something had happened that would wipe out all the past hour, all the ill-tempered argument, all the dropped bricks. This cancelled all other headlines – and Keith Crump was the saviour with the repreiving pencil.

Crump also was staring from face to face, working it out. He knew all the people present. With one exception, they were not his friends. As if he had sized it all up in his mind, he delivered them something to bite on, something real to write about at last.

'They've cut the road, just south of Shebiya,' he said, on a firm, controlled note. 'We were trying to get through, but we were ambushed. We lost two men, and I got hit myself.' The blood on his tunic challenged them to think otherwise. 'They've cut the road,' he repeated. 'It's just made for it, of course – thickest part of the bush – we'll need an army to get through ... God knows what's happening, up at Shebiya.' He paused again, then raised his head. 'Sorry to interrupt, David. But I've got to see you, immediately.'

IV

They were speeding southwards in the police jeep; David Bracken at the wheel, driving like a fury, and Keith Crump by his side, lying back exhausted and spent on a pile of blankets. The road was rough, but the jeep was designed for rough roads; though it bounced and swayed and jolted with mad persistence, yet it tore southwards with the speed of the wind, unrolling behind it a dusty yellow ribbon. For the first few miles, another car with newspaper correspondents had kept pace with them; then their pursuers had been left behind, and they were alone with the endless pitted road, the dust, and the sun casting long shadows across their pathway.

Their departure had been swift – so swift that there had been no need for secrecy. As soon as they were alone Crump had said: 'Got to see the Governor – telephone no good – got to see him, work something out,' and David, leaving two messages – one to be sent to Port Victoria, announcing their plans, the other for George Forsdick bringing him up to date – had led Crump out to the jeep, tucked him into the bucket-seat, sat down behind the wheel, and set course for Port Victoria. Since that moment, three hours ago, the jeep had never been out of top gear, and, no matter how vile the road, had never slowed below forty miles an hour.

Crump dozed, pale and exhausted, his wounded arm leaking a slow dribble of blood on to the seat beside him. David drove, with tension and pleasure intermingled; it was a wild ride, with fear behind them and doubt ahead, but his steely wrists commanded their progress, and their progress was ever southwards. The shadows lengthened;

evening drew a lowering canopy over their heads; soon it was time to switch on the lights.

Clouds of insects swarmed towards them, battered them briefly, and were lost behind; an owl with huge orbed eyes swooped low, and fled with a screech of alarm; once, an enormous python, stretching the full width of the road, interposed its evil twelve-foot length, glistening grey-green in the glare of their lights. But still they swept on; speed was their ally and their safeguard; speed, the curling yellow road, the whip and jolt of their passage, the tugging of the wind, and the tunnel of light ahead.

It was the fifth hour; one hundred and seventy miles of torn-up road behind them, a bare fifty to go. Crump groaned in his sleep, stretched awkwardly, and sat up.

David took his eyes for a moment off the road. 'How do you feel?' he asked.

'Stiff as hell ... Otherwise all right ... Where are we?'

'About fifty miles to go.'

Crump looked at the luminous dial of his wristwatch. 'Good for you.'

The jeep gave a jerk, jumping and slithering sideways from one scored-out track to another. Caught momentarily in the glare of the headlights, a group of oxen, outspanned by the roadside, turned slow and sleepy eyes towards them, their gaunt flanks made gothic by deep shadow. Then the jeep settled down, and the note of the engine climbed again. 'What happened?' asked David. 'Up at Shebiya?'

'Bloody shambles,' answered Crump. His voice came slowly, in jerks to match their progress, fighting the wind and the engine roar. 'This morning, we called Tom Ronald as usual on the police schedule ... Calling from Gamate, ten am routine ... Couldn't get any answer ... I didn't like the sound of that, so I took this old waggon – ' he kicked the side of the jeep, ' – and four of my chaps, and started to drive up to Shebiya ... All the way up, we kept trying to make radio contact ... Still no answer ... Then, when we were in the thick of the bush, a couple of miles south of the town, we were brought up short ... Big tree lying right across the road. We all got out to look, scouting around, and suddenly all hell broke loose.'

He was silent, for a full mile. 'An ambush,' explained Crump. 'Very well laid on, too ... Crossfire from rifles, a Sten gun somewhere, an old cannon blasting away at the jeep ... Missed it, luckily ... But two of my lads went down, for keeps ... I got a bullet through this arm, and something else nicked me on the head, as well ... We just turned tail and ran ... Nothing else to do.'

'But what's it mean?' asked David.

'Murder,' replied Crump briefly. 'The town's cut off – which means that something's happened up there that they don't want us to know about.'

'The Ronalds?'

'The Ronalds,' answered Crump. 'The late Ronalds ... And the late Father Schwemmer, unless I'm much mistaken.'

'Oh God!' said David. 'Was he there as well?'

'Went up two days ago.'

'But they wouldn't kill him. Everybody loves *him!*'

' "*Everybody*",' sang Crump, suddenly foolish, ' "*loves my baby*". Mr Bracken, at this very moment, they're probably loving him to *death* ... And Tom and Cynthia Ronald, as well.'

'But we must get through!' cried David, in anguish. His foot eased back off the accelerator. 'What the hell are we driving south for? We've got to go back, and get through to them!'

'We're driving south,' said Crump, in exhaustion and misery, 'because we can't drive north ... I haven't enough men to force a way through that road block, even if I could leave Gamate without a single policeman ... Which I can't

… So we're driving south to talk to the Governor. I don't want to sound like a bastard, but now it's *his* problem … I've done the best I can, with all the strength God gave me … Either we collect a lot of soldiers, and fight back up the road to Shebiya … Or we find some other way of getting through. And what the hell way *that* is, I wouldn't like to guess.'

'The soldiers are due here tomorrow.'

'Good for them,' said Crump. 'Just in time for the ceremonial burial party.'

Ahead of them, above the shadows and the oncoming brilliance of the road, there was now a vague yellow glow on the far southern horizon.

'There's Port Victoria,' said David. 'Just the loom of it. Thank God!'

'Eight o'clock,' said Crump, glancing again at his watch. 'There by nine.'

'But what can we do? How do we get through to Shebiya?'

'We swim,' answered Crump, his voice faint and hoarse. 'We swim, or we fly. We *know* we can't walk. There's a big tree and a lot of U-Maulas in the way.'

'I've asked you to come along,' said the Governor, 'because Keith Crump has just arrived – with some very bad news, I'm afraid – and I feel we ought all to know about it, and decide on a plan.' Opposite him, the clock on the ornate mahogany mantelpiece began to chime ten o'clock, and Sir Elliott Vere-Toombs waited, as if politely, for it to finish. His white dinner jacket was a focus of formal elegance in the shadowy room. 'I'm sorry it's so late,' he went on, as soon as silence descended again, 'but it really is unavoidable.'

No one spoke. Crump, still pale and spent, but with his head wound freshly dressed and his arm in a neat sling, sat back on the couch. Aidan Purves-Brownrigg was beside him; in two other armchairs, David and Captain Simpson completed the semicircle. Nicole Steuart was installed at a small desk just behind the Governor. She too was pale and tense, just as she had been ever since David had had a brief word with her, before the meeting.

Then, she had put her hand to her mouth, said: 'Oh darling ... Those poor Ronalds ...' and wound her arms round his neck as if to ward off all evil. But now, when her eyes met David's, there was nothing left of love in them. Love had been swamped by two things – discipline, and the fiercer emotions that went with thoughts of rescue.

The Governor raised his head again, looking at Keith Crump. 'Just bring us up to date, Keith, there's a good fellow. Start from this morning.'

Crump's account was succinct and precise; there was no trace in his voice of the murderous surprise of the ambush, still less of the horror that might be masked behind it. It was a list, neatly tabulated, set out in the proper order, with paragraphs A, B, C, and D: the radio silence from Shebiya, the expedition to find out what was wrong, the attack, the retreat. It was a police report, presented formally at the close of the day.

When he had finished: 'Thank you, Keith,' said the Governor. 'I think that's all quite clear ... I'm sure you were right to – er – break off the action, and go back to Gamate.' He cleared his throat. 'Before we consider ways and means, I'd like to complete the general picture for you.'

Now it was the Governor's turn to report, and (somewhat to David's surprise) his tone and manner were not vastly different from Crump's. Danger and doubt had sharpened his style, crisis had brought out tough qualities from an older, more effective past. He sounded resourceful and efficient, in the face of known and unknown adversity.

'This affair at Shebiya has come at a very bad time,' he began, 'when we were already stretched to the limit … We've managed to bring things under control, down here in Port Victoria; the strike is still in operation, but there's been very little further violence. We've recruited a civic guard, of sorts, from the Pharamaul Club, which is – er – doing valuable patrol work.'

In the pause that followed, David asked: 'Sir, is there any more news of Dinamaula?'

'Not that I know of,' answered the Governor. 'He's still here, of course, but still proving stubborn, and quite uncommunicative …' He looked at Crump. 'Have your people anything to add to that?'

'Only one thing, sir,' answered Crump. 'Zuva Katsaula, his cousin, called on Dinamaula a few days ago. Then he disappeared. He's rumoured to be up in Shebiya.'

'So Dinamaula may well have planned this Shebiya affair?'

'It's possible.'

The Governor nodded to himself; it was as if he were filing the intelligence away, against some future action – a reprimand, an enforcement of discipline, a show of strength. 'Turning now to Gamate,' he went on, nodding towards Crump again, 'the main body of the police force are, of course, in camp up there. They still have a great deal of unrest and rioting to contend with … I take it that we cannot afford to weaken that concentration, in any way?'

'No, sir,' answered Crump. 'Gamate is still very tricky. In fact, I took quite a chance this morning, detaching four men to go with me. And I lost two of them.'

The Governor nodded. 'Quite so. And that's really the crux of our dilemma at the moment. Because – ' he looked at each of them in turn, ' – the battalion coming from East Africa has again been delayed. They won't be here for at least another twenty-four hours. Then they have to disembark, and so forth.'

'They're coming by *sea*?' asked David, who had not known this.

Captain Simpson, the naval aide, answered him. 'Yes,' he said weightily. 'They're in a small troop transport, sailing from Mombasa. They've run into very heavy weather, rounding the Cape of Good Hope. Had to ease down to five knots ... I doubt if they'll dock here before tomorrow night. Disembarking will take another twelve hours or so. The dock strike is bound to slow things up.'

'But sir,' said Crump, in a taut voice, 'can't they *fly* troops in from Kenya?'

Now it was Aidan's turn. 'We thought of that, Keith, but it's no good. All the troops that can be spared for Pharamaul are stuck in the transport, coming round by sea. They simply haven't any more to send. We're still completely on our own here, for the next thirty-six hours.'

'And there you have it,' said Sir Elliott, picking up the threads as the room fell silent again, and the doom and knell of Shebiya sounded loud in every heart. 'Port Victoria is quiet, and possibly under control. Gamate is still highly explosive and dangerous. We really have as much as we can handle here, with our available resources, and no one to spare to force a way through to Shebiya. Isn't that so, Keith?'

'We certainly can't spare enough men to break through,' agreed Crump morosely. 'It would take a small army ... They're obviously well dug in, straddling the road about two miles south of the town. It'll mean a full-scale frontal attack, by a lot of men, properly armed. We can do it all right when the soldiers arrive. But in the meantime ...'

'In the meantime,' said the Governor, bridging the heavy silence, 'Shebiya has already been cut off for over twelve hours. We really have no idea of what may be happening up there …' The room suddenly seemed full of ideas, crude and bloody and tragic, of what could be happening up at Shebiya. 'I'm afraid we'll just have to wait.'

David caught Nicole's eyes on him, and her pale face, pleading for action. She was clearly in anguish, a woman in a man's cruel world mourning another woman who had been caught up in the same fearful web. He glanced sideways at Aidan, and saw a like reflection of horror and impotence. Sir Elliott was looking down at the blotter on his desk; Crump was lying back, an exhausted fighting man whose weapons had been stolen. It was true that there was nothing more to be done. In all good faith, they had given up three hostages – Tom Ronald, his wife, and old Father Schwemmer – and they could not retrieve them before the next two mortal sunsets.

Suddenly, inexplicably, Captain Simpson stood up. He was a tall man, and his bemedalled uniform was impressive; but now there was something in his bearing, something agleam in his ruddy, gin-flushed face, that focused all eyes. He was standing at attention, his arms stiff by his side. He spoke throatily, as if under heavy stress.

'Sir!' he intoned.

'Yes, Hereward?' said the Governor, taken aback.

'Sir, a cutting-out expedition.'

'I beg your pardon?'

'A cutting-out expedition.'

On the instant, there was throughout the room a general, deeply uncomfortable feeling that this was an unfortunate moment for the naval aide-de-camp to be drunk. But in fact Captain Simpson was not drunk, nor anything like it, and he made the point clear within a few moments.

'What exactly have you in mind?' asked the Governor doubtfully. Captain Simpson had a lot in mind; indeed, as soon as he started to speak, words and phrases tumbled and burst forth, propelled by history, by the Royal Navy, by the dear twin ghosts of Nelson and of Sir Hereward Simpson, Vice-Admiral of the Blue from 1816 to 1825. There were many different factors contributing to what Captain Simpson now said – the boredom of peacetime naval life, the burden of an ancient and honourable lineage, the simple wish to prosper in his career. But, strongest of all, he spoke from a deep need to quit himself well, in face of dire peril – peril to others.

'Sir,' he said, quickly, unevenly, yet irresistibly, 'a cutting-out expedition ... We can't get through to Shebiya by frontal land attack, but we can get through if we capture the village from the rear, while the people defending it are expecting us to come from an entirely different direction ...' His eyes glowed suddenly, emphasizing an amazing transformation. 'Sir, there have been all sorts of examples of this in the past, and they've always worked ... We can go round by sea, make our landing on the east coast opposite Shebiya, march through to the town, and be in full possession of it, before they've really woken up to what's happening. They're expecting us to come by road, from the south. We'll come by sea, and then through the forest, from the east.'

There was a large-scale map of Pharamaul, that tear-shaped and familiar island, hanging on the wall behind the Governor's chair. He turned towards it, and everyone in the room followed his movement and his eyes. There was no doubt that Captain Simpson's words, and especially his manner, had reopened the whole prospect of rescue, giving another chance to the guilt of their impotence. There was even a small and secondary guilt to be purged – for, after all, the naval ADC was talking sense.

'You mean,' said the Governor, narrowing his eyes, 'we could make a landing at Fish Village, and take the forest track up to Shebiya? How far would that be?'

'Not more than thirty miles,' said Crump, with awakening interest. 'I know the ground, sir. It's a passable road.'

'We could take the jeep,' put in Captain Simpson. 'Get through in about three hours.'

'We could take troop-carriers as well,' added Crump. 'I've got two of them available.'

'Just a minute,' said the Governor, reprovingly. 'What about a boat? We have nothing – '

'Sir, there's a boat in harbour at this moment which would just suit us.' Simpson was pressing forward again, eager, knowledgeable. 'She belongs to an American – I can't remember his name, but I went aboard her yesterday to look round. One of those luxury cruising yachts. Huge – about a hundred and twenty feet long. And she'll do fifteen or sixteen knots. We could make the whole trip in about twelve hours.'

'But she's not our boat,' objected the Governor.

'She could be,' answered Simpson stoutly. 'In this sort of emergency, we could certainly commandeer her. Or we could arrange it through Lou Strogoff, the American consul. Or we could just ask the owner. He was very friendly yesterday. I'm sure he'd play with us, if only for the fun of it.'

Now gradually the room was warming up again. Crump was on the edge of the couch, staring sideways at Simpson as if entranced by the prospect he had opened up. Nicole Steuart, her shapely head bent, was doing sums on the scribbling-pad in front of her – sums involving time, distance, and incalculable hope, sums that might add up to life instead of death. But it was Aidan who was the next to speak.

'Granted that we could land at Fish Village, and – ' he glanced up at Captain Simpson, ' – I think it's wonderful idea, the *only* idea – what about men? We'd certainly be taking the U-Maulas by surprise, capturing the village while they were still a couple of miles away, and looking in the wrong direction – but we'll still need troops to do it.'

Crump awoke to the last word, cutting in on Simpson. 'We wouldn't need nearly so many troops, this way ... I could take all the available men from Port Victoria.' He looked at the Governor. 'You said it's pretty quiet here, sir, and we've always got that civic guard to fall back on. That means that, for a few days at least, we could spare perhaps fifty armed policemen, the whole Port Victoria contingent. We've got Bren guns for them, in the armoury here ... If we could just achieve real surprise, and then wait for the people at the roadblock south of Shebiya to filter back to the village, and pick them off as they turned up ...'

He was seeing the whole course of the action in his professional mind's eye, and the others were catching the noble infection, and seeing it at the same time. Only Captain Simpson was frowning slightly.

'Of course,' he said, with odd formality, 'this is primarily a naval operation.'

'I don't mind what the hell it is –' began Crump carelessly.

Captain Simpson raised a formidable hand. 'It's a cutting-out expedition,' he said, with brisk decision. 'The troops to be landed by sea transport, and then led into action, as if they were Marines.'

'Oh,' said Crump, getting the point. He frowned, and then grinned in relaxation. 'I don't mind,' he said, 'as long as we get to Shebiya. It can be your show, technically, if you like, old boy.'

'Why *technically*?'

'All right – *actually*.'

There was a long pause. Suddenly, they were all looking at the Governor and Commander-in-Chief, and the Governor, who had been writing, raised his head.

'The landing is feasible?' he asked Simpson, precisely.

'Yes, sir.'

His eyes came round to Crump. 'You could get your men through? The surprise element might well work?'

'Yes, sir ... By God, yes!'

'Very well ...' Sir Elliott looked down at the piece of paper, and then began to speak, half reading, half talking; David, especially, was amazed at the quick incisive grasp, which must have been at work on details all the time that they had been discussing the project. 'A sea assault,' said the Governor. 'A cutting-out expedition. Captain Simpson in general charge of the whole operation. Keith Crump in field command of the police. David as second in command.'

There was a slight question in his voice. David looked up, and said: 'Thank you, sir.' Then he glanced at Nicole, and there was now love in her eyes, as well as all the rest.

'There are three stages to be covered,' went on Sir Elliott. 'One, arrange about the boat. Two, arm yourselves, and the policemen. Three, get on board, with your transport, and start out.' He looked at Simpson. 'Number one is yours, of course. It's a bit late, I know. But can you get in touch with the owner of the boat?'

'I think so, sir,' answered Simpson. 'He may even still be up at the club. I've just remembered his name, by the way. It's Loganquist.'

'Ah,' said the Governor. 'An American, you say?'

'Yes, sir. Very rich. He makes adding machines. But she really is a beautiful boat.'

'I'll leave all that to you, then. It may require some measure of diplomacy ... After all, there's no earthly reason why this Mr – er – should allow his beautiful boat to be used like this.'

'It'll be all right,' said Simpson confidently. 'I was on board for lunch yesterday.' He gestured. 'He's that sort of man ... He'll love it.'

'Very well ... Now for the police. Do you really feel up to this, Keith?'

'Yes, sir.'

'How long will you need to collect your men?'

Crump considered. 'I'll have to winkle them out, recall some of them from patrol, see about their arms, get them down to the clocks, and load the vehicles ... About six o'clock tomorrow morning, sir.'

'Will it be light by then?'

'Barely, sir,' said Captain Simpson. 'But it doesn't matter, anyway. In fact, from the security angle, it would be better if we sailed before dawn.'

'Very true,' agreed the Governor. He looked at Crump. 'You'll take care about that? – isolate your men? You know how quickly this sort of news travels.'

'We'll take care of it,' answered Crump grimly. 'If I have to tie them down with insulating tape.'

'Very well,' said the Governor. He consulted his notes. 'Communications?'

'The boat has a radio,' said Captain Simpson. 'Biggest I've ever seen ... We can organize a wavelength to fit the police schedule.'

'And when you land?'

'The jeep has its own set,' said Crump. 'As soon as we get ashore, we'll make contact, and keep on reporting.'

'Very well,' said the Governor again. 'That really leaves only one more thing. David?'

'Yes, sir?' answered David, in doubt and some anxiety.

'Just behind you,' said the Governor, with no change of expression, 'is a cupboard. In the cupboard are glasses, soda-water, ice, and a decanter of whisky. I suggest,' he said, with a wonderful, heartwarming air of shedding a heavy load on to men whom he trusted implicitly, 'that we all drink a quick health to the success of the expedition, the cutting-out expedition ...' As David rose, smiling, to obey, the Governor turned to Captain Simpson. 'Wasn't it your great-great-great-uncle,' he asked guilelessly, 'who brought off this same sort of thing, a few miles north of Corunna, in 1797?'

V

They slept fitfully, side by side, flank to flank in the narrow bed; the knowledge that the alarm clock was set for four o'clock, putting a curfew to sleep and to love, hung over them with grisly insistence. The threat of parting and separation, the danger on the morrow, killed sleep as if with a poisoned draught.

Their first embrace was ecstatic, their second full of a deep, sensual languor; then they drifted into sleep, then woke on the same moment to the needs and fears of an evil dawn. Nicole wept secretly, even as she received his body once more and fashioned it to her own; the sighing and shaking of her passion turned to sobs, while David was still unaware of anything save the familiar, longed for shuddering under him.

But when they were both spent, he discovered that her cheek beside his was wet, her bosom still heaving, her soft limbs trembling with more than the invasion of his body. For many rapturous minutes, she had been crying bitterly.

She felt him draw away, and said urgently: 'Don't put on the light.'

'But darling,' he said, 'I want to look at you.'

'I'm crying. You know that. You can feel it.'

'You mustn't cry, Nicole.'

'I can't help it. It's all so sad.'

'What's sad?'

'You leaving, just when you've arrived. And the Ronalds, up in Shebiya. And what's going to happen tomorrow.'

'But you were happy, a little time ago. And when we first made love …'

'When we first made love, it was just you and me, meeting after not touching or seeing each other for weeks. We know what that is like … But afterwards, things came crowding in … I'm sorry … So feeble … What's the time?'

David raised himself on one elbow, and looked at the luminous dial of the bedside clock. He was conscious of her body, warm alongside his, yet sad and forlorn at the same time. There were certain magics that two people could conjure up, certain aspects of despair that they could never surmount.

'Three o'clock,' he answered. He bent and kissed her, blindly yet certainly. 'A little time yet.'

'The littlest time in the world … What will happen tomorrow – today?'

'We'll go round by this boat, make a landing at Fish Village, push our way through the forest, and find out what's happened at Shebiya.'

'What do you think has happened?'

He lay back on the pillow, staring at a ceiling he could not see. 'God knows … Anything … I don't give much for their chances, I'm afraid.'

'So you'll be fighting?'

'We'll be fighting anyway.'

'Aren't you afraid?'

'I shall be.'

'But not too afraid?'

'No.'

He heard her sigh. 'Men are wonderful … Wonderful and awful …'

'Why awful?' He smiled, and tried to show it in his voice. 'I know about being wonderful.'

'Awful, because you go away so happily ... You leave us behind to do all the crying ...' Suddenly her voice had an edge to it which he had never heard before, a cutting edge, finely ground somewhere between hatred and despair. 'You make love to us, kiss us enough times to take care of the goodbye, give us enough orgasms to send us back to sleep, perhaps give us a baby to keep us quiet for the next nine months ... Was it like that in the war?'

'I wasn't married during the war,' he said, secretly shocked and ashamed.

'You're not married *now*.'

'Yes, I am ... As married as I can be ...'

She twisted her head aside, unappeased, still violent in her attack. 'Did you make love to me that third time, because you thought twice wasn't enough to make me go back to sleep? After you've gone away? Damn you! Did you?'

'Sweet,' he said, trying to knit the rags of the night together, trying to cover the appalling moment, 'I made love to you that third time because I wanted to, because I thought you wanted it, because I woke up, and you woke up, and you had an arm across my shoulder, and your breast in the curve of my neck ...' He turned to whisper to her, striving to exorcise the evil ghost between them. 'If you want to know the absolute truth, there was another reason. I made love to you the third time because, being the usual masculine show-off I wanted to prove that I could. And there you have it, in black and white and pink.'

After a long, long pause, he felt her hand come out, and slide gently into his. 'Darling,' she said, on a much smaller voice, 'I think I love you more than anything else in the whole world.'

'Just because of that third time?'

'Just because of that third time ... Sweetheart, I know you're wonderful, and I'm a bitch, but I *have* got a good reason ... Not any of those silly reasons I made up ... I'm miserably afraid, David. I don't want you to be killed. Basically, I don't care about Pharamaul or Shebiya or even those poor Ronalds ... I just care about you, and I don't want you to be shot or speared to death or drowned or lost in the jungle.'

'None of those things is going to happen.'

'They could.'

'They won't ... I'll just be gone for two or three days, and then I'll come back and we'll be in bed together again, like this.'

'And we'll be married?'

'And we'll be married. First thing next morning.'

'That will be lovely ...' Her hands, straying over his body, made their inevitable discovery. 'Why, David! ... Have you anything to tell me?'

He smiled in the darkness. 'There was a lot of defeatist talk about *three* times ... So long ago now.'

She turned to kiss him, with a soft and ready mouth. 'Just a big show-off, like you said.'

'Thank you for the adjective.'

'But darling, you *will* take care of yourself?'

'You take care of this, and I'll take care of me.'

VI

At the low ebb of five o'clock in the morning, David Bracken went aboard. The docks were dark and deserted, lit here and there by a naked, insect-clustered bulb at the corner of a building; in the shadows, nothing lurked save dogs and smells, waste paper, tangled coils of rusty wire, oildrums, baulks of wood, all the debris of the commercial seaside. He walked carefully, conspiratorially, conscious of animal fatigue, sadness, a wisp of Nicole's perfume from beneath his coat collar, and a growing nervous tension.

He walked towards a cluster of lights at the end of the main jetty, where many figures were moving, and a donkey-engine chugged busily, and the bows of a long white-painted ship emerged from the shadows like a trim ghost. At the top of the gangplank, Simpson and Keith Crump were standing; Simpson was watching a troop-carrying truck being manhandled aboard near the stern. Crump, white-bandaged, his arm in a sling, was speaking to one of his sergeants, tapping meanwhile on a piece of paper. There was an open case containing a dozen Bren guns at his feet.

They both looked up as David stepped off the end of the gangplank on to the white-scrubbed wooden deck. By contrast with the acrid air of the docks, the yacht smelled clean and new, too good for her murky surroundings, a lady among bedraggled whores.

'How's it going?' David asked.

'Very well, so far,' said Simpson rather grumpily. His manner was preoccupied; he was the expert, the man of affairs surrounded by amateurs and bohemians. 'That's the last troop-carrier. The men are all aboard, except the ones loading.'

'How do you feel, Keith?' asked David, turning to Crump.

'Better,' said Crump. He was still pale, but his air was brisk and confident. 'Much better.'

'Anything I can do?'

'Don't think so … We'll sail in about half an hour.'

'Forty minutes,' said Captain Simpson.

'This is quite a boat,' said David, looking round him. In the cold half-light, under the glare of the cargo clusters rigged overhead, the boat still looked elegantly luxurious. She was big; both fore and aft, she stretched out into the shadows. 'What's she called?'

'*Wander Lust*,' answered Captain Simpson, with distaste. There was a sudden noise from the stern, where the troop-carrier was being levered across the deck to a sheltered corner, and he called out: 'Quietly, there!'

'Where's the owner?' asked David.

'Up on the bridge,' answered Crump. 'You might go up and say hallo to him. He's an engaging old boy.'

'How does he feel about all this?'

'Mad keen,' answered Simpson. 'I knew we wouldn't have any trouble. He said "Yes" before I'd finished asking ... But his wife – Mrs Loganquist – is still asleep. I gather she hasn't been told what this is all about. We've got to reassure her when she gets up.'

'Oh ...' David looked about him once more. Within view there were two troop-carriers, and a jeep, securely lashed to the deck; a dozen Maula policemen in khaki uniforms; some piles of stores; one opened crate of Bren guns, and three still closed. Crump, also in uniform, had a bulging pistol holster, Simpson a Sten gun slung over one shoulder. 'What are we meant to be doing, then?'

'Elephant hunting,' said Simpson. 'Very hazardous occupation. Even the beaters are armed to the teeth.'

Up on the bridge, all was brilliance and light. The instruments gleamed, the glass was polished and dustless, the varnished woodwork immaculate. Just behind the wheel was a long-legged armchair, upholstered in light green nylon; and in it, playing idly with the controls, sat a small chubby man, middle-aged, cherubic. He was dressed in blue jeans, a hand-painted cream sports shirt with a motif of flying fish, and a red baseball cap with '*Wander Lust*' stencilled on the peak. At the sound of David's step, he turned.

'Hallo, there!' he said cordially. His spectacles gleamed an added welcome. 'Glad to have you aboard.'

'I'm David Bracken,' said David, holding out his hand. 'First Secretary at Government House. Mr Loganquist?'

'Mr Loganquist,' agreed the cheerful owner. 'Friends call me Logey ... Heard all about you, Dave.'

'You have?'

'Heard how you drove down from Gamate like a bat out of hell. Good for you, Dave!'

'Thank you,' said David.

Mr Loganquist hopped down from his chair. He was of short stature, and very round, his stomach only just held in check by an ornate gold-buckled belt. He seemed to be wearing some kind of cowboy footwear, high-heeled, ornamented with red tassels and white lacing.

'This is a wonderful assignment,' he said. 'I'm very grateful to the captain for suggesting it.'

'We're very grateful to *you*,' replied David. 'We had to have a boat, as you know, and this is exactly what we needed. She looks wonderful.'

'Just took delivery, two months ago,' said Mr Loganquist, demonstrably pleased. 'Built down at Providence, Rhode Island ...' He looked up at David eagerly. 'Bet you couldn't say how much she cost.'

'Well,' said David.

'Go ahead – take a guess.'

David looked round him. 'A hundred thousand pounds?'

'What's that in dollars?'

'About three hundred thousand.'

Mr Loganquist laughed delightedly. 'You're *way-y-y* off, Dave. Just over half a million bucks. What d'you think of that?'

'It's a great deal of money.'

'You can say that again ... Of course, I was robbed,' continued Mr Loganquist cheerfully. 'But what the hell, I always say. You can't take it with you.'

'What sort of crew do you have, Mr Loganquist?'

'Call me Logey, for God's sake … Crew of six – skipper, engineer, two deck hands, cook, steward … Steward's called Charlie – coloured boy from Jamaica. You'll see a lot of him, if you're any sort of a drinking man. *Are* you a drinking man, Dave?'

'Yes,' answered David. 'I think I am.'

'Good for you. How about a little snort, right now? Scotch? Rye? Let's start separating the men from the boys.'

David looked up at the clock on the bulkhead. It was five-fifteen in the morning. 'Not just at the moment, thanks,' he said, feeling somewhat boorish none the less.

Mr Loganquist waved his hand. 'Any time at all,' he said hospitably. 'Just ring the bell for Charlie.'

'I'll do that,' said David.

Mr Loganquist took off his long-visored baseball cap. Above the pink cherubic face, his bald head gleamed like the whitest, largest egg in the world. 'Well, if we're not drinking, I guess I'll go lie down for half an hour, until we start. There's just one thing, Dave.'

'What's that?'

Mr Loganquist looked secretive, and shy at the same time. 'Mrs Loganquist – Ella – doesn't know what the hell this is all about … I told her I was giving you boys a lift up the coast … You're on vacation, going on a big hunting trip. Understand?'

'Yes,' said David. 'I'll remember that.'

'Hunting,' repeated Mr Loganquist, as if he had come to believe it himself. 'Real English style – lots of native bearers, lots of beaters, plenty of guns and vehicles … That's what she believes. Ella's not a strong woman. I don't want for her to have any sort of shock.'

'We'll be very careful,' David assured him.

'We'd better play plenty of canasta,' said Mr Loganquist. 'Drink us plenty of scotch and rye. Do a little fishing on the side. Can you play canasta?'

'Yes,' answered David.

'Good for you, Dave … Well, I'll turn in. Ring for Charlie, if you want any damned thing at all.'

'I'll do that. Good night, Mr Loganquist.'

'Call me Logey.'

'Good night, Logey.'

'That's the boy! See you at breakfast, Dave. And just feel free.'

As with that other voyage, which now seemed so long ago – his first voyage by rail from Port Victoria to Gamate – David Bracken was never to forget the voyage by sea from Port Victoria to Fish Village, two hundred miles up the east coast of Pharamaul. The first train journey had been a true voyage of discovery, with everything new, everything unexpected; this one was also new, a journey into the unknown which had, all the time, a superb air of unreality.

The ship and the men she carried were headed for an assignment, slightly crazy, slightly melodramatic, whose sting in the tail might bring death and ruin to all of them; but the voyage itself was slightly crazy also, investing stern duty with the mad aspect of a circus. As it proved, they were not able to resist any of its lures.

The diesel yacht *Wander Lust*, 570 tons, cast off and set sail a little before six o'clock, sliding away from the jetty in tune with two low-voiced orders and a disembodied wave of the hand, turning astern in a wide half-circle, and slipping through the harbour entrance like a grey ghost obeying the curfew of cock-crow. It was not yet dawn, though dawn trembled on the pale threshold to seawards; behind their backs, the town slept, bleary-eyed and tawdry, while ahead of them the clean and limitless horizon beckoned them to their voyage.

Though that voyage must lead them to danger and to death, yet they freed themselves from the land, and embraced the sea, as if they were poor folk taking a rapturous holiday – a holiday with every last treat guaranteed by benevolent authority. Perhaps, indeed, it was that prospect of the grim future which persuaded them to indulge all later whims, accept offered blessings.

It grew light very gradually, as they cleared harbour and set course, first north-east and then due north, for their destination. The sea was calm, with a light fluting breeze from the south; as with a million dawns, daylight seeped imperceptibly across the surface of the sea and the sky, bringing hope and warmth in successive, wonderful instalments, transforming everything within view from black to pale grey, from pale grey to pinkish white, from pinkish white to a magical yellow gleam – the veritable gleam of sunrise.

As with a million dawns, this dawn seemed personal and miraculous, renewing the private hope of mankind; although not less than a thousand wakeful sailors afloat on this one single ocean must be sharing its commonplace repetition. For those aboard *Wander Lust*, it showed a placid sea, with the long curve of their wake spreading and surging behind them; a few seabirds hopefully following their trail, a smudge of black smoke marking the harbour they had left behind; an endless South Atlantic horizon on their right hand, and the low foothills and purple uplands of Pharamaul on their left.

But as well as these natural benefits, it showed the noble outlines of the ship that carried them. David, for the first hour of their passage, stood at the back of the bridge, on which two figures – a tall, taciturn man identified as the skipper, and an untidy deckhand at the wheel – guided their destinies. There was no doubt, from the very feel of her, that *Wander Lust* was a considerable craft; and now the rising sun filled in the details, as if from an expanding catalogue of virtue.

To begin with, she was brand new, with that particular gleam of brasswork and fresh paint impossible to achieve even with the most expensive subsequent refit. She shone like new-minted coinage; her decks were immaculate, her lines graceful as a vapour trail in the summer sky. She had obvious excess of power; her engines, steadily throbbing, drove her swiftly onwards, and the small seas were met and divided and pushed astern with a relentless thrust.

Looking round him with unprofessional eyes, as the light grew and the whole ship emerged, David was put in mind of the unworthy phrase 'No expense spared'; but for once it was expense in a good cause, it was luxury tutored to an explicit marine elegance. This was evident in small things as well as big; in the solid sweep of the deck, the multiplicity of instruments in the bridge-house, the spotless ensign, the fibreglass runabout hoisted amidships. At the back of the bridge was ranged a whole armoury of fishing equipment; long steel casting rods, delicate split canes, Penn reels like pithead winding gear, elaborate leather harness. There was a glass case of sporting guns, a rack full of assorted binoculars, a ship-to-shore radio like a minor broadcasting station.

The sun, heaving above the horizon, began to cast the ship's long shadow across the water on their left hand. David stood with braced legs apart, exulting in the feel of the deck beneath his feet, the warmth of the sun on his shoulders, the thrust and power of their advance. The long coastline of Pharamaul emerged from the pearly mist, stretching endlessly northwards. The skipper stared momentarily at something on the eastward horizon; the helmsman met a slight yawing of their bows with a deft twist of his hands upon the wheel.

Whatever lay ahead, hidden inland behind the northward coastline, it was good to be alive on such a morning … David stretched, felt his bristly chin, and walked a few paces to the ladder leading to the main saloon. When he entered this, a young negro in a smart white uniform poked his head out of the serving hatch, grinning a broad welcome.

'Good morning, sir,' he said.

'Good morning,' answered David. This must be Charlie – Charlie the steward. 'You're up very early.'

'This is going to be one of those long days,' observed the negro steward, unconnectedly. 'Will it be breakfast, or a Scotch-and-soda?'

David blinked. It was not quite eight o'clock in the morning. But he did want a whisky-and-soda, more than anything else in the world, and there seemed no point in pretending otherwise.

'I *would* like a drink,' he acknowledged.

'It's going to be a long day,' repeated Charlie the steward. His sharp eyes were busy, examining David with almost clinical care, while his hands, seemingly unco-ordinated, adroitly summoned up whisky, ice, and soda-water. 'It's been a long night, too. Scotch-and-soda takes care of everything.'

David received the proffered glass. He thought: I suppose it all shows in my face ... I think I shall always have a whisky-and-soda for breakfast, every time I make love to Nicole ... That's going to be a lot of whisky-and-soda ... He swallowed thirstily. The drink was very good.

'Where are you from?' he asked.

'Jamaica,' answered Charlie. 'God's own banana paradise. Tell me,' he went on, almost fiercely, 'just what are those nigger bastards doing, up-country?'

The whole of that day had the same inconsequent appeal as that eight a.m. whisky-and-soda; it was as if this preliminary stroke of classic immoderation set the tone of all that followed. At nine o'clock, Simpson and Crump came into the saloon, freshly shaved, briskly ready to lay the necessary plans for their landing; but they had scarcely settled down to discussion before their host and hostess put in an appearance.

Mr Loganquist was as David remembered him from their brief meeting of a few hours earlier; he had changed his shirt for a more subdued model made of tan corduroy, and he no longer wore a baseball cap, but he was as chubby, as cheerful, and as intent on significant living as he had appeared earlier. Mrs Loganquist supplied some of the reasons. She was a tall, tough-looking blonde, a good twenty years younger than her husband; her tailored cream slacks, elaborate hairdo, and brilliant make-up seemed to improve in the sunrise, by several degrees of light.

Vaguely, David remembered Mr Loganquist warning him that his wife was not strong, and must be safeguarded from shocks. But there must, he decided, be degrees of American anaemia scarcely perceptible elsewhere. Her first words were: 'Hi! Good to see you all!' and her next a raucous: '*Charlie!* Set 'em up!'

Charlie appeared, beaming, with a tray bearing five gin-slings. There appeared to be no choice, and no deviation possible; this was the mid-morning potion. When they had all taken their glasses, Mrs Loganquist raised hers, with a wide hospitable sweep of her arm which set the blood-red and gold costume jewellery clicking like castanets.

'Glad you came aboard,' she proclaimed, and drank deep. They all followed suit; and this drink also was excellent – cool, clean, tangy. Mrs Loganquist set her glass down with a clatter, and suddenly looked across at Captain Simpson. 'What's the matter, Captain?' she asked, as if disinclined for anything save one hundred per cent co-operation. 'Too early in the morning for you?'

'Not at all.' Simpson, who had indeed been gazing at his hostess with startled attention, recovered swiftly, and smiled. It was a cheerful, extrovert smile, owing much to gin – not just this morning's gin, but the last thirty years of solid naval toping, in wardrooms which had played host to far stranger female fish than this – ballet dancers, Lady Mayoresses, the wives of native chiefs, admirals' ill-tempered daughters. 'I was just enjoying my drink,' he explained. 'It's really delicious.'

'The English slay me,' said Mrs Loganquist to the world at large. ' "*Reallah delicious*",' she mimicked. 'No one else can say it like that … Tell you what. Let's all get fried.'

'Now, honey!' cautioned Mr Loganquist, with the air of a man who has said it many times before.

'Oh, stuff!' said his wife. 'I mean it …' She raised her frosted glass again, curving an elegant, deeply tanned forearm. ' "*Reallah delicious*",' she quoted, and drank once more. 'Let's all get fried to the eyeballs, and then we'll catch us some fish.'

The round of gin-slings was the first of many; reality retreated, Shebiya was forgotten, while the five of them sat in the luxurious, gently rocking saloon of the *Wander Lust*, and celebrated their northward passage with drinking, talking, and slightly vacuous smiles. Presently, spurred on by their host, they all went out on deck, into the midday sunshine; rods were broken out, lines baited with a magnificent variety of chromium spinners, plastic lures, and monstrous painted insects, and they settled down to fish. Charlie brought successive fresh supplies of gin-slings; after half an hour, Mrs Loganquist, obviously adept and skilful, struck hard into a fifty-pound tuna, played it briefly, and landed it in a flurry of foam, blood, and blue–green scales on the after-deck.

More drinks were called for, in celebration; later, David caught a mackerel, Crump a small and puzzled cod; Simpson went gently to sleep, and dropped his rod unnoticed into the sea. Mrs Loganquist surveyed the surrounding frieze of troop-carriers, guns, and chattering native policemen, and remarked caustically: 'Those animals sure must be *wild*.' Mr Loganquist, breathing into his glass, said: 'Now, honey!'

Wander Lust ploughed onwards, in steady power and pride; the final morning drink was served at three, and lunch (watermelon, curried eggs, and *crêpes suzettes*) at three-thirty. At five they tottered below, intent on sleep, though not before Captain Simpson had drawn David and Crump aside, and said, as if communicating the plans of D-day: 'We'll discuss you-know-what, a little later on.'

But a little later on it was time for canasta, and more drinks – this time mint juleps, made and served with dedicated care by Charlie the steward, who poured the jiggers of bourbon on to the crushed ice and diced mint as if he were laying salve upon a wound. Round each icy tumbler was a silver holder with a long curved handle; round each holder a kind of striped sock, green or red or blue, to insulate and identify the drink and its owner. The game grew careless and disconnected; Mrs Loganquist, a dashing performer, won seven pounds, exclaimed: 'Hell! You're all such lousy players!' and threw her winnings through the nearest open porthole. Mr Loganquist said: 'Now, honey!' Captain Simpson dozed off once more in his chair. Darkness came gradually, after a sunset of streaky, barbarous splendour which set the whole sea on fire. Presently the skipper stepped down into the saloon, surveyed the scene with sardonic approval, and said: 'Folks, we've run a clear two hundred miles, by log. Must be getting mighty close. Yes, sir!'

To which Mrs Loganquist replied: 'Cut out the crap, Captain!' for no attributable reason, and Mr Loganquist, stung into variety, said: 'Honey – *please!*'

Then they went out on deck, swaying gently, glasses in hand, to watch the nearing of the land, the mysterious growth of shadows, and the campfires of Fish Village come twinkling out of the darkness towards them. Charlie appeared, not without stumbling, bearing a final round of mint juleps. It was a merry farewell to the sea, a most cordial greeting to the task ahead.

VII

Suddenly all three of them were sober again; stone cold sober, watchful, and intent. As if impelled by some secret, well-remembered directive, they drew aside, under the lee of the bridge. There were plans to be made, and now it was amazingly easy to make them, and to plot their course, and to concentrate. The beguiling, necessary, and irresistible holiday was over. Now they were keyed high for their return.

'We'll lie offshore,' said Simpson, speaking quietly, his voice in the darkness sounding cool and authoritative. 'I'll take the launch – ' he gestured behind him, at the grey shadow of the *Wander Lust's* boat, still hoisted in its davits, ' – and Crump, and about half the policemen, as many as the boat will hold. We'll go ashore quietly, but as quickly as we can, make our landing on the beach, and put a cordon round the village so that no one can escape up the track to Shebiya ... For all I know, this lot may be friendly, but we can't take any chances. Then – ' he touched David on the arm, ' – I'll give you the signal by flashlight – one long and three short, the letter B – and you'll take control here and have this ship brought alongside the jetty. Then we'll unload our gear, and the rest of the policemen, and get on our way. Is that all clear?'

'Yes,' answered Crump, immediately. 'But there's just one thing. I know the layout of the village, and the actual hut of the man we want to find, as soon as we can. He's the headman, an old chap called Pemboli. Nice old boy, much respected. He won't be bloody-minded, I can guarantee. It's the odds and sods we have to worry about.' He looked at Simpson in the darkness. 'If you'll see to the outer cordon round the village, I'll go straight into the middle of it, with about six of my chaps, and nail Pemboli straight away. He's important, after all. We might have to get him to make a speech.'

'All right,' agreed Simpson, after a pause. David could almost hear him wondering if, in this variation, the roles were correctly assigned; if the classic lines of the cutting-out expedition – a strictly naval occasion – left a margin for such a military spearhead. It seemed that they did ... 'All right,' said Simpson again. 'But if you get into any trouble, fire three shots, close together, and we'll close in from outside.'

'Thanks,' said Crump equably. 'And if *you* get into any trouble, fire *four* shots, and we'll come running.'

Suddenly, David found himself shivering; the night air, the reaction from the drinks, the certainty of danger, all contributed to a cold sense of doom. In search of privacy, he turned aside, looking up at the stars, and the faint outlines of the rigging; *Wander Lust* was moving forward very slowly, edging inshore towards the thin lights of Fish Village, and the vast and deadly bulk of Pharamaul behind it. Wavelets rippled at their bows; an arc of phosphorescent water curved away from them, and was lost in the darkness. He heard Simpson's voice behind him.

'All right with you, David?'

'Yes,' David answered, turning back again. 'I wait for your signal, and then tell the skipper to bring her alongside the jetty.'

'It shouldn't take long.'

'But what if – ' David began, and stopped.

'Well?' asked Simpson.

'Suppose you run into trouble,' David continued, unwillingly. 'It's just possible that the people here – ' he gestured towards the darkness, ' – are the same as the people up at Shebiya. They may be on guard, waiting for us, ready to fight. Isn't that so, Keith?'

'It's very unlikely,' answered Crump. 'There aren't more than fifty families at Fish Village, and they've always been a bit self-contained. Pemboli is quite an old autocrat, and a good friend of ours. I don't think they'll have organized anything. Our principal worry is to make sure the odd straggler doesn't light out for Shebiya, and give the whole show away.'

'But if we *do* run into trouble,' said Simpson, with a certain grimness, 'you'll hear it, soon enough. Any sort of continuous firing will mean that there's real opposition. In that case, you must come in at full speed, and land the rest of the policemen. And to hell with secrecy. Make all the noise you can. Fire a few rockets – there are some up on the bridge. The more like an army you can sound, the better.'

'All right,' answered David. 'But I'd much rather come ashore first, in the launch.'

'Yes,' said Captain Simpson, with an odd satisfaction in his voice. 'Who wouldn't?'

In the event, it was easy. Burning dimmed navigation lights, *Wander Lust* cut her engines and came to a gentle stop, a hundred yards from the shore; Simpson, Crump, and twenty armed policemen crowded into the launch, and sped for the beach, cutting a swathe of rippling foam across the dark water as they made their swift passage. On the bridge, the skipper remarked: 'Nice going ...' Mr Loganquist poured himself a long drink. Mrs Loganquist, wearing a honey-blonde mink coat thrown carelessly over her slacks, said it was a hell of a way to hunt elephants, even for the English. David stood apart, staring through binoculars at the secret, unknown coast.

There was a long pause, of fifteen or twenty minutes; then – strong and clear against the flickering fires – a flashlight winked: one long beam, and then one, two, three short ones. David dropped his glasses, and turned to the skipper.

'All right,' he said. 'Let's go alongside.'

'Are you sure?' asked the skipper. 'There's half a million bucks tied up here. Not to speak of my nerves.'

'Certain,' answered David. 'They're waiting for us.'

'That's what I'm afraid of,' said the skipper. But his hand on the telegraph was ready enough, as he rang for half-speed.

Crump, his white arm-sling gleaming in the darkness, was waiting on the rough wooden jetty, and two of his men, ready to take their lines, and a tall old Maula – the headman Pemboli. The latter bowed as David jumped ashore.

'I greet you,' he said formally. 'You are welcome to my village.'

'Thank you, Chief,' said David.

'Everything's all clear here,' said Crump, in elaboration. 'They know what's happened up at Shebiya, and they don't want to get mixed up in it. Pemboli had a sort of local curfew imposed, long before we arrived.'

'Where's Simpson?'

'Here,' said Simpson. His tall figure loomed up from the darkness at the end of the jetty; light flickered momentarily on the Sten gun slung over his shoulder. 'Strictly according to plan.'

'How was it?'

'Piece of cake … Let's start the unloading.'

Beyond them was a ring of fires, and drifting smoke, and many watchful figures – men, old women, small children aroused from sleep. There was a deep gloom over everything, a waterfront murkiness interwoven with the acrid night-smell of Africa. At first, it seemed like a seaside village in the off-season, unavailable, sulkily private, closed for the duration. But as they began to unload the vehicles and the arms and the stores, men crept towards them, and stood watching, and presently began to help, carrying, hauling, coaxing heavy burdens away from the policemen. It was as if there were some guilt which they had to shrive, and this humble task was the only way to do it.

Everything was ashore, and loaded into the trucks, within half an hour.

To David's surprise, Mrs Loganquist kissed him warmly, by way of goodbye.

'Good hunting, honey,' she said. 'But take care of yourselves, with all those wild animals.'

'Oh, we'll be all right.'

'How about a little drink?'

'No, thank you.'

'OK,' said Mrs Loganquist. She leant towards him – perfumed, slim, a tough wild animal herself. She spoke softly. 'I'm so glad you didn't tell Logey what you're really doing. He has a heart condition.'

As a last farewell, Charlie the steward leant over the rail above them, undeniably swaying, teeth gleaming in an ebony face, and called out: 'Goodbye, Mr Bracken. And give those black bastards hell!'

CHAPTER FOURTEEN

❖

Captain Simpson rode in the first car, the police jeep, with Crump's senior sergeant, a gigantic grey-haired Maula, at the wheel, and ten armed men at his back, and a Union Jack flying oddly and bravely at the jackstaff on the radiator. Crump himself came next, in the biggest troop-carrier, a ponderous three-ton Chevrolet truck, crammed to the roof with thirty men, a dozen drums of petrol and water, most of the stores, and all the ammunition. David Bracken brought up the rear, with the remaining men, in the smaller troop-carrier; he drove it himself, with an eye on the twisting track and the two tail-lights ahead, an ear to the radio, and a rearguard of two Bren-gunners staring behind him, over the sights of their weapons, at the road disappearing into the darkness beyond.

It was midnight when the convoy left Fish Village; their advance was purposefully slow, timed so that they would reach Shebiya four hours later, at first light. But it would have been a slow journey anyway. The track was narrow, winding, and villainously rutted; few cars of any sort had ever attempted the passage that they were making, and their way led through an untamed, invading forest; a forest forced back from the road by a once-yearly tribal clearing operation, made by men with hatchets, long knives, and the driving force of freshly-brewed *kaffir*-beer … Sometimes these traditional men (they were called '*klembuki*' – 'way-makers') had been careless or lazy, missing a corner, giving up in despair before a thicket of trees, interlaced vines, fronded monsters of vegetation fit only for a museum of the unspeakably old.

Sometimes the rains had been busy, washing away a culvert or a poorly drained slope; sometimes the sun, burning day after day for more than a century, had roasted, melted, and ground the surface and the very foundations into a trough of axle-deep, ochre dust.

Now it was night, and the track, such as it was, was theirs. The jeep had its four-wheel drive, and could have gone up the side of a house made of underdone marshmallow; the troop carriers had their power, their double-banked rear tyres and their own ponderous weight to float them through. But the party still faced a heavy assignment. It was murderously hot, even at the low ebb of the night; the heavy trees, the age-old vines, caught and whipped at the cars as they lumbered onwards; swarms of insects, attracted by their headlights, converged upon them, fluttering, stinging, dying by thousands as they hit the lamps and the windshields. The thin crescent moon was no help; it had never penetrated this forest, and it would never do so.

They were all immensely isolated, in the middle of this pitch black, silent, ancient corner of Africa; three cars which must never fail, fifty men who must never falter before the pressing, clinging, foetid barrier, the primeval forest.

They drove towards Shebiya, at a grinding ten miles an hour; and Shebiya was always with them, like the insects and the dust and the pitted road. For what lay ahead of them was part of their ordeal. They were not driving through hell towards a respite. They were driving through the sixth department of Hades towards the seventh. And if they failed on the way, if an engine died or an ambush sprang its trap or the road was finally swallowed by the forest, their several bones would whiten for another year or another century, matching the suspected bones at Shebiya which were their foolish, morbid target.

Over them was an immense arch of sky, purple or deep blue, pricked by the Capricorn stars, stretching north to the Sahara desert, south to the bleak wastes of the Antarctic. But the night sky was rarely seen; the closer canopy of interlaced branches, the creepers, the tendril ropes from tree to tree above their forest pathway – these formed for the most part the only ceiling their eyes could reach. Under it, like insects under stones, wary fish under the sea-wrack, they blindly groped their way forwards.

By arrangement, the convoy halted at three o'clock, the three cars converging into a close-coupled unit as they came to a stop. David lifted his stiff arms from the wheel, scratched at an ankle bitten raw by mosquitoes, and jumped down on to the uneven track. No longer tempered by the wind of their passage, the heat of the forest was like a steamy embrace. Crump and Simpson were waiting for him as he walked forward to the jeep, standing within the rim of the headlights.

'Anything on the radio?' asked Simpson immediately.

'No,' answered David. 'Dead silence. Do you think we ought to try to make contact ourselves?'

Simpson shook his head. 'No, not again. They know well enough what we're doing, down at Port Victoria. The only worthwhile contact would be with Shebiya, and they've been silent for nearly two days now.'

Nearby, there came a murmur of voices from the biggest troop-carrier, the one with a reassuring platoon of thirty men. A few of these policemen now jumped down, to stretch their legs. There was some laughter as one small man tripped over a vine root and rolled away into the bush at the side of the road. But it was fearful laughter; the bush was too close, too avid; the man might be swallowed alive by it, with no more than a grunt of surprise, and never return to their sight.

Crump leant down to scratch at his bare knees, menaced by mosquitoes. From a crouching position he spoke: 'How far have we run? My speedometer hasn't been working for a long time.'

'Twenty-four miles,' answered Simpson. 'About seven to go, and an hour's more darkness. The timing is just right.'

'What's the plan?' asked David.

'We've got seven miles to go,' repeated Simpson, 'and we'll take them slowly.' His tall figure in the headlights seemed to exude strength and efficiency. 'After half an hour, we'll douse our lights, and move forward as quietly and slowly as possible – you could hear a car from two miles away, in this sort of country, on this sort of night, if you're properly alert ... When we get there, we'll make one quick dash for it. You – ' he looked at David, ' – will go straight to the police post. Find out what's happened to it. We had a corporal and four men there. If they're still alive, dig them out and take over the main square of the village. If they're not, stay where you are until we get back. You and I – ' he was now looking at Crump, ' – will sprint straight through, and down the road to the roadblock. We'll take them in the rear, and by surprise. If they fight, we'll shoot it out. If they surrender, we'll bring them back to the police post, and join up with David. Then we'll see what's happened to the Ronalds.'

Crump, who had discovered a tick clinging to his thigh, and had been busy burning it to extinction with a cigarette end, now straightened up.

'That all seems clear.' He was remembering the earlier consultation down at Port Victoria, and being very careful not to trespass upon the naval hierarchy involved in the cutting-out expedition. He felt in his bones that there was much gross and bloody work to be done; soon, it would not matter who was the man at the head of the column – all of them would be fighting for their lives, and splitting both the wounds and the honours equally ... 'But if this is to be our last stop, I think I'll get my chaps to check their weapons.'

'All right,' agreed Simpson. 'But as quietly as you can.'

From nearby a night bird screeched suddenly; further off, a colony of baboons deep in the bush set up a sudden growling and chattering. Crump called his men out from the three cars, marshalled them by the side of the track, and went through a brief arms inspection. The clicking of bolts, the slapping of rifle-stocks, the glint of light on polished barrels, were all reassuring elements in the murderous forest.

Standing apart from this military display, Simpson spoke suddenly. 'Have you done anything like this before?'

'Yes,' said David. 'I have.'

'Good,' rejoined Simpson. 'So have I. But it was a long time ago.'

'Where?' asked David. He was preoccupied and afraid, but he felt that he ought to ask.

'China,' answered Simpson, surprisingly. 'Pirates in the Yangtze Delta.'

'Mine was Italy, near Salerno. Italian *neo-fascisti*. But it's the same thing, really, isn't it?'

'Yes,' said Simpson. 'It's the very same thing.'

At that moment in the black, oppressive forest, they both believed that, with all their hearts. Yellow men in China, tanned romantics in Italy, black warriors in Pharamaul – they were all the same men, the men not on your side, the men who wanted to kill you, tear you into bloody strips. If you got there first, with guns blazing, trigger fingers light and ready as thistledown, you would be alive to talk big about it next morning. If not, not.

Suddenly, swiftly, they plunged through the last uphill mile, towards the dawn that was to show them their target, and the clearing in the jungle that was Shebiya. The pace quickened as the trees thinned; the track widened for them, until they were racing along at the full speed and power of the trucks, in a fierce effort to surprise and to strike. The steady roar and rasp of the three engines seemed to fill the forest; the drivers crouched over the bucking wheels, the armed policemen peered out, ahead and to the side and behind them, their weapons cocked, their fingers ready. Then there was a break in the line of trees, a stretch of smoother track, and the convoy burst out into the open clearing.

The village awoke all round them – men, women, dogs, goats, children, all coming to astonished life; then, just as swiftly, it stiffened into immobility again. The mangy dogs barked once and no more; the men who came running from their huts with spears froze against their doorways; the children stood still in their tracks, staring at the noisy and violent strangers. Light seeped through upon Shebiya; and with the light came guilty scruples, much prudent second-guessing … David's car, the last of the three, veered off sideways towards the police post, while the jeep and the big troop-carrier sped onwards, cutting a swathe through the dew and the spiders' webs, like the first invaders of Africa.

David watched them go, continuing full tilt across the clearing and disappearing down the southern road; he felt the fear of loneliness, but he felt the tautness of anger and decision as well. He brought his truck to a sharp stop, wheels skidding in the yellow dust; his men tumbled down, and turned outwards, as they had been trained to do, daring any human within sight to advance, or retreat, or play them false.

But no one stirred. Especially, at the police post, no one stirred at all; no flag flew, no sentry came forward; the windows in the whitewashed huts were blank. There was a sweet smell of death, a remembered smell, all over the post, all over the village square.

He posted his guards round the clearing, took two men, and walked up the pathway, his Sten gun clenched in his hands. Whatever I find, he thought, it can only make me angrier, and then I can do *anything*.

The two leading cars, the jeep with its Union Jack, the truck with its thirty men, roared onwards, lumbering and bucking like small ships in a twisting sea. Simpson's face was set, his hands ready on the trigger; in the second car, Crump found himself staring this way and that, watchful for ambush, and yet returning always to the road ahead, the downhill road that led to the enemy. Into the leafy forest, the dawn was now creeping; the dawn that showed it green and thick and secret. They ran a racketing mile, then another; their rendezvous could not be long delayed. Suddenly, at a sharp curve of the road, Simpson stood up and pointed wildly, and shouted: '*There they are!*'

There they were. It was a rough encampment, grouped round the fallen tree straddling the road; perfectly sited for an attack from the south, foolishly open to themselves. There were guns – an ancient cannon, two Brens on tripods, something that looked like an old Lewis gun – but the guns were pointing south, the wrong way, and the gunners were asleep, prone upon a circle of beaten grass and trampled earth. Singapore, thought Simpson instantly, clambering down, waving his arm for the advance, sighting and then toppling with a single burst of fire two men who ran out of a hut by the roadside: Singapore – the guns facing the wrong way, strong as Gibraltar to seaward, weak as a kitten for an enemy at their backs.

Crump's big truck stopped, wheel to wheel beside the jeep. The armed policemen jumped out shouting, their eyes rolling.

Other men jumped out – out of trenches, tents, leafy hideaways; men clad in blankets, scraps of forgotten uniforms, loincloths. They blundered forth in sleepy amazement, their eyes turning from the southerly road, whence the attack *must* come, to the innocent approach from their own village, where the scourging enemy stood. Simpson fired again, at a cluster of brave men trying to swing one of the Bren guns round, men who instantly died; Crump charged on foot at the head of his platoon, making for a clump of roughly built huts – the focus of the ambush, the headquarters. A fat man ran out, staring, a pistol in his hand.

'Puero!' shouted Crump, recognizing him. 'Stop where you are!' Puero, the gross, the slow-moving third Regent, faced him for a moment. Then he turned, his eyes squinting wildly. The nearest cover was the bush at the edge of the road, twenty full yards away. He made for it at a swift, snaking run, amazing for a man of his weight.

'Puero!' shouted Crump again.

There was no answer, only frenzied twisting. Crump had the broad back in his sights. He fired, missed, and fired again. Puero dropped, some yards from safety.

From the same hut, another man, smaller, came running. It was Zuva Katsaula, cousin of the chief. He also was armed. He loosed off a wild burst, six shots that whined over their heads. Now it was Simpson's driver, the big Maula sergeant, who fired. Zuva screamed, dropped his gun, cradled a right arm shattered at the elbow. He looked across at the invaders, with pain, sleep, and fear clouding his eyes. He called out: 'I surrender! Prisoner of war!'

The road and the clearing were now full of men, blundering into captivity, their hands above their heads: looking at the dozen corpses sprawled and displayed, they kept carefully aloof from their weapons, and from any taint of defiance. The cordon of police rounded them up, roughly, with free cursing and many blows; as the policemen cuffed and pushed, they barked their hatred of the mutineers, the despised U-Maulas. Presently their prisoners were all herded into a rough corral. There must have been four hundred of them, roused from sleep, shocked by the brief show of force, swiftly quelled, and now fearful and leaderless.

'One missing,' said Crump, glancing round him. 'The one we want.' He turned to the nearest of the prisoners, a thin trembling man. 'Where is Gotwela?'

The man was silent. Crump's Sten gun lowered until it was pointing at the man's stomach. He was breathing heavily, with the effort of running, the pain of his wounded arm, the tension of his anger. 'You know well that I will shoot,' he said, in the Maula tongue. 'Where is that Gotwela?'

The man looked at the gun, and then at his own stomach, his own precious genitals, but he would not speak. This man has taken an oath, thought Crump: he has sworn himself to silence, like any other prisoner of war – like a Yank in Korea, like an Englishman in the Western desert. This man's oath is vile and unspeakable, but it is the same sort of oath … From behind him, from the ranks of the prisoners, came a high and wheedling voice – the voice of Zuva Katsaula.

'Gotwela is in that tent,' said Zuva, pointing. 'He was drunk last night. He sleeps still … I claim my rights under the Geneva Convention.'

Simpson, as hard-breathing as Crump, but sweating and trembling from some inner force, raised his gun. He sighted the top of the tent, six feet from the ground, and fired a swift burst. It collapsed in a heap, the canvas smouldering. Then it heaved, and a man wormed his way out – a fat man, glistening with fresh sweat, naked save for the royal simbara, the lionskin, clasped loosely round his middle. It was Gotwela.

Gotwela blinked in the daylight, blinked at the guns and the new faces, scowled at his followers herded together and helpless, searched for the spears of his bodyguard and found them gone. Then his gross features settled themselves into a sullen cast of indifference. He stood stock still, outside his ruined tent, near the useless guns, out of reach of his defeated men. A policeman came forward to pinion him.

'Now, lionskin,' said the policeman, whose father and grandfather had been policemen, 'keep still, lest I am forced to flay you once more.'

Gotwela, his arms pulled roughly behind his back, spoke at last. He raised his heavy head, and his eyes searched among the corralled prisoners, and at length found Zuva Katsaula. He called out, in deep throaty contempt: '*Hé* – hyena! Did you not tell me that all the Maulas were marching to join us at Shebiya?'

Zuva looked steadily at the sky, and said nothing. It was as if he hoped to contract out of this unwholesome matter.

'You were right, hyena!' said Gotwela, after a pause. 'But you did not tell me they were policemen.'

'That's all!' said Simpson roughly. 'Cut out the bloody crosstalk! ... Now form up, and we'll all go back to the village.'

The long column gradually took shape, drifting into straggling order; Zuva and Gotwela bound with straps, the rest with their hands clasped above their heads. They started to march back to Shebiya, headed by the jeep, tailed by the troop-carrier. They moved slowly, a motley shambling crowd, no longer warriors with guns and spears, clutching their blankets and their shame. The way grew hot as the sun rose, but the prisoners were sweating with more than heat. They were sweating an enormous guilt, over something they had been hiding, something which must now come to light. Brothers in hideous crime, children trapped in a nursery anguish, they trudged back to be confounded by the facts.

Gotwela walked aloof, in fierce silence; Zuva stepped grudgingly, eyeing the protective bush, not daring to make a break for it. But he also must have been carrying in his head unspeakable things – much more than an ambush, more even than shooting with intent to kill. For he called out many times, to anyone who would listen, but principally to the jeep ahead and to the truck behind: 'I am a wounded prisoner of war ... I claim the Geneva Convention.'

II

David Bracken met them at the outer gate of the police-post; a grey-faced, shaken David, fresh from a view of hideous death which had struck him too early in the morning, too early in his life.

Simpson, from the front seat of the leading jeep, called out to him: 'Well?'

David, who had been waiting for a long and lonely hour, looked at him. He looked at the Union Jack, the long dusty line of prisoners with their hands queerly clasped above their heads, the thin ring of policemen pushing and cursing. Then he looked at his own small encampment; the deserted clearing which was Shebiya's main square, the spaced-out circle of his men standing guard, the pale sunlight flooding in to aid the reluctant eye. At his back, he felt penetratingly the police-post, with its bloodstains, its corpses sprawled like unswept rubbish, its sweet-and-sour odour of death. He said: 'Nothing much here … They've all been killed … All five … Probably two days ago … No one seems to know anything …'

The new mass of people before him began to take shape; Crump and his men shoved and herded the four hundred prisoners into the middle of the square, ordered them to squat down in close confinement, placed guards at intervals round the enclave. The dust gradually settled, the scene took on a jumbled order of its own. Simpson, a lone figure of authority, stepped down from the jeep and walked towards David.

'No one *here* knows anything,' he said grimly. 'But they will … Which way is the Ronalds' house?'

'There,' David pointed. 'But it's empty. I sent a policeman across.'

'Let's take another look at it …' Simpson turned, called out to Crump: 'We're going over to the District Officer's house.'

Crump, preoccupied with a knot of prisoners who, from some consideration of prudence or shame, wished to keep themselves apart from their fellows, raised his arm in brief acknowledgement. Leaving the transport and the guards, Simpson and David walked across the clearing to the Ronalds' house.

The small house was deserted, as David had forecast; silence hung over it like a pall – there was no movement, no sign of life, not even the corpses which both of them had feared. They stepped into the living-room, and then into the dining-room, Simpson leading the way. All was in perfect order, innocent, unstained. But just as, down at the road-block, he had thought 'Singapore', now he thought: *'Marie Celeste …'* Nothing was new, in the whole wide world; it was all part of history, all set down within the annals of disaster, on land or on sea.

The dining-room table was laid for three people; and the three people had clearly been snatched away from it without warning. Three sideplates with crumbled bread and butter confronted their eyes; three dusty glasses of water; three sets of knives and forks, still waiting to be used. The three chairs were thrust back from the table. But nothing was in true disorder. It was merely an interrupted meal for three. And not much of a meal, thought David, to die on.

Round them the little shabby house was silent. When they walked through into the kitchen, it was equally deserted. On the centre table was a dish of untouched, congealed curry; on the electric stove, a kettle with its bottom burnt through stood trembling on a red-hot plate. David switched off the heat, the only living thing in the house. When the red eye slowly died, utter silence returned.

'They certainly left in a hurry,' said Simpson.

David, sick at heart, scared of any imaginable future, had a sudden thought. It was inconceivable that within this stricken house there could be any living thing, anyone sharing their solitude, but the thought jolted him none the less. He raised his head, and then his voice: 'Anyone there?' he called.

Simpson said: 'Don't waste your time.'

'Anyone there?' David called again. And then, remembering: 'Samson ... Samson!'

Breaking the long deadly silence, above their heads, a beam or a floorboard creaked.

'Samson!' called David urgently, as if he were clairvoyant. 'Come down ... You remember me ... Mr Bracken. Samson ... Come down to us ...'

In the meagre hallway, set between the kitchen and the living room, a board creaked again. Quickly they walked through, and inevitably looked upwards. They looked up at the trapdoor into the roof – a trapdoor which now moved painfully aside.

'All right, Samson,' said David. 'You are safe now ... Come down ...'

In the gulf of darkness behind the trapdoor, a darker shadow moved. It took on the outlines of a black face – terrified, filthy, creased with fear and want. The small man who presently dropped through, and stumbled, and crouched by their side, was a grisly satire upon humanity.

It was Samson, the Ronalds' servant; a Samson grotesquely reduced by fear, his white suit creased and cobwebbed, his trousers stained with urine. He stood between them, bent nearly double with the stiffness of long concealment; his face was still consumed with panic, his tongue speechless.

'Christ!' said Simpson. And then: 'How long have you been hiding up there?'

In the grey-black face, the mouth opened; the tongue licked the lips, below a pair of eyes frenzied and livid. Samson spoke at last, whispering in the cracked voice of terror and extremity: 'Two day, *barena*.'

'Christ!' repeated Simpson. 'What happened?'

The syllables came slowly, as if sieved and extruded through pain. 'I ran away ... I came back.'

'But why did you run away?'

Samson opened his mouth to speak a third time, but he had expended already his brand new, miraculous quota of words. He rocked backwards, and collapsed silently at their feet.

'That's all we want to know,' said Simpson. 'The police will take care of him ... Now it's someone else's turn.'

'Give me a knife,' said Simpson, without emphasis; and when the tall Maula sergeant handed him an open clasp-knife, he brought the blade down to within an inch of Zuva's eye. The blade was steady, while the eye underneath it blinked wildly, and the pinioned man sought to writhe away, in a foretaste of agony. To the watchers, it seemed that the blade must within a moment penetrate and gouge the soft target. 'I will take your eye, and then your tongue, and then your balls, and then your life,' said Simpson, scarcely more than conversationally. 'Tell me what happened to the Ronalds.'

'I do not know,' said Zuva. He was in an extremity of terror, as well he might be. 'I have told you … I was not here …'

'You were here,' said Simpson.

'I took no part.'

Simpson advanced the knife a fraction of an inch. 'No part in what?'

'I took no part.'

'Are they dead?'

Zuva squinted up at the knife, and then beyond it to Simpson's pale, granite face. He strained back against his bonds, and the policeman holding him wrenched him upright again. The knife closed in, until it touched the very casing of the eyeball. Zuva screamed; a spray of sweat burst from his head and his neck.

'I took no part …' he panted. 'It was true I was here, but I took no part.'

'Are they dead?'

'Yes.'

Simpson caught his breath back, trembling; hearing the answer, he had been within an ace of plunging and twisting the knife, but he could not do it, even in hot blood. From the circle of men watching – David, Keith Crump, the sergeant, four or five policemen – came an echoing sigh;

they had heard what they feared to hear, they had found what they came to Shebiya to find. There seemed nothing else to do now … Simpson stepped back a pace, balancing the knife in his open hand. He stared at Zuva with a malevolent intensity. He said: 'Now that you have talked, talk some more … Where are they?'

'In the forest.'

'Whereabouts in the forest?'

Zuva hesitated. 'It is difficult – ' he began.

'*Don't give me that*!' Simpson suddenly roared, wildly angry, 'Or I'll kick your skull in …' He dropped the clasp-knife into his left hand, and with the right dealt Zuva a brutal slap on the side of his face. 'Tell me everything,' he shouted, 'or I will kill you now!'

Zuva's head fell to one side; the heavy blow had numbed his wits. When he spoke, it was more slowly.

'A half-mile from here,' he said. 'To the north. There is a clearing, a meeting place.'

'Who was killed there? Both the Ronalds?'

'Yes … And the priest.'

'What priest?'

'The small priest – Father Schwemmer, I think he is called.'

'Who killed them?'

Zuva raised his head, looking fearfully about him. 'Many people.'

'Who?'

'All the tribe.'

'Who was the leader?'

'There was no leader.'

Crump suddenly stepped forward. He wore the same expression as Simpson, tense, malignant, consumed by hatred and anger. He pushed Zuva roughly in the chest.

'I know all your secrets,' he said grimly. 'I know you have taken the oath, the filthy oath. But the oath will not save you. Nothing will save you. Look at the other people who have taken the oath. They are prisoners, and if they are murderers they will surely die. Some of them have died already. Puero, the false Regent, has died like a dog ... Who was the leader?'

Zuva looked past him, to where Gotwela sat on the rough ground.

'That man was the leader,' he said finally.

'Gotwela?'

'Gotwela.'

'How did they die?'

Zuva's eyes turned from the man he had betrayed, to the man who was questioning him. Suddenly, he was very small and very still, retreating into the protection of his skin.

'They died in different ways,' he said at last, with difficulty. And then: 'I am your prisoner ... I claim sanctuary.'

'Who saw them die?'

'All the tribe.'

Crump gestured behind him, at the prisoners sitting in their dusty open cage under the burning sun. 'All these?'

'Yes ... And all the tribe besides.'

'The women?'

'Yes.'

Simpson spoke. 'You were asked how they died, Zuva ... How did they die?'

Zuva looked at his feet. 'I cannot describe ... I cannot tell you in words ... But Gotwela was the leader, all the time.'

'What is this meeting place called, where they died?'

'Calavaree.'

'What?' said Simpson, startled by a faint ring of familiarity.

'Calavaree ... It is something in the lore of the tribe ... But that man was the leader.'

'Gotwela!' called Simpson loudly.

Gotwela turned his head.

'Get up,' ordered Simpson. 'We are going on a short journey ... You too,' he added to Zuva.

'I claim the protection – ' began Zuva.

'You too,' repeated Simpson. He turned to Crump. 'And all the prisoners, and any of the tribespeople you can round up. Form them into a column, the same as we marched them back from the roadblock. They're all going to take a second look at what they've done ... Gotwela!' he called again.

Gotwela, who was now standing, slumped between his two guards, raised his eyes. They were empty, expressionless, doomed.

'You will lead us,' said Simpson. 'Lead us all on the path to Calavaree.'

It was not a clear path, the path to Calavaree; it lay uphill for the most part, a track wandering at will through the same kind of jungle foliage which had led them from Fish Village to Shebiya. The column that now filled it was a long one; Gotwela headed it, with Zuva a few paces behind him; then came their guards; then some other village notables – the headmen, the witch-doctors, the cousins and heirs of Gotwela; then the jeep, the focal turret of strength; then the long file of prisoners; then the police, grim-faced, baleful, inexorable.

It was a long column, and it moved slowly; partly because of the difficulty of the way, which was not much trodden; partly because of the heat, pressing heavily at the approach of noon; partly because Gotwela and Zuva at the head, and the tribespeople behind, walked with the slow steps of men keeping a reluctant rendezvous with death. They knew what Simpson, and Crump, and David Bracken, and the policemen, did not yet know; they knew what they were going to find at the end of the journey. Their slow steps were the measure of their guilt, and their guilt was enormous.

Crump walked with the rearguard, the cream of his policemen; Simpson and David drove in the jeep, and the jeep's was the only noise in all the long column. The forest was silent; there was a constant brushing of undergrowth, a slurring of hundreds of feet on the dusty road, but there were no voices, and no other sounds. Both of them were preoccupied with their own thoughts; Simpson with the conduct of the operation – what he had done so far, what he might have left out, what could go wrong; and David with what they were going to find, when they reached their goal.

For him, the inside of the police post had been horrible – not because of the corpses, which were nothing new to a soldier who had seen war, but because of the barbarous, wanton carelessness with which the five policemen had been hacked to death and then left where they fell. He feared far worse things, and he did not want to see them, because he already knew what man, the most cruel animal, could do to man if he felt like it.

The column moved on, slowly, painfully. There were women in it now, trudging and shuffling alongside their menfolk; and others – men and women – were moving parallel to them in the forest, keeping clear of the track, which was evil, but compelled to be part of the pilgrimage. On all the triggers of all the guns – Simpson's, Crump's, the policemen's – fingers were crooked ready; but it was a formal readiness, because no one in this tribe would resist, or betray, or fight, for a very long time. They had had their happiest day, and this was merely the wan sunset of it.

Once more the trees began to thin, and the sun to burn hotter as the shade was left behind. They turned the last corner, and mounted the last slope of the hill. Gotwela slowed his stride, Zuva faltered and fell back another pace, trembling. Then they were in the open, the place of Calavaree.

It was a cleared space of a hundred feet square, and they filtered out upon it like players on a huge operatic stage, gathered for the last act. For a moment, black and white alike, they were not looking at what it contained; and then the range shortened, the focus grew sharp, and they were all looking.

Three human bodies, and two animal, were in the clearing; dead for two days in burning heat, they had lost the sharp outlines of life and were bloated and misshapen, but they were still to be recognized. Two of them were Tom and Cynthia Ronald, lying staring at the sky. The third was Father Schwemmer. The two animals were goats.

There was no discernible mark on Tom Ronald. He lay back naked, as if at rest, his strong legs splayed out on either side. The dark stains on the ground, the furious current of ants and flies, indicated that he had bled to death. From between his legs, white and yellow entrails flowed, like tentacles beneath the sea.

Cynthia Ronald lay in the same position, naked also, her legs splayed out for a different reason. Clearly she had died from the repeated impact of men upon her body, and they had left a sign manual of this. There protruded from between her legs a curious implement – a kind of spike, of dull unwrought yellow metal, narrowing at the entrance, blunted at the outer end, forced home and left in place like the staking of a claim.

Father Schwemmer hung skeleton-thin from a cross, in the classic attitude of agony. His body was less clear, less actual than the others; much of it hung in strips and tatters, as if many men had had their will of it with knives, purloining the flesh. On either side of his crude yellow-wood cross – seemingly according to some much older ritual – were two smaller crosses bearing, spread-eagled, two goats. The three crosses crowned with thorns the hill of Calavaree.

Crump, whey-faced, muttered: 'Christ Almighty!' David's stomach heaved; he turned aside and vomited, and then faced the fearful sight again, with stony determination. Within the circle, Gotwela and Zuva stood like cast statues; at their backs, the U-Maulas formed a guilty and infected ring, looking down steadfastly at their feet.

Simpson, the leader, stood alone, nearest the crosses and the bodies. His face was working violently, with pity and horror; there were tears wet on his cheeks, but they were not trustworthy tears – they could have been the tears of uncontrollable fury. When he had looked his fill, he turned back from the crest of the hill; and then, as if cutting many corners, forgetting many laws, he pointed a shaking finger at Gotwela, and said: 'Call your people.'

III

It was a happy lunch party, because the three of them were old friends, and the Ronalds were in love with each other, and Father Schwemmer always felt his spirits lifted, his faith renewed, when he visited this simple and contented household. While they drank their soup, they talked of the habitual things; the small changes in Shebiya since Father Schwemmer had paid his last call; the repairs to the mission house, now under way after long delay; and the child that was to be born some time next winter.

'I am so happy for you,' said Father Schwemmer. 'It will be a fine child, a boy. And you deserve it.'

'Why do we deserve it, Father?' asked Cynthia Ronald.

'Because you have married a good man,' answered Father Schwemmer readily, 'and the boy will have a good home.'

'Probably be a girl,' said Tom Ronald morosely. 'Ugly as sin, and rude to its mother.'

'Whatever it is,' said Cynthia, smiling, 'it will be ours.'

'Undoubtedly,' said Tom.

Father Schwemmer, watching the two of them, smiled also. His old face reflected their happiness – a domestic contentment he scarcely comprehended, but a wonderful thing in the world. 'What are you going to call it?'

Samson, the houseboy, came in, in answer to the bell, collected the soup plates, and went out again to the kitchen.

'We haven't really settled on a name,' answered Cynthia. 'There are so many to choose from, and we've both got loads of relatives too.'

They talked of names for a few moments, waiting for the next course. The rest of the house was silent; outside, in the garden, the midday sun burned relentlessly. Presently Tom broke off, and said: 'I say, old girl, are we getting anything to eat today?'

'Sorry, darling,' said Cynthia. 'It's curry, and you know how Samson – ' There was a vague noise in the kitchen passage, and she said: 'Here it is, anyway.'

But it was not Samson, nor the curry. It was a rush of padding feet, a dozen or more, and the bursting in of the door. Tom, who had his back turned, said angrily: 'Samson – what the hell? – ' and then he saw the horror in his wife's eyes, and the astonishment in Father Schwemmer's. He swung round, but the club hit him on the side of the head before he could rise, and he swayed and dropped to the floor.

'Darling!' screamed Cynthia.

The room was suddenly full of men – tall U-Maulas, half-naked, sweating, their faces set, their eyes glassy with alcohol. There was a high scream from the kitchen, and the sound of frenzied running down the garden path. Tom Ronald, regaining his senses briefly, muttered 'Shotgun – bedroom – ' but it was a foolish thought, with nothing to back it. The bedroom might have been a full mile away ... A man stood over Father Schwemmer with a menacing club; another man had wrapped his arms tight round Cynthia Ronald, in a revolting gesture somewhere between imprisonment and rape.

Father Schwemmer, an old man, said: 'God forgive you – what are you doing? Are you mad?' He made a trembling effort to rise, and the club came down, like a gentle tap on an eggshell, and he too fell to the floor. Cynthia screamed again as the man hugging her began to rub his heated groin against her thigh. The leader, a man known to them all as one of the headmen, laughed aloud at the sight, and said: '*Hé* – wait your turn!' and then, formally: 'Bind them all, and lead them out to the people.'

In the place called Calavaree, all was done in due order, although many of those taking part were far gone in liquor, having primed their spirits and their courage with a *bariaana* brew that had lain buried for many weeks. The three crosses had already been cut under the direction of the head priest who administered the old customs; one of them was large, and would occupy the place of honour in the middle, the other two were small and mean, fit only to bear the bodies of the 'thieves' – for so the sacrificial goats were named from long ago.

The turf round the crosses had been marked out in the semblance of a huge fish, and brushwood burned in a long shallow trench, so that the fish-emblem stood out, blackened and clear to all eyes, branded upon the living earth. Round the edge of this, the men and women of the

tribe were drawn up; at the centre, the oathtakers of the
first grade were waiting, thirty or forty men chosen for
their strength and courage. Standing apart in the forefront
were Gotwela, Puero, and Zuva.

There was a mounting roar as the promised prisoners
approached; for though this was a holy moment, yet it
contained the seeds of hatred and revenge, for which all
had waited for so long.

The old white priest shambled forward, half carried by
his guards; the girl strode proudly, looking at no one; the
man who had been the great man of authority walked
behind her, clasping a hand to the wound in his head.
When all were assembled, Gotwela stepped forward.

'The girl first,' he said briefly, as if further delay would
irk him. 'Before all the tribe, we will take the oath again –
the oath through the fish.' He looked at the girl with
glistening eyes. 'But today we have a live fish … Then I,
Keeper of the Golden Nail, will follow the custom and set
the mark of the U-Maulas upon her.'

At a sign the girl was stripped naked and thrown upon
the ground; the old white priest turned his eyes away,
while the man who had been married to her strained at his
bonds, and shouted and screamed in agony. Four men
stretched her out on the ground, like a white star; one man
to each hand, one to each foot. Other men, awaiting their
turn, fondled her breasts and the slim lines of her body,
while Gotwela the chief freed himself from his lionskin,
and threw himself down with heaving flanks.

He spent a long time upon the girl, because he was the
chief, and a man still in his lusty prime, and he enjoyed
women as he enjoyed food and drink. He ended with a
bellow of triumph that seemed to fill the forest. Those
watching laughed and stamped their feet; from the
containing edge of the fish, other lesser men sought to run
forward, but were forced back again by the spears of the

royal guard. Puero, whose eyes had become glazed as he watched, took the place of Gotwela.

The girl screamed many times, and clenched her body, and bit at her tormentors, but presently – after fat Puero, and Zuva who was quick and slim as a snake, and the head priests, and all the headmen, and another man who, wild as a bull, dived upon her body like a runner into a pool – after they had all enjoyed her, she grew faint, and lost her strength, and lay like a dead body on the ground. The old white priest moaned and prayed; the white man who had lost his authority and his wife cursed and shouted as if he were mad. But all around them the U-Maulas, men and women, watched their rulers proving their manhood through this living white fish, and stamped their feet rhythmically, and roared and shrieked their approval.

The thirtieth man rose from the girl. He looked at Gotwela, shaking his head.

'There is no life there,' he reported.

A priest came forward, to examine the girl, for the strongest magic would disappear if the girl were dead. He rebuked a man who was kneading her breasts, and another who was preparing to enjoy her. He said: 'It is true – the magic is gone. It is time for the Golden Nail.'

From its cover of white and fawn springbok skins, Gotwela the chief took the emblem of the Golden Nail – a huge spike of solid gold, hallowed by the ages, and won from the Maulas of Gamate more than fifty years ago. It was said that the chief of those Maulas still called himself, foolishly, 'Keeper of the Golden Nail', but the true Nail itself was here in Shebiya, and its strength belonged to the U-Maulas alone.

The old white priest had fainted, but the man who had been married still howled and raged as he watched. The ceremony of the Golden Nail was brief and quick, in accordance with the custom. The girl opened her eyes at the very end, so that she was not quite dead when the Nail entered her body, driven home by lusty strokes. But then she died.

Now that they had fulfilled their manhood, it was time for a special ceremony of dedication. The head priest told them again, as he had explained many times earlier, that it was the entrail drawn from a living man which must be used – a small piece, perhaps only a foot or two, but the man who gave it must be living. The white man of authority had gone out of his mind, and struggled so violently that he had to be cuffed and pounded by many hands until he was still; then the head priest produced from his robes the appointed instrument – a long peeled wand, forked at the end like the stick used for killing a snake.

With strong thrusts it penetrated the man's body from behind, and was twisted, and drawn down again. The first two times, though the white man screamed hideously, the stick came out unencumbered; then it took firm hold of the entrail, and this was drawn forth. While it was being drawn forth, the man still lived; but when it was cut he died.

Yet it was proper to say that the entrail drawn out was a living entrail; and when it had been pounded into a paste, and mixed with the blood of the goats, and the gourd passed from hand to hand, the oath-takers drank with the thirst of lions.

Father Schwemmer had prayed for unconsciousness, and even for death; and the sin of such a prayer was visited upon him promptly. He awoke to find himself in full possession of his eyes and ears, seeing all things with deadly clarity, including the manner of his death.

They guided him forward between the bodies of Cynthia and Tom Ronald, while the oath-takers pressed nearer, and the crowds lining the sides of the fish-emblem fell silent. They used no force upon the old man, because he knew what was to happen, and was compliant; indeed, he lay down upon the cross unasked, and stretched out his hands to suffer the nails as if his hands were now to receive what they had been born for … The priests chanted, in time with the pounding of the wooden mallets; the crowds sang, and knelt as they had been taught, and sang again; presently the cross was raised up, and on either side of it the two smaller crosses with the two 'thieves' – the goats that were also dying.

Father Schwemmer knew a cruel moment of agony as his hands and feet, pierced with rough-cut wooden pegs, took the weight of his body; then his mind clouded over, and he began to die.

Below him, like a tide washing round his pierced feet, the chanting went on, while the crowds, now released, walked to and fro, and men looked sideways at Cynthia Ronald, and laughed, and directly at Tom Ronald, and sneered. Above them, his head sunk on his chest, his old mind wandering, Father Schwemmer mumbled to himself a quotation which had been his favourite for fifty years, and now was coming to fresh birth: 'We owe God a death … He that pays this year is quit for the next …'

For a long time he could not die, though the sun beat mercilessly on his head and shoulders, and his thirst was terrible. But towards sundown he felt himself slipping away, and he turned his head briefly, looking at the two spreadeagled goats on either side of him, and he said in agony and delirium, fulfilling his own Scriptures: '*Heute noch wirst Du mit mir im Paradiese sein.*' It was then about the ninth hour. And when he had said this, he gave up the ghost.

When he was quite dead, the head priest took command again, and directed the cutting and sharing of the body. Not only the oath-takers, but all the tribe of U-Maulas, now gathered close; the small slices of flesh were passed round, and they spoke the hallowed words which had come down to them from misty times: '*Eat this in remembrance of me.*' They had long been taught that this was the very strongest part of the magic, and as they ate they bobbed and bowed to each other, and the priests chanted. When all had partaken, Gotwela strode forward, in full and gross manhood, the chief who was now far more than a chief, having taken his oath within the girl-fish, and drunk the goat's blood with the living entrail, and eaten the flesh before the whole tribe, and said: 'The ceremony is over. Now we are all brothers, and no one can be stronger than the U-Maula men of Shebiya. Tomorrow we march. But tonight – ' he grinned, swaggering, meeting their ready shouts and laughter, ' – tonight we feast, and drink, and enjoy the first fruits of victory.'

IV

'Call your people,' said Captain Simpson. With a rough and impatient hand he wiped away the tears from his cheeks; but it was the gesture of an iron man, and his eyes burned terribly as he looked at Gotwela.

'My people are here,' answered Gotwela indifferently.

'Call *all* your people,' said Simpson. His voice was shaking, but no one who heard it could have thought it the shaking of weakness. 'There are many in the forest nearby – ' he looked beyond them at the ring of trees, where here and there a face or a figure was to be seen, peering briefly from the shadows. 'Call them.'

'How shall I call them?' asked Gotwela, on a surly note of protest.

'We are your prisoners of war,' said Zuva, chiming in. His voice was higher, like a woman far gone in fear. 'You cannot force us – '

Simpson moved forward swiftly. The gun in his hand was trembling, but, once more, no one would have mistaken it for the trembling of a weak man. With the blunt muzzle of his revolver he prised open Gotwela's mouth, and forced the gun within. 'Call your people,' he said again, thickly, 'while you still have a tongue to call with.'

He withdrew the gun muzzle, wet and cloudy, and Gotwela swallowed. But he raised his voice: 'Come out,' he said, speaking towards the margin of the forest. 'Draw near.'

'Louder,' said Simpson.

'Come out!' repeated Gotwela. 'Draw near me!'

'Louder,' said Simpson.

'COME OUT!' said Gotwela, for the third time. He turned his head, shouting at the blank forest. 'DRAW NEAR!'

He repeated it many times, an eerie sound of command against the wall of the trees; and presently men and women began to flock fearfully out of the forest, closing their ranks with the prisoners who were already there. Insistently Simpson prodded Gotwela in the throat with the revolver, making him repeat the call again and again; David stared steadfastly at the cross; Crump looked down at his feet. This was all wrong, thought Crump, the police captain; but after all Simpson was in command … He himself had been very fond of the Ronalds … Father Schwemmer had been an old friend … It was all wrong, the things that were happening and the thing that was going to happen, but he could not bring himself to interfere, neither as a policeman nor as a man …

Presently the whole clearing was filled with people, edging forwards, overrunning and obliterating the burnt marks of the fish, surrounding the bodies and the crosses.

There must have been two thousand of them, staring, trembling, not uttering a sound. Captain Simpson, who had lost none of his sweating exaltation of rage, looked towards Crump.

'Translate for me,' he commanded. And then, turning to the main body of the people: 'Look now at what you have done!'

Crump raised his voice, and repeated the words in the U-Maula tongue. Every eye was focused obediently and fearfully on the bodies.

'It is the fault of all of you,' continued Simpson. David watched him, amazed; it was hard to identify this grim and avenging man with the hearty, gin-sipping naval aide he had known for the last few months ... 'You are vultures ... You are all guilty ... But the men most guilty are these two men.'

There was utter silence as Crump repeated the words.

'All those who are guilty will be tried,' said Simpson. 'But these two, the leaders – ' he gestured with his revolver, ' – will never be tried. The law is too slow for criminals such as these.'

All eyes were upon him now.

'You!' shouted Simpson suddenly, pointing at the nearest group of men. 'Come here!'

Five or six men stepped forward, slowly and unwillingly.

'Cover them up,' said Simpson, in the same loud voice, pointing at Tom and Cynthia Ronald. And as the men hesitated, not knowing how to obey, Simpson said 'God damn you! ... Take off your blankets ... Cover these two ...'

The bodies were quickly covered.

'Now take him down,' said Simpson, pointing at the torn body of Father Schwemmer.

It took some time to do this. The Descent from the Cross, thought David, viewing with horror the lolling corpse as it was lowered slowly from its cruel fastenings. Like Crump, he knew what was going to happen, as soon as this was all done, but he had not the smallest wish to arrest it.

The body of Father Schwemmer presently rested on the ground, covered by a blanket. Now the three shapes were ranged in the sunlight, decently hidden, restoring some order to the fearful scene. The air was the cleaner for it, but not yet clean enough.

In the silence, in the middle of the huge crowd, the click of Simpson's revolver was the loudest sound ever heard in the forest.

Simpson turned sideways to Crump. 'You can take a walk, if you like,' he said. It was as if he were talking in his sleep. 'This is my show ... If you hear a shot, it just means that my gun is in working order.'

Crump looked at him levelly, preserving his own discipline, abdicating the rest. 'I'm staying,' he said. 'You may be sorry afterwards ... But you know what you're doing ...'

'I shall never be sorry,' said Simpson, 'as long as I live. David?'

'I'm staying,' said David.

Simpson turned again. In the deadly silence, against the beating of a thousand hearts, he walked towards Gotwela and Zuva. 'You are murderers,' he said. 'Kneel down.'

Gotwela, sullen and resigned, obeyed without seeming to hear. Zuva also fell on his knees, but his was the attitude of agonized prayer, and as he knelt he twisted his body round towards Simpson, and screamed at him: 'You can't do this ... It is contrary to all law ... I demand a fair trial ...'

'A fair trial would condemn you to death, and you would be hanged,' said Simpson, in the same sleepwalking voice. 'Perhaps six months from now ... But you are not going to live so long. Turn round. Look up. Look at the cross.'

Gotwela's head was sunk on his chest, and his huge body was slack. By his side, Zuva still screamed and clasped his hands, and a babble of words poured from his lips. 'Democratic rights,' he mouthed, as if reciting a charm. 'Prisoners of war ... The Geneva Convention ...'

'Translate,' said Simpson again, looking up at the sky. And then, to those watching in terror: 'These two men, who were your leaders, are murderers ... Remember this moment, because it is a moment of swift justice ... You all know that they have killed a priest – ' he pointed down at the blanketed corpses, ' – and the District Officer, and his wife ... *Do any of you think that I will let them live?*'

Crump's voice as he translated was less taut, less filled with rage, but firm as a rock none the less.

'They are hereby condemned to death,' said Simpson. 'They are hereby executed.' His head came down, the revolver came up. Crump was still translating as the two shots rang out.

CHAPTER FIFTEEN

❖

The plane, a shabby old Dakota, bumped twice in the noonday heat, then settled down on its steady course, due east for Windhoek, and thence for Livingstone in Northern Rhodesia. The navigator, chewing on a sandwich, mumbled into his microphone: 'Port Victoria Tower – Port Victoria Tower – GAKC airborne – course oh-nine-oh for Windhoek – ETA fifteen hundred hours,' and then (in defiance of the regulations) switched off his radio. The pilot checked their altitude, set the automatic controls, and sat back in his seat, hands clasped behind his head. Another routine trip, Pharamaul to the mainland, was under way.

But this time it was not quite a routine trip, the pilot mused, glancing briefly downwards and to his left, where the eastern coastline of Pharamaul was already slipping away astern of them. For this was an official charter party, no less, with a secret take-off time and top Government priority; the plane reserved for Dinamaula, and the chap who was bear-leading him back to England. No other passengers allowed, no freight, above all no Pressmen ... It must have been an expensive job, to commandeer the whole plane, and throw a dozen fare-paying customers off it. Big deal, the pilot thought sourly: excuse my expense account … But presumably it was worth it, if only to make sure that Dinamaula got away without an uproar.

The pilot glanced behind him, through the open door into the main passenger space. Dinamaula, sitting by himself, was staring out of the nearest window; the man in charge of him also sat alone, across the aisle, reading some papers. Chummy little gathering. The pilot turned his head slightly, to wink at the navigator, and got an answering grin. The same thought had struck them both: that Dinamaula and his official guard weren't very likely to start chatting away like bosom pals, either now or at any other time on the flight to England. For one of them was being chucked out, and the other was the trigger-man.

Dinamaula had no thoughts, as he stared out of the plane window at Pharamaul's vanishing coastline, and the cloud-mottled grey surface of the South Atlantic; not even the bitter thoughts of an expatriate, not even the foreboding of a prisoner. This had been his mood for a long time now – a sort of emptiness of spirit and will – and he was carrying his vacuum with him into exile. Nothing had happened to him for many weeks past, while he had lain in his guarded lodgings at Port Victoria; there had been no sort of climax or crisis before he left; even the actual leaving of his homeland had been featureless.

Twenty-four hours later, in London, he was to read in the *Daily Thresh* that 'ten thousand loyal tribesmen stamped and wept, as their beloved chief was snatched away like a branded criminal'. But in sober fact no one had seen him off at Port Victoria, since no one save three or four Government House officials had known for certain that he was leaving.

He did not want to look back at Pharamaul; he did not want to feel anything; he did not want to think at all. For him, the last few months had been wholly pointless, and it was right that this moment should match them precisely.

He had come to Pharamaul with bright hope, stayed briefly and unhappily, and been ordered to leave. He was numbed, not by pain or grief or anger, but by the abject nothingness that pervaded his spirit.

He was looking down at the blank sea, because it was the thing nearest in view, the only available feature. He did not want to look inwards, anywhere within the plane, because the only feature *there* was David Bracken, and he did not wish to see any other human being, and David Bracken least of all, because Bracken was the man who held his leash.

David Bracken had many thoughts, almost too many to contain in one brain at one time; perhaps he had all the thoughts which Dinamaula did not have, as well as all his own ... Though it had happened a full week ago, the shock of Shebiya was still with him; his dreams at night had a disgusting clarity, his thoughts by day were loathsome and tainted. Indeed, there had been times during the past week when he had been obsessed by a physical revulsion against all black men, so that even the trusted Maula policemen at Gamate, or the ancient servants at Government House, were all lumped together in his mind as murderers, sexual fiends, deadly enemies. The task of acting as 'Conducting Officer' to Dinamaula had seemed grotesque and deeply offensive for that very reason, though now that the thing was in train, he simply wanted to discharge it smoothly, without mistakes or complications. But he did not specially want to talk to Dinamaula, lately head of that barbarous tribe.

The immediate past had been full of incident, and of work which came as a relief from thought. The journey down from Shebiya, where Simpson and Crump had been left behind to restore order and separate the true criminals from their hapless followers, had been swift; within half a day David had been back at Gamate – a Gamate sullen but quiet, resting firmly upon a brusque military rule. For now there were soldiers everywhere: standing guard on Government buildings, clamping down on meetings, enforcing strict curfew, patrolling at night – and also shaving in the open air while stripped to the waist, peeling potatoes, brewing tea, and spoiling all the children.

Their red sweating faces and honest, nasal Lancashire accents could now be seen and heard all over Gamate, as homely and reassuring as the police on a Liverpool street corner. On the night of their arrival there had been one minor riot on the *aboura* ground, swiftly and bloodily quelled, followed by a vast, night-long round-up of prisoners and suspects. After that, there had been nothing but good behaviour, the length and breadth of the town.

In Gamate, also, had been the assembled Press; and to them, David had given the first eye-witness account of what had happened up at Shebiya. He had told his story simply, with nothing left out, allowing the ghastly detail to have its effect; it was as if he were speaking from a raw, bruised memory which was still photographically clear. He did not say 'I told you so', nor even infer it; there was no fun in being right, when the cost was Cynthia Ronald and all the others … When he had finished, the questions were few, and markedly subdued.

'Can we get any photographs?' asked Clandestine Lebourget. 'People ought to see this.'

'I agree with you,' said David, from his position at the head of the table on the Residency *stoep*. 'But they've all been buried, and the crosses have been burned. There's really nothing left to photograph.'

'Can *we* go up?' asked Tulbach Browne.

'No,' answered David.

'Why not?' asked Axel Hallmarck.

Forsdick, the acting Resident Commissioner, sitting at David's side, answered for him.

'The whole Shebiya area has been closed off,' he said abruptly. 'Military precaution ... We're not allowing anyone in, till things are back to normal.'

'That's pretty high-handed,' said Tulbach Browne querulously. 'How do we know – '

'For Christ's sake!' broke in David, in a sudden blind rage. 'Can't you leave it alone, even now? The Ronalds and Father Schwemmer have been murdered, in this hideous way. The police are rounding up all the people responsible, and trying to make some sense out of the place. We don't want anyone or anything to get in the way of that process.'

In the pause that followed, David took a fresh grip on himself. It was beyond doubt that Shebiya must be isolated, until its guilt had been purged and its evil nature disinfected; but, to be absolutely fair, no one who had not seen the things that had happened there could be expected to appreciate their implications ... He had said nothing in detail about the execution of Gotwela and Zuva; he carried in his head the wording of Simpson's official report, the version they had jointly agreed to stick to: *Total casualties at the recapture of Shebiya were twenty – four U-Maula dead, including the three ringleaders – Gotwela, Puero, and Zuva.* Perhaps the true story would all come out one day, perhaps it would simply pass into tribal legend, and be lost to the censorious world ... When he had left the village, Shebiya had not been talkative, on that or any other topic.

The voice of Father Hawthorne broke in on his thoughts. The priest, his white cassock tastefully arranged over his knees, was leaning forward, a look of honest perplexity on his face.

'What I cannot understand,' he intoned, as if wrestling with a lowbrow devil, 'is the – er – unfortunate death of Father Schwemmer. That gentle, saintly man ...' He raised his clasped hands; it had always looked wonderful on television. 'You mean that they actually crucified him?'

'Yes,' said David.

'A deed of madness!' exclaimed Father Hawthorne. 'Those poor, misguided children!'

David looked at him. 'Yes, indeed. Misguided, *greedy* children.'

'What do you mean by "greedy", Mr Bracken?'

'I should have told you that they ate him as well.'

That had been the end of the Press conference.

Now the navigator walked back, down the aisle of the gently rocking plane.

'We're coming down for Windhoek, in South-West,' he said, speaking impartially to both David Bracken and Dinamaula. 'We've just got to fuel-up – take about ten minutes – and then we'll push on to Livingstone.'

'Thank you,' said David.

'You can stay on board,' said the navigator, 'or have a stroll around on shore, whichever you like.'

For the first time, David looked directly at Dinamaula, and their eyes met.

'Whichever you like,' said David, repeating the navigator's words. There was no change in the passive mask of Dinamaula's face. He did not care much either way, but he was remembering that Windhoek was virtually South African territory, and recalling his last visit there, when he had been roughly directed to the fly-blown cubbyhole labelled 'Non-European Lounge'.

'I would prefer to remain on board,' he answered, briefly and coldly.

'All right,' said David, and nodded to the navigator. 'We'll stay where we are.' He turned away from Dinamaula again, his palms suddenly sweating. To himself, he thought: *Bloody-minded bastard – the way you feel about me is nothing to the way I feel about you.*

After Windhoek it grew hotter, and the plane bumped and lurched without respite as it weaved its swift way into the heart of Africa. Their course was now north-east, across the seven hundred miles of barren scrub that separated them from Livingstone, where they would catch the London plane. Dinamaula still stared out of his window, preserving alike his silence and his indifference; below him, the grey of the sea had given place to the brown wilderness that was the northern edge of the Kalahari Desert.

There were dried-out watercourses, huge tracts of greenish swamp, stunted bush, dusty pathways leading from one hill to the next, hundreds of miles of ruffled yellow sand – all the arid defeat of nature that made up Northern Bechuanaland. It unrolled below him like an endless scorched ribbon, negative and worthless – a waste-product of Africa. But it was not more empty or more barren than his thoughts.

Out of the corner of his eye he saw that David Bracken was reading. He put his hand over his brow, shutting out the sunlight, and tried to sleep.

David Bracken was not reading; he was staring at a piece of paper which he had drawn by chance out of his briefcase, and seeing, beyond the typescript, its meaning in action. The paper was headed: '*Chief-Designate Dinamaula: Arrangements for Transfer to London.*' It was the bloodless, gutless word 'transfer' that had set him remembering again.

The Government Secretariat at Port Victoria had been tremendously busy during the last few days. Page-long telegrams went off to London, and were answered as copiously. Top-secret memoranda were drawn up; law books consulted; police reports correlated; tentative, conditional questions put confidentially to Crump at Shebiya, Forsdick at Gamate, the Army headquarters at Port Victoria, the town council, the headmen of outlying tribes, the two remaining Regents of the Maulas. Out of all these, and a hundred telephone calls, and a dozen inter-office discussions, and the final queries to the Scheduled Territories Office, and the final decisions, had come one single, anticlimactic answer.

On the appointed morning, there were assembled in the Governor's room, to hear this answer, the Governor himself, Aidan Purves-Brownrigg, David Bracken, a police sub-inspector, and Chief-Designate Dinamaula.

David wished that it might have been a more impressive ceremony, and he continued to wish this, with increasing embarrassment, right to the end. It reminded him of nothing so much as a prefects' meeting at school, convened to discipline some senior malefactor who secretly terrorized them all ... The Governor was ill at ease, and showed it by a fussy briskness of manner; Aidan, who had done most of the work during the last few days, was deadly tired, and lounged back in his chair like an elegant corpse; David was in one of those brand new, involuntary moods when he could not bear the presence of a negro ... Only the policeman, who stared at Dinamaula, and Dinamaula, who looked with sullen boredom at the Governor, were normal.

The Governor was not doing well; it was as if, at this season of his life, his fortitude and self-command ebbed and flowed by turns, and this was a time of ebb. He talked round the subject of the current unrest in Gamate for some ten minutes; then suddenly he went off at a tangent, trying to connect Dinamaula directly with the shambles up at Shebiya. The charge could not be made to stick, and he realized it; and it did not matter anyway, for a very good reason which David and all the others knew. But still he pecked away at it, like a bird obsessed by a false, unhatchable egg.

'We have information,' said the Governor laboriously, looking down at his papers instead of at Dinamaula, 'that your cousin Zuva called on you just before he left to go up to Shebiya. Is that so?'

Dinamaula nodded carelessly. 'Yes.'

'Ah … Did you give him any instructions?'

Dinamaula's eyebrows rose fractionally. 'How could I do that?'

'Perfectly easily. Because you are his superior – his chief.'

'That is not so.'

'Well, the chief-designate, then,' corrected the Governor testily. 'I hope we can dispense with quibbling … What exactly did you tell him to do, when he reached Shebiya?'

'I did not tell him anything. I did not know he was going to Shebiya.'

'What instructions did you give him?'

'None.'

'Or instructions to be relayed to Gotwela?'

'None.'

'His call on you, at that particular time, was simply a coincidence, then?'

'It was a call.'

The Governor sighed, fluttered some papers, tried again. 'What about the strike, then, here in Port Victoria? That was obviously organized under your direction.'

'No.'

'Oh, come now! The ringleaders are known to have called on you, shortly before the strike started.'

'I do not even know who the ringleaders are.'

'Are you pretending that this was another coincidence?'

'I am pretending nothing.'

This was getting them nowhere, thought David irritably; it was merely embarrassing – and the silly part was that they didn't need to get anywhere, as far as Dinamaula was concerned. He was trussed and bound already; all they needed to do was to pull the trigger. The Governor must have been struck by the same thought at the same moment, for with a suddenness equally unreal he stopped his cross-examination, and embarked straightway upon Act Two – the final one.

'Be that as it may,' he said, unexpectedly and nervously, 'I have come to the conclusion that you are and have been directly connected with serious disturbances in various parts of Pharamaul, that you are a focus of intrigue and indiscipline, and that you cannot remain in this country.' It was a painful moment; the Governor was not even looking at Dinamaula, but simply reading from a sheet of paper in front of him. The resemblance to that anxious head prefect grew stronger moment by moment. 'In pursuance, therefore, of the powers legally vested in me – ' the ridiculous phrase rolled off his tongue like a rehearsed line in a stilted play, ' – you are hereby ordered to leave the Principality of Pharamaul forthwith, and you are not to return save with the express approval of Her Majesty's Government.'

Like the policeman, David was watching Dinamaula at that moment, and for the very first time he saw a change in the other man's expression. So far, it had always been guarded, sullen, or indifferent; now for a brief and moving moment, the pain of the wound they were inflicting glowed in his face. There was an instant of absolute, hurt amazement; the mask slipped, showing them all a stricken man. Then Dinamaula said, with difficulty: 'But my rights as chief? My inheritance?'

'They are in abeyance,' said the Governor.

'For how long?'

'Indefinitely.'

Behind Dinamaula's shocked face, David tried to see the dead bodies of Shebiya, the white horror that had been Cynthia Ronald. He saw them, but not clearly; he tried to hate Dinamaula, but his hatred was not pure. Perhaps it was the Governor's fault – the unimpressive Governor who had started like an amateur inquisitor and ended like a spiteful nanny; perhaps it was the policeman's – the bovine, bunkered guardian of the law. Perhaps it was Aidan's – the smooth, weary political executive who had organized the machinery for this rout. Perhaps it was his own fault, because he realized, in spite of his hatred, that there were dappled shades of right and wrong in this matter, and that the only things in black and white were the people concerned.

Perhaps it was Dinamaula's fault, or his strength, or his cleverness, that he could not be hated unconditionally. This seemed especially true when Dinamaula said, 'Surely I have a right to appeal against this decision?'

'You can pursue that in London,' answered the Governor. 'However, I can hold out no hope.'

'But can I never return?'

'I really have no idea,' said the Governor, and rose to end the ceremony.

After that, it was simply office routine; and the routine had brought the two of them to this point of time and place, six thousand feet up, two hundred miles from Livingstone, on the crooked pathway to exile in England.

Like all airline pilots, from EL AL of Israel to Pan-American, whose routes took them anywhere near the Victoria Falls, a few miles south of Livingstone, this pilot circled the falls twice, at low altitude, before coming in to land. As David had expected, and indeed had been looking forward to, their plane made a double circuit, its port wing obligingly dipped to give them an uninterrupted view.

The view was the finest in Africa; trees, stray herds of game racing away from the plane's shadow, lush green vegetation, broad slow-moving water – and then the sudden majestic cleft in the surface of the earth, down which the water plunged in a roaring curtain nearly a mile across. At that season, the water was at a low level, giving them a clear vista of the whole falls, free from the blanket of mist that followed the rainy spell; but still the smoking clouds of spray and spume caught the evening sun, billowing upwards, towering above a gorge deeper than Niagara, wilder than Nature itself.

Before it, ranged in tiers, were other earlier gorges, incredibly old; an ancient framework dried out and disused when Africa itself was young, but still lending to these thunderous waters the awe of vast antiquity.

Both Dinamaula, and David who had moved across the plane to the seat behind him, watched entranced; no matter how many times one had seen this wonder, its massive power and torrential beauty made it freshly irresistible.

Dinamaula looked at the scene with wide eyes, roused at last from his lethargy. David, gazing his fill, was struck by one crystal-clear resolve: that, in spite of everything, he would never leave Africa.

It was after Livingstone that the two of them started to talk.

They started because it suddenly seemed foolish and artificial to do otherwise, and because they were now sitting side by side, in the big, comfortable BOAC plane, and silence at such close quarters was more awkward than speech. Above all, it seemed that silence was wasteful; they might be on opposite sides of a fence – black man and white, discredited chief and official warder – but they could still learn from each other, still lean over that fence and see what lay on the other side … As soon as they were airborne, the pretty blonde stewardess offered them drinks; David had a martini, Dinamaula a whisky and soda. Out of the corner of his eye, David saw Dinamaula's fingers clasped round the tumbler: he had a sudden vision of the same black hand resting on Cynthia Ronald's bosom – and then his brain cleared, and he said, to himself but almost aloud, '*This man did not do that*,' and he turned, and remarked out of the blue: 'I'd like to talk, unless you want to sleep.'

Dinamaula was not surprised, nor was there any need for elaboration, for he spoke his own thoughts straight away: 'I don't expect to sleep … I would like to talk, about anything at all … But I am not happy, and not very friendly.'

David grinned. It was the kind of answer he had hoped for, the kind that – given the necessary guts or pride – he would have wished to produce himself, in the same circumstances. 'Fair enough. I've got one or two reservations myself.'

Dinamaula sipped his drink. The plane droned on, steady as a ship in a calm sea; the blonde stewardess walked up and down the aisle, dispensing a many-phased largesse of alcohol, smiles, and a shapely turn of thigh and bosom.

'What are your reservations?' asked Dinamaula presently.

'Shebiya,' answered David. There seemed no sense in not going straight to the point. 'And before that, the riots at Gamate. And some of the things you said about running the country … What are yours?'

Dinamaula brooded, but his face was not sullen; it was simply young and hurt. 'Being kicked out, at twelve hours' notice,' he said briefly. 'Being treated like a child all the

647

time … Being patronized. Mr Bracken, can you tell me exactly where I went wrong?'

Kampala welcomed them, beautifully sited at the head of Lake Victoria, less beautifully sited on the exact line of the Equator at the height of summer. The night was unbearably hot, smelling of burnt grass and greasy woodsmoke; the small airport building was like an inferno. Inside it, some Americans bought leopardskin slippers and carved wooden antelopes, argued about the prices, changed their minds and thrust their purchases back at the Baganda salesman; a whining, suet-faced English child ran berserk among the coffee tables; a grey nun whispered to another grey nun, eyes downcast, fingers busy with beads. Above the tarmac and the waiting plane, the stars were cool and remote, aloof from the travellers pinioned to the burning earth.

'You brought it on yourself, and I honestly can't express it in any other way,' said David, pursuing his patient argument. The lights in the plane were going out one by one, as the passengers settled down to sleep. 'I'm not saying that your ideas aren't good ones, or that they wouldn't work out, but you tackled the whole thing in the wrong way, right from the beginning.'

'I only wanted to improve things,' said Dinamaula, not for the first time. 'The whole place seemed so out of date – like a museum, a museum of the nineteenth century. I wanted to make it take a step forward.'

'All right … So do we … But you've got to use the existing channels, you've got to fit your plans in with what's going on already. Andrew Macmillan, for example. You should never have got across him, the way you did.'

'He annoyed me, from the very first day. It was ridiculous, intolerable. He always treated me like a schoolboy.'

'Quite so. And what *you* did wrong was not to make allowances for him.'

'Allowances? Why should I?'

'Because he was an old-fashioned civil servant, near the end of his career ... Don't forget he was old enough to be your father – almost your grandfather ... Of course he was slow, he was schoolmasterish, he tried to discipline you ... But on the other hand, he did know the territory from end to end, far better than you did, and he did have its interests at heart. And, you see, once you turned awkward and unco-operative, from his point of view, he had to crack down. We all did.'

'You seemed to be enjoying it,' said Dinamaula sourly.

David shook his head. 'No – no one on our side could enjoy that sort of waste, that sort of destruction.'

Khartoum came, after the long, thousand-mile night haul over the desert and the foothills of Ethiopia. When the moon glinted, it glinted on the River Nile, a mile below them, its banks pricked here and there by nomad fires. At Khartoum, grave men in fezzes served them coffee; the spacious room was peaceful, the service quick and courteous. The blonde hostess bid them goodbye, smiling, saying: 'This is where I have to hand you over to a brunette ... I hope you're not going to talk *all* night.' She knew who Dinamaula was, as did all the crew; BOAC had been alerted some days before. But they had all looked at him with warm and friendly eyes; not like the tall Arabs of Khartoum, who, when they were not serving, stared at Dinamaula the negro with the rich contempt of a purer race.

After Khartoum, the chips were down.

'I had nothing to do with that horrible thing at Shebiya,' said Dinamaula. 'I only had a few vague hints about it from Zuva – nothing definite, nothing to go on. If I had known, of course I would have told you.'

'We still think it was partly your fault – a chain-reaction from the rest.'

'I know you do ... The strike at Port Victoria *was* my fault – I thought that was a good idea. And some of the riots at Gamate, too. I wanted to get my own back ... But of course the people who did most of the planning at Gamate were the Press.'

'They were no friends of yours,' said David, hardly.

'Perhaps not ... It was flattering, though.'

'There'll be a lot of that in London, too. I honestly think it would be a mistake to get mixed up with them.'

'Is that an official warning?'

'Sort of.'

Cairo, at dawn, smelt like an ancient sewer; the stink hit them instantly, as soon as the plane door was opened and a fat Egyptian official waddled in and began, with rare effrontery, to spray them with disinfectant ... But the airport bar on the upper floor was cool, and the view arresting; to the east, the desert dawn was just coming up, streaked with purple and pink and yellow. As they took off again, and rose above the Delta of the Nile, the new sun illumined a thousand streams and a thousand glistening mudbanks; and then suddenly the pure blue of the Mediterranean was the only thing in view.

'Pharamaul can't stand still,' said Dinamaula. 'No country in Africa can. We both agree on that ... But how is Pharamaul going to make any real progress in *any* direction, if you block new ideas all the time.'

'We don't,' said David.

'You blocked *me*.'

'Only because you wanted to move too fast … But, of course, in the future, it *will* make progress. It's bound to, and we all want it to.'

'I should like to see that get under way … Do you think I ever will?'

'I hope so.'

'As chief?'

'I honestly don't know.'

'I'd like to go back one day.'

'There would have to be all sorts of safeguards.'

'But even so … Tell them that, if you get the chance. I love that funny little country.'

'So do I.'

Rome on its seven small hills was elegant, sunlit, and noisy – noisy with planes taking off, turbo jets screaming as they warmed up, motor scooters weaving to and fro across the tarmac, Italian *carabinieri* and officials demonstrating their manhood and their influence at the tops of their voices. The little shops and boutiques were full of bright clothing, good-looking leather goods, jewellery, silk scarves. When the two of them sat on the terrace, waiting for their flight to be called, the morning air was magical.

'Only a few more hours,' said David, watching without guile a ravishing Air France hostess perched on the back of a Vespa motor-scooter, her legs as smooth and as tantalizing as her parted lips. 'Aren't you tired?'

Dinamaula smiled. 'Not at all … After all, we've only been talking for twenty-six hours … You should belong to *my* tribe, Mr Bracken. This would just be a preliminary chat.'

High above the Alps, level with the crest of Mont Blanc gleaming like a snowy sheath on their left hand, Dinamaula suddenly said: 'Of course, there never *was* an actual girl.'

'Girl?' repeated David, who had been watching the white encrusted hills and the wreaths of mist below.

'A white girl. The one I was supposed to be going to marry.'

David turned, surprised at last. 'Why on earth didn't you say so, then?'

'I told you – Macmillan annoyed me ... And also, I wanted to reserve my right to marry anyone I chose, black or white, *if* I wanted to. Why shouldn't I? There's no law against it.'

'But there's a tremendously strong custom. A mixed marriage would have split the tribe.'

'They would have come round to it. They *did* come round to it.'

'But it wouldn't have been a good idea, anyway. That's not the future pattern of Pharamaul.'

'Perhaps not. But don't you see? – I wanted to feel *free* – free to rule, free to marry, free to ignore nagging and criticism. After all, I was the chief. That is what a chief should be.'

'You really should have told us that there wasn't an actual girl.'

'It wouldn't have made any difference.'

London Airport was almost fogged in, with a cloud base at a mere five hundred feet; when they dropped through it, bumping and side-slipping, the thousands of wet-roofed houses, the thousands of streets, the sheer sprawling mass of the city took them by surprise. Could they really be poised in flight above eight million people? ... It would be raining in Whitehall, thought David; the murky gloom of the Scheduled Territories Office would be murkier still. He longed for Pharamaul, and dry sunshine, and his known friends, and Nicole.

Zipping up his overnight bag as they joined the disembarking queue in the aisle, he remarked idly: 'I shall be getting married when I go back to Port Victoria.'

Dinamaula asked, in a voice totally expressionless: 'Are you going to marry a white girl?' and they both suddenly burst out laughing.

They were both still laughing when they got off the plane, to be met at the barrier by a surging mob of Pressmen and photographers, hundreds of onlookers, and a deputation from the League for the Advancement of Coloured People, bearing dripping banners which proclaimed: 'WELCOME DINAMAULA, VICTIM AND DUPE OF COLONIALISM!' They were all held in check by a single policeman, who murmured: 'Spectators *behind* the white line, please.'

'Dinamaula was smiling bravely through his misery,' commented the *Daily Thresh* next morning. 'If there is any medal for men going into exile, he should have it tomorrow.'

'The ineffable Mr David Bracken,' said the *New Nation*'s most bile-ridden columnist, later that week, 'stepped off the plane wearing a somewhat inane grin, which he did not trouble to conceal. It could have been a grin of triumph. Whatever prompted it, it was in execrable taste. Is it too much to ask that when minor Government officials are entrusted ...'

II

All the newspapers were blazing, but they were blazing in different colours, with variations of heat, light, and smoke.

The arrival of Dinamaula was headline material, but it did not precipitate the hundred per cent universal row which would have greeted it a month or so earlier. For some stomachs, Shebiya had been too strong altogether; for others, too foreboding. Also, Dinamaula himself had proved curiously uncommunicative. He admitted that he was 'disappointed'. He said that he was 'sad to leave'. He declared that he 'still regarded himself as chief'. Then he stopped talking, and went into effective hiding.

Certain of the newspapers, however, held their course unwaveringly.

'The issue in Pharamaul is democracy versus colonialism,' said the *Daily Thresh*, editorially. 'It is as simple as right and wrong. If we exile Dinamaula, we are guilty, before the entire civilized world, of the betrayal of black mankind.'

'The issue in Pharamaul is crystal clear,' said the *News Intelligence*. 'We are using the mailed fist of officialdom to crush a simple, trusting people. But it is not too late to reverse this indecent process. Forget the past! Send Dinamaula back to his bereaved nation!'

'The issue in Pharamaul,' said the *Globe*, 'has never been clearer. Let Dinamaula claim his shapely white bride, and return in triumph for a glamorous, thrill-packed honeymoon under the tropical palms.'

'The situation in Pharamaul is a mess,' said the *New Nation*. 'Moreover, it is a mess of our own making. A handful of stuffed shirt jacks-in-office is sabotaging, in the sacred name of discipline, a gallant people on the verge of well-earned self-government. The least we can do is to send Dinamaula back with apologies – and plenary powers.'

'On page 4,' said *Glimpse Magazine,* 'a photograph of some goats at Gamate, taken by Lebourget & O'Toole – presumably to keep their hands in. It was as near to the famed "Shambles of Shebiya" as the British would let them come.'

But other newspapers were having second thoughts, for all sorts of reasons.

'The issue in Pharamaul demonstrates the need for firm handling at the summit – and the current lack of it,' said the *Onlooker.* 'This government of elderly ditherers is directly responsible for the atrocities at Shebiya. If we are going to rule, let us rule like men, not Etonian mice with drooping grey whiskers.'

'The issue in Pharamaul,' said the Earl of Erle (Gold Stick in Abeyance, Leader of the House of Lords) in a letter to *The Times,* 'is a classic example of too little and too late. It recalls India, and, to a certain extent, America. Firmness tempered with a due regard for the susceptibilities of a backward people should be our watchword.'

'We did right to sack Dinamaula,' said the Right-wing *Sunday Mirror.* 'He is hand-in-glove with the gang of perverts and communists who have made his country a hotbed of dirty-minded thuggery. Let him stay sacked!'

'As anyone with any knowledge of the national character might have forecast,' said *Clang,* 'Britain was second-guessing about Pharamaul. If he had done nothing else, hoofed-out chief Dinamaula had made them take a long, long look at their colonial responsibilities. Until last week, there had been nothing like it since the red-coats were routed at Bunker Hill.'

'The issue in Pharamaul,' said the *Daily Telegram*, 'is a delicate one.'

Above all, Parliament itself was thinking again. On the afternoon of Dinamaula's return, there was another long Question Time session on Pharamaul, the sixth in as many weeks; but it was neither as one-sided nor as awkward as the preceding ones. The horror of Shebiya, freshly reported in the newspapers, was in everyone's mind; and those who came to rant and roar about the blazing injustice involved in Dinamaula's removal found an unreceptive House and a firm Minister. It was even possible to detect the actual embryo of this unreceptiveness; the moment when the tide began to turn. It was, as so often in the history of disputation, a moment of laughter.

Emrys Price-Canning was on his feet, wagging a scornful finger at Lord Lorde, the Minister for the Scheduled Territories Office, and launching a series of supplementary questions which accused the latter of double-dealing with the electorate, bullying backward peoples, inventing atrocities, betraying Britain's historic mission of emancipation, and exiling a true martyr. But Price-Canning was not carrying the House, which had heard it all before, and he knew this, and it drove him to explore the realms of metaphor and simile. The flight was unfortunate.

'Since Pharamaul without its chief,' he began yet another question, 'is like a rudderless child – '

There was a titter, and then a loud burst of laughter which flooded the whole chamber. Price-Canning shook his head angrily, waited for the noise to subside, and then threw in: 'The laughter of fools ...' by way of rebuke. But he did not recover from the setback; his supplementary petered out into silence; and presently the topic itself ground to a halt, with nothing settled and no verdict given.

But the Minister had the last word, and he used it like a layer of slapped-on vanishing cream. The Government, said Lord Lorde, by way of graceful *congé*, realized that the need was not for the cut-and-thrust of debate, but rather for a dispassionate assessment of the known facts; with this in view, they would shortly table a White Paper on the origins and development of the disorders in Pharamaul, and their wider implications. The House and the nation could then see if the action over Dinamaula were not justified. Meanwhile ...

Meanwhile it was enough for the Parliamentary bookies, who presently, in the cosy hideaway of the Members' Bar, calculated the odds as even money against a full-dress debate, four to one against a Government retreat, and ten to one against Dinamaula's returning to Pharamaul within three years.

III

The Permanent Under-Secretary for the Scheduled Territories Office, Sir Hubert Godbold, strolled to the window, looked at the rain falling steadily on Whitehall, watched a bus recover from a skid as it rounded the sloping corner from Trafalgar Square, and then sat down at his desk again. The short walk was a sign that he was thinking at large, instead of dealing directly with papers. It did not mean that he had stopped working. Within this room, he never did that.

He was thinking about policy – policy in general, the framework of action; and, in thinking, recognizing for the thousandth time the pitfalls of formulation. It sometimes seemed to him little short of miraculous that a single clear-cut policy, on a single issue, ever emerged, out of the chaos of opposing interests and the pressing variety of contributors.

In his own Ministry, for example, policy was the product of a number of senior, overworked officials, ranging from glittering careerists near the top of the heap, to persuasive and devoted men five thousand miles away in the field. These were the immediate technicians; through himself, they advised their Minister, who in turn informed, cajoled, or knuckled under to the cabinet.

Round this inner ring was a wider one, often hostile, always critical; among it were ranged the working Press, the newspaper proprietors, and assorted members of Parliament – members on the make, members sincerely troubled, members with a sacrificial torch itching between their fingers. Behind them again was the general public, whether influential or miniscule – grumbling, bumbling, guessing, gossiping, writing letters to the newspapers, voting ... And out of all this, and genuine mistakes, and inaccurate estimates, and optimism, and political *mystique*, and Party expediency, must come a decision which everyone might shoot at, no one and nothing must wreck.

But as well as being viable and enduring, under this tough gauntlet, good policy must be something more; it had to preserve a balance between what was idealistic and desirable, and what was possible and expedient. The range was so enormous ... In Commonwealth and Colonial affairs, for example, it had to cover a people like the Maulas of Pharamaul, a predominantly simple race whom Britain was pledged to help, and who would take no undue advantage of it; and, on the other hand, other more 'advanced' races who, wise in the ways of democratic procurement, played Britain for a sucker while cursing her freely on all four corners of the world stage.

There were certain West Indians, for example, in the latter category – Godbold had been reviewing their somewhat squalid affairs on an inter-departmental committee that morning. Being within the Commonwealth, they were free to come to England, and there (if they could not get work) go on the dole forthwith, qualify for the free Health Services, and possibly live for the rest of their lives on the same broad back. Some were certainly worth having, others had proved themselves idle and vicious, with a sprinkling of whores and drug addicts. Was it fair policy to turn a bleak eye on this invasion, to resist it, to become selective – or should one shoulder the burden indefinitely?

Obviously in these restless tides, there was a time for compassion, and a time to be hardboiled. In formulating this particular facet of policy, you had to strike the right balance – and also persuade a huge number of amazingly different people that you were doing so. Your critics would range from stern Empire disciplinarians who cried for a dispersing whiff of grapeshot, to others who became starry-eyed as soon as a black man – any black man, from good citizen to sleazy rogue – came in sight.

It was impossible, of course, to satisfy more than a certain percentage of the onlookers and pundits, just as it was impossible to find a policy which everyone in any given 'dependent country' found adequate. If Britain granted independence too early, the country concerned became a prey to the corrupt – or, worse still, to the inefficient. If she held on too long, she might be blown out by thugs and replaced by political gangsters. If she held on indefinitely, she was pilloried as a colonial despot or fascist saboteur, reviled by half her own electorate, cursed by the

Americans, burned in effigy by the Indians, and self-taxed to extinction in order to pay for it all ...

Colonialism ... Godbold, pulling some papers towards him, smiled wryly at the twentieth century's favourite cant-word. Then he shrugged, looked down at the papers, identified them as the ones he wanted, and began to focus his thoughts nearer home. Policy in the round was one thing; now he had to find *a* policy – a policy for Pharamaul. In essence, it had to satisfy his own judgement, get past the cabinet and the House of Commons, stand up to Press criticism, possibly pass muster at UN – *and administer one hundred thousand Maulas fairly and hopefully, for the next ten or fifteen years.*

Being a methodical man, he had already written down an outline of this policy, and the way it ought to be presented. In addition, he was seeing David Bracken within a few minutes – partly because he always saw anyone who came back to London, whether on leave or on recall, as soon as they arrived, partly because he wanted to assimilate a few first-hand impressions.

There had been times during the last few months when the Pharamaul Secretariat had seemed incredibly remote, like the China or Peru of two hundred years ago, and their letters and telegrams had read like half-defaced hieroglyphics from another culture altogether. This might be an opportunity to reduce the distance, to clear the view. He also needed a factual report on Dinamaula, before their first difficult interview later that day.

He read again what he had written earlier, in the elegant Greek script which seemed to confer distinction on other people's drafts, even when reducing them to skeletal ashes of the original.

1. Since Dinamaula's arrival in Pharamaul, there has been continuous unrest:

(a) In Port Victoria (dock strike, riots, 2 murders)
(b) In Gamate (boycott of Governor's *aboura*, widespread defiance of authority, murder of European farmer and 2 children, 44 other deaths)
(c) In Shebiya (murder of District Officer, his wife, mission priest, and 5 policemen; armed insurrection).

2. These have all stemmed from:
(a) Dinamaula's first "Progress for Pharamaul" interview
(b) Dinamaula's reported marriage plans
(c) Press exaggeration (and provocation?)
(d) Division of tribe on (a) and (b).

3. Dinamaula persisted (inadvertently?) as centre of intrigue, disturbance, and resistance as long as he was in Territory.

4. He must therefore remain outside Pharamaul
(a) until complete order is restored (?)
(b) for a set term of years (?)
(c) indefinitely (?)

5. Government by Council of Regents should continue as soon as martial law is lifted: possibly Katsaula, and two younger men.

6. Neither the murderous activity in the Territory, nor these *interim* safeguards, should stand in the way of our progressive intentions for Pharamaul.

That was as far as he had got, in a brief which would furnish the basis for a cabinet paper, and later for the White Paper which had been promised in the House. It was still somewhat blurred round the edges, and conspicuously so when it referred to Dinamaula's future. Obviously the latter would have to be barred from the territory for a considerable time; martial law itself might be necessary for six months or so, and after that there would have to be a long period of rehabilitation, of the re-establishing of trust on both sides. Then, and only then, could they steer for the future.

But it might be that Dinamaula was too controversial a figure, or too explosive a personality, to make a satisfactory chief: that Pharamaul could never settle down while he was there; and that therefore he must remain in permanent exile. It would be a pity, because he seemed to have the makings of a good man; but good men had been sacrificed before now, in the interests of a more stable community, and the world still survived and even prospered ... When Godbold reached that point in thought, there was a knock at his door, and he called: 'Come in!'

His private secretary, an elegant blond young man very definitely on his way up, advanced and said, with the proper touch of disdain: 'Bracken, sir.'

'Good,' said Godbold. He smiled a welcome as David entered the room.

David had not been enjoying himself at all that morning. The Scheduled Territories Office had seemed darker and more depressing than ever, like an underwater cave to which light filtered down for a scant hour a day. Of course, a few months in Pharamaul's guaranteed sunshine was sufficient to destroy any patriotic taste for London in wintertime, but even so, had the office always been so dreary?

Had it, also, always been so superior? He had found himself progressively daunted by the arcana of power, by the sense of being an outsider admitted on brief sufferance to the mysteries. In the Information Department, a precise and humourless man had indicated a file full of Press cuttings, and said: 'You've been giving us a great deal of trouble lately.' In Establishments, he had been involved in an esoteric wrangle about his outfit allowance. 'You've been paid on a *sub-tropical basis*,' said a senior accountant, as if he could scarcely believe the evidence of the written page. 'Surely you must have realized you were tropical? Sign *here*, and *here*, and *here*, and give me a cheque for eleven pounds, fifteen shillings.'

When he had seen Crossley, the administrative head of his department, the gulf between London and Pharamaul had seemed bottomless indeed. He remembered an earlier meeting, before he had set out for Pharamaul, when Crossley, briefing him on the outlines of his job, had cautioned: 'We just need competent office work, within the normal pattern ... You'll be one of a team, of course ... Above all, no ugly enthusiasm!' He had smiled briefly as he said it, but David had realized that Crossley meant exactly what he said. Now, when they met again, Crossley had questioned him at length about Shebiya – but coldly and detachedly, as if Shebiya were a schedule of debts in a valuation for probate – and then added, as though on an afterthought: 'The PUS would like to see you for a moment – *since you're here*.'

At that moment, Pharamaul had seemed very far away, and inferior, and not worth the effort; good enough for the simple second-raters who might be posted there, not nearly good enough for the brains at head office. Would he ever be promoted? Would he ever make any headway? Or was it like the Vatican (or like he imagined the Vatican to be)? – like being a cardinal in England or America or China, instead of in Rome, obviously the only place to be a cardinal. For you would never grow up to be Pope unless you spent nearly all your time in Rome ...

He felt small, and depressed, and doomed to the colonial backwoods for the rest of his working life. But he began to enjoy himself as soon as he caught sight of Godbold's strong and lively face, as soon as Godbold started to speak.

'Sit down, Bracken,' said the Permanent Under-Secretary. He consulted his watch, and smiled a second time. 'We'll be able to have a gin in ten minutes – my secretary, who is very strict, doesn't like to see glasses on my desk before midday ... Now tell me first about Dinamaula. What sort of journey did you have, and what sort of mood is he in?'

It was such a reversal of form, such a contrast with the bleakness of his welcome so far, that David Bracken was momentarily taken aback. But the pause did not last more than a few seconds. He glanced swiftly round the solid, high-pillared, luxurious room, where great affairs were fitly conducted, and then back to Godbold again. The man behind the desk was wonderfully reassuring – he was like the room, but in addition, he had spoken his welcome aloud ... David leant back in his chair, and began to answer. After the first sentence, he did not need to search for words.

'It was a good journey, sir,' he said. 'Better than I thought it would be ... Dinamaula was very quiet, perhaps rather sulky, when we left Pharamaul. But it seemed silly to spend thirty hours together and not say a word, so I started talking, and I suppose he felt the same way, because he came to life almost immediately.' David grinned. 'We talked the whole way, in fact, sir – Livingstone to London.'

Godbold smiled also, leaning back, giving a heartening impression that he was not going to be bored. 'You must have covered a lot of ground ... I'm glad you got him to talk ... What was it all about?'

'Pretty well everything, sir.' David felt an absurd, almost schoolboyish elation as he faced Godbold; for some reason, compounded of relief, renewed self-confidence, even hero-worship, the whole thing was suddenly worth while again. Pharamaul was no longer a negligible dot on the map, it was part of an empire, and it was connected to this very room ... 'He was perfectly frank, and so was I.'

David set to work to describe to Godbold those five thousand miles of conversation, with their revelations, surprises, and occasional disagreements. It took a long time, because it was very fresh in his memory, and much of it seemed valuable; but, as at the beginning, Godbold gave a continuous impression that he was judging the time well spent. He only interrupted once, towards the end, when David mentioned Dinamaula's marriage plans.

'You mean,' queried Godbold, his eyebrows raised, 'he made the positive statement that there was no white woman?'

David nodded. 'Yes, sir. He said he originally made the remark to show his independence, and that when he was challenged on it later, he made up his mind not to back down. It was part of his reaction to discipline.'

'Discipline?'

'That was what he was feeling like, by then – as if he were being told to behave himself, or take the consequences ... I'm not saying, sir, that he might not still marry a white woman here, but he certainly hasn't got one in view, at the moment.'

Godbold considered the information, his lips pursed, the lines on his forehead deep. David could almost feel the other man's powerful mind catching his up in great leaps, seeing beyond one peak to the next.

'But it may still be an issue to the tribe,' said Godbold finally, almost to himself. 'They took sides on it, and in the end a majority of them endorsed it ... It's still there, as a disturbing element in his personality, if he ever goes back.'

'He might perhaps give guarantees on the point.'

Godbold's eyes suddenly sharpened. 'Did he say that?'

'Not quite. He said – or implied – that if there had to be certain safeguards governing his return, he would accept them.'

Godbold looked at him, and smiled, and said: 'Your journey was not wasted ... Go on.'

'I think that's really about all, sir. As I said, he was very sad at leaving, and rather surly, but he changed during the trip, as if he'd only just begun to realize what he'd lost, what had been taken away from him. I don't think it was calculated, or put on just to impress me, just to be passed along ... He was quite candid about the mistakes he'd made, and about trying to move too fast. He agreed that there might have been faults on both sides – '

'Agreed?' Godbold's eyebrows rose alarmingly. 'Did *you* propound such a proposition?'

'Proposition?' David was taken aback.

'That there were faults on *our* side?'

It was an awkward, even dangerous moment; in a single phrase, he might throw everything away. But it was also a moment to be honest; the man before him wanted a true account, and a true account included just such an element as this.

'I agreed with Dinamaula, sir,' he answered slowly, 'that if be had been handled differently, when he arrived – in spite of that silly newspaper story – all this later trouble might have been avoided. *He* agreed with *me* that he had gone about things the wrong way, giving the impression that he was going to put through a lot of radical reforms, no matter what the opposition.'

Godbold's expression remained formidably critical. 'I presume you made it clear that you were expressing a personal opinion.'

'No, I didn't, sir. It was – we were – ' David floundered, and then recovered. 'We were both trying to talk candidly, to tell the truth without scoring a lot of debating points. It was that sort of session.'

Godbold fell silent, and remained so for perhaps two minutes; it was his old, disconcerting habit, which was less a trick than an absolute insistence upon privacy for his thoughts. David stared down at the carpet, aware that he had blundered; the picture in Godbold's mind – that of a junior official giving away points to the enemy, in a large-hearted and fundamentally fatuous way – must be brutally clear. He would be recalling also that this was not the first black mark ... Bracken boobs again ... It came as another shock to hear Godbold saying, in a different sort of voice: 'Where did we go wrong – *who* went wrong – in our handling of Dinamaula, when he first arrived?'

David had a moment of pure panic: he wanted to say that he had changed his mind, that everything had been wonderful, that he had only been joking ... But he raised his head to find Godbold looking at him with the same steady interest as before, and he took heart. If he had really done wrong, then all that he had to say now was part of the same error, and he might as well unload the whole thing in one operation. As he was about to speak, Godbold suddenly held up his hand.

'I was forgetting,' he said benignly. 'Our drink ... Gin and tonic, or pink?'

It was difficult to judge whether the break was made on purpose, to give David time to collect his thoughts, or to assuage the earlier rebuke; whichever it was, it came as a grateful surprise. Drinks were poured, and presently, sipping his pink gin, David took up his theme again.

'I'm afraid it was Andrew Macmillan, principally, sir. Whatever he said to Dinamaula – I wasn't actually there – he must have put very bluntly and forcibly, giving Dinamaula no chance either to explain or to withdraw. On the plane, Dinamaula said he was made to feel like a schoolboy. Andrew himself told me he had given Dinamaula a flea in his ear ... That's surely wrong, even though there was such an age difference ... But I told Dinamaula that it was up to him to make allowances for Andrew as well – that he was old, and also very wise and very capable.'

'What did Dinamaula say to that?'

'He said "Yes".'

'What other mistakes did we make?'

'I think they all stemmed from that, sir – treating him like a little boy, instead of the incoming chief. Then everything got out of hand very quickly, and Andrew tried the same sort of thing with the Regents and the tribe, and *they* wouldn't stand for it either ...' David looked closely at Godbold. 'I don't want to seem to put all the blame on to Macmillan, sir – I think he was a wonderful man, and I wish to God he weren't dead. We *all* tried to deal with the thing in a rather – rather superior way, and it just didn't work. It was too serious.'

'And too volatile?'

David nodded again. 'Yes. It just blew up in our face. I think our Secretariat, and Andrew's people in Gamate, would have been good enough to handle that sort of crisis in ninety-nine cases out of a hundred. But the hundredth case was an exception, and we just didn't measure up to it. Of course, it was the Press who really put the lid on the whole thing. They made rings round us, right from the start. We should have taken a much stronger line with them.'

But Godbold was already shaking his head. 'If we were on firm enough ground, we should have been able to deal with them perfectly easily, without any "strong line". After all, you can't expect to operate in a vacuum. The Press must be free to observe and to report.'

'They did a lot more than that in Pharamaul, sir.'

'Maybe so. In fact, certainly so. I'm ready to admit that the Dinamaula story attracted not only the very worst newspapers, but the very worst men working on them. The reputable Press hardly touch it. But the things we do and say, in a place like Pharamaul, ought to be proof against *all* criticism, *all* slings and arrows. If we are fair, if we are honest, and if we are steadfast.'

There was another long moment of silence; and this time, Godbold rose and walked to the window. His back against the dull grey sky was a formidable monument. 'Fair and honest and steadfast' – the three fundamental words hung in the air between them, like banners in the stillness; strangely, they had the same weight and meaning here as they might have had in the centre of Gamate's *aboura*, or in Shebiya itself ... *Integrity*, thought David, with a flash of insight: it could start from cold in a room like this, and it could travel all the way to Pharamaul, and still arrive unbroached and entire. The sense of one-ness was stronger than ever now; he would never again regret his five-thousand-mile exile, when London and Pharamaul were thus incorporate ... Godbold was still standing by the window; presently he turned, and spoke firmly and quickly, as if reflecting truth.

'We have these same problems all over Africa, you know. There's no single answer to Africa. Out of our possessions or dependencies there, we can make - try to make – one of three things: a black dominion, a black-and-white partnership, or a purified white enclave ... I think we can write off the last alternative, as a matter of common sense. It goes directly against the historic trend; Africa is moving the other way. And in any case, if you inflict permanent subjection on a people, telling them that not only they themselves, but their children's grandchildren, will never have any political or economic advancement whatsoever, then there can only be one result – an explosion.'

Godbold walked towards his desk, sat down, took a drink, leant back. 'You and I both know these things,' he went on, 'but it's a good idea to restate them sometimes, particularly when you are wondering what to make of some specific country ... The black dominion is a perfectly feasible idea, if the people concerned are really ready for the test of complete independence in a very difficult world – which means, in effect, if we have been there long enough. It's already emerging in Nigeria and on the Gold Coast, as you know. My personal view is that we have moved too fast there, but I may well be mistaken. The most promising of all – ' he emphasized his words with a pointing finger, ' – is what they are trying to do in the Central African Federation. There's the beginning, there, of a genuine black–white partnership, with both races sitting down side by side to legislate and to govern. It's almost the only one in the world, and God prosper it! If that Federation scheme is a success, it may serve as a pattern for Africa as a whole, and that would be a very proud thing indeed.

'In fact,' said Godbold, 'it's *got* to be a success. When South Africa, the purified white tip of the continent, bursts into flames, and collapses in ruins – which may not be in your lifetime, or your children's, because South Africans are very efficient, and completely ruthless, and their white population, regardless of label, is ninety per cent on the side of white domination – but *when* that happens, it will be the test of what has been done, and what has not been done, elsewhere. If South Africa's neighbours catch fire from her, and burn also, they will have failed miserably. If they stand fast, and in due course, perhaps, export their ideas and their political structures back again to South Africa, they will have triumphed.

'But in all these changes,' said Godbold, ' – and this is important when we come to think of Pharamaul – there is one thing never to be forgotten, and that is the pace of Africa. It is not the pace of Europe, and God forbid it should ever be the pace of America! But it is a pace which we have always had to follow, in our colonial affairs. If we delay freedom, there is an explosion. If we hurry it, there is disaster.'

For the first time, David broke in. 'But which is Pharamaul, sir? They're ready for some things, not ready for others. There's already been an explosion – because of delay, I suppose. But they're not yet ready for independence, or anything like it.'

'I'll tell you what we're going to do in Pharamaul,' answered Godbold, glancing at his watch, 'and then I'm afraid I must keep my next appointment. We're going to forgive and forget, and *they* are going to forgive and forget, and we'll move on to the next step. It will involve more say for them in their own affairs, more power delegated to Regents and headmen, more local self-administration. Specifically, we'll keep the Council of Regents going, until a chief is ready to take over. That might well be Dinamaula – it all depends on events. Forsdick will move up as Resident Commissioner, I shall be reinforcing the Secretariat with one or two people from here. it's possible that there will be a new Governor, though that is strictly between ourselves at the moment. And you,' he said finally, smiling because he had so obviously kept it till the end, 'will take over at Shebiya, as District Officer.'

In spite of himself, David started. The word 'Shebiya' still produced the old reaction, of horror and disgust and fear. Godbold must have caught his glance, because he said instantly: 'In some ways, I realize, you have the hardest job of all, because you were there, and saw the horrible things they did. But you too have got to be part of forgive-and-forget ... It will be quite easy for us to forgive the Maulas, here in London; less easy in Gamate, which has had more than its share of murders and rioting; and hardest of all where you are going to be. But it must be done, because the whole of Pharamaul has got to take the next step forward – and we have got to grant them that step, and not have it forced out of us.'

David swallowed. 'I want to go to Shebiya, sir. In fact, there's nothing I'd like better. It's just that – surely they've got to be punished?'

'Some of them must be punished,' agreed Godbold. 'But when that is done, we've got to return, without equivocation, to the pace of Africa. The Maulas have outgrown Macmillan; they are ready for something else. They mustn't be prevented from attaining that something else, because a few of them tried to anticipate history.'

Godbold stood up, and smiled. 'Thank you for coming along, and for listening. A captive audience, I'm afraid ... I shall be seeing Dinamaula this afternoon, and I value your account of him, and your judgement. I think we might say, in the White Paper, that he will remain in exile until the state of the territory is normal and tranquil, when we will review the ban on him. Something like that ... We'll see how things develop, and in particular how he behaves here.'

'He could be of great value, sir. He's in a different mood now. You notice he hasn't been talking to the Press, and I don't think he will. Of course, a lot will depend – ' David paused, suddenly embarrassed.

'Yes?' asked Godbold. Then he noticed David's expression. 'Ah, yes – a lot will depend on how he is received here. Quite so.'

They walked towards the door. 'Thank you very much for the job, sir,' said David. 'And I'm glad the whole thing is settled.'

'*Settled*,' repeated Godbold, on a rueful note. 'Settled is a somewhat relative word ... There's a small matter of a cabinet meeting, at which our Minister, who doesn't really believe in positive action of any sort, has to convince a lot of other people who don't believe in it either. Then there's the White Paper, and a possible debate on it in the House. There'll be one row in the Press about keeping Dinamaula out, and another about letting him in again. Then there'll be a long tug-of-war in Pharamaul itself, after martial law is lifted. Apart from that,' he concluded, smiling, 'it's a – what do the Americans say?'

'A push-over?' hazarded David.

'Yes – a push-over.'

They were standing in the long alcoved corridor outside the Under-Secretary's room; the heavy overhead lighting shone down on polished marble, solid mahogany furniture, pictures and photographs of old proconsuls and forgotten tribal gatherings, bronze busts of the great, the adroit, the dreamers, the men of action. The vista of history thus enshrined was daunting and heartening at the same time.

'I won't see you again,' said Godbold, and held out his hand. 'Don't forget – that tug-of-war in Pharamaul is the only one that really matters. We can score goals and win matches in London, but they mean less than nothing, unless the result makes sense in places like Pharamaul.' He walked a few paces down the corridor with David, past a huge lithograph portrayal of the Delhi Durbar of 1911, and a marble bust of Cecil Rhodes. 'Once, either during or just after the American Civil War, Lincoln was asked why he did not destroy all his enemies, the men who were plotting or fighting against him. His answer was: "I destroy my enemy when I make him my friend." That's the only answer, in Pharamaul and a lot of other places. Make him your friend! Now go back to Pharamaul, and get to work.'

CHAPTER SIXTEEN

❖

Weddings from Government House were so rare that no one knew quite what to expect. The proceedings in church were decorous enough, though the second Stevens child, elected to officiate as a flower girl, took stage fright, trampled her bouquet underfoot, and raced incontinently out of the church followed by her mother, her elder brother, and her younger brother, all streaming astern like wild domestic tendrils. Aidan Purves-Brownrigg, the best man, produced the ring from his flowered brocade waistcoat with suitable aplomb; Sir Elliott Vere-Toombs, giving the bride away, played a monumental role. The organ thundered out the wedding march till the old church rafters shook. But after that it was a bit of a riot.

'Champagne!' Lady Vere-Toombs had decreed, adding privately to her friends: 'It's really our last chance, since our own little girl won't be getting married just yet.' (Anthea Vere-Toombs, having delayed in Port Victoria for a bare week after John Raper of the *Globe* departed – 'resting on her morals', as Aidan put it – had now taken off for London in brisk pursuit.) So champagne it was, by the glass, by the bottle, and by the case. It was a hot day, a good drinking day. Within an hour, Government House was afloat.

'Strolling on the spacious lawns,' scribbled Miss Tilly Sproule, Social Editress of the *Times of Pharamaul*, sprawling in a hammock discreetly veiled by jacaranda trees, 'the youth and beauty – yes, and the maturity! – of Port Victoria surrendered to the happy mood of the moment. The band regaled us with merry music, while the guests partook of the lavish hospitality of their host and hostess, Sir Elliott and Lady Vere-Toombs (so soon to leave us, alas!) who graciously stood *in loco parentis* to the lovely bride. I caught a glimpse of the newly arrived West German *chargé d'affaires* ...'

'I tell you funny English choke,' said the newly arrived West German *chargé d'affaires*, a stern bespectacled young man who had been ordered to make himself agreeable at all levels. He drew the just-married Nicole aside. 'It takes place at a wedding, like this, you understand. They stand outside the church following the ceremony. A man, an acquaintance, who happens to be passing by, sees them and says to the bridegroom: "Ha! Ha! What about tonight, *nicht wahr?*" ' He paused.

'That's terribly funny,' said Nicole, uncertainly.

'Ah, but there is more, much more,' said the West German *chargé d'affaires*, reprovingly. 'He says: "Ha! Ha! What about tonight, *nicht wahr?*" to the bridegroom, whom he knows. And following this the bridegroom answers: "Ha! Ha! What about this afternoon?" '

'Ha! Ha!' said Nicole. She looked round for David, but he was busy talking to someone else. 'Have you had a drink?'

'The time was about midday,' said the West German *chargé d'affaires*, in explanation. 'He is eager to anticipate – is that how you would say it?'

'I think so,' said Nicole.

'In Germany there would be no such choke,' said the West German *chargé d'affaires*, 'since all weddings take place in the afternoon. But in England such a choke is possible ...' He bowed stiffly, in military fashion, kissing her hand, and said: 'I hope you will be extremely happy in your new relationship.'

Miss Sproule took a fresh swig of champagne, moistened her pencil, and hurried on: 'The receiving line stretched from the steps of Government House to far back under the trees. Prominent among those waiting their turn to wish all health and happiness to the bride and bridegroom were Mr Quintus de Kok, the popular South African consul, and his wife, resplendent in oyster-coloured *peau d'ange*; Monsieur Kakowitz, the Honorary Representative for Poland; Mr "Twotty" Wotherspoon, Mr "Binkie" Buchanan, and their respective ladies; and Mr Louis Strogoff, the American consul.'

Mrs de Kok enfolded Nicole in a vast and motherly embrace; it felt like the collapse of a tent made of veal. 'What do you want to marry an Englishman for, eh?' she demanded, in a carrying voice. 'I hear they're no bloody good in bed, man – no bloody good at all!'

Nicole murmured that she was hoping for the best.

'Ach, you're crazy, eh? No Englishman ever did a damn thing properly ... Well, good luck, Nicole, and lots of kids, eh?'

The aged Representative for Poland, importing his own customs from a vanished century, carried a brimming glass of champagne with him along the receiving line. He bowed in a courtly fashion to the bride and groom, raised his arm elegantly, and drank down the champagne at one gulp. Then, dramatically, he hurled the glass away from him, aiming at a nearby tree. It described a feeble arc, and splintered against the wrinkled red neck of the French commercial counsellor. 'Assassin!' shouted the Frenchman, and hurled his own glass. A few drops of champagne found their target. 'Bolshevik rascal!' screamed the ancient Pole.

They glared at each other, mopping and trembling, until friends led them away.

'Let's not wait in this damned queue,' said Twotty Wotherspoon to Binkie Buchanan. 'I'm thirsty ...'
  'Must kiss the bride,' said Binkie Buchanan.
  'Do it later,' said Twotty.
  'She'll be busy later, what?'
  'And how ... Lucky man, young Bracken.'
  'Wish I were twenty years younger.'
  'Let's have that drink, and then come back.'
  'What about the girls?'
  'They'll understand.'
  'Lead on, Macduff.'

Lou Strogoff, the American consul, was talking to the Samuel Loganquists. The yacht *Wander Lust* was back in harbour, after a cruise round to Lourenço Marques, and the Loganquists had been readily bidden to the wedding.
  'Pretty girl,' commented Mrs Loganquist. '*Very* pretty ... You know, weddings make me sad.'
  'Let me get you a drink,' said Lou Strogoff courteously.
  'Logey will go ... Logey, fetch us about six glasses of champagne. In fact, bring the whole bottle back, and save yourself a lot of trips.'
  'Now, honey,' said Mr Loganquist.
  'Oh, hell, what are we here for? Don't see a wedding like this every day. This is quite a joint. Say what you like, you can't beat the British at putting on a show.'
  'Do weddings always make you sad, Mrs Loganquist?' asked Lou Strogoff.
  'Well, mine always have.'
  'Honey, *please!*' said Mr Loganquist.

It was cool and pleasant under the jacaranda trees; the music of the band sounded faintly and sweetly, mingled with the popping of corks and the muted roar of five hundred voices. Miss Sproule looked at what she had written, added a note about the bridesmaids ('bevy of beauty – *bouffant* skirts – sweetheart necklines'), and then refreshed herself again. She lay back in the hammock, and closed her eyes, humming gently with the band to the music of 'The Yeomen of the Guard'. The notebook dropped from her hand on to the grass. Presently she slept.

'Dead drunk!' said Miss Cafferata later. 'Disgusting! Snoring like a grampus! My dear, I positively *stumbled* over her.'

'That I can believe,' said Mrs Burlinghame.

'What do you mean by that, pray?'

'Just that I've been counting, dear.'

'Come off it, girls,' commanded Mrs Simpson. 'We're all a bit fried … Let's have another round, and I'll tell you a funny story about Malta.'

Nicole, David, and Aidan met under a tree in the centre of the lawn.

'Darling, I'm dead!' said Nicole, and gulped some champagne. 'We must have shaken a thousand hands. And that *photographer!*'

'A perfectionist,' agreed David. 'But not much longer now. Then we can catch the Johannesburg plane.'

'Everyone seems rather drunk,' said Aidan, looking round him.

'How lovely for them.'

'I too have not been idle,' said Aidan, draining one glass and catching another on the wing as a loaded tray went by. 'You know,' he said expansively, looking round him again, 'weddings are not *quite* my milieu, but there's no harm in getting into the act. I always maintain that *anyone* can get into *any* act. Did I ever tell you about the time I was in a terrible nightclub in Vienna, with a terrible orchestra of four old Jews? There were two RC priests getting drunk at one of the tables. They ordered bottle after bottle of champagne – heaven knows where the money came from – they must have just taken a *monster* collection ... But every time they ordered a new bottle, the four Jewish musicians marched over to their table and played *Ave Maria* ... Ever since then, I've never worried about being left out of things.'

'I don't believe that story,' said David.

'Nor do I,' said Aidan. 'It was a religious fantasy, suitable to the occasion ... You know, I shall miss you two children.'

'Oh, we'll be down here from time to time,' said David.

'That won't be much use to me,' observed Aidan. And as David looked mystified, he went on, 'I observe, Mr District Officer, that you have not taken the trouble to read your telegrams this morning.'

'Have a heart,' said David.

'If you had, you would have known about my posting.'

'Where to?'

'Washington.'

'Oh, Aidan!' exclaimed Nicole. 'How wonderful for you!' She kissed him warmly.

'Haven't drawn a sober breath since I heard,' said Aidan.

'Congratulations,' said David. 'That's terrific ... I wonder who we'll get in your place.'

'My dear, you *must* read those telegrams.'

'Why, who's it going to be?'

'A man from your office by the name of Crossley.'

'Oh, *no*.'

'I believe he's *charming*,' said Aidan. 'Now I'm going to have another drink.'

'What's the matter, darling?' asked Nicole anxiously. 'Is he awful?'

'He's a little – discouraging.'

'Oh well, we'll be miles away.' She entwined her arm in his, watching the people strolling to and fro round them, and the lengthening shadows on the Government House lawn. Under the trees, the magnificently robed Maula servants still worked like beavers, opening, pouring, bearing trays, weaving a swift cross-pattern against the noble backcloth of Government House. 'We'll be almost independent.'

'True,' said David.

'Don't let it spoil our wedding, anyway. It's been so lovely.'

'It hasn't even started yet … Darling, you look ravishing. You must always wear a wedding dress.'

'But I must take it off sometimes.'

'Now!' he said, and leant towards her.

Her eyes held his, soft and dreamy. 'I'm so glad it's legal … She squeezed his arm. 'Darling, what's it going to be like in Johannesburg?'

He winked at her, and said: 'Pretty much the same as it has been here.'

'Haven't you got rather a one-track mind today?'

'Haven't you?'

'Yes … I think,' she said, looking across the lawn towards a crowd of people unaccountably embarking on a square-dance, 'that we might start to fade out.'

II

In Shebiya, and Gamate, and Port Victoria, all was now very quiet. Visitors, observers, curiosity-seekers – all were gone; in their place, soldiers stood on guard, and officials ruled a silent people. It was not the silence of ill-omen, but the silence of guilt and second thoughts. The tide of violence had ebbed again, leaving the wreckage to be sorted by the dull professionals.

The ebb bore away the Pressmen as well; martial law had made it a very meagre dish for them, and no one seemed inclined to improve the fare at all. With scarcely a pause to pen a round-up word-picture of this rape committed on the prostrate body of Pharamaul, they took off for other beds and other battlegrounds.

John Raper of the *Globe* had already gone, leaving a decoy suitcase and an unpaid bill at the Hotel Bristol, and a note for Anthea which read: '*Darling, Wonderful while it lasted. See you one day, I hope.*' Little did he know ... Clandestine Lebourget and Noblesse O'Toole had also left, for New York via Paris, where they planned to do a series illustrating all aspects of French decadence. Pikkie Joubert was back in South Africa, reporting Rugby football matches, routine burglary, and minor outbursts of rape and murder in the native locations.

Axel Hallmarck of *Clang* received one of *Clang*'s cablegrams, signed by its foreign editor: '*Return forthwith,*' it read. '*Meet me lunch Antonellis one pm Thursday.*'

It was, he knew, the axe. *Clang*'s editorial lunches were in three tiers; at '21', at Toots Shor's, and at Antonelli's. '21' meant that you were celebrating a promotion. At Toots Shor's, you were holding your own, subject to an inspection and a pep-talk. Antonelli's, a glorified spaghetti joint on East 35th Street, was where you discussed your severance pay. There were no other gradations.

Father Hawthorne also tore himself away, from a country which (as he admitted on leaving) had grown very dear to him. But rumour had reached him from a totally reliable source of yet another diabolical injustice rampant within the Commonwealth, and he embarked hotfoot, cassock flying, to bring it under the microscope of world opinion.

This time, alas, it was in British Columbia, where hard-faced Canadian uranium barons were now known to be holding their workers in miserable peonage, aided by union spies, mounted Cossacks in red coats (these had actually been observed), and the usual loathsome democratic double-talk. By courtesy of Trans-Canada Airlines and the United Front for World Decency, he galloped to the rescue.

III

David Bracken walked slowly back from the police post, across Shebiya's main square, on his way home. Now and then he slapped ineffectively at the mosquitoes which hung in clouds round his bare knees and forearms – his khaki shorts and bush shirt were a long way from Government House rig, and further still from Whitehall, but they were the only thing to wear in the intolerable heat. Even so, his shirt clung stickily to his back, and his scalp under the wide-brimmed bush hat prickled and ran with sweat. Shebiya, just before the rains, was scarcely bearable.

He had been attending a small military ceremony – the formal lowering of colours, for the last time, at the police post, where the soldiers had been quartered.The two platoons of Lancashire Fusiliers had been stationed at Shebiya for five months; now they were on their way back to Kenya. The subaltern in charge, a keen young man who smoked a pipe and read nothing but the *Manual of Small Arms Drill*, would be coming over later for a farewell drink. After that, David would be on his own.

As he surveyed his small empire, he was content to have it so, whatever happened in the future. Though nothing in his life so far had been as exciting, as difficult, as fraught with fear and hope, as taking over the job of District Officer in this tightrope-walking corner of the world, yet now that he had made a start, he would not have exchanged his job for any other, on any conceivable horizon.

The U-Maulas were still, by turns, surly, neutral, or afraid, although they had long ago been purged of their Fish Oath, in an elaborate tribal ceremony of purification; and he himself still functioned as the sole native authority, since no candidates for the local Council of Headmen had yet come forward. But they would come, if not this year, then the next ... In the meantime, the spring sowing was not far off; he had made some friends; a new mission house had been built; a produce exchange system with Gamate had been established; and a full-width road was being cleared down to Fish Village on the coast, where – wonder of wonders – the harbour was even now being enlarged to accommodate Pharamaul's first fish-processing plant. The omens, for the most part, were good, the small future assessable.

But, of course, there could be no neat ending to this story, either here in Shebiya, or anywhere else in Pharamaul; there could only be slow progress, and hard work extending over a hundred hills into the future. No fairy, good or bad, would wave a wand and conjure up sufficient gold to keep each Maula man, woman, and child in affluence for ever; no wizard would grant them Parliamentary franchise and a seat at UN. The gold might be stumbled upon, a hundred years from now, by a man looking for something else; Pharamaul might conceivably be heard in the councils of the world, on some federal basis, in AD 2200. Such was the pace of Africa; and in the meantime, there was a garden to be cultivated, with the tools that were to hand.

There was no swift charm for friendship, either. It was not possible, *now*, to say, of any Maula or U-Maula, that he was your firm friend. They had all learned that, the hard way … For the white men who had been killed had all been the *helpers*: Oosthuizen, the farmer, strict but always paternal in his dealings; Father Schwemmer, the devoted Catholic priest who was as poor as the poorest of his flock; Tom Ronald, the administrator known for his fairness and straight dealing. It was the hospital at Gamate which had been the prime target of the rioters; it was the police who had attracted the hatred not only of bad men, but of all men. It had been Andrew Macmillan who had been goaded to his death …

Friendship also must be tied to the pace of Africa; and mutual trust emerged as the slowest growth of all.

There was a man coming towards him down the track, an old man in a yellow blanket and beehive hat. But for all his years he held himself proudly; and when he drew near, David saw that it was Pemboli, the headman from Fish Village, who was here to recruit labour for the work on the new harbour. That, in itself, was something fresh and hopeful; under Gotwela's hard rule, there had been perennial bad feeling between the villages.

'Well, Pemboli,' said David, saluting him.

'Jah, *barena*.' Pemboli raised his hat gravely.

'All goes well?'

'Jah, *barena*.'

'The men are coming forward?'

'Slowly.'

'Ask me if you need help.'

'Jah, *barena*.'

'*Ahsula!*'

'*Ahsula, barena*.'

My empire, thought David wryly: what will it become, what can I make of it, where does progress lie? ... He recalled the proclamation recently issued by the new Governor, when he succeeded Sir Elliott Vere-Toombs at Port Victoria. His aims, declared the new Governor, a shrewd, energetic ex-soldier with a reputation for decisive action, were 'to restore order, and work towards such degree of self-government for Pharamaul as Her Majesty's Government may from time to time approve'.

David, struck by a familiar ring, had thumbed through the manuscript of Andrew's book on the territory, which was now in his care. The new Governor's wording was almost identical with that used by the first Lieutenant-Governor, after the original troop-landing in Pharamaul, more than a hundred years earlier.

Things moved on, but only a step at a time. It was indeed an ordained pace, and it could not be challenged. Even the murderous disorder through which they had just passed was, in the life of this fabled continent, no more than an uneasy dream, a turning-over, a muffled groaning in the sleep.

Someone else was coming towards him. This time it was Nicole.

He watched her loved figure against the now familiar background of Shebiya – the dusty tracks, the thatched reed huts, the goats and the children running between them. It was the time of the evening meal; smoke from a thousand fires drifted across the sky, blunting the firm outlines, giving the whole scene a hazy dreamlike quality. He had thought that Shebiya would be a place of fear and loathing, poisoned by what he had seen there. So it had been, to start with. But Nicole had cured all that.

'Hallo, darling,' he said, as soon as she was close. 'What's for supper?'

'My romantic lover,' she said, kissing him.

'Eat first, make love afterwards,' he said. 'American plan.'

With his arm round her he turned and looked back at the way he had come. In the doorways of many huts, U-Maula men and women were standing. Some few of them were watching them, most were busy, intent on the evening tasks at the end of another day.

'How goes the empire?' asked Nicole, watching his face as he stared down the hill towards the police post and the bare flagpole. 'Did you have a good day?'

'Not bad … Lots to do, still.'

'Tired? Worried?'

'Not really. But I often wish we could move a bit faster. It'll be years before things get going here, years before Dinamaula comes back – *if* he comes back, years before we have anything to show for all the effort.'

'But Shebiya *is* settling down again. So is the whole island.'

'Oh yes …' He pressed her side, and then swung round, looking towards a much wider horizon. 'It'll be all right,' he told her, 'as long as we love each other.'

Aylmer Road, Province of Quebec.
May 1953 – January 1956

Nicholas Monsarrat

The Pillow Fight

Passion, conflict and infidelity are vividly depicted in this gripping tale of two people and their marriage. Set against the glittering background of glamorous high life in South Africa, New York and Barbados, an idealistic young writer tastes the corrupting fruits of success, while his beautiful, ambitious wife begins to doubt her former values. A complete reversal of their opposing beliefs forms the bedrock of unremitting conflict. Can their passion survive the coming storm …?

'Immensely readable … an eminently satisfying book'
Irish Times

'A professional who gives us our money's worth. The entertainment value is high'
Daily Telegraph

Richer Than All His Tribe

The sequel to The Tribe That Lost Its Head is a compelling story which charts the steady drift of a young African nation towards bankruptcy, chaos and barbarism.

On the island of Pharamaul, a former British Protectorate, newly installed Prime Minister, Chief Dinamaula, celebrates Independence Day with his people, full of high hopes for the future.

But the heady euphoria fades and Dinamaula's ambitions and ideals start to buckle as his new found wealth corrupts him, leaving his nation to spiral towards hellish upheaval and tribal warfare.

'Not so much a novel, more a slab of dynamite'
Sunday Mirror

Nicholas Monsarrat

Smith and Jones

Within the precarious conditions of the Cold War, diplomats Smith and Jones are not to be trusted. But although their files demonstrate evidence of numerous indiscretions and drunkenness, they have friends in high places who ensure that this doesn't count against them, and they are sent across the Iron Curtain.

However, when they defect, the threat of absolute treachery means that immediate and effective action has to be taken. At all costs and by whatever means, Smith and Jones must be silenced.

'An exciting and intriguing story'
Daily Express

'In this fast-moving Secret Service story Nicholas Monsarrat has brought off a neat tour de force with a moral'
Yorkshire Post

This is the Schoolroom

The turbulent Thirties, and all across Europe cry the discordant voices of hunger and death, most notably in Spain, where a civil war threatens to destroy the country.

Aspiring writer, Marcus Hendrycks, has toyed with life for twenty-one years. His illusions, developed within a safe, cloistered existence in Cambridge, are shattered forever when he joins the fight against the fascists and is exposed to a harsh reality. As the war takes hold, he discovers that life itself is the real schoolroom.

'… the quintessential novel of its time and an indictment of an age, stands today as a modern classic'
Los Angeles Times

NICHOLAS MONSARRAT

THE TIME BEFORE THIS

On the icy slopes of the great ice-mountain of Bylot Island, set against the metallic blue of the Canadian Arctic sky, Shepherd has a vision of the world as it used to be, before the human race was weakened by stupidity and greed.

Peter Benton, the young journalist to whom Shepherd tells his story, is dramatically snapped out of his cosy cynicism and indolent denial of responsibility, to face a dreadful reality. He discovers that he can no longer take a back-seat in the rapid self-destruction of the world, and is forced to make a momentous decision.

'In his wry and timely novel Monsarrat unfolds a tremendous theme with gripping excitement' Edna O'Brien
Daily Express

THE WHITE RAJAH

The breathtaking island of Makassang, in the Java Sea, is the setting for this tremendous historical novel. It is a place both splendid and savage, where piracy, plundering and barbarism are rife.

The ageing Rajah, threatened by native rebellion, enlists the help of Richard Marriott – baronet's son-turned-buccaneer – promising him a fortune to save his throne. But when Richard falls in love with the Rajah's beautiful daughter, the island, and its people, he find himself drawn into a personal quest to restore peace and prosperity.

'A fine swashbuckler by an accomplished storyteller'
New York Post

OTHER TITLES BY NICHOLAS MONSARRAT AVAILABLE DIRECT
FROM HOUSE OF STRATUS

Quantity		£	$(US)	$(CAN)	€
☐	A Fair Day's Work	6.99	11.50	15.99	11.50
☐	HMS Marlborough Will	6.99	11.50	15.99	11.50
	Enter Harbour	6.99	11.50	15.99	11.50
☐	Life is a Four-Letter Word	6.99	11.50	15.99	11.50
☐	The Master Mariner	6.99	11.50	15.99	11.50
☐	The Nylon Pirates	6.99	11.50	15.99	11.50
☐	The Pillow Fight	6.99	11.50	15.99	11.50
☐	Richer Than All His Tribe	6.99	11.50	15.99	11.50
☐	Smith and Jones	6.99	11.50	15.99	11.50
☐	Something to Hide	6.99	11.50	15.99	11.50
☐	The Story of Esther Costello	6.99	11.50	15.99	11.50
☐	This is the Schoolroom	6.99	11.50	15.99	11.50
☐	The Time Before This	6.99	11.50	15.99	11.50
☐	The White Rajah	6.99	11.50	15.99	11.50

ALL HOUSE OF STRATUS BOOKS ARE AVAILABLE FROM GOOD BOOKSHOPS OR
DIRECT FROM THE PUBLISHER:

Internet: **www.houseofstratus.com** including author interviews, reviews, features.

Email: **sales@houseofstratus.com** please quote author, title, and credit card details.

Hotline: UK ONLY: **0800 169 1780**, please quote author, title and credit card details.
INTERNATIONAL: **+44 (0) 20 7494 6400**, please quote author, title, and credit card details.

Send to: **House of Stratus**
24c Old Burlington Street
London
W1X 1RL
UK

<u>Please allow following postage costs per order:</u>

	£(Sterling)	$(US)	$(CAN)	€(Euros)
UK	1.95	3.20	4.29	3.00
Europe	2.95	4.99	6.49	5.00
North America	2.95	4.99	6.49	5.00
Rest of World	2.95	5.99	7.75	6.00
Free carriage for goods value over:	50	75	100	75

PLEASE SEND CHEQUE, POSTAL ORDER (STERLING ONLY), EUROCHEQUE, OR
INTERNATIONAL MONEY ORDER (PLEASE CIRCLE METHOD OF PAYMENT YOU WISH TO USE)
MAKE PAYABLE TO: STRATUS HOLDINGS plc

Order total including postage:_____Please tick currency you wish to use and add total amount of order:

☐ £ (Sterling)   ☐ $ (US)   ☐ $ (CAN)   ☐ € (EUROS)

VISA, MASTERCARD, SWITCH, AMEX, SOLO, JCB:

☐☐☐☐☐☐☐☐☐☐☐☐☐☐☐☐☐☐☐☐☐☐

Issue number (Switch only):

☐☐☐

Start Date:
☐☐/☐☐

Expiry Date:
☐☐/☐☐

Signature: _____

NAME: _____

ADDRESS: _____

_____

POSTCODE: _____

Please allow 28 days for delivery.

Prices subject to change without notice.
Please tick box if you do not wish to receive any additional information. ☐

House of Stratus publishes many other titles in this genre; please check our website (**www.houseofstratus.com**) for more details